D0007611

Free to Love

Books by Ivana Trump

For Love Alone
Free to Love

Published by POCKET BOOKS

IVANA
Free to Love
TRUMP

POCKET BOOKS

New York   London   Toronto   Sydney   Tokyo   Singapore

This book is a work of fiction. Names, characters, places, and incidents are either products of the author's imagination or are used fictitiously. Any resemblance to actual events or locales or persons, living or dead, is entirely coincidental.

POCKET BOOKS, a division of Simon & Schuster Inc.
1230 Avenue of the Americas, New York, NY 10020.

Copyright © 1993 by Ivana Inc.

All rights reserved, including the right to reproduce
this book or portions thereof in any form whatsoever.
For information address Pocket Books, 1230 Avenue
of the Americas, New York, NY 10020

Library of Congress Catalog Card Number 93-84537

ISBN: 0-671-74371-6

First Pocket Books hardcover printing October 1993

10 9 8 7 6 5 4 3 2 1

POCKET and colophon are registered trademarks of
Simon & Schuster Inc.

Printed in the U.S.A.

Once again I would like to dedicate this book to my three wonderful children, Donny, Ivanka, and Eric; to my dear mother, Maria; and in loving memory of my father, Miloš.

I would also like to thank my friend Camille Marchetta for helping me continue to tell Katrinka's story.

Acknowledgments

Thanks to Bill Grose, Jack Romanos, Anne Maitland, Kara Welsh, Paolo Pepe, and the whole staff at Pocket Books for their strong support and enthusiasm.

Thanks too to Robert Gottlieb, Marcy Posner, and Norman Brokaw from the William Morris Agency, for their continuing belief and friendship.

Finally, I would like to thank my friend and business partner, Riccardo Mazzucchelli, for his support and dedication.

Acknowledgments

The
Present

Fall, 1992

One

FROM THE BEDROOM DOORWAY, THE HOUSEKEEPER COULD SEE KATRINKA SEATED AT HER DRESSING TABLE, her hand clasped loosely around a bottle of perfume, the pale November sun filtering through the curtains, bathing the room in a milky light, robbing her face of color. Knocking gently, Anna called, "The car is outside, Mrs. van Hollen." But Katrinka continued staring blankly at a spot at the bottom of the mirror. She had arrived back from London like this—quiet, preoccupied, unsmiling, not like herself at all. "Mrs. van Hollen," she repeated. "It's after nine. Luther is waiting outside with the car."

Katrinka started. "Yes. Yes. Thank you, Anna," she said, her words a soft, quick rush of air. "Tell him I do come, right away." After almost sixteen years of living in the United States, Katrinka's English was fluent, though her Czechoslovakian accent remained pronounced and her grammar erratic, which charmed some and irritated others. Her former husband, Adam Graham, had been in the first category at the beginning of their relationship, and definitely in the second by its end.

Frowning with concern, the housekeeper left the room, while Katrinka turned back to the mirror and observed herself critically. Her eyes were rimmed with pink, her eyelids slightly swollen. Anyone could see that she had been crying. She picked up a large sable brush and stroked a faint trace of blusher along the high ridge of her cheeks, trying to relieve the pallor of her face. She considered using a darker

3

lipstick, then shrugged. Pride had got her this far, not wanting to appear in public any more worn and haggard than necessary, but there was no point in making herself up to look like a clown. She fixed the square-cut yellow diamonds into her ears and placed the matching pin on her lapel. Finally, she picked up a bottle of Fracas, dabbed herself with scent, stood, and surveyed herself in the antique cheval mirror that occupied one corner of the bedroom.

She was wearing a black wool Chanel suit with a fitted jacket, onyx buttons, and a ribbon trim that met in a bow at the waist. The perfect go-anywhere suit, she had thought when she saw it at the July collections in Paris. Now she regarded it with distaste. It *was* perfect. But she had not imagined that she would wear it for the first time to a funeral, to *this* funeral. How could she? The idea was inconceivable then. Now.

Oh, Mark, how I do need you, she thought. The image of her husband's handsome face floated between her and her reflection in the mirror. A Viking, she had thought him when they had first met: tall, with hair the color of corn silk and deep blue eyes, precisely chiseled features and sun-weathered skin. Handsome, *too* handsome, she had thought. But time had taken care of that. And life. Both had traced lines of character in his face. Why aren't you here? thought Katrinka as her eyes filled again with tears. She fought them back, reached for the black ribbon-trimmed hat that completed her ensemble, placed it atop her dark upswept hair, adjusted the veil to shield her eyes, picked up her crocodile bag and long gloves, and left the room.

Walking swiftly on high heels along the carpeted hallway to the elevator at the end of the corridor, Katrinka pulled open the door, entered, pushed four on the indicator panel, then fidgeted impatiently as the elevator creaked slowly into operation and lumbered upward. She was convinced it was faster to walk, and always took the stairs, but today she felt too exhausted even for that.

The fourth floor was the nursery floor, consisting of her daughter Anuška's bedroom, bathroom, and sitting room, the nanny's suite of rooms, a playroom, a small utility kitchen, and a large closet dubbed the "laundry" with an apartment-sized washer and dryer. Except for the nanny's quarters, the entire floor was decorated in the bright colors that specialists in child development now decreed essential for stimu-lating young minds.

Entering Anuška's suite, Katrinka found the baby's nanny, Marisol Colon, sitting on the striped sofa knitting. Marisol made sweaters and booties and pointed hats, which she either gave to Anuška or sent off in cardboard boxes to mysterious destinations. She made blankets and afghans, shawls and gloves, her constantly busy fingers reminding Katrinka of the women of her childhood in Svitov where she was born. A handsome dark-haired Salvadoran woman in her mid-thirties, Marisol spoke English with a faint Hispanic lilt. Calm, capable, honest, she had been a nurse in her own country before having to leave for reasons she gave as "political," but would not discuss.

"Mrs. van Hollen," she said, startled to see Katrinka entering. She dropped her knitting and got quickly to her feet. "I thought you had left."

"I did want to see the baby before I go."

"She's sleeping," said Marisol, a warning to Katrinka to move quietly.

Dropping her bag and gloves on a table, Katrinka gently pushed open the connecting door into her daughter's bedroom. The curtains were drawn and, except for a sliver of white light that appeared through a crack in the panels and danced on a crystal lamp opposite, the room was dark. And warm. Too warm, thought Katrinka, who believed it was not healthy to sleep in such a hot room. She never had. Her grandparents' house, where she and her parents had lived until she was eight, had been heated only by a single coal stove in the sitting room. It was left to die down at night: in Czechoslovakia, in the 1950s, fuel was expensive and had to be used sparingly.

Katrinka crossed to the antique brass crib that was once the property of a French princess. Instead of the usual lace it was draped with a vivid red, white, and black printed fabric with padded bolsters and a matching quilt, under which Anuška lay asleep on her stomach, her chubby fists poking out from a red flannel jumpsuit, one of them pressed against her smooth cheek, a red bow tied in her blond hair. She was long and fair like Mark, with Katrinka's slanted eyes and high cheekbones. She was seven months old.

Gently, Katrinka touched Anuška's small, clenched fist. As always, she felt a surge of love so great that for the moment it obliterated every other feeling. She had waited so long for this baby. Her first marriage had ended primarily because of her inability to provide her husband with an heir. The conception of this child, while she and Mark van Hollen were still lovers, had surprised them both, and shaken Mark badly. Both his sons and his first wife had died in a fire, and he was terrified, as he said, to provide Fate with another hostage.

Their histories had made both Mark and Katrinka overprotective parents. Downstairs in the staff sitting room was an armed security guard. Anuška never left the house without him.

If anything ever happened to Anuška, she would die, thought

Katrinka. Anything else she could bear and get on with her life as she had in the past, as she had when her parents had died so suddenly, when, wracked with grief and fear, she had given up her first child for adoption, when Adam had betrayed her and she had left him. As she would bear this, she thought, the swell of love for Anuška receding as she remembered the funeral she had to hurry to attend.

Retracing her steps, Katrinka turned down the thermostat on the sitting room wall, instructed Marisol not to let the baby's room get overheated, took her bag and gloves from the table where she had left them, and hurried down the three flights of stairs to the front door, where the butler, Josef, a quiet, fair-haired, unflappable man, appeared, with his usual flawless timing, holding her black cashmere coat.

As Katrinka slipped into it, the sound of dogs barking drifted up into the hallway from the staff quarters below. "There's no press outside?" she asked anxiously.

"No, madam," he said as he pulled open the heavy oak door.

The cause of the racket were the six Alsatians, part pets, part security system, named after the animals of Katrinka's childhood: Rosa and Rudolph, Bruni and Babar, Yana and Felix, the dogs who, along with her cousins, had been her companions during summer visits to her maternal grandparents' fruit orchards in northern Moravia. The barking grew increasingly frantic and Katrinka frowned. "Then tell Kelly to walk those dogs now," she ordered. There was a full-time staff member, a woman in her late twenties, whose job it was just to look after the plants and the animals. Unfortunately, she had developed a crush on Anuška's security guard and was becoming increasingly haphazard about her duties.

"Yes, Mrs. van Hollen," said the butler, inclining his head slightly as Katrinka stepped outside.

It was a typical November day, damp, cold, with a weak sun and biting wind. Katrinka pulled her coat close around her and started down the front steps. A passerby, a woman in a quilted jacket and cowboy boots, looked at her curiously, nodded in greeting as if they were acquainted, and moved on, her head automatically turning back to watch. People always recognized Katrinka, at least people in major cities did: over the past several years her face had been seen in so many newspapers and on the cover of so many magazines that it was virtually impossible not to.

Waiting at the bottom of the steps stood Katrinka's own security guard. Her driver, Luther Drake, who had been with her since the opening of the Praha Hotel, her first business venture in New York, was at the curb beside the gray Mercedes sedan. A tall, handsome black man, he was even bigger than the guard, and a lot more reliable in Katrinka's opinion. She always felt safe when Luther was with her. Already inside the car was Robin Dougherty, Katrinka's feisty red-headed assistant. Robin, too, had worked with her since the first days of the Praha, and the housekeeper, Anna, for even longer, since shortly after Katrinka's marriage to Adam Graham. She could not imagine life without the three of them.

Luther opened the rear door for her, and Katrinka settled herself next to Robin, who asked sympathetically, "Did you get any sleep?"

Katrinka shrugged. "A little," she replied. "Did you?" They had returned from London together the day before.

"Not much."

The passengers lapsed into silence as the security guard slipped into the seat beside Luther, who started the car and headed east.

The town house, which Katrinka and Mark van Hollen had bought immediately after their marriage, was on Sixty-second Street between Fifth and Madison, a short walk from the Praha Hotel and the duplex apartment Katrinka had once lived in with Adam Graham. That was the way of life in New York, at least among the most affluent. They tended to live in the same general area, go to the same few restaurants, attend the same gala events. It took a great deal of planning to avoid a former spouse, and most did not bother to make the effort once the financial settlement was agreed upon and the divorce granted. Katrinka had not even thought of moving somewhere more distant from Adam. For one thing, she had wanted to remain close to both her New York hotels. For another, by the time she and Mark had married, Adam was spending most of his time in Los Angeles, trying to make a success of his film company. She had thought he would continue to do that, but as usual she had misjudged his intentions—something that she had done from the beginning of their relationship, though she had not discovered it until the end.

That was a mistake she had been determined not to repeat with Mark. Mark. The thought of him brought instant anguish, followed immediately by anger. How could he do this to her! Again tears welled in her eyes.

Katrinka felt a hand touch her arm and, turning, saw that Robin was offering her a handkerchief, a lace-edged square of Swiss linen that had been a present from Katrinka some years before. "No, thank you, I do have one," she said, taking one from her purse. Robin, though somber, remained tearless.

Luther had turned the car up Madison, heading for the Campbell

7

Funeral Chapel at Eighty-first Street. But the heavy traffic and constant red lights did not irritate the usually impatient Katrinka, who, for once, was in no hurry to reach her destination. Looking out the car's tinted window, she saw the doorman at the Praha walk quickly to the curb to hail a taxi. It was time to replace his uniform, she noted, and repeated the thought aloud to Robin.

"Hmm," agreed Robin, as distracted this morning as Katrinka.

As the car crept slowly up Madison Avenue, Katrinka observed the shoppers in the street, bundled into their bulky coats, heads and necks covered, feet booted. They walked quickly, fighting the wind, anxious to get where they were going and find refuge from the cold. They looked pale and unhappy, as if they would rather be anywhere than here.

Not Katrinka. She loved New York. She found it exciting, stimulating, challenging. But then she had always been shielded from its harsher aspects. She had never had to pore over the pages of *The New York Times* on a Saturday afternoon, looking for an apartment that was both safe and affordable, hoping against hope to get to it before someone else did. She had never had to ride the subway to work, or walk terrified down a dark street late at night because there was no taxi to be found. She had come to the city as the bride of a rich man. She had lived in luxurious homes, had cars and drivers at her disposal, servants to do her bidding, enough money to buy whatever she liked. And when she wanted to escape, she did not have to book a package trip to the Caribbean or agree to share a house on Fire Island. She had only to request the Graham jet or reserve a seat on the Concorde.

Katrinka was lucky and she knew it. But she believed too that what she had she had earned. She had not been born into luxury. Her life had not been easy. Though her parents had adored her, their only child, they had nevertheless been strict with her. They had taught her to be honest, diligent, disciplined. As a result, all her life Katrinka had worked hard. From the age of five she had trained tirelessly to become a champion skier. After her escape from Czechoslovakia, she had worked first as a housemaid in a hotel to earn money, then as a model in Munich. With her savings, she had bought a small inn in Kitzbühel, in the Austrian Alps. Soon after she had made that a success, she had met and married Adam Graham, but even then she had not been content to remain at home, the pampered wife of a wealthy man. She had bought the Praha and turned it into the best small hotel in North America. By the time of her divorce, she was a wealthy woman in her own right.

Pragmatic, resourceful, generous, optimistic, Katrinka did what she could to help those less fortunate than herself, but it was not in her nature to let free-floating guilt spoil her pleasure. She thoroughly enjoyed what she possessed.

"Oh, oh," said Luther softly.

"Jesus Christ," added Robin. "Even here. They make me sick. They really do."

Making an effort, Katrinka pulled her thoughts back from where they had wandered and peered out the car window at the crowd in front of the funeral home. It seemed to consist mostly of photographers.

Katrinka shrugged. "They have to make a living, too," she said. "They just do their job."

Luther pulled the car to a neat, smooth stop in front of the funeral home's entrance. The security guard leapt out and opened the rear door. Robin got out first. Katrinka adjusted the veil of her hat and followed. A photographer spotted her instantly. "It's Katrinka van Hollen," he murmured to a colleague, remembering to keep his voice reasonably low in recognition of the solemnity of the occasion. The crowd whipped around toward the car and there was an immediate explosion of flash bulbs, but for once no raucous shouts, no pleas for Katrinka to turn her head, pose, or smile. The security guard cleared a path in front of her, and Katrinka, face blank, looking straight ahead, walked quickly through the throng and inside.

The chapel was just opening and there were few people in the lobby as yet, and, happily, none was press. Except Rick Colins, of course, but he was there strictly in his role as friend. "I'm so sorry, Katrinka," he said, taking her hand, bending his long, lanky frame to kiss her cheek.

Again fighting back tears, Katrinka hugged him for comfort. Rick understood, she knew, that despite all that had happened this past year, despite the distrust, the quarrels, the anger, her grief now was genuine. And he would never use that grief to boost the ratings of his television show.

Rick released her; then, steeling herself, Katrinka crossed the lobby to the viewing room.

The few mourners were already seated. Katrinka was dimly aware that among them were some of her best friends, the women who had helped her through every crisis of her adult life. She registered vaguely the pale face of her former mother-in-law, Nina Graham, for once neither cold nor contemptuous, but shocked and sorrowful. The coffin was banked with arrangements of flowers, hundreds of thousands of dollars' worth of flowers. The coffin. Katrinka's attention focused solely on it. Slowly she moved down the aisle toward it, then stopped.

It was closed. Of course it was closed. She should have known. Never again would she see that face. Never again would she hear that voice. Never.

Oh, no, she thought. It's not true. It can't be true.

"Katrinka," she heard someone call as the room suddenly whirled about her, as everything turned black, blacker than night, blacker than sleep, as black as death. "Katrinka," she heard again, from very far away, as she crumpled slowly to the floor.

The Past

❦

Winter,

1991–1992

Two

"HAVE YOU SEEN THE PAPERS THIS MORNING?"

"MOTHER, IT'S FIVE A.M. HERE. I'M NOT EVEN AWAKE yet." Phone nestled to his ear, Adam Graham extended a naked arm, turned on the bedside lamp, awkwardly propped a couple of pillows behind him, and resigned himself to listening to yet another of his mother's diatribes against what she called his "disgusting habit of appearing in the tabloid press," a failing which she made sound even worse, if memory served, than his wetting the bed at age two.

"Then I'd like to read you an item I came across in this morning's *New York Times*," said Nina Graham, her voice uncharacteristically urgent.

"Can't it wait, Mother? I've only had two hours' sleep," protested Adam, knowing it was hopeless. His mother was one of the few people he could not get to do exactly what he wanted. His mother and Katrinka, he thought, with the quick flash of irritation that these days always accompanied the memory of his former wife.

"It can't," said Nina Graham as he had expected she would.

Beside him, floating out from under the rumpled cotton sheet was a blond head. For a moment, Adam's mind was blank. Then he remembered: Courtney. He had met her at a party the night before. God, he had been drunk. These days he got so little sleep that even one glass of wine made him light-headed, and he had had at least three. He

13

hoped he had used a condom. Anxiously, his eyes searched the floor beside the bed. There it was, complete with a neat little knot at its base. The tightness in his chest eased. Relieved, he smiled and reached under the sheet to fondle the girl's shoulder.

"Married, Katrinka Graham to Mark van Hollen . . . " continued Nina Graham, cutting through her son's preoccupation with the problems of sex and alcohol in 1991.

"What!" said Adam, withdrawing his hand from the sleeping girl, sitting up straight in bed, no longer the least bit sleepy, his attention riveted on what his mother was saying.

Slowly, Courtney turned her head, opened her eyes, began to smile, and thought better of it. The man beside her, a man she really did not know, a stranger actually, looked ready to kill.

"In a private ceremony—"

"Mark van Hollen," muttered Adam, sounding like a man betrayed.

"In Manhattan—"

"Did you know anything about this?" he interrupted again.

"Certainly not. Katrinka has never confided in me," his mother added bitterly, as if she were a woman capable of greeting a confidence with either understanding or compassion, two qualities noticeably absent from Nina Graham's formidable character. Stunned, angry, Adam swore under his breath, but for once Nina failed to reprimand her son for his language. "There's more," she said. "Witnessing the ceremony was Mrs. van Hollen's son, Christian Heller."

"Son! What are they talking about? What the hell is going on?" As quietly as she could manage, Courtney got up from the bed, grabbed her clothes, and headed for the bathroom. Adam didn't notice. "How can Katrinka have a son that I don't know about?"

"That's precisely what I called to ask you."

Adam was silent for a moment, thinking. Then, more calmly, he asked, "Have you phoned her?"

"Of course. Her housekeeper informed me that Mr. and Mrs. van Hollen are away, on their honeymoon." Her voice dripped venom.

"Where?"

"Now, really, Adam. I could hardly ask that, could I?"

Knowing his mother, Adam was positive that she had indeed asked and had been met with the brick wall of Anna Bubeník's absolute loyalty to Katrinka. Anna must have orders not to reveal Katrinka's whereabouts, at least not to Adam or his mother. The same was undoubtedly true of Robin Dougherty, Katrinka's personal assistant. And you could pull Robin's long lacquered nails one by one from her tapered fingers, Adam knew, and she'd still never betray her employer.

14

"What are you going to do?"

What *can* I do? he thought. Katrinka and he were divorced. The final settlement had been arranged, the papers signed just two days ago. Two days. A wave of despair washed over him. It was an unpleasant sensation, happening with more and more frequency of late. "I'll let you know what I find out," he replied, avoiding his mother's question.

Adam set the phone back into its cradle, got out of bed, and walked naked across the granite floor to the bathroom. Through the large wavelike form of the mullioned window, he could see the curve of the balcony that swept around the house's upper level and, beyond it, the gray glint of the Pacific. The sky was beginning to brighten and soon brilliant sunshine would dance off the rolling surface of the ocean, and the sky rising above it would be a vast blue bowl, deceptively clear, apparently smogless. Hard as it was to believe on mornings like this, it was December. Christmas was only a few days away.

A perfect day for sailing, thought Adam, distracted momentarily by the prospect of taking his new Graham Marine twenty-nine-footer across to Catalina. But he had meetings scheduled all day. It was impossible, he decided regretfully as he opened the door into the white tiled bathroom. He stopped short. Courtney stood at the basin, completely dressed in last night's short tulle skirt and beaded denim jacket, peering into the mirror, applying gloss to the lips that Adam dimly remembered as having provided him with a great deal of pleasure. She looked beautiful, and very young, younger than he had thought, about eighteen or nineteen, he estimated. When she saw his reflection, she jumped. "I'm done," she said quickly, slipping the gloss wand back into its bottle and dropping it into her denim bag.

He had completely forgotten that she was in the house. "Take your time," said Adam, grabbing his white terry robe from its hook on the wall.

"No. No, really. I'm finished. I have to get going. I've got an early call. I'm doing a commercial," she added, sounding pleased, probably just to be employed.

That's right, he thought. She's an actress. He smiled, the slightly crooked Adam Graham smile that most women found irresistible. "In that case, you'd better run along. I can't have you holding up production. No matter how great the temptation," he added mechanically. Sex was the last thing on his mind at the moment.

"Well," she said, sidling past him with an awkward smile, "listen, it was great."

Not for a moment did it occur to him that she, an actress after all and reasonably ambitious, might be prepared to lie to the head of Olympic

Pictures about his sexual prowess. His smile broadened. "Terrific," he agreed, though he could remember little of the night's exploits.

"Well, 'bye," she said.

"We'll do it again," he responded, having no idea whether or not he meant it.

Courtney, of course, hoped he did. He scared her a little, but he was a very attractive, very sexy man. Young enough, too, only in his mid-forties. Rich. And divorced. Stranger things had happened to a young actress than to have a wealthy mogul fall in love with her. "I'd love it. I'll leave my number on that pad you've got by the phone. Okay?"

"Great," he said, trying to sound enthusiastic. She was, after all, a knockout and he might indeed want to find her again, later, when he was less preoccupied.

Adam watched her go, then turned to face the mirror. He wore his hair short now, in a brush cut, controlling its tendency to curl at the ends. Every day it had more salt than pepper, but it was still reassuringly thick. Otherwise, there was not much to be pleased about. Huge purple shadows hung beneath his dark eyes, his usually pronounced nose seemed to have sunk into his face, his skin was pasty under its tan. Taking off the terry robe, Adam regarded his body with equal displeasure. He had stopped exercising. He was also sleeping too little and eating too much. He had gained ten pounds he did not need. Time for a diet, he decided.

The image of Mark van Hollen's lean, athletic body and rugged blond good looks flashed into Adam's head, and again he found himself in the grip of unfamiliar and disturbing emotions: frustration and a growing sense of impotence. The man was everything that Adam despised. He had come out of nowhere, with nothing, had put together one of the most powerful newspaper empires in the world, and had amassed a fortune doing it. Many might have admired him for that, but not Adam. Money bought power, and, as Adam saw it, upstarts like van Hollen, the son of Dutch immigrants, threatened the power base of the old families, the ones who, like his, could trace their American roots back to the *Mayflower*. And if others of his kind were content simply to live on their dwindling capital with no more protest than an occasional disdainful sniff, Adam for one was not prepared to let the van Hollens of the world set *his* country's political and economic agenda.

How could Katrinka have done it? he wondered. Hadn't she learned anything in her years of marriage to him? He would have thought that, having lived with the genuine article for so long, she might have acquired some of his contempt for the copy. How could she not see that everything about Mark van Hollen was a little too polished, too perfect, too *new?*

But then, what was Katrinka herself, after all, but an upstart, an immigrant? Marrying a Graham did not in fact make her one, as his mother had repeatedly pointed out. When he had met her, Katrinka was a model, a Czech living in Munich, probably a communist (well, perhaps not actually a Party member, he admitted to himself, to be fair), but, in any case, definitely not in his class.

Adam turned on the shower, adjusted the water temperature, and stepped under the powerful spray. A son, he remembered. What had his mother said about a son? Katrinka's son? It was ridiculous. You couldn't be married to someone for over ten years and not know that she had a son. It was getting so you couldn't believe a word of what you read in the newspapers, not even a marriage announcement in *The Times.*

Tomáš, he thought, as the hot water struck his body in comforting bursts. Tomáš, who was the only one of Katrinka's friends who would talk to him, who *had* to talk to him, he would know what was going on. As soon as he dressed, decided Adam, he would phone Tomáš in Montreal.

"I don't care if he's in the middle of a take," said Adam, shouting into the phone. "You tell him I want to talk to him. Now."

While the assistant director who had had the misfortune to answer the phone on the set in Montreal, where *Marked for Death* was being filmed to save production costs, hurried to do the bidding of the owner and chief executive officer of Olympic Pictures, Adam sipped a cup of black coffee and paced impatiently back and forth across the polished floor of the library. It was only six, too early to leave for the studio.

Adam had rented the house the year before from a former Drexel Burnham trader who could no longer afford to keep it but did not want to sell until the real estate market in Los Angeles picked up. Designed by the foremost member of one of Los Angeles's leading architectural groups, it was a two-story, white stucco structure, built on a crest of land high above the ocean a few miles north of Malibu. It had white granite floors and gray granite fireplaces; steel-framed, floor-to-ceiling glass doors and windows looking out to the ocean; an indoor lap pool in black ceramic tile. The furnishings were spare, the decor subdued. He had moved in some of his own favorite pieces of art, including a painting by Cy Twombly and sculptures by Richard Serra and Dan Flavin. It was exactly the sort of house Adam preferred, as different as possible from the cluttered Graham family home in Newport where he had grown up, far more austere than the apartment he had shared with Katrinka in New York, more like the bachelor pad he had lived in before they had married. As soon as he solved some of his more pressing financial problems, he intended to buy it.

"Adam, how the hell do you expect me to finish this movie on schedule if you waste my time taking your phone calls?" asked Tomáš when he finally came to the phone. He sounded angry. But then he usually did. As they were fond of remarking in Hollywood, Tomáš Havlíček had an attitude problem. He hated directing exploitation films like *Marked for Death* and didn't care who knew it, including the head of the studio employing him. But Tomáš was not only a good director, he was not only reliable and fast, he was imaginative. He was that overused word, "creative." And the films he did made money, a lot of money. Consequently, people—Adam included—put up with him. Adam, who had given Tomáš his first American job, even considered him a friend.

"When *do* you plan to finish?" asked Adam.

"Friday afternoon. Sooner, if this conversation doesn't last too long." Though Tomáš had left Czechoslovakia years after Katrinka, thanks to the hours he had spent watching American films, his grammar was perfect and his accent hardly noticeable.

"How's it going?"

"Fine. Great," said Tomáš impatiently. "You've seen the dailies."

"Yeah," said Adam. "They look good."

"You've got a problem with something?" prodded Tomáš, after a brief silence. The faintest hint of anxiety had crept into his voice. It was unlike Adam not to get immediately to the point.

"Not exactly," said Adam.

There was another pause. "Adam," said Tomáš finally, "I've got a film crew standing around doing nothing, and a lot of expensive actors waiting for me to get back to the set. This is costing you money."

"Yeah, well, the thing is, I wanted to know about Katrinka."

"Oh?" said Tomáš, his voice wary.

"There's an item in this morning's *Times* saying that she got married."

"Uh huh," said Tomáš noncommittally.

"To Mark van Hollen."

"Yes," agreed Tomáš.

"You think she might have told me, instead of letting me read about it in a goddamn newspaper!"

"You're not her father, Adam. You're her ex-husband. She didn't have to come to you to ask permission."

"I'm not talking about *permission*. I'm talking about good manners."

There were a lot of things Tomáš might have replied to that: like your good manners fucking her best friend? Did you inform Katrinka before doing that? But he didn't.

"And what's this about a son?" continued Adam when Tomáš did not respond.

"That was in the paper, too?" asked Tomáš.

"Then it's true?"

There was a brief pause before Tomáš said, "Why don't you call Katrinka and ask her?"

"Do you know where she is?"

"If she's not at home in New York, then no, I have no idea."

"She's on her honeymoon," said Adam, sounding every bit as venomous as his mother had.

"Well, why not?" said Tomáš.

"Would you tell me what the fuck is going on, please?" said Adam, losing patience.

"Look, Adam, Katrinka invited a group of us to dinner the other night. The usual crowd. Only Zuzka wasn't there," he added, referring to his ex-wife. "Katrinka showed up with Mark and announced they were married."

"And the son?"

"He was there, too."

"For Christ's sake!" Adam still couldn't believe it.

"None of us knew anything about it beforehand. And we don't know much more now."

"Who's the father?"

"I think you should ask Katrinka that."

"I can't believe she kept something so important secret from me all those years."

"She kept it secret from all of us."

"All of you weren't married to her," said Adam angrily. "What's his name?" His mother had mentioned it, he remembered, but it had failed to register.

"Christian. Christian Heller," said Tomáš. He hesitated for a moment and then said, "There's one other thing that you should know, Adam. Katrinka's pregnant." It was better, thought Tomáš, that Adam should hear it from him instead of Katrinka when he found her. By then, maybe some of his anger would have dissipated.

"She can't be!" It was impossible. For years Katrinka had tried to have a baby and couldn't. If she had, their marriage would never have ended, or so he liked to think.

"She is. Three months pregnant." For the first time, there was a note of sympathy in Tomáš's voice. He knew how much Adam had wanted a child, how disappointed he, *both* of them, had been when Katrinka had failed to conceive. And if Adam's desire had been, above all, for an heir, for a son to continue the Graham "dynasty," well, who could say that everyone's motives for wanting a child were not, at bottom, a little selfish? Didn't every man find comfort in knowing that a part of him would live on when he died? Tomáš thought of his own son, Martin. No matter how difficult their relationship, he never for a moment regretted having him. "That's all I can tell you, Adam," he continued, refusing to get involved any further, even to spare Katrinka a bad time. "Now, if you don't mind, I think I'll get back to work. Somehow I don't think a phone call from you will cut it as an excuse if I don't make my pages today."

Tomáš replaced the receiver, but instead of returning immediately to the set, stopped at the long trestle table set up with urns of coffee and tea, bottles of fruit juice, and an assortment of bagels, rolls, cakes, and fruits, the breakfast the production provided for the cast and crew. He filled a paper cup with coffee and sipped it. The truth was, he agreed with Adam. Katrinka should have told them all about Christian years ago. At least, she should have told him. And Zuzka. It was they who had comforted her through the end of her affair with Mirek Bartoš, the Czech film director who had been Katrinka's first love and, according to what she had told them the other night, the father of her child. It was Tomáš who had acted as a go-between when Katrinka had ended her affair with the married director and refused to have anything more to do with him. If Tomáš had known then why Bartoš was so persistent, he might not have minded so much. As it was, he carried messages reluctantly, and only because, after his involvement in the Czech revolution of 1968—the Prague Spring—he would never have got a chance to direct films without the help of someone so successful and influential. He had owed his job at Barrandov Film Studios to Bartoš.

Tomáš remembered clearly how pale and drawn, how distraught Katrinka had been that summer of 1968, on her return from Munich where she had been working—or so they had thought—at a hotel to earn some extra money before the start of the national ski team's training season. He had never seen her look so ill, but that had hardly surprised him. Her parents had been killed in a car crash and she had been devoted to them. Never for a moment did anyone suspect that she was mourning not only them but the child she had borne in Munich and given up for adoption.

He understood, of course, why Katrinka had told no one. Tomáš had grown up in Czechoslovakia, in Svitov, the same town as Katrinka. He, too, had been raised in fear of the secret police, of the communist bureaucracy that regulated everyone's lives. He, too, had been taught to keep his mouth shut, to guard his secrets. Discretion had early on become a habit for all of them, one they found impossible to break unless absolutely necessary. He supposed, in Katrinka's case, she had not thought it necessary until, after more than twenty years of searching for him, she had finally found Christian.

Still, however much he understood, Tomáš could not help feeling a little hurt that Katrinka had not trusted him enough to confide in him, her childhood friend—hurt, but nevertheless filled with admiration for Katrinka's courage. Few people he knew would have been able to bear so much trouble, so much sorrow all alone.

Well, at least she had Mark now, Tomáš thought comfortingly. A good guy. Trustworthy. Reliable. Mad about her, too. Katrinka was going to need all the help she could get dealing with that son of hers, a bad apple if ever Tomáš had seen one.

"Do you want me to call everyone back to the set?" asked the assistant director as he approached the table, interrupting Tomáš's train of thought with a gentle hint that time and money were wasting.

"Where'd they go?" asked Tomáš, instantly alert and annoyed.

The AD shrugged. "You know what happens."

Tomáš took a last swallow of his coffee. "Get them back," he said. "I want another take on that master."

"What time will you be leaving for the studio, sir?" asked Carter, the English butler who ran Adam's life.

"What time's my first meeting?"

"Ten."

Adam hesitated a moment. He thought about the phone calls he needed to make to New York, to Miami, to Bremen, to Athens, to the long list of places where he had business interests. There was a stack of paperwork he needed to go through as well, and strategy to review before the meeting. John MacIntyre, his CFO and invaluable right-hand man, had flown out from New York the day before and was no doubt already on his way from his suite at the Beverly Hills Hotel to the studio. It would be a good idea to leave the house immediately, before the buildup of traffic on the Pacific Coast Highway. The problem was, he didn't want to.

"I'll leave in an hour," said Adam. "I'm going for a walk." It was a compromise decision. What he wanted was to go for a sail. Without even trying, he had found solutions to some of the most stubborn problems of his life while lying in the hull of a boat, hand on the tiller, the shoreline receding in the distance, the sea gulls circling overhead. He had asked Katrinka to marry him while sailing, he remembered irritably.

As he changed his custom-tailored slacks for running shorts and his Italian shoes for a pair of Nikes, Adam thought about the times he had, in the past, canceled meetings—to go for a sail, to make love to a woman, for the hell of it. But that had been in the days when the banks were lined up begging to hand him money, when companies had sat up begging to be bought. The world was a different place now. *His* world was a different place.

Going downstairs again, Adam crossed through the sparsely furnished sitting room, went out through one of the doors opening onto the terrace, took the slate path through the array of wildflowers that substituted for a lawn in the sandy soil, opened the gate at the far end of the garden, and descended the stone cliff steps to the beach. There was a small jetty there that had to be rebuilt each spring, and moored to it a twenty-nine-foot sailboat which, next month, Adam would ground until the Pacific storm season had passed. He headed north toward Trancas.

This morning's ten o'clock meeting was with Mike Ovitz, the man who had brokered Adam's purchase of Olympic Pictures several years before, to explore the possibility of selling the company. It was not something Adam particularly wanted to do. He liked being the head of a film studio every bit as much as he had expected. But something had to go if he was to climb out from under a mountain of debt. The yacht he had built for Katrinka shortly after their marriage was already up for sale. He would not sell the jet, of course. That he needed. There was no other way he could keep control of his far-flung business interests. And parting with the shipyards was out of the question: the Grahams had been building boats for hundreds of years, and Adam was not going to be the one to break that tradition. As for the tankers, they weren't profitable enough to attract the kind of money he needed, nor were the other companies he owned, including the cruise ship line that had a lawsuit pending, thanks to the drunken negligence of one of his captains. All in all, Olympic Pictures seemed the best bet. An Italian company was interested in buying, and if the deal went through, Adam would realize enough cash not only to pay off some debt but to begin exploring different and hopefully more lucrative ways of expanding, not to mention making the banks interested in playing with him again. You can't make money if you don't spend it, and it's always best to spend someone else's.

Abruptly, Adam stopped walking, sat on the sand, and stared out over the brightening ocean. Contributing to his financial problems, he thought, irritated by the unfairness of it all, was Katrinka. Just a few days ago, he had been forced to refinance the New York apartment that had once been their home in order to pay her her share of its worth. He had signed over to her the villa in the south of France, worth several million dollars. That she had wanted nothing else from him, not even alimony, or that he had never really liked the Villa Mahmed seemed suddenly insignificant to him when weighed against the fact of her sudden and infuriating marriage to a man who could easily have afforded to buy the damned villa for her.

The more he thought about Katrinka's marriage, the angrier he became. For reasons he could not quite understand, it seemed a betrayal to him, far worse than his betrayal of her with Natalie, who had not really meant very much to him at all. If Katrinka had only been patient, understanding, they might have picked up the pieces of their marriage and gone on together. He had even hinted at it once or twice, though she had still been too angry with him to consider it. Then. Or so he had thought. He had assumed that one day, when he made a big enough effort to win her, she would take him back.

But, no, that wasn't exactly true, he conceded as he watched in the distance a sailboat, looking as small as a child's toy on a pond, glinting in the sun as it moved gracefully across the horizon. A child. He had wanted a child, and Katrinka had failed to produce one. That had been the main problem in their marriage. The *only* problem, as he saw it. And now, he discovered, not only had she had a child years before they'd met, but she was pregnant again. Unreasonably, he felt as if Katrinka had deliberately withheld from him the one thing that he had desperately wanted. He felt as if she had played a terrible, a malicious trick on him. He felt as if she had made a fool of him.

But what was he to do about it? He lay back on the damp sand, his arms folded beneath his head. Above him, gulls wheeled and circled and dove for fish. He could accept defeat gracefully, of course. That was one possibility. But not a very attractive one. He didn't like to lose, ever, and certainly not to Mark van Hollen.

Mark van Hollen. Now, *he* presented any number of possibilities for revenge. Well, perhaps revenge was not quite the right word, corrected Adam. That smacked of a hot-headed, ill-conceived attack. Perhaps it would be more accurate to say that Mark van Hollen's newspaper empire presented an attractive business opportunity. What would it take, wondered Adam, to make a successful run at VHE? A lot, no doubt, but worth every penny to see Mark van Hollen on his knees, to make Katrinka realize the mistake she had made in marrying him. The thought of it made Adam feel a little more cheerful. He got slowly to his feet and headed back to the house, mulling over strategies in his mind.

Three

 THE PHONE RANG AND KATRINKA, LOOKING UP FROM THE SHEAF OF FINANCIAL STATEMENTS SHE WAS STUDY-ing, frowned and said, "Don't answer it."

Tempted, Mark hesitated. Then he shook his head. "It must be important." Not many people knew where they were and those who did had been instructed not to disturb them except in an emergency. Picking up the cordless telephone from the night table, he said hello, his voice curt, signaling to the unlucky caller that the interruption was not welcome.

Sighing, Katrinka let the papers fall onto the king-sized bed that was strewn with faxes, reports, file folders, yellow pads dark with hand-scrawled notes. She picked up the crystal flute from the bedside table, took a sip of the Cristal, and sat back against the soft pile of pillows, watching Mark's face, waiting to hear the bad news. To her relief, he began to smile. "What?" she asked as he dropped the receiver back onto its base.

"A computer, selling magazines," he said, starting to laugh. Katrinka quickly joined in. They were both a little silly with relief, delighted not to have their honeymoon cut short by some irritating business problem. It was going to end too soon to suit them in any case, in just a little more than a week.

When Carey Powers, van Hollen Enterprises's CFO and Mark's best friend, had offered them the use of his house, they had taken him up on it immediately. On the outskirts of Manchester, at the foot of the Taconic Mountains, it was a quick trip from New York by private plane. And unlike Aspen or St. Moritz, where they were likely to run into too many people they knew, it had the additional advantage of allowing them total privacy.

Usually, Christmas was the time of year when Katrinka particularly enjoyed crowds and parties. In her childhood, when religious celebrations had been frowned on by the communist regime, she and her parents had spent the holidays with the other members of the Svitov sports club at the *chata*, the club's ski lodge in Czechoslovakia's Krkonoše Mountains. It had been a festive if not particularly reverent time, with days spent on the slopes skiing and evenings in front of the fire singing traditional songs to the strains of balalaikas and guitars. As an adult, for both Christmas and the New Year (her birthday was on the eve), Katrinka had always been surrounded by friends at the small inn she had owned in Kitzbühel or, after her marriage to Adam Graham, as soon as they could decently get away from his family, in St. Moritz.

But this year she had wanted only Mark. The day after their wedding, as soon as her son had left for Munich to spend what was left of his school vacation with the Hellers, his adoptive parents, Katrinka and her new husband had boarded a small chartered jet and flown to Vermont.

Their days had been perfect. They rose at six, breakfasted lightly, phoned their European offices and dealt with business there. As soon as the lifts opened, they were out on Stratton Mountain or Mount Snow, not returning to the house until four, when they checked in with their offices, then fell into bed to make love and to nap, in no particular order. Afterward, they attended to whatever paperwork had arrived by fax or Federal Express, ate a light dinner either at home, prepared by Carey's housekeeper, or went into town for cocktails and dinner at the Equinox Hotel. Evenings they spent in front of the fire, reading, dancing to tapes of their favorite bands, talking. They found so much to talk about that they rarely went to bed before one, and then only to make love again. When housebound because of weather, only two days so far, they were just as contented, alternating between bed and hearth.

From the beginning of their affair, they had tried to keep out of the public eye, and had succeeded, retreating to obscure places to be alone together. Once, shortly after they became lovers, they had passed ten glorious days at Mark's tiny, isolated cottage in the Hebrides, off the coast of Scotland. Then, that had seemed a perfect time to them. But now, looking back, they could see that, while it had certainly been laden with all the romance and excitement anyone could possibly want, it had lacked the deep contentment, the sense of complete commitment that now marked their time together. Then, it had been all novelty and sexual passion. Now, it was passion strengthened by understanding, deepened by love.

"Do you want to eat in tonight, or go out?" asked Mark, dropping his files back into the leather briefcase beside the bed.

"I did send Mrs. Tucker home," said Katrinka regretfully as she put the empty glass back on the table and began tidying the bed, restoring her papers to the red expanding file she carried with her everywhere. It had started to snow and she had not wanted the woman stranded.

"I'll cook," said Mark. In the years living alone, before he had made his fortune, he had acquired all sorts of domestic skills. And after his wife and children had died, he had spent so much time in remote, even primitive, places, he had had a lot of opportunity to practice them. Now, no longer lonely or unhappy, he found that he actually enjoyed cooking.

Katrinka, on the other hand, did not, though she could. "What?" she asked, happy to take him up on his offer. She had no desire to leave the comfortable house.

"That depends on what there is."

"Eggs. Some cheese. A little ham, I think. An omelette?" she suggested.

"Hmm," considered Mark. "How about some pasta? Spaghetti alla carbonara? We have spaghetti, don't we?"

She nodded. "And wine."

"Who could ask for anything more," he said, pulling her across his lap. He bent his head to kiss her but stopped. "What?" he asked, not liking the sudden clouding in her pale blue eyes.

"I do love you so much," said Katrinka, "sometimes I'm afraid."

For a moment, Mark's face took on the bleak look that, in the year since they had become lovers, had all but disappeared. It was quickly replaced by one of annoyance. "Don't do this, Katrinka," he said. "It's crazy to worry about what we might lose. It's a waste of time. Just be grateful for what we have now."

He was right, of course. She laced her fingers through his silvery blond hair, pulled his head toward her, and began to smooth the frown lines from his face with her lips. She had so much to be grateful for. She had Mark. And, after years of thinking herself barren, she was pregnant with his child. That was miracle enough, but to have found

27

Christian, the son she had believed lost to her forever! She was a lucky woman, she knew. And usually, by nature, an optimistic one. "I don't know what is wrong with me," she said.

Mark, his anger gone as quickly as it had come, smiled and fondled the swell of her stomach. "Hormones," he said.

Probably, she thought. Her whole body seemed to have gone crazy. She, who normally ate little, was now hungry all the time. Favorite foods suddenly made her ill: she could no longer even look at crab without turning queasy. And she had developed cravings for things she usually did not like—chocolate, peanut butter, hot dogs. Perhaps it was no wonder that she often felt like crying for no particular reason, that she sometimes felt afraid.

But Mark was right. While fear had its uses (alerting you to danger, for one), Katrinka knew that left to grow without restraint it could crowd out all pleasure, all joy. Resolutely, she pushed away the nagging memories: of her parents' car hurtling off the side of a cliff, of Christian taken from her when she was too dazed with grief and drugs to withstand the pressure to give him up, of Adam betraying her with her best friend. Those events had taken her to the brink of despair. But she had always come back. And she would again, if . . . She pushed the thought away. "Love me," she whispered to Mark. "Love me."

"I do," he said.

As he untied the sash of her silk wrap, she moved her hands from his head, across his shoulders, down the muscled length of his arms. He was so strong, not just physically but mentally and emotionally. There was a solid core to him, a moral center, a sturdy practicality beneath his passion. Whatever was selfish in him was counterbalanced by insight and common sense, by compassion and decency. Katrinka trusted him as she had trusted no man before in her life, except perhaps her father.

"You're so beautiful," said Mark, admiring the suddenly lush curves of her body.

"Fat as pig," she replied, not unhappily.

"I like it." When he had learned Katrinka was pregnant, he had been terrified. Plagued by his own memories, for days afterward he had considered leaving her, cutting and running, giving up Katrinka and the child so he would not have to risk life's taking them from him. But that had turned out to be impossible. He loved her too much. He wanted their child. And, in any case, he was not a coward. Running away from possible trouble was not his style. He shrugged off his thick terry cloth robe, lay back on the bed, slipped Katrinka's wrap from her body, and pulled her on top of him. Arms around her waist, he nuzzled her full breasts. "I like it very much," he said, his tongue lapping at their dimpled brown tips, grown so much larger since the start of her pregnancy.

Straddling him, breathing softly into his ear, her lips tracing its shape, Katrinka could feel him swelling beneath her, growing harder, while she softened, dissolved with passion, liquefied, opened up to engulf him. He filled her entirely, her whole being, and yet, she thought, she would never get enough of him. Never.

Prior to leaving New York, Katrinka had moved her possessions from the apartment she had shared with Adam to another nearby, which Mark had taken to be near her in the months preceding her divorce. What she took were clothing and jewelry, personal gifts given to her by friends over the years, old photographs, and most treasured of all, mementoes of her childhood in Czechoslovakia. There was little else that she found she wanted, although she had decorated the apartment herself, with the help of the then unknown Carlos Medina. It had been a great success for them both, making the pages of *Architectural Digest*, establishing Carlos as a hot new interior designer and Katrinka, newly arrived in New York, as a taste to be reckoned with. She had felt justifiably proud of what they both had achieved. But the apartment had always somehow been more Adam's than hers. She was happy to leave it intact for him, to forget it, and move on to her new life with Mark.

But Mark had never liked his little apartment, considering it less a home than a temporary campsite, a place to drop off his things on his way to see Katrinka. He suggested that, instead of returning to it, they rent somewhere larger and more comfortable until the town house he had bought for them was ready.

"Oh, no," said Katrinka, horrified at the thought. While never really poor, she had worked hard all her life to get the things she wanted. She understood the value of money, and wasting it did not come easy to her. No way would she leave a prime New York apartment standing empty.

"Thrifty little *hausfrau*," said Mark, grinning. It was just the sort of thing that Adam's mother, Nina, might have said to her, a cool, appraising smile emphasizing the contempt in the remark. But in Mark's smile, Katrinka saw only amusement and appreciation. "I guess I don't have to worry about you putting me in the poorhouse."

They would be able to move before long, Katrinka knew. The town house on Sixty-second Street between Fifth and Madison avenues that Mark had bought a few months before their marriage was almost ready. Returning to New York from his current base in London, Carlos

Medina had again worked with Katrinka on the design and decoration. After completing three hotels and two houses together, she trusted him completely, which allowed her to keep in the background, to prevent word of her involvement with Mark from becoming public knowledge. She had been afraid that Adam would continue to delay the divorce if he knew she planned to marry as soon as she was free.

Workmen had already completed most of the structural changes in the house. Within days the plasterers would begin their work, and then the painters. Everything would be finished in little more than a month and, meanwhile, staying in Mark's two-bedroom apartment could hardly be considered a hardship, especially since, with their business interests abroad (Katrinka owned a hotel, the London Graham, off St. James's, near Piccadilly, while Mark had newspapers and publishing companies, binderies and paper factories throughout Europe and the Far East), they would as usual be spending a large part of their time in Europe, living either in Mark's house in London, or Katrinka's villa in St.-Jean-Cap-Ferrat.

"I would love a bath," said Katrinka, as she hung the Yves Saint Laurent jumpsuit she had worn on the plane in the bedroom's roomy closet.

"Mmm, me, too," said Mark agreeably. He looked at her briefly, gave a comical leer, and added, "Go run it, baby, and I'll join you," before returning his attention to the list of phone messages his secretary had faxed him.

"And afterward a hot dog with mustard and relish," she added.

"I'll call the deli in a minute."

Still wearing a silk teddy, Katrinka picked up her toilet kit, started out of the room, then stopped as she heard him swear. "What is it?"

"Three messages from Sabrina, and one from Carey Powers, marked urgent. What the hell is she up to now?" He picked up the phone on the writing desk and began to dial. Sabrina was his star columnist, noted for her wicked humor and acid pen, so internationally famous that she did not require a last name. Feared, hated, she was read with either amusement or terror by people all over the world interested in the antics of the rich and famous. Her column, which appeared in both *The New York Chronicle* and *The London Globe,* as well as most of the other newspapers in the van Hollen chain, contributed mightily to those newspapers' success. But her visibility made her, and the papers, good targets for lawsuits. There were usually several, in various stages of development, keeping Mark's team of litigation lawyers from enjoying too much free time.

"Cow," muttered Katrinka, who loathed her. Sabrina was the one thing that Mark and she quarreled about with any consistency, so far the only serious difference of opinion between them. Katrinka wanted Mark to fire her. She had seen her friends trashed, their sorrows used as food for a column always hungry for gossip, her own messy divorce played out in it. Until her involvement with Mark, Katrinka had been on the receiving end of Sabrina's most vicious attacks. But even Sabrina, who was afraid of little, thought it wise not to endanger her position by offending her boss. And it was as much to control her as profit by her that Mark refused to give in to Katrinka and let Sabrina go.

Katrinka continued into the bathroom and started the water running. She twisted her dark hair up on her head, pinned it, opened the toilet kit, took out a small tin of pads, and began removing her eye makeup. When she leaned over the tub to turn off the bathwater, she felt Mark slip his arms around her waist and bury his face in her neck. "It's started already," he said, his breath warm against her nape. "Trouble."

Katrinka twisted in his arms. "What is she doing now?" she asked.

"I just talked to Carey. Sabrina called him this evening, told him she's accepted an offer from Charles Wolf. She's going to work for *The Daily Register*."

"But *The Register* doesn't have anywhere near the circulation *The Chronicle* has."

"Not in New York. But Wolf's papers are big in the Midwest and California."

"And Europe?"

"Not yet," said Mark, wondering if this move meant that Wolf was planning to expand and, if so, what sort of threat that represented to VHE.

"*Ay yi yi yi*," said Katrinka, getting the point immediately. "You do think he's up to something?"

"Too soon to tell. But I'll keep my eyes and ears open." Mark was worried, and not just about Charles Wolf's plans. He was about to launch *The International*, a new weekly magazine, combining top journalism in an easy-to-read and entertaining format with color photographs and interesting graphics. It was designed to be the print version of CNN. Long a dream of Mark's, *The International* was turning out to be a very expensive reality, and his company could not at the moment tolerate any significant losses, any serious drop in circulation. Sabrina had an extensive and devoted following.

"I know this causes problems for you, but . . ."

"You're not sorry," said Mark.

"I hated knowing it was your money paying her to write such terrible things about people."

Mark shrugged. "She's out of my control. God knows what she'll say about us now that she has the chance." Mark hated publicity, personal publicity, even more than Nina Graham did.

"Well, at least fewer people will read it," said Katrinka.

Mark's mouth curved in something resembling a smile. "That's what I love about you. You can always find the silver lining in a cloud." He pulled her tight against him, kissed her, and let her go. "I better call Sabrina," he said. "I guess the honeymoon's over," he added as he turned to leave.

"Oh, no, it's not," she said, reaching out to stop him. She began to unbutton his shirt. "It will never be over. Not while we do have each other."

Four

THOUGH KATRINKA HAD AN OFFICE IN EACH OF HER THREE HOTELS AND COULD KEEP CONTROL BY PHONE NO matter where she happened to be, the nerve center of her business was on the Praha's second floor, in the executive suite. It was not yet eight o'clock, the morning after her return from Vermont, when Katrinka arrived at work. As she expected, no one was at the reception desk, but as she went into the interior office, though all the sleek secretarial workstations were empty, she could see a light in Robin's office. "Good morning," she called. The smell of brewing coffee filled the air.

Robin, dressed in a smart russet-colored Donna Karan suit that emphasized the red in her hair and the freckles on her creamy skin, came out of her office and grinned. "Hi. Welcome back. You look great," she said.

"It's marriage. I do recommend it."

"Some marriages, anyway," said Robin, who had lived through the years of Katrinka's growing unhappiness with Adam and the final heartbreak of the divorce. Just before Christmas, Robin had moved in with her boyfriend. Her stated plan was to save enough money for a down payment on a house before getting married, but she was beginning to suspect that what she really wanted was a chance to see how Craig and she managed under the same roof. "How are you feeling?" she asked, following Katrinka into her office, which—like all of the hotel except for the high-tech secretarial area—was furnished

33

with reproduction antiques, combined with traditionally styled modern pieces. The walls were painted a soft, flattering peach; a highly polished partner's desk was flanked by two Queen Anne chairs, and a flowered print Fortuny fabric covered the upholstered sofas that faced each other across an Italian glass-topped table.

"Fantastic," said Katrinka, dropping the file on the desk and collapsing into her leather chair.

"Want some herbal tea?" Robin had strict ideas about diet, and caffeine was not on her list of acceptable substances for pregnant women.

"Thanks, no. Not right now. I did have some at home."

"You ought to eat something."

"I eat all the time. Too much. Don't worry. How you doing? Everything okay? You had a nice Christmas?" And when Robin had filled her in on the difficulties of negotiating the holidays with her Irish-Catholic parents at war with her and her boyfriend over their living arrangements, Katrinka smiled sympathetically and said, "Be a little patient. Give them time. They'll come around. Craig's a good guy." Though Adam's family had not ever "come around" and accepted her, she was still optimistic enough to believe that others were less judgmental and more loving.

Robin grinned, as she always did when Katrinka used American slang. "Yeah," she said. "He's great. Let me go get my coffee and I'll give you a rundown on what's been going on while you were away."

Katrinka had not been out of touch while in Vermont. Every day, at least once, she had spoken either to Robin or to Michael Ferrante, her general manager, so that she was up to date with the performance of the Praha, the New York Graham, the London Graham, and the condition of the house in St.-Jean-Cap-Ferrat. "What do we do about the heating unit?" she asked Robin as soon as her assistant was seated in one of the chairs opposite her. She was referring to the villa's furnace that had broken down a few days before.

"They're having trouble finding a replacement."

"That's crazy," said Katrinka. "Everybody's freezing. It has to be fixed." She had a staff of five permanently in residence at the villa. Additional staff were hired as needed.

"You know the French," said Robin.

"Carlos will get it fixed in no time," said Katrinka. "Where's he staying?"

"At the Graham."

Katrinka, impatient as always to get a job done, picked up the phone herself and began to dial. "Carlos Medina, please," she said as soon as the hotel operator answered.

"Mr. Medina is not accepting calls at the moment," said the operator.

"It's Mrs. Gra . . ." She stopped herself. "It's Katrinka van Hollen," she corrected. "Put me through, please."

The operator heard the name Katrinka and did as told. A moment later, Carlos was on the line.

"Still sleeping?" said Katrinka, though she knew better. Like herself, Carlos needed only four or five hours of sleep to feel rested. "I thought you did have a house to finish."

"You're back," said Carlos.

"Last night."

"Guess my holiday is over," he said. He had in fact been up for hours, working on some sketches that he wanted to show Katrinka at their next meeting. "You planning to come to the house today? There are a few decisions you ought to make before I go any further. Now that you're married, I assume there's no need to keep anything secret."

"None," agreed Katrinka happily.

"Congratulations," said Carlos.

"I'll see you at the house at ten. Okay?"

"Great."

"But I do have a favor to ask first . . ." As she told him about the furnace for the Villa Mahmed, Katrinka heard her office staff beginning to arrive. Michael Ferrante, his thick curly hair in complete chaos thanks to the bitter January wind, stuck his head in the door and waved. See you when you're free, he mouthed. Katrinka nodded, held up five fingers, finished her phone call to Carlos, then ran down the week's schedule with Robin. "Chicago on Thursday?" she said, sounding distressed. She was set to deliver a speech there, at a breakfast meeting, to an association of businesswomen.

"Do you want me to cancel?"

"No," said Katrinka regretfully. She hated backing out of commitments and never did so unless absolutely necessary. And she enjoyed giving speeches, not just because she was paid well to do it, but because she liked the crowds, the excitement, the exchange of ideas in the question-and-answer period that followed. But, at the moment, she was very sorry to have to leave her new husband. "Call Mark's secretary and ask if it is okay I borrow his plane for the trip." She smiled. "And ask if maybe I can borrow him, too." If he didn't have anything else scheduled, she knew Mark wouldn't mind tagging along with her for the ride. "Tell her we'll be back by lunchtime Friday."

Nodding, Robin stood up, pointed to a folder on Katrinka's desk, and said, "You'll go through those invitations and let me know which you want to accept?"

"As few as possible," said Katrinka, opening the folder and staring in dismay at the pile.

"And we have to review plans for the Children of the Streets fund-raising drive."

"I did make some notes about that while I was away." Katrinka had taken over the organization when Daisy Donati had left New York after her divorce from Steven Elliott, and she had, since then, made it one of the most successful fund-raising groups in the country. There had never been any hint of scandal or accusations of corruption leveled at COTS, a record of which Katrinka was justifiably proud. And having given up her own child for adoption because she believed she could never support him on her own, it was the one charity that she, though she was cutting back on other commitments because of her pregnancy, felt she could not abandon. "Set a committee meeting for next week," continued Katrinka, as Robin turned to go. "And tell Michael he can come in now."

Robin, carrying her notebook and a sheaf of papers, headed for the door, then stopped as she heard the receptionist say, "I really should announce you." Katrinka looked up from the pile of invitations she had begun to sort through.

"Who the hell . . ." muttered Robin, starting forward again.

"Wait," said Katrinka, picking up the phone to dial security. If it were any of the normal visitors to the suite, the receptionist would not have sounded so upset. Through the open door, Katrinka could see the secretaries standing motionless, not knowing what to do, and Michael Ferrante heading to intercept the intruder. Though it was only a matter of seconds, it seemed to take forever for the connection to go through, for the phone to ring, for security to answer; but when she heard the guard's voice at the other end, she said suddenly, "It's Mrs. van Hollen. Never mind. There's no problem," and replaced the receiver.

"Good morning, Katrinka," said Adam, brushing past Michael, who had stepped aside but now waited, looking at Katrinka, for some indication of what to do.

"Good morning, Adam."

"Robin," said Adam pleasantly, as she moved to block his path.

Robin turned slightly to look at Katrinka, who nodded. "Good morning, Mr. Graham," she said finally. "Would you like coffee?" she added. "That is, if you're planning to stay."

"Nothing right now," he said, smiling (he hoped) disarmingly. "Just close the door on your way out."

Again Katrinka nodded. And, reluctantly, Robin stepped around Adam and out the office door. "Buzz if you need me," she said, closing it behind her, exchanging a look of dismay with Michael.

"I get the feeling she doesn't like me at all," said Adam as he sat in the chair Robin had recently vacated.

"What you are doing here?" asked Katrinka, ignoring his comment. "You're married."

"Yes."

"And pregnant."

For a moment, Katrinka's steady gaze faltered. The memory of the years she and Adam had tried to have a child came flooding back, and with it the pain of their disappointment. For a moment, she felt sorry for him. "Yes," she said finally.

"You might have told me." He couldn't quite keep the hurt from his voice.

"I did consider it. But then . . ." She shrugged.

"Why didn't you?"

If she told him why, that she had been afraid, if he knew, that he would try to delay the divorce, it would only provoke an argument. Again, she shrugged.

"You owed me that much, don't you think?"

"Owed you?" she said, trying to control the sudden flare of anger. "Owed you? No, I don't think so."

"We were married for twelve years, for Christ's sake. Doesn't that count for something?"

"Fourteen and a half," she corrected. "From start to finish."

"All right. Fourteen," he agreed impatiently. "God, we loved each other, Katrinka."

"That was a long time ago."

"Was it?" he said. He stood up, walked around the desk, and sat on its edge, leaning toward her. "It doesn't seem all that long ago to me."

I feel nothing for him, she thought, with some relief. Absolutely nothing.

He looked tired. And beneath his studied display of warmth, of seductiveness, Katrinka could sense the tension, the worry, the anger. Was it all to do with her, she wondered, or was something else to blame? She knew he had financial problems. Who didn't this year? Even the hotel receipts were down, though not as far as they had been the preceding January, as the world had waited for the Gulf War to begin. But if she respected little else about Adam, she still had enormous regard for his business instincts. She had assumed that he was on his way to recovery.

"How could you have done it?" he asked.

"What?"

"Married him."

"Why? Oh," she said, understanding suddenly. "You mean because his family did not arrive on the *Mayflower* with yours? Well, mine didn't either."

But, of course, Adam could not admit he meant exactly that, even to Katrinka. "That has nothing to do with anything," he said, irritated. "Feeling the way you do about his newspapers . . ."

"They're excellent papers," said Katrinka firmly.

"They're rags, and you know it."

"I don't want to argue, Adam."

He got up and walked back to the other side of the desk. "He turned Sabrina from a local nuisance to a world-class calamity, for Christ's sake. He made her the bitch she is today."

"I don't think Sabrina needed help," said Katrinka, standing.

"I understand she's quit."

"Has she?" asked Katrinka innocently, as she moved toward him. "And who did tell you that piece of news?"

"Who *told* me," corrected Adam, as he always did when irritated. "The verb has a past tense. Charles Wolf told me, as a matter of fact. I understand she's going to work for him."

"I didn't know you and Charles Wolf were friends." Why, she wondered, was the conversation suddenly making her not just irritated or unhappy, but somehow uneasy?

"I wouldn't say we were friends exactly," said Adam, his crooked grin less endearing than smug. "I'm building a yacht for him. Quite a nice one, about two hundred sixty feet. Lucia is designing it," he added. Lucia di Campo, a mutual friend, had worked with Adam from the beginning, before Graham Marine had acquired its reputation for producing grand luxury yachts.

"Then business is good?" asked Katrinka, unable to restrain her curiosity.

"Excellent," he said. "Sorry you didn't ask for alimony? Maybe then you wouldn't have had to rush into another marriage."

"I have everything I do need, Adam," she said quietly, ignoring the suggestion that her motives for marrying Mark had been mercenary. "Everything I do want."

"You used to think that all you needed or wanted was me."

"That, too, was a long time ago."

He reached out and cupped his hand around her neck. "Was it?"

"I think maybe it is time you should go," she said, moving out of his grasp.

"Yes, I suppose you're right," he said, backing up a little. "I have a morning full of meetings ahead of me. Tell me, was your husband very upset to lose her?"

"Who? You mean Sabrina?" Katrinka shrugged. "She sells newspapers. But I'm delighted she's gone." Again, she felt a flurry of unease, of suspicion. "You didn't suggest to Charles Wolf, maybe, that Sabrina would be a good acquisition for his chain?"

"Me?" said Adam, smiling innocently. Trust Katrinka, he thought, to get the point immediately. Over dinner with Charles Wolf a few days after Christmas, he had suggested just that. But while he did not mind Katrinka suspecting his involvement, in fact even relished the idea of taking credit for any upset caused Mark van Hollen, still he had no intention of confirming it for her. "You know I don't like Sabrina any better than you do. Why would I instigate anything of the kind, knowing she'd come out of it with a big pay raise."

Katrinka searched his face, not quite believing him. "I don't know anymore why you do half the things you do," she said finally.

"Well, trust anyway that I always have a good reason." He smiled, leaned forward, kissed her cheek, and said, "I'm glad we had this talk. We'll be running into each other here and there, and we might as well be civilized about it."

"Yes," she agreed. She watched him as he walked to the door. Something was bothering her. "Adam," she called after him. "You didn't wish me good luck."

"No," he said, turning back to look at her, his hand on the doorknob. "I didn't, did I?" He smiled again, a tight, bitter smile. "Oh, by the way, I almost forgot. I'd like you to stop using the Graham name." He had been planning that exit line for days.

"But I have," said Katrinka, not understanding for the moment what he could possibly mean.

"On the hotels," he explained.

"But Adam," she said, horrified by the amount of work, the expense involved in doing what he asked, "that's impossible. The cost . . ."

"It's my name," he said. "Not yours. Not anymore. I want you to stop using it. Don't make me fight you on this one, Katrinka, because I'll win, I promise you." Turning the knob, he opened the door. "Have a nice day," he said, a line he had picked up in his months in California where it was used everywhere in place of good-bye. It had a nice, ironic

39

ring to it. "You can go in now," he said to Robin, who hovered outside the door, not eavesdropping, just waiting to come to the rescue if needed.

Robin nodded coolly, then entered the office and saw Katrinka again seated behind her desk, her eyes filled with tears of frustration and rage. "Bastard," she muttered. "Bastard!"

Five

 "I HOPE YOU DID TELL HIM WHERE HE GO," SAID ZUZKA, WHOSE GRASP OF ENGLISH REMAINED UNCERtain and her speech heavily accented after almost seven years in the United States. Her son, Martin, spoke fluently and with no trace of an accent, a source of both pride and irritation, the latter with herself for being so slow to learn. Her former husband, Tomáš, had not had any problem at all, but then, as she frequently reminded herself, not only had he studied English in school but in the days before he had become a famous movie director he had spent every possible moment watching American films and television, leaving Zuzka to clean the house and prepare the meals in addition to her job. *"Čǔrák,"* she added in Czech for good measure, the short expletive summing up her present feelings toward Adam Graham, of whom, before he had broken Katrinka's heart, she had been very fond.

"I was tempted," admitted Katrinka, with a wry smile.

"Well, what are you going to do?" asked Daisy, dropping her fork, pushing away the Limoges plate, refusing to eat another bite of the delicious pasta primavera. Petite and always slender, Daisy's current method of maintaining her figure was to eat only half portions of anything she wanted. It was the only way, she insisted, to live peaceably with an Italian who had little patience with nibbling on lettuce leaves or chomping on celery and carrots.

Katrinka shrugged. "Change the names."

41

"Oh no," said Alexandra, disapproval registering on her beautiful face. She was tall and impossibly slender, with creamy skin and long red hair, once natural, now requiring hours of hard work by her hairdresser to approximate its original color. "You can't be serious. That will cost a fortune." Thanks to the faltering economy, Alexandra had recently lost the gallery that her keen eye and thorough knowledge of seventeenth-century Dutch art had made a success in the late 1980s. And her husband, Neil Goodman, CEO of one of the city's most influential brokerage houses, was fighting what often seemed to her a losing battle to keep his company afloat. Poor and resenting it for too much of her life, the daughter of an impoverished branch of an old and wealthy family, Alexandra thought that now was the time to begin pinching every penny. "Nobody can afford to throw away money these days."

"It does seem an awful waste," said Daisy.

"Well, I think you've made the right decision," said Lucia. Her chestnut eyes, rimmed heavily with black to make them appear larger, were serious.

Zuzka frowned. "Why you think that?" she asked. Though no one seriously doubted Lucia's loyalty to Katrinka, as one of Adam's oldest friends, not to mention his preferred designer, her opinion could be considered suspect.

"Because," explained Lucia with an impatient shake of her auburn head, "fighting him, Katrinka would run up endless legal fees; and, when the case got to court, as it probably would if I know Adam, there's a good chance she'd lose."

"Exactly what my lawyer said. And Mark." She had been furious when Mark had, as she saw it then, sided against her. "I suppose you do want me to call the hotels the van Hollen," she had said bitterly.

But Mark had only laughed. "The idea never crossed my mind," he replied, though he had admitted he was just as happy to have yet another reminder of Adam Graham removed from their lives.

Of course, as soon as she had calmed down, Katrinka had realized that both her lawyer and Mark were right: fighting Adam was worth neither the time nor the energy nor the money. "I will call them the New York and London Ambassadors," she told her friends.

"How perfect, darling," said Daisy enthusiastically. "You're an ambassador of goodwill if ever there was one. Though it is hard to believe that neither New York nor London has a hotel by that name," she added.

"I know," said Katrinka happily. "But I did check."

* * *

42

The friends were having one of their frequent lunches at one of their usual restaurants, Le Cirque, sitting at the banquette the owner, Sirio Maccioni, always reserved for their visits. It was in the front, near the door, where they could see and be seen by the other guests, among whom numbered a substantial number of influential people, from lacquer-haired DAR matrons to television talk show hosts. Next to them, Pepe Fanjul, resident of Palm Beach, owner of millions of acres of land in the Dominican Republic, the largest supplier (with his brothers) of sugar in the United States, sat talking with Jerry Goldsmith. Beyond them, Glenn Close was deep in conversation with someone no one knew, but everyone suspected was a foreign film director. Seated against the far wall, Richard Nixon was lunching with the head of the Russian delegation to the United Nations. Sabrina (and for this all the friends were grateful) had not put in an appearance that day. But Alice Zucker, who had replaced Margo Jensen as fashion editor of *Chic*, stopped by to say hello and to tell Katrinka that the layout in the March issue was looking great. It was of Katrinka, modestly pregnant, working out in the exercise room of what had been the New York Graham. Free publicity of the kind that *Chic* and the other magazines provided was worth a thousand paid adds and the issue would help to increase bookings at both the New York hotels and the one in London as well, since *Chic* had recently gone international.

"The hotel's name is the Ambassador," Katrinka warned her. "Be sure you make the change."

"She doesn't really have Margo's flair," said Alexandra, when Alice had moved off to join her lunch date. It wasn't just that the new fashion editor, an attractive petite blonde, lacked Margo's startling and dramatic good looks; she also lacked Margo's ability to ferret out what was new and original, and to spot, if not always to set, trends.

"I miss Margo," said Katrinka.

"New York's not the same," agreed Alexandra, "since she and Ted moved to Monte Carlo."

Alexandra, Lucia, and Daisy had not seen Katrinka since the dinner celebrating her marriage. Zuzka had been in Tokyo at the time with her lover, Carla Webb, who was conducting a golf clinic for the sports-mad Japanese. From there, she and Carla had gone to St. Moritz to spend the holidays with Daisy and her husband, Riccardo Donati. On her way home to Los Angeles, she had stopped off in New York specifically to see Katrinka.

"You know," said Zuzka, "I do think Martin has a crush on Pia." Her son, Martin, had also spent Christmas in St. Moritz, along with Lucia, her current lover, Patrick Kates, and her daughter, Pia. "Believe me," continued Zuzka, digging with enthusiasm into her crȩme brûlée, "I was so relieved."

"Relieved?" said Alexandra, polishing off the last of her New Zealand blueberries. She and Neil had just returned from Aspen to their Sixty-sixth Street town house, where they normally spent weekdays since their two children were in school, at Trinity. Weekends they spent at their estate in Pound Ridge.

"Why?" asked Daisy, who was in New York to see her pregnant daughter.

"Well, you know, he's been so moody. And I did think maybe with all the craziness—Carla, me—maybe he would hate women." Zuzka was a tall woman, though not so tall as Katrinka, with broad shoulders and a lithe, athletic build that fit compactly into a size eight. Her skin was clear and fair, and she wore little makeup except for mascara to darken her pale lashes and emphasize the shape of her large brown eyes. The long mane of blond hair was streaked to conceal the gray. The women now all dyed their hair, except for Katrinka, whose dark head still got only an occasional silver strand that she was able to pluck out without any trouble. Daisy, who was older, had already had a face-lift, a topic that took up more and more of their conversation of late.

"You thought he'd end up gay?" asked Alexandra, and, when Zuzka nodded, said, "I don't think being gay has anything to do with what your parents do or don't do."

"Rick Colins does believe he was born gay," said Katrinka. Rick, a newspaper columnist turned television personality, was a close friend and, once upon a time, Carlos Medina's lover. "Anyway, he did know it for sure when he was only eight years old."

"Have he and Carlos seen each other?" asked Daisy, pushing her unfinished chocolate mousse out of reach. She meant since Carlos's return to New York.

"I don't think so," said Katrinka.

"You think I was born gay?" asked Zuzka, returning the conversation to the matter uppermost in her mind. She still found the question of her sexuality very confusing. Until Carla, she had never been interested, physically, in a woman. Sometimes now she still could not believe she was. And she was certain that, if Tomáš had not been unfaithful, or, at the very least, if he had not been so obvious about his infidelity, she would never have left him. She had loved him passionately, she knew that. Did she love Carla the same way? Sometimes she thought yes. At other times, she wasn't sure. But she knew that Carla made her feel good about herself, something Tomáš had not done for a long time.

44

Katrinka looked uncertain. "Maybe," she said. "It does take some people years to realize it." She shrugged. "Anyway, what difference it makes? As long as you're happy now."

"Yes," agreed Zuzka. "But I want Martin to be happy. He has had difficult time." At thirteen, Martin would have died of a brain tumor, had Katrinka and Adam not arranged for him to be brought to the States and operated on by one of the country's leading neurosurgeons. And since Zuzka and Tomáš had defected to be with him, Martin, for a long time afterward, had felt guilty about costing Tomáš his career as a filmmaker in Czechoslovakia. Then, after years of unemployment, just as Tomáš finally got to direct a film, one that was to make him famous, Zuzka had left him for Carla. It was a lot for a teenage boy to have to deal with. "And soon he graduates from college, and I have no idea what he does afterward."

"I worry about Pia, too," said Lucia, who looked longingly for a moment at Daisy's mousse and then turned her eyes firmly away. After her separation from her husband, she had gained a great deal of weight, which had taken her a long time and a great deal of effort to take off. She had no intention of going through that torment ever again. "She's so silent, so withdrawn. I never know what's going on in her head. If she'd ever do anything as normal as get a crush on a boy, I'd be delighted. I'd love to see her happy, excited." Her eyes filled with tears. "We did a terrible thing to her, Nick and I."

"You did nothing," said Katrinka firmly.

"If anyone's to blame, darling, it's Nick," said Daisy. "You did the best you could in the circumstances."

Over the years, Nick Cavalletti's involvement with the Mafia, at first as a defense attorney, and finally, as some suggested, as *consigliere,* had brought him more and more notoriety. To get their daughter away from the increasingly sensational press coverage, Nick and Lucia had withdrawn her from school in Manhattan and sent her to a convent in Florence, not far from their vacation home in Fiesole. There Pia had remained, throughout Nick's trial and conviction on a number of felony counts, throughout her parents' separation and divorce. She was still there, at university in Florence.

"Sometimes I think I should never have sent her away," said Lucia.

"That's nonsense," said Alexandra, who had been horrified at the time by the abuse Pia was suffering at the hands of her classmates. "You had to get her out of that school."

"Anyway, you were in Fiesole all time when she was young. You did leave her only to go to meetings."

"She seems so sad to me sometimes, so lonely."

"She had good time with Martin, in St. Moritz," said Zuzka, who had been delighted to see the tense, unhappy look gone from Martin's face.

"Yes, she did, I think," said Lucia, smiling finally.

"Well, both she and Martin are invited for winter break in February," said Daisy, "if you think they'd enjoy a return visit so soon."

"That's very sweet of you, Daisy."

"Oh, you know how Riccardo and I love a house full of children. And none of his or mine are free in February." Daisy had hoped at least one of her sons could make it, but they were going to the Bahamas instead. And her daughter, of course, was in no condition to ski.

"Are you matchmaking?" asked Alexandra. "They're babies. Both of them." Martin would soon be twenty-one, and Pia twenty.

"Of course not," said Lucia.

"It was just good to see Martin laugh," said Zuzka.

"My two are growing so fast," said Alexandra. "Before you know it, they'll be dating." Her oldest, a girl, was eight. "Not to mention having sex," she added unhappily.

"One advantage of sending Pia to a convent school in Italy, I didn't have to worry about that. Or, at least, not very much."

The mention of sex reminded Daisy of Christian, who was by far the sexiest young man she had encountered in a long time. And, as one of the few people in the world willing to tackle head-on Katrinka's wall of reserve, she turned to her friend and said, "Now, tell us how that handsome son of yours is doing."

"I still can't believe it," said Zuzka, reverting to Czech for a moment. When Katrinka had phoned Zuzka to tell her about Christian, Zuzka, like Tomáš, had been shocked and hurt; but, in the weeks since, she had come to understand the reasons for Katrinka's silence.

"Sometimes neither do I," replied Katrinka, in English. "He's wonderful. Fabulous." He was difficult, too, moody, unpredictable, but that she preferred to overlook when she could. "I still can't believe I did find him."

After lunch, the women caravaned in their cars the two blocks to the new town house for their first look at it. Carlos conducted the grand tour, leading the five of them around sawhorses and paint cans, over electrical cables and toolboxes. Though the major construction was finished, the house was still a shambles, but each had had enough experience decorating to be able to see, at least dimly, what the final result would be. In any event, knowing Carlos and Katrinka, they trusted that it would be splendid.

Once the women had left, Katrinka spent half an hour going over fabric swatches and furniture designs with the designer. Then Luther drove her back to the Praha, where she chaired an executive committee meeting, and afterward began returning phone calls. She was in the middle of one, discussing with her accountant the cost of changing the name of the two hotels when Robin, who had been instructed not to interrupt, entered and handed her a note saying that Christian was calling and wanted to speak to her immediately. Katrinka could imagine the tone in which he had made his request, charming but insistent, leaving no doubt that he intended to have his way or raise hell. Tempted to have Robin tell him that she would get back to him as soon as possible, as she might have Adam, or even Mark, in similar circumstances, she nevertheless told her accountant she would phone him back shortly. Her relationship with her son was still too new and uncertain for her to take chances. Not only did she still have to win his love, she was sure she had yet to convince him of hers.

"Sorry," said Robin. "He said it was now or never."

Katrinka smiled reassuringly as she pushed the flickering red light on her phone. "It's not your fault. He's a brat. Christian," she said when she heard his soft breath on the line, "what is so important you have to be rude to Robin?"

"Did she say I was rude?" As usual, they spoke in German, Christian's native language and one Katrinka had learned to speak during her years working in Munich and Kitzbühel.

"I could tell from the look on her face."

"She has a lovely face, I remember. I would hate to upset her."

"Think of that the next time you phone."

"If I phone . . ."

Katrinka took a deep breath. It was the kind of blackmail Christian was fond of using, though in fact he had begun to call her regularly. "Why did you call?"

"Because I wanted to speak to my mother, who clearly is not so anxious to speak to me."

"You know that's not true, Christian," said Katrinka patiently. "But I was in the middle of an important conversation."

"Call me anytime, you told me. Anywhere."

"Christian, you're impossible," snapped Katrinka finally. "You know very well what I meant."

"That you'd get back to me when it was convenient for you?" All the pretense of teasing humor was gone from his voice. "That if it wasn't you'd get rid of me, the way you did when I was born."

On some level, Katrinka understood that Christian was trying to

47

manipulate her and knew that she ought to make some effort to resist. In more rational moments, the fact that she had been only twenty, grief-stricken, and pressured by an unscrupulous doctor into giving up her child for adoption, that she had regretted her decision bitterly from the beginning and had spent countless years and a considerable fortune searching for him, helped Katrinka to moderate her guilt. But, when confronted by her son in one of his moods, she was often overwhelmed by it. "You know that's not true," she said, defending herself. "You know I love you more than my life and I always have."

"I know nothing of the kind," he said, returning to his normal, rather cool, cynically humorous tone. "I know only what you say. And what you do. And that today you seem to be extremely irritated that I called you."

"I am delighted you called me. I always am. You know that," said Katrinka coaxingly, making an effort to shift the direction of the conversation. "I miss you. It seems so long since I've seen you. In fact, I have to go to London next week. And I thought, when I've finished my business, I'd come see you in Bonn." He was studying for his PhD in economics there.

"That would be very nice, of course . . ."

"But?" she said, hearing the hesitancy in his voice.

"My parents have forbidden me to see you."

"Then you've told them?" When he had left New York before Christmas, Christian had made it clear to Katrinka that he had no intention of informing the Hellers that he had met his mother until he was sure how he felt about her. That he had told them filled Katrinka with a sudden surge of happiness. And relief. He had made his decision then. He meant to stay in her life. All the rest was games. And those she could play, if she had to.

"Obviously," said Christian.

"And they're upset?"

Christian laughed, a not very pleasant sound. "Upset? Furious. They paid a great deal of money for me, you know. I'm a valuable asset. A handsome, intelligent son with an excellent future in front of him. They intend to keep me."

Katrinka did not believe him for a moment. Yes, the Hellers had bought Christian illegally from the doctor who had run the clinic where Katrinka had given birth to her son. But if they were as unfeeling as Christian said, why would they have gone to so much trouble and expense to get him? Surely, no matter how much he protested, his parents loved him, and that was reason enough for them to feel so

threatened by her sudden reappearance in his life. "And do you intend
to do what they say?" she asked, completely certain of his answer.

"In normal circumstances, of course, I would not dream of listening
to them."

"Why is it I hear another 'but' coming . . ."

"Well, you see, they have threatened to cut off my allowance."

It was Katrinka's turn to laugh, but with pure, unadulterated delight.
Her life had been so rich in other things, she had never felt poor, not
even when she had had little money. But she nevertheless had a good
sense of its worth, valuing it less for the luxuries it bought than the
freedom, and the power, it bestowed. "Do your parents have any idea
of how rich I am?"

"They are not my parents," he said quickly, obviously irritated, then
continued, as if genuinely curious, "Are you very rich?"

"Very," she assured him.

He laughed again. "Then, by all means, come to Bonn."

"A little blackmail?" said Mark when Katrinka repeated the conversation to him. They were at home, dressing for a dinner neither
particularly wanted to attend.

Katrinka stopped trying to twist her hair into a becoming knot on top
of her head and turned to look at Mark. "He did not mean it that way,"
she said, leaping to her son's defense.

"No, then how did he mean it?"

"It doesn't matter to him whether or not I have money." Mark raised
a questioning eyebrow and Katrinka, irritated, continued, "But he
knows how important it is for him to get that degree."

Mark considered a number of replies and thought better of them all.
"I don't want to argue about Christian," he said. The problem was he
didn't like the boy. The *man*, he corrected himself. Christian was
twenty-three years old, about to finish graduate school, about to enter
the high-pressure world of German business. And if ever he had seen a
person qualified to hold his own in that cutthroat arena, it was
Christian.

"Neither do I," agreed Katrinka, turning back to the mirror, picking
up her hairbrush, and resuming her efforts to coax her hair into an
upsweep.

"Leave it down," said Mark.

"It's such a mess."

"I like it."

Her eyes met his in the mirror and she smiled. "Anything you say."

"Anything?"

"Almost," she said.

Mark laughed. "Do you always tell the truth?"

"If I can't," she said, smiling at him happily, "I do try not to say anything at all." She got up, walked to her closet, and took the dress that the maid had left hanging on the door. It was a black velvet Oscar de la Renta ball gown. She stepped into it and went to Mark to zip up the back.

"Mmm," he said, as he raised the zipper. "You smell wonderful."

It was the most expensive perfume in the world, and Mark had given it to her for Christmas. "I am glad you do like it, considering what it cost you."

"Good enough to eat," he said, kissing the back of her neck.

She turned and faced him. "Will it always be this good?"

For a moment, he looked down at the growing bulge of her stomach, then gently rested his hand on it. "Probably not," he said, "but good enough. At least I hope so, and not just for our sake."

"Do you always tell the truth?" she said, smiling at him.

"I try to." He kissed her lightly on the nose, then stepped away from her. "Come on. Unless you've changed your mind and we don't have to go," he added hopefully.

"I promised," she said, regretting as much as he did that, instead of the opera at the Met they had planned to attend, they were to spend the evening listening to no doubt boring speeches and eating rubber chicken at a political dinner. "You know," she added as Mark helped her into her coat, then took her hand and led her toward the door, "I think I will ask Christian to come with us to St. Moritz for his winter break." They had rented a house for two weeks, across the road from Daisy and Riccardo's. "Pia and Martin will be there to keep him company. Anyway, it will be good for us all to spend time together."

Mark's first instinct was to protest, but he quickly buried it. He had no right, he knew, to come between Katrinka and the relationship she was trying to build with her son. "Why not?" he said. "There's plenty of room."

Six

"WHY, KATRINKA, HOW LOVELY TO SEE YOU, MY DEAR. AND, MARK, HOW NICE OF YOU TO COME," SAID NINA Graham, trying to force some warmth into her voice.

Hoping her surprise did not show, Katrinka smiled as politely as possible and leaned forward to kiss Nina's smooth, powdered cheek. Bouffant hair lacquered into place, she looked lovely in a gray Mary McFadden gown that exactly matched her eyes. The gown was one Katrinka remembered from many past galas: Nina Graham was not one to splurge on clothes. But surely she had had a face-lift recently? "Nina, what you doing here?" asked Katrinka. She had stopped calling her "mother" sometime before the divorce.

"Supporting my dear friend, the senator from Rhode Island," said Nina, sounding almost coy as she turned to the handsome, gray-haired man at her side in the receiving line and continued, "Darling, I'd like you to meet my former daughter-in-law, Katrinka, and her husband, Mark van Hollen."

"You're every bit as beautiful as Nina told me," said Russell Luce III, beaming at Katrinka, lying gallantly as befits a politician. On the subject of Katrinka, Nina was always less than flattering. "Glad to meet you, Mark," he went on smoothly, his handshake practiced, hearty. Tall, slender, with delicate pink-tinged skin and watery blue eyes, he was in his late sixties, Katrinka estimated, a few years younger than the woman at his side.

The four exchanged pleasantries for a few moments, then Katrinka and Mark moved on, their places immediately taken by another couple in the long line of wealthy New Yorkers who hoped that a contribution to the reelection campaign of the incumbent senator from Rhode Island might, in the future, sway a vote in the direction of their pressing business interests. What made Russell Luce particularly appealing to those who had gathered on his behalf, a group not noted for their willingness to support lost causes, was the certainty of his reelection: he had held his seat without serious challenge or hint of scandal for eighteen years, and he had had the good fortune not to sit on the controversial Judiciary Committee that had confirmed Clarence Thomas to the Supreme Court.

"If I did know she would be here, I would never have said yes," said Katrinka as she and Mark moved down the stairs from the gallery into the Plaza Hotel's white-and-gold baroque ballroom. She searched the room with anxious eyes. "Do you see Adam?"

"It doesn't matter," said Mark, slipping a possessive arm around her waist. They were bound to meet sooner or later and that night was as good a time as any, he supposed. "Nina called the senator 'darling.'"

"I heard." Katrinka shrugged. "But I did never hear her mention his name before."

"Well, let's hope she's getting laid. And that it mellows her out. Then maybe she'll stop bugging you." Since Katrinka's return from her honeymoon, Nina had called several times, each time to complain, with undiminished energy, about Katrinka's dishonesty in not only keeping Christian a secret from Adam and the "family," but marrying Mark without giving due notice to that same sacred group.

"Mark, shhh, someone will hear you," said Katrinka.

"Do you care?" asked Mark.

Katrinka looked at her new husband and considered his question for a moment. In his double-breasted Brioni tuxedo, he was the essence of elegance, a match for any man in the room, no matter how blue his blood or old his money. But it was Mark's underlying brashness that appealed to her most, that hint of the kid from the streets of Pittsburgh that both turned her on and made her feel comfortable. They were alike, kindred spirits, people from nowhere, who had made good because of intelligence, hard work, guts, and—they were both quick to admit—good luck. "No," she said, slipping her hand into his and following as he led her through the crowd to the table whose number the hostess, waiting at the bottom of the stairs, had given them.

An orchestra, for the moment playing background music, was seated on the stage at the far end of the room. The dance floor was surrounded by tables covered in gold-colored linen with centerpieces of cymbidium orchids. Each table was set for eight or ten, with a complement of delicate gilt-trimmed chairs. Theirs was a table for eight, noted Katrinka.

Alexandra and Neil had already arrived but were still standing, talking to Warren Buffett, who had been brought in to salvage the reputation of Salomon Brothers after the treasury bill scandal.

"Asking for advice?" whispered Mark as they approached the Goodmans. The word on the street was that Knapp Manning, Neil's company, was in trouble, though speculation ran that it was financial, not legal.

"I do hope so," said Katrinka softly. Alexandra was a good friend, and she was worried about her.

Not that there seemed to be much to worry about, if looks were anything to go by. Neil seemed solid and prosperous in his tuxedo, and amazingly sexy despite his thinning hair brilliantined back from his bald crown and his perfectly trimmed, bushy mustache. Alexandra was wild about that mustache, claiming it to be the best sex-aid device ever invented. She looked fabulous in a Bob Mackie gown with a high-necked beaded bodice, its long draped skirt slit to display a significant amount of firm, well-exercised thigh. Her long red hair was piled high on her head. A pair of diamond tassel pendants, a Chanukah present from Neil, hung from her ears, and on her finger sparkled a twenty-carat Winston diamond. She looked as rich and as happy as she had always longed to be.

Katrinka and Mark joined the group, which grew and contracted in turn as Buffett left but Carl Icahn and his wife, Liba, stopped to chat, then moved off again, and others came and went, until finally Katrinka heard the voice she had been dreading. "You look lovely, Katrinka," said Adam, bending forward to kiss her cheek. "A new dress?"

He looked better than he had when she had last seen him a few days before, far more rested. In fact, he looked very handsome, she decided, in the Armani tux she remembered going with him to buy. Though without Mark's almost perfect features, Adam with his salt-and-pepper hair, his long, narrow face, his close-set eyes, and crooked grin was a very attractive man, with all the sex appeal that charm and money could bestow. Thank God, none of that affected her at all anymore.

"Yes, brand-new," she said, pleased not to have to offer him an excuse or an explanation. For someone as rich as he, Adam had

53

frequently been resentful of the amount she squandered (as he put it) on clothes, even though it was often her own money that she spent and not nearly as much as he liked to think.

"You'd never even know you were pregnant, the way that sash falls. Hello, Mark."

The two men shook hands cordially as a number of people in the room turned to watch, hoping that the encounter might lead to something more dramatic than a polite exchange of greetings. From across the room, Sabrina, the columnist, observed them, her small eyes narrowed in concentration, her pudding face folding into a frown as nasty lines for tomorrow's column composed themselves in her head. Her gown, as usual, looked as if it could use pressing and her hair a shampoo. Katrinka saw her and barely suppressed a shudder. Sabrina smiled, nodded in the regal manner she liked to assume, and turned back to her escort, a young designer named Alan Platt, whose clothes Katrinka rather liked. Only one of a number of press sent to cover the event, Sabrina conducted herself as if she were there by special invitation.

"I'd like you to meet Tashi Davis," said Adam, drawing his date closer into the circle. Wearing a dramatic silver-beaded slip dress, she was instantly recognizable as one of the world's leading models. She was almost as tall as Adam, beautiful, and black.

"We've met," said Katrinka, who had been introduced to the model the year before in Paris. She smiled reassuringly at Tashi, who clearly found the situation a little awkward. It wasn't easy meeting ex-wives shortly after messy divorces, even when you weren't particularly involved with their former spouses. She and Adam had only just met.

Adam kissed Alexandra, shook Neil's hand, said he would be back later to claim a dance from each of the women, and ushered Tashi away, pausing briefly to hug the arriving Daisy, who watched with mouth slightly agape while Adam made his way through the crowd, his arm securely around Tashi's waist. "Well, well, well," said Daisy as she joined her friends, "I bet Nina is having a cow." Probably because everyone by now was convinced that Adam was incapable of love, no one for a moment believed that Tashi represented anything more to him than a new and intriguing way to annoy his mother, who was as bigoted a daughter of the American Revolution as it was possible to find.

Since Riccardo had not accompanied Daisy to New York, her escort for the evening was Dieter Keiser, a charming Swiss, fluent in several European languages, intelligent, exquisitely mannered, and with the gift of making himself infinitely agreeable to everyone. His divorce settlement from a Brazilian heiress paid for the necessities of his life. For the luxuries, Dieter relied on the kindness of his many acquaintances, including the Donatis. Katrinka found him amusing. Mark found him bearable in very small doses, since the charm of social parasites completely escaped him.

At Daisy's request, Dieter set about correcting the seating arrangement at the table, and was rewarded with a pleased smile. Known among her friends as "the little general," Daisy was always delighted to have matters arranged according to her own wishes, which always seemed to her to be so much more sensible than anyone else's. "I don't see any of you often enough to waste time speaking to people I don't care about at all," she said softly, before turning to welcome the arriving strangers with a cordiality and warmth that completely disarmed them. Her manners, passed down through generations of New England aristocrats, polished at the country's best finishing schools, were always perfect.

Despite the rearrangement of the guests, the table was too large and the room too noisy for consistent conversation. It splintered into subdivisions of two and four, each train of thought constantly interrupted as the focus shifted to the left or right as questions and manners dictated. The group compared holiday plans; they discussed mutual friends, Broadway shows, the previous night's Knicks' game; and, thanks to the presence of Senator Luce, they launched briefly into politics and found at least one point of agreement: no one at the table was at all happy with the way George Bush was running the economy.

Dinner was served. The senator made a speech, saying very much what he had been saying for all his eighteen years in office. Between courses, there was dancing, ballroom music for the older folks alternating with disco for the younger. Katrinka danced every dance.

"You've still got more stamina than I do," said Rick Colins, stopping in the middle of the dance floor and taking Katrinka's arm to lead her back to her table. "Even if you are pregnant."

"It's because I do take care of myself," said Katrinka, her smile not quite able to conceal the worry in her eyes. Heartbroken when Carlos Medina had left him for Sir Alex Holden-White, a curator at the Victoria and Albert Museum, Rick had finally seemed to pull his life together. He was writing and dating again, and had managed to halt the sag in the ratings of his cable television show. But no one was really convinced that he had recovered.

"A likely story," said Rick. "I bet you don't get more than five hours of sleep a night."

"Five or six," agreed Katrinka. "I don't need more."

"Neither do I." He was out every night, too late, making the rounds of the gay bars, and then he almost always brought someone home with him. Rarely did he get to sleep before dawn, if then. "Carlos is in town, I hear," he added, as casually as he could manage.

"Yes," said Katrinka. "He is working on my new house."

"Give him my love when you see him."

"I will," said Katrinka as Rick kissed her cheek, said good-bye to the others, and moved on to circulate, gathering gossip for his show the next day.

"You wore Rick out. Don't you think you should take it a little easy?" asked Alexandra, who had had two difficult pregnancies.

"So I keep telling her," said Mark, who was not sure whether to worry about the effect that Katrinka's boundless energy might have on her and the child, or be grateful for her continuing stamina and high spirits. His every attempt to coddle her ended in failure.

"I feel great," said Katrinka. She was positive this pregnancy would duplicate her last one, when she had barely shown until her eighth month and had kept active right until she gave birth to her son. The fact that she had then been nineteen and was now forty-three did not weigh with her at all.

Adam came and claimed his dance, unfortunately a foxtrot, which made talking possible. "You've decided to give in about the hotel names, I understand. You could have called and told me yourself," he added.

Katrinka, who had made up her mind never to deal with him directly unless absolutely necessary, ignored the comment. "It seemed a better idea than fighting you," was all she said.

"If only you'd always felt that way."

"Oh, I don't know," she said lightly. "I think I never really did fight you enough." With the single exception of his decision to buy Olympic Pictures, she had always cheered him on. Not that arguing with him would have had much effect, except perhaps that their marriage would have ended sooner. As it was, she reminded herself, it had ended at exactly the right time for her to be ready when Mark entered her life. The thought brought a brilliant smile to her face.

In response, Adam frowned, and for a moment Katrinka wondered what it was that she had done to annoy him again, since it was unlikely that he had read her mind. But then she realized he was not looking at her. "What it is?" she asked. Twisting her head to follow the line of his gaze, she saw Nina Graham dancing with Senator Luce, his body bowed to accommodate her five-foot-two height, his cheek resting against her lacquered hair.

"Nothing," said Adam, relapsing into silence until the song ended and he returned Katrinka to her table.

When Adam went off again with Daisy, Katrinka leaned across the empty chair separating them and said to Alexandra, "Is something going on between Nina and Russell Luce?"

Alexandra looked around to see who could overhear them, but there was no one. Dieter and Neil seemed to be enjoying each other's conversation, though what they had in common was difficult to imagine, and Mark was on the floor dancing with the wife of one of his business associates. "They're getting married," said Alexandra softly. Her mother, who was somehow distantly related to the Grahams, always managed to keep up with family gossip. "Adam and Clementine are having fits." Clementine was Adam's older sister, and, lacking the beauty and charm that took some of the sting from Nina's selfishness and snobbery, an even more unpleasant person than her mother.

"Why?"

Alexandra took a cigarette out of her gold case and asked, "Do you mind if I smoke?"

Katrinka did, but, knowing how Alexandra relied on cigarettes to take some of the edge off her anxiety, she shook her head and said, "They should be happy. Playing hostess for a senator would take a lot of time. Maybe she would stop interfering so much in their lives."

"Hmm," said Alexandra, taking a puff on her long filtered cigarette. "Part of it is the money."

Katrinka looked surprise. "But Kenneth did not leave so much."

"Not by Adam's standards, perhaps. But he doesn't like the idea of her wasting whatever there is on Russell Luce. And neither does Clementine. His wife died last year, of cancer. It was a long illness, and the word is that he used up all they had taking care of her." Alexandra shrugged. "Anyway, it costs so much to get elected these days, politicians never seem to have enough. Nina's picking up part of the cost of the dinner tonight. And she's thrown any number of parties for him over the past couple of months in Rhode Island."

Katrinka looked across the room and could just see Nina and Russell Luce, arms linked, talking to Henry Kissinger. "She does look so happy," said Katrinka, with an amazing lack of hostility toward the woman who had rarely treated her with anything other than coldness and contempt, resenting the "nobody" her son had dragged home from Europe and married.

"And she's older than he is, of course."

"At their age, it does matter? She looks fabulous."

"Who do you think did her face?"

"Who?"

"Steven Hoefflin. Last October when Nina was in L.A. supposedly visiting Adam."

"He did Daisy's."

"I know." Alexandra rested her fingers against her jawline and said, "What do you think? Is it time yet?"

"No," said Katrinka. "You look fabulous."

"Would you do it?"

"Absolutely," said Katrinka, who did not understand at all the people who took moral positions against it, or all the fuss that was made about it in the press. "My face and anything else that did need it. Why not look as good as you can?" She turned as Adam returned Daisy to the table and said, "Alexandra and I were just saying how happy your mother does look."

"Yes. She does, doesn't she? If you'll excuse me, I haven't introduced Tashi to her yet," he said, moving off.

"What did I tell you?" said Daisy as Dieter took her by the hand and led her back onto the dance floor.

However, Nina seemed completely delighted to meet Adam's new girlfriend. But, then, her social mask had been so well constructed, so carefully preserved, so polished after years of use, it was not likely to crack in public. "I've seen your face everywhere," she gushed a little, her small head tilted to take in Tashi's extraordinary height, "and thought how very beautiful you are. Trust my son to leave no stone unturned until he found you," she added, leaving Tashi to feel, despite Nina's smile and the apparent kindness of the words, that she had indeed crawled out from under some rock. Making others doubt that they quite measured up to her high standards was a skill that Nina Graham had honed to perfection.

"Pleased to meet you," said Tashi politely, mustering the smile that had dazzled countless readers of fashion magazines.

"It's good to see you looking so radiant," said Adam.

"Is it?" said Nina brightly. "I must say I do feel very, very well." She cast a fond look in Russell Luce's direction, then turned back to Adam. "I had no idea I would find politics so entertaining."

"I only wish the rest of us did," he said dryly, wishing he could make his disapproval of his mother's new romance more obvious. Unfortunately, Russell Luce had been useful to him in the past, steering defense contracts his way, and might be useful again. Adam didn't want to risk alienating him.

"You will be home this weekend, won't you?" asked Nina.

"Your birthday," said Adam, who had had a frantic phone call from Clementine about the weekend's plans. "Nothing would keep me away," he added, bending to kiss his mother's cheek. "And Tashi's dying to see the house, I've told her so much about it." He turned to Tashi, who nodded brightly in agreement, though this was the first she'd heard of it. "You can count on both of us." He smiled again and steered Tashi away.

Nina quickly banished the outraged expression from her face and turned to greet Sabrina, a person she would never have acknowledged if Russell had not asked her to be particularly nice to the press. Even for that she would not have done it, except that she had decided she would quite like to be a senator's wife. The Luces were an old and distinguished Rhode Island family, with a long history of service to their country. A Luce had attended the Continental Congress, another had been elected to the first state legislature, a descendant had served as secretary of state. Russell would make an admirable husband, she thought.

"I'm busy this weekend," said Tashi, as soon as she was out of earshot of Nina.

"Oh, are you?" said Adam, not sounding particularly unhappy to hear it. "Too bad." His decision to include Tashi in the birthday celebration had been taken without thought, prompted by a sudden urge to annoy his mother. Now, he weighed the pleasure to be had from upsetting his entire family, against the very uncomfortable weekend he would no doubt have in Newport if Tashi was with him, and decided against coaxing her to break whatever plans she had. "We'll do it another time, then. It really is a lovely old house," he added. Though Adam did not particularly like it, still to him it represented the Grahams, the family, and a long history of which he was very proud.

As Adam led her back onto the dance floor, Tashi smiled and said politely, "Sure," though even after such a brief meeting she could not imagine a fate worse than two days spent in Nina Graham's company.

Looking over Tashi's shoulder, Adam could see Nina talking to Sabrina, and when the steps of the dance turned them around, Katrinka and Mark, arm-in-arm, making their way toward the exit. Why didn't he feel happier? he wondered. More satisfied? So many things had gone his way that week. The negotiations with the Italians for the sale of Olympic Pictures were going well. Thanks to the seed he had planted in Charles Wolf's brain, Sabrina had left the van Hollen papers, causing Mark a few bad moments, he was sure, with more to come, if all went as he planned. And he had bluffed Katrinka into giving up the use of the Graham name, at great cost to herself and none at all to him. What more did he need? he wondered, disturbed by the discontent he felt. What more?

Seven

"THE GUY IS DRIVING ME FUCKING CRAZY," SAID ADAM, GLARING ACROSS HIS DESK AT LUCIA DI CAMPO, who looked more exasperated than angry. They were in Adam's New York office, which, like the house in Los Angeles, was decorated in the minimalist style he preferred, in subtle grays and black lacquer, with streamlined leather couches and Italian glass-and-chrome furniture. It was on the thirty-second floor of the Seagram Building, with a view overlooking Madison Avenue and the Racquet and Tennis Club of which Adam was a member, as his father had been before him.

"He's a little anxious, that's all," said Lucia.

"Anxious! He's hysterical."

"He wants to win, Adam. Surely you can understand that?"

"Well, tell him for me, the way to win is to keep your eye on the goal and, for Christ's sake, to stay calm."

"Tell him yourself," she snapped, starting to gather up the drawings she had strewn across Adam's desk.

"Where are you going?" he asked. "I thought this meeting was about Charles Wolf's yacht." He sounded as if it were her fault that somehow they had not yet reached that item on the agenda.

"So did I. But so far all we've done is fight about Patrick. And I'm sick of it, Adam."

Adam ran a hand through his hair. "Okay," he said. "Sorry. Not another word out of me. To you, that is," he added, seeing no point in antagonizing her further. "Anything else I have to say to Patrick, I'll say directly." Lucia and Adam had met at MIT, where they were both studying marine engineering. Briefly, they had been lovers. And that might have been the end of their relationship had Lucia not been such a talented designer. When he had bought his first shipyard, she had gone to work for him and had been part of the team responsible for making Graham Marine a success. Since going free-lance, she had continued to design for him, creating the interiors of some of his largest and most prestigious yachts, including his own *Lady Katrinka.* He respected her, more than he respected any woman, with the possible exception of his former wife. He also valued Lucia's friendship, which he had managed to keep despite her divided loyalties at the time of his divorce from Katrinka. As far as he was concerned, Lucia had only one real failing, her tendency to get involved with the wrong men (himself excluded, of course). Nick, her ex-husband, despite his law degree, was a gangster; and Patrick Kates, despite his impeccable ancestry, was a con man. "Only remember," said Adam, not able to resist another comment, "I *want* him to win the America's Cup. It's in my best interests that he does. A win would be a triumph for Graham Marine as well as for Patrick Kates. I am *not* trying to sabotage him."

"Adam," said Lucia, having had more than enough, "not another word, or I really am going to leave."

Lucia had resisted getting involved with Patrick Kates first because she was part of the Graham Marine design team building the yachts he would use to defend the America's Cup; then, and more importantly, because Adam was a major player in the syndicate underwriting the costs of the defense, and the two men had been at each other's throats, over plans, over money, almost from the beginning. Patrick repeatedly accused Adam of not using his connections in the yachting community effectively enough to raise financing and pressured him to make up the cash shortfall as backers failed to rally to the cause quickly enough, while Adam, for his part, adamantly refused to contribute more as his own financial condition worsened. Lucia, who knew the risks of mixing business with romance in the best of circumstances, had decided to keep well away from the battle. But, finally, she had allowed Patrick to convince her that her fears were foolish.

"You and Patrick have to work this out between you," she continued. "I refuse to be in the middle. I've told him that, and now I'm telling you."

But from the moment she had gone to bed with Kates, the middle was where she had been and where, unfortunately, she was doomed to stay, thought Adam as he smiled in apology. Kates was too much of a hothead to deal with directly. And there was no possibility of Adam's pulling out. Graham Marine had sunk too much money it could ill afford into the project already. Plus which, there was the very enticing prospect of winning the America's Cup in May. "My apologies again," he said. "And my lips are sealed. On the subject of Patrick Kates, at any rate. Let's have a look at these drawings," he added, beginning finally to pay attention to the sketches Lucia had made for Charles Wolf's yacht.

They bickered for a while over details, as they always did, Lucia giving in more often than not because she respected Adam's opinion, Adam conceding when Lucia stood firm because he trusted not only her ability but her taste. If his ego prevented him from feeling fortunate that he had such a talented designer working with him, at least he was willing to admit that they made a good team. When they had finished their discussion of the drawings, he looked up at her and smiled. "They're terrific. I think Wolf will be very happy. Once you've made the changes we've discussed."

"Of course," she agreed, returning the smile. "Where and when are we meeting with him?"

"He'll be in St. Moritz early next month. I thought that might suit all of us."

"When?" asked Lucia. And when Adam told her the dates, she said, "Perfect. I won't have to make a special trip. I'll be there."

"You're staying with Daisy?" asked Adam, hoping his curiosity did not show too much.

"Yes," she said. "Pia will be with me."

Adam didn't bother to inquire about Patrick, as he knew where he would be for most of February—in San Diego, for the second round of the defender selection series. "Daisy usually puts together a full house," said Adam, when Lucia didn't volunteer any more information. "Will her kids be there?"

"I don't think so. Neither will Riccardo's. But Martin Havlíček is coming. I don't know who else," she said firmly, refusing to satisfy what she knew was his curiosity about Katrinka and Mark.

"Don't tell me Katrinka won't be there," said Adam, since hinting had got him nowhere. "I can't believe she'd give up February in St. Moritz, even if she is pregnant," he added, not quite able to keep the bitterness out of his voice.

"Let it go, Adam," said Lucia quietly, though she had promised herself she would mind her own business.

"Let what go?"

"Katrinka. The marriage. Everything."

"I don't know what you're talking about."

"I just get the feeling that you've still got one foot in your old life, while Katrinka's moved on. That's all. I think it's time for you to move on, too."

"You think I'm still in love with her?" he said, his voice angry, belligerent.

"I hope not. Because if you are, what you did was not only cruel, it was incredibly stupid."

"I'm not," he said firmly.

"Good."

Adam watched as Lucia zippered up her portfolio, then said, "I hear you're designing Khalid's new yacht." Khalid ibn Hassan was a Saudi prince for whom Graham Marine had built two yachts, both designed by Lucia.

"Uh huh," said Lucia, looking wary, not quite sure whether Adam had tossed her a conversational ball or a live grenade.

"And Amels is building it?" Amels Holland was one of the world's top custom yacht builders and Graham Marine's chief rival.

"Yes," said Lucia.

"You tried to steer him my way, I suppose?"

"Adam, you've got to be joking. Even if I'd had the nerve to suggest it, do you think he would have listened? Khalid's fond of me, but not that fond. I'd have ended up losing the commission."

"And that mattered more to you than loyalty to me?"

Resisting the urge to point out that he was possibly the least qualified person in the world to talk about loyalty, she said only, "Please try for once to be reasonable."

"I am being very reasonable. Anyone else would have fired you from the Wolf project."

"Well, you've got a hell of a nerve trying to blame me for Khalid's taking his business elsewhere," snapped Lucia, losing her temper finally. "If you cared so much about keeping it, maybe you shouldn't have fucked his wife."

"They were divorced at the time, if you remember. They had been for quite some time."

"Oh really?" said Lucia, not trying to keep the sarcasm from her voice. "And you thought that made it all right? As charming, as intelligent as he is, as westernized as he seems, in Saudi, Khalid keeps his wives veiled and in a harem. Did you really think he'd put up with a business associate sleeping with one of them? Especially Natalie. He was crazy about her. He was devastated when she left him."

"That had nothing to do with me, and he knows it."

Lucia took a deep breath, then said more calmly, "If you don't get it, Adam, I don't know what more I can say to explain. But trust me on this, Graham Marine will never build another yacht for Khalid. Never."

"Convince him to meet with me."

"You want to see him, pick up a phone, Adam. Call him." As soon as she said it, she realized that Adam had no doubt already tried to reach Khalid. She also realized what his asking her to broker a meeting implied. "Just how much trouble is Graham Marine in?" she asked.

Again he ran his hand through his hair. "We're okay," he said, unable to admit even to one of his closest friends the extent of his financial worries. "But in this economic climate, I don't like to let anything slip through my fingers." He grinned. "I hate letting someone as rich as Khalid get away. There aren't a lot of customers for custom-built yachts these days."

"Tell me about it," said Lucia, who, since the stock market crash of 1987, had watched her commissions dwindle to few and far between. At the time of the divorce, everyone had told her she was crazy not to ask for some sort of settlement from Nick, but, as far as she was concerned, all Nick had was blood money, and she wanted no part of it. However, with a rich mother, and the income from investments she had made herself over the years, Lucia could afford the luxury of a conscience. She knew others were not so lucky.

As Lucia picked up her coat, Adam came around the desk to help her into it. "You should get Kates to buy you a fur," he said.

"If I wanted one," said Lucia, "I could get one for myself." She smiled ruefully. "And we both know Patrick only spends money on boats."

"You could do better," said Adam. Patrick Kates was the sort of old-money American Adam despised: spoiled, demanding, living on shrinking capital, not in the least inclined to work for a living, expecting everyone to hand him what he wanted on demand. But he was a good sailor. Adam had to grant him that.

"I'm doing just fine," said Lucia. Then, as she turned again to face him, unable to resist, she asked, "Do you still see Natalie?"

Adam hesitated and then said, "Yes, I see her. We've stayed friends. Romantically, she's a little too temperamental for my tastes, a little too neurotic."

A pity he hadn't realized that before wrecking his marriage, thought Lucia, with some bitterness.

"I must have been crazy to get involved with her in the first place," he added. Looking back on it now, Adam sometimes couldn't believe that he had done it, that he had let himself go to bed with Natalie, one of Katrinka's oldest and best friends, the former wife of one of his most valued clients. Of course, he had not expected anyone to find out about it, and still was not certain who had told Katrinka, though he had his suspicions. But once Katrinka knew, the opportunity was too good for Adam to miss. When she confronted him, he took it, not giving Prince Khalid or the possible business ramifications a thought, not really thinking at all, but moving instinctively to end his marriage. Why? Because he had felt bored, trapped. Because he believed he did not love her anymore. Because she could not give him the child, the *son*, he wanted to carry on the Graham name.

And now she was pregnant, by Mark van Hollen. The thought of it filled Adam not just with sorrow and envy, but with a fury he did not even try to understand.

"We talk on the phone every now and then, have dinner occasionally," continued Adam, turning his mind away from Katrinka to Natalie, whom some men might have seen as the source of all their troubles, the temptress who had lured them away from loyal and trusting wives, but Adam, to his credit, did not. "She's in pretty bad shape at the moment. That Australian she's been dating just told her he's getting married."

To her surprise, Lucia felt a stab of pity. Natalie seemed so alone to her. When she had left Khalid, she had fled to Los Angeles, which had seemed as far away as she could reasonably go to keep their son, Aziz, out of Khalid's reach. Natalie had known no one (which might have explained her flinging herself at Adam during one of his business trips). What remained of her family was in France, where she had been born. So, too, was the one man she trusted completely and relied on totally, Jean-Claude Gillette, her lover since she was seventeen. Then, her affair with Adam cut her off not only from Katrinka, but from the group of women friends who had welcomed her into their circle. To Lucia, all Natalie seemed to have now in the world was Aziz. And her business, of course, three boutiques in California that were reported to be doing well, despite Jean-Claude's recent withdrawal of his offer to take them over. "Has she found another investor to replace Jean-Claude?"

"That sonovabitch," said Adam, as if he had not ever been guilty of backing out of a deal with a friend. Then he shrugged. "The Australian's parting present was enough, apparently, for her to think about opening another store, in New York or Palm Beach. I tried to talk her out of it. Her West Coast boutiques are doing fine. I don't know why she can't be happy with that. Now's not the time to expand."

Lucia grinned. "I thought you were always in favor of expanding."

"Under the right conditions," said Adam, his eyes suddenly opaque, "why not?"

He was up to something, thought Lucia, who recognized the look. But what? Immediately, she suppressed her curiosity. With Adam, it was always better not to know.

His arm around her, Adam walked Lucia to the door of his office. "You wouldn't consider coming home to Newport with me for the weekend, would you?"

While her marriage to Nick Cavalletti had lowered Lucia considerably in Nina Graham's estimation, now that she was divorced she was deemed acceptable again. Though her father might have been nothing more than an immigrant Italian with pretensions to being an artist (or so Nina saw it), the Wainwrights, her mother's family, were old enough and rich enough to secure Lucia's pardon for her many sins, chief among which was her not giving a damn what any of them thought of her behavior.

"Why?"

"It's Mother's birthday. Clem will be there with Wilson and the kids. Assorted other family, I suppose. And Russell Luce, the third, God help us all."

"I suppose there's not a prayer he'll lose the election, is there?" said Lucia.

"I hope not. You know what a help he's been steering those government contracts my way." Orders for the Navy and Coast Guard had helped Graham Marine through more than a few rough patches. "But I'd still prefer that he not marry my mother. Come home with me. I'm not sure I can get through the whole weekend without some moral support."

Lucia shook her head. "Sorry. As much as I hate saying no to a favor, not a chance. Your mother will leap to the wrong conclusion and make my life hell."

"Mother is very fond of you."

"Not as a prospective wife for you. You're better off going alone."

Lucia was right, of course, given that Nina's prime qualification for a daughter-in-law at the moment was that she be young and fertile. Not only was Lucia in her mid-forties, she had only managed to produce one child during her marriage to Nick. "Maybe I'll just go for the party, and not stay the weekend."

"An excellent idea. The less time allowed for arguments the better." Lucia raised her cheek for Adam's kiss and said, "See you in St. Moritz."

The door closed after Lucia, and Adam returned to his desk, settled himself into his leather chair. There was a long list of phone calls waiting to be returned. Mac, his assistant, was waiting to discuss a few wrinkles in the deal with the Italians for Olympic Pictures. The managers of the shipyards in Bremen and Athens were concerned about falling revenues, while those in Larchmont, Miami, and New Haven had panicked. Still, he sat motionless for a few minutes, staring into space. Then, he reached into the wastepaper basket beside his desk and extracted the copy of *The Daily Register* that he had earlier tossed into it.

Instead of the single column Sabrina had been allotted in *The Chronicle*, she had the whole of *The Register*'s page seven. Featured in that day's edition were photographs taken at the dinner for Russell Luce: Luce with Nina; *Vogue*'s Shirley Lord with Alan Platt, the designer whose name Sabrina had recently made a point of mentioning in every one of her pieces, causing some speculation among insiders about a possible romance, as unlikely as that seemed; Henry Kravis and Carolyne Roehm; Robert and Georgette Mosbacher; Adam himself with Tashi Davis; and, of course, Mark and Katrinka, seemingly oblivious to the camera, deep in conversation with each other. The headline for once was harmless enough: "Gala Evening for Grand Old Man of Rhode Island Politics." In the article, Sabrina announced with absolute certainty that Nina Graham and Russell Luce III would soon be announcing their wedding, that her children, Clementine and Adam ("that handsome billionaire playboy"), were delighted with the match, that all Nina required to make her happiness complete was a double wedding with Adam and the prospect of a grandchild in the near future, all of which made Adam wonder just how many hysterical phone calls his sister was making to how many unreliable confidantes, since it certainly wasn't Nina talking. Sabrina's references to Adam were, considering the source, much kinder than they had been in the past and he suspected that Charles Wolf must have mentioned his name somehow in connection with her new job, though it was unlikely that he had given Adam credit for it. By now, Wolf was firmly convinced that he had thought of luring Sabrina away from van Hollen all by himself, which suited Adam perfectly. The less concerned Mark was about Adam's intentions, the easier it would be for Adam to carry them out.

But it was the photograph of Mark and Katrinka that held Adam's attention the longest. He studied it as if by staring at their faces he might be able to decipher their thoughts. Had he and Katrinka ever been so absorbed in each other, so totally oblivious to everyone and everything else? He supposed so, though for the life of him he couldn't remember when. What he did remember was that they had always confided their plans to each other, given good advice, supported decisions. Always, until the end.

She had a lot to be grateful to him for. But was she? He didn't think so. She seemed to have no real appreciation of how much he had done for her: marrying her and bringing her to New York, introducing her to a life of unbelievable luxury, encouraging her to go into business on her own, giving her the benefit of his financial expertise. That she seemed unaware of the enormous contributions he had made to her life irritated him. That she had turned so quickly from him to Mark van Hollen, as if they were interchangeable, offended him. The three years of their separation dwindled in his memory to no time at all as he reread Sabrina: "Mark and Katrinka van Hollen, married before the ink was dry on her divorce papers, are still apparently very much in love after a whole month of togetherness."

Lucia's words came back to him. Had Katrinka really moved on in her life while he remained stuck in the past? No, he decided, pushing the thought away. Lucia was wrong. His economic survival depended on a quick assessment of every trend. And no one who dealt as effectively with the problems he dealt with on a day-to-day basis could possibly be accused of living in the past. And if now he was more than ever determined to keep the Mark van Hollens of the world in what he perceived as their place, why should he deny himself the pleasure of adding the spice of revenge to what had always been his ambition? How could he resist demonstrating to Katrinka that van Hollen and he were not in the least interchangeable? That blood (that is, *blue* blood) and money would always triumph over money alone.

The buzzer sounded, interrupting his train of thought. Tossing *The Register* back into the basket beside his desk, he depressed the intercom button and said, "Who is it, Debbie?"

"Your mother, Mr. Graham."

Adam stifled a groan. "Tell her I'm in a meeting. And get me Charles Wolf."

"Yes, sir," she said.

Sitting back in his chair, Adam waited impatiently while Debbie dialed Wolf's number in Chicago. He was anxious to set the date of their meeting, next month in St. Moritz. He had a proposition to put to Wolf that had nothing to do with the new yacht and everything to do with Mark and Katrinka van Hollen.

"Mr. Wolf," said Debbie, her voice filtered through the intercom.

Would he take the bait? wondered Adam.

Eight

THE BELL 222 ROSE SLOWLY FROM THE TARMAC OF CELERINA'S SMALL AIRPORT, CLIMBED HIGH INTO AIR AS thin and clear as fine crystal, and headed for Piz Nair, a mountain peak a scant five minutes away. Peering out through the helicopter's Plexiglas window, Katrinka could see a ring of snow-covered Alps checkered with patches of stone pine and larch forest, above which the mountains towered bare and white, the faces of the glaciers sparkling in the bright sunlight. Between the mountains lay the bowl of the valley with the village of Celerina climbing haphazardly upward to meet St. Moritz. She could make out the tracks of the Cresta and bobsled runs snaking along the bottom edge of the slopes, and people lining the route watching what they could see of the practice, that split second when a Cresta rider on his toboggan whooshed by. The cables of the T-bars and chair lifts marked the white landscape like the sketchy lines of a small child's drawing. And the skiers, as the helicopter ascended higher and higher, faded to bright dots of moving color. Scattered here and there, on low snow-covered rises away from inhabited areas, were tiny churches with Gothic steeples and walled churchyards, relics of the plague years when it had been the custom to bury the dead outside the city limits and inside walls high enough to keep out wolves.

Smiling contentedly, Katrinka turned to Mark and said, "This was a brilliant idea." She meant the helicopter.

"I thought you'd approve."

They sat hand-in-hand, a picture of love gone right for a change, or at least for the time being, thought Christian cynically as he studied his mother and stepfather (new and—he had to admit—rather intriguing persons in his universe).

"Are you all right?" asked Katrinka, in German, turning her attention to her son. Though Christian clearly had wanted to be with her enough to quarrel with the Hellers and ignore their objections to his spending his semester break in St. Moritz, his expression was sullen, and he seemed, as always, to be more resigned than pleased to be in her company.

"Fine," replied Christian curtly. "Though you'll have to forgive me if my joy at life's blessings does not quite equal yours."

Katrinka knew that pretending to be a man of experience, unimpressed, world weary, was an act Christian put on for her benefit. But as much sympathy as she had for his situation, as hard as she knew it must be for him to forgive her, often she found the pose irritating. Life was too short to be wasted reliving the mistakes of the past, fighting old battles, righting old wrongs.

And then, inevitably, irritation would give way to guilt. "I would like you to enjoy yourself," said Katrinka softly.

"Oh, I am," said Christian, without a hint of sincerity in his tone. "Enormously."

What an impossible young man he was, thought Mark, so like Katrinka in looks, with the same prominent cheekbones, slanted eyes, and wide, full mouth; but his personality, his character, were as different from hers as his somber brown eyes were from her bright blue ones. What was his father like? wondered Mark. From Katrinka's description, nothing like Christian either. "We're almost there," said Mark cheerfully, forcing a smile, wishing he could like his stepson. Then he turned to discuss the landing site with the pilot.

Most of the people who skied Piz Nair rode the lifts to Corviglia, then took the cable car to the top. But the ski resorts in the Engadine Valley were among the oldest in the world and not quite so efficient as those in more recently developed areas. The cable cars were slow, always with long lines of people waiting to get on, each car as crowded as a New York subway at rush hour. Never willing to waste a glorious morning inside a dark hut, waiting her turn, when all she wanted was to be out on a slope, skiing, Katrinka occasionally took the helicopter service from Celerina or hitched a ride with Gianni Agnelli. This year, Mark had arranged for the helicopter he used to ferry him on short hops around Europe to be kept at Celerina while he and Katrinka were

71

there. Between their schedules and those of their friends, the Bell 222 was as busy as the local sport buses that transported passengers to and fro among the various ski areas at Celerina, St. Moritz, Silvaplana, Pontresina, and Samedan.

The helicopter sank slowly down, settling finally on a small, more or less square bit of flattened mountain top a few hundred yards from the cable car station. Leaving the propellers spinning and motor revving, the pilot leapt out, opened the door, and offered a hand to Christian, who ignored it as he dropped onto the snow and settled his goggles securely over his eyes. Mark followed him, turning to lift Katrinka out, swinging her through the air before placing her firmly on the mountain's icy surface. Despite the brilliant sun, it was cold, and Katrinka, wearing as usual only a pair of form-fitting black stretch pants that showed off her rounded stomach and a wool pullover under her short, pink, fur-trimmed jacket, shivered as she snapped closed the buckles of her boots, then hopped up and down to keep herself warm. What was taking so long? she wondered impatiently, though it took Mark and the pilot only a minute or so to maneuver the skis out of the helicopter and hand Katrinka and Christian theirs. She knocked the icy snow off her boots with her ski pole, stepped into the skis, tested to see that they were locked securely. "Ready?" she called as she turned, pointing her skis down the mountain.

"In a minute," said Mark, who had paused to give a few last-minute instructions to the pilot.

But she was too eager to wait. Over her shoulder, she called out the route she would follow, the words tumbling out in a rush, hardly finishing before she dug her poles in and pushed off, her skis gliding down Piz Nair's fast, icy surface. Jumping, she sailed over a mogul, landed firmly, and began traversing the fall line in neat, controlled parallel turns, heading toward Piz Grisch.

A momentary burst of pride lit Christian's face as he watched her, replaced a moment later by his more usual look of annoyance. Mark just laughed. As good a skier as he was, he knew he could never keep pace with his wife when she was in this kind of mood. "No point trying to catch up," he said to Christian. "If we lose one another, we'll all meet at the restaurant at one. Okay?"

Though Mark's German was fluent, he had spoken in English, which Christian knew and spoke well. "Fine," he replied, then set off in pursuit of Katrinka, not particularly wanting to catch her, but hoping at least to keep her in sight. As driven as he was to antagonize her when they were together, as impatient as he was then to get away, when they were apart, he felt anxious to be with her again. And then, irritated with himself for what he considered immature and unacceptable yearnings, he was even more impossible to her the next time they met. He felt sometimes as if he were being torn apart, the need to please his mother at war with his need to punish. He fled from her, home to Munich, to university in Bonn, to anywhere a friend would invite him, and then back again to wherever she was. What did he have to do to make her love him? was the question that preoccupied his subconscious — when it was not wondering how much she would take before refusing to see him again, how far he could push her before she said no more. His need for love warred with his desire for vengeance, his instinct to dominate with his longing to be comforted. Not that these were new feelings, new conflicts, for Christian. They had plagued him his entire life. But never before had they been focused so squarely on a single source, on a single person.

Mid-morning, at one of the lifts, Katrinka spotted Riccardo Donati's burly form and waved him over to join them. Martin and Pia, he told her, had driven to Corvatsch to ski. Daisy was somewhere on Corviglia with Lucia. Riccardo had left the house early, before the women had stirred from their beds. His time at St. Moritz, away from his studio in Florence, without the pressure of work, without the silent demands of the blocks of wood and marble, the formless pieces of metal waiting to be transformed into sculpture, was too precious for Riccardo to waste. "They're meeting us for lunch," he told Katrinka. "Not the kids, of course."

"Oh, that's too bad," said Katrinka, turning to Christian. "I wanted you to meet Martin. I've told you about him. He's the son of my friend, Tomáš." Though the two young men were so different, and Christian three years older than Martin, Katrinka could not help hoping that somehow they might become friends. The two boys were linked so closely in her mind. It was Martin's birth and all the latent maternal instincts it had stirred in Katrinka that had convinced her she must begin to search for her son. And since she had left the child in the West — in Munich — she had had no choice but to leave Czechoslovakia to do it. Without that goal she might never have dared to escape. And what would her life have been like then? She could hardly imagine. Reaching out, she touched Christian's cheek, something she rarely allowed herself to do for fear that he would flinch from her. He was so incredibly beautiful, she thought, as she felt her heart lurch with love for him. "You'll like Martin," she said. "He's bright, and good, and very handsome. All the girls are crazy about him, too."

73

"Then I expect we'll loathe each other," replied Christian, without much interest.

"Nonsense. You'll be great friends," said Katrinka with determined optimism as she climbed up into the chair lift next to him.

Corviglia, almost two thousand feet lower than Piz Nair, was in every other way more significant. It was the left chamber of St. Moritz's heart, the right being Badrutt's Palace Hotel. Reached by tram from St. Moritz or by gondola and chair lift from Celerina, on first sight it was nothing more than a flattened bit of snow-capped mountain dotted at intervals with ramshackle wooden structures. One of these housed the machinery for the cable car to Piz Nair. Several others were chair-lift stations to and from various other parts of the mountain. The largest was a vast multilevel structure that included the tram station, the ski school, public toilets, a deck where people sunbathed in full gear, a convenience stand, a cafeteria, and an excellent restaurant run by Hartley Matthis, master chef and restaurateur. But the most significant building, dropping off the mountain behind the tram station, almost out of sight, was the Corviglia Ski Club, considered by its members to be the most exclusive club in the Alps, perhaps in Europe, perhaps in the world. Numbered among them, distinguished by blood and money, were an assortment of titles: dons and barons, earls and viscounts, marquises and comtesses. Albert and Caroline of Monaco were life members; so was the Aga Khan, and the dukes of Beaufort and Marlborough. There were Rothschilds, Astors, Agnellis, Guinnesses, Hanovers, Niarchoses. Only a handful of Americans were included. Adam Graham was a member, as his father and grandfather had been; Mark van Hollen was not.

Both Katrinka and Daisy had good friends in the club, who arranged temporary memberships for them, which meant that they could dine in the restaurant, and that Katrinka, even after her divorce from Adam, could race with the Corviglia in the various competitions against clubs such as the Eagle from Gstaad. Katrinka had skied frequently in St. Moritz when she had been with the Czech ski team and she enjoyed her association with the Corviglia. It was all very comfortable, very familiar to her, not unlike the Svitov ski club to which she and her parents had belonged when she was a child. The two had the same sort of camaraderie, the same competitive edge. They shared the belief that their club was the best, that its members were without doubt superior beings, that its skiers could beat all competition.

Of course, there were differences: in the Corviglia everyone wore Bogner and Ellesse instead of hand-knit sweaters and caps; they ate *pâté de foie gras* instead of goulash, drank champagne instead of beer. But these to Katrinka seemed incidental. More to the point, anyone with five korunas to spare and an interest in skiing had been able to join the Svitov club. Becoming a member of the Corviglia was a little more complicated.

Unlike Katrinka, Mark had no real interest in joining. He skied for the pleasure of it, just as he climbed mountains. His competitiveness was, for the most part, reserved for business. And, unlike his gregarious wife, he was essentially a loner. He had no desire to be part of an organized elite who spent endless hours sitting around, as he put it, congratulating itself for being important. When Katrinka urged him to stand for membership, he refused.

Katrinka thought he was being very silly about it. Although her temporary membership allowed her to drop into the club anytime she liked, it did not permit her to take in guests, so Mark was unable to join her unless a member was willing to sign him in. The bylaws limited the number of times, otherwise there would not have been a problem, since Mark was liked and respected by any number of people in the club. While his family background left a lot to be desired, he was nonetheless intelligent, amusing, successful; he had impeccable manners; and, least important of all, he was rich. He also kept the sort of low profile they heartily approved. In many ways, he was a much more acceptable candidate for membership than Katrinka, or Adam for that matter, who had a knack for attracting publicity. But if Mark was not going to make the effort, then Katrinka felt she had to. She had no intention of racing with the Corviglia if Mark could not be there to celebrate her victory.

As Mark skied to a stop in front of the entrance to the ramshackle structure where Hartley Matthis's restaurant was located, he saw Katrinka, skis planted firmly, leaning on her poles, talking to Prince Dimitri of Yugoslavia and his friend, the model Carla Bruni. Katrinka saw Mark and waved, and he returned the greeting, but instead of joining them, took off his skis, placed them in the rack, and headed for the restaurant. He liked Dimitri, found him interesting, charming, and very knowledgeable about his work (he was with Sotheby's jewelry department), but he could guess what they were discussing and preferred to leave them to it. He had no objection to Katrinka's joining the Corviglia, but he saw no reason to try to help her achieve her goal. In any case, as he was the first to admit, she hardly needed assistance from him. Two members had already agreed to sponsor her. Now, all that was necessary was the approval of the committee, any one of whom could blackball her, though Katrinka, with her usual optimism, could not see why any of them would. Though capable of being a tyrant where work was concerned, she was essentially a democrat. If she believed in any aristocracy at all, it was the aristocracy of achievement. And her expectation was that she would be accepted on her merits, as she accepted others on theirs. It was this naive faith in the fairness of human nature that Mark found most endearing about her. He loved her blend of innocence and sophistication, femininity and ambition. He hoped she would not be too disappointed, or too hurt, or too angry, if she failed this time to get her way.

Looking back over his shoulder, Mark saw Christian ski to a stop beside his mother. Even at that distance, he could see how Katrinka's face glowed with love and pride as she introduced her son to the others. And, as always in company, Christian's face lost the look of petulance that marred it when he was alone with his mother.

Mark supposed that other men had worse problems to deal with in the early days of their marriages than difficult stepsons, but it was one he would have preferred to do without. He had never spanked his own sons, but he suspected that had he known Christian as a boy he might have been tempted. Now, unfortunately, it was too late, though just what to do about Christian's attitude was a problem he had yet to solve. Grin and bear it, he supposed. Leave it to Katrinka to sort out.

Riccardo halted in front of the restaurant, removed his skis, and racked them next to Mark's. "Is Daisy here yet?" he asked as he joined Mark.

"I only just arrived."

Leaving Katrinka and Christian still engrossed in conversation, the two men walked down the stairs, past the sun deck, along the line of vitrines displaying wares for sale in the St. Moritz boutiques, past the cafeteria, into the bright open space that was the restaurant. Crowded with simple pine tables, built-in benches, and movable chairs, the room was glass on three sides, giving views out over the mountain. As always, it was full, both with skiers on a break from the day's sport and people who had made their way up to the mountain top by tram just to lunch there. Reservations were always required.

Seeing the array of temptingly rich desserts at the tiered buffet table to the right of the entrance, Riccardo sighed regretfully. "I had the chocolate gateau yesterday, but on condition that today I would have nothing. Well," he said, "maybe just a little cheese." He was very fond of the rich creamy type called Vacherin, which was delicious served with caraway.

Since Mark knew cholesterol was a concept without any real meaning for an Italian, he merely grinned and said nothing.

"La Signora Donati è gia arrivata," said one of the waitresses, pointing to the table by a window where Daisy and Lucia had already been seated.

"Si, grazie," said Riccardo, who then launched into his order for a large supply of bullshots, giving his own recipe for the traditional combination of bouillon and vodka that was, in his opinion, the perfect pick-me-up after a hard day's skiing.

"Capisco," said the waitress, repeating the ingredients to reassure him. Most of the staff in shops and at hotels and restaurants in St. Moritz were multilingual, speaking French, Italian, and German, which were Switzerland's three native languages; English because it was the Victorians who had developed St. Moritz as a resort, and their descendants had been returning faithfully ever since; and Romansch, the local language, an ancient combination of Italian and German, in which St. Moritz was rendered *San Mureizzen,* and *casa* became *chesa.* *"Li porterò subito,"* she added, and hurried away as the two men continued through the crowded restaurant to the table where Daisy and Lucia waited.

"Where's Katrinka?" asked Daisy as Mark kissed her hello. Not a strand of her blond hair was out of place, and her makeup looked as perfect as it had the moment she had finished applying it hours before.

"She'll be here in a minute."

"She's talking to Prince Dimitri. Her son is here," said Riccardo, still sounding a little surprised that she should have one.

"Christian? How lovely," said Daisy. "I'm longing to get to know him better. When did he arrive?"

"Last night," said Mark with as much enthusiasm as he could muster.

"Oh, it's too bad we didn't know," said Lucia. "He could have gone with Pia and Martin to Corvatsch this morning."

"Well, we'll all have dinner this evening," said Daisy, the organizer, "and introduce the children to one another. How long will you be with us, Mark?"

"I'll be commuting, from London. *The International* is being launched next month." He had a lot of money riding on the enterprise, a weekly magazine designed to be global in attitude rather than American. Local journalists would be used rather than the traditional "foreign correspondents"; a central bureau would polish prose but not points of view. The venture, at its most idealistic, was an attempt to encourage international understanding and cooperation by reporting news as the natives of an area saw it, instead of sending in reporters who, with the best intentions in the world, often had little understanding of local

77

history or culture. *The International* had been a dream of Mark's for a long time, and that it was about to become a reality filled him with both elation and dread. He was too practical not to know that the venture might turn into a political, logistical, and financial nightmare. "I'm up to my ass in last-minute problems," he added.

"You'd never know it to look at you," said Lucia. "How do you manage to appear so calm all the time? And you don't even have an ulcer eating away at your insides, I suppose?"

"No," said Mark, grinning.

"Like me," said Riccardo. "He eats hard, works hard, plays hard. I don't have an ulcer. I don't believe in them."

"Riccardo doesn't believe in any illness," said Daisy, humor and affection mixed in her voice. "Consequently, I never get sick anymore. I don't dare. It upsets him too much."

"Hello, everybody. You order yet?" said Katrinka as she slipped into the seat beside Mark.

"Riccardo's ordered bullshots."

"Not for me," she said, then turned to Christian. "*Zlatíčko*, sit here, next to me. You know everyone, don't you?"

"Yes," said Christian, with the slight click of his heels and hint of a bow that advertised his years at Le Rosey, a Swiss boarding school. He took the offered seat next to Katrinka and answered the questions put to him with enormous ease and good humor: where he had traveled from; how long he was staying; if he had been in St. Moritz often before. He was at his most appealing, his handsome face undisturbed by so much as a hint of disdain. They were all, observed Katrinka with delight and Mark with surprise, quite charmed by him.

"What did Dimitri say?" asked Daisy as soon as everyone had finished trying to make Christian feel welcome.

"I'm a foot-in," said Katrinka, looking pleased.

Usually, her friends understood immediately when Katrinka, even after her long years in the United States, got an expression wrong, but this time they looked stumped. "I think you mean shoo-in," said Mark.

"Shoo-in," repeated Katrinka, not the least disturbed by the correction.

"You're joining the Corviglia?" asked Lucia.

Katrinka nodded. "After all, I was a member all those years with Adam."

"Speaking of Adam," said Lucia. She hesitated for a moment, reluctant to say anything to sour the atmosphere.

"What?" asked Katrinka.

"He's on his way. We have a meeting here the day after tomorrow."

"Well, he was bound to show up," said Daisy, being reasonable. "He always does."

Katrinka linked arms with Mark and Christian and said, smiling, "Who cares where Adam Graham goes or what he does?"

But Mark felt a small tightening in his gut. First Christian, now Adam. Some vacation, he thought.

Nine

THE HOUSE THE VAN HOLLENS HAD RENTED FOR THE
MONTH OF FEBRUARY WAS LOCATED ON THE ROAD FROM
Celerina to St. Moritz. Called the Chesa Konsalvi, it was built of stucco
painted a cheerful buttercup yellow, and set back behind a low stone
wall topped with iron railings, with a double gate of wrought iron
above broad stone steps and a wide path leading to a heavy wood door
recessed behind an arch. The windows too were deeply recessed and
set off by shutters painted a rich fudge brown. Over a foot of snow
covered the sloped roof and sat like huge square pediments atop the
gate posts.

The house, which dated from 1790, had six double bedrooms, a
sitting room, a dining room, and an enormous kitchen, plus a utility
room on the second floor. In the attic were two additional staff
bedrooms, hallways lined with cedar closets, and a large storage area.
Each floor had a luxurious bathroom and separate WC. Partly below
ground level were a wine cellar, laundry room, and playroom as damp
as a cave and with a beamed ceiling and enormous stucco fireplace. All
the main rooms had pine-paneled walls and ceilings. Brightly colored
Oriental rugs were scattered on the polished wood floors. The hallways
were wide, lined with antique tables covered with vases of flowers; the
white plaster walls were set with massive pine doors and hung with
landscape paintings and the horns of African gazelles. Deer antlers
served as chandeliers. The original owners of the house had been great

hunters and the carcasses of stuffed birds had swung from the walls in the dining room until Katrinka requested that they be removed. The present owner was a Swiss banker from Geneva, who was spending the month in the Cayman Islands.

The house was much larger than Katrinka and Mark needed, but it had the advantage of being across the narrow, curving two-lane road from the Chesa Mulin, Daisy and Riccardo's huge cream-colored house. It had a peaked roof and green shutters and was set on a piece of property large for an area where building space was limited by the mountains. Adjacent to it, rows of small houses climbed the hillside and white stucco condominiums with wood balconies had either just been completed or were under construction. Behind it ran the tracks of the "glacier express," the bright red train that had carried passengers across the Alps from Chur to St. Moritz for almost as long as the resort had existed, and still remained its chief means of access. There were no connecting airplane flights or direct trains from any Swiss airport. The trip was long, six hours from Zurich, with two changes of trains. Those who lived near enough, or could afford the high cost of renting a car, drove; the rich arrived by private plane or helicopter, owned or chartered.

What brought the wealthy to St. Moritz was the social life. Even the Europeans admitted that the skiing was better at Aspen and Vail; but neither of those Colorado towns had the variety of smart boutiques that lined the narrow streets of St. Moritz, nor the range of international glitterati (though more came to Colorado every year), nor the exclusive clubs, the assortment of excellent hotels and restaurants, the neighboring communities loaded with antique charm, nor, for that matter, for those genuinely interested in sports, the world-renowned toboggan and bobsled runs in addition to the staggering beauty of the Alps and the challenging pistes of Corvatsch, Corviglia, Furtschellas, and Diavolezza.

For Adam Graham, the social life of St. Moritz, all social life, was an extension of his business, a way to establish relationships, initiate deals, and close them. For Mark, and Katrinka, social life was a necessary relief from the pressures of work; but while Katrinka put the same limitless energy into enjoying herself that she did into running her hotels, or her homes, Mark could take only so much partying before he longed for solitude, which was why he owned a house in the Hebrides, why he went hill walking in the north of England and trekking in Nepal. It was not that he disapproved—he had no puritan guilt about having a good time; he had nothing against fun. In fact, he often envied Katrinka's ability to throw herself heart and soul into whatever she happened to be doing at the moment. His was simply a different sort of personality. And after ten days in St. Moritz, the ritual of tea at the Palace Hotel; the rounds of dinners, at private homes or in restaurants; the dancing afterward in the Palace's Grand Bar or Gunther Sachs's disco, Dracula; the fancy dress parties at the Chesa Veglia, where, inevitably, a drunken millionaire or two was escorted from the premises by security, Mark was beginning to long for a quieter, simpler life.

"Let's go to Méribel tomorrow," he suggested, as he guided the rented Citroën up the hill, past the Cresta run, toward St. Moritz. He knew she would enjoy seeing the Olympic events scheduled for the next day, and at least it was a change of scene.

Katrinka turned to look at him. "Are you bored?"

"Restless," he said, meeting her eyes briefly and smiling.

"You're worried about *The International*?"

"Not much. But it's always nerve-wracking when you get this close to the wire."

"The magazine's fantastic," she said enthusiastically. "It's going to be a big hit." The kind of magazine that Mark was in the last stages of planning had a huge potential market, and the advertising campaign he had launched was, in her opinion, brilliant, designed by the best minds on two continents.

He reached over and squeezed her hand. "One of the things I love about you," he said, "the idea of failure never enters your head."

"It does," she said. "But it doesn't frighten me. It doesn't frighten you either."

Mark laughed. "Not much, anyway," he agreed.

It was four in the afternoon, the sun was low in the sky, and all but a few fanatics had returned from the slopes. The Schoolhouse Plaza, opposite the tram station, was crowded with returning skiers, skis slung over their shoulders, boots clomping on the snow-covered streets, walking back to their hotels or waiting in long queues for the sports buses. Now that the stores had reopened after the two-hour midday closing, the streets were full of people wandering in and out of the boutiques, stopping to buy newspapers and postcards, pausing to admire the enormous snow sculptures that decorated the street corners, meeting friends at Hanselmann's for pastries, having coffee or beer at one of the many cafés.

As Mark turned the Citroën out of the square and into the maze of narrow one-way streets leading to the Palace Hotel, Katrinka turned to Christian, who was in the backseat of the car, observing the scene without much interest. "Would you like to go to Méribel?" she asked, taking it for granted that her son was included in Mark's plan.

For a moment, Christian was tempted to refuse the invitation. He felt too much like a third wheel when Katrinka and Mark were together. There was a bond between them that excluded him, and he resented it. But he could not say no. The desire to see at least some of the Olympics combined with the fear that Mark and Katrinka would just go off without him and he said, "It might be interesting."

"Good," said Katrinka, smiling with satisfaction. "We go."

Built in the last decades of the nineteenth century, the Palace Hotel looked very much like a medieval castle. It was an enormous gray-stone structure with pointed turrets and round towers, a distinctive green-tiled roof, and narrow recessed windows with red painted trim. The original architect had advised the owner against including private baths for each room, insisting that not many guests—most if not all of whom were expected to be wealthy—would pay extra for the luxury. Since then, the hotel had been in a constant state of renovation, with rooms combined to provide the private baths that had proved to be unexpectedly popular, each redone completely at regular intervals to ensure the hotel's reputation for luxury, and the public rooms on the ground floors enlarged or made smaller depending on the shifting demands for grandeur or intimacy. The hotel was set on a hill, its rear overlooking the lake, which in winter was frozen solid enough to double as a racetrack. The entrance was in one of St. Moritz's busiest areas, near the train station and tourist office, in a narrow street lined with designer boutiques.

Mark pulled the Citroën into the small forecourt of the hotel, which was crowded with parked cars, waiting taxis, people entering and leaving. Valets sprang to open the car doors, and Katrinka, Mark, and Christian climbed out. Pausing along the way to greet acquaintances, they entered the hotel, passed through the small lobby, turned right, and followed the corridor into the Grand Hall.

Once divided into smaller rooms—the Ladies' Bar, the Men's Smoking Room, etc.—the hall had been knocked into one great space, its feeling of intimacy maintained by the columns that ran from the carved wood ceiling to the carpeted floor, dividing it structurally into cosy seating areas. The walls were of white plaster with chair rails and decorative marble inlays. None of the furniture matched, but the odd assortment of round tables and tapestry chairs, as everyone remarked, "all worked." Beyond the hall lay the hotel's restaurants, and the two discotheques, one catering to the younger, another to the older crowd.

"There's Lucia," said Katrinka, spotting her friend's head of auburn hair. To the sounds of background piano music, tinkling glasses, and the soft hum of conversation, she led the way past the dessert trolley, weaving around the tables crowded with people, few of whom were having tea, most preferring cocktails or champagne with their chocolate gateau. Some still wore their ski outfits; others, like Katrinka and Mark, had changed into casual (designer, of course) clothes—slacks and sweaters, jumpsuits, an occasional dress or skirt. Everyone not in parkas wore furs. An animal rights activist would have had a heart attack on the spot.

"Who's that with her?" asked Mark.

"Pia and Martin," said Katrinka, sounding surprised that Mark should not recognize them.

"No, the one she's talking to."

But Lucia's head was in the way and at first Katrinka could not see to whom Mark was referring. Then, as Lucia sat back and out of her line of sight, she stopped. "Oh, my God, it's Khalid," she said.

"Another drama-packed afternoon at the Palace," muttered Mark.

"He can't still be mad at me," said Katrinka. Since she had helped Natalie run away from him, Katrinka and the prince had seen each other, but always at a distance, at a ball, at the races. They had never spoken. Nor did she and Natalie any longer, not since Natalie had repaid the favor by having an affair with Adam. It had been the worst betrayal of Katrinka's life. "And if he is still mad, he should stop. It does take too much energy to keep fighting old battles. Come on."

"What is it?" said Christian in German.

"I'll explain later," Katrinka told him, as she continued forward until she reached the table. "Hello, everyone. How you doing?" she said cheerfully, kissing Pia and Martin. "Khalid, how nice to see you." She offered him her hand, which he took, though reluctantly. "Have you met my husband, Mark van Hollen?"

"I heard that you remarried," said Khalid. He was wearing a white Ellesse ski suit, which complemented the rich almond color of his handsome face and made the silver in his dark hair shine.

"Like you," said Katrinka, not able to resist teasing a little. "Very happily." A year or so after his divorce from Natalie, Khalid had married an English beauty who had borne him another son, Jasim. He also had two Saudi wives and several daughters.

Again reluctantly, Khalid smiled. Then with more enthusiasm, he shook Mark's hand. "Pleased to meet you," he said.

"And this is my son, Christian Heller."

If Khalid was surprised that Katrinka should suddenly turn out to be the mother of a young man whom he had known for years to be the son of Kurt and Luisa Heller, he did not show it. "I know your father," was all he said. "Kurt Heller?"

"Yes, of course," said Christian noncommittally, bowing slightly as he shook Khalid's hand. Kurt Heller was in the German diplomatic service. His wife's father had been one of the country's leading industrialists and had left his daughter a fortune. The couple entertained lavishly, had entrée everywhere, and made it a point to know anyone with money or power.

But it was not Khalid ibn Hassan who interested Christian right then. When the conversation turned—as it was bound to do with Lucia and Khalid present—to yachts, Christian settled himself in the chair opposite Pia Cavalletti. Even if he had not found her beautiful, even if he had not been feeling somehow left out, excluded from the aura of contentment that pervaded any space inhabited by Katrinka and Mark, he might anyway have decided to make a play for her, egged on by the slight, involuntary frown with which Martin Havlíček had greeted his choice of a seat. "You were skiing Corvatsch today?" he said in his fluent but slightly hesitant English, smiling at her, making no attempt to include Martin.

"Yes," said Pia, her eyes not quite meeting his.

Christian thought she was exquisite, with heavy black hair, parted in the middle, framing her face, which had a high broad forehead and rounded chin. Dark brows slanted slightly upward above oval brown eyes. Her skin was a rich, creamy olive, her nose short and straight; her mouth full and perfectly shaped. There was a slight space between her two front teeth. Her manner was cool, guarded. To Christian, it suddenly seemed a great and interesting challenge to break through that reserve. "It was crowded?" he asked, though he knew the answer.

"The tram was. But otherwise . . ." She shrugged.

"A pity you didn't ask my stepfather to borrow his helicopter. I'm sure he would have been delighted to be of service to you."

There was a slight edge to the word "stepfather," and Martin caught it immediately. "It was no big deal," he said. "The wait wasn't all that long." If Christian had disliked Martin on sight, as he had expected to do, Martin was no less quick to sense a rival rather than a potential playmate. As nonchalantly as he could manage, Martin slipped his arm around the back of Pia's chair. "And Pia likes the tram," he added.

"If you can get next to the window, it's interesting," said Pia. "Especially at Corvatsch. The cable is strung so high above the forest, looking down the snow seems like white icing and the trees like green candles stuck in a birthday cake."

"We had a great day," said Martin firmly.

"My mother tells me you're an artist?" said Christian, ignoring him entirely.

"Yes," said Pia, "in a way."

"She designs jewelry," added Martin, refusing to be pushed out of the conversation.

"That pin?" asked Christian, referring to a delicate whorl of silver set with moonstone on Pia's black sweater. She nodded. "It's very beautiful," continued Christian. "Classic, yet also modern."

"Her work is very unusual," said Martin.

"I'd love to see it sometime, if I may."

"I only have a few pieces with me. Most are at home," said Pia discouragingly. "In Fiesole."

"Not an impossible problem to solve," said Christian, giving her the benefit of his most engaging smile. "There are planes, and trains, and automobiles, and any number of school holidays. You are still in school?"

She was, Pia told him. Christian was flirting with her, she knew, and though she liked it, she didn't respond. She never responded. And it wasn't just because of the years spent in convent schools in Italy, contact with boys kept to a minimum when not actually forbidden, with no chance to acquire a technique for social intercourse, but something deeper, a distrust of easy smiles, careless games. Her father had been a master of them, after all. Pia had adored Nick, and his conviction on so many felonies, including accessory to murder, when she had been at her most vulnerable, in her mid-teens, had left her not only heartbroken but embarrassed. And wary. It had made her cynical. And the sophistication, which she wore like a shield, was composed of nothing more than a mixture of disillusionment and pain. Almost no one, and nothing, touched her deeply; but the efforts that people made to get past her defenses, though she did not understand them, no longer surprised her. So the tension that hung in the air between her and Christian was familiar and not altogether uncomfortable.

Martin's reaction, too, was familiar and comforting. Pia had known him since a year or so after his arrival in the United States, when he was thirteen and she twelve. They had spent holidays together, aboard the *Lady Katrinka*, at the villa in Cap Ferrat, and more recently in St. Moritz, at Daisy and Riccardo's chalet. And when, after Nick's indictment and her removal from New York to Florence, Pia formed no really intimate relationships with the girls in her schools, she and Martin remained close. With him, she was never wary. There was no reason to be on guard, nothing to excuse or explain to him. And the same was true for Martin. Because of their mothers' friendship, they had always known everything about each other's odd family histories. They accepted each other without question, confided in one another, and considered each other best friends. And, if recently Pia had begun to feel that Martin wanted more from her than the friendship they had shared since adolescence, the prospect of a closer relationship rather appealed to her. At twenty, she had had some sexual liaisons, one with a ski instructor, another with the father of a schoolmate, a third with a married university professor. And if Martin, at twenty-one, had had more experience, his encounters had been equally unsatisfying. Both of them longed for stability, for a settled home life, and most of all, for love.

"Mother," said Christian, interrupting the conversation that had shifted to a discussion of the America's Cup, which did not interest him in the least.

Katrinka turned to him immediately, her face beaming as it always did when she heard him call her that. "Yes, *miláčku?*"

"I think Pia would enjoy coming with us to Méribel tomorrow."

"Are you going to Méribel?" asked Lucia.

"Yes," replied Katrinka.

"Of course," said Mark, answering Christian's question. "Pia's very welcome. And Martin," he added, though he knew it would not earn him any gratitude from Christian, who seemed to be interested in good manners only when it suited him.

"And Martin, of course," repeated Christian, as if that was what he had intended. There was no point alienating people unnecessarily, he supposed; and it mattered, for the moment at any rate, that Pia, and Lucia as well, consider him "a nice guy," as the Americans were so fond of putting it.

For a moment, Lucia was tempted to forbid Pia to go, though she knew her daughter was too old to be forbidden anything really, and certainly not something so innocent as a trip to see the Olympics with friends. But it was an instinctive reaction. She liked Christian. When he went out of his way to please, he was difficult not to like. He was handsome, as handsome as a movie star with his dark hair and slanted dark eyes; he was intelligent, charming, and—above all—he was Katrinka's son, and there were few people in the world Lucia admired as much as Katrinka. Yet she sensed that Christian could be trouble for a young girl, especially a girl as lonely and intense as Pia. Lucia sighed. She had hoped not to have to worry about her daughter during this holiday. She had been so happy to see that Zuzka was right, that Pia did actually enjoy herself in Martin's company. He clearly adored her.

And he was such a decent young man, as full of sound good sense as Zuzka, as fun-loving and creative as Tomáš. He looked like his father, with the same long Gypsy face, deep-set dark eyes, and wide, full mouth. Not beautiful in the way that Christian was, but attractive, and very sexy. If she had to choose, which one would she take? wondered Lucia, before pushing the thought firmly out of her mind. She did not approve of viewing her friends' children in an erotic light. Perhaps later she would warn Pia about Christian, gently, giving just a hint.

Catching the look on her mother's face, Pia said quickly, "I'd love to go." As uncomfortable as a day with Christian and Martin might prove to be, at least it would spare her having to spend time discussing either Martin or Patrick Kates with her mother. She did not know what, if anything, she felt about Martin, aside from friendship; and, more importantly, she was positive she did not like Lucia's current lover. She did not trust him either. Martin said that she was bound to distrust any man after what her father had put her through, but Pia disagreed. It was not a question of "any" man. After all, she trusted Martin completely. But as she was pointing that out to him, it suddenly crossed her mind that perhaps it was her mother she doubted, or rather her mother's judgment: any woman who could believe in Nick Cavalletti, and for as long as Lucia had, surely must have something very wrong with her bullshit detector.

"What's the event?" asked Martin, who had no intention of letting Pia go off to Méribel without him.

"The combined slalom," said Katrinka. "The women's."

"We may try to see some of the ice hockey as well."

"Sweden is playing Germany," remembered Christian, giving him yet another reason for wanting to go.

Daisy and Riccardo arrived as they were settling on a departure time. With them was Dieter Keiser, who immediately began pushing tables together at Daisy's request, reorganizing seating arrangements, and summoning waiters to take orders he had no intention of paying for.

"Where you did ski today, Dieter?" asked Katrinka.

"Nowhere, alas," he replied. "I only just arrived." He was staying with Daisy and Riccardo, making a convenient escort for Lucia, in Patrick's absence. "But tomorrow, I'll be out as soon as the lifts open. And Riccardo, too. No more loafing around for him."

"Loafing? I barely see him these days," said Daisy, without any real note of complaint in her voice. "He skies from the time the lifts open until they close." Daisy herself was a good skier, but a few hours on the slopes every day or so was enough to keep her happy. Her husband, however, was as obsessive about sport as he was about work. When they were at home in Fiesole, he would lock himself in his studio from early morning to late afternoon, not even stopping for lunch. Late in the day, when things had gone well, he was the best, most charming, most romantic, and attentive husband in the world. When they had not, he was surly as a bear.

Dieter turned to Riccardo, a look of mock accusation on his face. "Have you been neglecting Daisy? *Ma sei matto!* Do you know how many men would happily take your place?"

"Not if they value their lives," said Riccardo, in Italian, with a big, completely amiable smile. No one, however, doubted that he meant it.

"Is it any wonder that I love him?" asked Daisy as she linked her arm through her husband's. "He's so clearly mad about me."

The conversation went on like that for a while, light, bantering, occasionally flirtatious. No one took any of it at all seriously. At one point, Katrinka excused herself from the group to say hello to Vittorio Mosca, the president of Frette, who introduced her to the French novelist with whom he was having tea. Katrinka spent a few minutes chatting with them, then started back toward her friends, stopping along the way to greet a few other people she knew. She had almost reached them when Khalid stood up, said his good-byes, and turned to leave, coming face to face with Katrinka.

"You're going? So soon?" said Katrinka.

"Yes. I like to spend some time with my son before he goes to bed."

"Oh, your wife is here?"

"Of course," said Khalid, sounding surprised that she should think otherwise.

Of course, thought Katrinka. It was only his Saudi wives he left home. Natalie had always accompanied Khalid when he traveled. "Your son, he is well?" she asked.

"Very," said Khalid shortly, looking impatient to get away.

She should not have mentioned Jasim, thought Katrinka. Someone had told her—who was it? Lucia probably—that the boy had diabetes. Khalid would not welcome her prying. "I am glad to hear it," she said, smiling, starting to move away. "It was good to see you, Khalid." To her surprise, he put his hand on her arm to stop her. "Yes?" she said, turning back, a little startled.

Khalid hesitated, as if not quite certain what he wanted to say. "Do you speak to Natalie?" he asked finally.

"No."

"Does Adam?"

"If he does, he would certainly not tell me," said Katrinka briefly, not wanting to talk about Natalie, especially not with Khalid.

"No, I suppose not," said Khalid regretfully. "When I spoke to her last, she didn't sound . . . herself." He shrugged. "She didn't sound happy. I thought you might know what's wrong."

"Since when are you so concerned about Natalie's happiness?" asked Katrinka.

"She's the mother of my son," he said. "There are rumors." It was clear that he didn't like the discussion any more than Katrinka did. "That she's drinking. Perhaps taking drugs."

"I'm sorry, Khalid," said Katrinka sympathetically. "I know nothing."

"If the rumors are true, how can I leave my son with her? Katrinka, I'm worried to death."

"Then what you are doing here in St. Moritz?" she said impatiently. "Go to Los Angeles and find out what's going on. Don't expect me to do it for you. Or Adam."

Khalid took a deep breath. "Yes," he said finally. "Of course, you're right. If you'll excuse me."

As he walked away, Katrinka watched him for a moment. None of it was any of her business, she knew. It was Khalid's problem to solve, if indeed there was a problem. Still, she could not help being concerned. Though she could neither forgive the betrayal nor be her friend again, Katrinka's anger at Natalie was long gone. She wished her well. She wished her happiness. As for Aziz, she had always loved the little boy. If he was . . . but she did not want to think about that. There was nothing she could do to help. Absolutely nothing. And Khalid had ample time and money and power at his disposal to take care of his son himself.

Katrinka returned to the table and sat next to Mark, slipping her hand into his. He squeezed it gently, as if aware that she needed physical comfort. Turning his head, he whispered in her ear, "Let's go home."

"What a nice idea," she said softly.

Mark stood up. "We're off," he said. "See you all later." There was a costume party they were all invited to, thrown by a Spanish grandee and his most recent wife.

"Christian, are you coming?" asked Katrinka.

"Not if I can have a ride later," he said, looking at Pia. He could guess the reason for Katrinka and Mark's sudden desire to return home and had no wish to spend the next several hours alone in the house watching the Olympics on television.

"We can drop you," said Martin, who did not see a way to avoid the offer.

"Good," said Katrinka, waving cheerfully, then turning to leave. Again, Mark took her hand and Katrinka suddenly felt amazingly fortunate, wonderfully happy. Poor Natalie, she thought. Poor, poor Natalie.

Ten

ON THE WAY TO MÉRIBEL, MARK SAT IN FRONT WITH
THE HELICOPTER'S PILOT, LEAVING KATRINKA TO SHARE
the passenger cabin with Pia, Martin, and Christian, all of whom
seemed preoccupied, staring out at the snow-covered landscape,
watching as the helicopter climbed to clear the mountains, then
dropped again to pass over the stone-and-timber villages nestled in the
valleys. As if finally bored by them, no one pointed out remarkable
sights. The occasional comment sounded forced.

It's the noise, thought Katrinka at first. Soon, however, she realized
that noise did not account for the tension in the cabin. That, she
concluded after studying them a few more moments, crackled in the air
between Christian and Martin like electricity, invisible but potent.
Clearly, they disliked each other; and Pia, if not the only cause, was at
least the focus of their quarrel.

This was not what Katrinka had expected, and she felt not only
disappointed, but sad. Daisy's and Margo's children had been older
when she met them, with established lives of their own. She had had
no chance to build a relationship with them. But Martin she had
known since his birth, and Pia since she was four years old. Katrinka
was close to both; she loved both, and she had wanted Christian
included in their friendship. She had wanted it very much. It was as if
she hoped that such a friendship would be, in some miraculous way,

retroactive, blurring the line between present and past, incorporating Christian into Martin's and Pia's history, giving Katrinka the sense that she had reclaimed a piece of her son's childhood. Now, of course, she could see that she had miscalculated badly. She had not entered sex into her equation.

Why had she never before noticed that Martin was in love with Pia? wondered Katrinka. Because she was too used to seeing them together, she supposed. Because the attachment between them went back to the time they were hardly more than children. Because there had been no real hint of sexuality between them until Christian's entrance into the scene.

Christian. Katrinka had known him, too, since he was a child, though she had never (and this still continued to surprise her) suspected that he was her son. Over the years she had met him at one ski resort or another, at parties, at balls, at sporting events, which he had attended with the couple she had supposed to be his parents. Only last December had she discovered his real identity. Two months before: not very much time in which to build any sort of relationship, as Mark kept reminding her, let alone one between a mother and son. But patience had never been one of Katrinka's virtues. That Christian had not accepted her with the same instant and total love with which she had greeted his return to her life filled her with dismay. And frustration. How long was it going to take, she wondered, before he began to trust her? before his eyes lost their calculating expression, his face its coldness, his voice the hint of sarcasm when he spoke to her affectionately? He was not easy to understand, her son, not easy to reach at all.

Feeling her eyes on him, Christian turned to Katrinka and smiled questioningly. "You're very quiet this morning," he said in German.

"We all are," said Katrinka, her smile a little forced. "Maybe nobody got enough sleep?"

"But you didn't even come dancing with us."

More out of habit than desire, Katrinka had seconded Daisy's suggestion that they all go on to Dracula after the costume party, but Mark had said an emphatic no. In his opinion, a pregnant woman required more than four hours of sleep a night. And he was right. "I was out late every night for a week," she said. "Enough is enough."

Christian took her hand and, with a surprising display of tenderness, asked, in English, "You're certain you feel well?"

"I feel great," said Katrinka, suppressing a surge of irritation. It was not she whom Christian was trying to impress with his show of feeling.

And he did not care at all what Martin thought of him. It was all for Pia's benefit. "You did all have a good time at Dracula?" she asked, trying to bring the others into the conversation.

In response, Martin mumbled something that could be interpreted to mean anything. He had, in fact, had a rotten time. Though several girls he knew had tried their best to distract him, he had hardly noticed them, his attention focused always on Pia. Christian and she had danced together too often to suit him.

"There's nothing I'd rather do than dance," said Pia, meaning it literally. She was an amazing dancer, with a natural grace and a mesmerizing sensuality that brought to mind Mata Hari dancing for state secrets, or Salome for the head of John the Baptist. Dancing, Pia was out of control.

And watching her had made Christian think that, even without the pleasure to be had from annoying Martin Havlíček, Pia might be worth the effort he was making to interest her. "You dance very well," he said carefully, having noticed that obvious flattery caused her guard to come crashing down.

Martin's eyes darted briefly toward Christian, but he said nothing, which both Katrinka and Christian noted, and Pia did not. Martin's admiration was something she knew she had no reason to question.

"Adam Graham was at Dracula last night," said Christian, changing the subject, his face bland, his voice casual. Only his eyes betrayed any interest in seeing how Katrinka would react to the information.

"Oh?" said Katrinka calmly, refusing to rise to the bait. "You did say hello?"

"Of course," said Christian, who had met him any number of times, since Adam had, over the years, cultivated Kurt Heller's friendship, wanting the diplomat's influence at his disposal should he need any concessions from the Bonn government for the Graham shipyard in Bremen.

Pia frowned slightly. Not wanting to upset Katrinka, she had carefully avoided mentioning Adam. So had Martin.

"He asked about my father. Kurt Heller," added Christian helpfully, "not the other one."

His voice was so innocent, Katrinka was certain that no one but she suspected he was needling her. Christian knew very well the name of his real father. Katrinka had told him that and all the other details of his birth.

"He didn't stay long," said Martin.

"Not even half an hour," added Pia.

Both Pia and Martin were fond of Adam, and with good reason.

Whatever his other faults, he had always been amazingly good with children. But they were fond of Katrinka too, and, having seen how hurt she had been by Adam, protective of her.

"Some woman asked him to take her back to her hotel," said Christian dismissively, as if the subject was of no interest to him.

"It was only Sugar Benson," said Pia.

"Sugar?" said Katrinka, not able to stifle her surprise. Adam had never liked her. Both ruthless and greedy, Sugar Benson was not his kind of woman. He had thought Steven Elliott a fool for leaving Daisy to marry her; and his opinion was confirmed when Sugar had then divorced Steven for an aging Italian count, who had had the good fortune to die shortly before the scheduled wedding ceremony. Always enterprising, Sugar had pawned some jewels and used what alimony she received from Steven to go into business. She now ran one of the most successful "escort services" in London, and had recently opened another in Manhattan. Even had Adam been attracted to her, there was no way on earth that he would allow the Graham name to be linked with that of a known courtesan.

"They ran into each other at Dracula," explained Martin, after an angry glance at Christian.

"She wasn't his *date*," added Pia, with a hint of disgust at the idea.

Hearing the anxiety in their voices, Katrinka smiled. "It doesn't matter to me anymore who Adam does see, what he does do," she said. "That's all spilled milk under bridge."

Pia giggled, an unusual sound for her, and Martin laughed.

"What?" said Katrinka.

"It's water under the bridge," said Pia.

"And no point crying over spilled milk," added Martin.

Katrinka laughed, turned to Christian, and said with mock exasperation, "You see, Martin has been in the United States much less time than me, and already his English is perfect. No matter how I try, I never do get the expressions right."

"Not even you can do everything right," said Christian, smiling.

Although it sounded very much like a compliment, still Katrinka searched the words for hidden meanings, for clues to the way her son really felt. But she found none and had to be content with knowing that the laughter had finally broken the tension.

The 1992 Winter Olympics were being held in the French Rhone-Alps, the events distributed over thirteen different locales around Albertville in the Savoie province. Transportation to the region was by the usual train, plane, and automobile, with special buses ferrying spectators from place to place, and eight heliports spread out over the area to accommodate those arriving by helicopter.

Méribel, with its famous Roc de Fer run, was the site of all the women's alpine events as well as the ice hockey competition. Like St. Moritz, the village owed its development as a ski resort to the enthusiastic English, but much later, after the Second World War. Since then, a strict building code had allowed for a record number of lifts to be constructed, but had kept the village itself small, with low buildings in blond wood and gray stone set against a wild and difficult terrain.

Seats for five thousand had been constructed at the end of the ski run, and the area was crowded with excited spectators—sports enthusiasts and Olympic groupies alike; and, as the van Hollen party headed for their places, shortly before the first heat of the slalom at ten, a television reporter for CBS, on the lookout for celebrities, spotted Katrinka and signaled her crew in for an interview.

Since her marriage to Adam, when the two of them had been New York's rich young darlings, Katrinka's face had sold countless newspapers and magazines; she appeared often on television shows like "Lifestyles of the Rich and Famous" both before and after her divorce. She was used to being under siege by the media, and, as long as the press played fair, not going out of their way—like Sabrina—to be bitchy, Katrinka didn't mind posing for pictures or being interviewed. For one thing, she had learned from Adam that free publicity was much better for business than paid advertising. For another, the journalists were generally an interesting and amusing group, and Katrinka enjoyed their company.

Mark, however, despite his owning a large newspaper chain that included some very down-and-dirty tabloids, did not share his wife's appreciation of the limelight. His whole professional life, he had made it a practice to keep out of it. So, as the television crew moved in, Mark moved away. Recognizing some of his own reporters in the crowd, he stopped to talk to them. He frequently did, preferring not to rely on reports from his top editorial and management people to assess how things were going. It was also a good opportunity to let the photographers know that, if they wanted a picture of Katrinka, it was okay by him as long as they didn't overdo it. Their obvious relief made him laugh. "Never let it be said," he joked, "that I tried to restrict your first amendment rights."

As photographers from Mark's papers, *The Chronicle* and *The Globe*, joined those from *Hello, Paris Match,* and *Kicker,* jostling for a better shot, Christian stood a little apart, watching, resisting Katrinka's attempt to pull him into the photo op. "Can you believe it?" she said to the photographers, laughing. "My son, and he's shy!"

The journalists elbowed the photographers out of the way, hurling questions at Katrinka, about Mark, about Christian. "You come from a country where abortion is legal," called one. "How come you didn't get one? Don't you approve?"

How on earth, wondered Katrinka, could she compress all the conflicting influences, all the weeks of worry leading to her decision into a single quote she could stand by. Not that she had much chance of that. Experience had taught her that no matter how carefully she framed a reply, someone was bound to misquote it, someone else would pick it up and reprint it without checking, and months later she would be blamed for something she had never said. "I do believe in a woman's right to choose," she said carefully. "And my choice was to have my son. But I did think I would be able to keep him, and take good care of him. My regret is that I could not."

The questions continued, punctuated by the click of the camera shutters. Pia turned to Christian with a wry smile and said, "It's always like this with Katrinka."

"I know," replied Christian, who had in the past occasionally witnessed the same sort of frenzy. Then he had been merely curious about the woman who always attracted so much attention. Now, he was not certain what he felt. Amusement certainly. A dash of pride perhaps? Embarrassment? Contempt? Since December, his emotions had been in constant turmoil. Always so certain before of his motives, half the time now he didn't understand what he was doing. And he didn't like that. He linked his arm through Pia's. "Let's go find our seats," he said. She, at least, was a simple problem, one he knew how to solve.

"All right," agreed Pia, turning her body slightly so that Martin, who was talking to someone whom he knew from St. Moritz, was included in their group. She slipped her other arm through his. "Come on, let's sit down."

The edgy trio made their way toward their seats on the finish line, followed a few minutes later by Mark and Katrinka, who moved through the crowd at a slower pace, stopping to greet business associates, acquaintances, friends, people they ran into wherever they happened to be, people who—like them—went everywhere worth going.

They sat, drinking cup after cup of hot coffee, watching Carole Merle and Petra Kronberger compete for the gold. Katrinka, of course, cheered on the Czechs, though none of the team had a real chance of winning. The Czech ski team had never been able to compete often enough in international events to develop the edge necessary to take home a gold medal; but, with the economic problems that had plagued the country since the "Velvet Revolution," there was even less money available to fund sports than there had been under the communist regime. It was part of the price Czechoslovakia had had to pay for its freedom.

After the first heat, while Christian, Pia, and Martin went on to a hockey match, Katrinka and Mark headed toward the area reserved for the Olympic athletes so that Katrinka could see if any of her old friends were with the Czech team. And no sooner had she begun to explain who she was to one of the security people, when she heard her name being called. Looking up she saw a tall, weathered man, with thinning dark hair, coming toward her. It took her a moment to recognize him. "Vladislav," she said in Czech, "it's you. I don't believe my eyes." Vladislav Elias and she had once, when she was on the rebound from Mirek Bartoš, been lovers. He had been one of the leading skiers on the men's team. "Are you coaching now?"

"*Dobrý den*, Katrinka. How good to see you. Yes, yes, I'm coaching now. Come. You must meet everyone."

He led her into the enclosure and introduced her to the athletes. Standing among them, talking her native language, Katrinka, overwhelmed by memories, felt like a girl again, traveling with her teammates, her biggest dream getting to the Olympics. It was while training for the '72 Sapporo games that she had given up that dream in order to find her son, and had made her escape to Switzerland.

"I didn't see her myself," said Vladislav, telling the young skiers about Katrinka's mad flight from Cervinia to Zermatt, "but I heard about it that night. That was all anybody talked about for months. How crazy she was, and how brave."

One or two of them, Katrinka could see, did not approve, and she understood. What she had done seemed to them like treachery. "How crazy is right," said Katrinka, laughing. "But now everyone is free. Nobody has to try killing themselves to get away. It's a wonderful time for all of you. And for Czechoslovakia," she added with determined optimism. In addition to the financial problems, there was ethnic unrest in the country, with Slovakia wanting to leave the union. Václav Havel, the Czech president, had said that the situation would be resolved without bloodshed, and Katrinka prayed that he was right.

Would she be returning to Czechoslovakia to live? someone wanted to know. Katrinka explained that she had been returning regularly for the past two years, but that she was married to an American and, for the foreseeable future, New York would remain her home.

"Prague is too small a pond for such a big fish," said a voice that Katrinka recognized instantly.

The face, too, Katrinka recognized as soon as she turned. It appeared sometimes in the nightmares she had when she was upset, dreams of loss revolving around her parents' deaths, or Christian's disappearance. It was almost colorless, the eyes flat, like slate, the wispy blond hair now streaked with gray. *"Dobrý den,* Ilona," she said.

Ilona Lukánský had been Katrinka's chief rival, her only enemy, from the time they were children and had belonged to the same ski club. She had always been jealous of Katrinka, and Katrinka always a little afraid of her. Ilona had been vindictive, capable of doing anything to win, eager to spoil her rivals' chances. "Are you coaching, too?" asked Katrinka.

"Oh, yes," said Ilona, walking up to Vladislav and linking her arm through his.

Oh, my God, he married her! thought Katrinka. What interest Vladislav had shown in Ilona had always been to make Katrinka jealous. It was hard to believe that he had fallen enough in love to marry her. But then, thought Katrinka, she found it hard to believe that anyone could love Ilona, whose major talent was for making others miserable.

They spent a difficult few minutes exchanging biographies, but finally, to Katrinka's relief, Mark noticed the time and made their excuses. "What was it between you two?" he asked, as Katrinka and he made their way toward the Belvedere, the restaurant where they were having lunch.

"Which two?"

"Vladislav was a boyfriend," said Mark. "I figured that out."

"I wasn't in love with him," said Katrinka.

"What about Ilona? Was she jealous?"

Katrinka told him briefly about the rivalry that had sprung up between them from the moment they had set eyes on each other.

"You're the same age?" said Mark. "My God, she looks twenty years older than you."

"It's a hard life," said Katrinka. And for a moment, mixed in with her joy at how narrow, how lucky, how wonderful had been her escape from that small and restrictive life where every move was regulated, every reward reserved for those who followed the rules, was a surge of genuine sympathy for Ilona. "You can't imagine how hard."

They were nearing the restaurant, a small chalet in the woods near the Rond-Point, when Katrinka spotted a tall man and a much shorter woman, both wrapped in furs, moving slowly through the crowd. "Look," she said to Mark and, moving quickly ahead, fell into step beside Jean-Claude Gillette. "Jean-Claude, hello," she said, slipping her arm into his. "What a nice surprise. How you doing?"

"Katrinka!" He turned to her with a big smile, kissed her on both cheeks, and said, "Marriage agrees with you, *chérie*. You are looking very beautiful."

"How good to see you!" It had been months since they had last met, not since the L'Arc de Triomphe race in Paris the preceding October. Jean-Claude's hair, which he wore rather long, had a few more gray strands and it had receded perhaps a fraction, making his high forehead even more pronounced; but his eyes, black as onyx, were curious and keen, his handsome features remained well defined, his body agile and muscular. For someone who owned vineyards and specialty food stores, who claimed to be a gourmand, he was the epitome of slender elegance in a full-length Russian lynx coat and matching hat.

"Mark, congratulations," said Jean-Claude, extending his hand to Mark, as he joined them. "You're a lucky man."

"Luck didn't have much to do with it," said Mark, grinning. "It was persistence."

Pushing all thought of how hard and how long he had pursued Katrinka, Jean-Claude just laughed and said, "I can't think of anyone more worth the trouble."

Despite his complimentary words, for the first time since they had been introduced—by Natalie, who had then been his lover—there was nothing in the least flirtatious in Jean-Claude's manner toward her, noticed Katrinka. And it was not because of Mark's presence, since Adam's had never stopped him, nor because he had lost interest in her, since he was often seductive more out of habit than real desire. Curious, she turned to look at the woman at his side, who, as was the case more and more frequently, was not Hélène, his wife. But like her, this one was a pretty, dark-haired woman, much smaller than the long-limbed blondes and brunettes Jean-Claude usually preferred as "companions." She had large doe-shaped dark eyes, skin like café au lait, a long nose, full mouth, and a helmet of thick, black hair, worn parted in the middle. In her late twenties, she might have been Hélène's younger sister—or her daughter. She looked familiar to Katrinka, who could not quite place her.

"May I introduce Theadora Papastratos," said Jean-Claude, his arm encircling the woman's waist, propelling her into the group. "Katrinka and Mark van Hollen."

"How do you do?" said Thea. Her English had only a trace of an accent, the sort that multilingual Europeans who live all over the world eventually acquire. "It is a pleasure to meet you both, I've heard so much about you."

"And you," said Katrinka, who now recognized her. She took the delicate hand that was offered and was surprised at how limp it was in her grasp. Thea Papastratos was a noted horsewoman, owner of Thoroughbred stables in England and the United States, a "bruising" rider, as she was frequently described in the English tabloid press. It seemed unlikely that such a weak hand could control a high-strung stallion. Or the many business interests she had inherited from her father, who had made his fortune in the olive groves of Corfu. Sabrina liked to call her the "Olive Oil Heiress."

The four agreed to have lunch together and, before long, Katrinka began to wonder just what Jean-Claude was up to. He was attentive to Thea Papastratos in a way she had never seen before, not with herself when he had been hard in pursuit, or with Natalie when he had been most in love with her, or any of the countless other women who had hung on his arm over the years. Then, even with women whose intelligence he had respected, he had been, by turns, helpful, informative, charming, attentive, seductive, even passionate, but somehow never serious. All those subtle signs that wise women pay attention to signaled that, though Jean-Claude might be available for a long lease, it would be unwise to count on permanent possession. Natalie had understood that. Never had she expected him to leave Hélène and marry her, not even when she became pregnant with his child. But with Thea, Jean-Claude's manner was subtly different. He was actually thinking of marrying her, Katrinka suddenly realized.

"But why do you need a second apartment, *ma chère?*" asked Jean-Claude, with amusement bordering on exasperation.

Thea shrugged. "Need? What has need to do with it?" She owned one large apartment already in the Place Vendôme and was considering the purchase of another, next door to it. She also owned an apartment on Fifth Avenue in New York, a large horse farm outside Lexington, Kentucky, another in Berkshire, not far from the Newmarket race course, a pied à terre in Cadogan Square in London, and of course the family estate on Corfu.

"Real estate isn't a good investment in most places at the moment. I assume the same is true in Paris," said Mark.

"Perhaps not if you want to turn the property over immediately, for a profit. But that is not at all what I am talking about. In the long term, there is no better investment. An apartment in the Place Vendôme is always desirable."

"Like a beautiful woman," said Jean-Claude, taking Thea's hand and raising it to his lips.

"Exactly," said Thea, with a very small smile. "There is no more beautiful square in all the world."

"What you will do with it?" asked Katrinka, who understood the pleasure of buying and redecorating houses as well as hotels.

"Do?" Thea's manner indicated that she thought the question completely ridiculous. Thea had learned the forms of politeness, what fork to use, what words to say, but she had none of the genuine concern for others that was the basis of real courtesy. From the moment of her birth, her every need, every desire, every whim, had been satisfied as soon as she expressed it. She had been the center of the universe, never having to take another's feelings into account, never having to be agreeable if she did not feel like it. Rarely did she feel like it, and certainly not now, with these odd people who could be of no use whatsoever to her. Katrinka especially she did not like. She considered her somehow excessive, too colorful, almost vulgar. Mark at least had the saving grace of being a man.

"It does need a lot of renovation?" said Katrinka, who was not prepared to be patronized by anyone.

"You know the French," said Thea, without any apology to Jean-Claude. "The present owners have let it fall completely to ruin."

"You see what I have to put up with?" said Jean-Claude, smiling indulgently, as if confronted with the antics of an adorable child.

"And when it's done, will you lease it?" asked Mark, to help the conversation along.

"Lease? Oh no, not at all. I plan to combine the two apartments."

"Her present apartment has only twelve rooms," said Jean-Claude dryly.

"When I entertain, I can just accommodate fifty comfortably," explained Thea. "I would love to be able to manage a hundred."

"Thea gives extraordinary parties," said Jean-Claude. "Everyone is there: business people, politicians, writers, painters. It's like a Second Empire salon. You must come, the next time you're in Paris."

"We'd be delighted," said Mark, repressing a smile at how casually Jean-Claude issued invitations to a party he was not giving.

If we're asked, thought Katrinka, who smiled brilliantly rather than reply. She suspected that Thea did not like her any more than she liked the heiress, who reminded her, strangely, of Nina Graham. Thea seemed cold, unhappy, chronically discontented. Her smile never reached her eyes.

Katrinka thought of Natalie, of how beautiful and interesting, how wild and sexy, she had been, and how much fun. Jean-Claude certainly had thought so, rescuing her from her position as housemaid at his chateau, and not keeping her just as his lover, but promoting her up through the ranks of his Parisian department stores to chief buyer. What a pity, thought Katrinka, as she had often before, that he had not married her. They had been so well suited. And what a lot of grief every one of them would have been spared.

But Thea, of course, was a much better business proposition than Natalie had been. Her olive groves coordinated so well with Jean-Claude's vineyards and specialty food stores, her racing stables with his own. And Jean-Claude's passions were known to be money, horses, and women, in that order.

"I have business I want to discuss with you," said Katrinka to him as they were leaving the restaurant a little while later. She slowed her pace, so that Mark and Thea, who were discussing the publication of *The International*, moved slightly ahead and she had Jean-Claude to herself for a few moments. "Will you be in St. Moritz at all this month?"

"I hadn't planned on it," said Jean-Claude. "I have to leave for Montreal in a few days." Gillette CIE had stores in Canada as well as France and the United States.

"I'll call your secretary," she said. "We'll work something out. But do tell her not to be difficult."

"You weren't always so eager to see me," said Jean-Claude, smiling, apparently prepared to flirt just a little with Thea out of earshot. "When I think of how I pursued you, all around the world. And what came of it?"

"I do think we are friends," said Katrinka.

"Oh, that. Certainly," said Jean-Claude.

"And I do think you have other fish in the pan now," she added.

Without any pretense of not understanding her, Jean-Claude glanced ahead at Thea and back to Katrinka, his smile broadening. "I have always admired your beauty, *chérie*, but never more than your intelligence. What do you want to talk to me about?"

"Czechoslovakia," said Katrinka.

"You're not going to try to convince me that Prague is ready for my pretty little boutiques, or my gourmet shops, are you?"

Katrinka nodded. Havel, in an attempt to solve his country's economic problems, was trying to attract foreign investment capital. Katrinka was determined to do what she could to help. "I have a few ideas how it might work."

Jean-Claude groaned. "I have no money to throw away right now."

"Nobody does. But I do think what I have in mind could be a good thing for everybody. I'll call your secretary, okay?"

Her mission accomplished, Katrinka began to move more quickly, wanting to catch up with Mark, but Jean-Claude took hold of her arm. "I spoke to Natalie the other day."

"That is not news, Jean-Claude," said Katrinka impatiently. She knew the two were in constant touch. Though the love affair was long over, whatever the bond was between them continued to hold.

"She sounds all the time more and more . . . *distraite*. I think she could use a friend. A girlfriend."

"No," said Katrinka.

"Call her. As a favor to me?"

"What I want from you is a business deal, Jean-Claude, not a favor. One does have nothing to do with the other."

He stared at her a moment, then shrugged. "You don't forgive easily, do you?"

The absurdity of that almost made Katrinka laugh. Why should anyone be expected to "forgive" the woman, the *friend*, who had slept with your husband, destroyed your trust, betrayed you? But that was beside the point by now. "I'm not angry anymore, if that's what you mean. I don't want revenge. I do wish Natalie well. But she is not my friend. I'm sorry if she has problems, but they're no business of mine."

"Of course, *chérie*. I understand," said Jean-Claude, and he did, though it did not relieve his worry about Natalie.

"What did Jean-Claude say to make you so angry?" asked Mark, when they had left the other couple to return to their seats for the second heat of the slalom.

"You did notice?" said Katrinka. "I thought you only had eyes for the heiress."

"Jealous?" asked Mark.

"Very," said Katrinka happily, knowing she had no reason to be.

When she had told him about her conversation with Jean-Claude, Mark smiled sympathetically and said, "Baby, you're right, you know.

Natalie always struck me as a prize neurotic. No one can help people like that, until they're willing to help themselves."

"Don't worry," said Katrinka. "I have no intention of getting roped into that mess, whatever it is. What you did think of Thea?"

"Is that a loaded question?"

"No. You think she's pretty?"

"Beautiful," corrected Mark. "And cold. Not my type." He stooped a little to kiss her ear. "I prefer a more passionate kind of woman myself. The hotter her pants, the better in fact," he said, slipping his hand under her open fur coat and fondling her bottom. They both heard the motorized hum of a camera as its shutter clicked rapidly. "Oh, shit," muttered Mark, his arm dropping to his side.

"Hello, Mr. van Hollen, Mrs. van Hollen," said Sabrina, her mouth, smeared with lipstick, a wobbly red line in her pale pudding face. She was standing between Alan Platt, who flashed them an embarrassed smile, and the photographer who had snapped their picture.

"Hello, Alan. Hello, Sabrina," said Katrinka, making her usual attempt to be at least pleasant. "What you doing here?"

"My job," said Sabrina, cutting short Alan Platt's reply. "Lovely to see you," she added, turning away.

"What the hell," said Mark. "We can't be of much interest to anyone in Chicago, or on the West Coast." That was where all of Charles Wolf's newspapers were located. "With any luck they'll never print the picture."

"It's not such a bad picture," said Katrinka. A photograph from years before had flashed into her mind: Steven Elliott with his hand down the front of Sugar Benson's dress. "You're married to me."

"Another reason they probably won't use it," said Mark, sounding happier by the minute.

When Mark and she rejoined Christian, Pia, and Martin for the next heat of the slalom, Katrinka thought she noticed a subtle shift in their relationship. Instead of both boys casting frequent, covert glances at Pia, now both Pia and Martin could not keep their eyes from Christian. What had he done, wondered Katrinka with a blend of annoyance and admiration, to capture Pia's interest in so short a time?

The answer was, nothing. Realizing, finally, that paying attention to Pia only made her withdraw, Christian had stopped. And Pia, who, since she had met him the day before, had felt hot and uncomfortable in Christian's company, all of a sudden felt chilled, as if the sun had disappeared suddenly behind a thick cover of clouds. She could not understand what had happened, or what she had done to change Christian's attitude toward her. Not that she cared, she told herself: she was merely curious. Her eyes, when she should have been watching the skiers, strayed to him. And once, when he turned, as if sensing her regard, she smiled at him, she had to admit, with the sort of warmth she normally reserved for old and trusted friends, like Martin. But Christian, unaware of the honor she did him, merely nodded politely and returned his attention to the course. Pia could hardly help feeling annoyed.

Watching the exchange, Martin, instead of relieved, felt wary. He could not believe, however much he wanted to, that Christian's interest in Pia had disappeared so quickly, and for no apparent reason. If someone, something, had come along to distract him, perhaps then. But Christian did not strike Martin as the kind of person who would accept a rejection gracefully, who would just give up the chase when a woman expressed no interest in him. Martin might walk away if he got no encouragement, but he doubted Christian would do the same.

Suddenly, Martin wanted to leave, not just Méribel, but St. Moritz. He felt torn apart, by insecurity, by jealousy, by indecision. Should he or should he not tell Pia how he felt? Would it make any difference? Would it drive her away or draw her closer. Drive her away. The thought terrified him. He didn't know what to do. It was always so hard to know what Pia was thinking, what she was feeling, though he suspected it wasn't love for him, at least not the passionate, the *physical* kind he felt for her. He hated himself for being a fool and a coward, and Christian for being neither.

Perhaps he should leave? Go home, where he could think things through calmly, clearly. Yes, he decided, that's what he would do.

But no, how could he? Martin looked at Pia, his face bleak with misery. How could he go? How could he just abandon the field to Christian?

Eleven

"Honey, would you all mind paying just a little attention to me?" But the soft drawl, barely louder than a whisper, got no response, so Sugar Benson extended her foot under the table and gently kicked Adam Graham in the shins.

"What?" he said abruptly. Then, seeing Sugar Benson's quizzical face, he smiled. "I beg your pardon."

"Well, I hate to keep a man from thinking, but I'd hate people to get the idea you were bored by me. It wouldn't do my reputation the least little bit of good."

"It's been a rough day," said Adam apologetically. He had not yet unwound from the long trip to the Athens shipyard or the brief stopover at the financially strapped yard in Bremen. And Patrick Kates had awakened him in the middle of the night with news of torrential rains in California and a mast broken in a heavy wind during the preceding day's Cup defender trials. The calls from San Diego had continued nonstop, the last only minutes before Adam had left his suite at the Palace Hotel to meet Sugar. Kates's always rampant paranoia was at full flood: the yacht design had been lousy from the start; immediate modifications had to be made in the mast, in the bow, in the sails; Dennis Conner and/or Bill Koch, two of the leading Cup defenders, were trying to sabotage him, and so on. He wanted Adam to return to California immediately, which, of course, was out of the question, given his other unsolved problem of the day—Charles Wolf's

107

reluctance to fall in with his plans for Mark van Hollen's company. "I guess I need a bit of time to unwind."

"Given half a chance," said Sugar, "I'm awfully good at that, helping men unwind."

"I don't doubt it for a minute," said Adam, forcing as much interest into his expression as he could muster. He didn't know what the hell he was doing with her. An impulse he did not quite approve of had prompted his asking her to dance at Dracula the other night and suggesting this evening's "date." It was curiosity, he supposed, since it was hard *not* to be curious about someone with Sugar's reputation. But certainly he had no intention of going to bed with her. If having sex was beginning to seem to Adam more and more like playing Russian roulette, Sugar Benson was the bullet in the chamber as far as he was concerned. Steven Elliott, who had been a friend of his, though not a particularly close one by the end of his life, had died of AIDS not too long after his divorce from her. At the time, the gossip was that Sugar had been tested and found free of the virus that caused the disease, and gossip was always amazingly accurate. Still, there had been a lot of traffic through Sugar's bed since then; and while Adam didn't mind taking chances, he liked the odds, when he did, to be firmly in his favor.

"Don't look so worried, honey," said Sugar. "I'm every bit as careful as you are. Maybe even more careful. I have to be. It's my livelihood at stake, after all."

They were dining upstairs at the Chesa Veglia, one of St. Moritz's most popular restaurants. Tucked away in a narrow street near the Kulm Hotel, the restaurant was in a typical Swiss building, with a pitched roof laden with snow above walls of cream-colored stucco, deep window embrasures faced with wrought-iron grilles, and a massive wood door set into a rounded arch. Inside, there was a cloak room to the left, and directly ahead, stone steps leading up to a tiny, very narrow bar and a dining room with a wood floor, half-paneled walls, and tables covered in checkered cloths, all very cozy and informal, the sort of place to come for a pizza, which was a specialty, though everything on the menu was delicious.

"Now that you mention it," said Adam, "how is business?"

"Well, as you can imagine, the recession hasn't done us a lot of good."

"Not so many executives taking trips these days?"

"You know how it is," said Sugar, with an exaggerated sigh. "The boss gets to spend as much as he likes, on whatever he likes, but he sure as hell keeps an eagle eye on everybody else's expense account."

Happily for Sugar Benson's balance sheet, her small enterprise had a client list consisting of the world's wealthiest men—and women: heads of state, cabinet ministers, leading industrialists, CEOs of major international corporations, oil sheiks, rock stars, and a collection of bored, jet set Eurotrash. So, while the loss of lower echelon employees had reduced Sugar's gross income, her profits remained high enough to make worthwhile the risks of staying in business. "But I can't complain. All things considered, I'm doing very well."

The conversation stopped for a moment, while a waiter poured them each another glass of a 1978 Barolo from nearby Piedmont, then Adam asked, "Do your girls carry some sort of certificate with them when they go out on a . . . on an assignment?"

"A certificate of good health?" asked Sugar, and when Adam nodded, replied, "Of course. Unfortunately, we can't ask the same of our clients. Hardly fair, is it?"

"How often are they tested?"

"You're very curious about my business, aren't you?" Like Adam, for a moment Sugar wondered why she was wasting her time. But she quickly answered her own question: she had nothing better to do. She had come to St. Moritz with a few of her girls for a party hosted by the Duke of Cumber, one of Sugar's best clients, for some of his more adventurous friends. That over, she had decided to stay on for a few days of skiing. But while the Palace Hotel was still willing to take her money, the social doors that had been open to her as Steven Elliott's wife were now firmly closed. There were few people still willing to acknowledge her publicly. Adam was one of them. He was also an extremely attractive man. What a pity, she thought, that he seemed to have no sexual curiosity about her at all.

"Business is my passion, Sugar. You know that."

"I always knew we had a lot in common."

Sugar smiled, and for a moment Adam almost forgot his good intentions. She really was beautiful, with delicate features and honey-colored hair arranged in a neat upsweep of shining tresses, the heavy bun confined by a wide band of black silk. The body-hugging fabrics and plunging necklines she had worn when he had first met her had given way over the years to more sedate, classic styles, expensive and flattering, but far from overtly sexy. Why even his mother would approve of the ruffled organza blouse and velvet stirrup pants that Sugar was wearing. His mother. The thought of Nina Graham brought Adam back to reality. One of his great pleasures in life was crossing her, but even he was not prepared to go as far as Sugar Benson.

* * *

"Oh, no," muttered Daisy as she followed Dieter Keiser into the Chesa Veglia's dining room.

"What?" said Dieter, instantly attentive, turning his small, slender body toward her. "You have changed your mind? You would rather dine elsewhere?"

Daisy turned to Katrinka, who was immediately behind her, and said, "What do you think?"

"Something is wrong?" asked Katrinka. Then she spotted Adam and Sugar.

"We're staying here," said Mark, annoyed that anyone should think Adam Graham's presence mattered either to Katrinka or him.

"I never thought to ask him where he was having dinner," said Lucia apologetically.

"When you are all going to understand I don't care where he is, what he does," said Katrinka, her irritation even greater than Mark's. But she knew she was wasting her breath. After her divorce, Daisy had always been upset by running into Steven Elliott, until the end, when he had been so ill that she had returned to New York to take care of him. And Lucia, if Nick Cavalletti were to walk into the Chesa Veglia that minute, would run shrieking into the night.

Katrinka waved briefly, in the general direction of Adam and Sugar's table, then, despite Daisy's efforts to seat her with her back to Adam, sat in a chair facing him, with Mark beside her. Of the entire group, she knew that only they would be able to keep their eyes from straying to the couple on the opposite side of the room.

Christian, who had taken the seat on the other side of his mother, also resisted the temptation to look. He was curious about Sugar Benson. He had heard about her, of course, over the years: she was the subject of much international gossip. But he had only the vaguest memory of her from the time when she was welcome at the Hellers' parties. And the other night, at Dracula, he had paid attention only to Adam. Now, he regretted that. Though he had got over his fascination with prostitutes by the time he was seventeen, he thought he would quite enjoy knowing a world class madam.

"What is Adam *doing* with her?" said Daisy.

"*Cara, per piacere, stai zitta,*" said Riccardo.

"Sorry," said Daisy, keeping quiet as suggested, burying her narrow, aristocratic nose in the menu.

Riccardo summoned the waiter and requested several bottles of his favorite wine. Soon the dinners were ordered, the wine arrived, and the conversation retreated to what everyone hoped would be less dangerous territory.

Despite the casualness of the restaurant, not a pair of jeans or a sweater was in sight. All the men, including Christian and Martin, were in good wool trousers, sports jackets, and ties. The women were dressed informally, which in St. Moritz meant only that they were not in cocktail dresses. Each wore a recognizable outfit—by Missoni or Versace or Kors. Katrinka's was a two-piece Donna Karan pants suit with a detachable portrait collar on a jacket that flared at the hips to hide the slight bulge of her stomach. In no way would anyone's dress have been considered casual.

When the sommelier had opened the wine, and the waiters had poured some of the Castel Chiuro into each of the glasses, Daisy raised hers and said, "Well, bon voyage, though I wish you weren't leaving."

"So do I," said Lucia. She had had almost as many phone calls from Patrick that day as had Adam, who had finally suggested that she return to San Diego to assess what needed to be done, leaving him to follow as soon as he could. Why Adam could not be the one to leave, she did not understand, since Charles Wolf had accepted the revised yacht designs with enthusiasm and Adam had, as far as she knew, nothing more to keep him in St. Moritz. She, on the other hand, had Pia. "But apparently there's work to be done."

"You'd think, in all of Graham Marine, there would be someone else who could handle it," said Daisy.

"Not only Graham Marine," added Riccardo. "I read that there are over thirty scientists and engineers from all over the world working on the yacht design."

"Only a slight exaggeration," said Lucia, laughing.

"Then why you have to go rushing back?" asked Katrinka.

"To calm Patrick down, of course," said Pia, who, though she had been avoiding Lucia for days, was not pleased that her mother was cutting short her vacation.

"I hate leaving you, darling," said Lucia, who heard the reproach in Pia's voice, "spoiling your holiday. But—"

"I know," said Pia, interrupting. "It's business." She had been hearing that excuse from Lucia for as long as she could remember. Not that she held it against her mother—usually. However devoted Lucia was to her work, Pia had always come first, and she knew it. Had it been really important that Lucia stay, she would have told both Adam Graham and Patrick Kates to go to hell. It was just that Pia so disliked Patrick, she could not help blaming him for acting like a child and spoiling her mother's holiday. But not wanting to seem like a spoiled brat herself, she smiled reassuringly. "Don't worry about me. I'm old enough to look after myself."

"You always were," said Katrinka, who remembered the solemn and amazingly adult little girl Pia had been.

"Well, you certainly won't miss me much, not with Martin and Christian for company," said Lucia, relieved that Pia was making this so easy for her. Though, in fact, she was surprised at how reluctant she was to see Patrick. Not Patrick, she corrected herself immediately. She was just not looking forward to the display of temperament that would greet her. Damn Adam anyway, she thought.

Martin frowned. "The thing is . . . " he said. Pia and Lucia turned to him expectantly, neither able to imagine what he was going to say. "I have to get back to Los Angeles."

"Oh, you're not thinking of leaving, too," said Daisy, genuinely disappointed. "And the weather there is so awful now, with all those dreadful storms. I saw photographs of people swimming out of their cars on Burbank Boulevard."

"That's the problem," said Martin. "There were some mud slides at Carla's house. I think my mother can use some help."

"I did speak to her this morning. Everything's under control," said Katrinka, wondering why Martin seemed so anxious to get away. She would have thought Christian had something to do with it, but her son, since the trip to Méribel, had been paying no attention to Pia at all. But how stupid of Martin, she thought, to go and leave the field clear for Christian. She doubted her son would be able to resist the temptation.

"The storms aren't over yet." Undecided about whether to go or stay, the hint of panic in his mother's voice when he had spoken to her had made up Martin's mind. "Anyway, it's my last semester at Claremont. I need to start doing something about job applications. In fact, I hoped to be able to talk to you and Mark before I leave."

"Sure," said Mark, "anytime. When are you going?"

"I thought maybe I could hitch a ride in the helicopter to Zurich with Lucia tomorrow."

Mark nodded, then said, "Come by for breakfast before you leave."

"Tomorrow," said Pia, surprised out of her usual calm.

"I was scheduled to leave in a couple of days anyway," said Martin defensively.

Pia suppressed a surge of panic, which she did not at all understand. She was used to Martin appearing and disappearing in her life, with little or no warning. It had been that way since they were children, when their paths would cross briefly aboard the *Lady Katrinka*, or at the Villa Mahmed, or the Chesa Mulin, before they returned to schools thousands of miles apart in Los Angeles and Florence. What difference could it make to her this time whether Martin stayed or went? But it did. She glanced quickly toward Christian, but, deep in conversation with Riccardo, he seemed unaware, or uninterested, in Martin's change of plans. She looked back at Martin. Would he stay if she asked him? she wondered. For a moment, she was tempted; but, finally, for reasons she again did not understand, she said only, "Well, we'll be seeing each other at Easter, I suppose. That's only a few weeks away."

"Yes," agreed Martin, without enthusiasm. The time to Easter seemed like an eternity to him. He wished now that he had said nothing about leaving; or, better, that Pia had asked him to stay. Is that what he had been hoping for, he wondered, that she would beg him to remain in St. Moritz? But her attention was now focused on her salad, and there seemed little chance that she would.

"Try and get on my flight," said Lucia. She shuddered in mock horror. "A fourteen-hour trip. A nightmare. We can keep each other entertained."

"Martin just buries his nose in a book when he flies," said Pia, looking up. "He's not much company."

"Just like his father, when he was a kid," said Katrinka, smiling, "always reading, or going to films."

"I'm flying economy," said Martin, interrupting Katrinka. He was in no mood to hear fond reminiscences about his father, with whom he was always more or less at odds; and not just because of Tomáš's numerous infidelities, the cause, as far as Martin was concerned, both of the break-up of his parents' marriage and Zuzka's ridiculous affair with Carla Webb. Their problems dated back far beyond that.

"I'm only flying business," said Lucia. "We'll try and get you an upgrade. Who knows someone at SwissAir?" she called to the table at large.

"Dieter," said Daisy. "Dieter knows everyone, don't you, darling?"

"I try," said Dieter with what passed for humility. "What can I do to help?"

"You're leaving?" said Christian to Martin. "What a pity." He almost believed it was. Life would not be nearly so interesting in St. Moritz without Martin to annoy. On the other hand, he thought, casting a quick, surreptitious glance toward Pia, now he had not only motive but opportunity. It would have been much harder getting Pia to bed with Martin hovering around her like a lovesick nanny.

Daisy also looked at Pia, but she smiled. "At least you'll have Christian," she said comfortingly, "so you won't have to rely on us old folks for company."

"Perhaps it would be best if I left, too," offered Pia, who had a sudden urge to run away.

"Nonsense," said Daisy. "Riccardo and I would hate racketing around in that great house with only Dieter for company. Wouldn't we, darling?" she said, turning to Riccardo for confirmation.

"You're always welcome to stay with us, Pia, you know that," said Riccardo in Italian. "We love having you with us."

"*Grazie*," she said. Her panic receded as quickly as it had come, and she felt take its place a great surge of excitement. "*Ancora, se voi permettete . . .*"

"Good, good," said Daisy, who looked expectantly toward Christian, waiting for an offer of help.

Knowing what was expected of him, Christian obliged. "Pia knows I am completely at her service," he said politely and without any noticeable enthusiasm.

No man still breathing could be that nonchalant about being asked to keep a beautiful girl like Pia entertained, thought Mark, as he studied his stepson's handsome, bored face, even a man not desperately attracted to her. And until a few days before, Mark had thought Christian very attracted. What game was he playing now? wondered Mark.

But Lucia felt only relief. Christian was not the kind of man a mother could happily leave alone with her daughter. Charming as he was, he was too sexy, somehow too dangerous. "That's lovely," she said, in response to Christian's half-hearted offer. "I would have hated to spoil Pia's vacation, too."

After dinner, the party moved on to the Palace Hotel, Christian, Martin, and Pia to the King's Club, which, with its wildly muraled walls and rock music, catered to the younger crowd; the others went to the more sedate Grand Bar, which had more conventional paintings, comfortable banquettes, the Society Band, and Jocelyn, a slender chanteuse in gold lamé, whose dark mysterious looks hinted at hybrid nationalities and an interesting past.

"There's Tony Moreland," said Daisy as they came down the stairs into the bar. She had owned the estate next to his when, after her divorce from Steven, she had lived briefly in the English countryside.

Seeing them, Tony Moreland waved and called, "Daisy, Riccardo, hello. Come, join us." A short man with fair skin and silver hair, which he wore long, he looked like an Anglican vicar. In fact, he was a noted playboy, owning an art gallery in Cork Street to keep up the pretense of working for his keep, but in reality living on money inherited from a long line of extremely wealthy ancestors. "Katrinka, how lovely to see you again, my dear." He kissed her cheek and shook Mark's hand. "You, too, old chap. How's this new venture of yours coming? Magazine, is it? Heard a lot of good things about it. You know my wife, don't you? Priscilla?" He gestured in the direction of a petite blonde who looked a good ten years older than her husband, then turned to a distinguished man, tall with slicked-back gray hair. "And the Duke of Cumber?"

"We did meet. Good evening, your grace," said Katrinka as she shook the duke's hand. Nigel Bevenden, Duke of Cumber, was one of the wealthiest men in England, owning the parts of central London not already in the possession of the Queen, the Church of England, or the Duke of Westminster. He was also a regular client of Katrinka's London casino, where he was frequently seen in the company of Sugar Benson.

As usual, his grace of Cumber had trouble looking Katrinka in the eye as he greeted her. "Of course," he said, the words, even more so than Tony Moreland's, emerging half-strangled from his mouth in the affected style of the English upper classes. "Delighted to see you again." While he liked occasionally to flaunt his illicit pleasures, he was not at all comfortable in the company of those who had witnessed but not shared them.

"What's his problem?" whispered Lucia, as Daisy began to organize the seating plan.

"I did see him with Sugar," explained Katrinka.

"Well, at least his grace has the grace to be embarrassed," said Lucia, laughing.

"Is everyone drinking champagne?" asked Mark.

"Not me," said Katrinka, who allowed herself a glass only on very special occasions.

"A Campari and soda for me, please," said Daisy.

The music was loud, and conversation difficult, fragmented, changing shape and color as quickly as a kaleidoscope. They discussed friends, enemies, the Olympics, the weather, the Corviglia Club races to be held over the next few days, and whether or not Katrinka would take part in the slalom or the downhill. "But I'm not a member," said Katrinka, with an encouraging smile, hoping that Tony Moreland, who was on the committee, would cast a vote in her favor.

But Tony was not paying attention to Katrinka at that moment, she noticed. He was deep in conversation with Mark. "I'd love to give it a try," she heard Mark say.

"Good. Then come by the clubhouse Monday at about seven, and I'll show you the ropes."

"What you two are plotting?" asked Katrinka suspiciously.

"Nothing at all, my dear," said Tony, before Mark could reply. "Mark's just going to have a go at the Cresta."

"What!" said Katrinka, turning to Mark. She was horrified. "You are crazy! Completely crazy!" The Cresta Run was a narrow curving trail cut through high banks of ice from just below the St. Moritz clock tower to Celerina. It was a mad and dangerous sport, a lone man on a steel toboggan careening down an icy slope, around hairpin turns, completing a mile in just under a minute.

"When I first started, I used to be quite sick the night before a run," said Moreland agreeably. Katrinka's reaction was typically female, as far as he was concerned. There was no way she could possibly understand how thrilling it was to flirt so outrageously with death. "But there's nothing like it."

"It sounds like fun," said Mark.

Fun! thought Katrinka. The Sunday before, when they had watched the team known as "Shooting Party" win in competition with "The Young and the Restless," "The Grappa Seniors," and all the others, one of "The Tigers" had broken his collarbone. Katrinka had never met a member of the Cresta who had not at least once broken an arm, a shoulder, even his spine. But her years of arguing with Adam about the dangers of sailing had proved to her the futility of trying to get between a man and the sport of his choice. Or a woman and hers, she conceded, trying to be fair. Her mother, never a physically brave woman, had hated the idea of Katrinka's skiing, imagining all sorts of disasters for her only daughter. But once she had lost the argument with her husband and their headstrong child, she had never complained. She hadn't wanted to be a spoilsport. Eventually, Katrinka had reached that same point with Adam. And now, with Mark, she apparently had another set of dangers with which to come to terms.

"Excuse me for a moment," said the Duke of Cumber, scrambling past Daisy and Riccardo.

"Oh, shit," muttered Lucia, who watched him going to greet Sugar and Adam, who had just entered. "I thought we'd seen the last of them tonight."

"Dance?" whispered Mark in Katrinka's ear. She nodded, and he took her hand and led her to the dance floor. "Are you mad at me?" he asked, as he swung her into his arms for a fox-trot.

"Yes," she admitted.

116

"I can't do everything you want."

Why couldn't Mark understand how terrified she was, since her parents' sudden death, of losing the people she loved quickly, without warning? "Why not?" she asked, forcing herself to smile.

"Because you're a willful and demanding woman," explained Mark, with no hint of disapproval in his voice, "and if I let you ride roughshod over me, you'd lose all respect. You'd leave me, and I wouldn't like that."

"I would never leave you," she said. "I do love you too much. And I'm not demanding."

"You want everything to be perfect, you think you're always right, and you like to get your own way."

"So do you," said Katrinka. "So does every man I know."

Mark laughed. "You may have a point," he said.

How different he was from Adam, she thought with a surge of contentment: Adam never would have conceded her the argument. But not different enough, she decided a moment later with an equally strong surge of irritation. Like Adam, Mark too was going to do exactly as he liked, no matter how he worried her. "You're going to do the Cresta just to prove who's boss in our house? Is that it?"

"You really think I'm that dumb?" he asked.

"Are you?"

"No. Just dumb enough to think it might be fun. Now, are we going to dance, or argue?"

It was not an argument she had a prayer of winning, Katrinka knew. And if he did succeed in killing himself, she didn't want to have to live with knowing that they had parted on bad terms. "Dance," she said.

"Good." He pulled her as close as the mound of her stomach would permit and inclined his head until his cheek rested against hers. "We won't be able to dance like this for much longer," he said. The thought of this child had once terrified him: he hadn't wanted it. But now, he had to admit, he was as thrilled at the idea as Katrinka. He might not be any more able to protect this child from harm than he had his two sons. But life came with no guarantees. If you wanted to enjoy its riches, you had to risk losing even what you held most dear.

Mark felt Katrinka jump in his arms. "The baby moved," she said, lifting her head and smiling at him.

"I know." He pulled her close again and kissed her. "Don't worry," he said. "I have no intention of killing myself. I have too much to live for."

* * *

117

The Grand Bar's black ceiling and dim lighting made it difficult to see too far into the gloom, but Mark's height and head of silvery blond hair made him easy to pick out of the crowd on the dance floor. Watching him, Adam felt the familiar waves of anger and resentment begin to rise. It was bad enough before, having to witness scum like van Hollen exploiting the financial system, using cunning combined with greed to amass fortunes, trying to conceal their origins under assumed manners and custom-made clothes, thinking their money made them acceptable, expecting it to buy their entry into the clubs, into the *homes*, for Christ's sake, of those who really mattered. But now that van Hollen had claimed possession of one of Adam's most remarkable acquisitions, the young immigrant woman he had transformed into a leader of New York society, he found the situation really intolerable. Mark van Hollen had no business coming anywhere near Graham territory, abandoned or otherwise.

Though he could not be sure of where Adam Graham's attention was focused, the Duke of Cumber thought he could make a good guess. "You do know, I suppose, that your former wife has expressed some desire to join the Corviglia?" he asked. He took a sip of champagne and waited for Adam's response.

"Oh?" said Adam. Over his dead body, he thought. "I didn't know, but it doesn't surprise me. Katrinka has a lot of friends in the Corviglia. There's no opposition to her membership, I suppose?"

The duke as well as Tony Moreland was on the membership committee. "Not really. People seem in general to be quite fond of her."

"Yourself included?" asked Sugar, curious as to how this man with his odd sexual quirks would respond to someone like Katrinka, who, sensual as she seemed, did not appear to be in the least perverse.

"She seems a good enough sort," replied the duke politely, "if not exactly in my line." He turned to Adam with a smile. "Nor in yours any longer, I assume."

"Exactly," said Adam. "Not that I wish her anything but well. You can't go through a divorce without some bitterness, I suppose, but that's long over. As far as I'm concerned, she'd be an asset to the Corviglia, despite her unfortunate knack of attracting publicity."

"Yes," said the duke, a note of disdain coloring his voice. "She's certainly not camera shy, is she?" That Adam shared Katrinka's "knack" did not seem to occur to him; or perhaps it was just that making news seemed to him a man's prerogative. Like Nina Graham, the Duke of Cumber and his peers believed that a woman's name should appear in print only three times: when she was born, when she married, and when she died.

"And I don't suppose van Hollen will be around enough to bother anyone."

"Van Hollen?"

"Her current husband. Made his money in newspapers. His father was an immigrant. Some sort of laborer, I believe."

"Really?" said the duke, repressing the urge to smile. The Bevendens had arrived in England with William the Conqueror; the dukedom of Cumber dated back to the reign of Edward II. Viewed from the duke's perspective, the Grahams were very Johnny-come-lately. Still, one had to draw the line somewhere. "I had no idea."

So that's how it's done, thought Sugar with something approaching admiration, someone's fate settled neatly, with no more than a hint. And all because a husband had had the bad taste to have made and not inherited his money.

The duke stood. "I really must rejoin my party. A pleasure seeing you again, Graham." He leaned over and kissed Sugar's cheek. "And you, my dear. See you soon again, I trust."

"An interesting man," said Adam, watching as the duke threaded his way gracefully through the crowd, nodding a greeting, stopping to exchange a few words, on his way back to the Moreland table.

"You have no idea," said Sugar, exaggerating her drawl for effect.

Adam laughed. "Tell me," he said, his voice coaxing, inspiring trust. It was the one he used when negotiating difficult deals.

"Oh, now, I couldn't do that. A client's preferences are confidential, you know. But if there's something you'd like to tell me, some little whim you'd like to confess, some desire you want fulfilled . . ." She was too good a businesswoman to let any stone remain unturned, even one as hard and unpromising as Adam Graham. "My aim is to please."

"Thanks for the offer, but no thanks," said Adam. Fantasies were one thing. Acting them out, another. And paying for them, out of the question. He shook his head for emphasis. But, then, an idea occurred to him. He leaned toward Sugar and said. "Do you think any man can be seduced?"

"Yes," she said.

"Even me?"

She laughed. "I understand that's been done."

"Even him?" said Adam, gesturing with his champagne glass to the edge of the dance floor where Mark van Hollen stood, with his arm around Katrinka, talking to Prince Dimitri.

"A new husband, a pregnant wife . . ." Sugar took a sip of champagne, studying Mark over the rim of her glass. Then, she said, "Well, it would be quite a challenge, but I don't see why not."

"Would you be willing to try?"

"Oh, no, honey. For one thing, he knows me. For another, I really don't like to have to work so hard anymore."

"I didn't mean you, personally," said Adam. "But you do run a business, don't you? You have other . . . employees?"

Sugar's eyes widened slightly. "You're serious, aren't you."

"I'm always serious when discussing a business proposition."

"But why?"

"I don't think my motives are the issue here, do you? My ability to pay, and your ability to deliver the goods, that's all that matters."

Sugar sat silent for a moment, her mind calculating many things: whether or not she wanted to get involved; how much she could reasonably charge Adam, if she did; whether he was in as much financial trouble as she'd heard; if she knew a girl who had a prayer of luring Mark van Hollen away from his wife.

"Well?" said Adam impatiently.

"Why not?" said Sugar finally.

Adam smiled, his mouth quirking up at the corner in a way that had once made Katrinka's heart turn somersaults in her breast. "Why not indeed?"

Twelve

 "I LOVE YOU, PIA."

"I LOVE YOU, TOO. YOU KNOW THAT."

"Oh, Christ," said Martin, running a hand through his thick, dark curls. He got to his feet and began pacing back and forth in front of the huge open fireplace. A log splintered, fell through the grate, and for an instant the fire blazed higher. "I knew you wouldn't understand."

Sitting on the sofa, her bare feet tucked up under her, Pia watched him, her eyes anxious, unhappy. Without consciously knowing it, she had dreaded this moment since . . . well, for days. "Martin . . ." She began to speak, then changed her mind. Perhaps, if she said nothing, he too would keep quiet.

Martin stopped pacing and sat next to her again. Her hands were in her lap, her fingers toying nervously with one another. They were small, delicate, but Martin knew how strong they were, strong enough to wield a metal hammer or a blowtorch. He took her right hand and held it in his. Except to lead her across a street or onto a dance floor, he never had before. "I love you," he repeated. "I've loved you for years. I want to marry you, Pia."

They were alone, in the sitting room of the Chesa Mulin. Earlier, they had left the King's Club and gone on to Dracula, where Christian, as far as they knew, still was. By the time they had returned home, everyone else had gone to bed, except for the butler, of course, who had opened the door for them.

"Marry you?" said Pia. "But—"

Martin heard the distress in her voice and interrupted her. "I'm almost finished with school," he said, as if that were the issue. "We both are. And in a few months I'll have a job. I don't know where yet, but that won't matter to you, will it? You can work anywhere. You don't have to stay in Italy." He laughed nervously. "We could live in New York. That's more or less halfway for both of us. And if you crack the New York market with your jewelry designs, you'll have it made." He was talking too quickly, he knew, not giving Pia a chance to respond. But that was because he didn't want her to. He was afraid of what she would say. "It would all work out, Pia. I know . . ."

"Martin," said Pia finally, her voice firm. He stopped talking. "I can't marry you." Seeing all the animation fade from his face, the determination, the hope, all replaced by misery, she added, "I'm sorry. I really am sorry. But I can't."

"Why not? You love me," he said, pretending to have misunderstood her. "You said you did."

She pulled her hand away; her fingers began restlessly picking at one another again. "I didn't mean . . . I do. I do love you, but not like that. I love you like my friend. Like my brother." For once, Pia's guard was down. Her cultivated, cool facade had shattered. She moved toward him, slipped her arms around his neck, rested her face against his chest. About her father, she no longer knew what she felt. Now, except for her mother, there was no one in the world she loved as much as Martin. "I'd give anything not to hurt you."

He held her for a moment without speaking. Then he said, "I know."

Pulling back, she looked at him, her eyes sad, but with no trace of tears in them. "Forgive me?" she said. He nodded, and she went on, her voice urgent, "I don't want anything to be different between us. I want everything to be the same."

Nothing would be the same, Martin knew, even as he promised her that it would be. Unrequited love, thwarted passion, whatever name he chose to call it, would shadow them from that point on like a starved animal begging for food, depriving their relationship of the easy intimacy that had characterized it from the beginning.

More than anything, Martin wished that he had said nothing. Certain of how Pia would respond, that's what he had meant to do: just go, leaving everything between them as it had always been. But, despite all his good intentions, when it came to it, he could not, without first telling her how he felt. It had seemed, suddenly, because of Christian, too big a risk. And there was the chance, after all, that he had misunderstood the signs, that Pia loved him as much and in the same way, as passionately and completely, as he did her. But he had misunderstood nothing.

They sat up talking for another half hour or so, to reassure each other that nothing had changed between them. They promised to write, to see each other at Easter, at Katrinka's house in the south of France, where all her friends usually gathered for the holiday.

"Will Christian be there?" asked Martin, unable to help himself. He was not sure he could stand another holiday with Christian for company.

"I don't know," said Pia, her voice expressionless, as if the subject of Christian did not interest her in the least. "I suppose so, if he wants to come."

"Why wouldn't he?"

Pia shrugged. "Sometimes I get the feeling that he doesn't like any of us very much, Katrinka included. He's so odd, don't you think?"

Pia was obviously eager to talk about Christian, noticed Martin, who had immediately regretted mentioning him. "I don't know that I'd call him odd. Cold, calculating, maybe."

"From the moment you two met, you didn't like him."

There was no point denying it, so Martin said only, "But you do."

Again, Pia shrugged. "I find him interesting, I suppose. But more than that? I don't think so. He's a hard person to like."

"How about impossible?" said Martin. He leaned toward her. She did not move away, and he was happy for that much, at least. He kissed her cheek, then stood up. "I've still got to pack." But, instead of leaving the room, he remained looking down at her a moment, weighing whether or not to speak. Finally, he said, "Don't write off what I'm about to say, Pia, just because you think I'm jealous. Which I am. I admit it. But I care about you. Don't trust him, Pia, okay? Be careful."

"I always am," she said, almost regretfully. "You don't have to worry about me. Anyway, there's nothing to worry about. Christian has no interest in me. And I certainly don't in him." She stood up. "Do you want me to help you pack?"

"No," he said quickly. "It won't take me long." Just then, it was too painful to be with her. "You go to bed."

Silently, they left the sitting room, climbed the pine stairs, whispered goodnight when they reached the second floor, and entered their separate rooms. Hearing them, the butler sighed with relief, went into the sitting room, put out the fire, turned out the lights, picked up the tray of dirty cups and saucers and returned with it to the kitchen, where he left it on the drainboard to be dealt with in the morning. He turned out the remaining lights and hurried upstairs to the attic to bed, where his wife, the housekeeper, had preceded him. It was almost three, and they and the other servants had to be up by six-thirty to begin their morning duties.

If the butler got little sleep, Martin got none at all. In less than half an hour he had finished his packing, undressed to his shorts, and climbed under the down duvet. For the next three hours, he lay awake, not tossing restlessly but lying still, his hands under his head, thinking about Pia, about Christian, about his own future, which filled him suddenly with despair. When he heard the butler and housekeeper make their way back downstairs, he got up, put on one of the terry robes that Daisy and Riccardo supplied their guests, went to the WC, then into the bathroom to take a shower. The thing that amazed him about this house was that, no matter what hour of the day or night you were up, it was never cold.

By seven, Martin was knocking on the door of the Chesa Konsalvi. The housekeeper answered it and showed him into the dining room, where Mark and Katrinka were already at breakfast, both paying little attention to the basket of crusty Swiss rolls and homemade marmalade on the table in front of them as they studied the reams of faxes, sent overnight from their various offices.

"Martin, *zlatíčko*," said Katrinka, seeing Martin in the doorway. She was in a silk robe, her face free of makeup, her dark hair pulled up in a ponytail held with a rubber band. "Come in. What you want to eat? Eggs? Bacon? What else we have?" she asked, turning to the housekeeper, who had followed Martin into the room and stood waiting to take his order. A woman in her late fifties, the housekeeper lived in. Her sister came daily to help with the cleaning and laundry. Her brother-in-law acted as driver, general handyman, and butler for the dinner parties Katrinka and Mark hosted about once a week.

"Scrambled eggs, rolls, some coffee, if that's okay?" said Martin.

Despite Mark and Katrinka's continuing disagreement over the Cresta Run, there was a basic contentment in the room, a feeling of peace and security that felt vaguely familiar to Martin. It reminded him, he thought suddenly, of when he was small, before he had developed that tumor, when he and his parents had still lived in Prague. They had been happy then, he remembered, though even there Zuzka had had to work to help support the family and Tomáš had grumbled first about not directing at all and then about the kinds of films he was being made to do. When had everything changed? What had gone wrong? Had it really been his illness that had ruined

124

everything? Though Tomáš had never said so, not directly to him at any rate, Martin knew that's what his father believed.

"Is anything wrong?" asked Mark, seeing the disturbed, sad look on Martin's face. Not that there was a thing he could do to help, he thought, assuming that Pia was the root of Martin's problem. Pia *and* Christian. Young love was hell, he remembered, for the moment grateful that he'd never see twenty again.

"Wrong? Oh, no. Everything's fine." Martin attempted a laugh, which came out with a ragged, nervous edge. "I can't help being a little worried about the future, but, given the job market at the moment, that's only natural, I suppose."

"You will have your master's, though. That will be a big help," said Katrinka encouragingly. Graduates with only bachelor's degrees were going to have a rough time finding work for a very long time, she feared.

"Do you have any idea what you want to do?" asked Mark.

"That's what I wanted to talk to you about."

His mother, explained Martin, had offered him a job working with her, managing Carla Webb's various business interests, including the highly lucrative merchandising division that Zuzka had started soon after she and Carla became lovers. It was now worth several million a year, and she needed, or so she said, help running it. Martin, however, was very reluctant to become involved. He liked Carla well enough. And he had more or less come to terms with his mother's sexual involvement with her. But he did not want to be that embroiled in their lives. "I'm not really interested in personal management," he told Katrinka and Mark to explain his reluctance.

"I can understand that," said Mark, who thought Martin wise not to involve himself in such a potentially volatile situation. Working with lovers was never easy. "What *are* you interested in?"

The housekeeper returned with Martin's breakfast and, as he ate, he, Katrinka, and Mark discussed options, including the possibility of Martin's working for either of them, or for Adam. "You will take the best offer," she told him, with a big smile. Nothing gave her greater pleasure than setting a goal and achieving it, even for other people. But, after tossing ideas around for a while, it became clear, even to Martin, that what he really wanted was to work on the Street, something he had tried to put out of his mind, aware that, since the crash of October 1987, thousands of New York's whiz-kid investment brokers had helped raise the unemployment statistics.

"If you do want it, go for it," said Katrinka, always the optimist.

"You've got nothing to lose," added her husband, a little more cautiously. "God knows, there are plenty of people still making money. Lots of money." Mark, whose pleasure came, like Katrinka's, from starting a company, then watching it grow and prosper, or buying one and transforming it from loser to winner, did not quite understand the pleasure that others got from trading assets and liabilities they couldn't actually see or feel. Even playing roulette, you got to handle the chips, and winning, you could cash them in for money you put in your pocket. How could an electronic transfer deliver even that much satisfaction? He didn't get it. But others clearly did, and Martin among them.

"I'll talk to Neil Goodman when I get back to New York. Maybe he can find something for you at Knapp Manning," said Katrinka. "If he thinks it's possible, then you can talk to him." Martin had known Neil and Alexandra, too, since he was a child.

"Thanks, Katrinka, I'd really appreciate it."

"My pleasure, *zlatíčko*," she said.

"May I come in?" Christian stood in the doorway, dressed in ski pants and a sweater.

"Come in, come in," said Katrinka, her face lighting up as always at Christian's appearance. "I thought you would sleep all day, you got in so late."

"I never need much sleep," said Christian.

"Like me," said Katrinka quickly, with a delighted smile, like a detective still gathering evidence to prove they were mother and son, as if anyone seeing them together could doubt it for a moment. "Did you tell the housekeeper what you want for breakfast?"

"I'm not hungry," said Christian, reaching for the coffee pot and pouring himself a cup.

Martin stood. "I better get going," he said. "I don't want to make Lucia wait. Thank you both, for everything. You've been a big help already."

"I'll phone you as soon as I do talk to Neil," said Katrinka, as Martin bent to kiss her cheek.

Martin shook Mark's hand, then, since it was unavoidable, Christian's. "See you at Easter," he said, hoping to find out what Christian was planning.

Christian shot a quick glance at Katrinka, who said, "We usually spend Easter at the Villa Mahmed. Whoever wants to come." Katrinka loved the house, which Mark had not yet seen, since, until their marriage in December, they had avoided going anywhere they might be recognized.

126

"Of course," said Christian, with a faint smile. "Until Easter then." Martin nodded, turned, and walked to the door, then turned again as he heard Christian's voice. "It's not necessary to worry about Pia," he said in his slightly stilted English. "It will be my pleasure to look after her."

For an instant, Martin looked as if he would like nothing better than to hurtle back across the room and slug Christian. But he quickly got himself under control. "I'm not worried," he said. "Nobody knows better than Pia how to take care of herself. 'Bye." He forced a smile, managing one that looked relatively worry-free, and left.

Tension hung in the air. As Christian reached toward the wicker basket for a roll, Mark and Katrinka exchanged a glance. Then Mark stood. "I better start making some telephone calls if we want to get out on the slopes at a decent hour."

"We?" said Katrinka. "You think I wait for you?"

Grinning, Mark reached out and tugged the end of her dark ponytail. "Like I said, I better get a move on, or get left behind."

As soon as Mark had gone, Katrinka turned to Christian. "Were you deliberately trying to upset Martin?" she asked, though she knew the answer.

"Upset him? Not at all," said Christian, his eyes shining with innocence. "On the contrary, I was doing my best to be reassuring." As usual when they were alone, they spoke in German.

"I care about him and Pia very much."

"I've noticed," said Christian, wondering if perhaps that was one of his major incentives for tormenting the two. He did not like to share affection—or anything else for that matter. And even if he was not quite certain yet how he felt about this newfound mother of his, what he did know, absolutely, was that he resented anyone else's claims to her time or affection, any threat to his hold over her emotions. Her friends he disliked mildly; their children he detested, except for Pia, whom he viewed more as a potential acquisition than a rival; and he both loathed and feared Mark van Hollen.

Most people, finding them too frightening to acknowledge, buried such intense feelings, pushing them down layers deep into their subconscious. But not Christian. He had been in therapy for one reason or another, in one place or another, from the age of four until he had refused, at twelve, to continue. Not only had a few silent sessions at great expense convinced his parents then that there was no point in making him go on against his will, but everyone, the experts included, had agreed that Christian would resume treatment when he felt the need. That time had never come.

127

In those eight years of therapy, which Kurt and Luisa Heller now considered a great waste of money, Christian had learned to examine his actions and to understand what motives had produced them: in other words, he had got "in touch with his feelings." But since neither his actions nor their causes worried him in the least, since he, in fact, very much enjoyed being a "bad boy," he saw no advantage in changing, in trying to transform his dark passions into pale yearnings for what is sensible and good. Life then would not be nearly so amusing, he thought. All that his years of therapy had done for him, in the end, was teach him how to get exactly what he wanted without having to pay an unacceptable price for it. And because he was smart, usually he got off scot-free.

"They have both had difficult childhoods," said Katrinka.

"Harder than mine, do you suppose?" asked Christian as he covered a roll with marmalade.

"Much," said Katrinka firmly. "Compared to them, you've had an easy time of it."

"What do you know about it? What can you possibly know about what I had to endure as a child?" said Christian, sounding more contemptuous than angry.

"Only what you've told me," said Katrinka, refusing to lose her temper. Christian's stories of being sent away to school at six because of behavioral problems she took with a grain of salt. After all, how bad could a six-year-old possibly be? But that the Hellers had not been warm, loving parents, the kind she had wanted for her son, she believed and regretted. Seen in those terms, she understood her son's frequently stated dislike of them. And she shared it. But she hardly saw them as the demons Christian liked to pretend they were.

Christian smiled. "And if I've lied? What then?"

"Have you?" Frequently, she did not know whether or not to take him seriously, he so obviously loved playacting, his moods shifting so suddenly, with so little justification.

"This is a ridiculous conversation," said Christian, slamming his coffee cup back into its saucer. "What makes you think I have any interest in causing your little friends any trouble?"

"I've watched you the past few days. I've seen you go out of your way to annoy Martin and charm Pia."

"What if I like Pia? What if she likes me? What if we fall madly in love with each other?"

"I'd be delighted," said Katrinka, with a faint smile.

"You would?" Christian laughed. "How inconsistent of you, Mother."

"I have no problem with real feelings. It's playacting I hate. Hurting people for no reason, except that it amuses you."

"Is that what you think of me? That I enjoy causing people pain?"

"No, certainly not," protested Katrinka. "But you're thoughtless sometimes, Christian. You act without considering the effect it will have on others."

"If that is what you think of me," continued Christian, paying no attention to her protest, "perhaps I should leave St. Moritz now, before I do any further damage to these people you seem to care so much about, so much more than you seem to care about me."

He didn't mean it, Katrinka was certain, *almost* certain, of that. It was just his way of warning her not to presume on their relationship, which was too recent to withstand much strain. "I love you," she said. "The kind of love I have for you, I have for no one else in the world. I hope someday you'll believe that."

"I don't like your lecturing me."

"And I don't like doing it, believe me."

"Do you want me to go?" he asked, his voice belligerent, threatening.

"No," she said, her earlier assurance gone, frightened suddenly that he would leave. With Christian, it was always so difficult to tell what he intended.

He stood up. "Then this conversation is over."

Katrinka nodded. Though she knew she should not let him bully her, she didn't dare go further. For now, she had pushed him as far as she could.

Having won, at least for the moment, again Christian smiled. "Anyway, I don't see what you're worried about. I've hardly said two words to Pia since last Thursday."

That was exactly what she was worried about, thought Katrinka, as she sat silently, watching him go.

Thirteen

It was still dark when Katrinka heard Mark moving carefully around their bedroom, quietly opening and closing drawers and closets, doing without benefit of a light, his feet shoeless on the carpeted floor, obviously trying not to disturb her. "Where you are going?" she asked, caught somewhere between sleep and waking.

Mark came and sat on the edge of the bed next to her. "I have to meet Tony Moreland in the Cresta clubhouse at seven," he said.

Fear washed away the last remnants of sleep. "I did forget," she said, sitting up. "I'll go with you."

"You don't have to," he said. "The fax machine's been spitting out paper all night. You can get a little work done while I'm gone. And Robin wants you to call her in New York as soon as you can."

"I want to," said Katrinka stubbornly.

"Okay by me," said Mark, not prepared to argue the point. He leaned over and kissed the top of her head. "I'll wait for you in the dining room."

Mark left the room, and Katrinka got out of bed, pulled a bathrobe on over her silk teddy, and went into the large, pine-paneled bathroom for a quick shower. Fifteen minutes later she joined Mark at the breakfast table.

"Nothing to eat?" asked the housekeeper, who thought Katrinka ate barely enough to keep herself alive, let alone the child she was carrying.

"No, thank you," said Katrinka. She drank a cup of herbal tea, then turned to Mark. He was wearing a black one-piece Bogner ski suit. His skin was tan from the days they had spent on the slopes, his hair a silver-blond. Katrinka thought he was the handsomest man she had ever seen. He was strong, kind, gentle, loving, passionate, dependable, honest. Her list of words to praise him was endless. She respected him more than any man she had ever known, as much as she had her father, if without the same childlike belief in his infallibility. But he was as stubborn as . . . as she was, she knew both Mark and her father would say. She forced a smile. "Ready?" she asked.

"Not going to call Robin before we go?" Mark sounded surprised. Katrinka was not one to let business slip, no matter what else was going on.

Katrinka shook her head. "When we do get back," she said. She knew it was silly, but postponing the call made her feel as if the trip to the Cresta clubhouse was nothing more than an insignificant pause in a perfectly normal morning, a brief diversion without foreseeable consequences—like fractured skulls and broken spines. "If it was urgent, she would have said."

The day was beginning to brighten, the sky lightening to a robin's-egg blue. Except for a snowstorm the preceding week, the weather had been uniformly sunny and the days were becoming warm, almost balmy, which meant that ground snow tended to turn to slush by late afternoon, hardening into slick patches of ice overnight. "Careful," said Mark, as he helped Katrinka down the front steps, into the drive where the Citroën was parked. Despite the thick, ridged soles of her boots, she slipped once and would have fallen, had Mark not held her firmly. "Forget boots," he said, as he grabbed hold of the car and used it for a handhold as they made their way carefully around to the passenger side. "What we need are ice skates."

Katrinka laughed. "A lot of good that would do you," she said. They had gone skating at the nearby rink a few days before and Mark had spent most of the time flat on his backside.

"That's what happens when you have a deprived childhood," he said cheerfully. "You don't get to spend your free time ice skating, if you have any free time."

"You didn't have it so rough," she said.

It was a game they frequently played: whose childhood had been more difficult—Katrinka's in communist Czechoslovakia, or Mark's on the streets of Pittsburgh. When they had first started the game, the results had surprised them. More often than not, it turned out that Mark had had the rougher time. Raised in a close and loving family, all of whom held good and reasonably well-paying jobs, with the added benefits she had received from a young age because she was a star athlete, Katrinka had wanted for nothing. Mark's life had been very different. His father, watching as the Nazis increased their power, fearing the devastation of the war he was sure would shortly engulf Europe, had fled with his wife to Canada, where their first child, Mark's older brother, was born. Four years later, they entered the United States illegally, just in time for Mark to be born a citizen. The family had lived in a cramped three-room apartment in one of the poorest sections of Pittsburgh, barely getting by on the father's salary as a day laborer in a construction crew. Except for a television, there had been no luxuries, and certainly no holidays skiing. Mark's brother had died of acute appendicitis when his parents, worried about the cost, had failed to take him to a doctor until it was too late.

"Did you have skating lessons when you were a kid?" asked Mark.

"Everybody did," said Katrinka. It had been part of the sports program at school. "I was pretty good. But Tomáš was great," she added. "He could have been a hockey star, but he did spend all his time at the movies."

"You see," said Mark. "I rest my case."

The Cresta clubhouse was a tall, ramshackle wooden building towering over the narrow ice track that curved past its base. The top level was an observation deck, and, immediately below it, with almost as good a view, was a glass-enclosed bar. Nearby were several equipment sheds.

Mark parked the Citroën in the club's lot, then he and Katrinka crossed the narrow bridge spanning the track and entered the clubhouse in search of Tony Moreland, whom they met coming out of the office on the ground floor. The two men escorted Katrinka up to the bar, settled her with a cup of tea, then went off to get Mark signed in and outfitted for his run. In the bar, there were, as always, several people whom Katrinka knew, not only from St. Moritz, but from Paris, London, New York, Palm Beach, Cap Ferrat, from all the places the social set's calendar took them in the course of a year. Seeing her seated by the large glass observation window, acquaintances (all male, with the single exception of someone's wife) stopped by to chat. But, distracted by the sight below her of men in spiked boots, wearing knee and elbow and hand guards, carrying helmets and sleds, passing in and out of the various sheds adjacent to the clubhouse, she paid only halfhearted attention to the conversation, which was the usual cheerful nonsense about mutual friends, skiing conditions, and travel plans. Soon, amid the general hubbub of competing voices, she recognized Daisy's, greeting friends, as she made her way across the room. "There you are," she said, exchanging a kiss with the retired American army general who was hovering over Katrinka, then dropping into the seat opposite her.

"What you are doing here?" asked Katrinka, surprised and pleased to see her.

"I thought you could use some company." Daisy looked around at the group of admirers. "Not that you seem to be lacking it at the moment," she added.

"You could have come in the car with us."

"I walked," said Daisy, pleased with herself. "Uphill all the way. Wonderful exercise."

Katrinka felt the familiar rush of affection for the woman who had been her first friend in New York. A matron of impeccable social standing, Daisy had taken the immigrant bride under her protection, introduced her to everyone who mattered, helped her over the hurdles, steered her past the pitfalls, and established Katrinka as a reigning queen, first of New York, then of international society, simply because she had liked her. "Thank you," said Katrinka. "I'm worried sick."

"I thought you might be." She shook her head. "Men," she said, as if that said it all. Soon, due either to hormones, nerves, the thick cloud of cigarette smoke, or all three, Katrinka began to feel nauseated. "You're turning green," said Daisy. "Are you all right?"

"I do need some fresh air, I think."

Excusing themselves, they went upstairs to the observation deck. "Better?" asked Daisy.

"Much," said Katrinka, taking another deep breath. "It was all those cigarettes."

"Disgusting habit," agreed Daisy. "I wish Riccardo would stop. But there's no convincing him it's bad for his health."

"Alexandra won't stop either. She says she can't."

They stood looking over the rail, across the track, to where a group of trainees were assembling. "Look," said Daisy, pointing in the direction of the parking lot, "isn't that Christian?"

"Where?" Then she saw the cream-colored Mercedes 500SL that had been her Christmas present to him, its top down, pulling into an empty parking space near the bridge. Christian turned off the motor and got out, not bothering to lock the door, putting the key into the zippered pocket of his ski suit. "Yes, it is. What he is doing here?" Katrinka could not keep the anxiety from her voice.

"Come to watch, like us, I suppose," said Daisy, waving to attract his attention.

Either the movement caught Christian's eye or he could feel the intensity of their gazes. Looking up, he saw them, flashed a quick smile, and returned Daisy's wave. Katrinka beckoned him up to the deck, but he shook his head, and went instead to talk to Mark, and then to Tony Moreland, who was standing nearby.

"What he is doing?" asked Katrinka.

"There's really nothing to worry about," said Daisy reassuringly, though she was not quite certain that was true. "It's not a race. No one will take any unnecessary risks. And they do instruct them pretty thoroughly in the basics before letting them set off. I've never heard of a beginner getting hurt."

Feeling as if all the air were being sucked from her body, Katrinka moved away from the rail and went to sit down. Her throat and chest felt tight. Her heart was beating so strongly she could hear it. Daisy started to follow her, but Katrinka shook her head. "No, you watch. Tell me what's happening."

But nothing of moment happened for quite a while. Christian disappeared with Tony Moreland and, some time later, returned dressed for the run, joining the group of men assembled around an instructor wearing ski pants and parka who began to fill them in on the intricacies of tobogganing. Finally, Daisy said, "I think Mark's about to start. Do you want to see?"

Katrinka got up and returned to the rail. Looking down, she saw Mark, with the instructor's help, setting the dull red sled on the track. The sled was a lethal weapon, Katrinka knew. Made of pure steel, if it flipped and hit you as you came off, it could kill. Mark lay, chest down, on top of it, arms bent, hands grasping the front. There was no brake. Only the spikes on the boots and the motion of the body controlled the speed of the toboggan. Please, God, let him be all right, she prayed. Without fear for herself, she had no courage at all when the people she loved placed themselves in physical danger. Mark set off and a second later was out of sight around the bend a few feet below the starting point. Two other men followed him, and then Christian.

"They do this five times," said Katrinka. "I don't think I can stand it."

"You should have stayed at the chesa."

"I did think it would be worse."

What seemed an eternity later, Mark and Christian returned, set off again, then returned again. After the fourth run, they did not come back with the others. Katrinka's face grew paler, her breathing more labored. Daisy sent the army general, who had joined them on the deck, to the bar for a brandy. "Drink it," she commanded, when Katrinka refused. "I drank all through my three pregnancies, and have you ever seen healthier kids?"

"It's not good," insisted Katrinka.

"I know," agreed Daisy. "But this once won't hurt the baby."

Katrinka swallowed, and choked. She was for the moment so distracted she did not see Mark returning, alone. He crossed the bridge and entered the clubhouse, taking the stairs to the deck two at a time. As he came out into the bright sunlight, Katrinka saw him and opened her mouth as if to speak, or to scream, but no sound came out. "It's all right," he called, as he crossed the deck toward her. "I'm fine. Christian's fine." He pushed past the general, put his arm around Katrinka, and continued, "Christian came off the sled at the shuttle-cock." It was the worst turn of the run, and the bank above the track was lined with thick pads of hay to prevent injury. Coming off the sled just there was considered an important part of the initiation rite. There was even a club tie to commemorate the event. "He's got a few bruises but nothing serious."

"Where he is?"

"He'll be here in a minute, just as soon as he gets cleaned up." The strength went out of Katrinka's legs and she sagged against Mark. If he hadn't held her, for the second time that day she would have fallen. "He's all right, baby. There's nothing to worry about," said Mark reassuringly as he settled her in a chair.

Worried, Mark turned and looked at Daisy for help, but she glowered at him. "You ought to be ashamed of yourself," she said. "You and Christian both. Terrifying her like that, in her condition."

"I'm all right," said Katrinka, taking another sip of the brandy.

Mark resisted the urge to snap back at Daisy, and suppressed the growing desire to strangle Christian. It was not Christian's fault that Katrinka was upset, he reminded himself, nor his either, for that matter. Neither of them could go pussyfooting through life because her parents had died in an automobile accident. It was her fear, and she had to deal with it, though right now was perhaps not the best time for him to have tried to make that point, he admitted in a brief surge of regret. "I'm sorry, baby," he said, stooping to look into her eyes. "Forgive me?"

"It's not your fault."

"I know," he said, with a grin. "But try forgiving me anyway. It will make you feel better."

Katrinka tried a smile and some of the color came back into her face. By the time Christian joined them, she was her usual self and managed to greet him without hurling a single reproach in his direction. He had a bruise on his cheek and was carrying a shuttlecock tie. "What great fun!" He was smiling broadly, as if ignorant of the anxiety he had caused his mother. "You'd love it," he said to her. She was a superb athlete, and he admired her for it, and for many other things, though that did not prevent his trying to torment her.

Katrinka was not so sure she would love it, but she only smiled and said, "Maybe I will, on ladies' day." Women had been allowed to join the club in its early days, but the rules had since been changed.

They left the deck, and Mark stopped off briefly in the bar to thank Tony Moreland, then caught up with the rest of the group as they crossed back into the parking lot. "Did you drive?" Mark asked Daisy. She told him that she had walked, and he offered her a ride home. "We can send someone for your car later," he said to Christian, "if you'd rather ride with us now." He didn't think the boy was too shaken up to drive, but he thought he ought to make the offer.

"No, no, I'm fine," said Christian, setting off toward his car. But before they had settled into the Citroën, he was back again. "The key must have fallen out of my pocket," he said, as he unzipped each in turn, searching for the missing car key. "The zipper must not have been completely closed."

"Do you have another set?" asked Katrinka.

"In my apartment, in Bonn. I can have them Federal Expressed. They will be here by the day after tomorrow, at the latest." He looked unhappily at the car, not liking the idea of leaving it with its top down, completely unprotected, in a parking lot for a couple of days.

"I'll see what I can do," said Mark, climbing back out of the car and heading for the clubhouse.

"What can he do?" said Christian impatiently. "The key's lost."

Katrinka shrugged. "Probably nothing," she admitted. Mark returned a few minutes later, told them he had had a word with some of the officials and offered a reward to anyone who found the key.

"How much?" said Katrinka.

"Five hundred dollars."

Daisy whistled inelegantly and Christian said, his growing irritation showing, "How are they going to find the key? It's impossible."

Mark grinned. "Then I'll save five hundred dollars and you can start praying that it doesn't snow before the extra set gets here from Bonn."

When they got back to the Chesa Konsalvi, Katrinka and Mark went through the faxes they had received overnight and then retired to separate phones to place their calls. They had insisted on a second line being installed before they had agreed to rent the house.

Katrinka spoke to Robin, responding to that day's set of invitations; answering questions from Carlos Medina about the cornices in the new town house, firing off a list of instructions to be relayed to the staffs of her houses, to her lawyers, her accountants, the managements of her hotels. When she heard that the profits of the London casino had fallen, she told Robin to call Alistair Codron, its manager, and let him know she would be in London for the executive committee meeting on Thursday. She wanted to find out if anything more than the economy was to blame.

"I spoke to Alistair yesterday. He said it's nothing to worry about. Just a momentary blip, he called it."

Changing the names of the New York and London hotels from "Graham" to "Ambassador" was expensive. She didn't need a dip in profits to compound her problems. At the thought of it, she felt the usual surge of anger at Adam. "Tell Alistair, I do decide what I should worry about. I'll be there Thursday."

"I'll tell him."

"I'm going to London with you tomorrow," she told Mark, as they ate a light lunch in the Chesa Konsalvi's dining room.

Mark was surprised. "You're leaving Christian here alone?"

"I don't like it, but it can't be helped," she said, explaining the problem in London. "I'll only be gone a couple of days. He won't mind."

Mark wasn't so sure about that. Christian seemed to mind everything. But all he said was, "He'll think of some way to keep himself entertained."

After lunch, Katrinka changed into her ski clothes and set off with Mark, walking to the Celerina lifts, which would take them as far as Marguns. Once they had gone, Christian crossed the road to the Chesa Mulin. It had been agreed the night before that Pia and he would spend the afternoon together, but instead of skiing, he coaxed her into going with him to the skating rink. He was more shaken by his fall than he liked to admit. The steel sled had missed him by inches, almost grazing his head before landing in the hay at his side.

"You could have been killed," said Pia when he had finished telling her about his morning. They were walking downhill, toward the Celerina skating rink, sometimes together, sometimes in single file when the narrow walkway disappeared, avoiding the steady stream of traffic on its way to St. Moritz.

"Yes," agreed Christian, with an odd smile. "That's what made it so exciting." He had been warned. He should not have gone so fast, but he had been too caught up in the feeling, a heady mixture of exhilaration and panic, to surrender to his instinct for caution. "You have no idea how thrilling it was."

"You're not going to do it again," she said. Pia was not particularly brave, let alone foolhardy. Even as a skier, she was careful. She didn't believe in taking unnecessary chances; she didn't like getting hurt. That was why she felt so comfortable with Martin, who was as sensible as she. People like her mother, like Katrinka, like Christian, filled her with admiration, but also with fear.

"Of course," said Christian. "It was great fun. I'm having another try tomorrow." He saw the look on her face and laughed. "You look so worried, I think I should feel flattered. I had no idea you cared so much about me."

"Of course I care if you kill yourself," she said, annoyed.

"Oh, I won't kill myself," he said confidently. "At least not right now. I have too much trouble left to cause before I die."

Pia laughed nervously. Of course, Christian was only joking, but still . . . "You say such terrible things sometimes," she said.

His face became instantly contrite. "I know, I know," he said quickly. "I apologize. I never mean for people to take me seriously, but they do. You mustn't. Perhaps it's a language problem," he added as an afterthought.

"Your English is perfect." They were silent for a moment as a group of motor scooters roared past, then Pia asked, "Is Mark going to try the Cresta again?"

"I suppose not," said Christian, sounding suddenly bored with the conversation. "My mother doesn't approve."

"Then she can't like your doing it either."

"Do you always do what your mother wants?"

Pia hesitated a moment. "No," she said finally. "I don't."

He slipped his arm around her waist and, when the traffic broke, guided her quickly across the road to the entrance of the skating rink. "Good," he said. "Children aren't supposed to obey their parents. They must rebel. Otherwise they never grow up." He looked at Pia and smiled to show he was only half-serious. "In any case," he added, "I'm not quite used to her being my mother."

"It must have been an incredible shock when she told you," said Pia sympathetically.

"Oh, yes," agreed Christian. "A great shock. But not entirely unpleasant."

During their afternoon at the skating rink, Christian's attitude toward Pia kept shifting, as it had over the past several days, from attentiveness to disinterest and back again, keeping her constantly off-balance, not knowing whether he really wanted to be with her, or was there simply because Daisy had more or less coerced him into keeping her company. His attitude irritated her. Usually, men flocked to her, drawn by her looks, by her manner, begging for notice. Usually, she was the one keeping them at bay. And while she had often wished to be left alone, now that it seemed she might be, she didn't like it at all.

"Would you like to go dancing tonight, again?" asked Christian when he returned her to the Chesa Mulin. It would be their first night without Martin for company.

"No," said Pia quickly. "Thank you. But I really am tired. I'll just have an early night."

"Fine," agreed Christian, without any noticeable disappointment. "Maybe tomorrow?" he asked politely.

"Maybe," she said. "What will you do?"

"Oh, there's bound to be someone I know at Dracula. I'll go there, I suppose."

"Well, have a good time," she said, not quite managing to keep the irritation out of her voice. Why had she imagined he would stay home as well if she refused to accompany him? Because Martin would have?

"If you change your mind . . ."

"I won't," said Pia coolly. "I need a good night's sleep."

Christian nodded, bowed slightly, and said, "Then, until tomorrow." He waited until Pia entered the house, then turned and headed for the Chesa Konsalvi. He was smiling. Really, he thought, women were so transparent.

His smile disappeared as soon as he entered the house. "Christian, is that you?" he heard Katrinka's voice calling to him from the sitting room.

"Yes," he said, removing his parka and hanging it on the hook in the hall. He entered the sitting room and found Katrinka sitting on the sofa, her feet tucked up under her, a sheaf of papers in her lap, a broad smile on her face, his car key dangling from her outstretched hand. "Look," she said gleefully.

Instead of pleasure, all Christian felt was a surge of irritation. He looked at Mark, who was sitting in an armchair next to Katrinka, his feet up on the coffee table, reading a newspaper. "How could they have found them?" he said.

Mark didn't reply but Katrinka laughed. "With horses," she said in German. "I think they made the horses eat all the hay at shuttlecock until the key turned up."

"Is she serious?"

"It's as good an explanation as any I've heard," said Mark, trying hard not to smile at the absurdity of the thing. Christian would not appreciate it, he knew.

"Well, thank you," said Christian grudgingly, taking the key from his mother. "Thank you very much. Next time I will try not to be quite so careless."

"Oh, *miláčku*, it was not your fault," said Katrinka, not wanting the happy moment to evaporate before she had had a chance to enjoy it fully. "Anyone can lose a key."

"I'll not let it happen again."

With that, Christian turned and left the room and Katrinka looked at Mark. "We did something wrong?"

"He thinks he's an adult."

"He is," said Katrinka. She smiled ruefully. "In a few months he'll be twenty-four years old."

"And we somehow managed to make him feel like a child. He's a little embarrassed. It's not important," he said reassuringly. "He'll get over it."

"I don't think Christian does get over things easily, do you?"

"No," said Mark. "I don't." Suddenly, he was very glad to be leaving St. Moritz, doubly glad at the thought of having Katrinka to himself for a few days. While the prospect of fatherhood might terrify him, he knew it would be a piece of cake compared to stepfatherhood. Nothing, he was convinced, could ever be as difficult as dealing with Christian.

Fourteen

"VERY PRETTY," SAID ADAM, STUDYING A GLOSSY EIGHT-BY-TEN COLOR PHOTO OF A YOUNG WOMAN. HE put it aside and picked up another, then another. One seemed to surprise him. Curious, he turned it around so that Sugar could see it. "Not up to your usual standard, is she?"

They were in the sitting room of Adam's suite at the Palace Hotel, at opposite ends of the silk-covered sofa, a pile of photographs between them. The room had a soft golden glow, a result of both the luxurious furnishings and the morning sunshine that filtered in through the curtains of the long windows overlooking the frozen lake across which horses pulling sleighs carried tourists back and forth between the lower village of St. Moritz-Bad and the hotel.

Sugar glanced at the photograph and shrugged. "Well, not everyone's standards of beauty are the same, you know. And looks are not always what's most important to a client. Which is why we like to offer a variety of sizes, shapes, and . . ." She searched for the right word. "Talents."

"And what's her talent?"

Sugar grinned. "Her mouth."

Adam felt a stirring in his crotch. "She's that good?"

"Take it from me, honey, there's no one better."

Adam looked from Sugar back to the photograph and back again to

141

Sugar. Into his mind came the unbidden and enticing image of her and the woman with the talented mouth in a kaleidoscope of shifting erotic positions. Then he saw himself in their midst, part of the playful group, naked and having the time of his life. The stirring in his crotch became a definite leap to life.

"Interested?"

"No," said Adam firmly, getting control of himself. This was undoubtedly how it had begun for Steven Elliott—first Sugar, then Sugar and her friends, male and female, of all ages, sizes, colors: "Benetton sex" someone had called it. So hooked had Steven become on the perversity of the pleasures his wife had introduced him to that, even after the divorce, he was unable to give them up. "I'm a man of extremely simple tastes."

"Sex and food have a lot in common," said Sugar. "You have to sample a dish before you can be sure whether or not you like it. And sometimes, after only the littlest bite, you find you've gone and acquired a taste for some exotic specialty."

"I can believe it," said Adam, without much enthusiasm. He continued leafing through the photographs, got to the end of the pile, then rifled through them again quickly, stopping at the face of a lovely young woman with short brown hair, delicate features, and an expression that was both intense and intelligent. Turning the photo over, he glanced at the Xeroxed sheet that gave her vital statistics. She was of medium height, five-feet-five-inches tall, one hundred and ten pounds, a size six. "This one," he said, handing the photograph to Sugar. She was not the most beautiful of the women whom Sugar had suggested, but somehow he felt that she was the right one.

"Monica Brand. Good choice," said Sugar.

"Can she start immediately?"

"She's waiting for my phone call." Sugar smiled. "I had a feeling you would choose her. She's the one who looks most like his first wife."

Adam laughed. "You really are something, Sugar."

"Why, thank you," she drawled, smiling sweetly. "But I think when it comes to being bad, you have me beat by a mile."

"I'll take that as a compliment," said Adam as Sugar gathered up the photographs and restored them to her attaché case. "Now, when do we begin?"

"First things first," said Sugar. "We have a little business to take care of. We haven't discussed the terms of our agreement."

"You have something in mind?"

Sugar told him, and Adam whistled. "She's one of the best," said Sugar. "Beautiful, intelligent. Phi Beta Kappa—"

"Nobody appreciates the fine art of selling more than I do," said Adam, interrupting, "but don't start lying yourself out of a deal."

"It's the truth," said Sugar. "Phi Beta Kappa, and not from some dinky little playschool either. Monica graduated from Smith." At that, Adam let out a loud burst of laughter, and it was Sugar's turn to look annoyed. "I don't pick these girls up peddling ass on Broadway, you know."

"Where did you find her?" asked Adam, hoping he had restored a suitably serious expression to his face.

"She answered an ad I placed in *The Times of London*. If you want the best quality help, it pays to advertise in the best quality newspapers." After graduation, explained the madam, Monica had gone traveling through Europe with friends. When she ran out of money, she wrote a few magazine pieces, discovered how poorly that paid, and began looking for a temporary job to tide her over until she was ready to go back home to Connecticut and begin looking for permanent work. Being an "escort" had seemed a reasonable way to pick up a few extra dollars, and with the enticement of the mega-rich clients Sugar provided, the transition from purely social evenings to sexual encounters had not been difficult for her. After four years on the job, Monica still found what she did exciting, insisted Sugar with a hint of pride, was accumulating a sound investment portfolio, and no doubt hoping that one day, like a frog into a prince, a paying client would be magically transformed into an indulgent husband. That fairy tale had come true for more than one of her girls.

"Is Monica her real name?"

"Of course not."

"Is Sugar yours?"

Sugar smiled. "It's what my daddy always called me."

The phone rang. "I told them I didn't want any interruptions," said Adam, reaching for the receiver. "Excuse me." He listened for a few moments, then smiled apologetically. "It's my mother. Not even the Palace switchboard is a match for her . . . Hello? Mother?"

Always the soul of discretion, Sugar rose from the sofa and poked around the suite until she found the bathroom. She went in and, resisting the temptation to eavesdrop, closed the solid wood door firmly behind her.

"Adam, I have the most wonderful news," said Nina Graham, her voice almost girlish with excitement.

"What?" said Adam suspiciously.

"Russell and I are getting married next Saturday, the twenty-ninth, at home. A quiet wedding, with only the immediate family."

143

"That is a surprise. I thought you and Russell would both want a big wedding. Wouldn't that be better politics?" He was not able to resist adding.

"We're not thinking about politics at the moment," said Nina, the familiar disapproval back in her voice. Adam could imagine her seated at the antique writing desk in what she liked to call the "morning room" of the Newport house where he had grown up. It was there that Nina had always dealt with her correspondence and phone calls, wearing a simple, tailored dress, or a skirt and cashmere twin set, no jewelry but pearls, her hair and makeup perfectly done. "A big wedding would take far too long to plan. And we thought it would be rather sweet getting married in Leap Year, on the last day of February," she added. "So romantic. Though I suppose you think we're too old for romance."

"Not at all," said Adam, who was much less interested in his mother's love life than in her financial situation. He hated to see her squander what was left of her money, *Graham* money, on Russell Luce's political ambitions.

"I am pleased to hear that. Now, when can we expect you home?"

"Home?" echoed Adam, not at all happy at the thought of altering his plans. "I'm leaving for California in the morning. There may be a serious problem with the design of the Cup defender yacht. I have no idea how long I'll have to stay in San Diego." He also had another meeting with the Italians about Olympic Pictures, but he saw no need to confide that to his mother.

"Don't be difficult, Adam." Nina's voice was calm, assured, as if there was no doubt whatsoever that Adam would do exactly as he was told. "You can't possibly be thinking of missing this wedding. What would people say? In any case, you have to give the bride away."

"Can't you put off the wedding a couple of weeks?" asked Adam hopefully. The longer he could delay her, the better chance there was that she would change her mind.

"No, I can not," said Nina firmly. "Nor do I wish to. I am marrying Russell Luce on the twenty-ninth and I expect you to be there."

"Of course," he said. When Nina sounded like that, there was no point trying to argue with her. "I wouldn't dream of missing your wedding, Mother."

"I'm not asking much of you, you know," said Nina, not deceived by the change in Adam's tone. "Just to arrive in time for the rehearsal and stay until after the wedding lunch. Thirty-six hours, no more. That can't be much of an inconvenience for you, not with that seven twenty-seven at your beck and call. You do still have the seven twenty-seven?"

"It's no inconvenience at all," said Adam, ignoring her barely veiled reference to reports in the press that he was in financial trouble and beginning to dispose of assets. "I'll see you next Friday."

"Thank you, darling," said Nina, sounding satisfied to have got what she wanted. The satisfaction was temporary, Adam knew. His mother's chronic discontent would soon find something else to focus on, hopefully her future husband, though he suspected that with the wedding only ten days away, only afterward, when it was too late, would Russell Luce begin not to measure up to Nina Graham's very high standards.

"Is everything all right?" asked Sugar, returning from the bathroom and rejoining Adam on the sofa. "You suddenly look a little frayed around the edges."

"My mother has that effect on people," said Adam, with the boyish, crooked grin that even Sugar considered delightful. "It was good news actually," he added, deciding to put the proper spin on the event. "She's getting married."

"Why, how lovely for her. Russell Luce is a charming man."

Adam looked at her suspiciously. "You know him?"

"Adam, really," said Sugar impatiently. "I do meet men socially, you know, who have absolutely no connection with my business interests. For heaven's sake, he's one of the most respected members of the United States Senate."

"You haven't heard anything about him?"

"Not a word. Cross my heart and hope to die."

It would have been too good to be true, thought Adam, as he returned to negotiating the deal for Monica Brand's services. When they had agreed on the details, Sugar and he shook hands on it, "a gentlemen's agreement," as she called it, without a trace of irony.

"When do we begin?" asked Adam.

"Katrinka returned to London with Mark this morning. It's probably wiser to wait until she leaves him there alone."

"Katrinka went with him! But Lucia told me she was remaining here." His annoyance, he was sure, was at having to delay putting his plan into operation. It was an ingenious plan, he thought, one designed to cause a scandal that would both undermine van Hollen's hold on his board of directors, paving the way for the takeover, and destroy his marriage: two birds with one stick, as Katrinka always said.

"They're still newlyweds," said Sugar. "Can't bear to be apart for a moment, I suppose. I told you this would be a challenge."

"Well, let's hope it's not too big a challenge for Miss Brand," said Adam dryly.

"Don't worry, honey, if anyone can break up that marriage, it's Monica."

"For this amount of money," replied Adam as he signed enough traveler's checks to cover the down payment, "you ought to throw in the Archbishop of Canterbury's for a bonus." He felt suddenly restless. It occurred to him that he ought to have brought a companion with him, a female companion. When he had left New York, he had been preoccupied with business, the necessary trips to his various shipyards, his meeting with Charles Wolf, the hope of resurrecting his relationship with Prince Khalid, who was still refusing to take his phone calls. He had thought that having a woman around would be more of a nuisance than a pleasure. But now he was not so sure. St. Moritz was full of people he knew—he had hardly spent a moment alone—and still he felt this rush of . . . what was it? Loneliness? The idea made him uncomfortable, and he pushed it quickly away. What he needed, he decided, was to get laid.

As soon as he had ushered Sugar from the room and the bellman had collected the coffee service, Adam settled himself on the sofa and began telephoning. There were still a few items of unfinished business to be taken care of before he left St. Moritz—that afternoon, he decided suddenly. There was nothing more to keep him there. He called his pilot, in Zurich, and told him to get the jet ready, asked the concierge to charter him a small plane for the flight out of St. Moritz, then phoned his secretary in Los Angeles and gave her a list of women, in order of preference, to call and invite to dinner on his behalf the following night. That done, he confirmed his lunch date with Charles Wolf, who was finally beginning to sound interested in a move on VHE. His final call was to the Duke of Cumber.

Without Katrinka and Mark to distract him, Christian devoted himself entirely to his pursuit of Pia. The first thing he did was *not* call her, though he had implied he would when they had parted the day before. Instead, he spent the morning skiing with some people he knew who had been schoolmates of his at Le Rosey, and then joined them for lunch at the Corviglia Club, where they were members.

Quite an impressive group was gathered within the club's hallowed walls. Tony Moreland was there, lunching with Dick Cowell, one of the few American life members, and his wife, Jackie. Spyros Niarchos, who had been at Le Rosey a few years before Christian, was with Robert Millbourn, the club secretary. "Delighted," said Millbourn, when they were introduced. He was an attractive Englishman with grizzled hair and an easy smile who liked to dance. "Know your father." Then an unwelcome thought occurred to him, and he added quickly, with only the faintest trace of embarrassment, "Kurt Heller," as if Christian might be in some doubt as to who that was.

His friends, some of whom had known him since his first year at Le Rosey, when he was six, were agog to know all about the new and interesting twist in Christian's life, though of course, even under torture, none of them would have admitted to it. Twelve years in one of the world's best boarding schools had taught them nothing if not superb manners, and questions of a personal nature were simply not asked. But Christian had no problem relieving their nonetheless obvious curiosity. In fact, he rather enjoyed it. His illegitimacy added another dimension, he thought, to the bad boy image he delighted in cultivating. It gave those who distrusted him, the parents of some of his friends, for example, another reason to consider him unacceptable, without quite allowing them to cut him. Their dilemma amused him. The Hellers were too important, too well connected, to risk offending them by insulting their adopted son; and Katrinka and Mark van Hollen were too rich.

"Katrinka van Hollen," said one of his English friends, Viscount Egerton. "Lucky sod. Though I think I'd much rather date her than call her 'mum.'" As pleasantries in that group went, it was pretty mild, but Christian's face, to their surprise, registered neither appreciation nor amusement, but rage. "Sorry, old man," said the viscount instantly. He had always been a little afraid of Christian, without quite knowing why, beyond a vague sense that, when pushed, Christian was capable of anything. "Bad joke. I do apologize."

Christian blinked and the fury was gone from his eyes. Could they have imagined it? wondered his friends, as he regarded them with his most charming smile and said, "Not at all. I felt that way myself at first."

Everyone laughed, the tension passed, and the conversation reverted to the safer topic of sports. How had he liked the Cresta? they wanted to know. Two of them were members, a few of the others were curious about trying it. As he recounted his adventure, Christian noticed Adam Graham across the room, having lunch with a balloon-shaped man with thinning hair. Their eyes met for a moment and each of them nodded slightly in acknowledgment. For reasons neither of them saw any reason to explore, what they felt for each other was mingled curiosity and distrust.

"Do you know Adam Graham?" Christian asked the viscount later, as they were leaving the restaurant.

"Of course."

"Who is he lunching with?"

Egerton glanced quickly in the direction of Adam's table and then said, "I have no idea. I've never seen the chap before."

"It's Charles Wolf," said one of the others in the group. "He owns some newspapers in the United States. My parents had him to dinner the other night."

No one of any importance to him, decided Christian with another quick glance in Adam's direction. The Duke of Cumber had stopped at the table and was shaking hands with Wolf, who seemed almost overcome with the honor of touching aristocratic flesh. A social climber, thought Christian dismissively, following his friends back out into the brilliant afternoon sunshine.

On his way home later that day, Christian stopped at the local drugstore to replenish his supply of condoms. And when the house-keeper at the Chesa Konsalvi opened the door, she informed him that Mrs. Donati had invited him to join her for tea at the Palace, saving him the trouble of having to make the next move in the chess game he was playing with Pia. There was no need to phone, the message had continued. He was just to go across the road when he was ready. Daisy always carried on as if she were in charge of everyone's social life, though, unlike most controlling people, she was remarkably good-humored about accepting refusals.

Pia was alone in the sitting room when Christian arrived. "What a beautiful necklace," he said, before she managed a word of greeting. "Did you make it?"

"Yes," said Pia, her fingers going immediately to the chain of antique buttons strung with delicate bands of filigreed silver.

"It's exquisite."

Pleased at the compliment, Pia was almost willing to forget that she had been neglected all day. She smiled. "Thank you," she said. "Do sit down. We're almost ready to go. We're just waiting for Daisy to finish dressing."

"I'm ready. I'm ready," said Daisy, stopping in the doorway. "Christian, hello, my dear. I'm so pleased you could join us. I was afraid you'd be desperately lonely now that Katrinka and Mark have left."

"I've hardly had time yet," said Christian, laughing, as he and Pia followed Daisy into the center hall. "They've only been gone a few hours."

"You've managed to keep yourself busy, I take it?"

"He had lunch at the Corviglia," said Dieter, coming down the wide stone steps into the hall, trailed by Riccardo.

Daisy looked at Christian and laughed. "He's terrifying. One can't make a move without his knowing it."

"Some friends of mine, from Le Rosey, are members."

"*Andiamo*," said Riccardo, already in his parka, Daisy's fur slung over his arm. "*Ho fame.*"

"After that enormous lunch you ate, how can you possibly be hungry?" said Daisy, slipping into her coat. "Everyone ready?" she asked, as she led the way out past the massive front door.

When they arrived in the Grand Hall, with Dieter's none too subtle assistance Christian managed to seat himself next to Pia and to monopolize her attention despite the steady stream of visitors to the table and the constant ebb and flow of conversation. But before he could ask her to join him for dinner, Daisy again saved him the trouble by suggesting it. She and Riccardo and Dieter were invited to a party at the Agnellis and she did not want Pia to feel abandoned.

"Oh, I don't mind at all," said Pia. She smiled at Christian. "If you have other plans . . ."

Instead of disinterested, detached, Pia for once seemed almost flirtatious. He had made great progress, thought Christian, very satisfied with himself. "None that I wouldn't be delighted to change," he assured her.

In Christian's Mercedes, they drove to Pontresina, a pretty stone village in one of the highest of the Upper Engadine valleys, and dined in a small Italian restaurant, staying afterward to dance for a bit in its disco before returning to the Palace's King's Club to see what was happening there. They ran into the viscount and two others, but when, smitten by Pia and her dancing, his friends began being a little too attentive, Christian whisked her away. By one-thirty, they had returned to the Chesa Mulin. "I'll phone you in the morning," said Christian as he walked her to the door.

"Will you?" asked Pia.

"Of course."

"You didn't today." She had not intended to mention it, but the words somehow slipped right past her guard.

"I hadn't promised I would. I never break a promise," he added, with more conviction than truth. "In any case, I wasn't sure you wanted me to. I wasn't at all sure you liked me."

Pia smiled, this time a shy, almost embarrassed smile. "And now you are?"

"I'm more hopeful," he said, with a laugh. He kissed her cheek, then rang the doorbell to summon the butler, who opened the door almost immediately. "I'll call you in the morning," repeated Christian, as Pia entered the house. She turned and waved, then the door closed behind her. Smiling, Christian returned to his car to drive it the short distance home.

As soon as he awoke, Christian placed the promised phone call to Pia and insisted the butler wake her when told she was still asleep. "I've been thinking about what we should do today," he said when she finally came to the phone.

"And what is that?" She sounded sleepy, but not in the least annoyed.

"It's a surprise. I'll pick you up in, what? an hour? Is that enough time?"

"Yes. But what shall I wear?" said Pia quickly, before Christian could hang up.

"What does it matter? You look beautiful in everything."

"Christian, thank you, that's lovely, but not very helpful." She was trying to sound stern, but he could hear the pleasure in her voice.

"Something that will take you from day into night. And I'm not saying another word. See you in an hour."

"Where are you off to?" asked Daisy a while later when she found Pia and Christian in her front hall, preparing to leave.

"It's a surprise," they answered simultaneously.

"For whom?" asked Daisy, laughing.

"He won't tell me where we're going," said Pia. She had worn long black boots, a short, flared black wool skirt, and a fitted tartan jacket, an adaptation of an Yves Saint Laurent design, which she had found in a boutique in Florence. It would, as Christian had suggested, go anywhere.

She was almost unrecognizable, thought Daisy, so full of interest and enthusiasm, not at all like her usual, cool self. "What a treat!"

"Will you be late?" asked Riccardo, coming into the hall, zipping up his parka, about to leave for a morning's skiing. The butler followed him, carrying his skis.

"Yes," said Christian. He smiled reassuringly at Riccardo. "But don't worry. I'll take good care of her."

"Of course you will," said Daisy, who felt a sudden, guilty pang about Martin. But she dismissed him instantly from her mind. Pia deserved to have a good time after what her wretched father had put her through, and if Christian could provide it, well, that was wonderful.

Riccardo's feelings were more complex. Christian was Katrinka's son, a high recommendation, and Riccardo had no reason to distrust him. But Pia was a young girl entrusted to his care by her mother. She was, so to speak, his responsibility, and he did not quite like her going off alone for who knew how long with a young man he did not know at all well. Still, if Daisy did not think there was anything to worry about . . .

"Perhaps you'd better take a key," said Daisy. The butler immediately propped Riccardo's skis against the wall, took a large key from the rack on the wall near the front door, and handed it to Daisy. "Thank you. There's no point your losing more sleep than necessary," she said to him, then handed the key to Pia, saying, as she kissed her cheek, "Have a lovely time."

"Drive safely," called Riccardo, watching from the doorway as Christian helped Pia across the patches of ice in the drive and settled her in his car.

"I will," said Christian, who was beginning to be annoyed by Riccardo's parental concern, though he managed not to show it. He got behind the wheel of the Mercedes, started the motor, waved, then pulled out of the drive.

"Dieter's leaving this afternoon," said Daisy, linking her arm through her husband's, tilting her small, perfect head up to see his face.

"So that's why you were so anxious to get the children out of the way," said Riccardo, with a teasing smile.

"Of course not," said Daisy indignantly. "I'm just so pleased to see Pia happy. Though it will be nice to have you to myself for a change."

Riccardo bent down and kissed her. "*Mangiamo a casa questa sera, si?*"

"Oh, yes," said Daisy enthusiastically. "A lovely candlelit dinner, just the two of us." She looked in the direction of the disappearing car. "You do think it was all right to let them go off alone like that?"

Riccardo sighed. "Pia's old enough to take care of herself," he said without much conviction. He shook his head. "I'm glad I never had daughters."

* * *

It was another day of brilliant sunshine and balmy, spring temperatures. There was almost nowhere that Christian could have chosen to
go in the vicinity that would not have been interesting and beautiful,
no one place particularly more so than any other. His keeping the
destination secret served no purpose really but to add a dimension of
mystery, of excitement, to turn what, for the Alps, was an ordinary car
ride into an adventure. "Are we there yet?" said Pia, when they had
been on the road for no more than ten minutes. Surprised, Christian
looked at her, but before he could reply, Pia laughed. "It's a joke. It's
what everyone claims American children say endlessly to their parents
when they start off on a trip. It drives them crazy."

"I can believe it," said Christian, smiling at her, delighted at the
change he saw. He reached out, took her hand, brought it to his mouth,
and kissed it. That embarrassed her a little, he noticed, and he let it go
immediately. "Have you ever been in love?" he asked.

"No," she said. "Have you?"

"Never." He turned his head and looked at her. "I've been waiting
for the right person." He smiled and looked away again. He turned on
the radio and moved the dial until he found a station playing American
soft rock. "Oh, I love this music, don't you?" he asked. Not waiting for
an answer, he began to sing along. "'I heard it through the
grapevine . . .'" The words sounded strange, in his odd, precise
English.

She had never known anyone like him, thought Pia, as she watched
him. His moods changed so quickly, from dark and somehow threatening to light and full of fun. She never knew where she stood with
him, and that made her feel both uncomfortable and excited. Christian
turned again to look at her, and, smiling, she too began to sing.

They drove through mountain passes, around hairpin curves,
climbed steep grades, and dipped again into the valleys. In every
direction, the Alps marched away toward the horizon. Sometimes in
the distance they would see, etched against the snow, the black power
lines of the chair lifts or a hut nestled into the hillside. Clusters of
houses with peaked roofs and stenciled trims occasionally appeared at
the side of the road; and once they saw a turreted *schloss* perched on a
cliff above a narrow gorge through which ran a clear rush of gray-green
water.

In Bellagio, they stopped for coffee at a café overlooking Lake Como.
Pia thought that was their destination, but she was wrong. Afterward,
Christian ushered her back into the car, and they continued their
journey, driving until they reached Milan.

To come from the serene beauty of the Engadine Valley into the bustle of a major city like Milan, and in February, might not seem like much of a treat, but after two weeks in the mountains it at least had the virtue of novelty. And there was not much else Christian could have suggested that Pia had not done first with Martin.

They had lunch in a small café in the glass-and-iron domed Galleria overlooking the Duomo. Afterward, they had a quick look inside the cathedral, and, when Pia remarked that Leonardo's *The Last Supper* was one great Italian painting she had not yet seen, they bought a guidebook, went searching for it, and found it finally—faded and partly obscured by scaffolding—in the ancient Dominican refectory next to the Church of Santa Maria delle Grazie. Pia was so naively grateful to him, as if he had fought giants and slain dragons for her, that for a moment Christian was almost ashamed of his ulterior motives. But not quite. In an antique shop on the Via Solferino he bought her a delicately worked silver thimble because she admired it, and later, in the Via Monte Napoleone, an Hermès scarf. The gifts were small, thoughtful, not at all in the same league as a diamond bracelet or a fur coat, which she would have had to refuse, but Pia was thrilled with them, not because she particularly wanted to be showered with presents, but because she found Christian's efforts to please her very touching and, of course, flattering.

Since La Scala was considered a must on any trip to Milan during the season, Christian had considered taking Pia to the opera, but he had discarded the idea when he realized it meant getting back to St. Moritz very late, which would interfere with his plans for the rest of the evening. Instead, they went to dinner at a small restaurant he knew in the Piazza Mercanti where they ate pasta with tiny clams, followed by osso buco and gelati for dessert.

By the time they returned to the car to begin the journey home, Pia was in a mellow and contented mood. If her guard had not completely dropped, it had lowered significantly. She was inclining toward trust, an unusual position for her.

As they retraced their route through the mountains in the magical silvery light cast by the full moon, the lilt of a Mozart violin concerto white noise in the background, they talked softly, exchanging life histories, Pia telling Christian, in outline form, skating across the surface of her feelings, about the onslaught of publicity that had resulted in her being sent abroad to school, trying to make light of her embarrassment, her loneliness, her fear. Christian too presented his childhood carefully, keeping the bitterness from his voice when telling her of being sent away to boarding school, his feelings of alienation, of isolation, of unhappiness. He wanted her sympathy, but he was careful not to let her see too much of his anger, his bitterness, for fear they would frighten her. What he told her was as much of the truth as he was willing for her to know.

By the time Christian and Pia reached St. Moritz, they understood each other a lot better, liked each other a lot more than when they had left. Even Christian, who had set out on a thoughtless campaign of seduction, found himself genuinely moved, admiring Pia's courage and style, her refusal to give in to self-pity. But that changed neither his mind nor his motives. Having decided that breaching Pia's defenses and taking her away from Martin would be amusing, discovering that he liked her, in addition to wanting her, made the prospect of succeeding that much more appealing. What might be good for Pia did not at all enter into Christian's calculations. But then, concern for the woman's welfare was hardly the priority of most men in the presence of a woman they desired.

Instead of taking Pia directly home, Christian drove the Mercedes directly into the driveway of the Chesa Konsalvi and invited her in for a drink. She hesitated a moment and then accepted. Christian had nothing more in mind than friendship, she was fairly sure, and if she was wrong, she was an expert at handling men who wanted more from her than she was prepared to give. In any case, the day had been so perfect, she did not want it to end.

The housekeeper, looking as if she had been awakened from a nap, opened the door after the second knock. Christian requested a bottle of champagne and, when she brought the Cristal, a bucket of ice, two cut-glass flutes, a jar of caviar, and some crackers, told her to go to bed. "Don't be foolish," he said in German, when she protested, "I'll take Miss Cavalletti home, then lock the door and put out the fire. There's no need for you to wait up to do that. Not when you have to be up so early in the morning." He kissed her on both wrinkled cheeks and, turning her around, propelled her out the sitting room door. "Go to bed," he ordered. "And don't worry. I promise not to burn the house down." When she had gone, Christian looked at Pia and said, smiling broadly, "Now I have you all to myself."

But his leer was so comical that she only laughed. "You've had me all to yourself all day."

"And a great pleasure it's been, too." He opened the champagne, lifting the cork with a small, satisfying pop, and splashed the fizzing liquid into the crystal glasses.

"That must be why yellow diamonds are so popular," said Pia, watching him.

"Because they look like frozen champagne?" said Christian, as he offered her a glass. "Do they make women feel light-headed and happy?" He sat next to her on the sofa, close, but not enough to seem threatening.

"I suppose that depends on who they're from."

They clinked glasses, took a sip of the champagne, and sat for a moment quietly looking into the fire. Then Christian reached for a cracker, smeared it with caviar, and gave it to Pia. "Try this. It's very good. Some American general sent it to Katrinka, a thank-you for a dinner party. I prefer it to flowers."

"You do?" said Pia, who shared Katrinka's love for flowers, whether cut in elaborate arrangements, or growing wild in fields.

"You can't eat flowers," said Christian, with a laugh, biting into the cracker, then sighing with appreciation. "Excellent."

"You've been so different today."

"I have? How?"

"You've seemed so relaxed and . . . happy, I suppose."

"So have you. Not like yourself at all."

She put down her glass and looked at him. "I am usually very happy," she said firmly.

"Are you? Well, you don't look it. Usually you look very prickly and uncomfortable, like a . . ." He searched for the English word. "What are those animals with the short sharp spines?"

"A hedgehog?" she said, sounding annoyed.

Christian nodded, then smiled. "A very beautiful hedgehog." He took the champagne from the ice bucket and refilled their glasses. "It made me afraid to get too close," he said, not looking at her.

"I don't think you're afraid of anything." She picked up the flute and took another sip.

"Everyone's afraid of rejection," he said, as if admitting a painful truth.

About to protest that she doubted he had ever been rejected by anyone, Pia remembered the circumstances of his birth. Though her reading on the subject had been casual, articles in women's magazines found in doctors' offices and hair salons, she knew enough to understand that there was no rejection so basic, so painful, as that of a child given up for adoption by his mother. And added to that was Christian's having been sent away to boarding school at such a young age. Suddenly, she felt overwhelmed with compassion for him: poor little baby abandoned by his mother; poor little boy deprived of the love and comfort of a real home. At least she had been spared that. Her life had been so much easier than his. She felt near to tears and wondered if she had already had too much champagne to drink. "I'm sorry I seemed so unfriendly. Everyone tells me I'm a very reserved sort of person. And I think that's all right. I mean, it's my personality, and I don't think there's anything wrong with being quiet, or shy."

"I was not criticizing," said Christian quickly.

"But I'd hate people to think that I'm an angry or a hostile person."

"I didn't think that. I just thought you didn't like me."

"You were so friendly at first. Then you changed completely. Got so distant, so withdrawn. Is that why?" Christian nodded, and Pia reached out to touch his hand. "I'm sorry," she said.

He leaned toward her. "There's nothing to apologize for. Someone as beautiful as you can't help making a man suffer. You do it simply by being there and not being his." He kissed her lightly on the mouth, and when she jumped back as if startled, he stood up. "Let's dance," he said. He crossed the room to the sound system, rifled through the tapes Mark and Katrinka always traveled with, snapped one of slow, danceable ballads into the player, then returned to the sofa, took Pia's hand, and pulled her to her feet. They moved slowly across the carpeted floor, arms around each other, Christian's cheek resting against Pia's, his warm breath riffling the dark hair that covered her ear. The champagne had done its work. If Christian were not anchoring her to the floor, Pia felt she would float off into space, up through the roof, and into the moon-filled night. Soon the breath against her ear became a mouth feathering kisses, then a tongue tracing its shape, licking the tender spot beneath it, leaving a trail of fire to where the neckline of her jacket stopped its progress. Dropping her hand, he undid the jacket's top button and kissed the hollow of her throat. Her eyes were closed when he reached her mouth, kissing her gently, then exerting more and more pressure, until her lips opened and his tongue met hers. Slowly, he opened the remaining buttons of her jacket, pushed it aside, and slid his hand under the lace of her bra to touch her breast. He could feel her body stiffen and he let his hand rest where it was, not moving. "Don't ask me to stop," he whispered against her mouth. "Please don't ask me. You feel so good. I want you so much. Pia, *liebling*, please . . . You're so beautiful."

She relaxed against him, kissing him, letting her tongue slide into his mouth. Slowly, in time to the music, he moved her back to the sofa, removing her clothes as they went, her jacket, her skirt, the black silk slip, until she wore nothing but her garter belt and panties, her black stockings and her high black boots. "Everything about you. So beautiful," he said, leaning over her, looking at her, reaching into his pocket for the condom he had been carrying all day.

They were still lying together naked on the sofa, feeding each other caviar, taking turns sipping from the same glass of champagne, when Christian heard the fax machine begin to hum. Curious, he got up, draped Pia's fur coat over her for warmth when she protested, and went to see what had arrived. He did not expect it to be for him, but he never could resist the urge to pry. That was one of the Hellers' many problems with him.

The fax was from Zuzka, a scrawled outraged note to Katrinka followed by a copy of a column from a Los Angeles newspaper. She apparently did not know that Katrinka had left for London.

The column was Sabrina's. The headline read: "Katrinket Black-balled from Elite Club." It went on to report, in Sabrina's usual snide tone, that although the new Mrs. van Hollen had lobbied diligently to become a member of the prestigious Corviglia Club, its aristocratic members had considered her and her husband too *nouveau riche* to be acceptable. "They didn't even inherit their money," an anonymous source was quoted as saying to explain the committee's decision.

"What is it?" asked Pia.

Christian returned to the sofa and showed her the fax. "What does this 'Katrinket' mean?" he asked.

"It's what Sabrina always calls Katrinka. She's such an awful woman."

"Will Katrinka be very upset about this?" asked Christian, realizing that he did not really know very much about his mother and how she felt about things.

"Oh, she'll be furious at first. She hates negative publicity. But she'll calm down. She really doesn't care very much about this kind of nonsense. Clubs and things. As long as nobody tries to stop her from doing what she likes. How stupid people are," she added, getting angry herself as she thought about the implications of the column. "And vain, and foolish, to treat working hard and earning money as if they were some kind of crime!"

"You really like Katrinka, don't you? I mean, for herself, and not just because she's your mother's friend."

"Katrinka? Of course, I do. She's been so good to me. Anyway, she's such a lot of fun."

"I don't really know her very well yet," said Christian. "I'm sorry if this will upset her," he added, surprised to find that he actually meant it. "I'll wait until morning to send it to her."

Pia sat up, the coat slipping to her waist as she began rummaging for her discarded clothes. "Where do you think you're going?" asked Christian, stopping her.

"Home. Before Riccardo alerts the police."

"I forgot about Riccardo," said Christian. He looked at his watch. "But I think we have a little while before he gets really worried." He leaned toward her and rested his mouth against her naked breast.

"I think—" she began.

"Don't," he interrupted. "It's never a good idea at times like this."

The
Past

Spring, 1992

Fifteen

TRYING TO CURB HER USUAL IMPATIENCE, KATRINKA FLIPPED AGAIN THROUGH THE PAGES OF THE MARCH edition of *Chic,* stopped at the spread of herself working out in the New York Ambassador's exercise room, and surveyed it critically. She looked a little fat, she thought, but that was to be expected: she had been three months pregnant when the photographs were taken. No one but herself seemed to mind. The pages had been designed to advertise her hotels, and they had succeeded. Occupancy in all three was up slightly.

Replacing the magazine in the pouch in front of her, she forced herself to relax into the Mercedes's comfortable leather seat and go over in her mind the list of things she still had to do that day. In addition to the luncheon scheduled to start in approximately forty-five minutes, she had the usual correspondence and telephone calls to deal with, after which she had to revise a speech she was giving to a group of small hotel owners in Houston the following day; meet with the manager of the Ambassador about the new menus for the cocktail lounge; attend a cocktail party at Kenneth Lane's; and afterward join Alexandra and Neil Goodman for dinner with Gordon and Ann Getty. The Gettys had been interested for some time in getting into business with Mark, and Neil's company, Knapp Manning, stood to receive a large fee if a deal was made.

It would be close to midnight by the time she and Mark returned to the house they had moved into just a week before—at Mark's insistence, without the big party she had wanted to give to mark the event; and not until the following Tuesday, when they had tickets for *Le Nozze di Figaro* at the Met, would they get to spend an evening alone.

Katrinka sighed. She wished they had more time for each other. But Mark's schedule was always hectic; and as hard as she tried to cut back on her commitments it still seemed as if every waking minute of her day was filled. But her energy remained high, despite her being six months pregnant. Her spirits were excellent. And, as before, when she was pregnant with Christian, she had gained little weight. Then, of course, she had been trying to conceal her condition and had worried continually about her size. Now, Katrinka was so delighted to be pregnant that she sometimes regretted she did not show more, a regret that passed quickly. Even at nineteen her last month of pregnancy had not been fun. What would it be like this time when she was forty-three?

"There's Mrs. Havlíček now," said Luther, Katrinka's driver, as he saw the doorman spring into action and Zuzka emerge out of the apartment building, pulling her mink coat close around her, hurrying through the brisk March wind toward the car.

Zuzka was looking very good, thought Katrinka, watching her friend approach. In fact, her physical appearance had changed little over the years, except that recently, for the first time in her life, Zuzka had begun to look less like the robust and beautiful athlete she had been when Katrinka and she had skied for the Czech national team than a rich, pampered member of the monied class.

"*Andělíčku, dobrý den,*" said Zuzka, climbing into the car and kissing Katrinka on both cheeks before settling back against the seat. "Thank you for picking me up," she added, as Luther got back into the driver's seat, started the car, and headed back to the Praha, where Katrinka was hosting a luncheon for the mayor of Prague and several of his associates who were in the United States on a trade mission.

"No problem," said Katrinka, replying in Czech, which the two tended to speak when alone together. She had had a meeting with her lawyer about the purchase of the Prague hotel, and stopping by Zuzka's apartment had required only a short detour. "It was on the way. But you look fantastic. What have you been doing to yourself?"

"I've been at the Canyon Spa Ranch," said Zuzka. "Next time Carla and I go, you should come. It's great." She studied Katrinka fondly. "Not that you look as if you need a rest. You look incredible."

"I'm happy, that's why," said Katrinka. "So happy, I feel blessed."

The momentary worries about her relationship with Christian, about his safety, about Mark's, about the inevitable problems of business, of daily life, were just that—momentary. She refused to dwell on them, to let them burrow deep inside where they could gnaw away at her pleasure and contentment. Her life was good, and she was the first to admit it.

"Then you weren't too upset by that article? I wasn't sure whether or not to send it."

"You know how I am. At first, I wanted to strangle Sabrina. But . . ."

"*Kunda,*" muttered Zuzka.

Katrinka laughed. "Well, she is. But this time she was right. I *was* blackballed. Somebody on the committee at the Corviglia Ski Club didn't want me as a member."

"But why?"

"I don't know. And I don't care. I will still go to St. Moritz because I like it there. I will still enjoy myself because I have many good friends. To me, the Corviglia is not that important."

Zuzka hesitated a moment and then said, "Do you suppose maybe Adam had something to do with it?"

"Adam?" She considered the idea for a minute, then said, "No, I don't think so. What difference would my being a member make to him? And there's no reason for him to be so mean. He's the one who had the affair. I never did anything to hurt him."

"You're happy. For some men, that's all the reason they need to try to make you miserable."

"Some women, too," said Katrinka, to be fair.

"Yes," admitted Zuzka glumly. "Women are not so different."

Katrinka recognized the note of unhappiness in her friend's voice. She had heard it before, in the last few years of Zuzka's marriage to Tomáš.

While Katrinka considered whether or not to ask if there was a problem with Carla, Zuzka changed the subject. "Martin tells me he has an appointment with Neil Goodman next month."

"Yes. He's coming to New York to see Neil during his Easter break."

"Katrinka, I want to thank you. Not just for phoning Neil. I suppose I could have done that myself, if I had known that's what Martin wanted," she added with just a hint of bitterness. "But talking to him, you and Mark both, and helping him come to some decision about his future. He wouldn't discuss it with me."

"*Zlatíčko,* don't be silly. You don't have to thank me. You know I would do anything for Martin. And sons don't talk to their mothers. At least not the ones I know," she added, thinking of Adam and his strained relationship with Nina, hoping that her own relationship with Christian would not follow that same awful pattern.

"I had wanted him to work with me . . ."

"He told me . . ."

"But maybe this way is better, after all."

Again Zuzka's voice had that worrying tone. Something was definitely wrong. "The business is doing well?" asked Katrinka.

"Wonderful," said Zuzka brightly. "We're still making a profit, in spite of the economy."

After the Havlíčeks had left Prague and settled in Los Angeles, Zuzka had gone to work in a large sporting goods store to help support her family while Tomáš had tried to establish himself as a film director. Later, when she had become involved with Carla Webb, Zuzka had put her knowledge of sports clothes and equipment to use, not only by acting as a manager and getting Carla jobs endorsing the best on the market, but by starting a company that created and sold top quality golfing merchandise under Carla's name. It was the success of that company that had made Carla Webb a rich woman, and presumably Zuzka as well.

"Thanks to you," said Katrinka.

Zuzka shrugged. "Without Carla, there would be no business."

Up to a point, Zuzka was right; but she was, as usual, seriously underestimating her own part in the company's success. She had a talent for business, which everyone realized but Zuzka, who saw her contribution simply in terms of hard work and good luck, refusing to acknowledge her ability because of what? wondered Katrinka. The usual female posture of deference toward the more powerful mate? Katrinka, too, had often felt the need to walk a pace or two behind Adam, like some royal consort. Thank God, with Mark, she no longer had to do that. He didn't expect it, though Katrinka doubted that, at this point in her life, she could manage to appear acceptably submissive even if he did.

There was no point pursuing the subject, so Katrinka changed it to something else that had been on her mind. "How is Martin doing?" she asked, and when Zuzka shrugged again, continued, "He's upset about Pia?" It was less a question than a statement.

Zuzka nodded and said, "I didn't know he cared so much about her."

"We all misjudged the situation. Lucia, you, me." When she had returned from London to St. Moritz and seen Christian and Pia together, Katrinka knew instantly what had happened. Pia had positively glowed with love, and Christian with . . . satisfaction was the only way Katrinka could describe it. Her first reaction had been anger, with Christian for ignoring her warning and taking advantage of the situation, with herself for underestimating her son's charm, with Pia for being an idiot. But eventually Katrinka had calmed down. Martin, after all, was not the first young man to lose the woman he loved, or Pia the first girl to sacrifice devotion for excitement. First love was more often than not destined to end in disappointment, as her own affair with Mirek Bartoš amply illustrated. She had recovered, as would Martin, and Pia, too, should there ever be anything for her to recover from. For the moment, her relationship with Christian was going well. He had flown to Florence to visit her the weekend before, and they would be spending the Easter holiday together at the Villa Mahmed. "But what could we have done even if we had known?" asked Katrinka. "As much as we want to spare our children pain, we can't in the end."

"I know."

"It seems sad, though, that Martin won't be with us in the south of France next month."

"He has friends. He'll be all right, I suppose. Maybe he'll spend some time with his father." She turned to Katrinka, grimaced, and added, "Anyway, I'm not sure I can make it to Cap Ferrat this year."

"Oh, Zuzka, why not? You know how you love it there." Katrinka was not only disappointed, but also a little bit worried. "Are you sure everything is all right?"

"Everything is fine," said Zuzka firmly. "I'm just very busy right now."

Katrinka did not believe that for a moment, but before she could ask any more questions, the Mercedes pulled to a stop in front of the Praha. Luther climbed out and moved to help the women from the car, and the doorman, seeing he was not needed at the curb, waited at his post until the women drew near, then pulled open the hotel's heavy glass door. "Good afternoon, Mrs. van Hollen," he said.

"Hello," she said, greeting him by name. "How you doing? Your wife feeling better?"

The doorman's wife, too, was pregnant, but unlike Katrinka, seemed to be suffering terribly from one thing or another. "Oh, yes," he replied, lying politely. "Much. Thank you for asking."

Zuzka followed Katrinka upstairs to her office, where they both repaired the damage the wind had done to their hair before going back down to the small ballroom that had been set with tables to accommodate the luncheon guests.

"How's it going?" asked Katrinka as she entered the ballroom and spotted Robin shouting into a phone.

"We're short one flower arrangement, Mrs. van Hollen," explained the banquet manager, who was overseeing the waiters scurrying around the room making final preparations.

Katrinka glanced quickly around. The rococo room was not enormous, but it felt spacious, its size enhanced by its domed ceiling and mirrored walls set in arched panels of white painted wood trimmed in gilt. Each of the tables, which were set with burgundy-colored linen and Royal Worcester gilt-edged china, had a bowl of white roses accented by red and purple freesia in its center. Except for one. It was the only flaw that Katrinka's expert eye could detect.

Robin slammed the phone down and turned to Katrinka. "They're not sure they can get another arrangement here in time."

As problems went, it wasn't much of one. Katrinka remembered seeing a similar arrangement in the dining room; one of the bellmen brought it down, Katrinka made a few adjustments, and, stepping back to study her work critically, said, "I do think no one will notice the difference."

"Don't worry," said Zuzka in Czech. "Everyone will be too busy trying to figure out who got the better table to notice the flowers."

Katrinka laughed. "You're right. The seating plan was a nightmare, believe me."

"There's Michael," said Robin, pointing to where Michael Ferrante, the hotel's general manager, stood in the doorway, looking elegant in a dark Ralph Lauren suit, for once every strand of his thick curly hair in place. He motioned to them and, when they were closer, called, "The mayor's here."

Somewhere in his late thirties, attractive, with light brown hair, dead straight, which he wore long, the mayor of Prague had the look of a classical musician or an aging intellectual. His English was limited, but his two associates, a man and a woman, spoke fluently. Katrinka, who had met them on her last trip to Prague, introduced them to Zuzka, and to Mark, who was the next to arrive, looking unusually harried.

"Something is wrong?" whispered Katrinka as he kissed her hello.

"Nothing serious," he replied, with a reassuring smile.

A flood of guests came in Mark's wake, all of whom moved politely down the receiving line—Neil and Alexandra Goodman; Henry Kravis; Robert and Georgette Mosbacher; Richard Gere and Cindy Crawford; New York's Mayor Dinkins; Vincent Tese, the state's director of economic development, and his wife, Joyce; Rinaldo and Carolina Herrera; Liz Smith of *Newsday*, Billy Norwich of the *Post*, Alice Zucker of *Chic*; Bill Blass; Oscar de la Renta; Rick Colins; Sabrina and her usual escort, the designer Alan Platt—while Katrinka, in an amazing feat of memory, managed to get everyone's name as correct as her imperfect English would allow.

"If you'll come this way, please," said Robin, steering the guests reaching the end of the receiving line toward one of Katrinka's assistants, who was standing at the entrance to the ballroom with the seating arrangements.

"I don't know how you manage it," whispered Alexandra, falling into step beside Katrinka when the line had come to an end. "I forget my own name half the time," she added, exaggerating for effect. Alexandra was an accomplished hostess. "Really . . ." She stopped speaking mid-sentence and her face seemed to pale slightly. "I don't believe it," she said finally. "That bastard. How could he?"

"What?" said Katrinka, spinning around. But all she saw was Jean-Claude Gillette walking toward her, not a sight to upset either Alexandra or herself. In fact, Katrinka was delighted. As a follow-up to a brief discussion they had had about the possibility of going into business together in Prague, she had particularly wanted him to meet the mayor. But what had upset Alexandra had clearly disturbed Zuzka as well. Muttering in Czech, she abandoned the aide to whom she had been speaking and placed herself firmly beside Katrinka, now flanked by two of her best friends, both of whom were clearly prepared to do battle.

When she had time to think about it later, Katrinka supposed that she had not immediately recognized Natalie Bovier not only because her attention was so fixed on Jean-Claude just then, but because her former friend was the last person in the world she expected to see at a private party she was hosting, where she had had complete control of the guest list. And though she knew there was not much Jean-Claude would not do just for the devilment of it, she would not have imagined even him to have been capable of this.

"Katrinka, *chérie*." he said, extending his arms to embrace her, "*comme tu es belle!*"

"Hello, Jean-Claude," said Katrinka, taking a step backward instead of into his arms.

"Katrinka, it's good to see you," said Natalie in her soft French accent, a hesitant smile on her face. Her blond hair was a shade or two darker than it had been; the purple shadows under her green eyes were not completely hidden by makeup, but she was as lovely as ever, and her figure as youthful. She had the same erotic aura that men, including Adam Graham, found irresistible. "I hope my coming does not inconvenience you. But Jean-Claude insisted." She did not dare extend a hand, but turned to look at Zuzka and Alexandra, extending her greeting to them, her smile fading instantly when she saw the loathing in their eyes.

"Jean-Claude did not say he would bring a guest," said Katrinka coolly. "So it will take a minute to find a place for you. If you'll excuse me, I'll arrange it." As Katrinka turned away, so did Alexandra and Zuzka, without speaking a word either to Jean-Claude or Natalie.

"I told you it would do no good," said Natalie, fighting back tears.

"One must begin somewhere," said Jean-Claude. Knowing Natalie was in New York to look at a possible location for a new boutique, he had not been able to resist the temptation of bringing her to the luncheon. Seeing Katrinka's face, he had, for a moment, doubted the wisdom of his decision. His confidence, however, was returning. He was certain that he had made the right move. Taking care of Natalie was an old habit, and one Jean-Claude had no interest in breaking, as long as it did not seriously inconvenience him. He did not like seeing her so lonely, so unhappy, and because he knew Katrinka was the only woman Natalie had ever seriously liked, the only person aside from himself Natalie had ever completely trusted, he wanted to help her regain Katrinka's friendship.

Succeeding would not be without some benefit to him, of course. If the women were friends, Katrinka then would have to shoulder some of the concern, some of the responsibility for Natalie's welfare. As Jean-Claude had so many other delicate situations to deal with at the moment, that would be a great relief to him. "Consider this a first step," he continued, as he put his arm around Natalie's waist and gently propelled her after Katrinka. "The next will not be so hard, for either of you."

"Are you all right?" asked Alexandra, watching as Katrinka made a desperate effort to get her feelings under control.

"Yes," said Katrinka, trying to find just the right smile for her face.

"Tell her to get lost," said Zuzka.

"Natalie doesn't matter. I'm just mad at Jean-Claude for making such a stunt."

Katrinka's friends were so used to her confusing expressions, Alexandra did not bother to explain that it was either "making a scene" or "pulling a stunt" but merely nodded in agreement, saying, "I always knew that man was dangerous."

"He is prick," said the forthright Zuzka, this time in English so no one would miss the point of her remark.

"We do need another place," said Katrinka, when she had reached

Robin and the assistant who were still waiting at the ballroom door to greet latecomers.

"Oh, Christ," said Robin. "Not another one. I already had to find somewhere for a woman named Monica Brand. Ever hear of her?"

"No," said Katrinka.

"Me neither. But she had an invitation, the envelope addressed to her and everything. Beats me." Then she saw Natalie and her face froze. "Jean-Claude can't be serious." She turned to Katrinka. "*You* can't be serious."

"I don't want to argue," said Katrinka. "Please find her somewhere to sit. And somewhere nice. I don't want people saying I stuck her in the kitchen."

Robin looked at Zuzka and Alexandra, but they only shrugged helplessly. "Shit," muttered Robin, as Katrinka, a warm smile fixed firmly on her face, finally entered the ballroom.

"Well, well, well, look who's just arrived," whispered Alan Platt into Sabrina's ear when he spotted Natalie. She had been one of the first to buy his clothes for her West Coast boutiques and, as much as Alan was capable of feeling grateful to anyone, he was to her. Much more so than to Sabrina. Since Sabrina was not the sort of woman he usually looked at twice, it was his opinion that by making love to her he more than paid for all the supposedly "free" publicity she gave him in her column. Not that he looked at many women twice. With a few notable exceptions, he much preferred men. Natalie was one of those exceptions. "Looking good, don't you think?" he said generously, though Natalie had never shown much interest in him. Not rich enough for her, he supposed, though with Sabrina's help that would soon change. "She has quite a way with clothes."

"Because she likes yours?" said Sabrina dryly, watching as Natalie took a seat at Alice Zucker's table.

Sabrina was wearing one of Alan's designs, which she thought a great compliment. On her, of course, it seemed to sag instead of hang and it had somewhere, somehow, acquired a small tear on the cuff, though he had checked it thoroughly before letting her put it on. He sighed. Sabrina, too, had a way with clothes, a disastrous way. "It's one of the things I admire most about women," said Alan honestly.

"Hmm," murmured Sabrina, not really paying attention to him as her eyes traveled to Katrinka to gauge her reaction to Natalie's entrance.

But Katrinka only glanced briefly at Natalie, registering no emotion, then returned her attention to the mayor, who was seated at her right.

When Jean-Claude interrupted them, before taking his place at the next table, a warm smile lit her face as she introduced the two men. Not much there to spark a column, thought Sabrina gloomily. But her disappointment was replaced almost immediately by irritation. Really, if people wanted to see their names in print, you would think they'd try a bit harder to make themselves interesting. As it was, she had to do all the work, inventing here, embroidering there. Charles Wolf had no idea what hard slog it was earning that six-figure salary he had so grandly agreed to pay her.

"I can't wait to read what you make of this," said a soft voice very close to Sabrina's ear.

Looking around, Sabrina found her old rival, Rick Colins, leaning over her, smiling smugly into her face. She would like, she thought, nothing better than to grab the ends of his signature bow tie and pull them until his hazel eyes popped out of his bland preppy face and his breathing stopped altogether. Rick's lanky boyish charm was completely lost on her. "Whatever it is will be more interesting than the drivel you talk on that awful show of yours," she said, her voice dripping venom.

Rick's voice was far more cheerful. "That awful show of mine, on its worst days, has a larger audience than all your syndicated columns combined."

Did he also make more money than she? wondered Sabrina as she felt her gut twist with envy. And he had just signed a contract with a major publishing house to do a book on the old East Coast aristocracy. The fact that no one would buy the book did not console her in the least. Her lips curved, like a candy orange-slice smile in her flat, pudding face, and she said sweetly, "I'm sure that fact is of great interest to anyone interested in quantity rather than quality."

"And you'd never be so crass, would you?" he asked, not in the least offended. He'd match the quality of his show against the best of Sabrina's columns any day, and win. And that wasn't just his opinion. The critics, by and large, reviewed him favorably, and the ratings were still climbing, giving Larry King something to worry about. It was all very satisfying. These days, despite the hours he spent cruising rough-trade bars for sex partners, work was the only real, satisfying pleasure Rick had.

"Now, my dears," said Alan warningly, "let's not have a catfight. We don't want to spoil Katrinka's party."

He certainly did not, thought Rick, getting himself quickly under control. "Don't choke on your lunch," he said, starting away toward his own table.

"Drop dead, faggot," muttered Sabrina as she watched him.

"Did you say something?" asked Alan.

"Yes. Pass the butter, please."

The mayor gave a short speech, assisted by a translator, outlining the wonderful business opportunities in Prague, to which Katrinka, following Nancy Reagan's approach to political life, appeared to pay rapt attention, though she had heard a draft of it the night before. Later, she noticed the Mosbachers talking to the mayor and thought they looked charmed, which boded well for American/Czech trade possibilities, if the Republicans kept the White House after the November election, which, according to the latest polls, looked likely. Katrinka herself acted as translator to Ace Greenberg and Henry Kravis, both of whom had some pointed questions to ask about how the Czech government was prepared to deal with the profits of its foreign investors. Jean-Claude's remarks were much more general, though he spent a long time in conversation with an aide afterward, no doubt hoping to get more detailed information. Always willing to help out when needed, Mark, who spoke Czech with reasonable fluency, translated for Vincent Tese, when Katrinka, acting as a sort of unofficial trade delegate, felt it necessary to mingle with her other guests, answering questions as best she could, calling on the mayor's aides for assistance when the conversation strayed into areas of government policy with which she was not familiar. Sometimes, she caught sight of Natalie— talking to Alan Platt and Sabrina, her arm linked through Jean-Claude's, then deep in conversation with Ronald Perelman and Claudia Cohen—distracting her until, with a great effort of will, Katrinka blotted Natalie from her mind and returned to the business at hand.

"I'm sorry, *chérie*, if I upset you," said Jean-Claude as he was leaving. He did not look in the least repentant. "But I thought it was time to bury the hatchet, as the Americans say."

"It is none of your business, Jean-Claude," said Katrinka, smiling so that no one would suspect they were arguing.

"Forgive me?"

"I'll think about it."

"And if I promise to consider seriously going into business with you in Prague?"

Katrinka laughed. "You know you would do that only to make money, not to make me happy."

"Don't underestimate yourself, *chérie*," he said, as he kissed her on both cheeks, then turned to Mark, as he joined them, and added,

171

"We've settled our differences; there's no need to do battle on your wife's behalf."

Slipping an arm around Katrinka's waist, Mark smiled at Jean-Claude and said, "I wouldn't dream of it. Katrinka doesn't have any problem holding her own . . . in a fair fight."

New husbands were such fools, thought Jean-Claude, so overprotective. He vowed that he would never, never permit himself to behave in such an idiotic fashion when he got around to marrying his lovely Greek heiress. *"Ouff,"* he said with a very Gallic shrug, "but then fights are not very often fair, are they?" He extended a hand for Mark to shake, then smiled at Katrinka, *"Au revoir, chérie. Je te téléphonerai demain."*

Mark watched him cross the room, take Natalie by the arm, and guide her toward the door.

"If your hotels go bust," said Mark, "you can always get a job acting."

Katrinka laughed. "You wouldn't think so if you did see me in a movie." She had made two films with Mirek Bartoš, playing small parts in each, one when she was a child, another just before they became lovers. Her face grew solemn again and she shrugged. "I don't feel angry at Natalie anymore. But the only hatchet I do want to bury right now is one in Jean-Claude's head."

"That's what I meant," said Mark, laughing. "A great actress. The mayor thinks he's your best friend."

Katrinka smiled again. "When I'm not mad at him, I like him very much," she said grudgingly. Then she saw the mayor and his entourage beginning to move toward the door. "I suppose I should say good-bye. Thank you, *miláčku,* you were a big help today."

"Make my excuses, baby, okay?" said Mark, kissing her cheek. "I've got to get back to the office."

Katrinka remembered that he had arrived looking worried. "There's a problem?"

"Not really. Somebody's buying my stock and I want to know who, that's all. Carey's been doing some checking while I've been out," he said, referring to Carey Powers, his CFO. It occurred to him it might be the Gettys.

"Will you make the cocktail party?"

"I'll let you know." He started to move away, but felt a hand on his arm. Turning, he saw the dark-haired woman with whom he had spent a few minutes talking earlier in the day.

"I didn't want to leave without saying good-bye," she said.

"Oh? Well, thank you," said Mark, smiling at her. She was a very

172

pretty and obviously a very sweet young woman. "Do you know my wife?" he said, turning to Katrinka, who shook her head. She had no idea who the woman was, which was odd, she thought, since everyone at the luncheon (with the exception of Natalie) had been personally invited by herself. "Katrinka van Hollen, Monica . . ."

"Brand," finished the woman when Mark hesitated. She smiled shyly at Katrinka. "Your husband and I met at the opera in London last month."

"The one you didn't go to with me," said Mark to Katrinka. Because of Christian, she had decided to return to St. Moritz as soon as her meeting had ended, rather than wait for Mark. "Somehow Ms. Brand ended up in your seat."

"We use the same ticket agent," said Monica. The agent, one of Sugar Benson's contacts, had received a substantial fee to let Monica know the minute Mark's secretary had turned back the extra ticket. "Mr. van Hollen was kind enough to buy me a drink during the intermission." There had been three intermissions, but she saw no reason to belabor the point.

Which Katrinka, in any case, got. But if there was one thing in the world she was sure of, it was Mark. "You do live in London?" she asked.

"Part of the time," said Monica evasively. "I'm a free-lance journalist. I go where the stories are."

"And the story was here today?"

"That depends." She looked at Mark. "I was hoping to talk Mr. van Hollen into letting me interview him."

"I don't give interviews," said Mark, but in a much softer tone than he generally used when asked.

"Which is why it would be such a coup."

Katrinka laughed. "I wish you good luck," she said.

"Yes, well, I was warned it wouldn't be easy. But I don't intend to stop trying."

"You're wasting your time," said Mark.

"Maybe," said Monica Brand. "Maybe not. See you around."

"Nice girl," said Mark, watching as Monica's attractive, well-rounded body made its way toward the door.

"Hmm," said Katrinka. "I do wonder how she got an invitation."

"Probably bribed the help," said Mark, who had no way of knowing how right he was. Monica had bribed one of the cleaning staff to filch an invitation from Katrinka's desk. "You know how journalists are. See you later, baby," he said, kissing Katrinka's cheek again and following Monica's path to the door.

Sixteen

"SORRY TO HAVE KEPT YOU WAITING," SAID ADAM, NOT LOOKING IN THE LEAST REPENTANT. "ONE OF THOSE mornings. Want some coffee? Tea? Nothing? Well, I'd like another bottle of Evian, please." He glanced briefly at Heather, his secretary, before turning back to Tomáš, inviting him into his office, offering him his hand to shake. Snatching the photographs that Tomáš had just retrieved from Heather's grasp, Adam looked quickly through the stack as he retraced his steps across the carpeted floor. "Cute kid," he said, hiding the regret he always felt at the sight of someone else's child, smiling amiably as he sat in his executive leather chair, behind his chrome-and-glass desk, its surface marred only by a telephone, a Mark Cross pen set, and one file folder. The messy stacks of scripts, the books, the piles of contracts that decorated the offices of most film studio executives, in Adam's were concealed within the wall of lacquer cabinets behind him. The opposite wall was glass, covered with narrow strips of dark blinds past which filtered the flickering image of cars moving along the 134 Freeway and, beyond that, the Santa Monica mountains. On a third wall hung a large painting by Francis Bacon, enough to put most people off work. It was a reminder, said Adam, of just how brutal the film business could be.

"Thanks," said Tomáš, taking the photographs and tucking them securely in the pocket of his jacket, which was standard studio issue with the Olympic Pictures logo stamped on the front and *Marked for*

174

Death, the name of Tomáš's most recent film, emblazoned across its back.

"A new baby, at your age," said Adam. "You're old enough to be a grandfather."

"It's never too late," said Tomáš cheerfully, aware that he was about four or five years younger than Adam. He settled his briefcase at his feet, then sat back in the chrome-and-leather chair and tried to appear relaxed. "That's what's so great about being a guy."

"Sure is," said Adam, who did not sound as if the thought cheered him very much. "What did you call her?"

"Alenka," said Tomáš. "It was my grandmother's name." His father had deserted him shortly after his birth, his mother had been an alcoholic, and his grandfather difficult, sometimes even violent. In all his family, his grandmother had been the only person Tomáš had loved, and she had died when he was seven. If it had not been for Katrinka and her parents, who had lived in a neighboring apartment, his childhood would have been one of unrelieved misery.

"How's Lori doing?"

"She's terrific."

"And Martin?" Tomáš shrugged and Adam said, "I hear he's got an appointment with Neil Goodman next month." Alexandra had told him. If the subject was not too obviously concerned with Katrinka's personal life, which Alexandra considered off-bounds, he could usually get her to tell him anything he wanted to know.

"Yeah," said Tomáš. "It seems he wants a job on Wall Street when he gets his MBA."

"He could have come to me if he needed help."

Was that hurt in Adam's voice? wondered Tomáš as he said, "You've done so much for him already."

"So has Katrinka." It was ridiculous of him to mind, Adam knew, and he certainly didn't want gratitude for having saved Martin's life, calling in favors at the State Department to cut through red tape, having Martin flown from Prague to Boston in the Graham jet, picking up the tab for the surgery that could only be done in the States. But he had always liked Martin, from the first time they had met, when Martin was just a little kid in Prague. He had thought that Martin returned his affection, that he trusted him, that he felt free to ask when he needed help. But instead he had gone to Katrinka. And Mark.

"If you think I know what goes on in my son's head, you're wrong. He doesn't tell me anything, and I've learned not to ask." Tomáš frowned and added, "Zuzka says he's pretty upset about Pia."

"What about Pia?" Alexandra hadn't mentioned her.

175

"Martin was in love with her, which none of us had figured out. And now she's dating Christian."

"Christian Heller?"

Tomáš nodded. "It happened when they were all in St. Moritz." He shook his head. "Love," he said.

"What do you think of him?"

"Christian?" asked Tomáš and, when Adam nodded, replied evasively, "I only met him once."

"He's a cocky sonovabitch," said Adam, then he smiled. "I didn't mean that literally," he added.

Tomáš did not return the smile. "No, of course not."

The office door opened and the two men fell silent for a moment as Adam's secretary crossed the room, carrying a bucket of ice, a cut-crystal glass, and a bottle of Evian on a silver tray. "How's the editing going?" asked Adam, ignoring the young woman as she placed the tray in the niche provided in the lacquer cabinet. She poured him a glass of water, placed it on the desk at his right hand.

For all of her quiet efficiency, Heather was not unaware of her sexual attraction, thought Tomáš, who resisted the urge to turn his head to watch the roll of her bottom in its short, tight denim skirt as she exited. With admirable control, Adam's eyes flicked in its direction for only a moment, before returning to Tomáš's face. He was waiting for an answer. "It's never easy," said Tomáš.

"I like what I see," admitted Adam, with the hint of a smile. He may or may not have been referring to Heather's ass.

"Good. Good," said Tomáš, choosing to believe that Adam meant the cut versions of several key scenes he had recently watched.

"You'll be finished on schedule?"

"Absolutely."

That was a relief, thought Adam. He wanted the movie in the theaters before *Lethal Weapon III* and *Batman Returns*, to capitalize on the first surge of summer movie frenzy. There was not a doubt in Adam's mind that this film, which recombined all the elements of the studio's earlier (and only) successes—that is, scriptwriter, star, and director—would be a major hit. It had to be. If the deal with the Italians hadn't closed by then, if they were (as Mac suggested) stalling until *Marked for Death* opened, the first weekend's box office returns needed to be big enough to convince them that Olympic Pictures was a potential gold mine. "So, then, what's the problem?" asked Adam. "I'm assuming you didn't call up and ask for a meeting just to tell me everything's going great."

"No," said Tomáš, reaching for his briefcase, a nervous smile playing on his face. "I would have called and invited you to lunch for that." He opened the briefcase, took out a script, and handed it to Adam. "A client of Lori's wrote this. She thinks it's great. So do I. We hope you will, too."

Stifling a groan, Adam took the script. "Is there coverage on it?" Every studio employed readers to report on literary material—the galleys of books, plays about to be produced at some regional theater, original screenplays churned out by neophyte writers and old hacks alike—in the hope of making a fortune. The reports, averaging about three pages, were called coverage. Executives rarely read anything longer.

"I don't want the opinion of some junior assistant you're underpaying, Adam. I want yours."

"It's that good?" asked Adam, turning to the title page. By B. D. Howe, it said. The name meant nothing to him.

"It's the film I've been dreaming of making for years."

That was exactly what Adam feared. He knew the kinds of films that Tomáš wanted to make, had heard about them endlessly over dinners, long before he had thought of acquiring a movie studio. Small, dark dramas, like *Closely Watched Trains*, the 1960s hit by another Czech director, Jiří Menzel; or expensive costume pieces like *Amadeus*, which made money only by fluke; or politically relevant films, like *Bob Roberts*, which never made money at all. Why couldn't Tomáš be satisfied directing the exploitation movies that the public loved? What did it matter if the critics hated them? Couldn't Tomáš just cry all the way to the bank and stop tormenting himself and everyone associated with him? But all Adam said was, "Who's B. D. Howe?"

"She's never done anything you've heard of."

"She?"

"Beth Howe," said Tomáš. "I don't know what the 'D' stands for."

All Adam's worst fears were confirmed. A screenplay by a woman. It was bound to be not only small, but soft, sentimental. If he made it, it would most likely get respectable, possibly even glowing reviews; if he controlled the budget carefully, it might even make a respectable profit. But it would never be the kind of blockbuster he needed. "What's it about?" he asked.

"It's a hundred and twenty pages. Read it, Adam. It'll take you an hour. An hour and a half, if you don't skip too many words."

"I'll read every line. I promise," said Adam, his mouth curving in the foolproof crooked smile he hoped would make Tomáš feel secure.

"Then I won't waste any more of your time. Or mine. I've got to get back to the editing room." Tomáš snapped his briefcase shut and stood up.

"How soon can you begin prepping *Low Flying Planes*?" asked Adam, as he got to his feet and walked around the desk to escort Tomáš to the door. That was the working title of Tomáš's next film, and Adam wanted its status updated on the production reports for his next meeting with the Italians.

"In four weeks. As soon as I get back from Cancún." Tomas saw the look on Adam's face, and continued quickly, "I'm tired, Adam. I brought *Marked for Death* in on time and on budget. And I've been editing night and day since I got back from Canada."

"I know. I know," said Adam, trying to force some sympathy into his voice.

"I promised Lori."

"Okay. Go to Cancún. But just watch what you eat and drink. The last thing you need is an attack of Montezuma's revenge. All right?" said Adam, hoping his voice did not betray the urgency he felt.

"And I'm going to Palm Beach for the weekend. To the Goodmans."

Adam was about to protest, but thought better of it. Tomáš's face looked particularly belligerent. "Yeah, well, I'll be in Europe so I can't make it. Have a good time."

Tomáš nodded. "The break will do me good. Give me a fresh p.o.v. In case you haven't noticed, the script still needs work," he added, firing the warning shots in the battle that would, inevitably, soon be waged.

Adam laughed. "Scripts always need work. According to directors, at any rate."

"In this case, the director is absolutely correct."

"You'll get your new script. Don't worry about it." Scripts were always rewritten, and rewritten again, as many as fifteen or sixteen times, at enormous expense, with the final draft (at least in Adam's limited experience) rarely any better than the first. When he had taken over the studio, Adam had made an effort to limit the rewrites, in an attempt to cut costs, but directors had sulked, stars had walked off projects, and his head of production had pointed out to him the folly of expecting anyone to buy into a project without, so to speak, first fingering the goods. Nobody was happy unless the rewrite ritual was followed. Not that anyone was happy afterward.

The two men shook hands. "You'll be hearing from me," said Adam. He was careful not to specify when and Tomáš did not ask.

"Come around for dinner some night," said Tomáš. "Meet the baby."

"I will. Tell Lori to call and invite me."

"See you tomorrow," said Tomáš. Adam was scheduled to see another cut scene in the morning.

Adam closed the door after Tomáš, returned to his desk, poured himself another glass of Evian, then sat and opened the script again. B. D. Howe. The name was no more promising than before.

The intercom sounded, interrupting his train of thought. "My mother first," said Adam, when Heather had finished reading him the list of calls he still had to return. Nina and Russell had just returned from honeymooning at a friend's condo at the Seaview in Bal Harbour, hobnobbing with the Bakers and the Doles and other political buddies. And she sounded, thought Adam, as girlishly happy as she had before the wedding, which was just as well since, short of death, there was no politically correct way of terminating the marriage.

While he was on with his mother, Heather brought in a fax from his lawyer and Adam brought the conversation to a quick stop by promising to put in an appearance at a fund-raising dinner planned for the following month. The wedding out of the way, the campaigning for the Senate seat was beginning in earnest. Replacing the receiver, Adam scanned the fax. The news was not good. With all delaying tactics exhausted, the lawsuit against the cruise ship line would come to trial within thirty days; and since there was no guarantee that Adam would win it, perhaps now was the time to think about a settlement? Now was definitely *not* the time, insisted Adam, as soon as he had his lawyer on the line. He didn't have the money for a settlement. "Think of something else," he ordered. "Find another reason to delay. That's what I pay you for, isn't it?"

When he returned Charles Wolf's call, the news was no better. Apparently nervous about the rapid movement of his stock, Mark van Hollen had started buying VHE shares; others had smelled a quick profit and started buying, too, driving the price up higher and faster than anticipated. What did Adam want him to do now? asked Wolf.

"Keep buying," said Adam.

"The stocks are overpriced."

"That'll keep the shareholders happy."

"This is crazy, Adam."

"Nobody ever made money by being too sane. Keep buying. I'm footing the bill, aren't I?" Knowing that any move by him against VHE would put Mark van Hollen on instant alert, Adam had needed a front man for the takeover attempt, and Charles Wolf, with his newspaper chain, was perfect for the job. But Wolf had finally agreed to go along with the plan only if Adam provided the financing.

"Okay," said Wolf, "but I'm glad it's your money and not mine."

What they were doing was illegal, of course. But then so much of business was, they hardly noticed the fact. Charles Wolf was blinded by the prospect of rivaling Rupert Murdoch without risking a cent of his own money; and Adam, driven by the desire to get Mark van Hollen, seemed worried only about how to close the studio deal so that he could pay for the scheme. Graham Marine's debt burden was so great that he could not raise a dime at the banks. The cruise ship line couldn't be sold until the lawsuit was settled; no one wanted the tankers, and the shipyards, the heart of his empire, were not for sale.

Under the circumstances, someone else might have backed off the takeover plan, but giving up was not Adam Graham's style. When he made up his mind to accomplish something, he did it. One way or another, he would secure the financing; then, when Monica Brand had succeeded in compromising Mark van Hollen, undermining his control of the VHE board of directors, Adam would move in for the kill.

At the thought of Monica Brand, Adam frowned. All she had to show for the time and effort and money that particular venture had so far cost were two brief encounters—not much, though Sugar Benson was certain that Mark was attracted enough to take the bait. Soon, hoped Adam, who wanted to see a quick return on that investment.

The intercom buzzed again and Heather announced Lucia, who was in San Diego, trying to keep Patrick Kates happy—an impossible task. Now that the problem with the mast had been resolved, he was worried about the design of the keel. Reports of innovations being tried by the New Zealand challenger team had him making life hell for the designers, who were working around the clock trying to come up with solutions to the always vexing problems of increasing the yacht's speed without decreasing its maneuverability and safety.

Though Patrick was so far not pleased with the way things were going, Adam was. From what he had seen of the trials so far, he thought *The Valiant* could win, and that it could take the cup in May, if Patrick kept his head and sailed a good race.

Adam wanted to win, for practical reasons certainly. What better publicity could there be for Graham Marine? But he had another, more powerful motive. He wanted the glory. Graham Marine had not designed a winning yacht in over a hundred years. His father had lacked the necessary resolve, perhaps even the skill, to make his dream of winning the cup a reality. Adam had no intention of repeating the disappointment, of following in his father's footsteps, of being a failure in this way or any other. If Kates didn't win the America's Cup this time, Adam was determined to do it himself next time.

"When are you coming down?" asked Lucia.

"I think I liked it better when you were in love with Nick Cavalletti."

"I didn't," said Lucia, her voice growing cold.

"I'll be there in the morning. About ten. All right?"

"That's terrific." All the warmth came flooding back into her voice. "I'll see you then."

Adam replaced the receiver, buzzed Heather, told her to charter a helicopter for the trip to San Diego, then sat back in his chair thinking about Patrick Kates until his eye fell again on the script Tomáš had left behind. Even without reading it, Adam was certain it was good. He trusted Tomáš: at least, he trusted his artistic judgment and his taste. He also liked Tomáš. At one time, he would even have said that they were friends, though friendship was a concept that Adam had difficulty understanding. Most of his relationships with men were with people like Mac, who worked for him, or Neil Goodman, with whom he did business. There was no one with whom he spent time simply for the pleasure of his company, because they shared common interests, laughed at the same jokes, enjoyed the same pastimes. Even the men with whom he sailed were either hired to crew or were business associates he was out to impress.

Adam's record with women was better. Despite his having been, according to them at any rate, selfish, inconsiderate, and unfaithful during their affairs, afterward Lucia and Alexandra had remained his friends. Even Natalie had forgiven him for breaking off their relationship. Adam was intelligent, powerful, sexy, and charming, they said. He was also generous, remembering birthdays, sending flowers, even expensive little gifts. They had acquired the habit of forgiving him everything, even betrayal, whether it was of themselves or his wife.

Having managed to patch things up with his former girlfriends, Adam sometimes wondered why he could not do the same with Katrinka. But the reason was simple, though it never occurred to him. Neither Lucia, nor Alexandra, nor Natalie had ever trusted him. Katrinka had, totally. He had betrayed her trust, and for that she would never forgive him.

Because they were mutually dependent, Adam and Tomáš had both preferred not to investigate too deeply the effect of the Graham divorce on their own relationship. Tomáš had taken the position that "these things happen" to everyone, including himself. Warily, he tread along the battle line drawn by Adam and Katrinka, careful not to stray too far over it in either direction.

But for all that he noticed and appreciated the effort Tomáš made to be fair, Adam misunderstood his motive. While he did not doubt that Tomáš cared for Katrinka, he was not sure what Tomáš felt for him: affection? friendship? loyalty? Not unreasonable emotions to have for the man who had saved your son's life, rescued you from poverty, given you your first American feature to direct, turned you into a star. But Adam suspected, completely misjudging him, that Tomáš had not come down firmly on Katrinka's side only because he was trying to protect his position as Olympic Pictures's number-one director. And Adam minded.

Depressing the intercom, he told Heather to hold his calls. He leaned back in his leather chair, picked up the script, and began to read. An hour and thirty-five minutes later he had finished, having read every word as he had promised Tomáš. The script was good. Very good, in fact. But Adam had expected that. It was also powerful and gutsy, which he had not expected. It was about a Chinese family in San Francisco at the end of the last century, a period piece with strong political overtones. It was called *Westward, Ho*, an ironic reference to a popular American classic about the settling of the western frontier. In Adam's opinion it should have been called *Death at the Box Office*. In the best of circumstances, if the studio had been steadily profitable, if Adam had felt inclined to keep Tomáš happy, he would not have seriously considered making such a film. It was the equivalent of committing suicide.

He would not, however, tell Tomáš that, since he wanted to keep his temperamental director in a good mood throughout preproduction on *Low Flying Planes*. Instead, he would instruct his business affairs department to begin negotiating to acquire the rights to the screenplay; then, once shooting on *Planes* had started, when Tomáš was safely out of town on location, Adam could let the whole matter drop.

Leaning forward, Adam again depressed the buzzer of his intercom and asked Heather to come into his office. "Take this," he said, when she stood in front of him, eager to do his pleasure. He handed her the script. "Get some coverage on it. Call Don in Business Affairs. Tell him I want to see him, whatever time I've got free tomorrow morning. When Lori Havlíček phones to invite me to dinner, make a date. I don't care what you have to clear from my calendar to do it." He smiled, causing Heather to wonder again just what she had to do to make him that eager to have dinner with her. "And buy something nice for the baby. Something nice and expensive," continued Adam. "Let's keep the Havlíčeks happy."

Seventeen

"HOW DID THE SPEECH GO?" ASKED MARK.

"FANTASTIC," REPLIED KATRINKA, A SATISFIED SMILE lighting her face. At a breakfast in Miami that morning, she had spoken to a group about the perils and pleasures for a woman of owning and operating a business. "I did get a standing ovation. And you?"

"And me," said Mark, sounding relieved, pleased, tired. "They loved the magazine, or so they said. It looks great, baby. Really great." *The International* was about to hit the stands and Mark was in London for its launch. Earlier that day, at a champagne reception, he had shown the first copies off the press to a select group, including his board of directors and principal stockholders. "It's a winner. I know it. The multinationals love it. The only real problem's going to be keeping up this standard of journalism."

"It won't be easy, *miláčku*, but you'll do it. Most of the time anyway," she added.

Mark laughed. "I'll do it," he said.

"I wish I was there with you."

"Me, too, baby. I miss you." They had discussed Katrinka's accompanying him, but not only had she accepted the speaking engagement in Miami before the magazine's publication date was set, but both of them agreed that, until the baby was born, she ought to give up the two- and three-day exhausting transatlantic trips that had been a part of her itinerary for years. "I hope at least you're getting some rest, to make my sacrifice worthwhile."

"Don't worry. All I do this afternoon is lie by the pool." A hired limousine had brought Katrinka from Miami to Palm Beach, where she was staying with Alexandra and Neil for the weekend. Mark was expected the next day. "You do sound exhausted, though, *miláčku.* Don't stay out too late tonight."

"I'll have dinner, and come right home," said Mark. "Which reminds me. Do you remember that cute young woman, that journalist who wanted to interview me?"

"Journalist?" echoed Katrinka, trying to remember whom he meant.

"She came to the luncheon you gave for the mayor of Prague. Monica Brand."

"Oh, yes."

"She turned up at the opera again the other night. She was with a girlfriend. Carey was with me and we had drinks with them during the intermission. And last night she was my partner at dinner. At Tony Moreland's."

"How funny," said Katrinka.

"Quite a coincidence," agreed Mark. "She asked me for a job."

"Doing what?"

He laughed. "She sounded eager enough to do just about anything."

"And you said?" Even Katrinka was surprised to hear the edge in her voice.

"You're not jealous," said Mark, as if not quite believing his ears.

"No," said Katrinka, after an almost imperceptible pause. "I do trust you. But that doesn't mean I'm stupid enough to trust every woman who flirts with you."

"Well, I have to admit I enjoy it."

There was a teasing note in his voice, but he meant it. "Yes, I did notice," said Katrinka dryly. And why shouldn't he? She liked it when men flirted with her. That didn't mean she thought, even for a moment, of going to bed with any of them.

"But in this case, I think *Ms.* Brand really does just want a job. She seems bright, and ambitious."

"You are going to hire her?"

"She dropped some of her clippings off today at the office. The ones I've read so far are pretty good. We're meeting for lunch tomorrow to discuss it, before I leave for Palm Beach."

"Lunch?"

"Yes," he said. "Lunch."

Katrinka recognized the note in Mark's voice. It was the one used to announce that her husband, seeing absolutely nothing wrong in what he was about to do, would not change his mind. She had heard it many times, including the few days before he had tried killing himself on the Cresta Run. "Fine," she said shortly.

"Katrinka, if I objected every time you had lunch with a man I'd be in big trouble. You have nothing to worry about. I love you."

"I do know that."

"So?"

She sighed. "I'm not sure. I think I don't like Monica Brand."

"Well, she speaks most flatteringly of you. You should hear her. Maybe I'll tape our lunch," he said, with a laugh. "Just to prove what a good boy I am."

"I do trust you, *miláčku*," she said, meaning it.

"I should hope so. I better get going, or I'll be late for dinner. Tony is taking Carey Powers and me to White's. My socialist father must be turning over in his grave." One of the oldest of the famous English men's clubs, White's was in St. James's Street, not far from the intersection with Piccadilly, its facade discreetly unmarked, recognizable to those who cared about such things by its famous bow window. Its members had once included, among others, the Duke of Wellington and Beau Brummell. "'Bye, baby. I'll see you tomorrow."

"Don't come too early," said Katrinka, finally mustering a laugh. "Or you'll catch us all in face masks and hair curlers." Alexandra had planned what she called a "spa day" for her girlfriends.

"I'll be there around six."

"'Bye, *miláčku*," said Katrinka. She always hated that moment, the end of a long-distance phone call, the finality of it. The sudden quiet reminded her of death.

That day, the feeling was worse than usual. Sighing, Katrinka replaced the receiver. What was wrong with her? It was not like her to be so moody. Or so jealous. She did not at all like the idea of Mark's having lunch with Monica Brand. Hormones, she decided finally. Her pregnancy was causing her to react in uncomfortable, unfamiliar ways. She was being "emotional," which was annoying, but unfortunately to be expected.

Getting up from the delicately painted writing desk, Katrinka took off the short-sleeved pink Scaasi suit that she had worn to the lecture and stood studying herself in the mirror. Her face seemed fuller, and her breasts; from just above her waist, her stomach rose like a domed cover above a serving plate. Mark said he loved the way she looked. Would he change his mind soon, she wondered, when she blew up like a balloon?

Not liking the direction her thoughts were taking, Katrinka turned away from the mirror and walked naked to the Vuitton suitcase that lay open on the floor, rummaged for a moment, then changed into the backless, skirted La Perla bathing suit that was one of several she had brought with her. But instead of going immediately to the pool, she sat down again at the writing desk and phoned New York to take care of business before finally allowing herself to relax.

As she spoke to Robin, Katrinka looked about her, studying the results of Alexandra's handiwork with a critical eye. The room was delightful, she decided, with its walls sponged a muted pumpkin, giving it a warm, golden glow. A tapestry spread covered the bed, which had a frame of elaborately carved wood. There was a sofa upholstered in rose brocade against one wall, with paler fringed draperies on the arched windows and fringed shades on the table lamps. A chandelier of pink-and-turquoise Venetian glass dangled from the ceiling, Venetian mirrors hung on the walls between oil paintings of Italian street scenes.

Designed by Marion Sims Wyeth in the early 1920s, the entire house resembled a Venetian palazzo, with a near-flat red-tiled roof, columned loggias with pointed arches, and recurring patterns of rectangular and curved windows. It had a marble entry hall, tiled floors, coffered ceilings, and walls paneled in carved wood. On the Lake Worth side of South Ocean Boulevard, just down the road from Mar-a-Lago and the Bath and Tennis Club, the Scampo Dolce, as it was called, was decorated almost entirely with Italian antiques, some bought with the estate from the previous owner, one of the Woolworth heirs, some found by Alexandra on European hunting trips.

Society in Palm Beach was not easy to break into, but Alexandra's family connections (both Graham and Ogelvy) had helped her to overcome some of the resistance and to bridge the gap that ordinarily existed between the city's Wasp and Jewish communities. Still, no matter how well connected Alexandra might be, no power on earth could get Neil Goodman (who had had the misfortune not only to have earned his money instead of inheriting it, but to have been born Jewish as well) accepted into either the Everglades or the Bath and Tennis Club.

But being excluded from hallowed halls by the old guard did not necessarily mean being left out of the fun. The old fogies were dying off. A new, more inclusive generation was moving in and establishing a separate but equal social scene. And while the Wasp hierarchy might one day pack up and go, abandoning the field to the *nouveau riche*, as it had in other places many times before, meanwhile, in private homes and on neutral territory, the two groups mixed freely.

Having learned at her mother's knee that the way to a city's heart was through its charities, Alexandra had immediately involved herself in Palm Beach's fund-raising circuit, and that year, for the first time, was chairwoman of the gala for Planned Parenthood, which, despite the growing national controversy about abortion and sex education, not to mention the dominant presence of rich conservatives in the area, remained one of the town's most popular causes. The ball was on Saturday night at the Flagler Museum. Katrinka and Mark had promised to attend, as had Margo and Ted Jensen, who had come from Monte Carlo for a week's visit. Tomáš and his family were expected later that day. But Daisy and Riccardo Donati had sent their regrets; so had Lucia; and Adam Graham, to Katrinka's intense relief, was on a business trip out of the country.

Her conversation with Robin finished, Katrinka returned two urgent phone calls—one to the manager of the casino in the London hotel about a bookkeeper whom he suspected of fiddling with the books, which might have, at least partly, accounted for the drop in profits the preceding month; another to Carlos, who was visiting friends in France and thought he had found the perfect bed for the baby's nursery in an antique shop in Champagne-sur-Seine. When those were completed, she slipped into her crisp white cotton cover-up, put on her straw hat, picked up the copy of *All Around the Town*, the Mary Higgins Clark novel she was currently reading, and went down to join Margo and Alexandra, who were already lying on white Tropitone lounges beside the long turquoise pool.

Although the property in the front of the house was extensive, that in back was not, and the area from the rear loggia to just beyond the pool was decked in stone and brick, with only a narrow band of lawn between it and the balustrade that edged the property at Lake Worth. Nearer the house, there were planted areas with towering palms, umbrella-shaped jacarandas, lipstick-red hibiscus, soft-pink geraniums, and scarlet bougainvillea. To the south was a grove of fruit trees: orange, grapefruit, tangerine, and kumquat. The latter made wonderful marmalade and was delicious pickled or served coated with chocolate. There were two inner courtyards, separating various wings, one with a cool patch of green lawn and bougainvillea climbing the columns of the cloistered walk; another shaded by a giant banyan tree and paved with coquina stone. More than once, their disapproving nanny had caught the children scrambling to play in the fountain in its center.

"It's about time," said Alexandra, when she looked up and saw Katrinka coming down the wide brick steps from the loggia.

"We thought you'd fallen asleep," said Margo.

"I was talking to Mark," said Katrinka, as she adjusted the position of the lounge next to Margo to get the full benefit of the sun.

"He is coming, isn't he?" said Alexandra, sitting up straight, sounding anxious, as if anyone would notice one person more or less at the huge ball on Saturday night.

"Of course. He'll be here tomorrow." Katrinka checked through the bottles of sunblock and tanning oils in the basket on the table beside her, chose one, then sat and began spreading the lotion over her body.

Alexandra relaxed. "Good," she said as she settled back into the lounge and lifted her face to the sun.

Margo looked from her to Katrinka. "I can't believe you two," she said.

"What?" asked Katrinka, picking up her book.

"With everything that's been written and said about skin cancer, look at you, lying there, as if there's not a thing to worry about." Margo was completely covered by a long-legged, long-sleeved Pucci suit, her hair tied up in a scarf, a large open umbrella shading her.

"It feels so good," said Katrinka.

"I look better when I have a tan," insisted Alexandra.

"How you dare," said Margo, "with your red hair and fair skin, is beyond me."

"Margo, stop," said Alexandra, with a groan. "This is the first time in days I've had a minute to relax. Don't ruin it." She had not stopped smoking yet either and a lighted cigarette was burning in an ashtray beside her.

"Sorry," said Margo, picking up her copy of *Chic*, shifting her critical attention from the havoc caused by sun to the work of Alice Zucker, who had replaced her at the magazine. "What did you think of the layout Alice did of you?" she asked Katrinka.

"Not bad," said Katrinka diplomatically, wondering how much Margo actually missed working now that she and Ted had retired to Monaco. "Except I did look fat."

"I wish I looked as fat as you when I'm pregnant," said Alexandra.

A butler in black pants and white coat emerged from the house with a tray holding two pitchers of iced herbal tea and tall plastic glasses. As he served them each a glass Margo asked, "Did you read the piece on Elizabeth Taylor?"

"Yes," murmured Katrinka.

"I would *never* have done the two of you in the same month."

"She looked terrific," said Alexandra. "I have to get that photographer to take some pictures of me. What's his name? Patrik Andersson."

"It's the name of her plastic surgeon I want," said Margo when the butler was out of earshot.

Alexandra sat up straight in her lounge again. "You're thinking about plastic surgery?"

"Every woman pushing forty is thinking about plastic surgery. And I'm fifty-six."

"But you do look wonderful," said Katrinka, also sitting up to look at her friend.

There wasn't a lot of Margo visible at the moment. Her frizzy halo of charcoal hair was concealed by her scarf, her brilliant dark eyes and arched brows hidden beneath large sunglasses. But the strong jut of her nose, the cheekbones rising prominently under a thick layer of pale makeup, the lines etched at the corners of her full red mouth, seemed essentially unchanged. And Margo's looks, after all, had never been conventional. Her attractiveness lay in the combination of startling features and strong personality. By force of will alone she had convinced the world that she was a beauty, and it was difficult to understand how surgery could better that.

"Now's the time to act," said Margo, "before everything falls completely apart." She dropped the magazine into her lap. "Anyway, I have to do something, and I don't know what else to try."

Both Katrinka and Alexandra felt the sudden shift in mood, the quick injection of misery into the previously tranquil and happy afternoon. "Something is wrong?" asked Katrinka.

"What's happened?" asked Alexandra.

The usually talkative Margo for once seemed at a loss for words. Trying to speak, she couldn't. When no sound came out of her open mouth, she closed it again. Grabbing a paper tissue from the box on the table, she pushed her sunglasses out of the way and wiped her eyes. For a moment, her two friends were equally speechless: Margo never cried.

It couldn't be anything to do with the children, reasoned Katrinka. If the idea of plastic surgery made Margo cry, it had to have something to do with Ted. "You have a problem with Ted?" she asked, even though the idea was absurd. They were the most devoted couple she knew. They adored each other. But then, she reminded herself, she had once thought that about Daisy and Steven, about Adam and herself.

"Ted?" echoed Alexandra, as shocked by the idea as Katrinka.

Margo nodded. "He's . . . he's having an affair," she said finally, forcing the words out.

"You're sure?" asked Alexandra.

"Positive." Margo blew softly into the Kleenex, crumpled it, tossed it onto the table, and pulled the sunglasses down over her eyes. "He told me," she said.

"But why?" asked Alexandra.

Neither of the other two women misunderstood the question. Men had affairs. Men of Ted's age, even if they had managed to stay faithful before, frequently gave in to temptation, a final fling, a last grab for youth. The question was, why had he admitted it to Margo?

"He wants to marry her," said Margo.

"He doesn't mean it," said Katrinka.

"I think he does," said Margo morosely.

"After all you've done for him," said Alexandra, sounding outraged, remembering how Margo not only had resigned her job at *Chic* to nurse Ted through the depression and alcoholism that had plagued him after a fire had destroyed his Seventh Avenue factory, but had rebuilt the business sufficiently for Ted, once he was recovered, to sell it for a small fortune.

"That's the problem," said Margo. "He says he won't leave me if I ask him not to, because of how much he owes me." She began to weep again. Pulling another tissue from the box, she blew into it loudly. "But I don't want him to stay unless *he* wants to."

"You didn't tell him that," said Alexandra.

"Yes," said Margo, sobbing. "But I don't think I can live without him. I never have. Not really." It was Ted who had first appreciated her quick mind, her sense of humor, the beauty behind her homely facade. Except for Ted, and possibly her father, no man had ever loved her. "And I'm too old to start now."

"We all do feel that way," said Katrinka, "at first. Look at Daisy. Look at me. But I don't believe Ted will leave you."

"It's only a fling," said Alexandra. "Don't do anything crazy. Don't, whatever you do, agree to a divorce. Or a separation. He needs time to get over it."

"Who is she?" asked Katrinka.

"Her name's Gigi," said Margo. She started to laugh. "Do you believe it? Gigi!" The other two joined in. Suddenly they were like teenagers at a pajama party.

"It sounds like the name of a *Penthouse* centerfold," said Alexandra.

"She's an officer in the bank where we have our account," said Margo, the laughter fading from her voice. "Thirty-four, divorced, with a nine-year-old daughter. Very cute little girl, Ted says," she added bitterly.

There was quiet for a moment as both Katrinka and Alexandra searched for something to say. If Gigi had been younger, nineteen, say, they might have mustered an argument against her being a serious threat to Margo's marriage, though, of course, she would have been: anyone young and beautiful has to be considered a serious, a *dangerous*, threat. Had she been a waitress in a café, a shopgirl, an aspiring actress, they could have dismissed her as a "bimbo," which, however untrue, would nonetheless have been reassuring. Then, should the marriage actually fall apart, Margo would have the cold comfort of feeling superior to her rival in every way but age.

A bank official, however, was something else entirely: the position implied someone adult, mature, intelligent, substantial—a woman not easily dismissed. "Gigi," said Alexandra finally, "that's a very frivolous name for a banker, isn't it?"

"Her real name's Gabrielle. 'Gigi' is what her mother calls her. And her *close* friends."

"How long it's been going on?" asked Katrinka.

For months, Margo told them. A business meeting had led to a lunch date, a couple of lunch dates to a dinner, dinner eventually to bed when Margo had been in Paris with Daisy and Alexandra for the collections at the end of January.

It was a familiar pattern, recognized Alexandra. That was how Neil and she had begun their relationship. She had worked at Sotheby's, specializing in seventeenth-century Dutch art, and Neil had been an avid collector. But it had taken years for Neil to make the final decision to leave his wife. "Ted's *not* going to leave you," said Alexandra with as much reassurance as she could manage.

"How can you say that? Men always leave their wives."

"That's not true," said Katrinka.

"Of course it's true," said Margo. "Look at Steven and Daisy. And what about Neil?" she asked, not even the dark lenses able to hide the bitter glare she focused on Alexandra.

"That was completely different," said Alexandra defensively. "Neil didn't love his wife. They had no life together at all. Ted adores you. Even now, it's obvious that he does." Was that quite true? she wondered. Had she noticed a slight difference in their relationship at dinner last night? It was hard now to be sure.

"Maybe our group is not such a good example," said Katrinka. She searched her mind for a successful marriage, one that had worked, one that she could use to demonstrate a point, but none came readily to mind. "But some marriages do last," she added lamely.

"Our parents' marriages lasted," said Margo. "Ours don't."

"Men are such fools," said Alexandra, despite the fact that she owed her very pleasant existence of the moment to just the sort of foolery she meant. She knew perfectly well that Neil might leave her someday, as he had left his first wife, though without such a good excuse. Alexandra made it her business to keep her husband happy.

Katrinka thought about Mark and his coming lunch with Monica Brand and felt her stomach knit with an unfamiliar anxiety. "Not all men," she said.

"Well, not Mark certainly," agreed Margo, who remembered how devastated he had been by his first wife's death. He would never be crazy enough to jeopardize his second chance at happiness. Would he? He had to know Katrinka would never forgive him.

"Not Ted either," said Katrinka firmly. "He'll get over this Gigi. You must be patient. Understanding." She was giving advice she had not been able to follow with Adam, whom she had left as soon as she discovered he was having an affair. That had been the right decision for her, she was sure of it, but somehow it did not seem the right one for Margo.

"Understanding!" said Margo. "Oh, I understand well enough. The old goat!"

"Margo," said Alexandra, trying not to smile. "Ted's only, what? Fifty-seven? That's not so old." Neil was a lot older than that.

"Old enough to know better," she said. "Oh, Christ, I must be out of my mind to think a face-lift would help. As if dropping ten years would matter."

"If it would make you feel better, then do it," said Katrinka.

"You think so?" There was a note of hope in Margo's voice, a desire to believe that a plastic surgeon might work a miracle in her life.

"Why not?" said Katrinka. "When you do look and feel your best, it's easier to do whatever you have to. Talk to Daisy. She'll tell you all about it." After her divorce from Steven, when she had gone through a brief period of having affairs with younger men, Daisy had had her face and body variously nipped and tucked.

"I'll have my face done and I'll leave him," said Margo. "I'll do what Daisy did. I'll find myself a young lover. Oh, goddamn him," she said, beginning to cry again.

By the time Ted and Neil returned from their afternoon of golf at the Palm Beach Country Club, Margo was again in control of her emotions, which made pretending that everything was all right much

192

easier for Alexandra and Katrinka. Then, soon after, Tomáš arrived with Lori, Alenka, and Alenka's nanny, focusing attention on the squalling infant, who was eventually fed and quieted, cooed and fussed over, declared adorable and the image of Lori.

"She hardly ever cries," said Lori apologetically.

"Don't worry," said Alexandra. "If she cries, we won't hear her." She had put the baby and the nanny in a suite in the wing overlooking the fruit orchard, where they would be least likely to disturb her other guests.

"The walls are incredibly thick," said Neil. "We never hear our two, no matter what they get up to." Their boy was six, their girl eight. They occupied a separate suite of rooms on the ground floor.

"You're here to have a good time, so just relax and enjoy yourself."

Lori looked around and smiled happily. "This sure beats a weekend at Club Med," she said.

The jury was still out on Lori, who was as petite and dark as Zuzka had been big and blond. Attractive, intelligent, hard-working, ambitious, Lori had a lot in common with Katrinka and her friends, but she seemed more nakedly aggressive than they, her manner even more brash than Margo's, as direct as Zuzka's without the compensating warmth. She was not an easy person to like, though everyone, for Tomáš's sake, was making an effort.

"Well, I don't know," said Alexandra, laughing politely, "I hear the accommodations are really very comfortable. And the one in Morocco is said to be beautiful." Even at her poorest, she would never have done anything as middle class as take a Club Med vacation.

"I did read in *The Wall Street Journal* that Club Med has a deal with Adam's cruise ship line," said Katrinka, changing the subject.

"Yes," said Neil.

"Saved his ass," said Ted. Unlike Neil, who had helped broker the deal, Ted had no reason to be discreet.

"Shit, I was just joking," whispered Lori a few minutes later, as she and Tomáš followed a footman carrying their luggage down the long corridor to their second-floor room.

"About what?" asked Tomáš.

"Club Med."

"You were?"

Lori sighed, then smiled ruefully. One of the disadvantages of marrying a man whose native language was different from your own was that frequently your sense of humor completely escaped him. He might get the jokes when they were announced in advance as such, but wry statements often just went flying over his head. Why the others (Katrinka excepted, she supposed) had not understood her remark about Club Med, she wasn't at all sure. But she did remember that once, when she had taken an American producer and an English writer out to dinner, to test the chemistry before trying to make a deal, she had spent the entire evening saying, "That was a joke . . . He was just kidding . . ." over and over like some sort of mantra. But East Coast versus West? She had not thought there would be such a vast cultural difference between the two. "Yes," she said. "I was. I don't think your friends like me."

"Of course they do," said Tomáš.

"As much as Zuzka?"

Tomáš hesitated, then said, "You have to give them time. They've known Zuzka for years. They just met you."

"Fuck 'em," said Lori. If they couldn't like her as much as some Czech lesbian, who needed them? She had plenty of friends of her own. "Why did they invite us anyway?"

"Because I'm a hotshot Hollywood director," said Tomáš, grinning.

"And I'm a hotshot Hollywood agent?"

"Because you're my wife," said Tomáš, again not getting the joke.

"I know, I know," said Lori, with mock sadness. "Nobody cares about agents unless they're named William Morris." Then she followed the footman into the bedroom and stopped talking. "Oh, my God," she said, when she had caught her breath.

"Thank you," said Tomáš to the footman as he put the bags down and turned to go.

"Would you like one of the maids to help you unpack?"

Tomáš looked at Lori, who shook her head. "Thanks. I think I can manage."

The footman's head bobbed slightly. "If you find you need something pressed, just phone down to the butler's pantry. Someone will come to get it." He pointed toward the writing desk. "There's a list of extensions beside the phone."

"Great," said Lori. "Thanks."

The footman's head bobbed again, and he left, closing the heavy door behind him. "Shouldn't you have tipped him?" asked Lori.

"When we leave," said Tomáš.

Lori nodded, then began to move slowly around the room, picking up items, and examining them. "Look at this place, it's a fucking fantasy land." The walls were turquoise, the sofa and draperies a paler shade of pink, the design of the chandeliers and the painted motifs of the furniture slightly different, but the overall effect was the same as that of Katrinka's room. "It's gorgeous."

"You think this is a fantasy land," said Tomáš. "Wait until you see Katrinka's place in the south of France."

"Oh, my God," said Lori, thinking of their own home in Santa Monica, which, though small when measured against Bel Air mansions, she had always considered large and airy and comfortable. "Will we ever be this rich?"

"Not if Adam agrees to make our movie." He knew better than to expect the same fee for directing a small film as for one of the studio blockbusters.

Lori sighed. "It's a bitch, isn't it? Always the same choice. Art or money." Then she smiled at Tomáš. "But who cares, right? If we're happy. And we'd be very happy to make that movie."

"Very," said Tomáš, putting his arms around her, nuzzling his face into her neck. She was so unlike anyone he had ever known before. And he did love her.

"Do we have time before dinner?" she asked, as he pulled her down onto the brocade bedspread on the wonderfully comfortable queen-sized bed. He might not always get her jokes, but he was smart as hell, handsome, talented, sexy; he was her husband, the father of her child, and, boy, did she love him.

"Do you want me to hurry?"

"Oh, no. They can all just keep their caviar on ice until we're good and ready."

Because of the ball the following night, instead of taking their guests to the elegant Club Colette or the trendier Café L'Europe, the Goodmans had decided to have a quiet dinner at home. A table for nine was set in the cloister, with Washington lace table linen, flowered Spode china, and antique blue Venetian glasses with a delicate design of pale pink apple blossoms. Served by a butler and two footmen, there were stone crab claws from Joe's in Miami as an appetizer, followed by roasted Rock Cornish hens, wild rice, and red cabbage, with fresh fruit salad in Grand Marnier for dessert. In Palm Beach, the Goodman children, except for formal dinner parties, were always allowed to dine with the adults.

Dinner was served early, at seven-thirty, and by nine, everyone had gathered in the library for a screening of *Meet Me in St. Louis*, the old Judy Garland musical. Afterward, when the children had gone off to bed, Neil, who considered himself quite a dancer, suggested an excursion to Au Bar, which was even more popular after the William Kennedy Smith trial than before. No one seconded the idea. Alexandra wanted an early night to prepare for the long, difficult day in front of her. Katrinka, who a few months before would have led the way to the car, decided it was wiser to follow Alexandra's example and get a good night's sleep. Both Margo and Ted had reached the limits of their ability to pretend that everything was perfectly fine. And Lori, who wanted to see as much of Palm Beach society as she could while she was there, did not like to insist in the face of everyone else's lack of enthusiasm. "I'll check on the baby," she said, resigned to the early night, as soon as the Goodmans and the Jensens had retreated to their rooms.

"I'll be up in half an hour," said Tomáš. He turned to Katrinka. "*Zlatíčko*, feel like taking a walk?"

"A short walk," said Katrinka, smiling at him happily. He was her oldest and best friend and they had not seen each other in months.

The night was warm, with a hint of rain in the air, and a full moon hanging like a silver disk against a sky of dark blue silk. Careful not to trigger the security devices, Katrinka and Tomáš took the tunnel under South Ocean Boulevard and emerged into a sea of platinum light, the moon's rays dancing up from the white sand and hanging, shimmering in the air. Katrinka removed her shoes, and carried them in one hand, and with the other took hold of Tomáš's. "It's so good to see you," she said in Czech. "It's been too long."

"You look beautiful," he said.

"And you, you look so happy. Are you?"

"Unbelievably."

They talked quickly, in a flood of Czech words, with the ease and intimacy their native language always brought them, about Alenka, about Martin, about Zuzka.

"I think there's trouble between her and Carla," said Tomáš.

"Me, too," said Katrinka. "But she's said nothing."

"Well, she wouldn't say anything to me, certainly, or Martin, but I hear gossip. Rumors are flying around Los Angeles about Carla."

"Another woman?"

Tomáš nodded. "You know her reputation. Worse than a man's. Once the conquest is made, the boredom sets in. She's chasing some German girl at the moment."

"*Ay yi yi yi*," said Katrinka. "Poor Zuzka."

"Don't say anything," warned Tomáš.

"I wouldn't."

Tomáš told her about the script he had given Adam to read. "He got

6666666

back to me the next day, said he thought it was terrific, that he wanted to make the picture. I could hardly believe my ears."

"It doesn't sound like his kind of movie," said Katrinka doubtfully.

"That's what's so great. That he's willing to take this kind of chance. I didn't think he would, but I felt obligated to give him the first shot. To be honest, Katrinka, if he'd said no, I'd have tried to set the film up someplace else. That's how much I believe in it. And I'm just so sick of directing nothing but shit. I need to do something good before I lose all faith in myself."

"You're in negotiations on the deal?" asked Katrinka, still not quite able to believe that Adam was serious.

"Not yet," said Tomáš. "Lori and Olympic's head of business affairs have been playing phone tag for the last couple of days."

"Be careful."

Tomáš laughed. "I like Adam. I can't help myself. He's done so much for me, *zlatíčko*."

"I know," said Katrinka, "but . . ."

"But," said Tomas, "I know better than to trust him."

"Good," said Katrinka. She told him about Mark and how excited he was about *The International,* about Christian and her feeling that slowly, very slowly, their relationship was getting better.

"I hear he has another pretty girl on his mind at the moment," said Tomáš.

"Pia." Katrinka sighed. "But you know, if it wasn't that their relationship made Martin so unhappy, I would be delighted. It brings him closer to me, into my world. Do you understand, Tomáš?"

"Yes," he said. "Don't worry too much about Martin. He'll be all right."

"So I keep telling myself," said Katrinka.

By the time they crossed back through the tunnel and were making their way along the brightly lit path toward the house, they had left personal matters behind and were talking about Czechoslovakia, and what might happen if Václav Havel, the president, was unable to hold Czechs and Slovaks together in some sort of confederation. "I'm going next month, to Prague," said Katrinka. "For a business meeting with Jean-Claude Gillette and members of the department of trade. If we can just get the economy moving fast enough, the rest of the problems may solve themselves."

"God, I hope so. That beautiful country. The thought of war . . ." He left the sentence unfinished.

"It's terrible," agreed Katrinka. "There won't be a war," she added with determined optimism.

They walked upstairs and along the corridor to their bedrooms. "Can you and Lori come to the Villa Mahmed for Easter?" asked Katrinka.

Tomáš shook his head. "I'm starting another movie right away. *Low Flying Planes*," he added, a note of disgust in his voice.

"Try. I know Lori would love it."

He laughed. "I already told her that." Outside her door, he kissed her on both cheeks, "Goodnight, *zlatíčko*," he said. "See you in the morning."

Once inside her Venetian bedroom, Katrinka realized she was not in the least bit tired. The bed had been turned down and a vase of fresh hibiscus blossoms placed on the writing desk. She changed into a silk teddy, removed her makeup, and brushed her long, dark hair. What she wanted, she realized, as she stared at the pink hibiscus, was to phone Mark in London. She was aching to talk to him. She looked at her watch. It was only five in the morning there. How could she wake him up when he had sounded so tired?

Instead she climbed into bed, opened her book, and tried to read. But her mind kept searching for the face of Monica Brand. Was she dark or fair? Dark, she thought, with short hair, but she wasn't really sure.

This was nonsense, she told herself. She was being a fool. Monica Brand was not the first woman Mark had lunched with since their marriage. Why was she making such a big deal about it? The same answer as before came back: hormones.

I am not, she told herself, going to make myself miserable about this. Putting down the book, she picked up the television remote, and turned on the set. She watched a little bit of Johnny Carson, then the news on CNN. Finally, watching *Green Card* on The Movie Channel, she fell asleep.

Eighteen

BREAKFAST AT THE SCAMPO DOLCE WAS SERVED IN THE ORANGERY, A RECTANGULAR ROOM WITH A MARBLE floor and a south wall of arched panes of leaded glass overlooking the orchard. It was a bright and airy space and, when the weather was poor, lunch was served there instead of in the loggia or on the patio at the rear of the house.

Katrinka, feeling much better after five hours of sleep, was the first down the next morning. She picked up copies of *The New York Times* and *The Wall Street Journal* from the selection on one of the sideboards, asked the waiting footman for breakfast, then sat and began her morning's trek through the world's political and economic news, none of it any better than usual to judge from the front pages. By the time the children arrived at eight, she had worked her way through *Newsday* and *The Chronicle* to *The Palm Beach Daily News,* catching up on the local gossip, which was the latter's sole offering. A former editor claimed to have been fired for trying to incorporate news of national and international events into its pages. Even reports of local issues were frowned upon: not a word was to be found about sewer rates, falling SAT scores, or rising unemployment in the area. Still, Palm Beach's residents were addicted to it, searching through it for photographs of themselves, for descriptions of parties they had attended, for advance notice of events to which they might or might not receive invitations, calling it affectionately—because of its incredibly expensive newspaper stock and ink guaranteed not to come off on either fingers or Porthault table linen—"the shiny sheet."

Looking as if he had not slept at all, Neil arrived for breakfast in time to see his children before they went off for a tennis lesson. Then Tomáš and Ted, dressed in shorts and T-shirts, put in an appearance, Tomáš relaxed and happy, Ted a little haggard despite his tan. When the men began to discuss how best to spend the morning, Katrinka excused herself and returned to her bedroom, sat at the writing desk, and looked at her watch: eight hours at least before Mark would arrive. Never had she felt so anxious to see him. She looked at the phone. Christian and Pia were spending the weekend skiing in Kitzbühel, so she did not even consider trying to find her son; but she called her housekeepers in New York and Cap Ferrat, and then the managers on duty at her hotels in New York and London. There were no pressing problems anywhere, and Katrinka, who normally would have been delighted at the prospect of a long, lazy Saturday, was wondering how she could speed up the passage of time, when there was a knock on her door and Alexandra, wearing a short-sleeved Escada suit, her long red hair pulled back in a ponytail, swept into the room and announced that she was on her way to take care of some last-minute preparations for the ball, and Katrinka, in her absence, was to keep Margo cheerful and Lori entertained.

Shopping was not something that Katrinka normally enjoyed. But what Lori Havlíček wanted to do most was check out Worth Avenue and, since Margo had no objection to it, Katrinka agreed. Alexandra had taken the Cadillac, so one of the staff drove the three women into Palm Beach in the silver Rolls, leaving them at the beginning of the Esplanade arcade, on order to return for them at twelve-thirty. Lunch was to be served at one.

The Esplanade was a two-tiered enclosed shopping arcade running from a valet car park at one end to Saks Fifth Avenue on the corner of South County Road. Its two levels were lined with the usual upscale shops, as was Worth Avenue itself. Martha, Gucci, Valentino, and similar name-brand boutiques bordered the street, along with a number of art galleries, the popular restaurant Ta-boo, and a department store by the name of Frances Brewster in the space once occupied by the bankrupt Bonwit Teller. At intervals, charming "vias," pedestrian alleys, led off the main thoroughfare past rows of smart shops, antique stores, restaurants like Bice and Renato, to Peruvian Way, the parallel street, where the Club Colette was located. The shopping ended a short way from the ocean, at the Everglades, where the

Duchess of York had once lunched, causing another firestorm of bad publicity because its membership was restricted.

"This is it?" said Lori when, after an hour's wandering in and out of a number of shops and galleries, they reached the end. The whole of Worth Avenue, with its stucco facades, red-tiled roofs, and galleried walks, extended no more than three blocks.

"This is it," repeated Margo. "Disappointed?"

"Well," said Lori hesitantly. "It's very pretty. But somehow not what I expected." The Scampo Dolce had raised her hopes too high, she realized. She had expected a street as extravagant, as opulent as the house she was visiting. But Worth Avenue looked just like a lot of streets in a lot of middle-class California towns. Only the names on the storefronts were different.

"Someone did tell me," said Katrinka, "that next to St. Moritz, Palm Beach is the most expensive place in the world."

Lori thought of the new pedestrian walk in Beverly Hills, constructed to resemble a European street, and said, "I guess this is what you'd call old money understatement." There certainly wasn't much of that on the West Coast.

"We should start back, or we'll be late," said Katrinka, who wished she had had the foresight to tell the driver to meet them at the entrance to the Everglades.

"What do you think," said Lori, "should I buy those Kenneth Lane earrings we saw?" She had been debating whether to be sensible or extravagant.

"Well, they did look great on you," said Katrinka.

"And they'll really jazz up the gown I'm wearing tonight," said Lori, willing to be swayed.

"Buy them," said Margo, "what the hell." Palm Beach was not a town that encouraged caution.

The purchase was made quickly and the three women came out of the store into the bright midday glare, heading back toward the waiting car. It was then that Katrinka noticed what somehow she, and Margo too, had missed on their first pass by: an open door, a shop empty except for construction workers, and a notice in the window announcing that "Trends" would be opening soon.

"Alexandra did say something about this to you?" Katrinka asked Margo.

"Not a word," replied Margo, looking from the sign to Katrinka.

"What?" asked Lori.

"She probably had no idea," said Margo, not really hearing Lori. "She's been so preoccupied with this damn ball."

Katrinka began walking again, the others falling into step beside her. "We do know the owner," she said to Lori.

"Trends?" Lori thought a minute, then said, "Natalie Bovier? You know her?" As soon as she asked the question, she remembered. Natalie Bovier was the woman who had broken up Katrinka and Adam Graham's marriage. She could have kicked herself. "I mean, of course, you know her," she said, sounding apologetic.

"Uh huh," said Margo neutrally. She turned to Katrinka. "I wonder where she got the money? I thought when Jean-Claude decided not to back her that would stop her expansion plans for a while."

Katrinka shrugged. She really didn't care about Natalie or her store. It was just the surprise of stumbling across one here, when she wasn't expecting it.

"Do you suppose Adam's decided to go into the retail business?"

Katrinka shook her head. "Right now, I don't think he has any money to risk, and retail's not exactly a safe bet."

"But boutiques like Trends are making money," said Lori, who never liked to be left out of conversations. "Great stuff by new designers, kind of off-beat and interesting. Reasonable prices. Everyone shops there."

Katrinka smiled at Lori, whom she was beginning to like very much. Tomáš's new wife was not afraid to say what she meant, and Katrinka preferred that to polite deviousness any day. "Natalie's very talented," said Katrinka. "I do wish her well."

"Not me," muttered Margo, who was not in the mood to be forgiving about women who stole other people's husbands.

"Isn't that her?" asked Lori as they crossed South County Road. "Coming out of Saks."

"Oh, my God, so it is," said Margo.

But ever since she had seen the store, Katrinka had been prepared for a meeting, assuming that Natalie might be in Palm Beach to supervise the work. "Hi, Natalie, how you doing?" she said cheerfully as the startled woman came face to face with them. Was it her imagination, wondered Katrinka, or had Natalie gained weight? And the circles under her eyes, were they darker?

"*Oh la la*, Katrinka, Margo. I didn't know you were in Palm Beach. How nice to see you."

"I'm sure," said Margo dryly.

"I'm opening a new boutique here. A better risk than New York, I thought."

Though Katrinka's pace had slowed, she had never quite stopped moving. "Yes, we just saw it. Good luck," she said, as she brushed past Natalie and continued on, followed closely by the others.

Natalie, turning to keep them in view, called, "Katrinka, *chérie.* Margo, perhaps before you leave, we could have lunch? I have some new photographs of Aziz . . ."

"So sorry," said Margo, "but we haven't a minute to spare. You know how it is."

Katrinka said nothing since Natalie was not someone to whom she felt it necessary to apologize.

Margo turned to Lori. "Forgive us for not introducing you. . . ." When Lori assured her that was fine, Margo looked at Katrinka. "Why did we bother to say hello?"

Katrinka shrugged. "It's certain that we run into her sometimes, and it makes life easier for everyone just to be a little polite. I would have liked to see the photographs of Aziz," she added sadly.

"I know how crazy you were about that kid," said Margo sympathetically. "Well, we all were. Cute little guy. I thought she looked terrible, didn't you?"

"A little heavy," said Katrinka. "And pale." She thought of Jean-Claude's reports of how unhappy Natalie was, about Prince Khalid's obvious worry. Then she pushed the thought away. Natalie's frame of mind had nothing to do with her.

"I thought she looked like shit," said Lori, summing up everyone's opinion.

After lunch, Neil took Tomáš and Ted, who had spent the morning spear-fishing in the ocean, for a cruise on Lake Worth with the two children, while the women began their preparations for that night's ball. Alexandra had hired a team from the Bonaventure Spa in Miami; one of the upstairs loggias and an adjoining room were declared off-limits, and the four women spent the afternoon taking turns being massaged, having facials, manicures, pedicures, their hair washed and set, their makeup applied. "Oh, God, I love this," said Lori, as the masseuse smoothed fragrant oils into the soft skin of her back. The temperature was in the mid-seventies, with not much moisture in the air. The only sounds were the chirp of birds and the hum of insects; the sweet smell of frangipani drifted up through the thick canopy of the banyan tree from the courtyard below. "I never want to go home."

"Hmm, it's lovely," agreed Margo, her hair wrapped in a hot towel, her face covered with mud. "I think I may have forgotten how miserable I am."

"The next time we do go to the Saturnia or the Canyon Spa Ranch, you come with us," said Katrinka, whose long nails were being coated with light pink lacquer.

"I'd love to," agreed Lori, though she wondered if Tomáš and she were rich enough to keep up with the life-styles of his friends. Suddenly, her body stiffened. "Is that Alenka crying?" she asked. She had waited until she was thirty-four to have a baby, waited until she had found Tomáš, the perfect father; but she wondered sometimes if it wouldn't have been smarter to have done it earlier, before she had known just how many awful things could happen to an innocent child.

"She's with the nanny," said Margo reassuringly.

"Just normal baby fussing," said Alexandra, whose long red hair was being curled onto large rollers.

"Nothing to worry about," said the masseuse, who had two of her own.

Katrinka, who had never raised a child, said nothing, though she listened intently, as she did to any exchange of information, hoping to pick up pointers that might come in handy later on.

Alenka had already stopped crying. Forcing herself to relax, Lori stretched out again on the table and gave herself up to the masseuse's magic hands.

In three months, thought Katrinka, she would be listening to her own baby cry. It was such a happy thought, she felt suddenly like crying herself. Those hormones again.

"You know," said Alexandra, "I think I ought to order just one more crate of champagne."

"Everything will be fine," said Katrinka reassuringly. "Stop worrying."

Alexandra took a deep breath. "I wish I could."

By five, except for having to put on her ball gown, Katrinka was completely ready for the evening—showered, manicured, made up, hair done—giving her two hours completely to herself before having to put in an appearance for cocktails on the patio at seven. She lay on the brocaded sofa in her bedroom, wearing a flowered silk wrap over a cream-colored merry widow, a garter belt, sheer stockings, and lace-trimmed silk panties that stopped just below the prominent mound of her stomach. A porcelain tea service rested on the table beside her, along with a heap of magazines, topped by the perennial yellow pad covered in notes scrawled with a felt-tip pen. When she got to the end of the novel she was reading, she dropped it onto the floor, took a sip of the tea, picked up the yellow pad to add to her list of things to do as soon as she returned to New York, then heard the door open, and, looking up, saw her husband, smiling, looking tired but delighted to see her. "Oh, baby, do you look good."

As always, she felt a rush of excitement that was a combination of admiration, desire, and happiness. He was, she thought again, the handsomest man she had ever seen. *"Miláčku,"* she murmured.

"Just leave everything right there," said Mark to the footman, who had followed him into the room with the luggage.

"You do need your tuxedo pressed?" asked the always practical Katrinka, stopping Mark in his rush across the room toward her.

"Oh, yes," said Mark impatiently. "It's in that one," he said, pointing. The footman heaved the large case onto the luggage stand, and Mark opened it, took out the required clothes for the evening, and handed them to the young man. "What time are cocktails?"

"Seven, sir."

"I'll need them at quarter to."

"Yes, sir," replied the footman, understanding that his presence would not be desired a minute before then.

When the heavy door swung closed, Mark crossed the distance separating him from Katrinka, bent to kiss her on the mouth, then sat on the sofa next to her. "Hello," he said. "Hmm, you look good enough to eat."

"Thank you," she said. She reached up and touched his face. "You do look tired. Bad flight?" She was referring to the weather, since it was otherwise impossible to have a bad trip on the luxurious VHE Gulfstream IV.

"No. It was okay." He bent his head again and kissed her neck. "You smell good, too."

"You did bring a copy of the magazine?"

"Uh huh. I'll get it for you in a minute." His hand slid under her wrap and rested on her stomach. "You're bigger," he said.

She laughed. "You always say that."

"And it's always true."

"How was your lunch?"

"Lunch?"

"With Monica Brand."

"Okay," he said. She had been as bright, as entertaining, as attractive as he had expected. There was something about her looks, about her style, that appealed to him. Once during lunch, some gesture of hers had made him think of Lisa, his first wife, something he did not do very often anymore. It had touched a tender place, caused a flood of warmth. He supposed, if he wasn't so in love with Katrinka, that he would seriously consider pursuing his attraction (as much as he hated to admit it, that's what it was). But, as matters stood, it was out of the question. "She's a very interesting young woman, bright, talented . . ."

205

"You are going to hire her?"

"No," he said.

The smile that lit Katrinka's face was one of obvious relief. "Good," she said.

Mark laughed. "I don't know whether to feel flattered or insulted," he said. "But don't get a big head. I'm not turning her down because of you. She's talented enough . . . she has an intelligent, rather witty style . . . but no experience, and it shows. I haven't got a place for someone like her right now."

Katrinka knew well enough that when any man, her husband included, wanted to pursue a woman, they made a place, made time, moved mountains to get whoever it was they desired. Mark didn't want Monica Brand, that much was clear, and that made her very happy. She wrapped her arms around his neck, drew his head down to hers, and said, "Promise you'll always have a place for me."

"Always."

She slid one hand down and rested it against his chest. "Here?"

"Forever," he promised, then kissed her again. Her hand returned to the back of his neck, and he felt her mouth open beneath his, the tip of her tongue against his teeth. Raising his head, he studied her elegantly coiffed head, the dark hair coiled into intricate patterns, the perfectly applied makeup on her face, and said, "I suppose I'm not allowed to mess you up?"

"Who did say that?" Her voice was playful, coaxing.

He opened her wrap and dropped his head to kiss the full breasts, supported but barely concealed by the merry widow she wore.

"You don't want to take a little nap?" she asked.

"No," he said, his hand moving slowly up her stockinged leg, across the soft flesh of her thigh, to the ruffled silk strip of her bikini. She separated her legs for him, and Mark found he did not have to push her panty aside to reach her. It was slit, allowing easy access. He felt himself growing harder, threatening to explode against the zipper of his fine wool pants. He raised his head to look at her. "Let's go to bed." When she nodded, he helped her to her feet, then, his arm around her, led her to the carved bed, stripped down the tapestry cover, and lay beside her on the linen sheet. He watched her face as his fingers again found the slit in her panties. She seemed to soften beneath him, to melt with desire, and, when finally she felt him inside her, she gasped.

"I was waiting for this all day," she said. "All day, I was waiting for you."

Nineteen

THE FLAGLER MUSEUM, WITH ITS RED-TILE ROOF, WHITE STUCCO FACADE, DENTILLED CORNICES, AND COLONnaded porch, seemed to relate to no particular architectural period or design and was described in books on the mansions of Palm Beach rather vaguely as "European-style," as if the continent of Europe was one undifferentiated mass, with no delimiting characteristics except for its happening not to be "America." Inside, however, the fifty-eight-room mansion was more or less consistently French, all highly decorative, with a lot of marble and gilt in evidence—and lampshades with pink tulle rosettes. Originally known as Whitehall, it was built at the turn of the century, as a wedding present for his third wife, by Henry Morrison Flagler, the Standard Oil tycoon who created Palm Beach out of swampland. The mansion was later a hotel, and, finally, in 1960, it opened as a museum, with many of its original furnishings restored. Since then, with the ballrooms at The Breakers, it had become a primary site for the one-hundred-plus charity functions held in Palm Beach each year.

On the night of the Planned Parenthood Ball, the museum's brilliant white facade was floodlit and its wrought-iron gates open, admitting a procession of long white Cadillacs, silver Rolls-Royces, some Lincolns, and a few Mercedes. A storm was threatening. The air was heavy with moisture and the date palms bent gracefully in the gusts of heavy wind that sent the dark clouds sailing at a mad pace across the night sky. A few large drops of warm tropical rain had already fallen, and valets armed with large black umbrellas stood at the bottom of the museum's wide steps to open car doors and escort ladies inside without damage to their elaborate hairdos and expensive designer gowns. Standing in the Marble Hall to greet the arriving guests, Alexandra had finally found an outlet for her anxiety: the weather. "Rain," she muttered, turning to her husband. "I don't believe it."

Neil smiled at her reassuringly. "Look on the bright side," he said. "No one will leave until it stops. You've got a captive audience."

"True," said Alexandra, immediately cheering up. The focal point of the evening was to be an art auction, the proceeds of which were to go to Planned Parenthood.

"How lovely you look," said Alan Platt. Unlike Arnold Scaasi and Calvin Klein, Alan did not own a home in Palm Beach, at least not yet. He was staying at The Breakers with Sabrina, who, instead of saying hello to Alexandra, had stopped to pay her respects to the regal Alyne Massey, one of the leading ladies of Palm Beach society.

"And how nice of you to say so," said Alexandra, ignoring Sabrina's snub, smiling warmly at Alan, "even though I'm not wearing one of yours." Her dress was a form-fitting black widow with a plunging neckline and sheer beaded chantilly lace skirt and sleeves. Her long red hair was plaited into an elegant French braid and around her neck she wore a diamond and natural pearl choker that Neil had bought for her at a Sotheby's sale the year before. It had once belonged to a local grande dame.

"I'm not the jealous type," said Alan insincerely.

"But I am looking forward to your show next month," continued Alexandra. "Your clothes are such a delight to wear," she added, hinting that she was planning to buy, though Neil had warned her she could not spend too much money this year. However, thinking she might would most certainly encourage Alan to bid on a painting, if only one of the smaller ones. "You scratch my back, and I'll scratch yours," was the underlying theme of all social and business intercourse in Palm Beach as well as New York.

Waiters in tails, from C'est Si Bon Catering, circulated from room to room carrying silver salvers holding delicately cut canapés and crystal flutes of champagne. "Do you think I should go rescue Alyne?" said Margo, hesitating only briefly to pick up a canapé from a passing tray before continuing on her way with Katrinka across the Marble Hall toward the music room where the paintings to be auctioned were on display.

"I think she can take care of herself," said Mark, as he offered Katrinka a glass of champagne, which she refused. And, as if to prove his point, Alyne Massey saw her chance, inclined her lovely blond head in a gracious farewell, and turned decisively away from Sabrina to greet a newly arriving couple.

"My God, that's Nina Graham, isn't it?" asked Margo.

"Yes," said Katrinka, not quite able to restrain a sigh, though Alexandra had told her that Nina and Russell would be there.

"Well, let's go look at those paintings," said Margo, quickening her stride, "before she spots us."

Katrinka laughed and followed her, saying, "I do have to say hello sometime."

"Why?" asked Mark, who could not understand how Katrinka could still consider Nina "family." He had never met anyone who seemed to him less like a mother.

"It's polite," said Katrinka.

Mark slipped an arm around her waist. "Such a good girl," he teased.

"You know what they say," said Margo. "Good girls go to heaven, but bad girls . . ."

"I know, I know," said Katrinka. "They go everywhere."

Laughing, the three of them entered the music room, which was beginning to fill up with people passing through for a look at the paintings before moving on to the terrace or dining pavilion. Its silk patterned wallpaper was peeling in places, noticed Katrinka, its furniture needed recovering, the gilt touching up, and the plaster cupids in relief above the cornice were badly in need of a coat of paint. Some of the museum had recently been refurbished, but clearly not this room. As always when faced with so much beauty in disrepair, Katrinka had an urge to phone Carlos and set to work with him putting everything right, a thought she banished immediately from her mind.

In the center of the flame-patterned solid wood floor, the Havlíčeks stood talking to Rick Colins, his date for the evening—a society matron whose husband was out of town, and Jackie and Dick Cowell, whom Tomáš had met once or twice before over the years. Katrinka was very fond of both the Cowells. Some ten years older than Katrinka, Jackie was blond and beautiful, perennially tanned and an expert athlete, water-skiing with the Italian team in Palm Beach, and skiing winters in St. Moritz. Dick was tall and slender, with the weathered good looks of the sportsman. One of the few American members of the Corviglia and Tobogganing clubs in St. Moritz, he told riotous stories about the Cresta's exploits, and his own, including one about the time he had water-skied from St. Tropez to Portofino. The two groups joined and stood chatting for a moment, then Chan and John Mashek, leading members of the younger Palm Beach crowd, said hello as they passed by. Margo excused herself to go look for Ted, who had disappeared in search of a cigarette, and Katrinka and Mark moved off to study Alexandra's exhibition.

The museum's usual collection, including a large portrait of Mrs. Flagler, had been replaced by the paintings that were to be auctioned. These included a wide range of periods and styles, donated by people who, for one reason or another, wanted the charitable deduction for tax purposes. Though Alexandra's trained eye and boundless tact had kept the quality high, only a few were of museum quality, one a small still life by Willem Kalf, which Neil Goodman had taken from his collection, possibly for the deduction, possibly—at Alexandra's insistence—to spur others to contribute. No one who knew him doubted that giving it up had caused him a great deal of pain. Next to Alexandra and his children, there was nothing Neil loved so much as his paintings.

Flowing with the social current, Katrinka and Mark made their way slowly around the perimeter of the room, stopping to chat with people whom, if Katrinka didn't know, Mark did, acquaintances from New York, London, Paris, St. Moritz, Cap Ferrat, everywhere. Palm Beach in March was a date on everyone's social calendar. They said hello to Ambassador Guilford Dudley and his wife, Jane; to Pat and Ned Cook; to Cathy Tankoos and Dennis Ross; to Anne and Howard Oxenberg; to the people whose photographs would appear the next day in the "shiny sheet" or later in *Palm Beach Society*, the weekly social magazine. They discussed sports, travel, local gossip, even the pictures on the wall, but kept clear of anything controversial like the economy or politics. "All they do in Palm Beach," some local wit had once told Katrinka, "is eat, sleep, party, and make love." According to the more sensational of the local novelists, this endless round of mind-numbing activity caused such boredom that, to relieve it, many of the town's most respected citizens indulged in wildly exotic sexual activity, which was hard to believe, thought Katrinka, when seeing them at an event like the Planned Parenthood Ball, the gracious women in their sedate designer gowns and the elegant men in their well-worn tuxedos. Even the missionary position seemed too undignified for that group.

And even if the stories about booze and drugs, wife-swapping, group sex, and sadomasochism were true, Katrinka suspected that the scene was becoming less wild, not only as paranoia about AIDS increased, but as the younger crowd moved in and took control. They were still working, and hard, to keep the fortunes they had made. They were not in the least bored. And while sex, God knows, was not about to become extinct, it was less likely to be as rampant and perverse. Or was she being completely naive? she wondered. And why was she so preoccupied with sex?

"What you think, we bid on that one?" said Katrinka to Mark, who was no doubt the reason, pointing to a small oil of a Moroccan street scene by a nineteenth-century English painter.

"If you like it," he said agreeably.

"Don't you?"

"I don't *dislike* it." Mark's interest in art was minimal. He had had no exposure to it as a child and little time to develop a taste for it as an adult. Unlike music, to which he responded instinctively, he had to work at appreciating a painting, and preferred representational works with images that struck an emotional chord in him, like those of Winslow Homer or Edward Hopper. His taste was decidedly American, which, as the son of immigrants, he thought was understandable.

Katrinka, on the other hand, responded to form and color, whether in paintings or design, and she liked a great variety of periods and styles, though not the more severe minimalist art that Adam found so appealing. "Well," she said, "we do have to bid on something, and it would look very good at the Villa Mahmed."

That conversation was interrupted by a tanned and smiling Prince Dimitri, who introduced them to Princess Sybil de Bourbon Parme, a local resident, with whose party he had come. When they had moved on to join another group, Mark said, "If you really want the painting, I'll buy it for you."

"You don't have to," said Katrinka, who had planned to buy it with her own money.

"I want to," said Mark. "A gift."

"You give me so much," protested Katrinka.

"I haven't given you a thing since your birthday," said Mark. That was true only if the new town house and its furnishings, the flowers, the silk scarves, the bottles of perfume, the cashmere sweater he had just brought her from London, were not counted. But there had been no significant pieces of jewelry, fur coats, or designer gowns. What little she had ordered from the collections in January, she had paid for herself.

But Katrinka had not expected, nor wanted, any gifts, knowing how much Mark was spending not only on them but on getting *The*

International launched. Then, too, there had been the expense of fighting off that sudden, inexplicable run on the van Hollen stock. She fingered the necklace of cabochon rubies and diamonds that had been her birthday present from him and said, "This was more than enough to last me. At least until my next birthday," she added with a smile.

"And very nice it looks on you, too, baby," he said, smiling at her happily. The necklace and matching earrings went perfectly with Katrinka's gown, a flower-printed Dior with an enormous segmented bustle and a knife-pleated flounce at the bottom. His wife looked very beautiful, he thought, stylish and elegant, and completely "at home" among this group of old-money Wasps. That was one of the things he loved about her, that she seemed at home anywhere, from his small, rough cottage in the Hebrides to a garden party at Buckingham Palace. He wondered if he did, not that he cared particularly. "But I'll buy the painting," he insisted. Since Katrinka and he were going to be spending time there, Mark felt the need to make his mark on the Villa Mahmed, which had once belonged to Adam Graham; a painting, however small, was at least a beginning. "Okay?"

"Okay," she agreed, linking her arm through his.

"Go and sit down," whispered Alexandra as she glided past them. "It's almost time for dinner."

"Ladies and gentlemen," echoed one of the butlers standing in the doorway. "Please take your seats. Dinner is about to be served."

The sound of Peter Duchin's orchestra began drifting through from the custom-designed tent overlooking the lake, where tables to accommodate the three hundred guests had been arranged. Katrinka and Mark began to make their way slowly through the mansion's gilded rooms toward it, stopped occasionally by bottlenecks in the traffic flow, finding themselves, as they entered the pavilion, finally face to face with Nina and Russell Luce. With as much warmth as she could manage, Katrinka smiled and said hello.

"Why, Katrinka, how nice to see you," replied Nina, who surprised even herself by meaning it. Oddly, over the years, she had become respectful, admiring, and possibly even fond of the daughter-in-law she had once despised, though she would never have admitted it, not even to herself.

Mark shook hands with the couple and made a few vaguely complimentary comments. He didn't like Nina, and Russell he considered a lightweight, a windbag, with no real convictions, no moral center. And while, when he was younger and hotheaded, he would have despised himself as a hypocrite for standing there with a polite smile plastered on his face, he had learned that letting true opinions show, at least in social situations, produced nothing more productive than an awkward scene and hurt feelings for all concerned.

"You're looking lovely, my dear," said Russell as he looked at Katrinka admiringly.

There was something unpleasant about him, Katrinka thought, despite his handsome face and aristocratic manner. But he did look every inch the besotted bridegroom, and Nina was radiant in a simply cut, very elegant blue Geoffrey Beene gown, which set off her delicate complexion and pouf of white-gold hair. "Well, look at you two," said Katrinka with a forced enthusiasm. "Marriage obviously does agree with you."

"He's just a wonderful man, as close to perfect as they come," said Nina, which was the most positive comment anyone had ever heard her make. "He spoils me dreadfully."

"Only because she's such a darling," said Russell smoothly, patting the small, manicured hand she had placed on his sleeve, "and such a pleasure to spoil."

A darling? Nina Graham? Katrinka could not *wait* to report this conversation to Alexandra and Lucia, and everyone else who had suffered from Nina's barbed comments over the years.

"And a real trooper," continued Russell in his hearty, insincere manner. "Out stomping the state with me, helping to get out the vote for the primary. And fund-raising. Why, she's the best little fund-raiser I've ever had. No one can say no to her."

"Yes," said Katrinka, smiling broadly, unable to resist, "I did notice that."

"Oh, you managed," said Nina, with a smile that was almost warm. But the smile faded quickly. At least when Adam was married to Katrinka, she had known more or less what he was up to, thought Nina irritably. Now, she had no idea at all. Why had the foolish girl left him, dragging the Graham name through the newspapers in that unacceptable way? For a moment, Nina completely forgot the grandchild that Katrinka had failed to produce. Then she remembered and grew even more annoyed. Like her son, Nina sometimes felt that Katrinka's inability to have a child had been deliberate and that her pregnancy now was a sort of revenge against the Grahams, an act of retribution for all the snubs, all the criticism, for Adam's final betrayal. She looked Katrinka up and down, her eyes resting for a moment on the bulge below Katrinka's waist, minimized by a panel in the skirt, and said, "What a lovely gown. So . . . flamboyant. And a new necklace, I see." The hint of disapproval was back in her voice.

"A present from Mark," said Katrinka, refusing to be offended. For years Nina had implied that she had no sense of the value of money, that she threw it around in a thoroughly vulgar manner: Katrinka was used to it.

"Oh, of course," said Nina, her meaning perfectly clear: What can one expect of someone from his background? Her gaze rested assessingly on Mark, noting the perfect features, the silver barely visible in his thick blond hair, the tall, well-exercised body. He looked like the prince in a fairy tale, except for the deep lines cut into the planes of his face; he looked more the aristocrat than anyone in the room, she thought, finding more surprise than pleasure in the idea. But his manner was too cocky and his tuxedo too new. He couldn't quite pull it off, she decided, wouldn't quite pass. It never occurred to her that he might not want to.

"Cost me a fortune," said Mark cheerfully, knowing it was exactly the sort of remark to offend the sensibilities of someone like Nina Graham Luce, who thought any public discussion of money indecent.

Nina smiled icily and said, "That's obvious. But then I wouldn't have expected anything else of someone like you." She turned to Russell. "Come, darling. We really ought to find our places." She nodded her head graciously. "Good-bye," she said, as she steered her obedient husband away. Russell Luce seemed to be no more a match for her than any other member of her family.

Katrinka sighed with relief, then turned to look at Mark, who was patting the front of his tuxedo jacket with both hands. "What are you doing?" she asked.

"Searching for the knife," he said.

Katrinka laughed. "She really is impossible. She did upset you?"

"No," said Mark reassuringly. He knew as well as Katrinka that the necklace was not at all ostentatious. It was as delicate as it was possible for a ruby-and-diamond necklace to be, exquisitely set, and certainly as tasteful as the triple-strand opera length pearls with the sapphire clasp that Nina was wearing. "But I don't like her taking potshots at you."

"At least she does do it face to face. Not like Sabrina."

Mark laughed, patted his chest again, and said, "You're almost as good at throwing knives as your former mother-in-law."

But Katrinka smiled and shook her head. "I hope not," she said. "People like that make themselves more unhappy than anybody."

"We're at the same table," said Rick Colins as he passed by, his arm firmly under his matron's elbow. "It's over here." Rick was welcome everywhere. Though his career as a gossip columnist and television celebrity might have made him suspect, he, like Alexandra and Nina, was distantly related to many of the people in the room. "Follow me," he called, his slender figure cutting gracefully through the crowd. Despite his graying hair, he looked like a schoolboy on vacation from Exeter or Choate.

Their table was for ten and included some of the cream of Palm Beach society, as did every table in the room. Alexandra, surveying the scene, had every reason to feel content. Princes and princesses had shown up at her invitation, viscountesses, a sir or two, the elite of old Palm Beach society, and the newer crowd from Wellington, several miles inland, where the golfers and polo players tended to congregate. The tent was decorated to look like an artist's studio, with half-finished canvases lying among incomplete statues. Place cards were set on miniature easels and centerpieces were copies of floral still lifes, from early Dutch flower paintings to Van Gogh's irises. Alexandra had even arranged for an artist and a discreetly draped model to work quietly in a corner as dinner was served, and curious guests took time out from eating and dancing to watch as a painting slowly materialized before their eyes. Everyone seemed to find it all delightful. Now, if only the art auction went well, the evening would be deemed a great success. But at the thought, though the brilliant smile remained firmly fixed on her face, Alexandra felt her stomach tighten once again in apprehension.

"Would you like to dance, honey?" said Ted. He had excused himself from his dinner companion and now stood politely behind his wife's chair, waiting to pull it out for her when she agreed.

"Love to," she said with a smile, getting to her feet. "And don't call me honey," she added in a whisper as she took his arm and followed him to the dance floor. She was being impossible, she knew, but she couldn't help herself.

Ted said nothing. Any reply was bound to provoke a discussion he did not want to have. Instead, he put his arms around her and pulled her close, though not so close as they used to dance. Margo would have stepped on his foot if he had tried that, or kicked his shin. She was hurt and angry; she was furious with him, and she had every right to be. He deserved whatever abuse she decided to heap on him. Never had he imagined that he would treat anyone so badly, and certainly not Margo, his wife, whom he had loved wholeheartedly for practically as long as he could remember. *Still* loved. That was the hell of it all. And he was more unhappy than he had ever been before in his life.

On the other hand, he was also happier—at times—than he had ever been before in his life. That was the hell of it, too. He thought of the "lunch" dates with Gigi when instead of a restaurant they spent the hour in a room in a hotel near the bank. He remembered the exquisitely erotic feel of their soaped bodies rubbing against each other as they showered before she returned to work and he went home to Margo. He remembered the day they had flown to Paris, when Margo had been away somewhere, and the sexual frenzy that had led them to the Ritz instead of the Musée d'Orsay, where they had meant to spend the afternoon. He felt younger now than he had in years, more alive than he had ever felt. And he should not be thinking about any of this when dancing with his wife, he realized, as he felt the blood begin to pump through his cock, making it throb against the shiny black fabric of his tuxedo trousers.

"Is that for me?" whispered Margo, pulling back a little in his arms so that she could see his face. But instead of desire, what she saw was guilt. "You sonovabitch," she muttered, twisting out of his arms, leaving him standing in the middle of the dance floor, unable to move for a moment until he recovered his equilibrium and could follow his irate wife. But before he could reach her, to try to make whatever feeble excuse he could think of, she had asked Rick Colins to dance, and instead Ted made his way outside for another cigarette, thinking that he must have been out of his mind to agree to accompany her to Palm Beach.

What a fool Ted was, thought Neil, observing the scene from the arms of a Palm Beach matron he was steering across the floor in time to the music. Alexandra had told him the whole story, and he could hardly believe it. Imagine confessing to your wife that you were having an affair, and before you even knew what you meant to do about it! The man must be half out of his mind with lust, decided Neil, who remembered the lengths he had gone to in order to keep his first wife from finding out about Alexandra. And she had never suspected a thing, not up to the moment he had announced he was leaving her. That had had its problems too, of course: the shock, the anger, the hysteria. But secrecy and deceit, no matter how unpleasant, in his opinion, were the best policy. At the very least, they saved months of useless recriminations. And, strangely, he and his ex-wife had ended up friends again, talking at least once a week on the phone, something Alexandra did not know. It seemed to him sometimes that Alexandra resented the affection he still had for his ex-wife and their children; and though he had pointed out to her the unreasonableness of expecting him to blot so many years (and many of them very happy ones) out of his mind, she never seemed to understand.

There was so much Alexandra seemed not to understand lately. For

216

example, whenever he tried to discuss the situation at Knapp Manning with her, she either refused to take it seriously, criticized him for not taking more decisive action, or became so upset at the idea the company might actually fail that Neil ended up having to reassure her with words not even he believed. When he asked her to cut back on expenses, she tried, for a while, but soon she was back to spending as if the supply of money was endless, which it certainly was not. He understood why: after years of penny-pinching, of being the poor relative, of standing with her nose pressed against society's window, Alexandra could not bear the idea of slipping back again into that position. It would not come to that, he assured her constantly, but the very thought seemed to send her scurrying to Tiffany's or Bergdorf's to shop, as women of another class might have run to synagogue or church to pray.

"Would that be all right with you?"

"What?" Neil glanced down at the trim blonde in his arms. "I'm sorry. I didn't quite get that. The music . . ." he said, hoping that would be a sufficient excuse for his not having any idea what she was talking about.

"The next time I'm in New York, if I could call you?" she repeated. "For investment advice," she added when she saw the startled look on Neil's face.

He remembered that her husband was somewhere in his late seventies. She was, he guessed, about thirty-five. "Of course," he said gallantly. Alexandra, he noticed, was dancing with a dark-haired, dark-eyed Argentinean, one of the polo crowd from Wellington. She seemed to be having a wonderful time, not in the least worried any longer. "Though you understand I may not be of much help. It's not what I normally do."

"Oh, I understand you usually deal with much bigger fish. But I would be grateful. Arthur's mind isn't as keen as it used to be," she said, putting it mildly. "And sometimes I think his advisers are taking us for a ride. An impartial, informed opinion would be very helpful."

Her look was so trusting, so full of admiration, that he felt flattered. "I'd be delighted," he said. Only a lunch, he promised himself. She wasn't even his type.

The pace of the music quickened from old-fashioned swing to rock. "Let's dance," said Katrinka, taking Mark's hand and pulling him toward the floor. After a while, they switched partners, Katrinka moving off to join Tomáš, as Lori, shaking her Kenneth Lane earrings, wiggling her Scaasi-clad bottom, stepped into the beat with Mark.

"How do you like it so far?" said Mark, making an effort to be heard over the music.

"Only a jewel thief could like it better," said Lori, closing in on him, shouting into his ear, making Mark laugh. "Some of these rocks could cause blindness."

The music kept on for what seemed a very long time. Katrinka danced with Neil; then, when she saw Ted sitting alone, went and pulled him onto the floor to keep people from speculating about why he was looking so morose. Finally, exhausted, she sat down to catch her breath, while Mark politely asked Rick's elderly matron to dance to the fox-trot the band had just begun.

Left alone with Katrinka, Rick immediately began pumping for news of Carlos, as Carlos always pumped her for news of Rick. "It would make my life much easier, if you two would just talk to each other," she said, sounding a little exasperated.

"We do," said Rick. "But we don't tell each other anything that matters."

"I do see him when he's working," said Katrinka carefully, "and you know Carlos. That's when he is happiest."

"Or craziest."

Katrinka laughed, then reached over and touched Rick's arm. "Why you don't forget him?" she said. "Why you don't just find someone else and start over?"

She wasn't talking about the black leather and heavy metal types he continued, against his better judgment, to pick up at bars, Rick knew. He smiled at her weakly. "We don't all have your strength, Katrinka. Or your energy. Maybe not even your love of life."

"That's nonsense," she said.

"If something happened with Mark, could you just forget him and start over?"

"What could happen with Mark?" she said, knowing she sounded defensive and unable to help it. She had been too worried for days not to let Rick's comment bother her.

"You see."

"Yes, yes, I would," said Katrinka emphatically after a minute, watching as Mark returned from the dance floor. "I would be unhappy for a while, maybe a long time, but then I would get over it, and begin again."

Rick stood to help the matron settle into her seat, and Mark said, "Get over what?"

"Losing you."

"Are you planning to lose me?"

"It was . . . how you say, a pretend situation?"

"Hypothetical?"

"Yes."

"One that would *never* happen."

"*Might* never happen," corrected Katrinka, who was in no doubt about the meaning of the word.

"In this case, never is correct," insisted Mark.

"I do believe that," said Katrinka, leaning forward and brushing his cheek with her lips. Then, she stood up. "If you excuse me, please." She wanted to get to the powder room before the auction began. Moving quickly, she threaded her way through the tables, smiling hello but not stopping to talk to any of the people trying to waylay her, noticing among the crowd some interesting couples: Sabrina talking to someone who under any other circumstances would have had nothing to do with her, Sue Whitmore, the Listerine heiress; and, at the same table, Russell Luce chatting to Alan Platt. About what? wondered Katrinka, not able to imagine the senator discussing fashion, or the designer politics.

In the powder room, to her dismay, Katrinka found Nina standing at the mirror, applying lipstick to her perfectly shaped mouth. "What can Alexandra have been thinking of?" she said, the minute she saw Katrinka, "seating that awful Sabrina at our table? I of course have been politely noncommittal, but she hasn't let poor Sue Whitmore be for a minute."

Katrinka looked around quickly, saw they were alone, and said, "Maybe she did think some publicity would help Russell."

"He doesn't need that sort of publicity," said Nina. "No one does."

"Every politician needs it," said Katrinka. The value of publicity was another old argument between them. "How you do think the president won the last election?"

"George Bush won because he was the best man for the job," said Nina, whose mind on the subject was firmly made up. "And he will win this year for the same reason."

"If you think your husband can win an election without getting his name in the papers, Nina, you're wrong," said Katrinka, who did not want to get sidetracked into presidential politics. What she did want was to caution Nina, though she was not sure whether her motive was to spare her former mother-in-law an unpleasant surprise down the line or to have one last try at winning an old dispute.

"I understand that perfectly well," said Nina. "And I have no objection to publicity, whatever you may think. Up to a point, that is."

But that point was beyond anyone's control. That was what Nina could not understand. Once the publicity machine got started, there was no stopping it, no boundaries it wouldn't cross. "Well, I do hope everything goes the way you want," said Katrinka.

"It will," insisted Nina. "One simply has to take a firm stand."

Nina left the powder room and a few minutes later Katrinka followed her. As she slid into her seat beside Mark, Alexandra introduced Stanley Rumbough, the president of Planned Parenthood ("a man who needs no introduction"), to the crowd and, after a few brief remarks, he in turn introduced the Sotheby's auctioneer, whom Alexandra had invited to conduct the sale. The auction was slow to get started, but soon everyone got into the mood, and amid much good-natured jeering and cheering the paintings were sold. Mark paid seventy-five thousand dollars for the Arab street scene and, in the only controversial move of the evening, Neil bought back his Kalf at an exorbitant three hundred twenty-five thousand, outbidding Alfred Taubman, Sotheby's chairman, and MaryLou Whitney. It was worth far more, of course, but neither of the others was passionate enough about having it to keep bidding. Some, however, thought that Neil should not have put up such good a fight. There was something unpleasant, they felt, about such naked possessiveness, such naked greed. Aware of the sentiment, on some level even sharing it, Alexandra watched as the sheen of her evening dulled. If Neil had cost her a place in Palm Beach society, she thought, she would never forgive him.

But Neil left the Flagler in triumph, his painting under his arm, not even worried yet about having spent money he could ill afford. That would come the next day.

The rain had stopped, but the wind was still gusting and Katrinka put a hand up to smooth her hair back into place. "I do love it," she said, watching as the chauffeur put her painting into the Cadillac's trunk, next to Neil's. The Goodmans' Rolls was parked behind it, waiting to catch the overflow of guests.

"Now wouldn't be the best time to tell me if you'd changed your mind," said Mark, grinning.

"Can we go now?" said Margo, coming down the museum's steps. Her eyes were bright from too much champagne, but otherwise she seemed to be all right.

"Sure. Why not? Where's Ted?" asked Mark.

"Who cares? I hope I never see the sonovabitch again as long as I live."

"I took Mr. Jensen home a little while ago," said the chauffeur politely.

"I think he should leave in the morning," said Margo.

"We're all leaving tomorrow," Tomáš reminded her.

"More's the pity," muttered Lori.

"We're all leaving *after* the polo match," said Margo. The next day's plans included lunch in the clubhouse and an afternoon of polo at Wellington. "I want him gone before. I don't intend to be seen in public with him again."

No one knew what had happened to set Margo off, and no one wanted to ask. "You discuss it with him when you get back, okay?" said Katrinka. "I'm sure he'll do whatever you want."

"He better," said Margo as she got into the Rolls, followed by Lori and Tomáš.

"Do hurry, Neil," said Alexandra impatiently, as Neil readjusted for the third time the position of the two paintings in the trunk. "I'm exhausted." She climbed into the back of the limo, sat back, and closed her eyes. She felt a headache coming on. The evening had been a success. People had enjoyed themselves, and well over a million dollars had been raised for Planned Parenthood, no mean accomplishment in a depressed economy. Her praises would be sung for days, possibly even weeks to come. Nevertheless, instead of elation, Alexandra felt a strange sense of unease.

"That's all right now," Neil said, signaling the chauffeur to close the trunk. He turned and waited for Katrinka to get into the car, then, as soon as Mark had settled into one of the jump seats, he got in and took the other.

Waiting for the chauffeur to start the car, Katrinka settled back against the Cadillac's leather upholstery. Looking out the window, she saw Sabrina standing on the floodlit steps of the museum, looking from the Rolls to the Cadillac and back again, her expression changing from speculative to satisfied, as if she had finally solved some troubling puzzle. What did she see? wondered Katrinka. What awful stories were taking form in her nasty mind? How many of them would turn out to be true? She shivered.

"Are you cold?" asked Neil, who was sitting opposite her.

"No," said Katrinka, resisting the urge to make the sign of the cross, to ward off the evil eye as she had seen the old women in Svitov do. "I'm fine."

Twenty

WHAT SABRINA SAW AT THE PLANNED PARENTHOOD BALL, ACCORDING TO HER COLUMN ON THE FOLLOWING Monday, was a lot more exciting than anything witnessed by others who were there. "Dance Floor Brawl Shocks Stately Palm Beach," ran her column head, as if spousal murder, messy divorces, and rape trials were unknown in the town. For those who had, by blinking, missed Margo Jensen stalking away from her husband in the middle of a fox-trot, Sabrina went on to describe the scene and to hazard a guess that more trouble was brewing in a marriage that had so far survived Ted's severe drinking problem and his company's near bankruptcy. Was there a woman in the picture? she asked coyly, only guessing, but knowing the odds favored her being right.

With an ability to read minds that would have put a psychic to shame, Sabrina also noted Alexandra's displeasure at Neil for taking home the painting he had donated, put two and two together, and got Knapp Manning's financial difficulties as the reason. She took passing shots at the Taubmans and the Masheks, described Russell Luce as a charming gentleman and his bride as beautiful. Katrinka she referred to briefly as having been "as usual, the most flamboyantly overdressed woman in the room," presumably because she had overheard Nina's remark. It was unthinkable that Nina might have repeated it to her.

While Sabrina's column was characteristically waspish, Rick Colins's report of the ball on his Monday television show was good-natured and full of praise for, as he put it, "the superb job done by Alexandra Goodman in raising much-needed funds for a widely respected organization currently under siege by right-wing extremists." In private, Rick could be even bitchier than Sabrina. He could reduce his friends to near hysteria with cutting comments about the exploits of the rich and famous. But in print or on television his attacks were never personal and he never slammed what he considered good causes. Instead of meanness, he relied on intelligence and wit to keep both his television shows and newspaper columns entertaining. People who watched him and read Sabrina could easily have believed that each had attended a different event the previous Saturday night in Palm Beach.

The harm Sabrina could do, however, was limited. By leaving the van Hollen chain, she had reduced her reading public. Her column no longer appeared in papers in New York or in any of the European capitals, and in Los Angeles it attracted little attention. Her prey were the international glitterati, and Hollywood was interested only in its own.

All this she should have foreseen but had somehow overlooked in her desire both to earn more money and to be out of Mark van Hollen's control. She had since tried to get her column syndicated in the international press and failed. Increasingly frustrated, Sabrina felt sometimes as if she had crawled into a coffin and shut the lid on herself. What she had to do, she realized, was get out before someone else nailed it shut—not an easy feat to accomplish.

To her relief, Charles Wolf so far seemed unaware of the fact that he was not getting value for money, that Sabrina would probably not sell one extra copy of his newspapers anywhere they circulated, that the people she wrote about—the people who dazzled each other in the capitals of the world—were of little or no interest to the inhabitants of Paris, Idaho, or Manhattan, Kansas. So far he appeared to be absolutely delighted with what he still considered his coup against Mark van Hollen. When he had, at their last meeting in New York, taken Sabrina to lunch at La Grenouille, he had treated her like the queen of the hive, something her former employers had never done. He had also hinted at a future full of new and exciting prospects. What those could be had baffled her at first. But then she remembered the recent run on van Hollen stock. Again, she put two and two together and this time came up with a takeover. Not wanting to jeopardize whatever Charles Wolf was up to, she did not, however, mention this suspicion in her column; she did not even mention it to her lover, Alan Platt, who was beginning to think he could manage without her help and was therefore no longer controllable. But she did tell her broker to buy VHE stock. Mark van Hollen out of a job, Charles Wolf in control of van Hollen Enterprises, her column back in the world's prime markets, and a killing on the stock market: it was all too delicious to contemplate.

When Zuzka read Sabrina's column on Monday morning, she faxed a copy to Katrinka, then called her in New York to find out what had really happened in Palm Beach over the weekend. Katrinka, in a rapid uninflected Czech that had lost little of its fluency in the years she had been living out of her native country, filled her in on what she knew. When she finished, there was silence on the other end of the line. "Zuzka, are you there?" she asked.

"Yes, yes. I'm here," said Zuzka. "I am just so sad for Margo."

It *was* terrible, agreed Katrinka, to watch people who had once loved each other circling, with daggers drawn, each waiting for a chance to strike the deadliest possible blow. It was a bloody business, the breakup of a marriage.

"Not just marriages," corrected Zuzka. She sounded worn out.

"Zuzka, is everything all right with you?"

"Yes. Everything's fine," replied Zuzka quickly. She was lying, and they both knew it. "I was thinking of you and Mirek Bartoš, that's all. How unhappy you were when that affair ended."

Katrinka and Zuzka had been raised in a communist society where any deviation from accepted opinions or policy could cost you a place to live, food to eat, a job, sometimes your life. From an early age they had learned to keep their mouths shut, to guard their secrets. If Zuzka did not wish to tell her what was wrong, Katrinka was not going to insist. All she said was, "I got over it, the way you got over Tomáš."

"And you got over Adam."

"Exactly," said Katrinka. "The important thing is not to cry over milk that's spilled, but mop it up and go on," she added, battering the old proverb in translation, but this time getting the general sense of it correct.

"Yes," agreed Zuzka, who did not yet sound totally convinced. "Margo's sensible. She'll be all right."

"She'll be fine," said Katrinka firmly. She had great faith in the emotional resilience of all her friends. Whatever life handed out to them, they could take. Except for Natalie. The thought came unexpectedly into her mind, and for no good reason. The Natalie she had known was neurotic, yes, but independent, intelligent, resourceful. So

Katrinka pushed her former friend from her mind and said, "Margo's a strong woman. Like all of us, *zlatíčko*."

"You think we can do anything," said Zuzka, laughing. "And who knows? Maybe you're right. How's the new house?" she asked, changing the subject. "I can't wait to see it."

The new town house was, everyone agreed, fabulous. Katrinka and Carlos had steered clear of the fussy and ostentatious. There was no gilt, no fringe, no cabbage roses. It was not necessary to walk sideways to avoid colliding with furniture, or to keep wayward arms from knocking Ming vases and Fabergé eggs from cluttered surfaces. Yet it was in no way as austere, some said cold, as the apartment they had created together for Adam Graham to live in. Instead, a feeling of opulence had been created by combining pale colors, rich textures, and exquisite workmanship. A white marble floor with timber insets ran throughout the ground floor of the house, unifying sitting room, hallway, dining room, and library. Heavy curtains in cream corded cotton hung from wood rods at the windows. Comfortable contemporary furniture in monochromatic colors mingled with the rich finishes of antique tables and chests. A seventeenth-century tapestry in a lush pastoral design hung on the wall in the sitting room, and each panel of the *faux marbre* walls in the dining room held framed architectural drawings.

The rooms on the second floor showed the same restraint. Katrinka and Mark's bedroom was done in a variety of off-white fabrics, which hung on the walls and the windows, and curtained the bed. Mark's office had an antique desk and leather chairs, while Katrinka's was completely feminine with a sofa and armchairs covered in ivory linen with pink piping, framed color prints of roses by Redouté, the French artist, and a crewel rug on the hardwood floor. The two master bathrooms were done in marble, while those of the guest suites on the third floor were either onyx or tile. The nursery suite on the fourth floor was the only one decorated in vibrant primary colors, though the nanny's rooms again returned to the more restrained style. The fifth floor was an enormous playroom, with oversized sofas, a pool table, a built-in stereo system, large-screen television, and doors leading out onto a roof garden with flagstone decking, stone sculptures, and ornamental shrubs in containers. The garden at ground level had a patch of grass, a Japanese fountain, and another stone sculpture. The wood-and-slate kitchen was on the lower ground floor, as were the pantry and staff rooms.

Now that it was finished, except for the few items of furniture still to be delivered, including the antique bed for the nursery that Carlos was sending from France, Katrinka was showing off her newest creation to her friends one at a time or in small groups at intimate dinner parties; and she had said yes to a feature in *Architectural Digest,* which had previously run pieces on both her hotels and her homes.

"What a pity *Chic* didn't get in first," said Margo, who, instead of returning to Monte Carlo, had flown from Palm Beach to New York with Katrinka and Mark on the VHE jet. "The house is fabulous."

"You were comfortable? You had everything you did need?" asked Katrinka, as she entered the library, a cosy paneled room on the first floor overlooking the garden. At her heels were Bruni and Babar, two of the Alsatians that Mark had recently purchased as combination pets and guard dogs.

"Everything. Anna took excellent care of me. Sweet baby," said Margo, stretching out a manicured hand to pet Bruni.

Katrinka sank gratefully onto the wide sofa, kicked off her heels, and put her feet up. "I am worn out." Except for a lunch with her accountant at The Four Seasons, she had spent the entire day at the Praha, most of it in a long argumentative meeting with an advertising agency about the campaign to highlight the New York Ambassador's cocktail lounge, the Starlight Club, which was scheduled to start offering entertainment in the middle of May. Katrinka was hoping the club would become an uptown hangout, along the lines of the Oak Room at the Algonquin or the Village Vanguard. "Bruni, Babar, down," she ordered when she saw that Margo was about to be overwhelmed by their attentions, then she stretched luxuriously. "It's good to be home. You did stay in all day?"

"Actually, I've been a busy little bee."

Katrinka studied her friend for a moment, then said, "What you been up to? You're in a much better mood than this morning."

Margo's dramatic face was flawlessly made up, her skin pale, almost white, a backdrop for her full red mouth and prominent dark eyes, fringed by thick false eyelashes. The eyes now glowed like coals, with only a hint of pink surrounding the irises, the result of days spent crying. "Can't keep a good woman down," she said, her full mouth broadening in a smile.

"Not for long," agreed Katrinka. A knock at the library door interrupted the conversation, and the plump, pretty, gray-haired housekeeper entered carrying a silver tray with a Spode tea service and a plate of Italian cookies from Balducci's. "Anna, thank you," said Katrinka in Czech, "just what I needed."

"I brought a cup for Mrs. Jensen, but she may prefer something else."

"Margo, do you want herb tea? Wine? Some champagne?" asked Katrinka, switching to English.

"Tea is fine. If I drink, I'll just start crying again."

Anna poured the tea, handed a cup to each of the women, and then left. As soon as she had gone, Katrinka turned again to Margo and said, "Well, tell me . . ."

She had lunched with her children, Margo told Katrinka, both of whom were working in Manhattan, her daughter as an editorial assistant at *Chic* and her son as a junior editor at one of the large publishing houses. Both had first been surprised that their mother was in New York, and then worried. Not wanting to cause the kind of family war that had erupted among the Elliotts when Steven had left Daisy, Margo had not told them much, only that she and Ted were going through a difficult patch and had agreed to spend a little time apart. She had not mentioned the word "separation." Later, when they were used to the idea, she would tell them what was really going on. "Well, not everything," said Margo. "I don't want them to hate their father. Well, maybe just a little," she corrected herself. "After lunch, I called him."

"Ted?" asked Katrinka. Margo nodded. "What he did say?"

"He was furious I told the kids." She laughed bitterly. "Isn't that just like a man? Wants to eat his cake and have it too. He said nothing was decided. I told him maybe not for him, but I'd made up *my* mind."

"Have you?"

Margo shrugged. "I suppose. I don't know. I never thought this would happen to Ted and me." For a moment, she looked on the verge of tears again, but she shook her head and continued brightly, "And then I had cocktails with the publisher of *Chic*." She sounded very pleased with herself. "I called him, just to say hello. He suggested we get together. We met in the Oyster Bar at the Plaza." She paused for a moment and then added, "I got the feeling he hasn't been exactly pleased with the way things are going at the magazine."

"Circulation is down?"

"No. But advertising is. And this duel between *Vogue, Harper's,* and *Savvy* is making him nervous. He's worried that they'll tie up all the major talent."

"I did hear that Liz Tilberis offered Helmut Newton a fortune to switch to *Harper's.*"

"He thinks nobody on staff now at *Chic* has what it takes to deal with that kind of competition. And he's right."

"He did offer you a job?"

"Not exactly," said Margo. "But he asked if the idea of returning to work ever crossed my mind."

Katrinka reached for the Spode pot and poured another cup of tea for Margo and herself. "And you did say?"

"Several times a day lately." Margo bit into a cookie, then said, "If Ted and I can't work things out, I'll need something to keep me busy or I'll fall apart."

"You'll work things out," said Katrinka, with more optimism than she felt.

"I don't know," said Margo doubtfully. "Even if he gives that . . . that *bank clerk* up, I'm not sure I can forgive him."

"People forgive each other all the time."

"You didn't forgive Adam."

"He did never ask," said Katrinka quickly.

"Would you forgive Mark if he was unfaithful?"

The idea of it caused such pain that Katrinka started. "I don't know," she said unhappily. "Maybe. It would depend."

At first surprised at the distress her question (a perfectly routine question, as far as she was concerned) had caused, Margo then remembered Katrinka was pregnant. "Are you all right?" she asked.

"Yes," said Katrinka, not quite telling the truth.

"I didn't mean to upset you."

"You didn't. It's the hormones." Katrinka laughed weakly. "They make me so moody. I don't know how Mark can live with me."

"Because you're a sweetheart," said Margo, forcing herself to sound cheerful. "Guess what?" she added, changing the subject.

"What?"

"I called Steven Hoefflin's office, in Los Angeles. I've made an appointment to see him. I can't go back to work looking like an old hag."

"You look great," said Katrinka, exaggerating a little. "But if plastic surgery will make you feel better, then go ahead."

"Do you think Zuzka would put me up for a few days?"

"Of course," said Katrinka. "She would love it." She reached for the phone extension and picked it up. "Let's call her now."

Margo's attack of cheerfulness did not survive dinner. After a weekend of partying, no one was in the mood to go out, so the van Hollens and their guest dined at home, on *svickova*, a beef in cream sauce, prepared by the chef because it was one of Katrinka's favorite Czech dishes. Margo had finished her second helping and was in the middle of declaring it the best thing she had ever tasted when she burst suddenly into tears. "I'm sorry," she muttered, dabbing at her eyes with a napkin. "It's the wine."

"Do you want me to make myself scarce, so you two can talk?" asked Mark.

"No, no. I've bored Katrinka enough for one day."

"You haven't," protested Katrinka.

"Anyway," said Margo, "I like you, Mark. You almost restore my faith in men."

Mark laughed. "I'm flattered, I think."

"Just don't turn into a shit, okay?" And she burst into tears again.

By the time dessert arrived, Margo had quieted sufficiently to indulge in a strawberry dumpling; and afterward, rather than try to keep a conversation going, Mark suggested they see a movie, so they took the elevator to the fifth floor playroom and watched *Robin Hood, Prince of Thieves*, a videotape interrupted only by the van Hollen staff arriving periodically with bowls of freshly popped corn, diet sodas, glasses of wine, bottles of Evian, cups of espresso with lemon. "You two really know how to live," said Margo appreciatively.

"You mean Katrinka knows how to live," said Mark, who never failed to marvel at his wife's talent for organization. Left to his own devices, he never got such good service, not at home at any rate.

"If you pay people well and treat them decently, they don't mind working hard," said Katrinka.

"That's not been my experience," said Margo, who had no idea how difficult and demanding she was. People either loved her for her brilliance or loathed her for her autocratic manner. "I liked Errol Flynn better," she said later, when the movie was over.

"Who?" asked Katrinka.

"He was an actor, popular before you were even born," she said, laughing. Then she stopped laughing and her eyes filled with tears. "Oh, God, I'm so old."

Margo's mood continued to seesaw from extreme to extreme during the remainder of her visit, and it was with some relief that Katrinka joined her in the center hall on Thursday morning to say good-bye.

"You've been an angel," said Margo, hugging her. "Thanks for letting me cry on your shoulder."

"Anytime," said Katrinka. "Call me from Los Angeles. Let me know how you're doing."

"I will," said Margo, as she turned to follow the butler carrying her bags down the front steps toward the waiting limo.

Ignoring the curious glances of the passersby, Katrinka stood on the doorstep, two of the Alsatians at her heels, watching as Margo settled the skirts of her Saint Laurent suit to avoid creasing.

Margo rolled down the electric window and called another good-bye. Katrinka waved, watched until the car pulled into traffic, then went back inside, leaving the butler to close the door. The two dogs padding along behind her, she crossed the center hall, then followed the corridor to a small conservatory overlooking the garden, where she and Mark normally had breakfast and lunch when they were at home. "Stay," commanded Katrinka, as she entered, and the two dogs immediately fell to the floor, one on either side of the door. "That Kelly is a wonderful trainer," said Katrinka to Mark, who was still at the table. "Look at those dogs."

"Is Margo gone?" asked Mark, looking up from his copy of *The Wall Street Journal* as Katrinka sat opposite him and poured herself a cup of tea from the pot on the table. When she nodded, he smiled and said, "Peace, at last."

"She's so unhappy."

"I like Margo, but . . ." He shook his head. Lately, he had had enough trouble trying to keep up with Katrinka's constantly shifting moods. Dealing with Margo's as well had left him feeling irritable. "She can be pretty demanding."

One of the footmen entered bringing Katrinka's breakfast, and as soon as he had gone, she said, "Margo's been a very good friend to me."

"I know."

"I did have to offer her a place to stay."

"You offer everyone a place to stay." Sometimes, like now, it seemed to him that he and Katrinka never had time alone together anymore. Sometimes, not often, he wished it were possible to return to those months before their marriage, when they had hidden from the world.

She looked at him accusingly. "You mind?"

"Not usually. No. Not if it makes you happy."

"How can I be happy, if you're not?"

"Katrinka, did I say I was unhappy?"

"I don't know. Did you?"

Mark took a deep breath. "Baby, let's not quarrel. Okay?"

"I don't want to feel guilty about inviting my friends to my home," said Katrinka stubbornly.

"Then don't feel guilty."

"Especially when they've got problems," continued Katrinka, as if he had not spoken.

"Ask anyone you like," said Mark, sounding annoyed.

"I didn't think you would mind."

"Jesus Christ," said Mark. "Can we just end this conversation?"

"No," said Katrinka. But before she could say anything more, Mark was on his feet, heading out of the room. "Where are you going?" she called after him.

"To work," he said. "I'll phone you later."

Mark didn't phone as he promised, but at eleven that morning a bouquet of champagne-colored roses from Salou arrived with an unsigned card that said, "We'll talk later. I love you."

"Now why doesn't Greg do things like this when we fight?" asked Robin, as she watched Katrinka arrange the flowers in a vase of etched Czechoslovakian crystal. "All I get is an apology, which half the time he doesn't mean."

"It's better if you don't fight in the first place," said Katrinka.

"Everybody fights," said Robin. "It's normal."

"My parents didn't fight."

"Of course they did," said Robin. "You just don't remember."

Did her parents fight? wondered Katrinka when she was alone again and supposedly checking the casino figures from the London Ambassador. She could not remember one quarrel, though, after a while, she decided Robin had to be right and her parents must have quarreled sometimes. But when? She wracked her brain trying to summon just one incident. Perhaps when she wanted to join the ski club? She remembered how opposed her mother had been to her racing, afraid that she would get hurt. But Katrinka could recall no angry words, no shouts, no tears. All she could remember was the love, the feeling of security. She wanted to give that to her child, to this baby that Mark and she had created together; and she wanted to make up to Christian for all the years he had been deprived of it. Christian, her difficult son. She depressed the button on the intercom. "Would you call Christian, please, at the number in Bonn," she told the secretary, who responded. "If he's not in, keep trying until he does answer." However much she promised herself that she would not spoil him, that she would give him the space he needed to grow to love her as much as she did him, sometimes she could not resist showering him with gifts, sometimes she just had to hear his voice, to convince herself that, after all her years of searching for him, he was really there. She picked up the sheet of casino figures to study while waiting for her call to Christian to go through, but her eyes focused instead on the roses that Mark had sent. Champagne-colored, they were Katrinka's favorites, as he knew. All at once, her good sense returned and balanced her emotions. Robin was right, of course. Everyone quarreled. It meant nothing. It was normal. What mattered was that Mark and she loved each other, that they were honest with each other, that they were committed to working out whatever problems they had together. She suddenly felt much better, and when the phone rang and her secretary announced that Christian was on the line, she picked up the receiver, smiling, and said, "Christian, *zlatíčko*, how good to hear your voice . . . No, no, everything's fine . . . I just wanted to confirm when you will be coming to Cap Ferrat . . ."

Once he had told his secretary to send Katrinka some flowers, Mark turned his mind to business. Although *The International* had been well received, the advertising revenues still fell far short of where he needed them to be. So he spent most of the morning telephone conferencing with advertising and promotion executives at VHE newspaper offices around the world. The equipment used for this, the latest in visual telecommunications, was one reason why the new magazine was so deeply in debt. But Mark believed that this heavy investment in technology, which made exchanging ideas throughout the company as easy as walking into the next office to tell a buddy your latest brilliant idea, would eventually pay off in greatly increased profits.

However, eventually could be a long way away. In the meantime, Mark had to head off, while it was still in its preliminary stage, what he still suspected was a takeover move on his company. And with the large amounts he had spent to launch *The International* and to buy up stock shares to stop the last run, he did not have a cash reserve large enough to make him feel secure about fending off another, more serious attempt.

"Don't you think you're being a little paranoid?" said Carey Powers when Mark raised the subject with him as they headed back along the corridor from the conference room in the VHE building on Avenue of the Americas to Mark's office, which was large, comfortably furnished, and very untidy, with newspapers, magazines, books, and stacks of files cluttering every surface.

"About what in particular this time?" asked Mark, grinning. Short, muscular, with a gently receding hairline and a genius for numbers, Carey was not only Mark's chief financial officer but his best friend. It was thanks to him that van Hollen Enterprises had stayed afloat in the terrible years after the death of Lisa and the boys, when Mark had spent most of his time in remote parts of the world, trying to come to terms with his grief.

"This takeover you seem to expect. They've gone out of fashion, in case you haven't noticed. The eighties are over. No one's got the money anymore."

"That's what makes what's happening seem so strange."

"Maybe nothing's happening," said Carey patiently, hoping this time Mark would get his point.

Normally, he trusted Carey's opinion implicitly, but this time Mark just shook his head. "I've got this feeling . . ."

"What feeling?"

"Like I'm walking down a dark alley, after midnight, and suddenly I hear footsteps . . ."

"Mark, I've asked everyone I know if someone's on the make, and the answer comes back negative every time."

"Because nobody sees anything doesn't necessarily mean that no one's there."

"Granted . . ."

"When you're raised on the street, you develop this instinct . . ."

Carey laughed. "An instinct for survival? Believe me, you develop it at the Wharton School, too."

"You really think I'm crazy?"

"Yeah. This time, I really think you're crazy."

"Okay," said Mark finally. "We'll sit still for a while. But let me know if you hear anything. Anything, you understand? No matter how unimportant you think it is."

"I'll keep my eyes and ears open." The intercom buzzed and, as Mark reached for the phone, Carey stood and headed for the door. "Catch you later," he said.

"Yeah?"

"There's a Monica Brand on line three," said his assistant, a young man named Josh Allen, who had dreams of running the company one day.

"Oh, shit," muttered Mark. "Okay, I'll talk to her." He depressed the button on the third line, feeling guilty for doing even that much. He knew Katrinka, if he told her, would not like it. She was completely irrational on the subject of Monica Brand. "Hi, Monica. You in New York?"

"Uh huh. Just got here. And I'm very happy to find you. I thought you might be off somewhere on business."

"No, I'm here for a while. How are you doing?"

"Okay. Pretty well in fact. Even though you won't give me a job."

It occurred to Mark that he really didn't know how she earned the money to pay for the stylish clothes she wore. Certainly not writing the few articles he had read. "I wouldn't put it quite that way," said Mark evenly. "If there's an opening, something you might be qualified for . . . who knows?"

"I've got a pretty good idea," she said, with a laugh. "Anyway, I didn't call to hound you about a job. Or even about that interview of you I'd like to do."

"Well, I can't say I'm not relieved."

"I called to ask a favor."

"Sure."

"Don't you even want to hear what it is?"

"Fire away."

"I'd rather tell you in person."

Her voice was low, melodic, sexy. For a moment, Mark considered seeing her. Once upon a time, not too long ago, he would have. But he had been single then, he reminded himself. Now he was married and in love with his wife. Who would have his head on a plate if he shared so much as an Evian with Monica Brand. "That's kind of hard to arrange at the moment. I've got a pretty full schedule."

"Mark van Hollen, you're not scared of me, are you?" Now the sexy voice was teasing, tempting.

"Being scared of you is probably a very smart move, and I pride myself on being a very smart guy."

"One little lunch? What harm can it do?"

"Don't wheedle, Monica. I told you, I'm busy."

"And I love spending time with you. There aren't a lot of men like you, you know. Intelligent, successful . . ."

"You obviously don't hang out in the right places."

"Sexy and so good looking," she continued.

"Monica, I'm flattered. I really am. It's not every day a woman as beautiful as you calls me up to heap compliments on my head. To tell you the truth, at another time, I'd be in a taxi by now on my way to wherever it is you're calling from . . ."

"The Carlyle," she said quickly.

"But at the moment, and for the foreseeable future, I am very much otherwise engaged."

"A pity," she said softly.

"Yeah," he agreed. He did not want Monica Brand in any active, compelling way. His desire at the moment seemed to be centered firmly on his wife, which for many reasons was an enormous relief. Still, the idea of it, the idea of lust for lust's sake, had its appeal, as did those well-worn concepts, the thrill of the chase and the satisfaction of conquest. He was, after all, only human. "Now, that favor you wanted?" he asked, promising himself that if it involved him any more deeply with her he would refuse.

"A letter of recommendation I can use to get a job with someone else?"

Mark couldn't quite see how a letter from him, since she had never been employed by VHE, would help Monica, but it seemed petty to refuse so small a request. "Sure," he said, "I'll have something for you by the morning."

"I'll stop by and pick it up. What time would you suggest?"

He was about to say he would send it by messenger to the Carlyle, when he realized how petty *that* would sound, not to mention cowardly. "Any time after ten." He would just tell Josh to keep her away from him. "See you," he said.

"You bet you will," he thought he heard her reply before he hung up.

When he got home that night, Mark did not mention the phone call from Monica Brand. He had enough to do, he had decided, just explaining his quick exit that morning without introducing Monica into the conversation. The butler greeted him at the door, took his coat and briefcase, and told him Mrs. van Hollen was in her room. Ignoring the elevator, Mark took the stairs to the second floor, entered their bedroom, walked through to Katrinka's bathroom, and found her standing naked in front of the mirror, applying makeup. He put his arms around her waist, cradled her stomach with his hands, and kissed the back of her neck. "Hi," he said. "Have a good day?"

"Yes, very good," she replied, surprising him. "Did you?"

"Not as good as I could have if I'd known you weren't mad at me," he said, releasing her.

She turned around and faced him. "Who did say I'm not mad at you?"

"I can always tell," he said.

"I'm not mad at you," she agreed, kissing him lightly on the mouth. "Now go and change before we're late."

"Late?" He sounded more dismayed than surprised.

"We do have that fund-raiser tonight. For Cerebral Palsy. Didn't Josh remind you?"

"Yes," said Mark, frowning. "This morning. But I conveniently managed to forget again."

"You don't want to go?"

A good way to patch up that morning's quarrel, thought Mark, was to say yes, change his clothes, and accompany his wife. But that was a short-term solution. At the moment, he was more interested in long-range planning. "No," said Mark. "I don't want to go." He turned away, and, starting to remove his jacket, headed back into the bedroom.

Pulling on a silk wrap, Katrinka followed him on bare feet, across to his dressing room, where Mark was stripping off his clothes, preparing to shower. "You go if you want to," he said when he saw her. "I think I'd rather just stay home and read."

"I don't want to go without you," she said.

"That's silly." When he was naked, instead of continuing on into the bathroom, Mark put on a terry robe, took Katrinka's hand and said, "Let's talk a minute." He led her back into the bedroom, settled her in an armchair, and sat on the edge of the bed facing her. "I've been thinking about us all day, on and off."

"Me, too."

"The way we lived the year before we got married kind of gave us the wrong idea about each other."

"You mean, you did never realize what a party girl I am?" she said, smiling, though her eyes were serious.

"Exactly. And you never realized what a stay-at-home I am."

"That's not true," protested Katrinka. "You do love to party."

"When I'm in the mood. The problem is, I'm not always in the mood, and you are."

"If you're trying to say we're"—she searched her mind for the English word—"incompatible," she said finally, "that's nonsense. We're not. We have very much in common."

"I'm not saying that. I'm just pointing out that I have a house in the Hebrides for a reason."

"But I love it there."

"I know. That's what had me fooled." She was about to protest, but he stopped her. "Look, any new marriage requires adjustments. You know that. And what you and I have to do is work out a way to live that suits us both."

"Going to a party alone does not suit me," said Katrinka stubbornly.

"And going to every goddamn fund-raiser in New York doesn't suit me. So, what are we going to do about it?"

Katrinka sat quietly for a moment, feeling the love, the sense of security that had comforted her only that morning in danger of slipping away. "I don't know," she said finally. How stupid! she thought. She ought to be able to think of something.

"I need time to myself," said Mark, "time to be alone. I don't want to go out every night. I don't want a house always full of guests. I want us to have time to be alone together."

"So do I," said Katrinka, beginning to feel more cheerful. She started to smile.

"What?"

"This is easy problem. We compromise."

"Easy?"

"We go over plans together. We decide what we want to do, and we do it."

"And if I don't want to go to something and you do?"

"If it's important, you come. If it's not, I ask someone else, or I don't go."

"Do I get to ask someone else to things you don't want to attend?"

"That will never happen," she said, smiling happily. "Unless I'm sick, and then you should stay home to take care of me. Anyway, I never get sick."

Mark laughed. "And what if I don't agree with you about what's important?"

"We fight. It's normal," she said. "We do have to fight sometimes."

Mark reached out, took her hand, pulled her to her feet and onto his lap. He buried his face in her neck. "I do love you."

"I know." She wrapped her arms around his neck and kissed the top of his head.

"Tonight we stay home?"

"Tonight we stay home," agreed Katrinka. "It's no big deal. We did pay for the table. That's enough."

Mark moved his mouth along the line of her throat, to her chin, then to her lips. "Would you like to take a shower with me?" he asked as he kissed her.

"I just did have a shower," she said, her voice teasing.

He rolled her off his lap and onto the bed. Leaning over her, he opened her silk wrap and pushed it aside. "What if I make you all hot and sweaty? Would you reconsider?"

"Oh, yes," she said, as she felt his mouth tugging at her nipple, his hand moving up the inside of her thigh. "Absolutely."

Twenty-One

NOTHING WAS GOING QUITE ADAM GRAHAM'S WAY.
HIS LAWYERS HAD WORKED OUT A SETTLEMENT IN THE
class action suit against Graham Marine's cruise ship line and were
advising him to pay thirty-four million dollars rather than risk going to
court.

Lucia had phoned to report that Patrick Kates had lost his second
race in the Cup Defender semifinals in San Diego, which meant that
Patrick would probably not make it to the match, resulting in a
potential loss of business for the shipyards well into the millions of
dollars.

Less serious but somehow more irritating, not only had Adam's plan
to weaken Mark van Hollen's position with his board got nowhere, but
Charles Wolf's efforts to acquire VHE had so far been as tentative as a
teenage boy's debut performance in a brothel. More money was
needed to push Wolf to move more aggressively, but where was Adam
to find it? He doubted he could even come up with the cash to cover the
settlement.

Here it was, April, and not only were the Italians still stalling, but
there seemed to be no one else interested in acquiring a film studio, at
least not *his* film studio. And, although his business affairs people were
running rings around Tomáš Havlíček, instead of accepting it as
business per usual, Tomáš was starting to make noises about taking his
pet film project elsewhere, as if any studio executive in his right mind

would consider making a period piece about Chinese immigrants. But if *Marked for Death* was the studio's only chance to make a profit this year, *Low Flying Planes* was the only project on the Olympic Pictures's production schedule that looked like a solid money-maker for the following one. So Adam wanted a happy director to show off to the Italians: a happy director, a script full of sex and violence, a star with proven appeal—the necessary ingredients, so conventional wisdom went, for enormous box office returns.

But the studio was the least of his problems, thought Adam, as he lay on the Clarence House banquette in the library of his Fifth Avenue apartment, staring out at the dusk slowly descending on Central Park. At least Olympic Pictures was in reasonably good financial shape; and even if it had not been, there was always a rich fool somewhere (he did not, of course, include himself in that category) wanting to get into show business. Eventually, there would be a taker. What he was much less optimistic about were the chances of selling the tanker fleet or the cruise ship line, his yacht or the apartment, not unless he was willing to take enormous losses. But if he did not sell something, and soon, would he be able to avoid declaring bankruptcy to protect what he could of his assets? That was the billion-dollar question.

The thought of parting with any of his holdings was not pleasant, except for the apartment, which he was anxious to get rid of. It was too big and too expensive to run. More to the point, he hated it. Every inch of it had been decorated to suit his taste and cater to his comfort, and still he hated it. Though he had waited impatiently for the divorce to become final and Katrinka to leave, when he had finally moved back in last December, instead of the elegant home he had once loved, what he had found was an apartment as haunted with memories as any Gothic mansion.

The phone rang, but Adam did not reach to answer it, knowing that one of the staff somewhere in the apartment would pick it up. Instead, he walked over to the bar, opened another Perrier, added some ice from the always ready chrome bucket to his glass, and returned to his seat on the banquette. But no sooner had he stretched out again than Carter, his butler, entered to tell him that his driver was waiting downstairs with the car.

"Tell him I'll be down in fifteen minutes," said Adam, as he got resentfully to his feet.

"Shall I call to say you'll be late?" Being English, Carter had a profound respect for social rules.

"That won't be necessary," said Adam, heading across the hallway toward the corridor leading to the master bedroom suite. It didn't at all matter that he would be late for his seven o'clock appointment, and he fully intended to be on time for dinner with his mother and stepfather. He wanted Russell's help pushing another much-needed defense contract to Graham Marine: his mother's remarriage was not without its blessings. In any case, he did not want Carter to know where he was going. "Why don't you move some of the furniture around while I'm out?"

Carter looked startled. "But where . . . ? I mean, did you have something specific in mind, sir?"

"No," said Adam curtly. "Just move it."

Since everything in the penthouse had been designed especially for it, Carter looked around uncertainly, wondering how he was going to do as his employer ordered without reducing the place to a shambles. "Yes, sir," he said finally, knowing better than to argue when Adam was in one of his moods.

It was because nothing had changed visually since he and Katrinka had lived there together that Adam felt so strange, so uncomfortable, being there without her. Sometimes he expected Katrinka to come walking through a door, any door, asking a question or announcing a plan in that absurdly ungrammatical English of hers. Had she felt the same, he wondered, expecting him to reappear magically at any moment, after their separation, when she had returned alone from Europe? If so, he thought bitterly, the feeling had not lasted for long. Entering the bedroom, he eyed the king-sized bed with distaste, imagining not only Katrinka in it but Mark van Hollen as well. Feeling the familiar rush of rage, he turned away and began to strip off his clothes. A shower was what he needed. It would clear his head.

Fifty minutes later, Adam Graham's Mercedes sedan slid to a smooth stop in front of an apartment building in the East Fifties. Dave, his driver, got out and opened the rear door.

"I'll be about half an hour," said Adam.

Dave nodded, then closed the car door. What's he up to now? he wondered as he watched Adam enter the building, search the directory, ring the button on the entry phone, wait a moment, then push the door open, and go in. The street was a perfectly respectable one between Lexington and Third Avenues, and the building the sort of bland tower that had sprung up all over the city in the fifties and sixties. Though it had no doorman, it was clean, well tended, ordinary. That was the problem. It was *too* ordinary. Not at all the sort of place that Adam Graham usually visited.

Adam was thinking the same thing as the elevator doors opened and he saw the narrow corridor lined with linoleum. He consulted the arrows on the wall, turned left, stopped in front of apartment 7C, rang the bell, and waited impatiently, wondering why he had thought this was a good idea.

"Don't you look handsome," drawled Sugar Benson as she pulled open the apartment's green door. Touching a lapel of his Fioravanti suit, she added, "Mmm, nice."

"I'm glad I meet with your approval," he said, pushing past her almost rudely, wanting to get inside before someone who might recognize him from newspaper and magazine photos spotted him in the hallway.

"Why do I get the feeling I don't quite meet with yours?"

"How can you say that?" he asked, kissing her briefly on the mouth before sitting on the wide peach-colored sofa. "You look stunning as always." Her hair was hanging loose to her shoulders in a flow of enticing curls. She was wearing a beige double-breasted coat dress, cut in a deep V with wide lapels, reserved enough to appear businesslike, yet hugging her body in a flatteringly sexy way. She could have been a television anchor rather than a notorious madam. "Sorry I'm late," he said, not really giving a damn. "We're alone?"

"Just as you requested. I've sent the girls out for an early dinner."

"Good." Meeting in his office or apartment was out of the question. And he did not want any phone number associated with Sugar appearing on his bills regularly enough to cause comment, should anyone begin asking questions. He was not being overly paranoid. Almost every day *The New York Times* ran a story on some Wall Street broker or company CEO under investigation by one government agency or another. You never knew, these days, who was accessing your computer files, studying your phone bills, going over your accounts. A quick visit to Sugar's "office" seemed the safest bet. He looked around at the comfortable room, done in tones of peach with blond wood and white accents. He remembered hearing somewhere that peach was a very flattering color for a woman. Certainly it did Sugar no harm, he thought, as he ran his eyes from her Charles Jourdan–clad toes back up to her honey-colored head. "Nice place," he said.

Sugar's company headquarters, so to speak, were in London, but a branch office had been in existence in New York for the past several months, operating out of this apartment. Residential rather than commercial space was essential, given the long and erratic hours of business. It was the usual sort of two-bedroom place, with kitchenette. One of the bedrooms was used as an office, complete with computer, copier, and fax machine. Here as in London, records were kept in elaborate code, which Sugar was reasonably certain no one could break. The key to the code was well hidden, in this case in a safe in the recess above the fake fireplace, a little awkward to get at, making it that much more secure. The office manager lived in, and the two assistants shared another apartment in the same building. It was all very friendly, very efficient, and unlikely to cause suspicion among the neighbors, who in New York did not usually tend to be nosy. Most of the business was handled on the phone, in oblique conversations that were far from incriminating. Unless there was a problem, the girls, who commuted on business between Europe and the States, and sometimes Asia, stopped by the apartment rarely, usually to settle accounts. They took Visa, MasterCard, American Express, and cash; checks were accepted only from preferred customers. For IRS and Inland Revenue purposes, Sugar Benson ran a computer dating service; and, remembering what the French had done to poor Madame Claude, she was careful about keeping phony records and paying what seemed reasonable amounts in taxes to both the United States and British governments.

But seeing the place from Adam's point of view, Sugar repressed her usual feelings of pride and satisfaction and said only, "It serves its purpose. Would you like something to drink?"

"No," said Adam. "Nothing. Thank you." These days he needed a clear head. "I haven't got a lot of time."

Sugar sat in an armchair opposite him and crossed her long slender legs, giving Adam a glimpse of bare thigh above the stocking top. He was tan and looking better, she thought, than when she had seen him in St. Moritz, as if he was working out again. The haggard look was gone from his face, but still she sensed a tension in him that had not been there when she had first met him. But then, he had been climbing toward the peak of his success, and now he was on the way down. "You might have bought me dinner," she said, but her tone was teasing rather than offended.

"Unfortunately, I'm dining with my mother this evening, and I don't think either of you would enjoy the experience."

"Oh, I don't know. I've been told I'm quite good at handling tight-assed old ladies."

For a moment, Sugar thought she might have gone just a little too far: the Grahams did tend to take themselves very seriously. But then Adam laughed. "Perhaps another time," he said, not meaning it, but intrigued nonetheless with the image of Nina Graham and Sugar Benson slugging it out over the onion tarts at Lutèce.

"Perhaps," agreed a smiling Sugar. "But in the meantime, why don't we take care of business, so you can run along and meet your mamma.''

"An excellent idea," said Adam. He pulled a billfold of American Express checks from his inside pocket, put it on the coffee table in front of him, then took the Montblanc pen that Sugar handed to him. He did not, however, begin signing. Instead, he sat back in the sofa and looked at her. "Have you noticed that I've been paying you a great deal of money for very little service?"

"It isn't all profit, you know," said Sugar, a pleasant smile on her face. She looked and sounded like an ad executive trying to keep an account, or a politician defending a less than adequate record. "We've paid out a fortune in bribes, phone calls, theater tickets, plane tickets . . . Poor little Monica's been working her tail off."

"Seems to me she's been having a holiday, at my expense."

"I told you it wouldn't be easy," said Sugar, for the first time sounding defensive. It was not, after all, as if Mark van Hollen had lived his life like a monk. Between the death of his first wife and his marriage to Katrinka, he had worked his way steadily down the list of the world's most beautiful and eligible women. And Sugar was beginning to take it personally that one of her girls could not manage to seduce someone so obviously a player.

"What is he?" said Adam. "Some kind of fucking saint?"

"Nonfucking saint is more like it."

Adam didn't bother to laugh. He ran a hand through his short salt-and-pepper hair and said, "Maybe it was a rotten idea to begin with."

"Do you want to settle accounts and call it quits?" asked Sugar. "That would be fine with me. But I would like to point out that I never have yet met a man who didn't eventually give in to temptation."

"Eventually can be a long way off and cost a great deal to get there."

"As I said, honey, it's up to you." Sugar uncrossed her legs, sat back, and waited for the decision.

Adam sat motionless, considering his options. He was spending a lot of time thinking about Mark van Hollen, and a lot of money trying to ruin him. Should he just cut his losses and call a halt now? But as soon as he asked himself the question, he knew he couldn't. Not yet, at any rate. And it wasn't just because of Katrinka, he assured himself. In fact, she had very little to do with his desire to humble Mark van Hollen. Even before her, Mark had brought out Adam's worst competitive instincts. His mother would say that Mark was an upstart who needed to be put in his place. That phrasing was too old-fashioned for Adam, who didn't in any case need to justify his actions to himself. Rivalry

243

was something he had understood and accepted for as long as he could remember, whether over a toy, a girl, getting top grades at school, or winning at sports. It didn't have to be either explained or excused: it was enough to know that Mark van Hollen irritated the hell out of him, and, somehow or other, Adam was determined to get him.

Finally, he began to see a way. His lips curved in a crooked grin that was very boyish and appealing. "Doing right isn't good enough," he said. "You have to *appear* to be doing right."

Sugar nodded. "So they say. But what's that got to do with our little problem?"

Adam leaned forward and began signing the travelers' checks. "Let me explain," he said.

Twenty-Two

DAISY CAME DOWN THE VILLA MAHMED'S STAIRCASE, INTO THE LARGE TILED HALL. HEARING NO SOUNDS OF life anywhere, she began peering into the rooms she passed as she made her way toward the patio, where, in good weather, breakfast was usually served. She found Katrinka in the study, on the phone with her London office. Daisy waved and continued on her way, but no sooner had she settled herself at the breakfast table than Katrinka joined her "Where is everyone?" asked Daisy.

"On the boat." Katrinka grabbed a stack of newspapers from a nearby side table and sat opposite her. "Except for Margo. She's asleep."

"Do I have time for breakfast? I'm famished."

Katrinka nodded. "I did tell them we wouldn't be there until ten."

"Be where?"

The voice came from the doorway and Katrinka and Daisy, turning to look, saw Margo standing poised on the threshold between the open glass-and-iron doors, as if deciding whether or not to brave the bright sunlight. She was wearing a cotton jumpsuit in a bold jungle print. Her hair was wrapped in a scarf, on top of which rested a wide-brimmed straw hat. Large dark sunglasses concealed most of her face.

"We thought you were still asleep," said Daisy.

"I can't sleep," complained Margo, sounding weary.

"We're going to San Remo for lunch," said Katrinka. Mark had

245

chartered the eighty-six-foot motor yacht *Bella Rena* for ten days, and while it was nowhere as big or as luxurious as the *Lady Katrinka*, it was comfortable and more than large enough to ferry the van Hollens and their guests on brief trips around the Mediterranean during the Easter holidays. "Why you don't come?"

"I don't think so," said Margo. "I'd really just like to stay here and relax."

"You won't be bored?"

"Or depressed?" asked Katrinka.

"No. I'm fine, really. You know how I love this house." It was like something out of *A Thousand and One Nights,* a more or less Moorish fantasy built by an English noblewoman who had fallen in love with a Bedouin sheikh. A near ruin when Katrinka had discovered it, she and Carlos had faithfully restored all its intricate inlaid wood and exquisite tile work, had refinished the antique furniture, and replaced what was irreparable with new pieces brought from North Africa, Spain, and Italy. Those who saw it either loved it or hated it, considering it either an elaborate joke or a work of genius. For Katrinka, it was a retreat, a place of peace and comfort that she loved to share with her friends. "I just want to sit for hours and stare at the ocean."

"You really ought to come," said Daisy, who was not happy unless she had organized everyone into doing what she thought was best for them.

"Well, maybe I'll read a little, too," said Margo, with a faint, teasing smile that faded so quickly it might have been imagined. She had been warned against smiling.

Thanks to a patient of Steven Hoefflin's coming down with a cold and canceling her appointment, Margo had been able to go from initial visit to completed face-lift in record time. The surgery had been done in his private clinic, and when it was over, Margo had been taken by chauffeured limousine to a small luxury hotel in Beverly Hills, where she had spent the next few days, her face swollen and bruised, being cared for by a competent and understanding staff, who had catered to her every whim. Since Zuzka had made it clear she would be grateful for the company, when she was released, Margo had returned to the house in Benedict Canyon. While she was there, Carla had left Zuzka for a twenty-year-old German countess and all hell had broken loose. Phone calls had raged nonstop between Los Angeles and New York, Los Angeles and various European cities. The lawyer Katrinka had referred Zuzka to, after calming her down, had told her not to move out of the house or stop going to work, advice she was diligently following, one reason why she had not accepted Katrinka's invitation

to spend Easter in Cap Ferrat. But after three weeks of holding Zuzka's hand (and vice versa), Margo had felt well enough to travel and had flown to Nice, where she was met by Katrinka and Mark's driver and brought to the Villa Mahmed. Her face was still a little swollen, but the scars left by the tiny stitches on her head, her face, her body, had all but disappeared. She looked the same, but younger. People who hadn't seen her for a while could not quite put their finger on what was different. "You look wonderful," they said. "So rested."

Margo walked to the edge of the courtyard, which was laid in a herringbone pattern of sand-colored bricks, and looked out past the pool and the changing rooms to the long galleried walk that overlooked the Mediterranean. "I really feel too lazy to budge from here today." She turned back and said to Katrinka, "Could someone take a lounge down to the cloister for me?"

"No problem," said Katrinka. "Just ask Anna. She'll arrange it." Katrinka had brought some of her staff with her from New York to supplement the local help.

A young dark-haired man in a white jacket came out of the house carrying a tray from which he took bowls of fruit salad to set at Margo and Daisy's places, complete china coffee and tea services, tiny dishes with butter and jam and marmalade, and a basket filled with crusty rolls and croissants. As usual, he had ridden the motor scooter into the village early that morning to buy the household's food for the day. "You would like something else?" he asked in accented English.

"Non, non, merci. Ça me suffit," said Margo, who was pleased with how fluent her French had become since her move to Monaco.

"This is lovely," said Daisy, picking up a croissant, breaking off a piece, and dabbing it lightly with marmalade.

"Anything interesting in the papers?" said Margo, as Katrinka finished leafing through a copy of *The International Herald Tribune* and dropped it on the table.

"Interesting, yes, but not good," said Katrinka, sounding frustrated. "This war in Yugoslavia. It's terrible."

"Are you worried the same thing will happen in Czechoslovakia?" asked Daisy.

"It will never happen," said Katrinka emphatically.

"Well, here's good news, anyway," said Margo, who had been scanning *Figaro*, with little real interest. "Patrick Kates won another race yesterday, after losing two last week."

"Adam must be delighted," said Daisy.

"And Lucia," added Margo. She turned to Katrinka. "Have you heard from her?"

Katrinka nodded. "Two days ago. She called to talk to Pia."

"Does she think they have any real chance of winning the Cup? How does she sound?"

"Fed up, I would imagine," said Daisy. "That man would be enough to drive anyone crazy."

"Don't you like him either?" asked Margo.

"No," said Daisy. "I do not."

Margo turned to look at Katrinka, who smiled ruefully and said, "I think he is a big pain in the butt."

"He's so completely different from Nick," said Margo.

"Only in appearance," said Daisy. "Otherwise, they're as alike as peas in a pod."

"Peas in what?" asked Katrinka. Daisy laughed and explained what she meant and Katrinka looked at her soberly and said, "You think Patrick is dishonest?"

"Well," said Daisy, "I don't think I'd go that far. But I think he'd bend a lot of rules to get what he wants."

"Oh," said Margo dryly. "In that case, he's just like everyone else we know." Katrinka frowned and Margo looked at her and said, "What? You don't agree?"

"Not everyone does lie and cheat."

Daisy, who, like Katrinka, was thinking of her husband, nodded in agreement. Mentioning husbands, however, did not seem like a good idea in the circumstances, so she said, instead, "We don't."

"We're not men," replied Margo, her voice full of disgust.

"*Ay yi yi yi,*" said Katrinka, with a laugh. "You do sound like a real man-hater. But I know better. I saw you flirting with that waiter at the Chèvre d'Or last night."

"I was not," said Margo indignantly, but she began to smile. "I was merely trying out my new face."

They all laughed, and now that some semblance of Margo's good humor was restored, Katrinka stood up and said, "We better get going or we'll be late. You're sure you don't want to come, Margo?"

"Positive, thank you. I'm going to have a nice, lazy day, all on my own." She watched as Katrinka and Daisy crossed the courtyard, then called, "Just bring back some of that delicious pesto," as they disappeared into the house's dark, cool interior. Was she making a mistake by not joining them? she wondered, considering whether or not to change her mind. But she really did not, just yet, want to set eyes on Monaco, not even from a yacht at a safe distance.

* * *

In the Porsche 911 that she kept at the villa, Katrinka drove Daisy along the Boulevard Général de Gaulle, past the stucco houses painted cream, peach, pumpkin, rose, with brown or turquoise shutters and roofs of orange tile. The sky overhead was a deep indigo blue, with traces of wispy white clouds floating high above the tops of the tallest pines. Along the side of the road grew scarlet bougainvillea, pink and white oleander, purple trumpet vine, and pink geraniums. Everything was clear light and brilliant color. The only sounds were the soft hum of the car's motor and birds calling in the distance.

Turning right into the Avenue des États Unis, Katrinka followed the road down into the small village with its narrow streets and rows of shops—a bank, a hardware store, bookstore, grocery, deli, bakery—past the Voile d'Or Hotel, and into the harbor. Katrinka and Adam had been married in a church not far from here, but she thought of that rarely these days, though she still avoided visiting either the tiny bare church or the wonderfully baroque cemetery next to it. She had once thought them charming; now the sight of them brought back only unhappy memories.

Katrinka pulled into a parking space on the dock, next to the BMW Mark had driven down earlier. As she and Daisy got out of the car and headed across the narrow strip of tarmac to the *Bella Rena*'s gangplank, Riccardo saw them coming and waved. *"Ah, bene,"* they heard him say as he turned and called to someone out of sight. *"Sono qui."* He was wearing white duck trousers and a striped T-shirt and his thick silver hair was wind-blown. Extending a hand, he helped the two women onto the boat. "We were thinking you would never come."

"It's only five to ten," said Katrinka indignantly.

"Don't pay any attention to him," said Daisy. "He's always late." Thanks to Riccardo, she had arrived at a banquet in London after the guest of honor, who happened to be Princess Margaret, causing an uproar in the tabloid press. The matter was settled with a polite exchange of notes between Daisy and the princess.

Pia and Christian, wearing bathing suits, were in the bow, keeping out of the way of the crew, who were getting ready to cast off. They, too, waved but otherwise did not move. Rick Colins, who was staying with the van Hollens at the villa for a few days before going on to Paris and London, was sprawled on one of the banquettes in the stern reading a copy of *The New Yorker*. His face was already beginning to turn pink. "Good morning," he said cheerfully. "What a perfect day."

"Perfect," agreed Katrinka, who was pleased to see him looking so happy. He rarely did of late.

"Bless you for inviting me." He took her hand and kissed it, then looked from her to Daisy and said, "Well, you two are looking gorgeous this morning." Katrinka was in her seventh month and though she still carried most of her added weight in her stomach, no one could now mistake the fact that she was pregnant. She was wearing black Lycra leggings under a crisp white beaded tunic. Her dark hair was pulled into a ponytail and covered by a large black straw hat. Daisy was in a blue-and-white sailor outfit, with a peaked cap set at a pert angle on her blond head. "You'd never know you were up to all hours last night." After gambling at the casino for a while, they had all gone on to Jimmy's to dance, except for Margo, who had insisted on returning to the villa, a stroke of good luck, since they had run into Ted and his Gigi there. Ted had been very embarrassed and had left soon after their arrival.

One of the crew appeared to ask if they would like something to drink, and after ordering iced tea, Katrinka and Daisy went below to stow their gear. There, in the lounge, they found Mark studying charts. When Katrinka went over to kiss him hello, he pulled her onto his lap. "What kept you so long?" he asked.

"Me," said Daisy. "I wanted my breakfast."

"We did get here five minutes early," protested Katrinka.

"It's always like this when I'm away from you," he said, laughing. "It feels like forever."

Daisy looked at them, beaming with approval. "Aren't you sweet," she said.

"Very," agreed Mark, releasing Katrinka, who got up but did not move away from him.

"You do know where we're going?" she asked, peering over his shoulder at the chart.

"Yes. And so does the captain. Go and relax." He patted her stomach gently. "Don't worry about a thing. Everything's under control."

"Yes, sir," said Katrinka, happy to leave the day's planning to him.

By the time Katrinka and Daisy returned to the deck, the *Bella Rena* had backed out of its mooring and was heading north along the Côte d'Azur toward the Italian border and San Remo.

It was cool and the humidity was low, but lying in lounge chairs on the deck, out of the wind, it was warm enough to sunbathe. Ignoring the stack of magazines at her side, Katrinka stretched lazily and gazed out at the moving landscape: the limestone cliffs of the southern Alps, plunging from time to time to the sea, creating the coves where the Riviera's tranquil bays and sandy beaches nestled; the lush pine-studded peninsula of Cap Ferrat giving way to the more arid coast near Beaulieu; the village of Eze perched on its hilltop; the omnipresent cranes of Monaco testifying to the boom that crowded more and more buildings into the tiny principality.

"Isn't that Khalid's villa?" asked Daisy at one point as they rounded Cap Martin.

Katrinka looked at the large, white house with its round tower and tiled roof and nodded. They had spent many happy times there before Khalid and Natalie's divorce.

"She's doing all right for herself," called Rick. "The store in Palm Beach is quite a success."

"I did see her there," said Katrinka to Daisy.

"How did she look?"

"Terrible."

The thought of Natalie led almost inevitably to the subject of Jean-Claude Gillette. "Have you heard anything about Jean-Claude and Thea Papastratos?" asked Rick.

"You're on vacation, Rick," said Daisy, with a laugh. "Try to relax."

"You can't blame me for being curious," said Rick, with no animosity.

"We're all curious," said Daisy.

"Not me," said Riccardo. "I have sufficient troubles of my own."

"What troubles?" asked Daisy.

"How to keep you happy, *cara*, for one."

"Jean-Claude's coming to Prague with me next week," said Katrinka.

"Business or pleasure?" asked Rick.

"That's my wife you're talking to," said Mark, with mock severity. "Watch it."

"Will you be going with Katrinka?" asked Rick. After years of being a gossip columnist, he could not, even when on vacation, stop himself from asking questions.

"No," said Mark. "I can't."

"And it's going to be so much fun," said Katrinka. There was to be a reception at Hradčany, the presidential palace. But the rest of her time in Prague would be spent doing business, with and without Jean-Claude. She also wanted to look for a house or apartment to buy, since she hoped that Mark and she would be spending more time there in the future. That was the principal reason she had wanted him to go with her, but anything to do with *The International* took precedence these days over everything else, or so it seemed.

"If I get my business finished in time, I'll join you," said Mark.

"If you need an escort," offered Rick, "you know you can always count on me."

From where he was lying in the bow, Christian heard the laughter, raised his head, looked over at the cheerful group, and frowned. "I don't know how Katrinka stands that guy," he said. Words like "guy" always sounded strange when used by Christian; his English was so formal and correct.

Pia propped herself up on her elbows and said, "Rick? But he's an old friend. Everyone likes him."

"Have you noticed the way he looks at me?"

Pia seemed startled. Then she shook her head. "You mean, you think he finds you attractive?"

"That's one way of putting it," said Christian.

Pia smiled, lifted one arm from the lounge and reached out to stroke his muscled back. "Well, why not? You're very handsome."

"Don't do that!" said Christian sharply.

"Sorry."

"Oh, God," said Christian, with a groan. "I detest it when you sound like that."

"Like what?" asked Pia, her voice small and hurt.

"Like a martyr."

Pia dropped back flat onto her stomach, turned her head away, and fought back tears. There was no point saying anything because it could never be the right thing, not when Christian was in this sort of mood. The mood would pass—it always did—and he would be charming to her again, attentive and loving. But while it lasted it would be hell, leaving her feeling that somehow she had failed him, that she had done something unutterably awful to cause his sudden withdrawal of affection, his silent rage, his icy contempt. All her old insecurities, her old fears came flooding back through the hole in her defenses that she had allowed Christian to make.

Once, Pia had tried to discuss all this with Christian—his withdrawal, the effect it had on her—but he had refused. "I grew up without learning how to love," he said. "Nothing is your fault. Or mine, I suppose. I do the best I can. Like you."

On a trip to Bonn to visit Christian one weekend, Pia had met his parents, Kurt and Luisa Heller. Kurt Heller had officially retired from diplomatic life but continued to serve as a special envoy of the German government to various world trouble spots. The Hellers lived for the most part in Munich, though they spent a portion of each year in their palazzo in Venice and a considerable amount of time at ski resorts around the world. In Bonn not to see their son but on government business, they had taken Christian and her to dinner in the Steigenberger Hotel, where they were staying. The Venusberg restaurant was beautiful, with a view overlooking the hills, and the meal was excellent, but Pia had not enjoyed herself. Under the Hellers' charm, she had sensed a great coldness and a barely concealed disapproval ("dislike," she had thought at one point) of their son. With them, Christian had behaved in a way she had never seen before, going out of his way to shock and offend. And the more he tried to be disagreeable, the less notice the Hellers took of him. The meal had been a nightmare.

After that, Pia had understood a little better Christian's sudden changes of mood, the attacks of anger, the melancholy alternating with euphoria. Nevertheless, they still disturbed her and made her anxious. She no longer knew, if she ever had, how to please him. The more she tried, the less she succeeded. Only when she withdrew from him, when she retreated back inside her shell, did he relent and beg her forgiveness.

Lying next to her, his eyes closed, trying not to notice the annoying babble of conversation coming from the lounges in the stern, Christian wondered what to do about Pia. She was in love with him, desperately in love with him, which was what he had wanted; but, instead of pleased, he felt stifled. She wanted so much more from him than he was willing to give, so much more than he was *able* to give. When he was with her, he wanted only to get away. The longing in her eyes, the mute anguish, the silent reproach, made him feel restless and bored.

Usually, when Christian had reached this point with a girl, he ended the relationship, but he was unwilling to let Pia go. And when they were apart, he was filled with the need to make certain that he had not lost her, that she remained constant and loving, that she worshipped him no matter how little he deserved it.

Sometimes Christian thought he held on because his intimacy with Pia made him feel less isolated, not as love affairs usually do, by weaving separate lonely lives together, but by threading himself into the old bonds that tied Pia to Katrinka. Sometimes he thought it was because no one had ever loved him quite like Pia, with such unselfishness and purity.

Opening his eyes, he saw Pia's head turned away from him, her back stiff, her long legs rigid. He felt nothing coming from her, not love, not anger, not pain. It was as if she had gone away somewhere and left only a shell behind. He felt the small, irritating surge of anxiety her withdrawal always caused him. "Pia," he said softly, and when she did not answer, he sat up, leaned over her, and said again, "Pia, *liebling*."

She turned over onto her back and looked at him. "Are you angry with me?"

"No," she said honestly. It was not anger she had felt, but fear.

"I'm sorry."

"It doesn't matter."

"It does. That crazy homosexual upset me, and I took it out on you."

"You shouldn't mind, Rick," she said. "He's a sweetheart, really. He'd never do anything to hurt you. Or Katrinka."

"Ah, yes," he said. "My sweet mother. How we all long to make her happy."

Sometimes when Christian spoke about Katrinka, there was something approaching admiration in his voice; at other times there was an edge Pia could not quite understand. It wasn't the same sort of coldness she could hear when he spoke about the Hellers; still, it was unpleasant. "Rick wouldn't hurt anyone actually."

Christian leaned forward and kissed her, slipping his hand under the strip of bikini covering her breast and squeezing it gently. "You have such a beautiful body," he said when he lifted his head. "I don't know why you wear this thing. Everyone on the Riviera goes topless."

"Not Daisy and your mother."

"They would if they looked like you," he said, leaning down to kiss her again.

The captain radioed ahead for permission to dock at the marina in San Remo, and, when the *Bella Rena* was safely moored, the passengers went ashore, had lunch in one of the port restaurants, made a brief side trip to buy the pesto that Katrinka's chef would use on the pasta appetizer that night, and then reembarked. After about an hour, at Mark's request, the *Bella Rena* again came to a shuddering halt. The anchor was dropped, and Mark, as if to demonstrate that he really did have Viking blood, ordered the Zodiac and fifteen-foot Boston whaler to be dropped. He and Riccardo and Rick, Pia and Christian donned wetsuits and water-skied for a while, but Riccardo, who had enormous tolerance for cold on the ski slopes, hated it in the water, and gave up, followed quickly by Pia, Rick, and then Mark, who knew Christian would never stop until he did. As her son climbed aboard, Katrinka picked up a towel from the stack the steward had set out and, as he took off his wetsuit, told him to turn around so that she could rub his back dry. It was not often that she got an opportunity to touch him and she could not resist. "That's how cold the pool was in the gym in Svitov, when I was a kid. I did swim all the time. And did I hate it!" she said, smiling happily.

Christian turned, took the towel from her hand, said thank you, and kissed her cheek.

Katrinka felt her heart stop for a moment. Christian usually did not offer spontaneous signs of affection. *"Miláčku,"* she murmured, touching his wet, dark hair, so like her own. "You water-ski very well."

"Not as well as Mark," he admitted grudgingly.

"Thanks for the compliment," said Mark, pretending not to notice the resentment in it. "You've made an old man very happy."

"Old man," said Riccardo. "Listen to him. Wait until you turn sixty."

"Gladly," said Mark. "As long as I can."

Katrinka laughed with the others, relieved that Mark and Riccardo both knew how to deal with an awkward moment. That son of hers, he was like a great dark cloud, seizing every opportunity to blot out the sunshine.

The equipment was stowed and the *Bella Rena* weighed anchor, while her passengers, served strong drinks or cups of steaming coffee, tried to get warm again.

"I'm going to change," said Pia.

"Wait, I'll go with you," said Christian, following Pia below.

Katrinka watched them for a moment, allowing herself to feel pleased at the way things were going. Maybe, hopefully, she had been wrong and Christian would not make the poor girl miserable.

What a beautiful young man, thought Rick with a pang. And a real prick. Nothing but trouble. "They make a great-looking couple."

"Oh, to be young," said Daisy.

Mark sat in the lounge chair. "I'm exactly the age I want to be," he said, pulling Katrinka down on top of him. "Hmm, keep me warm," he murmured, kissing the back of her neck.

By five that afternoon, all the guests at the Villa Mahmed were back in their luxurious bedrooms. Margo was polishing her nails a brilliant shade of red; Daisy and Riccardo were napping; Christian and Pia were making love; Mark was on the phone with his New York office; and Katrinka was relaxing in a bubble bath that splashed over the sides of the tiled tub every time she moved.

"Was there any mail today?" asked Mark when he had finished his call.

Katrinka opened her eyes and saw him standing in the doorway. He was wearing a terry cloth robe and his hair was wet from the shower he had taken a short while before. "None did I see. Ask Anna." He turned to go, but Katrinka stopped him. "What you do think about Pia and Christian?"

"Like Rick said: they're very good-looking."

"And?"

He came back into the bathroom and leaned against the wall, looking down at her, his eyes serious. "Why don't you just tell me what it is that's bothering you."

"I worry that they'll hurt each other." She looked at him questioningly.

"Katrinka, I know you think I can do anything. And it's very flattering, baby. But I have to confess that foretelling the future is not one of my talents."

"Tell me what you think," she insisted. She was not going to let him off the hook.

"I think that Pia is crazy about Christian. I think that Christian is flattered to have such a beautiful woman in love with him. I think it will probably end with Pia heartbroken and Christian consoling himself with someone else." That's as honest as he was prepared to be.

"That's what I did think at first," said Katrinka, nodding in agreement. "But now I'm not so sure."

"Well, in this case, I'd be happy to be wrong." Katrinka opened her mouth to speak, then closed it again without saying a word. "What?" said Mark.

"Nothing." She had been going to ask if Mark liked Christian, but had decided it was pointless. If he did, that was wonderful; if he didn't, she really did not want to know, at least not right now.

"I'm going to see about that mail," said Mark, turning away.

As Katrinka picked up the hand shower to wash her hair, she could hear Mark's voice from the bedroom, talking to Anna on the house phone. When she had finished, she climbed out of the tub, wrapped herself in a large white towel, dried her hair, then slipped into a silk robe. As she entered the bedroom, there was a knock at the door. Mark was lying on the bed, talking on the phone, to London this time. All around him were scattered the usual faxes, newspapers, files. "Come in," she called.

The door opened and a white-jacketed footman stood on the threshold. "The mail, madame," he said, in his accented English, offering her the small stack he carried.

"Thank you," said Katrinka, taking it from him. "Will you let everyone know dinner is at nine?"

"Yes, madame," he said, and left, closing the heavy carved-wood door behind him.

Katrinka rifled through the mail, sorting hers from Mark's. Most of it had been forwarded from their various offices, nothing urgent or it would have been sent by Federal Express. There were what looked like invitations from local addresses, including one from Lynn Wyatt, the Houston socialite who had a villa nearby. Katrinka recognized Zuzka's handwriting on one envelope, but another, a square-shaped lavender one, heavily scented, was addressed in a sloping feminine hand that wasn't familiar to her. There was a second similar envelope addressed to Mark. Neither had a return address.

"Phew," said Katrinka, when Mark finished his call. She handed him his stack of mail, the lavender envelope on top, and sat on the bed next to him. "If I didn't get one, too, I would think someone is writing you love letters."

"Who are they from?" asked Mark.

"The stamp is English, but there's no address on the envelope," said Katrinka, tearing hers open. She began to read, but at first none of it made sense to her. Then, as she began to understand, the color drained from her face. She felt dizzy, as if she was about to faint.

Mark, who had ignored the lavender envelope to open the mail from his New York office, looked up when he heard Katrinka cry out. "What is it?" he said. He took one look at her face and grabbed the sheet of lavender paper from her hand. "What does it say?"

"It's terrible."

Mark scanned it quickly. "Jesus Christ," he muttered, turning almost as pale as his wife. "It's not true," he said, when he reached the end. "Katrinka, none of it is true."

"Why she would write something like that?"

Dear Katrinka, the letter said, *I feel I can call you that because I feel I know you so well from all that Mark has told me about you. This is such a difficult letter for me to write, you have to believe that, and I know it will be a difficult one for you to read. But I have no choice. I'm in agony. I love your husband. And he loves me. He has told me so over and over. He has given me no reason to doubt him. But now he is refusing to see me because, out of guilt, out of pity, he feels he cannot leave you while you are pregnant. I understand his feelings, and I wish I could do as he asks and simply wait quietly until after the baby is born. But it is such torment to be without him, to love him and not be able to see him, to touch him. You have so much, Katrinka. You're successful, rich, beautiful. But I have nothing, nothing but him.*

It went on like that for two pages, giving dates and details of their meetings. It recounted an incident, in London, when she had helped Mark choose a cashmere sweater for Katrinka, and how, when he saw she was upset at his leaving to return to New York, he had bought her one as well, in the same style and color. It was signed Monica Brand.

"It's not true," insisted Mark. "Katrinka, I swear it."

257

"But why?"

"Because she's crazy. I don't know. I don't care. I just want you not to believe her. Katrinka, please . . ." He reached to pull her into his arms, but she resisted him.

"What yours does say?" she asked, her voice flat.

Mark hesitated, tempted for a moment to destroy his letter without reading it. But that would solve nothing. Katrinka was capable of imagining worse than anything she would read in it. He tore the envelope open, took out the sheet of lavender paper, read it quickly, then handed it to her.

Mark, darling, it said. *How can you do this to me? How can you do this to us? Love like ours doesn't happen every day. It's never happened to me before, nor to you either, if I can believe what you told me. And I do, I do believe it, my darling, with all my heart. Which is why I will fight to keep you, no matter how wrong you think I am, because I know that nothing in life is worse, that there is no greater sin, than to betray the love two people have for each other.*

Again it went on, the lavender sheet covered front and back with dates, times, places, incidents, recalled in loving and intimate detail.

As she read, tears she was not aware of poured down Katrinka's face in a constant stream. Never in her life had she read anything so terrible.

"Tell me you believe me," said Mark, when she had finished the letter.

"Is it true about the cashmere sweater?" she asked.

Wanting desperately to lie, Mark hesitated, but then he said, "Partly. It was after our lunch in London. The one we had to discuss her coming to work for me. Afterward, I mentioned that I wanted to buy you a present before leaving for the airport. She suggested a shop in the Burlington Arcade, which was nearby, and volunteered to come with me. She helped me choose the sweater, that's all. We said good-bye at the exit to the arcade, I got in the car, went to the airport, and got on the plane."

"You didn't buy her a sweater?"

"Of course not," said Mark impatiently. "And if I had, it wouldn't have meant a damn thing except that I felt sorry for her."

"How she does know all those things about you and me?"

Mark shook his head. "I don't know," he said.

"Oh, God," she said, the words leaving her mouth in a wail.

"Katrinka, baby." Mark reached for her again, and this time succeeded in pulling her to him. He lifted her into his lap and cradled her against his chest. "Baby, I love you. You've got to know that. What she said is all lies."

"You never made love to her?"

"Never. I swear it." Waves of emotion surged through him, concern for Katrinka, guilt at allowing himself, even for a moment, to think Monica Brand was attractive, anger at being placed in this situation. "Jesus Christ," he said, "how could you think I would do something like that to you?"

If she hadn't been so upset, she might have laughed. How? The same way Adam Graham had. And Steven Elliott. And Ted Jensen. All of them had seemed like loving husbands. All of them had betrayed their wives. Behavior like that did not encourage trust.

When Katrinka didn't answer, Adam went on, "I'm not saying that I would never give in to temptation. Circumstances change. People are weak. *Men* are weak. They're at the mercy of their cocks a lot of the time, not their heads. And I'm not a fucking saint, for Christ's sake. But right now, I have no interest in anyone but you. I love you. And if I did ever cheat on you, baby, I'd tell you. I'd have to. I'm not a liar."

The shuddering sobs stopped, and then the tears. Katrinka lifted her head and reached for a Kleenex, wiped her nose and eyes, then rested her head again on Mark's chest.

"Do you believe me?" he asked.

"Yes," she said. It occurred to her that she was quite possibly being a terrible fool, but nevertheless she did believe him.

He took her head in his hands and raised it so that he could see her eyes. "You're sure?"

She nodded. "Yes," she repeated.

He lowered his hands and picked up the letters, tore them to bits, and put the pieces on the bedside table. "If she pulls another stunt like this," he said, "I swear I'll strangle the bitch."

Twenty-Three

IN HER ENTIRE LIFE, KATRINKA HAD BEEN TOTALLY OPEN ONLY WITH MARK, AND THOUGH, SINCE MEETING HIM, she had become a little more candid with her friends, still she did not confide easily in anyone, especially when she was troubled. Then, her instinct was to smile, to work, to carry on as if everything were perfectly fine, while her mind searched for solutions to the problem.

Not that she considered Monica Brand a real problem. She believed Mark. But would her friends? She could imagine the looks on their faces should she tell them about the scented lavender letters, about the accusations in them and Mark's denials. When their own husbands and lovers had proven to be such liars, how would they be able to accept that hers was not? And, when they remembered how easily she had been deceived by Adam Graham, Katrinka's own confidence in Mark would count for nothing. Not wanting to have to fight their doubts as well as her own, she kept quiet.

And she did have doubts—small, insubstantial, fleeting, but doubts nonetheless. No matter how honest a husband or trusting a wife, dismissing a direct accusation of infidelity was not easy. It took a lot of courage, a lot of resolution, and a total disregard for the laws of probability.

So Katrinka bathed her eyes in cold water, put on makeup, and went down smiling to join her friends for cocktails in the Villa Mahmed's sitting room. Mark, who had the successful businessman's ability to bluff through a meeting, also seemed relaxed and good-humored. Anyone who caught him, at dinner, throwing an occasional, anxious glance down the table toward Katrinka wrote it off as the normal anxiety of any loving husband for a very pregnant wife. Whatever dark clouds hovered in the air were firmly fixed over Margo's head. Even Christian seemed to be in an unusually good mood.

Early on the Monday after Easter, the villa began to empty of guests. Christian left for Bonn, Rick for Paris, and Pia set off with Daisy and Riccardo, in their car, for Florence. Later in the day, the van Hollens' chauffeur drove Margo the half hour to her home in Monte Carlo, supposedly to pick up the last of her clothes. She phoned Katrinka the next morning. Sounding exhausted but hopeful, Margo told her that Ted and she had agreed to a reconciliation. "I walked in," she said, "and his mouth dropped open. He told me I looked terrific. The fool doesn't even realize I've had surgery. He thinks being away from him took years off my life! That's given him food for thought, I can tell you."

Mark had also intended to leave on Monday but postponed his departure so that he could have some time alone with Katrinka. Never had he been so reluctant to leave her, not even in the first days of their relationship when he had been far from sure of her, or later when their passion had reached such a level of frenzy that even a separation of a few hours had felt like an eternity to both of them. Though the passion was still there, the frenzy had gone, leaving in its place a comforting sense of security. Or so he had thought. The letters from Monica Brand had hurt his marriage, just how much he was not yet sure, but certainly the unquestioning trust that had been its basis was gone. Now, there were plenty of questions and, until they were answered, he did not like the idea of being away from Katrinka.

But both of them had commitments elsewhere. Mark's presence was required in London, not only to sort out some of the expected early problems with *The International*, but because van Hollen stock had started creeping up in price again, which meant that another takeover attempt was in progress. And Katrinka had business in Prague that could not, in her opinion, be postponed.

So, when the last of their guests had gone, Mark and Katrinka spent what remained of the day by the pool, then in the cloister, sitting on the carved wooden benches that lined the tile walls, looking out over the sea. Monica Brand's name was not mentioned, though the thought of her intruded from time to time, causing brief lapses in the conversation, until one or the other would introduce another topic: who might be trying to acquire VHE, how to run a business in Prague from New York, what to name the baby, what to do about Christian.

"Why do we have to do anything about Christian?" asked Mark, who considered Katrinka's son more than able to fend for himself.

"He will get his degree next month."

"Yes. And with a PhD in Economics from Bonn University, he ought to be able to get a job anywhere he wants, in Germany at least."

"But what he wants is to come to New York."

"He wants that, or you do?"

"Both of us."

"He's told you?" asked Mark, still not sure whether or not it was wishful thinking on Katrinka's part. Christian's wishes, and his motives, were often hard to figure out.

"He didn't ask. You know what he's like. But he did mention how Neil Goodman is helping Martin Havlíček."

So much had been going on in his own life that Mark had understandably forgotten all about Martin. "Wasn't he supposed to have a meeting with Neil sometime soon?"

Katrinka nodded. "Last Thursday. And Neil did offer him a job at Knapp Manning, starting in June." Zuzka had phoned for advice about her escalating battle with Carla and had told Katrinka the news about Martin. She was upset about that, too, not wanting Martin to move so far away.

"And you told Christian."

Katrinka nodded. "Then I did offer him a job, but he turned it down. He's not interested in hotels."

Although he was certain he was not going to like the answer, Mark asked, "What is he interested in?"

Katrinka smiled. "Newspapers."

Mark did not return the smile. "What's it about newspapers he finds so fascinating?"

"Not the newspapers themselves," explained Katrinka, "but van Hollen Enterprises. It's a big, multinational corporation. You own newspapers, publishing houses, printing plants all over the world. You see how appealing that would be to someone as ambitious as Christian."

"Yes," said Mark, who did indeed see.

"I have only three hotels. So far." She smiled again. "I can't compete with you."

Mark stared out at the horizon line, watching as the bright orange ball sank slowly into the sea. He did not want Christian working for him. He did not (and he was almost ashamed to admit it, even to himself) like Christian. Nor did he trust him. And though Mark was certain Katrinka would not hold a refusal against him, at that moment he felt the need to do anything in his power to make his wife happy. And giving Christian a job, getting him to New York, was something she would appreciate far more than the sapphire necklace he had planned to buy her as soon as he reached London. "All right," he said. "But it won't be a big job, you understand. I'm not going to start him anywhere near the top."

"Of course not," said Katrinka indignantly. "That would be very bad for him. He's spoiled enough."

"One other thing . . ."

Katrinka turned her head so that she could see his eyes. "What?"

"He can't live with us. You can rent him a place, buy him one, anything you like . . ."

Katrinka understood immediately that it was a non-negotiable condition; and as much as she wanted to keep Christian as near to her as possible, she knew that Mark was right. "We'll buy something, I think. I can decorate it for him. I would love to do that."

Having won the most important point, Mark decided not to argue that one.

Neither wanted to go out that evening for fear of running into someone they knew, so they dined in the villa's candle-lit dining room on trout bought fresh that morning in the village. Afterward, in the study, lying on the wide, comfortable divan that Lady Marina, the villa's original owner, had imported from Morocco, they watched television for a while, until the end of the "CNN World Report." Then they went to bed and made love.

"Don't stay away too long," said Mark, afterward, as they lay quietly in each other's arms.

"Just to the end of the week," said Katrinka.

"Do you want me to wait for you in London?"

"If you can. Then we can fly home together."

"I'll try," he said, hoping that nothing would come up in the next few days requiring him to be elsewhere.

"I love you," she said, then turned away from him so that they could nestle together spoon-fashion without her stomach getting in the way.

Mark moved in close to her, until her bottom pressed against his stomach and his left hand rested on the large mound jutting out in front of her. Then, as he drifted off to sleep, the baby moved and jolted him awake. As always, he was filled with love, and awe, and terror. He kissed the back of Katrinka's neck. "I'll wait for you in London," he promised.

Completely at odds with the beautiful city it serviced, Prague's air terminal was a large, barnlike structure with no distinguishing features beyond its complete utilitarian blandness. Still, as Katrinka entered through the electric doors into the central lounge, she felt a surge of pleasure having nothing to do with the badly dressed people seated at the many bars eating sausages and drinking beer while waiting for their flights to be called, or the long line at the currency exchange where unsmiling bureaucrats changed foreign money into Czech crowns for arriving tourists and reversed the procedure for those departing. Though she never regretted leaving Czechoslovakia, returning always made her happy.

Since she was being met by a hired car and could change money later when it was more convenient, Katrinka avoided the line at the exchange, went through passport control, and continued on to collect her baggage, letting one of the attendants hoist her two Vuitton cases onto the trolley provided and pushing it herself into one of the tiny cubicles where a single stern customs inspector checked baggage. Katrinka held a U.S. passport and she was ushered through quickly, with no problems, after a brief flurry of Czech conversation. Tourism was an important and growing industry and people able to spend hard currency were most welcome.

Her driver was waiting immediately beyond customs together with one of the aides who had accompanied the mayor on his trip to the States. Both recognized her immediately. If not the only well-dressed woman arriving, she was by far the most distinctive, in a short chartreuse balloon coat, the only spot of bright color in the place. The aide, a tall, slender man with light brown hair and wire-rimmed spectacles, smiled as they shook hands, then relieved her of the Vuitton bag that held her files as the driver took over the trolley and continued pushing it toward the exit.

On the trip from the airport to the hotel, the aide ran through her schedule for the next few days, but Katrinka's attention was focused on the landscape, and she paid little attention. "Everything is written down?" she asked finally.

"Oh, yes, of course," he assured her.

"Good," said Katrinka.

The highway from the airport passed through the usual flat, dull industrial landscape common to all airports in all cities. But soon the "thousand" spires of Prague could be seen in the distance, and shortly after that the car crossed the Vltava River and drove along the cobbled embankment toward the hotel. The memories, as always, came flooding back. On the left was Charles Bridge, one of the most beautiful in the world, a Gothic structure lined with baroque statues (mostly reproductions of the weather-damaged sandstone originals) and a tower at either end. As a student at Charles University, Katrinka had lived not far from there, in a small house in a narrow street in the Malá Strana. Her son, Christian, had been conceived in that house.

On the right, a little farther on, was the National Theater, and, across the street from it, the Maxmilianka café, where Katrinka had introduced Zuzka and Tomáš, where Mirek Bartoš, Christian's father, had recognized her face from a magazine cover and offered her a part in a movie. How much time they had all spent there, talking, laughing, singing, drinking beer. Until the death of her parents and her decision to give Christian up for adoption, her life had been a very happy one.

A few doors down from the Maxmilianka was FAMU, the film school Tomáš had attended. For a brief period before the Russian invasion of 1968, FAMU had revolutionized the Czech movie industry. Films by Forman and Menzel, Passer and Kadar, had been acclaimed throughout the world, and the hope of one day achieving the same kind of artistic success had obsessed Tomáš. No wonder he was so miserable making exploitation films, thought Katrinka, as her car, caught in heavy traffic, drove slowly past, and she peered through the building's open door into its dark, shabby lobby. The "F" was missing from the hanging brass letters spelling out the school's name.

"That's FAMU," said the aide helpfully.

"Yes, yes, I know," said Katrinka, turning to him with a smile. "I went to university here in Prague."

The car turned into Curieových Square and drove around its perimeter until it came to a stop in front of the Intercontinental Hotel. A large, nondescript modern building, it was far from the most beautiful hotel in Prague, but it was comfortable, offering every modern convenience including good water pressure. It catered to the international business set, who were coming to Prague in droves, with and without the government's specific invitation, to assess Czechoslovakia's investment potential, to determine how helping the Czech recovery could line their own corporate pockets. The hotel's service was of high quality, surprising to those expecting it to live up to the usual surly Eastern block standard.

The aide accompanied Katrinka into the hotel and turned her over to the manager, who checked her in and escorted her to her suite. Not only was he familiar to her from past visits, but he came from the same part of Moravia as she and they knew many of the same people. "If anything is not to your liking," he said as he opened the door and let her precede him inside, "please let me know." The suite was attractively furnished, scrupulously clean, and the bathroom was well stocked with soaps and lotions, shampoo and facial tissue, the sort of things that make guests feel as if they are being treated royally. It also had the only hot tub in the hotel. She was certain everything would be fine, Katrinka assured him, and he smiled as they shook hands. "We checked the Jacuzzi before you arrived to make sure it was in good working order," he said as he left. "Enjoy your stay."

Half an hour in a hot tub was just what she needed, but that, with alcohol, was banned during pregnancy, so she would settle for a bath, decided Katrinka, whose body had acquired unfamiliar aches and pains in the past few weeks. She turned on the water, but, before undressing, returned to the sitting room to read the cards on the three flower arrangements that had been awaiting her. One was from the mayor, another from Jean-Claude. The third was from Mark. "I miss you already," said the card. Except for addressing his "to the adorable Katrinka," Jean-Claude's card was much more pragmatic. "Call me," it said, which meant that he had already arrived in Prague.

Later, thought Katrinka, as she began stripping off her clothes.

Jean-Claude was also staying at the Intercontinental, and as soon as she was dressed and ready, Katrinka phoned his room and coaxed him into accompanying her to see the hotel she was in the process of buying. It was located not far from Vaćlav Square, one of the city's main tourist attractions. A little larger than her other hotels—just over a hundred rooms—it had an eye-catching baroque exterior badly in need of repair and an interior requiring extensive renovation. As soon as the final papers were signed, which Katrinka hoped would be before her departure from Prague, she and Carlos would set to work.

An astute businessman who had parlayed his family's vineyards into a multinational corporation, Jean-Claude was quick to see the possibilities. The building undoubtedly had charm, and, having witnessed the amazing transformations that Katrinka and Carlos had wrought on other properties, he did not doubt that they would soon transform this seedy little hotel into a small jewel. About his own part in Katrinka's plans, he was not quite so sure.

"I agree, *chérie*," he said, "the hotel is certainly lovely—at least it will be—but I don't see why you need me."

She did not, really. But part of the commitment she had made to the

Czech government was to help attract investment money into the country, and Jean-Claude was not someone who normally would have thought of expanding in that direction. "I don't know if *need* is the right word, Jean-Claude," she said honestly. "But I think it could be very good for both of us."

"Ouff," he said with Gallic disdain as they came out again into the street, looking disapprovingly at the passersby in their dowdy clothes, "I don't know who in this city would buy anything I'd care to sell."

Katrinka laughed. "Japanese businessmen to start with, for their wives. And Germans and Americans. Maybe even a few Czechs. Some have money, you know."

Over dinner that night, Katrinka continued trying to persuade Jean-Claude of the wisdom of her idea to open both clothing and specialty food boutiques in the Ambassador. Initially, he would capitalize on the same business and tourist trade as she, Katrinka explained, but eventually, as the economy improved, he could expand into other parts of the city and perhaps even to Brno and Bratislava. By then, not only would he get preferential treatment from the government because of his initial early investment, but his name would be known to consumers. "And so," she finished, "you get a big head start on all your competitors."

Jean-Claude laughed. "So, *chérie,* you are suggesting this expensive and risky scheme all for my benefit?"

"It's not risky," she said. "Not long-term. The economy here will improve, if enough seed money is invested."

"I thought Americans only cared about the short-term?" he teased.

That made Katrinka laugh. "You know, Jean-Claude," she said, "at heart I am just a thrifty European housewife, planning for the future."

They were dining in the Golden Prague, the Intercontinental's penthouse restaurant with its exquisite view of slanting tile roofs, baroque cupolas, Gothic spires. As they talked the vibrant colors of the city, the sands and roses, the ochres and greens, gradually faded while the sky deepened in color to an intense midnight blue, against which the buildings, when the lights went on, shone like a fairy city made of gold. "Oh, look," said Katrinka, who never tired of the sight. "Look how beautiful it is."

"Very," said Jean-Claude, his eyes never leaving her face.

"Oh," she laughed, when she turned back to him. "You're impossible."

But in fact Jean-Claude was not in his usual flirtatious mode. For him, he was on very good behavior, and Katrinka was certain that Thea Papastratos was responsible for it.

Jean-Claude himself brought up that subject, once Katrinka had decided it was politic to let the matter of the boutiques rest awhile, and after she had firmly refused to discuss Natalie. "Why don't you and Mark come to Kentucky in May?" asked Jean-Claude. "Thea has a horse running in the Derby. You can stay with us, at the farm." Thea owned a stud farm there as well as one in England and another in Ireland. "By the way, we are thinking of forming a syndicate to buy another. Would you be interested?"

"Right now, I am only interested in hotels." She patted her stomach. "And babies. But if I can, I would love to see Kentucky."

"Good," said Jean-Claude. "I want you and Thea to be great friends."

Based on her few encounters so far with Thea Papastratos, Katrinka thought that unlikely. But she nodded agreeably. "That would be very nice," she said, with a polite smile.

"Thea was planning to come with me, you know," he volunteered. His shoulders lifted in a typical French shrug. "But one of her prize mares is about to foal."

"She thinks there will be a problem?"

"No. No more than usual, that is. But she is anticipating great things from this foal, and she wanted to see it immediately. Thea is not a very patient woman. Anticipation does not add to her pleasure."

"To put up with you she must have a great deal of patience."

Jean-Claude did not smile in response to Katrinka's teasing. "Whatever she had is gone . . . pouf . . . *fini.*" He sat staring at the view for a moment and then added, "She is threatening to leave me."

"And you don't want her to?"

"No."

"You love her?"

"Love," said Jean-Claude. Again he shrugged. "I suppose so." Once, when she had asked him that same question about Natalie, Jean-Claude had responded with a great deal more enthusiasm. "We have many interests in common. We enjoy a lot of the same things. Thea is a beautiful, interesting woman. I'm happy . . . well, content, when I am with her. And miserable when I am not. Is that love?"

"It could be."

"But not necessarily. You see my problem. All I know for certain is that I have no intention of losing her."

Which meant that Jean-Claude really was going to divorce Hélène, something he had not considered for a moment even when he was most in love with Natalie, even when she was pregnant with his child.

But then, thought Katrinka cynically, whatever her other attractions, Natalie had not been a Greek heiress.

The next few days were hectic for Katrinka. She delivered a lecture, entitled "The Entrepreneurial Way to Success," to a small group of businessmen from all over the country. Working with a small committee, whose formation she had discussed with the mayor during his New York visit, she helped draft plans for seminars to be led by the world's most knowledgeable business people, part of whose commitment would be to remain involved with the project as consultants. Designed to teach the basics of running a business, the seminars were to be a sort of short course for those without the time or money to get MBAs from Wharton or Harvard. It was a project that everyone, including Katrinka, was very excited about.

Additionally, she spent hours with lawyers and government officials discussing the contract for the purchase of the new hotel. Dragging Jean-Claude along, she went house-hunting, and put in an offer for a large apartment with a view overlooking the Petřín Gardens. She also took him gallery-hopping, encouraging him to buy paintings by Czech artists as she was doing. The pleasure of Jean-Claude's company aside, it was a way to familiarize him with the wonders of the city, to help him understand its many possibilities. And she made sure, as well, that he met all the most important government and business people in Prague. Her tactic succeeded. By the night of the reception, not only had he agreed to open boutiques in the Ambassador, he was beginning to talk optimistically about expanding, as if it were his own idea.

Jean-Claude was Katrinka's escort for the night and, while he was perhaps not as taken with the extraordinary beauty of the castle as Katrinka herself, he announced himself duly impressed. Begun in the tenth century, Hradčany had, over the years, incorporated almost every architectural style into its construction. Within its massive walls were a Romanesque church, Gothic cathedral, renaissance palazzo, medieval alley, and baroque palace. Its multicolored buildings shone in daylight with a lustrous patina; and at night, under the lights, it took on a golden glow. Like Venice, it often seemed too beautiful to be real.

The president's official residence was within the castle walls, and though Václav Havel himself preferred to live quite modestly and dress in T-shirt and jeans, as a dramatist he understood the need for spectacle in public life. Immediately upon taking office, he had redesigned the uniforms of the castle's guards and had begun extensive renovations on its many buildings, including the palace, once a royal residence, where the reception was held. The food was excellent, as was the music, two orchestras playing Strauss waltzes and Czech polkas. The guests included government officials, foreign ambassadors, important businessmen, artists, and the country's leading intellectuals, as well as the president himself. Havel seemed, Katrinka thought, quite tense, as who wouldn't be given the growing Slovakian nationalism and the National Assembly's increasing resistance to his programs? Still he smiled and expressed optimism, complimented Katrinka on her gown (the same "flamboyant" one she had worn in Palm Beach), and thanked her for all she was doing. That pleased her more than anything.

"Will he last?" asked Jean-Claude when their conversation with the president ended.

"The people are becoming impatient. They admire him, they know he's a good man, but there's less work and more crime. Not a good combination." Then, preferring as always to look on the bright side, Katrinka smiled, adding, "If the economy begins to improve, yes."

"The eternal optimist," said Jean-Claude.

She looked around her at the beautiful long hall with its delicate Gothic vaulting, at the well-dressed smiling people, all of whom had enormous power to do good—if they wished—and her smile broadened. "Why not? Who knows what can happen when people try? Certainly when I was a student here in Prague, I did never think I would see Czechoslovakia free. I did never dream that one night I would dance in the presidential palace."

"Is that an invitation?" said Jean-Claude.

"Oh, yes," said Katrinka. "I do love to dance."

The next day there were photographs of the reception in all the local newspapers, many of them featuring Katrinka. And as she continued her busy schedule, she found that as well as the curious glances her haute couture clothes and stylish good looks usually attracted, she was greeted with the same surprised and welcoming smiles as in New York or London or St. Moritz. Katrinka smiled back, returned greetings in Czech, and hurried on. She was trying desperately to get everything done in time to meet Mark in London by Saturday, at the latest.

They spoke every day, once and twice a day. "Are you getting enough rest?" he asked.

"Yes," she lied. She was not napping at all, and was sleeping, at the most, five hours a night. "Don't worry so much."

"I know you," he said.

"Tomorrow I sign the papers for the hotel," she said, changing the subject. "The ones for the apartment can be sent to us in New York. I want you to see it, *miláčku*. It's large and full of light, with such pretty views."

"So you can leave tomorrow afternoon or Saturday morning?"

"Absolutely."

"Let me know what time you're arriving. I'll send the car to meet you," he said. "Better yet, I'll come myself."

"I can't wait."

"Neither can I. I miss you."

"Dobrou noc, miláčku."

" 'Bye, baby. See you soon."

Feeling that same reluctance as always to end the call, Katrinka waited until she heard the line go dead before hanging up the receiver. But no sooner had she put it back in its cradle than it rang again.

"Katrinka? Katrinka? Is that you?" said a voice she did not recognize. It was a woman, speaking Czech.

"Yes. Who is it?"

"You don't know me. That is, we've never met. I'm Zuzanka, Mirek's daughter."

Oh, yes, thought Katrinka. Zuzanka. The film director. "Oh, Zuzanka, hello. How are you?" she said, since nothing else came to mind.

"I saw your photo in the papers this morning. My father saw it, too, somehow. His nurse showed him, I think. I . . . I know this is a great deal to ask, but he would like to see you. I told him how busy you were, but he insisted that I call to ask if you would come. I couldn't refuse. Katrinka . . . he's dying."

Dying? But, of course, Mirek was an old man now, not the handsome, robust fifty-year-old who lived in her memory. "Of course I'll come," said Katrinka, flooded with nostalgia, pity, regret, and an overwhelming sadness. "The first thing tomorrow. Tell me where."

Twenty-Four

After a night of restless sleep, Katrinka rose early, showered, dressed, then sat at the writing table in the suite's sitting room, sipping tea, trying to focus her attention on her notes for an eleven o'clock meeting, waiting impatiently for it to be time for her to leave to visit Mirek. Finally, the antique clock on the mantel registered eight-forty and she picked up her purse, slung a light coat over her arm, and went down to the lobby where her driver was waiting for her.

Mirek had lung cancer; he had been in and out of the hospital for the past several months, his daughter had explained, but now, since there was nothing left to do but wait for the end, he was at home being cared for by his children and the elderly housekeeper who had been with the Bartošes for years.

Katrinka had not needed directions to the apartment. As her car pulled to a stop in the wide boulevard, in front of the large art nouveau apartment building not far from Charles Square, she remembered the time when, shortly after she and Mirek had become lovers, she had driven past slowly in her little blue Fiat. She had wanted to know exactly where it was he went each time he left her in the middle of the night to "go home." The experience had been painful, and she had never repeated it.

The concierge announced her and Katrinka rode up in the elegant etched-glass elevator to the sixth floor. As she emerged into the corridor, Katrinka saw the door to an apartment open and a woman on the threshold beckon to her. She wore a long full skirt and a blouse with a Peter Pan collar. Tall and broad with graying dark hair and large brown eyes, she was unmistakably Mirek's daughter. *"Dobrý den,"* she said, extending her hand to shake Katrinka's. "Come in. I'm so pleased you would come," she continued in Czech. "I'm Zuzanka." In her worried face, Katrinka, to her surprise, caught fleeting glimpses of Christian.

Her brother and sister-in-law, who lived with Mirek, had left for work, explained Zuzanka. She had just finished editing her last film and was not yet preparing her next, so she had more time to spend with her father during the day. Her children, one of whom was at Charles University, the other at FAMU, stopped by to see him between classes. "There's not a lot we can do now but be with him," she told Katrinka. Her mother, who had suffered a stroke several years before, had died nine months ago.

"I'm sorry," said Katrinka.

Zuzanka shrugged. "It was time. Her life was terrible. But still it's hard."

"Yes," agreed Katrinka.

"Would you like some coffee? Tea?" asked Zuzanka.

"No, thank you," said Katrinka, shaking her head. "If I could see him?"

"Yes, yes, of course," said Zuzanka. She led Katrinka along the hallway, past the dining room, sitting room, study, giving Katrinka glimpses of the life she had wondered about so often. As Mirek had told her, the apartment was full of treasures he had accumulated on the trips that he made abroad to promote his popular films: French and Bavarian porcelain, Italian furniture, Venetian glass, Swiss clocks. Seeing Katrinka's eyes taking it all in, Zuzanka said, "My father always came home from abroad with crates full of contraband." Then she blushed. "But of course you knew that." However discreet her parents had tried to be, somehow Zuzanka and her brother had always found out about their lovers.

Katrinka nodded but said nothing. Mirek had brought her stylish French dresses, perfumes, makeup, American jeans, a Swiss watch. He had got away with his large-scale smuggling not just because he was the country's leading popular film director, responsible for earning large amounts of hard currency, but because his wife's father held a high position in the Czech secret police.

Zuzanka opened the door into a large bedroom, full of art nouveau furniture, the rich wood gleaming in the soft morning light filtering through the lace curtains. The large bed with its carved tulip motif dominated the room, and, lying amid its embroidered white cotton sheets, Mirek Bartoš looked very small and frail. As she drew close to him, Katrinka had to fight back tears. Mirek's sex appeal had come not just from his obvious charm but from his size, his power, his enormous energy. It was awful to see the toll that life had taken.

The housekeeper, who was sitting in a chair beside the bed, got up as Katrinka approached, nodded in greeting, and moved out of the way. On the far side, standing where a night table should have been, was a tank of oxygen with a tube connecting it to the device in Mirek's nose. It was the only piece of medical equipment in the room.

Katrinka stood looking down at him a moment. His cheeks were sunken, his skin like ancient parchment stretched over his bones. "Mirek," she said softly.

Slowly, his eyes flickered open and stared at her blankly. Then he smiled. *"Miláčku,"* he said. "You came." His voice was hesitant, labored.

"Of course," she said.

"Sit," he commanded, and Katrinka sat in the chair the housekeeper had vacated and took his hand. "You look more beautiful than ever."

"Don't talk," she said.

He nodded. "Tell me everything."

Katrinka told him what she was doing in Prague, about the hotel and the apartment and the committee she was so excited about. She brought him up to date on Tomáš, who had been his protegé, describing what she could remember of the film he was trying to convince Adam to make, telling him about Tomáš's remarriage and the new baby.

His eyes flickered open again and he looked at her. "And you, *miláčku?* You're pregnant?"

Her A-line dress was cut so full, she thought perhaps he had not noticed. "Yes," she said.

His eyes filled with tears. "I regret . . . so much . . . still."

"It's all right," she said reassuringly. "Mirek, I've found him. It's all right." She felt his fingers squeeze hers and she saw his lips move, but could not make out what he was trying to say. Then his eyes closed again. Katrinka turned anxiously and looked at Zuzanka, who had remained hovering in the doorway.

"Talking exhausts him," she said. "He's just fallen asleep."

Katrinka sat with him a while longer, holding Mirek's hand as he slept. When she stood up finally to leave, the housekeeper slipped into the empty seat, and Katrinka retraced her steps along the hallway until she found Zuzanka, seated on a sofa in the sitting room. She was crying. Feeling Katrinka's presence, she stopped, dried her eyes, and stood up, smiling wryly. She had never been able to forgive her mother for the string of lovers for whom she had ignored her children; forgiving Mirek had been easier. "He was not a good father," she said. "But I loved him."

"He had so much charm, so much vitality," said Katrinka. "He was very lovable."

Zuzanka sighed. "One way and another, he hurt us all very much."

"May I come again?"

"Yes. Please."

From Mirek's apartment, Katrinka went to her lawyer's office, where, in the presence of the banker who had helped arrange the financing, she signed the final papers and received the deed to the hotel. A secretary brought in a bottle of Moravian champagne, which the lawyer opened with a flourish. "To Katrinka van Hollen," he toasted gallantly.

"And the Prague Ambassador. Success to both," added the bank manager.

To be polite, Katrinka took a sip of the forbidden champagne, then instructed them to proceed with the purchase of the apartment and to keep her informed of developments. After thanking them for their help, she excused herself. Feeling unusually tired, when she returned to the Intercontinental, she lay down on the king-sized bed and tried to nap, but sleep would not come. Instead, she kept turning over in her mind, like snapshots in an album, her memories of Mirek, from their first encounter, when he had approached her mother outside a butcher shop in Svitov to ask that the five-year-old Katrinka appear in his movie, to the time, years later, in a corner of the Maxmilianka when he had urged her to forget about the son she had given up for adoption and get on with her life; and, finally, their last meeting, a little more than two years before, when she had returned to Prague after the revolution. She had not known until then how much he had regretted the loss of her and their child.

Sitting up in bed, she reached for the phone, and, when she got the hotel operator, asked her to try Christian's number in Bonn. Of course, he was not in; and it was not until later in the day, after her final lunch with Jean-Claude, who was leaving for Paris immediately after, that she succeeded in reaching her son. He listened without comment to her hurried, formal German, until she had finished speaking, and then said calmly, "I have plans for the weekend."

She should have expected the response, she knew; nevertheless, the coldness in his voice shocked her. "Your father is dying, Christian. Didn't you understand me?"

"Yes. Perfectly."

"What could be more important than that?"

"He's nothing to me."

"He's your father."

"Father. Is the word supposed to bring sentimental tears to my eyes?"

Katrinka could imagine her son's dark eyes, so like Mirek's in color, but narrowed and brooding, his handsome face with its strong jaw and full lips sullen with annoyance. "I think you should come," she said. "You'll never get this chance again. And it would be awful if later you regretted missing it. But suit yourself."

The silence went on for so long that Katrinka began to think that perhaps Christian had hung up; but finally, he agreed to come.

"Good," she said, unable to keep from her voice the satisfaction that she knew would irritate him.

"Not for any sentimental reason," he said coldly. "But because I'm curious."

She thought it wiser not to comment. "Call me back when you've made your travel plans," she said. "I'll send a car to meet you at the airport."

As soon as the line went dead, she signaled the operator again and placed a call to Mark in London. Like Christian, he listened to her summary of the events of the past twenty-four hours without comment. "You understand," she said, when she had finished, "why I can't leave tomorrow?"

"Yes," said Mark, sounding unusually irritable. "I suppose so." He knew it was unreasonable of him to worry about being separated from Katrinka for a few more days, but nevertheless he was. He also knew it was unreasonable of him to resent Mirek for choosing this particular time to die, but nevertheless he did. "I'm just disappointed. How much longer do you think you'll stay?"

"I'm not sure. A day or two. *Miláčku*, I'm sorry."

"I know. So am I." He hesitated a moment, and then said, "Do you want me to come?"

"No." For once, she did not want Mark with her. Mirek and Christian were about all she could deal with at the moment. "I will have my hands full, and you won't like it if I ignore you."

He laughed. "You're right. I won't."

"It's better if you take care of business. Everything is all right there?"

"Yes. Fine. We've decided to issue eight million more shares of VHE stock. That ought to slow down any takeover attempt." He laughed again. "And raise some money."

They talked business for over an hour, neither one of them wanting to end the phone call; but finally, Mark's secretary interrupted with an emergency call from Carey Powers in New York. "Gotta go, baby," said Mark.

"I love you."

"I'm counting on it," he said. Then the line went dead.

Christian arrived later that same evening. Katrinka, who had been waiting impatiently in her suite for the driver to return with him to the hotel, raced to answer the door as soon as she heard the bell ring. "Zlatíčko, I'm so glad you're here. Come in, come in," she said, hugging him.

"Good evening, Mother," responded Christian without much enthusiasm as he kissed her cheek politely. He was wearing gray flannel trousers, a black shirt, a white scarf draped around his neck, and a black-and-white checked Givenchy jacket. His longish dark hair was wind-blown. His face was exactly as she had imagined it—petulant, like that of a spoiled brat forced by a determined parent to perform some chore he felt beneath his dignity.

Katrinka, as usual, ignored his mood. "Are you hungry? I waited dinner for you. I'm starving."

"Then, of course I'll keep you company," he replied politely.

Katrinka showed him his room, where he dropped his duffel bag before going into the bathroom that connected it with Katrinka's. She returned to her seat on the sofa and began leafing through a copy of *Chic* while she waited, trying hard to see things from his point of view, wishing she did not find his attitude so irritating, especially as there was little she could do about it but to keep trying to break through his reserve and to hope that one day he would forget his grievances . . . as Zuzanka had hers. She hoped Christian would not wait until she was dying. She sighed. Dinner would be a nightmare, she expected.

It was not, however, as bad as Katrinka had feared. Christian seemed quite taken with the restaurant, the food, the view. He declared Prague a beautiful city. He volunteered that his plans for the weekend had not included Pia. "After all," he said, "we just spent all that time together at the Villa Mahmed. We both need to breathe." Then Christian deflected any further questions on that subject by asking her to tell him about Mirek. Pleased at his interest, Katrinka filled in the rather brief outline of his father that she had presented to Christian in the past. She told him how Mirek had liked her pigtails and offered her a part in a movie; about how successful and admired he was as a director; how Tomáš and she had argued over his abilities for years afterward; how she had met him again as a student in Prague, where again he had offered her a part in a movie; how she had fallen in love with him; and how his fear of his father-in-law's position with the secret police had kept him from leaving his wife to marry Katrinka.

"So he told you at any rate," said Christian cynically. "And you were such an innocent you believed him."

"You have no idea what it was like," protested Katrinka. "People were often arrested for no good reason—only because they had offended someone important—and sent to labor camps in the Soviet Union. Felix Mach was a very powerful man. We were all a little afraid of him."

Christian shrugged, unwilling to be convinced. "And so you gave me up for adoption."

Katrinka nodded and continued her story, emphasizing the part Mirek had played in arranging the travel visas for herself and her parents; making all the arrangements for her care in Munich; and later trying to help her find their son when he saw how heartbroken she was at having given him up. "He called the doctor . . ."

"Zimmerman," said Christian, his voice full of disgust. Dr. Klaus Zimmerman had been a friend and business associate of the Hellers. He had supplied them with a child; they had supplied him with political favors that had kept him safe from the law until his death.

"Yes," said Katrinka, her loathing as obvious as Christian's. "But Zimmerman would tell Mirek nothing."

"And that was the end of your affair."

"Yes. I thought I could never forgive him."

"But you did?"

"Finally. When I saw him here two years ago."

"And now you expect me to?" Christian's heavy eyebrows rose quizzically and a faint smile touched his mouth.

"That would be best," agreed Katrinka, ignoring his irony. "For you. For Mirek, I don't think it matters anymore."

The first thing the next morning, Katrinka called Zuzanka, this time at her own home, to ask when it would be convenient for her to stop by to see Mirek.

"My brother is staying with my father this morning. Though I think his wife has other plans. I will phone them to ask what time would be good."

Katrinka volunteered to do that herself but, when Zuzanka insisted, agreed that it might be simpler for all concerned if Zuzanka made the call. "My son has arrived in Prague," said Katrinka, before letting Zuzanka go. "And I would like to bring him with me."

"Your son?" asked Zuzanka.

"Yes," said Katrinka firmly, "my son." As always, she was reluctant to say anything more than necessary. "I know it would make Mirek happy to see him."

Zuzanka hesitated a moment as she considered the implications of this bit of news, and then said, "I'm sure that's no problem. I'll telephone my brother now."

Within fifteen minutes Zuzanka had phoned back to let Katrinka know what time she and Christian were expected. She sounded upset, but, since that seemed only normal in the circumstances, Katrinka thought no more about it until the door of Mirek's apartment was opened not by his son or housekeeper but by Zuzanka herself. She was wearing a long shirtwaist dress. Her eyes were red and her face set in a stubborn expression that reminded Katrinka both of Mirek and Christian. Katrinka introduced her to Christian, a procedure complicated by the fact that Christian spoke no Czech and Zuzanka only limited German and English. But Christian was all deliberate charm and conscious sex appeal, clicking his heels slightly and bestowing on her his warmest smile. Katrinka could see that Zuzanka was quite taken with him.

"Would you like some coffee?" she asked as she ushered Katrinka and Christian through the apartment.

"No, thank you. Nothing at all." Seeing them together, their similarity was even more pronounced, but only to someone looking for it, thought Katrinka with relief. On the whole, Christian looked overwhelmingly like her.

Mirek's bedroom was at the far end of the corridor, but just before they reached it, the door of another of the rooms opened. The man who had been about to storm into the corridor stopped in his tracks when he saw them, his face registering dislike and the desire to retreat without a greeting. Good manners, however, prevailed and he continued toward them, his eyes cold with dislike.

"My brother, Felix," said Zuzanka, who dutifully performed the introductions.

"*Dobrý den,*" said Katrinka, extending her hand to shake the one Felix reluctantly offered.

He was in his early fifties, the same age Mirek had been when Katrinka had fallen in love with him. But Felix was nothing like his father. Not only did he resemble his mother physically—he was slender, elegant, and blond—but he lacked all of Mirek's vitality, his sexuality. Felix looked like the petty government functionary he was. And clearly he was in no mood to forgive Katrinka for having been his father's mistress, or to consider her presence in the family home anything but an affront to good taste. "*Dobrý den,*" he responded, then offered his hand to Christian, eyeing him with even greater suspicion and dislike.

To Katrinka's astonishment, Christian's face lit with a warmly angelic smile that she would not have believed him capable of producing. "I am so pleased to meet you," he said, shaking Felix's hand. "Brother . . ." he added.

"What?" said Felix, who was not sure he had understood Christian's German correctly.

"I have dreamed of this moment ever since I was a child and discovered I was adopted."

"What are you talking about?" asked Felix.

The smile on Christian's face faltered. "You mean you didn't know? I'm Mirek's son."

"Christian," said Katrinka, in English. "That's enough."

Katrinka turned to Zuzanka apologetically but before she could say anything, Zuzanka shook her head and said, "I suspected as much." She turned to her brother. "We'll discuss this later, if you don't mind."

Without another word, Felix turned and stormed away down the corridor. "I apologize," said Katrinka. "It seemed, in the circumstances, a good idea to say nothing."

Again Zuzanka shook her head. "It's best there are no more secrets. We've all lived with too many of them." Then she touched Christian's arm. "Come and meet your father," she said.

Christian nodded, and the smile he gave Zuzanka seemed to Katrinka to be genuine. "I'm sorry if I upset you," he said.

Returning his smile, Zuzanka replied in her halting German, "Normally, I detest surprises. But in your case, I make exception." She kept hold of his arm until they reached Mirek's bedroom, then she stepped aside, allowing Katrinka to enter first, then Christian. Again, the housekeeper stood up, nodded a greeting, and, after exchanging a glance with Zuzanka, left the room. Zuzanka remained in the doorway, watching, feeling she ought to leave, unable to bring herself to do so.

Katrinka stood by the bed and looked down at the frail figure lost among the crisp white sheets and down covering. The only sounds in the room were the faint hiss of the oxygen and the labored wheeze of Mirek's breathing. His eyelids were almost transparent. "Mirek?" she said softly. "Mirek, *zlatíčko*? Are you awake?"

Slowly, his eyes fluttered open and, when they finally brought her into focus, he smiled and reached for her hand, carrying it slowly to his lips.

"I've brought someone for you to see," she said, taking a few steps forward so that Christian could move into Mirek's line of vision.

Mirek shifted his gaze to the young man. At first he looked distressed, as if worried that Christian might be someone he ought to know but had forgotten, something that had been happening with increasing frequency in the past few months. But, gradually, he began to make sense of the assortment of features on the somber face staring down at him.

"This is Christian," said Katrinka, forgetting she had never told Mirek their son's name.

"You're as beautiful as your mother," said Mirek, the words coming slowly and with difficulty. "But you have brown eyes. A pity," he added. He had always imagined the child with Katrinka's brilliant pale blue eyes, not his own more ordinary brown ones. He squeezed Katrinka's hand, then let it go. He gestured to Christian. "Kiss me," he said.

Overwhelmed by a feeling of repulsion, Christian hesitated. This sick old man, too weak and feeble to hate, meant nothing to him. He did not know him, did not care about him. He had come merely to satisfy his curiosity. And now that he had, he wanted only to get away, to leave behind this airless room and its sweet smell of approaching death.

"Kiss me," repeated Mirek.

Katrinka said nothing, and Christian turned and started away. But when he caught sight of Zuzanka standing in the doorway, he hesitated, then turned back again. Leaning over, he brushed Mirek's dry, hot cheek with his lips.

"Thank you," said Mirek, his voice hoarse. "God bless you."

Again, Christian turned and, without looking at either Katrinka or Zuzanka, left the room.

"He has a lot to forgive us for," said Katrinka, "but he will."

Mirek nodded. "For your sake, I hope . . ." The words trailed off and his eyes closed again.

Katrinka drew the housekeeper's chair closer to the bed and sat with

Mirek a while longer, without speaking. Finally, she rose, leaned over, and she kissed his cheek. "Good-bye, *miláčku*," she whispered. "Rest well."

As on the previous day, she found Zuzanka in the sitting room, but there was no sign of her son. Looking up, Zuzanka saw her and said, "Christian's waiting for you in the car."

"I didn't mean to upset everyone," said Katrinka. "But I thought it was important to bring Christian. I thought he should know his father."

Zuzanka smiled. "You upset only Felix. And you have no idea how easy that is to do. I'm glad you brought him. I'm glad I got the chance to meet him."

"Thank you. You're very kind."

"Rubbish," said Zuzanka. She grinned. "As Christian pointed out to Felix, he is our brother. Will you come again?"

"If you'll let me. Maybe on Monday, when your brother and sister-in-law have returned to work?"

"Yes. Yes. That's a good idea. I'll see you then." She shook Katrinka's hand; then, impulsively, she kissed her cheek. "I know you've made my father very happy today."

As soon as he spotted her walking through the lobby, Katrinka's driver got out of the waiting car and opened the rear door for her. Christian was already inside, sprawled in the far corner. "What a joke," he said.

"Thank you for coming with me," said Katrinka, resisting the urge to smack him. She leaned forward and told the driver to take them first to the apartment she was in the process of buying and then to the hotel, by way of some of Prague's landmarks so that she could point them out to her son. "I want you to see what I've been up to," she said to Christian as she settled back in the seat.

"Don't tell me you're not upset about that prick Felix," said Christian, refusing to leave the subject.

Katrinka shrugged. "I thought you'd have enough sense to keep quiet. But I should have known you'd never be able to resist the urge to make trouble."

"So you are angry?" It was more of a challenge than a question.

To his surprise, Katrinka smiled. "I was. But I got over it. Everything turned out for the best." She reached over and touched his hand, half expecting him to snatch it away. "You liked Zuzanka, didn't you?"

Christian shrugged. "Where did she get that awful dress?"

"I would say it's the way everyone dresses here, but her mother was always one of the best-dressed women in Prague. I suppose it's a form of rebellion." She looked at Christian pointedly. "Children do that, I'm told."

Christian didn't reply and Katrinka let the subject drop. Instead, she focused her attention on keeping her son entertained, making the most of the time they had together. He planned to return to Bonn the next day.

They spent the afternoon sight-seeing. In addition to the apartment and the hotel, she showed Christian where she had lived as a student; she pointed out the scattered buildings of Charles University, where she had attended class, and FAMU, where Mirek had occasionally taught. She even had the chauffeur drive them the eight kilometers to Barrandov Studios so that Christian could see where his father had made so many of his films. By the time they returned to the hotel, Katrinka was exhausted. While Christian showered, she spoke briefly to Mark, who told her that Carey Powers had a position opening up in his department, if Christian wanted it. Then she napped for an hour, saving the news to tell him later.

For dinner that night, Katrinka took Christian to U Zlaté Hrušky, one of the restaurants that Mirek had introduced her to. In an eighteenth-century house, near Hradčany, its cuisine was strictly Czech. After they had ordered, she told him about Carey Powers's offer.

"Doing what?" he asked.

"You'll be one of his assistants. And before you say you would never consider it, remember that he is the company's chief financial officer."

"I suppose I would learn a lot," said Christian grudgingly.

"Yes," agreed Katrinka, "an enormous amount."

"All right, then."

"You'll phone Mark and tell him?" asked Katrinka, who thought she had done enough.

"Of course," said Christian. "I am not completely without manners."

"By no means," said Katrinka, who resisted the temptation to point out that he had not yet thanked her for her help.

"And I will have to call my parents and tell them, I suppose." Kurt Heller was currently in Lima, on a special diplomatic mission. He was considered by the Bonn government, after his years serving as ambassador to one South American country after another, to be the best man to talk sense to Fujimori, who had declared martial law and disbanded the assembly shortly after his election as president.

"Certainly," said Katrinka. Then a thought struck her. "You have discussed this with the Hellers? Your wanting to come to New York, I mean?"

"Not yet."

As little liking as she had for Kurt and Luisa Heller, still Katrinka had no desire to cause them pain. She was not trying to take their son away. All she wanted was to share him. "You should have discussed it with them."

"There didn't seem to be much point until it was settled."

"I hope they won't be hurt," she said.

"Why should you care?" he asked, sounding genuinely bewildered, as if he could not understand this concern for someone else's feelings.

"I don't like to see anyone hurt," she said.

"Well, don't worry," said Christian comfortingly. "They'll be only too happy to be rid of me."

Katrinka looked at him suspiciously. "I thought they disapproved of your spending time with me."

"That was true," said Christian. His smile was not pleasant. "Until they realized its advantages. After all, they haven't lost a son—he's merely gained a fabulously wealthy mother."

"Is that why you agree to see me?" asked Katrinka, though she knew she would not get a straight answer. Christian's motives always were too complex to be understood by anyone, including himself.

"Oh, Mother," he said, taking her hand and leaning forward in his chair so that he could kiss her cheek. "Mother, *liebling,* how could you even ask such a thing?"

It was close to eleven when they returned to the hotel, but the message waiting for Katrinka said that she was to call Zuzanka no matter what time she returned. While she waited for the operator to place the call, Katrinka went over in her mind all the possible reasons for Zuzanka wanting to speak to her: but the most obvious one she refused to consider until she heard Zuzanka's voice. She knew then, even before Zuzanka spoke the words.

"I'm sorry," said Katrinka.

"Yes, yes, I know. Thank you," said Zuzanka.

"If you'll tell me, when you've had time to make your plans . . . And if there's anything I can do."

"Yes, of course," said Zuzanka. "Thank you for coming so quickly. It meant a lot to him."

"To me, too," said Katrinka. They exchanged a few more words, the conventional words of comfort that do as well as any others, then Katrinka replaced the receiver. "Christian," she called.

A moment later, her son stood in the bedroom doorway. "Yes?" he said, and then, when he saw her face, "He's dead."

"Yes. He died at about ten. They were all there. His children and grandchildren."

How touching, Christian was about to say, but he bit back the words. As he had with Zuzanka earlier, he gave into a sudden, unfamiliar feeling of concern. He crossed the room and sat on the bed beside Katrinka, taking her hand. "Are you all right?"

"Yes. Just a little sad. But I'm happy you're here," she said. "Very happy."

Twenty-Five

FUNERAL SERVICES FOR MIREK WERE SET FOR TUESDAY MORNING AND, AFTER DISCUSSING THE MATTER WITH Zuzanka, Katrinka decided to stay in Czechoslovakia in order to attend. Felix and his wife might not approve, but Zuzanka did, and Katrinka did not doubt that Mirek himself would want her there.

When Katrinka phoned Mark in London to tell him of her change in plans, he was disappointed, as she knew he would be, and upset as well. He could not think of one former lover whose funeral he would have either wanted or felt it necessary to attend.

"He was very important to me once," said Katrinka, trying to explain.

"Once," repeated Mark. "A long time ago."

"I want to do this, Mark."

"Is Christian staying, too?" he asked, realizing he could not change Katrinka's mind.

"Yes," said Katrinka. To her surprise, Christian had insisted on remaining in Czechoslovakia with her. "He will miss just one seminar." She laughed. "He did tell me he will get a degree with honors in any case."

Arrogant bastard, thought Mark, though if there was one thing about Christian he did not doubt it was his intelligence. "I'm sure he wouldn't do anything to jeopardize his future," he said, his tone neutral. "You don't have to worry about that."

"I'm happy he's staying. For his sake."

"Don't get your hopes up too high, baby," said Mark. "Don't expect this to knock all the chips off Christian's shoulder."

Katrinka laughed again. "No, you're right. I will settle for just one or two."

This time Mark didn't offer to fly to Prague to be with her. For one thing, he really could not remain in Europe any longer. For another, he knew he would not be of any real use to her. She did not seem overly upset by Mirek's death, just saddened. She also seemed to have her own agenda concerning Christian.

Mark's understanding of the situation, however, did not mean that he was happy with it. His frustration continued to build; and he could not shake the idea that now was a lousy time for Katrinka and him to be apart. Though why he should feel that was becoming increasingly unclear to him. Katrinka seemed to have forgotten all about Monica Brand and the letters, and if they were not preying on his wife's mind, then they certainly ought not to be of any great concern to him. But he could not quite rid himself of the desire to wring Monica's lovely neck.

Of course, Katrinka had forgotten neither Monica nor the letters; she was just not the sort of person who could brood for long. When her parents had died, she had begun training for the ski team the day after their funeral. When Adam and she had separated, she had thrown herself into her business with an intensity that had kept the hotels profitable despite the growing recession. When she was in pain, she had either to work or to go crazy. But this time she was not in pain; she had not believed Monica Brand's allegations, and between the rush of business in Prague, then Mirek's illness and Christian's arrival, she had banished them to the back of her mind.

Instead of staying in Prague until the funeral, Katrinka suggested to Christian that they hire a car and drive into the countryside. It occurred to her that she might never get the opportunity again to have her son completely to herself for a few days, and she wanted to use it, as always, to try to close the gap between them, to make him feel closer to her by giving him access to her memories. Christian again agreed quickly. He was in the grip of emotions he did not quite understand. Curiosity was what he was most acutely aware of feeling: about Mirek, about his reactions to Mirek; about Felix; about Zuzanka; and, most of all, about Katrinka and everything that touched her. There was rage as well, always there, always ready to swell suddenly as it had the other day with Felix. And a surprising, inexplicable affection for Zuzanka, whom ordinarily he would have dismissed as a frumpy Eastern

European housewife (conveniently forgetting that she was generally acknowledged to be a talented director). Finally, he was aware of an unpleasant confusion, a vague discomfort caused by fleeting hints of other deeper and more disturbing emotions. But they flitted by him too quickly for him to be sure what they were, and he saw no reason to pursue them. They were nothing he cared to know about.

With just an overnight bag for each of them, they set off early on Sunday morning in a rented Škoda, taking the two-lane highway out of the city south toward Moravia. Traffic was light, mostly passenger cars, a few trucks and buses.

"Did you have a car when you were a child?"

"Not at first," said Katrinka, pleased at the interest Christian was showing. "But my mother went back to work when I started school and we had a little more money. We bought a Škoda. Then, when I was a student, with what I made modeling, I bought a little blue Fiat Six Hundred. I loved it."

She had told him about the magazine cover that had brought her to Mirek Bartoš's attention for the second time, but still Christian looked puzzled. "I don't understand who it was you were modeling for," he said.

"There was a state-run fashion industry," explained Katrinka. "Some of the designers were very talented, some were hopeless. But no matter how bad they were, if they were members of the Communist Party they kept their jobs, got the best promotions, and earned the most money. That's the way it worked."

The outskirts of the city with their sprawling development of bleak apartment complexes gave way finally to gentle green countryside, the road lined with birch trees, behind which the pines marched in tight formation toward the summit of the hills. Occasionally, the forests would halt before fields of rape seed, or villages of ochre and gray two-story houses topped by red-tile roofs, church steeples rising above them like arrows marking the spot. There was an occasional old-fashioned farm or dismal modern factory. Everywhere there were signs of continuing renovation, scaffolding going up, houses being painted.

They stopped for gas and drinks in one of the highway's service centers, which had a sprawling wooden restaurant serving hot foot and cold sandwiches, soft drinks, as well as wine and beer. "Try a *plzenske*," Katrinka urged Christian. "It's the best beer in the world, made right here in Czechoslovakia, in Bohemia. Your grandfather used to love it." For a moment, Christian seemed not to understand whom she meant.

"My father," she added. She touched his arm. "You would have liked him. Everybody did."

"I think I'll just have a coffee for now," he said.

Beyond Brno, they turned into a single-lane highway and, despite the relatively light traffic, the going was slower, the faster cars trapped behind lumbering trucks and buses until it was safe to pass. At one point they drove through a village of low ochre buildings surrounding a large manor house. "Pretty," murmured Christian.

"This is Austerlitz," said Katrinka. Its name was currently Slavkov, changed long after Napoleon had won his famous victory there.

"Really?" said Christian, sounding startled. "I had no idea Austerlitz was in Czechoslovakia."

"In Moravia," said Katrinka, to be precise. She laughed. "And you were educated at supposedly one of the best schools in the world."

Christian smiled reluctantly. "Napoleon's victories don't matter to anyone but the French."

"And Hitler's?"

"Hitler is talked about as little as possible," he said dryly.

"*Ay yi yi yi*," said Katrinka, "what a world."

Soon they reached Svitov, and, like a tour guide in love with her subject, Katrinka showed Christian the sights: the city square where the lovely old baroque buildings now faced rows of jerry-built shops in a garish pumpkin color, its central garden torn up and replaced with cobblestones, all in the name of modernization; the low cement block that housed the cinema where she and Tomáš had spent so many hours of their adolescence; the sports complex where her father had been assistant manager. "He should have been manager," she told him, "but he would never join the Party." They stopped for lunch in a large cafeteria in the main street, ordering open-faced sandwiches at the counter. Christian this time agreed to try the beer.

From the city center they drove the few blocks to the red brick building where Katrinka had gone to elementary school. She showed him the path across the railroad tracks and the steep stairs set into the hillside that she and Tomáš had climbed every day, then drove him into the hills above the town, pointing out the semidetached house where her grandparents had lived and the four-apartment complex to which her family had moved when she was eight years old. "Tomáš lived downstairs," she told Christian. "With his mother and grandfather. We lived upstairs." Nothing had changed since her childhood. The houses and apartment complexes that ranged the hillsides, running down to the city and up to the forest's edge, were still well kept, each with a square of garden, either front or back, with slate walks running between the vegetables and wildflowers. There were borders of roses and irises and tulips just coming into bloom. On her first return visit, Katrinka had knocked at the door of her grandparents' house, but the residents had been so suspicious, fearing that she planned, as so many were doing, to reclaim the property from the government, that she had left without seeing its interior. This time she did not even bother to ask.

"This is the gymnasium where I went to high school," said Katrinka, referring to several long low buildings, rather like army barracks, that occupied the highest developed point of the hillside. Above it was only forest, with sprawling stands of oak and hornbeam, with paths for hiking and clearings used for soccer practice. Students with canvas book satchels on their backs walked to and fro between buildings. "Not like Le Rosey, is it?"

"Not at all," agreed Christian. Again, he smiled. "But I am sure I enjoyed myself much less at Le Rosey than you did here."

"Were you very unhappy?" she asked, as she turned the car around and headed back toward the city center.

He stared out the window at the rows of neat apartments. "I was not within walking distance of home," he said, and then he shrugged. "Not that home was any better. There was no such place, not in physical terms at least, since we traveled so much, from one embassy to another, from one country to another. And our *family* bore no resemblance at all to the cosy little picture you describe. No, I suppose, all in all, I preferred being at school."

"Did they beat you?" she asked, remembering all the stories she had heard about boarding schools.

"Where? At home? Of course. And at school, too, though nothing as brutal as you are probably imagining."

"That's terrible," said Katrinka, outraged.

"There are worse things than beatings," said Christian, sounding, as he sometimes did, like an adult explaining something unpleasant to a naive child.

Once again, Katrinka was not certain exactly how much of what Christian implied was true, how much exaggerated for effect. She did not like the Hellers, she never had. Over the years, when they had met, she had found them cold and blindly ambitious, but she had never thought them either decadent or brutal.

"You don't believe me, do you?" asked Christian, who had turned from studying the landscape to look at her face.

"Of course I do," protested Katrinka. "Sometimes I think you exaggerate a little, but mostly I think you tell me the truth."

He smiled, and for once it was an expression totally without pretense or cynicism. "Perhaps I do exaggerate a little," he said, in one of those lightning changes of mood that Katrinka found always both startling and welcome.

He told her more about his life at Le Rosey: the demanding scholastic requirements; the loneliness, not only of himself but of most of the boys; the discipline problems, inevitable among a group of spoiled rich kids whose wealthy parents were too busy or too lazy or too involved in divorcing and remarrying to take care of them.

"Were there a lot of drugs at the school?"

"No more than at other schools. And less now, I suppose, that there are weekly urine tests." He looked at her quizzically. "Are you asking whether or not I used them?"

"Yes," she admitted.

"I tried everything, marijuana, hashish, cocaine. But I didn't like the effect. I like to be in control." He paused for a split second, then asked, "Do you believe me?"

"I told you," she said. "I always believe you."

He was, up to a point, telling the truth. What he did not add was that, although he had not habitually used drugs, he had been one of the school's primary suppliers. Son of a diplomat, traveling often between South America and Europe, young, handsome, and well dressed, he had made an excellent courier. From the age of eleven, he had made a great deal of money, both for transporting the drugs and for dealing to his schoolmates. But he had not done it for the money—he had always received a generous allowance from the Hellers. It was the danger he liked, the excitement, the sense of power it gave him as he watched his friends become hooked while he remained completely in control. Only once had he come close to being caught. A schoolmate named Christian as the supplier of his drugs, but he denied the charge, insisting that the boy was the dealer, lying because he was jealous of Christian. Since no drugs were found in Christian's possession, since no one had ever seen him anything resembling high, and since a large part of the student body supported him (not wanting to cut off their own supply), the other boy was expelled and Christian got off with a warning to stay out of trouble.

When they returned to the city center, it was only mid-afternoon. They checked into the only hotel, a large unattractive building but reasonably comfortable inside, then walked over to the street market to stretch their legs. As she did each time she returned there, Katrinka ran into people who had known her parents and grandparents. She smiled, shook hands, introduced Christian, easily evading the obvious questions since everyone was more interested in her pregnancy than in the origins of the handsome young man at her side. When she had bought the bouquets of flowers that had been the real object of the walk, she hurried Christian back to the car and drove the ten minutes out of town to the cemetery where her parents were buried. She turned into the rutted lane that cut through the forest and continued until she saw the familiar markers and stopped the car. "This is it," she said. Neat rows of marble tombs were laid out in alleys between the trees. Some had marble slabs lying in front of the headstones, others just a raised patch of earth planted with flowers and surrounded by borders of stone. On top of the slabs were vases of flowers, potted plants, votive candles. The tall trees blocked all but occasional rays of sun, which, like arbitrary spotlights, gave prominence to some details and ignored others. The air was soft and warm, the light a pale chartreuse. The only sound was of birds calling.

Here Katrinka felt close to her parents. She lay the bouquet of flowers across the marble slab and stood silently for a few minutes, not praying but remembering them. Then, she moved on the few feet to where her grandparents lay buried and did the same. "They were good people," she said.

Christian watched Katrinka, saw the unquestioning simplicity of her feeling for her parents and her grandparents, the purity of it, and wondered if she loved him in that same uncomplicated way. He doubted it somehow. He looked at the forest, listened to the birds, waited to see what he felt. Tired, he decided at last. Hungry. It had been a long day.

And it was not over yet. That night, Katrinka and Christian had been invited for dinner to the home of Ota Černý and his wife, Maria; Katrinka had telephoned them from Prague to say that she was on her way to Svitov. "Uncle" Ota had been a friend of her father's and Katrinka's ski coach both on the provincial level and later when she had skied for Czechoslovakia in international competitions.

Maria was Ota's second wife, a cheerful, affectionate woman the complete opposite of his first wife, Olga. Having learned all of Katrinka's favorite dishes, Maria prepared them: roast pork with hot sauerkraut and dumplings; and for dessert, *palačinky*, thin crepes rolled with raspberry jam, covered with whipped cream and hot chocolate sauce. "This is the last time I'll eat for a week," murmured Katrinka, contentedly patting her stomach. "If I'm not careful, this baby will be born as fat as a little pig."

"What foolishness," said Maria. "You're like a rail. You should have seen me when I was pregnant with my children. Big as a cottage I was." One of the great joys of Ota's remarriage was that he had acquired not only Maria but her children and grandchildren.

Ota turned his attention to Christian. "Has your mother told you what a great skier she was?" he asked in his heavily accented German. Katrinka had written to tell him about Christian months before, and he had expected to meet a bright, optimistic young man, open and affectionate, like his mother. But Christian's darkness went deeper than his looks. He had a brooding, cynical quality that was surprising in one so young. Perhaps he took after his father, thought Ota. But the few times he had met Mirek Bartoš, he had seemed an outgoing and charming man.

"Yes," said Christian, who was becoming bored with being polite. What was he doing here, he wondered, with these tedious old people whose only interest was in reliving the past?

"It almost broke my heart when she left Czechoslovakia. I was counting on her to win an Olympic medal for me in Sapporo in '72."

Despite his age, Ota still looked vigorous and healthy, a handsome seventy-year-old. It was hard to believe that he was the same age as Mirek. "I thought you had forgiven me for that," said Katrinka, her voice full of affection.

"I did, zlatíčko," he assured her, reverting to Czech. "A long time ago." His gaze as it rested on her was troubled, and as he kissed her good-bye he urged her to take care of herself.

"Don't worry," said Katrinka. "I've never felt better in my life. I haven't been this happy since I was a child."

"Happiness comes and it goes. That's how life is."

"If it goes, I'll manage."

"I know you will," he said. "Na shledanou, zlatíčko."

"Dobrou noc," she replied, hoping it was indeed only good night rather than good-bye. "Maria, thank you very much," she said, kissing the old woman's plump cheek. "I'll see you both again soon."

"He didn't like me," said Christian as he fastened his seat belt.

"Why should he?" said Katrinka, sounding irritated. "You behaved like a brat with no manners."

"But you do?" he asked, reaching out and touching her arm lightly.

Katrinka turned to look at him, then smiled reluctantly. "No, I don't like you," she said. "Not all the time. But I love you. And I am so happy to have you in my life."

"That will do," he said.

After breakfast the next morning, Katrinka and Christian set out on the next leg of their tour. From Svitov, she drove the half hour along the familiar route to the sports club's mountain chalets. "We did this every Friday," she told Christian, "first by bus, then by car when we bought one, all winter long. My mother hated it but she came anyway to please my father and me."

At first the countryside was gentle, with hills rising gradually behind the two-story houses lining the road. The majority were constructed entirely of stucco, usually with three horizontal stripes in shades of gray or cream; some were half timber or stone. Even the plainest had at least a decorative trim surrounding the windows. A few of the hillsides were planted with vegetables, and once they saw a woman in shorts hoeing between the rows. Most, however, worked in long dark dresses and stout shoes, the older ones wearing kerchiefs on their heads and popover aprons to cover their clothes. Old men in peaked caps rode bicycles pulling carts full of hay. One drove a horse and carriage. Cows and sheep grazed in hillside pastures and geese waddled across front yards. Crossing a stream, they saw a boy with a crook tending a gaggle by its banks. These were scenes from another age, deceptive scenes that gave no hint of the hardship behind the images of pastoral tranquillity.

Soon the houses disappeared, then the fields of wildflowers. The forest grew dense, and the hills gave way to the Javorníky Mountains. Crossing the provincial border into Slovakia, the car began climbing more steeply. "We used to park here," said Katrinka, pointing out a patch of level ground with a shed at the far end, "and walk the rest of the way. In snow," she added. The car wound up the narrow road, around the mountain to the top, where the two wooden chalets, set on adjacent hills, commanded the view.

Katrinka parked the car on the shoulder of the road, then she and Christian got out to walk along a thick carpet of sloping green grass studded with buttercups. "That was ours," she said, pointing to the nearer of the two chalets, which were still some distance to the west. "It was called the Orlik. It means eagle." There were twelve lifts linking the surrounding slopes. To the east, in the distance, the High Tatras were towering gray shadows; and, in front of them, the Low Tatras, darker and more distinct, rounded humps covered in dense forests from which swatches of pine had been cut out for lumber. Nestled in the valleys between the Tatras and the Javorníky, red-roofed villages sparkled in the sunlight, their church steeples jutting up from stands of trees into the clear blue sky.

"Come," said Katrinka finally. "We have more driving to do." It did not occur to her to ask if he was tired or bored. Perhaps because she did not want to know, so intent was she on showing him everything.

They crossed back into Moravia and headed north, stopping once along the way for gas and something to drink. By twelve-thirty, they were beyond Olomouc, once the capital of Moravia, on the way to Mohelnice, when Katrinka turned the car into a side road, continued a short distance, then stopped in front of a gate.

"Would you open it for me, please?" asked Katrinka.

"Is this it?" he asked.

"This is it," she assured him.

Christian got out, opened the gate, waited until Katrinka drove through, then closed it behind her before climbing again into the car. The gate and fence were newly painted, noted Katrinka, as was the trim of the rambling stucco farmhouse. Again Katrinka was assailed by memories, of long summer vacations spent here at the farm, playing with her two cousins, climbing the trees in the fruit orchards, swimming in the pond, singing at night by the fire. It had been owned by her mother's family, the Novotnýs, for generations, and had somehow managed to slip through the bureaucratic cracks when collectivization was decreed after the communist takeover.

As the car stopped, three German shepherds came bounding across the yard; the front door of the house opened and a plump woman came running out, her arms extended, calling, "Katrinka, zlatíčko, dobrý den." Her fading blond hair was twisted up on top of her head. She wore a long dress and no makeup. It was hard to believe she was a few years younger than Katrinka.

"Olinka, how good to see you," said Katrinka, hugging the woman. "This is my cousin František's wife," she said to Christian, in German. "And these are the dogs. There are always dogs." Then she repeated what she had said to Olinka in Czech.

"And chickens and pigs," said Olinka, laughing. "Come in, come in. How handsome your son is. He looks just like you. Ah, too bad my boys aren't home." They were both in Brno, at the university. "Only Milena is here. She'll be home from school in a little while."

"And where is František?"

"Working in the orchards. But he'll be here any minute for lunch."

Katrinka and Christian followed Olinka inside to the giant kitchen where a table was set for five. An old woman, her gray hair neatly braided, sat rocking in a chair by the hearth. When she heard the footsteps, she called, her voice thin and excited, "Katrinka, is that you? Look at you," she said, when Katrinka stood in front of her. "A baby at your age! God bless you. Come, give your old aunt a kiss."

"Aunt Zdeňka, how good you look," said Katrinka, kissing the old woman's wrinkled cheeks. Zdeňka and her mother had been sisters.

She patted Katrinka's stomach. "It will be a girl," she said.

"What's wrong with your foot?" asked Katrinka, noticing the cast resting on a footstool.

"So stupid," said Zdeňka impatiently. "I climbed on a chair to get a jar of preserves from the shelf, and I fell. Now I have to sit here all day doing nothing."

"We keep her busy peeling potatoes and carrots," said Olinka, her voice teasing.

"Is this your son?" asked Zdeňka. "How good-looking he is. *Zlatíčko*, come here. Give me a kiss."

"Kiss her," instructed Katrinka, in German.

"With pleasure," said Christian, with more warmth than he usually displayed. "I'm always delighted to kiss a beautiful woman. How are you, aunt?" he inquired politely.

"What did he say?" asked Zdeňka.

Katrinka translated and Zdeňka laughed. "He has a tongue made of honey, like your father," she said.

In a few minutes, František came bounding in. A tall man, with broad shoulders, he enveloped Katrinka in a bear hug. "Welcome, welcome," he said. "It's been too long."

"The trouble he got me into when I was little," she said to Christian, laughing. She had worshiped František and his brother, Oldřich, who was now teaching at the university in Brno—and would have followed them to hell had they suggested it.

They laughed all through lunch, Katrinka and her family catching each other up on recent news and reminiscing about the past. From time to time, Katrinka translated for Christian or one of the others would try a halting sentence in German or English, while he sat back eating the homemade sausages and freshly baked bread, observing the scene as if it were a film he was watching for which he had to write a review at some later date. Occasionally, it crossed his mind to wonder what he was doing in such a strange place, so far from the palatial homes, the exclusive schools, the trendy nightclubs that were his usual haunts. But, for the most part, he was intrigued by the image of his sophisticated mother, someone who hobnobbed regularly with the world's richest people, whom he had seen dancing at a party in St. Moritz with King Juan Carlos of Spain, perfectly at home in the kitchen of a farmhouse in an Eastern European country. He certainly could not imagine either of the Hellers in this setting. Would he ever understand Katrinka? he wondered. He hoped not, for while he was not prepared to admit that he cared very much about her, he could certainly acknowledge that she interested him, and so long as she did, he was happy enough to have her in his life, and even (more or less) to do as she wished. In the meantime, he refused to think about why he found the possibility of her *not* being in his life so disturbing.

After lunch, František returned to his work, Olinka insisted she could tidy up on her own, and Katrinka took Christian on a tour of the farm. She showed him the orchards where the different fruit trees, peach and plum, apricot and cherry, were in various stages of bloom, their soft flowers surrounding the treetops like clouds tinged with the colors of sunrise. They sat for a while by the pond, not talking much, Katrinka lost in memories, Christian content just to watch her.

By the time they returned to the farmhouse, Milena was home from school. She was of medium height, and slender, with pale skin and delicate features. Her fingers were long and elegant, her hair a brilliant red, falling in loose waves to her shoulders. "How beautiful you've grown," said Katrinka when she saw her.

"She looks just like your mother as a girl," said Zdeňka.

Milena blushed, the rush of blood into her face tinging her pale skin with pink. With an obvious effort, she thanked Katrinka for the compliment and said how nice it was to see her again.

"What's the matter with you?" said her mother, turning to Katrinka to add, "She's not usually so shy. You should have seen her yesterday when she heard you were coming."

"You should have seen me," said Katrinka, with a laugh. "I was so happy at the thought of being here."

"If you'll excuse me?" said Milena, heading for the door. "I have some English homework to do." While the others loved Katrinka as a member of the family, Milena idolized her. She was the one who had gone away, who had done extraordinary things, and the girl longed to be just like her.

Christian watched her go regretfully, but he did not have long to wait for her return. The lure of Katrinka was too strong for Milena to remain in her room, pretending to study. An hour later, when she came into the kitchen, she found Katrinka helping to prepare the evening meal, while Christian sat at the table, leafing through an old magazine. "You're in the way, *miláčku*. Why don't you go inside and read?" said

Katrinka, as she brushed past him. Unable to resist, she touched his hair. "Or watch television. Unless you care to help Aunt Zdeňka shell the peas," she added teasingly.

"I think I'll watch television," said Christian. He stood up. "Unless Milena would like to practice her English."

"No, thank you," said Milena quickly. Christian had spoken in English and she replied in the same language. She really did not want to be alone with him. Something about him disturbed her. He was not at all like her brothers, who were as open and easy to read as a child's storybook. She knew she would never know what to say to him. "I will stay and set the table."

"You do speak English very well," said Katrinka.

"Very," agreed Christian. He smiled at her. "Maybe, then, later you will teach me a few words of Czech?" Milena nodded nervously. "Good," said Christian, who excused himself and left the room.

Dinner that night was a reprise of lunch, full of laughter and conversation. As Katrinka spoke, Milena watched her almost hungrily, and Christian in turn watched Milena. She was beautiful. A pity she was so shy, he thought.

When dinner was finished and the kitchen tidy, František brought out the guitars, handing one to Katrinka. Milena disappeared for a few moments, then returned carrying a balalaika. Then, as they had done almost every night at the farm that Katrinka could remember, they sat around the hearth and played the old folk songs, the waltzes and polkas, while everyone sang. But soon, Katrinka became aware of an unfamiliar quality to the sound and stopped playing. František followed her lead, then Olinka and Zdeňka stopped singing. Milena continued, strumming her balalaika, her voice true and sweet, gentle at times, then powerful. For a long time, she seemed oblivious to what had happened, then suddenly her eyes opened, she saw everyone watching her, the blood again rushed into her face, and she stopped playing.

"Oh, no," said Christian, "don't stop."

"You're wonderful," said Katrinka.

"She sings like an angel," said her doting grandmother.

"There are pop stars with voices not half as good as yours," said Christian.

"What?" asked Olinka.

Katrinka translated what Christian had said and added, "It's true. She's very good."

"Yes, yes," said Zdeňka, smiling broadly and nodding.

"I dream of being a singer," said Milena, her voice wistful.

"It's no life for a good girl," said František, frowning. "Madonna . . ." He shook his head.

"Not everyone is like Madonna," said Katrinka.

"Have you ever been to a concert?" asked Christian, ignoring the others, his attention focused on Milena.

"No," said Milena. "There are no concerts here. And I've never been anywhere else." She bit her lip, debating whether or not to say anything more. Then, realizing it might be her last chance, she said, "Katrinka said I could visit her in New York sometime."

"What a good idea," said Christian.

"What?" asked Katrinka, turning her attention back to the two young people.

"For Milena to visit you in New York." Katrinka looked startled, and Christian continued, "She said you promised her."

"Yes, I did. I said she could come when she was older." Then Katrinka smiled at Milena. "Well, I suppose you are older."

Milena nodded. "I'm almost eighteen."

"She's starting university in the fall," said František, who did not like the direction the conversation was taking.

"Perfect," said Christian. "She can spend a few weeks in New York this summer before she starts." He turned to Milena. "Would you like that?"

"Oh, yes," she said.

Christian turned to Katrinka and waited. She hesitated a moment, torn between irritation with Christian for forcing the issue and her desire to give Milena the gift she so obviously longed for. Then, she said. "If your parents agree, I'd love you to come."

All shyness forgotten, Milena jumped out of her chair and flung herself at Katrinka. "Oh, thank you."

"Don't I deserve some of that?" said Christian, but when Milena looked at him anxiously, he was smiling so sweetly, that she blushed again.

"Thank you," she said shyly, but keeping a safe distance away.

"What is going on?" asked Olinka, for whom the shifts of language had been too quick for her to understand exactly what was being suggested.

Katrinka explained, and soon the conversation degenerated into chaos. Only Christian and Milena remained silent, Christian not understanding a word of the rapid Czech being fired around the room, Milena following the arguments avidly, knowing her future was at stake, both absolutely convinced that Katrinka would eventually win and Milena would spend the summer in New York.

"We don't have to make a decision now," said Katrinka finally. It was always a good idea to give people a chance to get used to an idea. "We should all think about it a little. It's another six weeks before school is even finished. All right?" She looked at Milena, who hesitated a moment, and then nodded. "I'll phone you from New York in a few weeks."

"It's kind of you to offer," said František, gracious now that the pressure of making a decision was off.

"I would love to have her," said Katrinka. "And I think it would be a good experience for her." As František seemed about to start arguing again, she added quickly, "But enough has been said." She turned to Christian. "It's time we should be going."

"Yes." Christian stood, shook František's hand, then kissed Olinka and Zdeňka's cheeks, thanking them for the day. As he leaned toward Milena, she withdrew slightly, then stopped herself, smiling at him shyly. "Don't worry," he whispered as he kissed her cheek. "My mother always gets what she wants. And so do I."

"I'm grateful," she said, "for your help."

"My pleasure," he said, with a small, courtly bow.

"What a good boy," said Zdeňka, when Katrinka and Christian had left. "So handsome, and charming."

"Imagine her keeping him a secret for so many years," said Olinka, with a small shake of her head.

"Katrinka could always keep her mouth shut," said František admiringly, remembering the times his cousin could have told tales on him and hadn't. But the smile quickly faded from his face. Katrinka must have been Milena's age, maybe a little older, when she got pregnant. He shook his head again. He was not sure whether it was Katrinka or Milena he did not trust, or possibly just life itself, but he did not at all like the idea of his daughter going to New York.

"Well, you did certainly set the dog among the birds," said Katrinka, as usual hopelessly confusing the terms of the old proverb.

Christian, who did not quite understand the expression, nevertheless got its general meaning. "Don't you want Milena to visit you?" he asked innocently.

"What I don't want," she said, "is to upset my cousins." However, she sounded more resigned than annoyed.

"It would be a pity to waste so much talent."

She looked in front of her again. "Would you be so concerned about her talent if she was homely. Or a boy?"

Christian laughed. Neither Milena's looks nor her sex had led him to intervene on her behalf—after all, she was not the only pretty girl he had ever met. His primary reason had been to make her pay attention to him: he disliked being ignored. "Probably not," he said. Katrinka smiled, a little grimly, then yawned and shifted uncomfortably in her seat. "Why don't you let me drive?" he asked.

"It's not so far," she said.

"You've been driving for days. You must be exhausted."

"Thank you, *miláčku*. You're right." She pulled the car to the side of the road, then she and Christian changed places, Katrinka adjusting the passenger seat until her legs were comfortably extended and some of the pressure on her back relieved. "Oh, that's much better," she said.

"Try to sleep a little. I promise not to get us lost." He was joking: the run to Prague was reasonably straight and the roads clearly marked.

Katrinka smiled. "I trust you," she said, closing her eyes.

It was close to one in the morning by the time Christian pulled up in front of the Intercontinental. He shut off the motor and turned to look at Katrinka. She was fast asleep. Getting out of the car, he went around to the passenger side and got there just as the doorman reached it. "If you'll take care of the luggage," said Christian, opening the car door and taking Katrinka gently by the arm. "Mother," he said. "Wake up. We're here."

Katrinka's eyes opened slowly. She saw Christian's face and groaned. "I feel awful."

"How awful?" he asked anxiously.

With a reassuring smile, she said, "Just tired."

He helped her from the car and together they went into the lobby and stopped at the desk, where the clerk on duty greeted them by name and handed Katrinka two Federal Express envelopes, a stack of faxes, and the telephone messages that had arrived in her absence. There was also a message for Christian, which he read quickly, then crumpled and threw into a wastepaper receptacle on the way to the elevator. "From Pia," he said in response to Katrinka's quizzical glance.

"I'm going to have a hot bath," said Katrinka, as they entered the suite.

"I'll start the tub for you."

"Thank you, *miláčku*," she said, touched by his concern.

From her bedroom, as she changed out of her clothes, she could hear Christian in the bathroom, starting the tub, flushing the toilet, running water in the basin. "It's all yours," he called when he had finished.

"Don't forget, the funeral mass is at nine." It occurred to her suddenly that she had Mirek to thank for this time she had had alone with Christian. Dear, dear Mirek, she thought, the last remnants of her anger toward him evaporating before her gratitude for this son he had given her. "Goodnight, *miláčku*," she called.

She heard Christian's response, then, picking up the stack of mail, she took it into the bathroom with her and set it on the side of the tub as she took off her robe and climbed in, sinking low into the soothing hot water, letting it rise over her stomach and partially cover her full breasts. She sat that way a few moments, her eyes closed, then straightened and reached for the mail.

There were several faxes from Robin with reports of the past few days' business activities. Nothing had happened requiring her immediate attention, Katrinka was pleased to see. There was another from Carlos, in reply to hers letting him know that she had signed the final papers on the hotel and was ready to begin work. And one from Mark asking her to phone him in New York as soon as she got back to Prague. The phone messages were from Margo, from Zuzka, and several from Mark, who had apparently been trying to reach her all day. She began to feel more annoyed than flattered by his worry. She opened one of the Federal Express envelopes and looked quickly through the sketches Carlos had sent, frowning slightly: she did not think he had quite captured the look they had discussed earlier. She dropped them onto the pile of faxes on the marble floor beside the tub and opened the second Federal Express envelope.

Inside were photographs, with no covering letter, no note, nothing to identify the sender. The first photo was of Mark's house in Chapel Street, in London. The second a closer shot of the front door. Vaguely in the background, behind the glass, she could just make out two figures. In the third photo, the door was partially open and a man—no, *Mark*—was starting to walk out. Again, she could see the shadowy figure behind him. The fourth photograph revealed the figure to be a woman, following closely on Mark's heels, reaching for his hand. He had reached the bottom of the front steps in the fifth photograph and the woman was holding his hand firmly. In the sixth, they were kissing, and in the seventh, and the eighth, the woman's arms by now wrapped around Mark's neck, his hands on her hips. The ninth showed Mark getting into a waiting limousine. The tenth was of the woman alone, crying, a close-up of her face. It was Monica Brand.

No, no, thought Katrinka. It was impossible. It couldn't be true. She had to talk to Mark. Right away. Dropping the photos onto the floor, she stood up, reached for the hotel's terry robe, stepped out of the tub, put it on, and started to move toward the door. The marble was slippery under her wet feet as she hurried, and suddenly she felt her legs slide out from under her. She reached for the basin to steady herself, but missed it. "Christian," she shouted as she fell. Then her head hit the floor.

The sound of Katrinka's voice calling to him mingled with the other disturbing voices in Christian's dream: Milena singing, Pia crying, Luisa Heller scolding him for some unmentionable offense. The thud of her body against the tile was the sound of his falling, trying to evade the butler who was to bring him to his father for punishment. It took a moment for him to swim up out of the depths of his sleep, to begin separating fact from nightmare. He saw the light still on under the bathroom door. "Mother?" he called. When there was no reply, he got out of bed, pulled on his robe, went to the door, and knocked. "Mother?" he called again. The silence worried him. Slowly, he pushed the door open. He saw the filled tub, the pile of papers beside it, Katrinka lying on the floor, blood seeping out from under the hem of the terry cloth robe. God in heaven, he murmured, racing to the prone form. He knelt beside her. "Katrinka," he said. She was breathing, he could see that. "Mother," he said more insistently. She didn't respond. He got up again and went to the phone. "Mrs. van Hollen has had an accident," he told the operator. "Call an ambulance. Immediately, do you understand? An ambulance!"

"Yes, yes," repeated the operator. "An ambulance, right away."

He ran to the door of the suite and opened it so there would be no delay when the emergency team arrived. Then he returned to the bathroom and sank down on the floor beside Katrinka. He didn't know what to do, didn't know how to help her. Getting up again, he grabbed the towels from the rack, then knelt beside her, stuffing them between her legs, trying to stop the bleeding. He sat back and pulled her partially onto his lap, holding her, praying that help would come soon.

Twenty-Six

THINGS WERE DEFINITELY LOOKING UP, THOUGHT ADAM GRAHAM, AS HE OPENED HIS DESK DRAWER AND caught sight of yesterday's edition of *The Daily Register*, which he had put there for safekeeping. It would have been even better, of course, if the paper had a wider circulation, but Sabrina's column had seemed the obvious choice. Liz Smith never would have used the story in *Newsday* without checking its source, and Rick Colins was too good a friend of Katrinka's to have used it at all.

"While Katrinket Plays, Her New Hubby Strays," ran the headline. To illustrate the column, Sabrina had used two photographs: one of Katrinka, elaborately gowned, entering Hradčany for a reception, hand-in-hand with Jean-Claude Gillette; the other of Mark kissing Monica Brand in front of the Chapel Street house. Sabrina quoted rumors floating around Paris that Jean-Claude was finally going to divorce the long-suffering Hélène, suggesting that he had marriage to Katrinka in mind, a theme she had been playing off and on for years; she described Monica as a "beautiful and talented free-lance journalist," who had recently been seen in Mark van Hollen's company. For the Hollywood crowd, Sabrina threw in the information that Katrinka had formerly been married to "film tycoon" Adam Graham.

For the pleasure of it, Adam read the article again—it could not have been better if he'd written it himself. Then he studied the photograph, looking for flaws. But it looked very incriminating, even to him, and he knew it was a setup.

By now, Adam speculated, Katrinka would have returned to her hotel in Prague and called back her good friends, all of whom would have tried to break the news to her as gently as they could. She would have spoken to Mark. But what could he say to explain away the contents of that Federal Express package? Nothing convincing. Adam could imagine her rage. Katrinka was very beautiful when she was angry. Her spine got very straight, making her seem even taller, more formidable, like an avenging goddess, her pale blue eyes glinting as coldly as an arctic sea. Inevitably, she would start to cry and spoil the effect, but at first, it was stunning. If his own experience was anything to go by, within twenty-four hours Mark van Hollen would be given his marching orders and the marriage would be over.

And that would be just the beginning of the end, if all went as expected. The scandal should succeed finally in undermining Mark's control of his board, making them more receptive to a handsome offer from a reputable source—that is, Charles Wolf, who was quietly accumulating, at Adam's expense, more and more VHE stock. And as Mark threw money away trying to defend his company, Adam's finances steadily improved. He had signed a lucrative deal with Club Med to provide cruise ships for the club's Caribbean holidays; the package tours the line had once offered in tandem with Katrinka's hotels were now to be promoted through the much larger Ciga chain, owned by the Aga Khan. The Italians had finally stopped haggling: except for the signatures on the contract, the sale of Olympic Pictures was a done deal. Even the New York apartment was in escrow, and Adam had made an offer on a town house in Sutton Place, not far from where he had lived before marrying Katrinka.

The only cloud in Adam's forecast was Patrick Kates, who had been eliminated in the finals at the end of April, leaving Bill Koch to defend the cup against the Italian team, winner of the Challenger trials. Kates, of course, was laying off blame right and left: on his crew, on the design team, on the shipyard. And there was enough blame to go around certainly, but there was no doubt that Kates deserved the major portion of it. Constantly outguessing the designers, changing specifications on whims that he referred to as "gut instinct," he had failed to inspire confidence, trust, or loyalty in his crew. Kates was a good, possibly a great, sailor ruined by an out-of-control ego.

Adam had had little cash tied up in the venture, but his company's prestige had been on the line. And while a win would have meant millions of dollars in needed business for Graham Marine, the loss would end up costing the company a fortune in lost clients.

Patrick Kates, however, would not be one of them. He was insisting that Graham Marine refit his old yacht, the one-hundred-eighty-foot *Beautiful Dreamer*, at a bargain price. Lucia had already agreed to do her part of the work for nothing and was adding her voice to her lover's hectoring for a deal. The hell of it was that business was slow at the Larchmont yard, and however pleasing the prospect of getting rid of Kates permanently, it was worth taking on the project just to avoid laying off more people.

The intercom buzzed, interrupting Adam's train of thought: his mother, his secretary informed him. As he picked up the receiver, like a child trying to conceal incriminating evidence, he dropped the copy of *The Daily Register* back into the desk drawer, which he closed firmly. "Good morning, Mother," he said.

"What is this I hear about Mark van Hollen?" asked Nina, who did not waste time on polite chitchat when there was something she wanted to know.

"Now, how would I know?" responded Adam innocently.

"You mean you haven't seen it?"

"Seen what?"

"There was an absolutely appalling photograph of him in some newspaper yesterday, in that dreadful Sabrina's column. He was kissing a young woman."

"I don't believe it," said Adam.

"Well, I wouldn't have either," agreed Nina, in whom disbelief, shock, distaste, and curiosity were fighting for supremacy. "But a friend arrived at the breakfast this morning—we had a fund-raiser for Russell—waving a copy of the paper. Dodie Wainwright. You remember her? We were at school together." She made it sound like only a year or two before, as opposed to the half century it nearly was. "I find the whole thing terribly upsetting."

"Why? It has nothing to do with you."

"You can't be that naive."

"I wouldn't have thought so," said Adam dryly.

"Surely you can see," continued Nina, sounding as if she were explaining something perfectly obvious to a particularly dense child, "that anything concerning Mark involves Katrinka, and that naturally leads to you, and to me, and now, and this is really most unfortunate, to Russell."

"I really think you're exaggerating the importance—"

"Please allow me to be the judge of that, Adam. You have absolutely no idea how trying this whole business of campaigning is. There's this appalling young man running against Russell, making the most awful accusations. All nonsense, of course. I mean, he has actually counted how many votes Russell has missed during his years in the Senate. Can you imagine anything so paltry? He knows Russell's wife was dying of cancer for a lot of that time. And this is only the primary race. These accusations are coming from within his own party! Think what it will be like in the summer when poor Russell will be running against a Democrat! And to make everything worse, Mark van Hollen, whom I must say I credited with better sense, has to go and make a fool of himself."

"I don't imagine he was thinking about you, or Russell, at the time."

"There's no need to be sarcastic," said Nina.

Adam took a deep breath, then said calmly, "Mother, Mark van Hollen's affairs have nothing to do with me, or you, or Russell. This mess can't possibly affect his campaign. And the story will die quickly in any case. You can be sure it won't make any of the van Hollen papers, for a start—"

"I suppose you're right." She still sounded doubtful.

"Certainly, I'm right."

"Poor Katrinka," said Nina, finally sparing a thought to the person most directly involved.

"Yes," said Adam. "Two failed marriages would be hard for any woman to take, even Katrinka."

"Not to mention two husbands without the sense or the decency to conduct their affairs discreetly. Of course," she added, "if she knew how to handle her men properly . . ."

If there was a knock at the door, Adam didn't hear it. But suddenly it was flung open and Lucia, looking pale, her short red hair disheveled, stood on the threshold. There were smudges on her fingers, and one on her cheek. She had been working in an office down the hall and had obviously raced out of it without a thought to how she looked. Jesus Christ, thought Adam, what the hell did he pay his secretary for if not to keep people from barging in on him? He held up five fingers, hoping Lucia would take the hint and go away until he was ready to see her. But she shook her head adamantly, refusing to budge. He frowned, but said, "Mother, something's come up. I'll call you if I hear anything." Ignoring Nina's protest, he replaced the receiver and glared at Lucia. "If this is about Patrick Kates, save it. I'm not in the mood right now."

"No, no," said Lucia. She seemed on the verge of hysterics. "It's Katrinka."

"What?"

307

"She's had an accident. She's in a hospital, in Prague."

Afraid that Lucia was about to faint, Adam was up from his seat and around his desk in an instant, grabbing her by her arms, settling her in one of the leather armchairs. "What kind of accident? How serious? Is she going to be all right?"

"I don't know. Nobody knows," said Lucia, responding only to the last question. "She's in critical condition."

"And the baby?"

"The same. It's a girl," continued Lucia. "They did a caesarean."

For a moment he felt as if a sailboat he had believed himself to be fully in control of had capsized suddenly, without warning, trapping him underneath. Fighting through to the surface, he took a deep breath. "We both need a brandy," he said quietly, going to the bar concealed in the lacquer cabinets covering the far wall. When he had brought her the drink and she had taken a sip, he said, "Tell me what happened."

"She slipped in the hotel bathroom. Christian was with her. He called an ambulance. I don't know much more than that. We'd all been trying to reach her because of that awful photograph, but she had taken Christian on a trip somewhere. Apparently, there was a Federal Express envelope with that photo and others waiting for her at the hotel when she got back. Christian found them beside the tub. She must have opened her mail in the bathroom, seen them, gotten upset, climbed out of the tub, and slipped. Thank God she had time to shout for Christian before she passed out."

"Who told you?"

"Christian called Mark. He called Robin. Robin called the rest of us." She took another sip of the brandy, choked a little. The color came flooding back into her face, relieving her terrible pallor.

"Where's Mark?"

"He should be in Prague by now."

"That sonovabitch," said Adam. The rage he felt was genuine, but it was obviously not because he believed Mark to blame for Katrinka's fall, the premature birth, the critical condition of mother and child. He knew better. But this was not the way he had planned things. Katrinka was supposed to be hurt, yes, but not physically. And if anyone was to run to her aid, it was supposed to be himself, not Mark van Hollen.

Suddenly, Lucia started to cry. "I'm sorry. I'm just so worried."

"Do you want more brandy?"

"No," she said, reaching into her pocket for a handkerchief. "I'll be all right."

Adam got up, returned to the lacquer cabinet, poured himself another drink, took a long swallow, then crossed to his desk and depressed the intercom button. "Get me Robin Dougherty."

"Yes, Mr. Graham." The disembodied voice, coming from the speaker, sounded startled, curious.

"I just spoke to her," said Lucia.

Adam didn't reply. He sat and waited the few seconds until the intercom buzzed and his secretary announced, "Miss Dougherty on the line."

"Robin?"

"Hello, Mr. Graham." Her voice sounded wary, as it had in every conversation since his separation from Katrinka.

"Lucia told me what happened," he said, cutting through the first round of verbal fencing. "Have you had any more news?"

"No," she said. "Katrinka and the baby are still listed in critical condition."

"If you hear anything, you'll let me know?" It was more an order than a question, and when she didn't respond immediately, he shouted, "Robin, for chrissake, I'm worried."

"Yes, yes, I'll let you know. I really can't talk anymore. I'm sorry." The line went dead.

Adam replaced the receiver, then put his elbows on the desk, and buried his head in his hands.

"I don't understand," said Lucia, shaking her head in bewilderment. "I don't understand at all. Mark's crazy about her. Why would he—"

"Just shut up, Lucia. Please. Just shut up."

"Mr. van Hollen, would you like some coffee?" A plump, smooth-cheeked, middle-aged woman, the nurse looked at Mark with concern as she held out the metal tray with the steaming mug of thick, dark Turkish coffee favored by the Czechs. He looked absolutely exhausted, she thought, almost as pale as his poor wife.

"Thank you," said Mark, taking the mug. He had already had too much coffee. It had kept him from sleeping on the plane trip over and strung his nerves as tight as catgut ready to snap. He had come close to hitting Christian, who had tried to bar his entry into Katrinka's room. If a doctor hadn't come along. . . . But a doctor had, thought Mark gratefully. He didn't want a brawl with Christian added to the list of things he had to explain to Katrinka if . . . *when*, he corrected himself, she regained consciousness.

"So many lovely flowers," said the nurse, continuing in Czech, looking around the room at the vases covering every available surface.

The clinic in Charles Square to which Katrinka had been taken catered mostly to foreigners, and its staff was multilingual, so the nurse's English was good; but Mark's Czech was even better. "She must have a great many friends."

"Yes," agreed Mark. And at least one terrible enemy. But who? Who could have sent her those photographs?

"You should go back to the hotel. You need to sleep," she continued. "If there's any change, I would call you."

"I'd rather stay," said Mark. "But thank you."

The nurse resisted the urge to smooth Mark's hair and left, thinking how lucky Mrs. van Hollen was to have a husband who was so handsome and so obviously in love with her. Her own husband had left her two years before.

Once the nurse was gone, Mark turned his attention back to Katrinka, who lay pale and motionless in the white bed, a monitor connected to her heart, an oxygen tube in her nose. Her dark hair was matted with dry sweat. She looked helpless, frail, almost unrecognizable with all her restless energy stilled. He took her hand. "Katrinka, baby, can you hear me?" he said softly. When there was no response, he sat back in his hard chair, picked up the mug of coffee from the nearby table, took a sip, then closed his eyes, and waited as he had since his arrival at the hospital at one o'clock that afternoon.

Within half an hour of Christian's call, Mark had been on his way to Kennedy Airport. By eleven o'clock the previous night, he had been airborne. And then time had stood still. The plane trip to Prague had seemed interminable. Mark had tried to read, but couldn't concentrate. He had gone into the master cabin to lay down on the queen-sized bed and try to sleep, but it was impossible. Returning to the main cabin, he had continued to drive his pilot crazy with requests for position reports. By phone, he had stayed in constant touch with the hospital in Prague, monitoring Katrinka's condition and the baby's. He was sick with worry. And with guilt. Though logic told him that what happened to Katrinka was not his fault, still he could not stop blaming himself. He had known it was not a good time to leave her alone. His instincts, the ones on which he prided himself, the ones that had brought him so much success, had warned him to stay close to her, and he had ignored them. He had allowed them to be overrun by business concerns. He'd been a fool. He should have gone with her to Prague. At the very least, he should have flown to meet her once she had delayed her return. To hell with her private agenda, to hell with her plans for Christian, to hell with his being an understanding husband. He should have been with her.

And now he was, and there was nothing for him to do but wait. It was driving him crazy. He tried to remember the relaxation techniques he had learned in Tibet, one of the places he had gone after the death of Lisa and his two boys. But he could not concentrate even on that. Had he ever known how to pray? he wondered. His family had not been religious, and, except for weddings and funerals, he never attended church services. His eyes opened and he looked again at Katrinka. Nothing had changed. She hadn't moved so much as a finger.

Standing up, he stretched. Thinking a shave might make him feel better, he reached into his leather overnight case, took out the kit, and carried it down the hall to the WC. The worried family members of other patients ignored him, and harried nurses smiled at him as he passed, but he saw no one he recognized, no one he could ask the same question he had been asking since the previous night: when would they know?

He peed, washed his hands and face, then began to shave away the stubble. His eyes were red with strain and gritty with fatigue. He felt as if he hadn't slept in a week.

When he returned to the room, he found Katrinka just as he had left her. He had no illusions. He knew she could die. He knew the baby could die. He was incapable of optimism. Life had robbed him before, and might again, with as little reason. But if optimism eluded him, so did despair. Just as arbitrarily, Katrinka or the baby or both might survive.

Replacing the shaving kit in the leather bag, he went back out into the corridor in search of the small office with the phone he had been granted permission to use. When he found it, he asked the dour bureaucrat behind the desk, in his most polite Czech, if he could make two calls, then phoned Robin to report that nothing was new, and his office, speaking to both his secretary and Carey Powers. "Everything's under control here," Carey assured him. "I'll let you know if there's anything I can't handle on my own. Okay?"

"Okay," agreed Mark. Impatiently, he listened to Carey's well-meant expressions of reassurance, tried to respond as if he believed them, then hung up and went to the nursery to have a look at his daughter, who seemed unbelievably small to him as she lay in her incubator, her tiny body connected by numerous wires to monitoring machines.

"She's doing well, very well," the nurse on duty told him.

Mark did not know whether or not to believe her. "She's so tiny," he said.

"Not so tiny," contradicted the woman. "I have seen babies under three pounds. Five pounds two ounces is a good size."

Yes, thought Mark, taking some hope from that. The baby was only about six weeks early. That didn't seem too terrible to him. He remembered Katrinka's telling him that she had been born prematurely. How much had she weighed? he wondered.

"Would you like to hold her?"

Mark was startled. Was that allowed? If only they were someplace where he trusted the medical procedures, like St. Luke's or Columbia Presbyterian, instead of in an Eastern European country where the techniques had to be years behind the times. Still, he had to admit that so far he had no reason to complain about the care Katrinka and the baby were receiving. Everyone seemed kind, caring, and—most important of all—knowledgeable. "Yes," he said, "please. I would like to hold her."

The nurse removed the baby from the incubator, crooned to her in a spate of Czech endearments as she wrapped her in a blanket, then placed her in Mark's arms. "See," she said. "She's quite an armful."

The baby squirmed a little, screwed up her pink monkey's face, then settled back to sleep. Mark could see no resemblance to Katrinka or himself, yet the minute he took hold of the small, unfamiliar, miraculous body of his daughter, he knew he was connected to her by bonds much stronger and much deeper than the slender wires connecting her to the monitor. Tears pushed at the backs of his eyes. His heart seemed to be melting inside him. "Yes," he agreed, "quite an armful."

By the time Mark got back from the nursery, Christian had returned from the hotel, where he had gone for a few hours rest, and was seated in the chair beside Katrinka's bed. "Has she been awake at all?" he asked as Mark entered the room.

"No. She hasn't moved since I got here."

"You should go rest. I'll stay now."

"No," said Mark. "We'll both stay." He asked one of the orderlies for another chair, then sat beside Christian. The air between them vibrated with suspicion, with animosity. Christian had seen the photographs and wanted an explanation. Mark had refused to give him one. The argument that had started on the phone the night before had almost come to blows when Mark had arrived at the hospital. But, for the moment at least, Christian seemed prepared to let the matter rest.

"Zuzanka called," he said.

"Who?"

"Mirek's daughter. He was buried today. She wanted to know what had kept us away."

"Oh," said Mark noncommittally. He felt curiously detached from that part of Katrinka's life.

"She said to tell you she was sorry. And that she hoped Katrinka and the baby would soon recover."

"That was kind of her," said Mark. Then, for a moment, something other than worry about Katrinka and the child occupied his mind. "Are you okay about missing the funeral?"

"Okay?"

As always, Mark found it difficult to read Christian. "Did you want to be there?"

Christian shrugged. "He meant nothing to me."

They lapsed into silence. Though the two in fact had many interests in common, there was no ground on which they could meet, so guarded were they with one another. Christian disliked Mark as he disliked anyone whom he saw as a rival. He also blamed him for what had happened. His phone call to Mark the night before had been made in panic, before he had stopped to think, and he had regretted it ever since. He did not want Mark there, and would not have felt in the least guilty had he succeeded in keeping him away.

And Mark, who was wary of Christian, distrustful of his motives, afraid of the hurt he might one day do Katrinka, could not get past his own fear, his own fatigue, and deal with Christian as if at least the possibility of affection existed between them.

Occasionally, one of them would stand up, stretch, and go for a walk along the corridor. At eight-thirty, at the doctor's insistence, they left the hospital briefly to get something to eat, dining together in near silence, neither wanting to discuss his own feelings, or intrude into the other's. In less than an hour they were back at Katrinka's bedside.

The minutes ticked by slowly. Mark's eyes closed and sleep began slowly to overtake him. Then, he was jolted awake suddenly by Christian's voice, speaking softly. "I think she's moving."

Mark's eyes snapped open. Without even realizing he had moved, he was on his feet, leaning over Katrinka, watching as first her hand, then her head, finally her leg, shifted position. Her eyelids fluttered slowly open, her eyes for a moment as flat and dull as pieces of old blue tile. Then they seemed to focus.

"Christian, *miláčku?* Where am I? Mark, what you are doing here?"

"You had an accident," said Christian. "You fell."

She remembered and her face clouded with pain. "The photographs," she said.

"I'll explain," said Mark, "when you're stronger. For now, all you have to know is I love you."

"The baby?"

Perhaps she hadn't heard him, thought Mark. Perhaps she didn't care. "She's going to be all right," he said, and for the first time felt certain that was true.

"She?"

"We have a little girl. She weighs five pounds, two ounces. More than you did, if I remember right."

"Much more," agreed Katrinka. Her eyes were beginning to close again, but she forced a smile and reached for Christian's hand. *"Miláčku,"* she murmured.

"I love you," repeated Mark. "Katrinka, do you hear me?" She nodded. "Do you believe me?" She nodded again. I love you, repeated Mark, this time not aloud.

As soon as the doctor pronounced Katrinka out of danger, Mark returned to the hotel to sleep, leaving Christian to sit with her for a while longer. When he returned to the hospital the next morning, he found Christian still there, and Katrinka, though pale, wide awake and having breakfast. "You look great," he said, leaning over her to kiss her cheek. He could hear the relief in his voice.

"My stomach hurts, but otherwise I do feel terrific. The doctor said in a little while I can go see the baby."

"You're not thinking about walking," he said, making it clear he did not approve.

She shook her head. "They will take me in a wheelchair." She laughed. "We do have all the modern conveniences here."

"Whatever, they have saved your life, and I'll be eternally grateful." He turned to Christian, feeling almost fond of him for once. "Did you get any rest?"

"I feel fine."

"I want him to go to Bonn today. He's lost enough days on my account."

"I'll think about it," said Christian.

"You'll go," said Katrinka.

Mark laughed. "I can obviously stop worrying about you. You're back to your normal, bossy self." He reached into his pocket and took out a wad of cables and faxes that had arrived at the hotel for her. She took them reluctantly, he thought. "They're all from friends," he said. He had read them, to be sure they contained no unpleasant surprises.

"And so many flowers," she said.

As soon as the breakfast tray was cleared, a nurse entered with a wheelchair, then, with Mark's help, lifted Katrinka and settled her in it.

"Are you okay?" asked Mark.

"Fine, fine," said Katrinka impatiently. "Let's go."

Flanked by Christian and Mark, the nurse wheeled the chair along the corridor to the nursery. There were five or six babies in hospital cribs, some squalling, some sleeping, one being changed by a nurse. There was only one incubator and Katrinka's eyes went immediately to that as the nurse wheeled her nearer. "She's so small," said Katrinka.

"She's bigger than you were," Mark reminded her.

"It's hard to believe." Katrinka looked at the nurse. "Can I hold her?"

The nurse picked up the baby, waking her from a sound sleep, and placed her in Katrinka's arms. "Holding is good for babies. It helps them grow."

Katrinka wasn't aware of it, but tears were streaming down her face. Mark took the handkerchief from the breast pocket of his blazer and wiped them away. "I can't believe this," she said. "It's like a miracle." She turned to Christian. "You were born early," she said, "but not so much. You already weighed seven pounds."

Looking down at his mother and little sister, Christian smiled dutifully, but in fact the charming picture they made didn't touch him at all. Mother and child. It was too predictable, too sentimental. Not his kind of thing at all. It was as if, in the past several days, he had used up whatever supply of feeling he came equipped with, and was finally numb.

"Andelíčku," crooned Katrinka to the baby. "Moje zlato."

He would definitely do what Katrinka had asked, decided Christian, and return to Bonn that afternoon.

It was not until after lunch, when Christian had gone, that Katrinka and Mark finally decided to stop postponing the conversation they knew they had to have.

She had awakened from a short nap and Mark had looked up from the book he was reading to find her watching him. "Tell me," she said.

For a moment he remained absolutely still, then he got up, dropped the book on the chair, and sat on the bed beside her. He took her hand. "It's not a very believable story," he said. "But it's true."

"Tell me," she repeated.

"I was on my way to the airport. My bags were already in the car. The butler had taken them down while I finished up a phone call. When I got out of the elevator, Monica was there, in the lobby. Maybe she got in when the butler opened the door. I don't know. But there she was. She began talking, all nonsense, about how she was in love with me, how she needed to see me, on any terms, she didn't care. I guess, at the beginning, maybe I found her interest flattering, but I swear, Katrinka, by that point I thought she was nuts. I had never done a thing to encourage her. I couldn't imagine what she was doing there, carrying on like that. If anything, I was a little stunned. I said something, I don't even remember what, and started out of the building. She came running after me. She must have grabbed my hand. I don't remember. At the bottom of the steps, I stopped to tell her she had to cut it out, leave me alone, that I was sorry if I'd given her the wrong impression, but I was not interested in any kind of relationship with her, physical, social, or business. She let go of my hand, but instead of backing off, she put her arms around my neck and kissed me. I felt like a fool. There I was, in the middle of Chapel Street, a beautiful woman kissing me, and all I wanted to do was cut and run. I was terrified someone would see us. But I never spotted the photographer. I would have killed him if I'd seen him. I pushed her away. I told her she ought to get professional help. And I got into the car, and told the driver to get the hell out of there."

Instincts were certainly peculiar, thought Katrinka, as she sat listening to Mark. But were they trustworthy? She remembered the way, when Jean-Claude had suggested that Adam was being unfaithful to her with Natalie, as unlikely as the story had been, her husband and her best friend having an affair, she had believed it. Now here was another husband, Mark, denying a much more familiar story, a completely believable one about his involvement with a younger, beautiful woman, and she believed him, too. Was she out of her mind?

"You have to believe me," he said.

"I do. I think I am very crazy, but I do."

"I swear it's the truth."

"I believe you," she repeated.

He felt the weight he had been carrying for days suddenly lifted. Happiness washed over him. "Oh, baby, thank you," he said as he leaned toward her and kissed her ear, her cheek, her mouth. "I was so scared."

"But why Monica would do something like that?" she said. "Why she would send me those photographs? It's so crazy, so terrible."

"I don't know," said Mark. "I really don't know. But I intend to find out."

Twenty-Seven

WITHIN A WEEK, KATRINKA WAS ABLE TO LEAVE THE
CLINIC; BUT THE BABY, WHO WAS DOING WELL, STILL
weighed too little to be released. It was not an arrangement designed to
make Katrinka happy, especially since, for the first few days after her
return to the hotel, she was too weak to visit the child. However,
though Mark knew he ought to return to New York to deal with the
problems the newspaper stories had caused with the more conservative
members of his board, he left it to Carey Powers to soothe the outraged
morals and smooth the ruffled feathers. He remained in Prague,
spending hours every day in the nursery, holding his daughter, and
what remained of his time reassuring his wife about the baby's health.
It was certainly a period of great stress, but it was also a time of peace
and contentment. They were together, they loved each other, they had
a child who every day was growing stronger: they had survived the first
great crisis of their marriage, and both were relieved and grateful.

For Katrinka, there was one additional source of pleasure. Christian
called almost every day, all the coldness, the cynicism, the manipulativeness, gone from his voice. "You saved my life, *miláčku*," she said to
him once.

"I called an ambulance," he responded dismissively. "Don't make
too much of it." But Katrinka was certain she heard affection in his
reply. She did not yet dare to hope it was love.

* * *

317

By the time it was necessary for Mark to leave Prague, not only was Katrinka able to manage the trips to the clinic on her own, but Carlos Medina had arrived, and the time she did not spend with her daughter, she spent with the designer revising plans for the new hotel, choosing colors, wallpapers, carpets, furniture, helping him to assemble a crew for the start of construction. She also talked several times a week with Jean-Claude about the food and clothing boutiques, and every day with Robin and the general managers of her hotels, keeping a firm hand on business despite the distance. Faxes and Federal Express packages went to and fro with plans, budgets, ad campaigns, promotional material—anything that needed Katrinka's approval.

Her continuing presence in Prague also resulted in a quick exchange of contracts for the new apartment; and she of course attended meetings of the committee she had helped establish to arrange and conduct business seminars. But, happy enough to have dinner alone or with Carlos, Katrinka refused most business and social invitations, except for one from Zuzanka to meet her husband and children. It was an odd evening, spent in the family's bleak modern apartment in one of the new developments on the outskirts of the city, not far from the Barrandov Film Studios. Everyone was a little uncomfortable at first, but gradually the strain lessened and by the time Katrinka left she was no longer "that rich American" or even "one of grandpa's girlfriends," but a friend of the family.

"Next time, if it's possible, I would like Christian to come. I would like him to meet my children," said Zuzanka as she escorted Katrinka to the door.

"I'm not sure when he will be back, but I know he would like to see you again," replied Katrinka, with more confidence than she usually felt when trying to judge Christian's feelings. She had never seen her son respond to anyone so immediately, without any trace of duplicity or self-interest.

From London and then New York, Mark phoned several times a day and a good deal of his conversation centered around his begging, and then ordering, Katrinka not to work too hard; but she insisted that she was enjoying herself. And she was. She was eating well, sleeping more than usual, getting massaged every day to help strengthen her weakened muscles, and starting gradually to exercise. With her worries about the baby growing less as each day the child grew stronger and healthier, Katrinka soon felt on top of the world. That is, she did as long as she kept busy. When she grew restless or bored, she began to brood, spending too much time thinking about what might have happened if Christian had not heard her cry out, letting her anger at Monica Brand build until it threatened to explode. Would the woman let them alone now or would she try something else? Just how crazy was she? The many unanswered questions were worrying.

For Mark, too. On his return through London, he had tried to find Monica, but her phone number was out of service, and the mailing address that she had given him, the one that had been on the cover sheet of the articles she had asked him to read, did not exist. She was not listed in any of the London phone books and the magazines that had published a few of her short pieces had long outdated information. Remembering that she had been his dinner partner one evening at Tony Moreland's, Mark called Tony to ask how to find her, but Tony had no idea: she had simply arrived with one of his other guests—the Duke of Cumber, he thought. But the duke, when asked, said he did not recall anyone of that name. Knowing his reputation with women, Mark didn't doubt that one could easily get lost in the crowd.

Monica might almost have been a figment of his imagination, thought Mark—except for the photographs, which proved conclusively that she existed, perhaps not in London, perhaps no longer using the name Monica Brand, but somewhere. Finally, in desperation, he called Sabrina.

"Surely you don't expect me to reveal my source?" said the columnist in response to Mark's questions. Her accent was at its most British and disdainful, as if she were staunchly upholding First Amendment rights rather than merely protecting her own rear. She had no source. An envelope with photographs and a story had simply appeared on her desk one day. They had been too delicious not to use.

"Your source is a liar," said Mark.

"I have reason to believe otherwise."

"Tell Charles Wolf I'll feed him to the sharks for this," said Mark before slamming down the phone.

As far as Sabrina was concerned, that was Charles Wolf's problem. She kept up the attack. According to her, Mark had "abandoned" Katrinka in Prague while their child was still in critical condition in the hospital. Distorting information supplied by a hotel operator she had bribed, Sabrina reported that Katrinka was in constant communication with Jean-Claude Gillette, begging him to return to her as soon as possible, although Jean-Claude, torn between "the imperious Katrinket" and "the fabulously wealthy" Thea Papastratos, seemed in no hurry to obey the summons. And, after Mark's phone call, which appeared in Sabrina's column as "a plea for help," Sabrina hazarded the guess that, fearing retribution from the "possessive Mrs. van Hollen," Monica Brand had gone into hiding.

As usual, Rick Colins jumped into the fray and used his television show to refute the stories. In a brief on-the-air telephone interview, Katrinka denied them vehemently; and Mark, although it was against his principles, gave Rick a quote to use. He felt he owed it to Katrinka to declare publicly that the stories were a lie.

The charges and countercharges made all the tabloids, American and European. Even the van Hollen newspapers were forced to mention them, though they did so briefly and in positions not likely to attract attention. To control damage, Mark got Katrinka to agree not to read the trashier papers and called her friends to ask them not to pass on any gossip to her. "You can believe me or not believe me," he told them. "I don't give a damn. It's not the issue. The issue is helping Katrinka get back on her feet. There's a limit to how much of this shit she can take at the moment."

Zuzka and Daisy did in fact believe him, as did Tomáš, though Alexandra, Lucia, and Margo took Mark's denials with a grain of salt. All of them, however, agreed to stop passing on to Katrinka any nasty bits of gossip they might read or hear. And happily (for Katrinka and Mark at least), the continuing saga of Princess Di's unhappy marriage and the antics of the Duchess of York absorbed a great deal of the public attention that might otherwise have been focused on two rich and famous Americans.

When Mark thought about the progress of his relationship with Monica Brand—those first few coincidental meetings, the lightly flirtatious phone calls, the equally flirtatious lunch, then that sudden mad leap to scented letters full of accusations, hysterical scenes, incriminating photographs—things seemed to him not to add up. For one thing, Monica had appeared to him to be a cool, and if not calculating, at least savvy young woman, not particularly neurotic, not in the least "disturbed." For another, on reflection, such a long string of "coincidences" was very hard to buy. And what could possibly account for her sudden and complete disappearance? It began to seem likely to Mark that someone was out to get him and Katrinka.

While Mark did not want to discuss the full extent of his worries with his wife, he did tell her that he thought it important to find Monica and declaw her, to eliminate the possibility of her making trouble in the future. Katrinka agreed and suggested that he contact Paul Zeiss, the detective who had located Christian for her. So, on his way back to join

Katrinka in Prague, Mark stopped over in Paris, going directly from Charles de Gaulle Airport to the detective's offices overlooking the Pompidou Center.

Though he had heard much about him not only from Katrinka but from news reports about the success of Zeiss Associates in tracking down political hostages, kidnap victims, corporate executives who had absconded with company funds, etc., Mark had never met the man before, and his first impression was not favorable. It occurred to him later that he must have been expecting Sean Connery or Sylvester Stallone. What he found was a small gray man who looked more like a minor government official than anyone's idea of an international private eye. But after a few minutes of conversation, Mark revised his opinion upward. Paul Zeiss clearly knew what he was doing. In his overly careful English, he questioned Mark closely, making a note of every detail, no matter how minor. He glanced at the articles, the letters; he studied the photographs of Mark and Monica intently, turning them over and back again.

"Do you recognize her?" asked Mark.

"No, not at all," said Zeiss. "But the photographer clearly knows what he is about."

"So I thought," said Mark. "But there's no shortage of paparazzi around."

Zeiss shrugged. "It is a place to start." He put the photographs back in the envelope and looked at Mark. "Is there anything else you would like to tell me?"

"You mean, was I fucking her?" Zeiss inclined his head a fraction of an inch. "I wasn't even thinking about it," said Mark.

"You gave her no reason to believe you might be interested?"

"Not intentionally. But then I'm not dead yet."

"And you can think of no reason why she might have sent you these?" asked Zeiss, indicating the pile of papers and photographs on his desk.

"None. Except . . ." His suspicions suddenly seemed very farfetched to him and for a moment he hesitated.

But Charles Zeiss finished the sentence for him. "That someone else put her up to it?"

"Exactly," said Mark, relieved to see that Zeiss had come to the same conclusion.

"Whom do you suspect?"

Mark shook his head. "I can't think of anyone who hates Katrinka or me that much. I can't see what anyone would gain from a stunt like this."

They talked for a while longer, then Mark looked at his watch, said his plane was scheduled to take off soon, and stood up to go.

"I am not a miracle worker," warned Zeiss, as he always did when ending a meeting. "The work is tedious, and it will take time."

"My wife has great faith in you," said Mark as he shook Zeiss's hand.

"And in you apparently," replied Zeiss dryly.

"I hope so." Mark smiled faintly. "When will I hear from you?"

"Reports are sent out regularly once a month. I'll phone you should I learn anything of interest before then."

"I want her found before she does any more harm."

"I understand," said Zeiss. "Perfectly."

The day after Mark returned to Prague, the baby was declared well enough to leave the clinic, and Mark and Katrinka went together, if not exactly to bring their baby "home," at least to return with her to their suite at the Intercontinental. The following Sunday morning, Anna Milena van Hollen, named after both her grandmothers, was christened at St. Vitus Cathedral in Hradčany. Her godparents were Carey Powers and Daisy Donati. Afterward, Mark and Katrinka threw a party at the Golden Prague restaurant for the godparents, their spouses and children; Christian; Katrinka's cousins and their families; Zuzanka and hers; Carlos Medina and his lover, Sir Alex Holden-White; the mayor and his wife; the doctors who had treated Katrinka and the baby; and several of the nurses. Anuška (as the baby was to be called) slept peacefully through the entire celebration. It was a happy day. Katrinka wore the sapphires Mark had bought her. Christian was on his best, most charming behavior, completely captivating Zuzanka's children (his "niece and nephew" as he insisted on calling them), treating both Katrinka and the baby with extraordinary tenderness. The only tense moment came when he urged Katrinka to repeat her invitation to Milena, who had avoided him for most of the day, intimidated not only by the charm that worked so well on everyone else, but by the suspicion that he expected something from her, though it was unclear to her just what.

"Invitation?" repeated Mark, who was standing with Katrinka when Christian raised the subject.

Suddenly Katrinka remembered that she had promised Mark not to invite people to stay with them without consulting him first. "So much was going on, I did forget to tell you. Milena wants to visit us for a few weeks this summer."

"Oh?" said Mark, who was not pleased with the news.

"I'm sorry," said Katrinka softly. "There was really nothing I could do but invite her. I did promise her years ago."

"It was entirely my idea," said Christian apologetically, though he did not seem in the least regretful. "I'm sorry if it's inconvenienced you in some way."

"Are you very mad?" asked Katrinka.

"No," said Mark, after weighing the possible inconvenience of Milena's presence against his desire not to upset Katrinka just then. "But that's it. No other guests."

"Except for me, of course," said Christian smoothly.

"You're not a guest," said Katrinka. "But I do think you would like your own apartment. Right?" she asked, hoping that Christian would agree.

For a moment, just for the pleasure of annoying Mark, Christian was tempted to say he much preferred staying with them, but then decided that would not suit him at all. His own place was definitely preferable. "That's very kind of you," he said. "Of both of you," he added. "You are being very generous."

"We are happy to do what we can for you, *miláčku*," said Katrinka. "You know that."

And Mark, grateful to Christian for saving Katrinka's life, for once did not disagree.

Instead of returning immediately to New York, Mark suggested that Katrinka spend a few more weeks in Europe, recuperating at the Villa Mahmed with little Anuška. It was not only the pressure of business Mark was trying to shield her from, Katrinka knew, but the public scrutiny and nasty innuendos that would greet her on her return. For the same reason, hiding out a while longer did not seem such a bad idea to her either. She gave in without too much of a fight.

Together with a young Czechoslovakian nurse, Jiřina Král, whom they had hired as a nanny, Mark and Katrinka and the baby flew in the van Hollen jet from Prague to Nice. Mark remained with Katrinka at the villa until the housekeeper, Anna Bubeník, arrived, then turned his wife and daughter over to her care. "Don't worry about a thing," said Anna reassuringly. "I'll make certain Mrs. van Hollen doesn't overdo things."

"I know you will. Why else do you think I sent for you?" asked Mark, smiling fondly at the plump motherly woman. It had been a great relief to Mark to discover that Katrinka's loyal housekeeper was among the small group of people who had not believed any of the rumors. "I'll be back next Friday," he told Katrinka before he left.

"Promise?" she asked. That was ten days away, an eternity. For some reason, she felt close to tears and hoped that her hormones were not still being crazy.

"Barring a disaster," he qualified.

"Don't even joke," she said. "I did have enough disasters so far to last forever."

"I'll be all in one piece, I promise," he said as he kissed her good-bye.

Katrinka stood in the gravel driveway, watching Mark's car disappear from sight, having second thoughts about staying behind, not totally convinced that the villa's quiet was really what she needed just then. Being left to herself, with too much time to worry, suddenly did not seem like such a good idea.

Coming from one of the open upstairs window, the sound of the baby's crying interrupted the gloomy train of Katrinka's thoughts. Turning, she went back inside and up the tile staircase to Anuška's room, where she found Jiřina changing the baby's diaper. "She's very hungry," said the Nanny, a pretty blond girl with a broad face and statuesque body.

"I'll feed her," said Katrinka, picking up her daughter as soon as Jiřina had finished buttoning the one-piece terry jumpsuit. Despite the baby's red face, the features contorted with anger, the open mouth emitting a sound brash as a bugle call, Katrinka thought her perfect. "Ssh, ssh, ssh," she murmured as she let her lips trail along the baby's soft round cheek into the folds of her neck. She smelled sweetly of lotion and talcum powder. "Food is coming, *andelíčku*. Just be a little patient." Katrinka looked at Jiřina and said, laughing, "She's just like me; she hates to wait." Sitting in an armchair, Katrinka cradled the baby in her arms, took the bottle Jiřina handed her, and ran its nipple around the baby's lips until the tiny mouth closed around it and began to suck. Katrinka was not, in all truth, sorry she had been unable to nurse Anuška. She was doubtful she would have found it as physically pleasurable as some people insisted it was; and she knew she would have resented the leaking breasts and the necessity of being available when the baby was hungry. But, without doubt, there was nothing in the world as comforting, as satisfying, as holding her child in her arms. She felt her spirits begin to lift. Two weeks at the villa, with no office to run or social commitments to eat up her time, suddenly seemed to Katrinka like heaven.

But no sooner had Katrinka reconciled herself to a peaceful, lonely existence than Margo phoned, asking if she could come to stay for a few days. "How you did know I was here?" asked Katrinka.

"I called Robin to see how you were, and she told me. Is it all right? Do you feel up to company?"

"I feel great," said Katrinka, who suspected Margo did not. "Come when you like."

"I'll be there in an hour," said Margo, who arrived fifteen minutes ahead of schedule, with two large Vuitton cases. Despite the face-lift, the layers of carefully applied foundation, the kohl-rimmed eyes, the bright red mouth, the startling bursts of color on her cheeks, Margo's misery was painfully obvious.

"What did happen now?" said Katrinka when she saw her friend's haggard face.

"I don't want to talk about it. I just want to see the baby. Oh, God, she's adorable," said Margo, when Katrinka had taken her up to the nursery to show off her sleeping daughter. "I love babies." She extended a finger and gently touched the soft down on Anuška's head. "I wish my kids would get married and produce a couple of these. I think I'm ready to be a grandmother."

Katrinka smiled. "Sometimes I do find Mark, standing just like you, leaning over the cradle, staring at her. You should see him with the baby. He's so cute."

At the mention of Mark's name, Margo stiffened slightly, but she said nothing except, "Cute as a button, I'm sure." She might not trust him herself, but she did not think it would be helpful, just then, to point that out.

Not that Katrinka failed to notice Margo's reaction: she had been expecting it. She knew most of her friends thought she was a gullible fool to believe her husband innocent. Sometimes she even thought it herself. But not for long. She trusted Mark completely.

That had to seem like idiocy to Margo, who had had all her faith in Ted, after twenty-five years of marriage, wiped out, destroyed, reduced to rubble. "He's still seeing that tramp," she told Katrinka later. "He promised he'd keep away from her, but he can't. He just can't."

"Maybe you should both leave Monte Carlo," suggested Katrinka. She was sitting on a leather pouf, sipping a kir royale, watching as Margo threw clothes haphazardly into an antique Moorish chest in one of the guest bedrooms.

"You think I didn't beg him to leave?" said Margo. "I pleaded with him." Her voice cracked and tears began to cut deep channels through the makeup on her cheeks. "I threatened to kill him. I threatened to kill myself. As if he'd care. He'd probably be delighted. Then he could marry the bitch." She grabbed a Kleenex from the filigreed box on the bedside table, wiped her eyes, leaving charcoal smudges in the tissue's wake, blew her nose, then said more quietly, "Everything was going fine until she started seeing someone else. He couldn't stand it."

"Maybe she'll fall in love with this other guy," said Katrinka optimistically.

"I hope she does. I hope she falls madly in love and dumps Ted. I hope she makes him miserable. I want her to make him suffer the way I've been suffering." She closed the suitcase, stuck it in the closet, and threw herself on the bed. "I can't believe this is happening to me."

"You did decide what to do?"

Margo raised her head. "You mean after I cut his heart out? After I cut off his balls? After I make sure he hasn't got a penny left to his name?"

Katrinka smiled. "Uh huh," she said.

"No," said Margo, letting her head fall back against the soft pillows. "That's as far as I've gotten with my plans."

"Maybe you should think seriously about returning to work?"

Margo shrugged. "Oh, Katrinka. You think work's a cure for everything."

"Not a cure. But it helps."

"I think I'd rather do what Alexandra's doing: find someone pretty to distract me."

"Alexandra? What you are talking about? What is Alexandra doing?"

Margo sat up. "You don't know?"

Katrinka shook her head. Though she had not seen Alexandra since March in Palm Beach, Katrinka had spoken to her often, at least once a week, more since Anuška's birth. But in all their conversations, Katrinka had heard no hint of trouble beyond Neil's continuing problems at Knapp Manning. The company, for some time, had been overrun with SEC investigators, which was pretty much business as usual on Wall Street in recent years.

"Remember that polo player she met in Palm Beach in March?" said Margo.

"The one she did spend so much time dancing with at the ball?"

"Yes," said Margo. "Gabriel de Mellor. She's been seeing him."

"What you mean, *seeing*?"

"What do you think I mean? She's been spending time in Palm Beach with him. He's even been to New York to visit her a few times."

"Maybe they're friends."

"Katrinka, for someone as sophisticated as you appear to be, sometimes you are incredibly naive."

"Why? Because I do find it hard to believe my friend is cheating on her husband?"

Margo didn't respond to that directly. Instead, she said, "De Mellor is very wealthy. A huge ranch in the pampas. An apartment in Paris. A house on Mustique. It's not just cattle. It's oil, and God knows what else."

"Alexandra loves Neil," said Katrinka stubbornly.

"Neil is a sinking ship."

"I can't believe it," said Katrinka, even as she began to suspect that Margo might be right. She took another sip of her drink, then said, "How you do know all this?"

"It hasn't made the columns yet, but everyone is talking."

"Gossip," said Katrinka distastefully.

"And Alexandra practically came right out and admitted it the last time I spoke to her. You've probably had too much else on your mind to notice how often de Mellor's name crops up in her conversation."

"*Ay yi yi yi*," said Katrinka sadly.

"Neil hasn't got any real money, aside from his salary—what with alimony for his first wife and the way he and Alexandra live. If he loses his job," predicted Margo, "he'll lose Alexandra too." She didn't report any of this with satisfaction. The idea of other people's problems didn't make her feel any better about her own. She was just doing her duty, keeping a friend informed. "Oh, Christ," she muttered, settling back against the pillows again. "Mark will have my head for this. He said I wasn't to upset you. I'm sorry."

"It's okay."

"Listen, maybe I'm wrong. It won't be the first time. Shit! Why can't I ever keep my big mouth shut?"

It wasn't often that Katrinka regretted extending hospitality to a friend, but this time she was beginning to think she had made a mistake letting Margo come to the villa. Her story about Alexandra and Gabriel de Mellor had been upsetting, and certainly Margo's unhappiness about the state of her own marriage was no fun to witness, but that was the least of it. Ted called the villa at all hours, alternately pleading with Margo to understand or begging her for a divorce. The constant jangle of the phone, the shouting, the crying, soon got on Katrinka's nerves. "Tell her to go," Mark shouted at her, when she told him about the continuing scenes. "Tell her to get the hell out of there. Put her on the phone, let me talk to her!"

"No, no, I'll deal with it," Katrinka said, not wanting to add to Margo's problems by having Mark rage at her.

"You better," said Mark. "Or I will."

"Don't shout at me," said Katrinka, shouting back.

"You're supposed to be there resting."

"I'm sick of shouting. Stop it."

Hearing that she was close to tears, Mark calmed down. "All right. I'm sorry," he said quietly. "But she has to go, baby. I won't have her upsetting you."

"I told you, I'll take care of it."

But before Katrinka could think of a tactful way to broach the subject, the phone calls stopped (because Mark had phoned Ted and shouted at him, Katrinka found out later) and Margo herself suggested leaving. "This is crazy," she said to Katrinka the next morning at breakfast. "I've got to get out of here. It's too close to home. I'm going to New York. Who knows? Maybe I'll take your suggestion and try to get my old job back. Fighting with *Vogue* and *Harper's* ought to take my mind off fighting with Ted. What do you think?"

"I think it does sound like a great idea," said Katrinka.

Margo heard the relief in Katrinka's voice and laughed. "I've really been a bitch to have around, haven't I?"

Katrinka smiled regretfully. "You haven't been easy."

"Well, you've been an angel to put up with me. And I'm grateful. I really am. Would you do me one more favor?" she added apologetically.

"What?" asked Katrinka, sounding wary.

"Keep my car here until I decide what to do with it. I don't want Ted to have it." She began to cry. "He gave it to me for our last anniversary."

Margo was packing and Katrinka was in the nursery feeding Anuška when she heard the sound of a car on the gravel drive beneath the open window. Since she wasn't expecting any visitors, she made no attempt to move, but sat contentedly watching the baby in her arms suck sleepily at the almost empty bottle, knowing that Anna or one of the staff would deal with whoever it was: someone lost, no doubt. From the hallway below drifted the faint sound of voices, a little louder than usual, followed quickly by silence. She waited for the sound of the car driving off, but it didn't come. Instead there was a soft knock on the door. Expecting to see Jiřina returning with the baby's ironed clothes, Katrinka looked up, smiling, and found Adam Graham looking at her. "Very pretty," he said. "Like a painting. Madonna and child." There was a sarcastic edge to his voice, despite which he meant every word, though he would not have liked Katrinka to know how moved he was by the sight of her and the baby. How moved, how frustrated, how angry.

"I'm sorry, Mrs. van Hollen," said Anna, appearing suddenly behind Adam in the doorway. "But Jacques answered the door and didn't know . . ."

"Tell him not to do it again," said Katrinka.

"Hello, Anna," said Adam, smiling at her warmly.

"Mr. Graham," she said curtly, brushing past him and going to Katrinka. "I'll look after the baby, if you like. Jiřina will be here in a minute."

"It's all right. She's asleep," said Katrinka, getting to her feet. She walked to the cradle, put Anuška down, then turned to look at Adam, who had moved nearer to see the infant.

"She doesn't look like you," he said.

"No, I think she'll be fair, like Mark. Would you like something to drink?"

"Yes, please. Some mineral water, anything you've got."

"I'll have a glass of white wine," said Katrinka, to Anna. "We'll be in the library."

Anna hurried away to get the drinks, and Katrinka led Adam down the stairs. "Thank you for the flowers. And the stuffed animal for the baby."

He remembered the flowers, but not the gift. He must have told his secretary to send something from F.A.O. Schwartz. "I hope she likes it."

"Oh, she will. When she gets a little bigger. It's huge. What you are doing here?" she asked, as she settled herself in one of the library's leather armchairs.

"I always hated this room," said Adam, looking around at the walls of carved and inlaid wood, the mosaic floors, the Oriental carpets, the Moorish furniture. It was all too ornate for his taste.

"You always did hate the whole house," said Katrinka. "What you are doing here?"

He wasn't sure himself what he was doing there. Stopping had been an impulse, an irresistible impulse. "I was worried about you. So, I thought I'd drop in and see how you're doing. I'm on my way to Athens."

"I'm doing fine. Thank you."

"You're looking well. No, you're looking beautiful." Katrinka nodded graciously, but didn't reply. "And the baby?"

"She's wonderful," said Katrinka, biting back the impulse to elaborate. Like herself, Adam had wanted a child desperately; and though some would have said it was for all the wrong reasons—to carry on the family name, to have an heir, perhaps even to prove his manhood—Katrinka was not certain that she agreed. Adam had always been very good with children. Again, she found herself feeling sorry for him. She was so lucky: she had Mark and Anuška. And Adam, what did he have? Nothing but an old name and a fortune he had to fight day and night to keep from losing. "It was nice of you to come. I know how busy you always are. But you could have called. To warn me a little?"

"I was afraid maybe you wouldn't see me."

"Why not? I am too happy to stay mad at you."

The dark-haired Jacques entered with the tray of drinks and a Meissen bowl full of peanuts. He looked embarrassed and worried. "I'm sorry, Mrs. van Hollen," he said apologetically.

"Yes," said Katrinka. "You won't let it happen again?"

"No, madame," he said, serving the drinks quickly and retreating from the room.

"I'm still not used to hearing you called 'Mrs. van Hollen,'" said Adam when they were alone again.

"I did get used to it very fast."

"How much longer do you think you'll keep it?" asked Adam, annoyed suddenly by the depth of Katrinka's obvious contentment, by his own irrational feeling that Mark van Hollen had stolen not only his wife but his child.

Katrinka's eyes narrowed. "What you are getting at?"

"You left me fast enough when you found out I was having an affair."

"You shouldn't believe all the nonsense you read. You should know better."

Adam laughed. "How trusting you've become."

"I have always been trusting. With some people too trusting, for too long."

"You mean me? Well, you're wrong. I never cheated on you a few months after we were married."

"No? How long you did wait exactly?"

"Christ! Aren't you ever going to learn to speak correctly?" It was one of the things that had driven him crazy in the last years of their marriage.

"Maybe when you stop trying to torment me," said Katrinka, her voice rising finally to match his. "Why you don't stop this? Why you don't leave me alone?"

"I'm hurt, that's why. I'm hurt that you trust that sonovabitch, and you didn't trust me."

Katrinka could hear in his voice how true that was and felt all the fight go out of her. "You did never deny you were sleeping with Natalie," she reminded him, lowering her voice.

"And if I had, would you have believed me?"

She thought for a moment, then said, "No."

"Why?"

"Because you would have been lying."

"Jesus Christ!" muttered Adam. "And you really think he's not? What did he do? Hypnotize you?"

"I don't want to talk about this with you anymore."

"You're such a fool!"

"I want you to go away."

The door to the library opened and Margo entered, saying, "I'm finished packing. Can I borrow Jacques to drive me . . ." She saw Adam and stopped. "What the hell are you doing here?" she said.

"He's just going," replied Katrinka.

"Hello, Margo."

Margo eyed him with suspicion. He was handsome, he was charming, and he was smiling in a way she had always found irresistible. Until recently. "Did you come to cause trouble?"

"I came to see Katrinka. I was worried about her. But she assures me she's fine."

"Happy as a clam," said Margo.

Adam stood up, kissed Margo's cheek, and said, "I'm delighted to see you, too." Then he went to Katrinka, reached down, and took her hand. "I'm sorry if I hurt you. I hope you believe that much."

She shrugged as she got to her feet. "Spilled milk under the bridge," she said.

Adam shook his head and laughed. "Sometimes I don't know how I stood you as long as I did." He kissed her cheek. "It must have been love. Take care of yourself. And the baby."

"Thank you," she said.

She watched him leave the room, then sat down again. "I'm worn out," she said.

"To think I used to like him," said Margo, frowning.

"So did I," said Katrinka. "I did love him very much." Though she knew what she said was true, at the same time it seemed incredible to her. What could have happened to all that feeling? Where could it have gone? Had it just evaporated, gone up in steam from all the boiling fury she had felt for so long, leaving nothing behind but a dim memory? "And now, all I do feel is anger sometimes, and pity."

The
Past

Summer, 1992

Twenty-Eight

THE SOUND ON THE FORTY-FIVE-INCH SONY WAS MUTE AND, THOUGH ONE OF THE BOYS IN BLUE WAS CROSSING home plate and the crowd in the stands was going wild as the Los Angeles Dodgers racked up a rare victory, no one in the Havlíček den was paying any attention. Lori and Martin could not tear their eyes away from Tomáš, whose attention was focused completely on the voice at the other end of his remote telephone. The baby, Alenka, was on her stomach on the floor, trying to master the art of crawling.

"Yes . . . Yes . . . Certainly . . . I don't have a problem with that," said Tomáš. "I have his word on it," he added, after listening for what seemed a very long time. Then he laughed. "Okay, for you, I'll see he signs a contract . . . That's great. Great! See you Monday." He replaced the receiver, then leapt to his feet and let out a whoop.

"What? What?" said Lori.

"Is it a deal?" asked Martin.

"It's a deal," said Tomáš.

Startled by the commotion, Alenka began to cry and Lori swooped down, picked her up, and said, "I don't believe it. Oh, God, this is so wonderful. Ssh, sweetheart, it's okay. Everything's okay. Your daddy's gonna make a movie."

"What's going on?" said Candy, the Guatemalan housekeeper, as she ran into the room, looking anxiously around, expecting to find disaster. "What happened to the baby?"

335

"The baby's fine. Everybody's fine," said Tomáš. He began singing a Czech folk song and, grabbing Candy, began to polka around the room with her.

"We just scared her," said Lori as she patted the baby's back and made soft, soothing noises.

"Dad got a green light on a film," explained Martin.

Finally, Tomáš released Candy, who, laughing and out of breath, said, "You're all crazy," and retreated to her kitchen, where some semblance of sanity reigned.

"What did he say?" asked Lori, settling into a chair, the baby on her lap.

"He" was Spencer Ross, head of an independent film company. "That everybody loves the script, loves the cast, loves me. We start shooting September one." That was six weeks away.

"And?" asked Lori, who had been in the business too long not to expect a glitch, no matter how small.

"We need to make a few changes in the script. Nothing much. A little more heat here and there."

"And Beth gets to do them?" Tomáš nodded. "Sounds good to me," said Lori, relaxing finally, a big smile lighting her pretty face. Who could ask for anything more? she thought: a charming (albeit small) Spanish colonial house in Santa Monica, a beautiful baby, a real sweetheart for a stepson, and a green light on a film written by one's very own talented client, to be directed by one's very own handsome, desirable, talented husband. Whoopee, indeed.

"It's a great script, Dad. You'll make a terrific movie," said Martin.

Tomáš looked at Lori and said, "You see, I told you he had good taste." He turned back to Martin. "One of these days I'll be coming to you to arrange financing for my films, instead of some Hong Kong bank."

"Is that where Ross got the money? Hong Kong?" asked Martin.

"Most of it," said Tomáš.

While Tomáš did his best to explain the complicated deals as he understood them, Lori excused herself to take the baby upstairs for a bath and Martin listened with interest to the subtleties involved. He had recently started working at Knapp Manning and was trying to accumulate practical knowledge to supplement what he had learned at Claremont, alma mater of Henry Kravis, among others. "It's amazing," said Martin when his father had finished a financing saga almost as long and far more complex than the film he wanted to make. "How much time did it take Ross to put it all together?"

"Four months."

Martin whistled in appreciation. "That fast."

"It's what I like about him. He gets a move on."

"So, what's your schedule now?" asked Martin. "First you do *Low Flying Planes*, then this?"

Tomáš didn't answer for a moment. Then he shook his head. "I can't do both."

"You mean, you're not going to make Adam's movie?" Though he tried, Martin could not quite keep the note of disapproval from his voice.

"The two conflict. They're both scheduled to start shooting in September. And you know what will happen if I push this one off—the whole deal will collapse."

"Adam's not going to like it."

Tomáš shrugged. "I gave him a chance to make this movie. I'd never have gone to Ross in the first place if he had just said yes, instead of jerking me around for months."

"It's not exactly his kind of film, is it?"

Tomáš laughed grimly. "To put it mildly. Well, it's my kind of film, and I'm going to make it. Fuck Adam Graham."

Why was it, wondered Martin, that he could never be one hundred percent on his father's side? Why did his loyalties always have to be divided? He stood up. "I better get going," he said.

"Aren't you going to stay for dinner?"

"I promised Mom I'd have dinner with her." He was only in Los Angeles for the weekend, and his primary reason for returning had been to see Zuzka.

"How is she doing?" asked Tomáš.

"Okay," said Martin evasively, reluctant to betray his mother's confidence.

"If she needs anything, you tell her, just to call and ask."

"Why don't you tell her?"

"I did. But maybe she'll listen to you."

"It's this lawyer," said Martin finally. He needed to talk this over with someone, and who else was there but his father? "I think Mom wants to settle. I think she wants this whole thing over and done with and out of her life. But he keeps talking her out of accepting any deal that Carla offers."

"Sure. He's getting a percentage, isn't he? The longer he can keep this going, the more he can get out of Carla, the more he stands to make."

"I've told Mom that. She says she trusts him. She says she knows he only wants what's right for her."

"Do you think I should talk to her?"

"You can try, Dad. I don't know if it will do any good."

"I'll try." He walked with Martin to the front door, then turned to face him. Sometimes it still shocked him to have a son two inches taller than he. And always it saddened him that somewhere along the way, somewhere between Prague and Los Angeles, he and Martin had lost the closeness they once had shared. "Look," said Tomáš, "I know you think I owe Adam a lot, that we *both* owe Adam a lot, and I agree with you. I'm grateful to him. For saving your life, for giving me a chance to direct. I'll always be grateful to him for that. But you have to see this from my point of view. I've paid my debt. I've made him money. That's all Adam really cares about. And now, for the first time in my life I have a chance to make a film I really believe in. I can't let that opportunity pass me by."

"Believe me, Dad, I understand. I know this is something you have to do. I'm just sorry Adam may get hurt in the process."

"Are you going?" called Lori, as she came down the stairs into the foyer.

"He has to," said Tomáš.

"When will we see you again?"

"I'll let you know," said Martin, as he kissed Lori good-bye.

"Keep in touch," said Tomáš, extending his hand. Then, on impulse, he pulled Martin close for a hug. "Good luck," he said.

Martin returned his hug, then said, "I may need it. Things seem pretty shaky to me. At Knapp Manning, I mean."

"All over," said Tomáš, trying to be reassuring. "You'll be okay."

"See you," said Martin, as Tomáš opened the heavy wood door for him. He walked down the clay path, then turned to wave.

"Did he say anything about Pia?" asked Lori, watching as Martin got into the Honda he still kept at his mother's.

"No."

"She's moved to New York. Katrinka told me." Lori had called her to find out how she and the baby were doing.

"To be near Martin?"

"No, Christian."

When Martin's car turned the corner and passed out of sight, Tomáš put an arm around Lori and drew her back inside. Pia had always seemed too cool to Tomáš, too aloof. He couldn't help feeling his son was better off out of the relationship. "Well," he said, "nobody gets through life without a broken heart."

* * *

Tomáš considered taking the coward's way out and phoning, or sending a letter, but finally decided that, as unpleasant as it would be, he owed it to Adam to tell him to his face that he was pulling out of *Low Flying Planes*. So, the following Monday, as soon as his meeting with Spencer Ross was over and Tomáš was as certain as it was ever possible to be that the deal would not fall apart on him, he called Adam's office and arranged a meeting for mid-afternoon.

For once, Adam did not keep him waiting, the usual politics of power put on hold in deference to what Adam assumed was Tomáš's hectic schedule preparing Olympic Pictures's next blockbuster for production. He greeted Tomáš like the old friend he was, offered him a drink which Tomáš refused, poured himself a Perrier, and, instead of sitting behind his desk, took a seat in a leather armchair and asked how everything was going.

Everything was on schedule and going well, Tomáš assured him. The script needed another rewrite, but that was pretty much business as usual. The set designs were incredible, the director of photography they wanted had agreed to do the film for less than they had been prepared to pay him, and a "yes" by Mel Gibson was expected at any moment. There was only one problem, added Tomáš; he hoped Adam would understand; these things happen; conflicts can't always be resolved; he would not be directing the film.

Adam's first reaction was that he had not heard correctly; his second that Tomáš was making a bad joke; his third was fear, followed immediately by rage. This was not a question of just another film. The contracts for the sale of the studio were scheduled to be signed on Wednesday. If the Italians learned of this before then, who knew if they would go through with the deal. What didn't panic them panicked their backers, especially the English merchant bank putting up the money.

"You're out of your mind if you think I'll let you get away with this," he told Tomáš.

"You don't have a lot of choice, Adam."

"I don't? Who the fuck do you think you are, waltzing in here, telling me you're off my picture. I decide who's on, who's off. And you're not. You're not walking away from me on this one."

"What do you plan to do? Get somebody to smash my kneecaps?"

"You've got a contract with me."

"I don't have a contract," said Tomáš quietly.

"You what?"

"I didn't sign it." While Adam tried to work out the ramifications of that, Tomáš continued, "I was pissed off at the way you were jerking me around and I didn't sign. I meant to, eventually. But . . ." He shrugged.

"That's irrelevant," said Adam, when he had figured out his next step. "You've been working under its terms, just as if you had signed. That makes it binding." He wasn't sure whether or not that was true; he'd have to check with his lawyers, but it sounded reasonable.

Tomáš stood up. He didn't look happy. "As they say in the business, so sue me."

"This is crazy," said Adam, his mind racing, trying to find a way to salvage the situation. "I don't want to sue you. We've got a relationship, Tomáš, a good relationship. I don't want to screw that up. Postpone the other movie, that's all you have to do. Direct *Low Flying Planes*, and I'll make the other one for you, I swear it," said Adam.

"You won't even own the goddamn studio by then," said Tomáš, his voice full of disgust.

"I'll get an undertaking from the Italians—"

"Maybe I'd take you up on that, if I thought there was going to be a worldwide shortage of toilet paper. Come on, Adam, who do you think you're talking to?"

"I thought maybe a friend."

"Bullshit. If you'd been a friend, you wouldn't have had your contract people string me along for months, pretending you were going to make the film, when all along you had no intention—"

"I don't understand," said Adam, tacking back, "why you can't just do *Low Flying Planes* first, then the other. Why is that so impossible?"

"I've got a cast, I've got a crew, I've got money. But you know it could all fall apart in a minute if I tried to stall."

"And your commitment to me? to Olympic Pictures? They don't matter at all?"

"They matter, just not as much. Sorry, Adam, but that's the way it is."

"You know, I can fix it so you'll never get another job directing." Adam was exaggerating. But it was certainly true that he could make it harder for Tomáš by labeling him temperamental, unreliable.

Not to be offered bad films to direct, not to be tempted by money, not to have to hate himself for saying yes: what Tomáš felt was not fear but relief at Adam's threat. "Fine," said Tomáš. He turned away and headed for the door.

"But I won't," said Adam, though he was not quite sure it was true. He had to think about it. But, in the meantime, he had a problem to deal with. "Just do me one favor, okay?"

"What?"

"Keep quiet about this until the end of the week."

"Sure," said Tomáš, guessing that the Italians were going to sign sometime soon. "Why not?"

"Thanks," said Adam, without much enthusiasm.

Tomáš shrugged. "It's the least I can do."

As soon as Tomáš left, Adam called Mac in New York and filled him in on what was happening. Usually, Mac could be relied on for a cool assessment of any situation, but this time he blew, predicting disaster, shouting invectives into the phone, threatening Tomáš with the loss of essential pieces of his anatomy. And the angrier Mac got, the calmer Adam became. By the end of the phone call, he had a plan worked out.

"What are you going to do?" asked Mac.

"Tap-dance," said Adam. "Don't worry. It'll be okay."

"Adam, for chrissake—"

"Talk to you in the morning," he said, then pushed the button of the intercom. There was information he needed, phone calls to make, no time to waste. Mac was right to be worried. If the studio deal fell through, the shock waves would inevitably hit Graham Marine, which was still seriously overburdened by debt despite the improvement in business over the past few months. Adam had been moving money around as fast as a sidewalk con artist in order to cover payments. The sale of Olympic Pictures would, at the very least, get rid of a sizable loan and put some distance between him and his nervous bankers. It would also provide the cash needed for the final move against van Hollen Enterprises.

Adam rarely stopped to consider what he would do with a publishing empire once he got his hands on it, except get richer. He'd let Charles Wolf buy him out, he supposed, at a handsome profit. Or, visions of Si Newhouse and Walter Annenberg dancing in his head, he'd hold on to his shares, let Wolf run the show, and ride along on the gravy train. Either would suit him, as long as he won and Mark van Hollen lost. Whatever regret Adam felt for the harm he had done to Katrinka and her child stopped short of his plans for her current husband. He had called off Monica Brand, paid for her to disappear (she had taken a trip to Hong Kong, Sugar had told him, where the hunting for rich businessmen was good), but that was as much as he was prepared to do; and, according to the gossip he was hearing, the scandal had already had the desired effect on the van Hollen board. Ruining Mark, to him, seemed a separate issue. Katrinka had money of her own, after all, and Mark was an old, old rival.

341

To a large extent, Adam had always been an impulse buyer, getting into a deal because his "instinct" told him to, without really paying much attention to the financial consequences. He had become a billionaire ignoring good advice. And if selling a studio to reduce debt, only to acquire more by taking over a publishing company, did not, to someone as cautious as Mac, seem a particularly good idea, to Adam everyone's reservations only served to convince him that once again he was doing the right thing. They were accountants, he was a visionary. That's why they worked for him, and not the other way around.

Since his secretary had undoubtedly heard enough of his conversation with Tomáš and Mac to figure out what was happening, Adam took her into his confidence. And, by the time he left the office that day, Heather had supplied him with a list of top directors, their credits, availability, and price; a copy of the latest revised script of *Low Flying Planes*; a budget update; and a preproduction report on the film. He had phoned Mel Gibson personally to see if he could get a sense of how deeply he was committed to the film (very — if the director and the money were right); and he had canceled his dinner with Tashi Davis, the top model whom he had been dating on and off for months, for one hastily arranged with Ridley Scott, the director of *Blade Runner* and *Thelma and Louise*.

As he had told Mac he would do, Adam tap-danced his way through a dinner overlooked by dragons, Buddha heads, and cranes in Chinois on Main, in Santa Monica. Tomáš might possibly withdraw from the film for "personal reasons," he told Scott. (A nervous breakdown? cancer? AIDS? what? wondered the director.) If he did have to leave the film, there was no one Adam would rather have replace him. Mel Gibson was ready to commit, the moment Scott did. If Scott wanted him, that is. Harrison Ford was also interested, and Don Johnson. He told Scott the story, and, when the director responded positively, gave him the script to read. They promised to be in touch with each other in the next few days.

All in all, thought Adam as he drove north past Malibu, the evening had gone well, and the day was ending much better than he had expected. At the very least, if the Italians found out about Tomáš, he could tell them that Ridley Scott was ready to sign on. No one would deny it. There wasn't an agent in Hollywood who would deny that a client was about to start work on a big-budget, blockbuster film.

His good mood did not last long. As he was heading home along Pacific Coast Highway, his car telephone rang. It was Natalie Bovier, hysterical, almost incomprehensible. All he could make out in the

confusion of French and English coming at him along the crackling phone line was that she needed to see him.

"Natalie, I'm exhausted. I've had a rough day. I'll stop by in the morning," he said calmly, hoping to cut through the note of panic in her voice.

"Adam, please," she begged, sobbing. "It's Aziz."

"What is it? What's happened?" he asked. As far as he knew, her son was with Khalid in Cap Martin for the summer.

"I can't stay here by myself, waiting . . ."

Her affair with an Australian real estate developer had ended months before. She had other lovers, Natalie always did, but no one who mattered. Katrinka had been her one female friend, and they no longer spoke. The only people in her life to whom she felt close, aside from Aziz, were two of her former lovers, Jean-Claude Gillette and Adam Graham; and Jean-Claude, at the moment, was on Corfu with Thea Papastratos.

He had little hope, Adam realized, of finding out anything while Natalie was so frantic. "I'll get there as soon as I can," he said. "It should take me about twenty minutes."

Making an illegal U-turn, Adam headed back along PCH to Sunset, then turned east. He was worried. Natalie was neurotic, she was emotional; she certainly liked drama, but only enough to add a little spice to a love affair. This sort of scene was unusual for her. At least it had been until now. Had she finally slipped over the edge that all alcoholics reach sooner or later?

Within fifteen minutes, Adam pulled his car into the drive of Natalie's mock-Tudor house in Brentwood, got out, and moved quickly along the flagstone path to the front door. The maid must have been on the watch for him, because she flung open the door before he had a chance to ring the bell.

"Where is she?" asked Adam.

"In the sitting room," said the maid, her plump brown face pale with worry.

"What's going on?"

"Adam, *chérie*, is that you?" called Natalie.

"Yes," said Adam, starting for the other room. But Natalie came hurtling across the carpeted floor toward him, her eyes swollen, her face mottled. She looked like hell, he thought, as she flung herself into his arms, murmuring in French, which he did not understand. Adam turned to the maid. "Bring us some brandy, Maria, please." Then, his arm around Natalie, he led her back into the sitting room, sat with her on the oversized sofa, and held her as she cried. When the maid returned with the brandy, Adam pulled away a little and offered her the drink. Natalie took it, gulping it down, choking a little as she swallowed hurriedly.

"Tell me what's happened," said Adam.

"*C'est horrible, incroyable . . .*"

"In English, Natalie," Adam reminded her gently.

"Aziz has been kidnapped," she said, and burst into a fresh flood of tears.

She was clearly terrified. And, to make matters worse, she had been drinking. Afraid to give her more brandy, Adam held her again until she quieted, then listened as, between bouts of tears, Natalie told him disjointedly what had happened.

As he did at some point every summer, Khalid had set off on his yacht from his villa in Cap Martin for Sardinia. In addition to Aziz, with Khalid were his other son, Jasim, who was two and a half, and Jasim's mother, the Englishwoman who had replaced Natalie as Khalid's third wife. (His two Saudi wives and their children were in Riyadh.) On the way to Sardinia, the yacht had docked at Cargèse in Corsica, where Khalid and his wife had gone ashore to have dinner with friends, leaving the boys on board with their nannies and the crew. No one was quite sure whether the bandits had been forewarned that the yacht was to dock there, or whether they had on impulse decided to take advantage of a golden opportunity, but about twenty men had boarded the boat, overpowered the crew, and made off with the boys.

"When did this happen?" asked Adam.

"Tonight, at about nine." With a nine-hour time difference that would have been about noon Los Angeles time. But Khalid had not returned to the yacht until after three in the morning. It was then that he found the crew and the nannies tied up and locked in one of the cabins and the boys missing.

"Has he had a ransom demand?"

Natalie shook her head and began to cry again. "No. He waited before calling me, hoping he would hear something. Oh, God, Adam, I'm so frightened."

He was frightened himself, he realized. And angry, as he always was when he felt helpless. Aziz was a bright, handsome, moody boy Adam had become fond of during his affair with Natalie. Having none of his own, Adam inevitably became fond of his friends' children: it was one of his most appealing qualities. He would have done anything to help

344

the boy. The hell of it was, there was nothing at all he could do. "They'll be in touch with Khalid," he said to Natalie, sounding calmer than he felt. While not exactly common, kidnappings in Corsica were not unheard of, and—unlike those on the Italian mainland—were usually motivated by money, not politics. "They want ransom, that's all."

"He'll pay anything they ask. He won't argue. Jasim has diabetes. He needs medicine. Khalid just wants the boys back, before . . . before . . ." Her voice broke.

"He'll get them back, don't worry," said Adam, hoping he was right, hoping that the kidnappers would not overplay their hand. Did they know about Jasim's diabetes?

"Don't leave me," pleaded Natalie.

"I won't," promised Adam. "I'll stay with you until Khalid calls. Until he tells you he has them safe."

While waiting for Adam to arrive, Natalie had put through a call to Jean-Claude, who was with Thea Papastratos at her estate on Corfu. And it was Jean-Claude who, the next morning, telephoned Katrinka to tell her about the kidnapping. She was still at breakfast, in the conservatory of the New York town house, when Jean-Claude phoned. Mark, sitting opposite her, scanning *The Wall Street Journal*, heard her gasp and looked up, saw her pale and thought that she was about to faint. "Oh, God," she murmured softly. She seemed to recover, listened quietly for a few more moments, and then said, "You'll call me when you do hear something? . . . Thank you, Jean-Claude." She replaced the receiver and met Mark's eyes. Hers were full of tears.

"What is it?" Katrinka told him and Mark shook his head in disbelief. "There's not a thing in any of the papers about it."

"Khalid is keeping the story quiet. He's afraid."

"Yes . . ." He thought of Anuška, in her nursery upstairs; of his two sons, dead now for close to ten years; of the terrifying uncertainty of life. "How much time does he have?"

"I don't know exactly. But Jasim did get his last dose of insulin at six last night. It's almost twenty-four hours."

"Khalid should release the story to the papers," said Mark. "To all the media. It's the only way to let the kidnappers know they have a serious problem on their hands."

"He was to tell no one. That was the message they did leave with the crew."

"He can't afford to wait."

"I know," said Katrinka. "Someone should call Khalid and tell him."

"Someone has to," agreed Mark.

It was Adam who made the call.

Knowing of no other way of finding out how to reach Khalid, Katrinka called Natalie, something she had promised herself never to do. But then Katrinka had never imagined circumstances like these: they made all her grievances seem trivial in comparison.

The maid answered, but it was not Natalie who came to the phone to speak to Katrinka (she had finally fallen asleep), but Adam. And so preoccupied were they both with the kidnapping that neither seemed surprised by the other's presence at the other end of the line, the irony of the situation completely escaping them, at least for the moment. Even when she had told Adam what Mark suggested, and he had agreed to call Khalid to urge him to do it, Katrinka did not think anything beyond how typical it was of Adam, not generally a considerate person, to turn into the best kind of friend when a child's life was involved. And Adam, for his part, never once thought of ignoring the suggestion that came from a man he loathed.

For that matter, Khalid, who had not spoken to Adam since the beginning of his affair with Natalie, took his call, listened to the advice, and agreed to contact the media.

The story made the afternoon papers around the world. Within hours, it was being broadcast over Corsican television and radio stations. The local police, perhaps not as rigid in their ideas about negotiating with kidnappers as law enforcement agencies in other places, made it clear that they would do everything in their power to expedite matters, if the kidnappers would just come forward with their demands. Still, there was no word.

Katrinka had gone to her office at the Praha, but unable to concentrate, had returned home before lunch. Mark couldn't concentrate either, hardly paying attention to the restructuring plan Carey Powers was suggesting as a hedge against the takeover bid that every day seemed more imminent to him. Finally, they postponed a decision on the plan until the next day.

"Is anything wrong?" asked Christian when he saw Carey Powers returning to his office, a worried frown on his face.

There was plenty wrong. It was clear that Charles Wolf was buying VHE stock, though his holdings had not yet reached the five percent mark that would require his making a formal declaration to the SEC. Nor had he made an overt takeover bid, which at the very least would have resulted in everyone's knowing exactly where everyone else stood. As it was, Powers felt he was shadowboxing, and wearing himself out in the process. But he only said, "Do you know Prince Khalid ibn Hassan?"

"Why, yes," said Christian, wondering what Prince Khalid had to do with van Hollen Enterprises. "He's a friend of . . ."—for a moment, he hesitated, then continued—"my parents," since that seemed to cover everyone, the Hellers and Katrinka.

"His sons were kidnapped, by some bandits, on Corsica."

"How awful," said Christian politely.

"What a world." Powers shook his head in dismay, then said, "Do you have those figures I asked you for?" changing the subject back to business, where he always felt more comfortable.

Christian indicated the folder he was carrying, inside which was a printout of year-to-date advertising revenues from all the van Hollen newspapers and magazines. "That's what I was on my way to see you about. They look good."

"They do?" Powers sounded surprised, and relieved. Picking up a pile of pink message slips from his secretary's desk, he glanced through them as he said, "Well, come in, and let's see what you find so optimistic."

"A few markets are down," said Christian, following him into his office, ignoring Powers's ambitious young assistant, who glared at his retreating back, seeing him as her chief rival. "But overall, in the past few months, there's been a steady trend upward."

"Good." Expecting a hard time dealing with the spoiled brat stepson of the company's owner, Powers had nevertheless agreed to take Christian on because only a fool would have said no to someone with an advanced degree in economics from Bonn University. But though admittedly it was early days yet, just three weeks since Christian had started at the company, Powers was impressed with him. He found Christian intelligent, brilliant with numbers, hardworking, willing to do whatever he was asked. In fact, he found Christian very likable, and wondered why Mark seemed to have such a difficult time with him. "Where are we down the most?"

"Where you would expect. Where the economy is worst. England. Spain. But in Germany we're holding steady."

As soon as his meeting with Carey Powers ended, Mark sat thinking about the security guards Katrinka had used during the heyday of the publicity surrounding her divorce from Adam. After her marriage to Mark, when life had grown increasingly domestic and quiet, she had discontinued their services. But the rumors surrounding Anuška's premature birth had sparked new publicity, which had not quite died out. Katrinka and the baby, and to a lesser extent himself, were now very much in the public eye. It was easy enough to say that the United States was not Corsica, and that a kidnapping could never happen here; but then it was only necessary to think of the Exxon executive taken from the driveway of his home in New Jersey.

Mark knew that whatever he did to ensure his family's safety, there could be no guarantees. Fate always managed to penetrate even the most secure defenses. Still, he had to do something. He buzzed Josh, his assistant, and when he answered said, "Call Robin at the Praha and ask her the name of the security firm Mrs. van Hollen used. Then get me the president of the company."

It was times like these, thought Adam Graham, that made him almost grateful not to have children. Watching Natalie sitting pale and silent by the telephone, hour after hour, waiting for news, he knew he was lucky. As upset as he was, as terrified, he knew his anguish did not come anywhere near hers. There was no one, nothing, in the world who mattered to Natalie as much as her son.

Through most of the day, Adam stayed with her, taking care of business by phone. Late in the afternoon, he showered and changed into the clothes Carter had brought him from home, and left briefly to attend a meeting with his lawyer. Natalie spent the entire time he was gone on the telephone with Jean-Claude, provoking his first serious quarrel with Thea, who said later that she was fed up with the amount of time he spent talking to and about his ex-mistress. If he didn't stop, she added, she would leave him, a threat Jean-Claude did not take seriously. Thea was pregnant. He told her that when she had a child she would understand. And he thought, perhaps, he would then, as well. Horrified as he was in the abstract by what had happened to the two boys, his concern really was for Natalie. Love of a friend, of a woman, he understood. Love of a child was a mystery to him. Thea's child would be his first, the first he had ever allowed to be born. It occurred to him sometimes that he must be getting old to want to put in his bid finally, and a little late, for immortality.

When Adam returned from his meeting, he could see that Natalie had been drinking, enough to take the edge off her fear, not enough to make her drunk. He asked the maid to prepare something light, then insisted Natalie at least taste a bit of the chicken. She managed only a few mouthfuls before she pushed the plate away and said the food was making her sick. How much longer could they stand this? wondered

Adam. He turned on the television, tuning to CNN. Neither of them paid much attention, but at least the noise of it helped drown out some of their own thoughts.

The phone rang from time to time: Adam's secretary with a question, the managers of Natalie's boutiques wanting to know how she was. Late in the evening, Katrinka called and, when Adam told her there was still nothing to report, she asked to speak to Natalie.

"It's Katrinka," he said. "Do you want to talk to her?"

"Oh, yes, yes," she said, taking the phone and bursting into tears. "Katrinka, *chérie*, it's so terrible. You can't imagine. Poor Jasim. And my Aziz."

"I know. I am so sorry, Natalie."

"I would do anything to have him back. Anything."

"He'll be all right. You must just be patient, and not give up hope."

The other line rang and again Adam answered. This time it was Khalid. He did not want to speak to Natalie, he said. He couldn't just then. Talking to Katrinka, Natalie hardly noticed as Adam stood quietly listening, his eyes from time to time glancing in her direction, then away again. "Yes, I'll tell her," he said finally. "Khalid, I'm . . . I'm sorry. I'll phone you in the morning. If there's anything I can do . . . Yes. Yes, I will." He hung up, crossed the room, and sat on the sofa next to Natalie. She looked at him and knew immediately something was wrong. "Was that Khalid? What did he say?"

"Aziz is all right," said Adam. "Khalid has him, and he's well. He hasn't been harmed."

"Oh, thank God," she said, then speaking into the phone, she told Katrinka, "Aziz is safe. He's all right." Then, she remembered. "And Jasim?"

"He was in shock when they got him back. It was too late. He died a few minutes ago."

"Oh, my God," she wailed.

Adam gathered her into his arms, then took the phone from her and said, "Katrinka, I'll call you back later."

"It's Jasim, isn't it?" said Katrinka. "He's dead."

"Yes."

"Poor Khalid." She could not just then even remember his wife's name.

"I'll call you."

"Yes. Let me know if there's anything I can do."

Adam replaced the receiver in its cradle. "It's over," he said, stroking Natalie's hair. "It's over."

Twenty-Nine

HE'D BEEN WRONG, OF COURSE, ADAM TOLD KATRINKA ON HIS NEXT TRIP TO NEW YORK. IT WAS NOT OVER FOR Natalie. "The odds were always in favor of the kidnappers letting Aziz go once they had the ransom. But Khalid will never give him up now."

They were having lunch at Le Cirque. Adam had called to suggest it, making it clear that the subject under discussion was to be Natalie; and Katrinka, both too curious and too concerned to turn him down, had said yes without considering possible consequences. The moment she entered the restaurant she had realized her mistake. She saw the thoughtful glances, heard the buzz of conversation, and understood instantly that Adam, who, in her own mind, was history, in the public consciousness remained a player in an ongoing soap opera with herself and Mark as the other key characters. Since she could not, however, turn around and leave without adding more spice to the gossip, she let Adam take her arm as they followed Sirio, Le Cirque's unflappable owner, to their table.

Throughout the lunch, the elegant, mirrored room reflected their image to the sidelong glances of the restaurant's other patrons, all busy speculating among themselves the probable causes for such an unlikely lunch. They weren't quarreling, that much was obvious. But were they dealing, or dating? And, most intriguing of all, did Mark van Hollen know what was going on?

350

"But Khalid did promise," said Katrinka softly, doing her best to ignore the public scrutiny.

In reply, as if explaining a problem in simple arithmetic, Adam said, "Jasim was alive when Khalid made that promise. Now, Jasim is dead."

"Poor Natalie," murmured Katrinka.

"Poor Khalid," said Adam.

Katrinka looked at him. "You think it is right, what he did? To me, he seems as bad as the Corsican bandits." Prince Khalid had taken Aziz home with him to Riyadh and left it to a flunky to tell Natalie that, when she wanted to see the boy again, it would have to be in Saudi Arabia.

Katrinka's constant expectation that people would behave well, which persisted in face of all odds, never ceased to amaze Adam. "I think it's foolish to expect that Khalid, after what's happened, would surrender custody of his son, his *only* son, to anyone, let alone someone like Natalie."

"What you mean, someone like Natalie?" said Katrinka, annoyed, both with Adam for taking Prince Khalid's side, and herself for leaping to Natalie's defense. "What is so wrong with her?"

"A single woman. Living on her own. With a string of lovers."

"You do sound like your mother," said Katrinka, with disgust. "Like Russell Luce," she added, as if it was the worst insult she could think of.

"Who drinks too much," said Adam, ignoring her criticism, continuing his chronicle of Natalie's shortcomings.

Khalid had told her that months before. And Jean-Claude, too. But Katrinka had put it out of her mind. Natalie had hurt her so badly, Katrinka hadn't wanted to think about her. Now she couldn't seem to help herself. "She is drinking so much?"

"More than is good for her."

"And drugs?" Khalid had mentioned something about that, too.

Adam nodded. "A little marijuana, a little cocaine, when it's around. I don't know how big a problem it is."

"This will only make it worse."

"That's what I'm afraid of," said Adam. How had his relationship with Katrinka ever reached the point, he wondered, that they could discuss Natalie so calmly, without anger or recriminations? But rather than pleased, Adam felt irritated by the change. It occurred to him that he preferred Katrinka jealous. Leaning toward her, he let his hand rest lightly on hers on the white tablecloth. "I'm glad we're not fighting anymore," he said.

The busboy appeared then so that Katrinka had an excuse to slide her hand away and sit back in her chair, allowing him to remove the Limoges plate that still contained at least half her arugula salad. When he had gone, she turned to Adam and said coolly, "We have nothing to fight about. Do we?"

The image of Monica Brand flashed into Adam's mind, but he pushed it firmly out again and smiled reassuringly, "No, thank God. I like it much better when we're friends."

Katrinka would not have gone that far. She did not consider Adam Graham her friend, not now, probably not ever. Still, she had to admit it was a relief not to be at war with him. So, she changed the subject, and, over the chicken paillard and grilled swordfish, tried to keep the conversation firmly confined to safe territory.

His mother had loved being in Houston for the convention, Adam told Katrinka when she asked about Nina. Though her fondness for publicity had not increased, she was coping with it well enough, probably because she actually enjoyed political life, not just hobnobbing with George and Barbara and the Washington in crowd, but the challenge of the game itself. Since there was nothing Nina Graham Luce liked better than winning a fight, she was invaluable to Russell, not just raising money, but plotting strategy. She was being credited for the defeat of Russell's opponent in the Rhode Island primary; and, since no one associated with Russell's campaign (including Russell himself) dared oppose her wishes, when he retained his Senate seat in November, which seemed certain, she would get credit for that win too. "If Mother has her way, we'll all wake up one day and find Russell president," said Adam. As always when talking about Nina, her son sounded both amused and annoyed.

"He is too old, no?" said Katrinka, too horrified at the thought to realize Adam was joking.

"Well, there is always the possibility that he'll die first."

Adam was equally caustic about Patrick Kates. "I should have known," he said, "that if Lucia was sleeping with him, the man had to be nothing but trouble."

"You did always like Nick," said Katrinka. She had never cared for Nick Cavalletti herself, but Adam and he had been friendly, and not just for Lucia's sake.

"Nick's a hustler, but at least he's amusing. Patrick Kates is nothing but a pain in the ass." Having sat around on his family fortune for years, not noticing as it dwindled away beneath him, when it was gone, instead of setting to work trying to rebuild it, Kates had contented himself with conning other people out of their money. And while Adam detested self-made men like Mark van Hollen, at least on some level he respected them. For Patrick Kates, a loser, he had nothing but contempt.

"Why you are refitting his yacht, if you feel like that?"

"Because it's cheaper than keeping the Larchmont yard idle. And because Lucia talked me into it, I suppose. He's got her working for nothing. I wish she'd get rid of the sonovabitch."

"So do I," agreed Katrinka. She and Mark had spent an evening with Lucia and Patrick a few nights before and it had not been pleasant. Patrick had been boastful about his own accomplishments, which were few, and scornful of Lucia's, which included designs for some of the most beautiful yachts afloat. "He's a pig," said Katrinka. "Lucia could do much better than him."

"So I've told her. But, so far, she's not taking any good advice." Adam laid his knife and fork across the top of his plate, then added. "She's too upset about Pia, I gather, to think about her own life."

"Yes," said Katrinka shortly, not wanting to pursue that subject.

"Apparently, Pia was under the impression that Christian and she were to live together once she got to New York."

"He did never tell her that," said Katrinka, leaping to her son's defense.

"Perhaps not," said Adam. "But he clearly led her to believe—"

"I don't want to talk about this," said Katrinka. Whatever she felt for Pia, which was a great deal, her son was still her prime concern. "Pia and Christian are old enough to work out their problems themselves."

Not wanting to end the lunch with a quarrel, Adam agreed and instead asked politely how Christian was getting along at van Hollen Enterprises. That led to a discussion of Martin's progress at Knapp Manning, and from there, inevitably, to Tomáš's new film. On that one, they again came close to quarreling but, before the conversation grew too heated, agreed to disagree. "The Italians signed. I've sold the studio. I suppose Tomáš hasn't really cost me anything but a few sleepless nights," he said, adding, "Thanks for not saying, 'I told you so.'"

Katrinka had not wanted Adam to buy the studio, one of the few times in their marriage she had argued with a business decision of his. "I did think you would lose your shirt. You didn't. So maybe I was wrong," she replied graciously.

"You see," said Adam, "we can be civil to one another, if we try."

"I was always trying," said Katrinka.

"Well, maybe I wasn't always," said Adam, with the crooked grin that Katrinka had once found irresistible, "but I am now."

They left the restaurant together, stopping on the way out to greet people whom they knew—Barbara Walters, who asked if they would like to share with her the reason for their lunch; Eleanor Lambert, who consistently put Katrinka on her list of best-dressed women; Hal Prince, who was preparing a new Broadway musical—Adam doing his best to fuel speculation about their meeting, Katrinka trying to make little of it.

Outside, the August weather that had been hot and humid all morning had turned to rain. Katrinka's car was waiting at the curb, her driver and security guard in the front seat, sheltering from the downpour. Seeing them in the entry, the guard opened the rear door, while Luther grabbed an umbrella, got out, and hurried to meet them. "Good afternoon, Mr. Graham," he said politely.

"Hello, Luther, good to see you again. How's your wife? And the children?"

"Fine," said Luther. His wife, he knew, would never believe this: if he were ever unfaithful to her, she'd cut out her tongue and his heart before she'd talk to him again.

Since Adam had walked to the restaurant, Katrinka offered him a ride, which he accepted on condition that they drop her first, since she had a three o'clock meeting at the Praha. The hotel, in any case, was nearer.

As he settled in the back of the car next to her, Adam asked her about the guard and Katrinka explained Mark's paranoia since the kidnapping. "Overreacting a little, isn't he?" asked Adam.

"He did already lose two sons," she explained.

"I'd forgotten," said Adam; then he apologized because it seemed the thing to do.

"And I worry too, not about me, but about Anuška."

"You always did worry too much."

"Maybe," said Katrinka. But he had reminded her of something that had crossed her mind earlier in their conversation and she said, "You know, I was thinking, when you were talking about Patrick Kates, that maybe you should compete in the next America's Cup race."

Adam laughed and said, "Does that mean you don't care anymore whether or not I drown myself?" She had always been terrified of his sailing when they were married.

"Don't even joke like that," said Katrinka. "I just think you would like it."

"I would," he said. "But it takes a lot of time. I have to think about whether I can afford to take it."

"Maybe the economy will improve after the election," she said optimistically.

"I said time, not money." It annoyed him that anyone might think he could not afford to do anything he liked.

"No one has time when business is bad," said Katrinka calmly, as the car pulled to a stop in front of the hotel. "Well, thank you for lunch," she said, extending her hand.

Adam took it, but leaned forward to kiss her cheek. "Let's do it again."

"Sometime," she agreed vaguely.

As the doorman came to the car, his umbrella ready, a young girl in a beige raincoat, carrying a clear plastic umbrella, stopped under the hotel's awning, waved, and seemed to be waiting for Katrinka to get out of the car. Adam noticed her and asked, "Do you know that girl? She looks a little familiar, but I can't quite place her."

"She's my cousin František's daughter, Milena Čermák. She is spending the summer with Mark and me." Adam had never met her cousins.

"That's it," said Adam. "She looks like you. It's the red hair that confused me for a minute."

"She does look like my mother really. She is named for her."

"She's lovely."

"Yes," said Katrinka. "And very sweet."

Instead of remaining in the car and continuing on his way, Adam followed Katrinka out. She introduced him to Milena as Adam Graham, not adding any explanation. But Milena of course knew from the letters Katrinka had written to her family over the years exactly who he was. She smiled at him shyly, surprised to find him on such good terms with Katrinka and a little embarrassed, as if she had caught them somehow in a compromising situation. *"Dobrý den,"* she murmured, then corrected herself, "I mean, I am so pleased to meet you."

"You speak English," said Adam.

"Better than I do, I think sometimes," said Katrinka, smiling proudly.

"That wouldn't be hard," he said, but rather than irritated, he sounded amused, as he had been in the early days of their relationship when he had found Katrinka's sometimes odd English very cute. "Are you enjoying New York?" he asked, turning his attention back to Milena.

"Very much," she said.

"Katrinka's been showing you around?"

"Oh, yes. With Mark, and Christian, too, I have been everywhere."

"Christian?" said Adam, looking at Katrinka. "So that's why he's been avoiding Pia."

"That does have nothing to do with it," said Katrinka firmly. She smiled at Milena and said quickly in Czech, "We should go in. It's getting late." Then, she added in English, to Adam. "Milena is helping me here in the hotel a few hours a day. So she doesn't get bored. Well, thank you again, Adam."

"My pleasure," he said, then extended his hand to Milena and added, "Perhaps I'll see you again before you leave New York."

"That would be very nice," she replied as she shook hands with him, blushing a little at the intense way he was studying her face, though for some reason she really didn't mind. When Christian looked at her in the same way, it made her nervous.

"I'll send the car back right away," promised Adam, returning to the Mercedes.

"He seems very nice," said Milena curiously as she followed Katrinka into the hotel.

Despite Adam's occasional kindness to friends, Katrinka had long ago stopped considering him "nice." But she merely murmured something noncommittal and changed the subject.

Christian stood in front of the mirrored wall in his bathroom, completed knotting his Hermès flower-patterned tie, returned to the bedroom, put on the cream-colored jacket of his Armani suit, then went back to the bathroom for another look. Running his fingers through his longish dark hair, he adjusted the carefully designed rumpled wind-blown look. He studied his handsome, moody face and lean body with thoughtful eyes. All a little informal for the opera, he decided, but this was New York, and August. At least he would be reasonably comfortable.

Last year at this time, he had been in Sardinia. The Hellers had rented a villa there, as they had every summer since Kurt Heller had retired. And since it had never occurred to his parents to insist he get a job (or to him for that matter), he had spent his days sailing, swimming, diving, water-skiing, and his nights dancing and making love. What a difference acquiring a new mother had made in his life.

It was not that Christian had any real desire to be a playboy. He was too ambitious for that. No, he had no objection to working hard, as he was doing, long hours for ridiculously little money, so long as the pay-off down the line was a big one. It was just that, in his experience, there were few places in the world as unpleasant as New York in August.

With so much of their winter and spring having been spent in Europe, Katrinka and Mark had decided not to return there for any extended period over the summer. Occasionally, Mark had to fly to London on business; and sometimes Katrinka and the baby would join him, continuing on to spend a few days at the villa in Cap Ferrat. As a junior executive at VHE, Christian's work schedule had not allowed him to join them for any of those excursions; but Mark had taken a summer house in East Hampton for the family and, even when Katrinka and he were away, Christian drove there weekends in the Mercedes he had had shipped from Europe, sometimes with Pia, usually with old school friends who were in New York briefly on business and happy to accept his invitation to escape Manhattan for a day or two. He had several times asked Milena to join him, but she had always refused, preferring to explore Manhattan, finding its hot, empty weekend streets oddly intriguing, like a deserted fortress, she said. He had the feeling that she preferred not to be alone with him. He more and more wished that Pia felt the same.

The house phone rang and, when he went to answer it, as if his thoughts had summoned her, the doorman announced that Pia was in the lobby. "Tell her I'll be right down," he said.

He returned to the dresser in his bedroom, opened the bottle of Dior's Sauvage, poured some of the scent into his palms, and patted his face with it. When he had finished, he picked up his keys and headed out of the apartment. If he took too long, Pia would fight her way past the doorman and trap him in the apartment, making him late for the opera.

The apartment was in the Dakota, the most sought-after building on Central Park West. Though it had only one bedroom (a small study doubled as a guest room, if necessary), its rooms were large with high ceilings, giving an impression of infinite space, enhanced by the picture window overlooking the park. Katrinka had bought the apartment shortly after her return to New York in the spring and it had been ready for Christian's arrival in late June. He might have preferred to be consulted about the decor, but he had to admit that it suited him. It was both masculine and comfortable, cozy and uncluttered, with neutral honey-beige walls, large overstuffed sofas and armchairs in Schumacher burlap with kilim accents, a comfortable blend of contemporary and antique furniture, and, on the walls, modern Czech paintings by artists Katrinka had recently started to collect. He suspected that Katrinka would sign the apartment over to him as his Christmas gift. Certainly, he couldn't think of a nicer one.

When he reached the lobby, Christian saw Pia, a large sample case at her feet, seated on one of the sofas, impatiently watching the elevators, waiting for Christian to appear. Looking both apprehensive and embarrassed, she stood up as he approached. Despite his annoyance, Christian gave his usual faint hint of a polite bow, then asked, "What are you doing here?"

Pia recoiled slightly but her face remained impassive and she said coolly, "I was hoping to talk you into having dinner with me."

"You should have called first. As you can see, I'm on my way out."

"Yes," she agreed. "I know I should have." She forced a smile. "But I wanted to surprise you."

"You've come all this way for nothing," he said, hoping he sounded convincingly regretful, both for the effort she had made and his own unavailability.

"Oh, I didn't come specially to see you." It was only half a lie. "I was showing my jewelry to some of the shops on Columbus Avenue. I've had quite a good afternoon really. Two have agreed to sell it so far, on consignment. Still, it's a beginning." Her desire to start building a career as a jewelry designer had been the reason she had given Christian, and her mother, for wanting to come to New York. Milan or Paris might have done as well, of course; but Christian had been in neither place. Nor did Lucia keep an apartment in either city, while in Manhattan she owned a two-bedroom co-op in the East Fifties, where Pia was resigned to living until she could convince Christian to let her move in with him. So far, though she had failed miserably with Christian, she had made some small progress attracting interest in her jewelry designs. "And I've an appointment with a buyer at Bendel's tomorrow. Mother arranged that."

"Good, I'm pleased to hear everything's going so well," said Christian, picking up Pia's sample case, taking her by the arm, and steering her toward the door. "Taxi, please," he said to the doorman. It was too hot to walk, even the short distance to Sixty-seventh Street. "You can drop me at Lincoln Center on your way home," he added to Pia.

"I'm not going home," she said, pulling away from him, not volunteering any more information. "You're going to the theater?"

"No, to the opera. The Mostly Mozart Festival, with Katrinka and Mark." He saw no reason to add that Milena would be joining them.

He didn't have to. Pia knew that she would have been invited if

Milena had not been going. Pia was developing an intense dislike for the young Czech girl. "Have a lovely time." She leaned forward and kissed his cheek. "I'll see you . . ."

Pia had not for nothing spent years cultivating a cool facade behind which to hide her turbulent feelings. She was so good at disguise that, for a moment, Christian actually believed she didn't give a damn. "Where are you off to?" he asked as a taxi pulled to a stop at the curb and the doorman opened its door.

"I told a friend I might meet him for dinner. As long as you're busy . . ."

"What friend?"

"Martin. I ran into him at Tatou the other night."

It must have been the night he had taken Milena to see *The Phantom of the Opera*. Christian could imagine the scene: the trendy disco, looking like the interior of an old movie palace; the loud music; Pia dancing, lost in some world of her own, oblivious to the hot eyes following her every move: Martin's eyes. Hit by a sudden wave of possessive jealousy, Christian said, "I should be home by midnight."

"Aren't you having dinner after the opera?"

Christian nodded. "Yes, but you know how Mark is, wanting everyone home and safely tucked in bed at a reasonable hour. He thinks Katrinka doesn't get enough rest."

"I'm not sure I'll be free by midnight."

He put his arms around her and kissed her, letting his tongue flick just once, lightly, against her lips. "Try," he said, when he released her.

"I'll see," she responded, as if it didn't matter to her one way or the other.

"Better make it twelve-thirty," he said, as he settled her into the waiting taxi, handing her sample case in after her, "just to be safe." He closed the door, then waved.

As her taxi pulled away from the curb, Pia turned back to watch Christian, standing at the curb, waiting for another cab.

"Where to?" asked her driver.

She was going home. Even if she did manage to summon the energy to call Martin to tell him her plans for the evening had changed and she was free after all, she still had to shower and dress for the date. What she should do, she knew, was go dancing and forget all about Christian. What she should *not* do was appear at his apartment later that night like some high-class call girl. But she knew she would. From wherever she was, at the appointed hour, she would take a taxi back to Christian's. Having finally fallen in love, Pia did not know how to stop.

* * *

Whatever his reservations about Pia, it was satisfying for Christian to know that he had unsettled any plans Martin Havlíček might have made for the evening. The idea of Martin rankled somehow. He was too generally considered to be thoughtful, intelligent, decent—exactly the sort of young man who most irritated Christian, so worthy, so admirable, so completely unlike himself. Worse, Martin was attractive, though without Christian's classic good looks; he was rugged and athletic and possessed a healthy sexuality that even Christian had to admit was very appealing to women. What Christian did not want was Pia running to Martin for comfort.

His satisfaction at having prevented it, for that evening at least, lasted through the obscure Mozart opera featured that night at the festival and dinner afterward at the Russian Tea Room, making Christian seem unusually lighthearted, without a trace of the cynicism or manipulativeness that sometimes made others uneasy in his presence. He was at his best and most charming, even Mark conceding to himself that his stepson could be very good company when he made the effort, and Milena for once genuinely enjoying his attention, untroubled by the subtle pressure she usually felt in his company.

"Oh, this is so good," said Milena, taking another bite of her blini.

"I will send you home fat as a pig," said Katrinka, laughing.

"Am I getting fat?" she asked, looking at Katrinka, her eyes worried.

"Of course not. I was just joking."

"All the food is always so delicious."

"You look beautiful," said Mark. "Who was it anyway who said women have to be flat as planks?"

"You think I'm too skinny?" asked Katrinka, with mock indignation.

"Not in all the right places," said Mark.

"It seems sad that Milena has to leave," said Christian, "when she is enjoying herself so much."

"I start university in September," said Milena quickly. "Anyway, I would never want to outstay my welcome."

"You could never do that," Katrinka assured her, relieved that Milena did not seem reluctant to go. "But your parents would have my head if I kept you here." She took a bite of blini and added, "You know what I have been thinking?"

"Oh, oh," said Mark, who recognized the look on his wife's face. "What scheme have you been cooking up now?"

"One everyone will like," she said firmly. "How you would like to perform in public?" Milena had several times entertained Katrinka's guests at home after dinner parties, and everyone had been charmed by the music (a combination of old Czech folk songs, and more current European and American pop music) and impressed with her talent.

"In public? Where?"

"At the Ambassador. In the Starlight Club." The hotel had started booking acts into the cocktail lounge the preceding winter, and so far the venture had been successful, with more and more celebrities putting in appearances to catch the shows, bringing celebrity-watchers in their wake.

"What a wonderful idea," said Christian.

"There is a jazz trio performing there now, the Waverlys. You would be a good contrast. I thought maybe you could fill in during the breaks, at least for the next few weeks before you go home. It will give you some experience." Milena was hopeless in an office, with no real business or even organizational skills. It seemed silly to make her continue working at the Praha, answering phones or cleaning rooms— as Katrinka had done at her age—just to keep her occupied during the long summer days, when, instead, Katrinka could give her the thrill of a lifetime.

"Oh, God, I'd love to," said Milena. Then she stopped, frozen by a horrible thought. "Do you think I'm good enough?"

"If I didn't, would I ask you?"

"You're wonderful," said Christian. "You have enormous talent."

"What if I get"—she hesitated, couldn't think of the English word, then completed the sentence in Czech for Katrinka—"stage fright?"

"You won't," said Katrinka. "When you start singing you forget anyone else is there."

Milena laughed and said, "Yes, yes, I would like it very much."

"Has she said yes?" asked Christian, who had not followed the lapse into Czech.

"She has," said Mark, who did not sound as elated as everyone else with the idea.

"Do you think it is a bad idea?" said Milena, sensing his lack of enthusiasm.

"He thinks it is a wonderful idea," said Katrinka, who could not imagine Mark disagreeing with her about this. "I phoned your parents today, and even they think you should do it, if you want to."

Mark, knowing it had all gone too far for him to stop without hurting Milena, said only, "I think *you're* terrific. And it's probably a good idea for you to find out whether or not you like performing in public before you waste too much time dreaming about it. But if you find you don't, you tell us, okay? Don't worry that you'll hurt Katrinka's feelings. You won't."

"Of course not," agreed Katrinka. "I want you only to do what makes you happy."

What worried him, Mark explained to Katrinka later, as they were getting ready for bed, was not just that Milena was young and innocent, inexperienced and naive, but that she was, at least temporarily, their responsibility. He would prefer that she put off any growing up she had to do until she was back home with her parents.

"What you think will happen to her?" called Katrinka from her bathroom. She came back into the bedroom, wielding a hairbrush, wearing only a black silk teddy. Weeks of strenuous exercise had done its work and her figure was back to what it had been before her pregnancy, only her breasts a little fuller. But Mark liked that. "Men will flatter her. Maybe turn her head a little. Maybe she'll fall in love. That is so terrible?"

Mark was lying on the bed, wearing only a pair of cotton shorts, his hands clasped behind his head, a book lying open, face down, on the mat of blond hair on his chest. "No," he said. "I suppose it's inevitable. I just would like it all to happen in Brno next year, when she's at university, not this summer in New York."

"Poor Anuška," said Katrinka, laughing as she brushed her hair. "What a time she is going to have growing up, with you for a father."

Mark thought of his daughter as he had last seen her a few minutes before, contented and safe, sound asleep upstairs in the antique crib that had once belonged to a French princess. Katrinka was right, of course. He wished to keep her that way forever. "You think I'm being a little overprotective?"

Katrinka nodded. "When I was Milena's age I was traveling all over Europe with the ski team. I was just a little older when I started modeling and acting."

"And look at the trouble you got into," said Mark, proving his point.

"I grew up, that's all. I don't regret anything."

"Let me do that," he said, motioning Katrinka to the bed beside him. Sitting up, he put the book he had been reading on the bedside table, took the brush from her hand, and began stroking it through her long dark hair. "Milena's not you. She doesn't have anything like your strength, or your courage."

"Nonsense," said Katrinka. "She's a sensible girl."

"She is that," agreed Mark.

"And it did seem so mean not to give her a chance."

"I know." Mark pushed aside Katrinka's hair and kissed the nape of her neck. "Promise me one thing?"

"Anything," she said.

"Now, that's what I like to hear." He dropped the brush on the floor and pulled her back against him, lifting her onto his lap, reaching in front of her to fondle her breasts through the thin silk of the teddy.

There had been no more letters or photographs. Except when the monthly report arrived from Paul Zeiss, stirring old worries, Monica Brand was forgotten, the pain she had caused in their marriage completely healed by Anuška's birth and by the trust, the commitment, the passion that, after two years, so far showed no signs of fading from their lives.

Katrinka leaned against her husband, almost mesmerized by the feel of his hands on her breasts, of his mouth against her shoulder. "What you want me to promise?"

"If Milena has any second thoughts, let her back out. No pep talks. No encouragement. Just let her find her own way in her own time, okay?"

"Okay," agreed Katrinka.

His hands slid down her body from her breasts, to her hips, then along her legs, coaxed her knees back to her chest and apart, coming to rest for a moment on the band of fragile black silk between them. "Buttons," he said, "how convenient," as she turned her head to take his tongue into her mouth.

Milena had no second thoughts. She was nervous about singing in a public place, worried that sophisticated New Yorkers might find her music either quaint or dull, afraid that her voice would go or that her fingers would find only the wrong strings on her balalaika. But though her dreams had extended only as far as Prague, she had always, for as long as she could remember, wanted to perform on stage, in front of adoring fans, on television, in movies. She had wanted to make records and hear herself on the car radio as she drove through the Czech countryside with her parents and brothers, or, better yet, with a handsome movie star who was madly in love with her. Living on a farm, on the outskirts of a small town, in a sheltered environment, lacking resourcefulness if not ambition, Milena had not had any idea of how to make her dream come true. And then Katrinka had come to visit. Milena had not dared to hope that Katrinka would help her, but she had, first by inviting her to visit, now by giving her this once-in-a-lifetime, this not-to-be-missed opportunity to sing in New York. Milena was determined not to miss her chance.

Over the next few days, Milena ran through her repertoire, choosing songs she thought would make the best impression, checking her choices with whoever happened to be handy: Katrinka, Mark, Christian, the housekeeper, Anuška's nurse, the dog walker, the security guard, the cook. She stopped going to the Praha with Katrinka and stayed home to rehearse. By Friday, the day chosen for her premiere, she felt she was as ready as she was going to be. That evening, in front of the Ambassador's usual crowd and a few friends Katrinka had gathered together for the occasion, Milena did her first show. It was thirty minutes long, and five minutes into it, Milena was as relaxed as if she were performing in front of her grandmother, losing herself in the music as she sang, shyly grateful for the applause when she finished. The audience loved her, finding her fresh and appealing, original and exciting. She was something completely new to talk about.

"She's a delight," said Margo, who was in New York but not finding it as easy to reclaim her old job as she had imagined. She was generally considered too old to battle the competition.

"Everyone will be talking about her," said Alexandra. She had come with Gabriel de Mellor, in town for a week or so on business, he said. Neil was in Washington for meetings with some people at the National Association of Security Dealers, all of which made Alexandra extremely nervous since he had not told her why, but had palmed her off with platitudes about the meetings being routine and nothing to worry about.

"What if I invite her to appear on my television show?" suggested Rick Colins.

"You would do that? How wonderful," said Katrinka, but when Mark shot her a warning glance, she added, "Talk to her. If she says yes, that's fine."

"Have you heard from Carlos?" asked Rick, placing himself on the banquette next to Katrinka so that no one else could get near her.

"Yes," said Katrinka carefully. "I did speak to him today."

"Is he all right?"

Carlos was not all right, in fact. He had had a telephone call from London, informing him that his lover had been arrested for soliciting a minor. After phoning Katrinka to tell her he would be leaving Prague, he did not know for how long, Carlos had handed over all the work at the hotel to an assistant and taken the next available flight to Heathrow. "I think so," said Katrinka, not wanting to carry tales between the two former lovers.

"I know all about it," said Rick. "Alex wasn't in jail for more than five minutes before people were calling me to let me know. Poor sonovabitch." It wasn't clear whether he meant the dignified Sir Alex Holden-White or Carlos himself. "How did Carlos take it?"

"He was upset. He was hurt. Worried. You know Carlos."

"Give him my love when you talk to him."

"Why you don't call him?" suggested Katrinka.

"You think he'd like to hear from me?"

"When there's trouble, everybody needs friends."

"Yes, you're right. I will phone him," said Rick, who then excused himself to go invite Milena to appear on his talk show.

"Well, what you think?" asked Katrinka, sliding into the next booth, beside Lucia.

"Not exactly MTV material," said Patrick Kates, removing his hand from under Lucia's skirt as he leaned forward to kiss Katrinka's cheek. "Thank God," he added.

"She's lovely," agreed Lucia, with a worried glance at her daughter.

"And very talented," added Pia graciously. She had not enjoyed the show. Christian had not taken his eyes from Milena the entire time she was singing, and had excused himself to go congratulate her as soon as she had finished.

"She's going back to Czechoslovakia in a few weeks," said Katrinka. "But I thought she should enjoy herself a little first."

"I didn't know she was leaving," said Pia, her relief obvious.

"Oh, yes," said Katrinka. She was not sure that would be of any benefit to Pia, but she knew the girl was unhappy: let her take what comfort she could in knowing Milena would soon be out of her way. "She starts university in September. I'm glad you did enjoy yourselves," she said, having accomplished what she intended. She made her excuses and moved on to another table.

"Shall we go?" asked Lucia.

"I haven't finished my drink yet," said Pia, looking anxiously across the room at Christian, wondering if he ever planned to return.

"Pia . . ." began Lucia, but she took one look at her daughter's stubborn face and decided to keep quiet. The last thing she wanted to do was provoke another quarrel about their dislike for each other's boyfriends.

Christian offered to take Milena somewhere to celebrate her debut, but when she decided to return home with Mark and Katrinka, he made his way back through the thinning crowd toward Pia. As he approached the table, he saw her gather up her purse and begin to slide out along the banquette. "Are you going?" he asked.

"We were just leaving."

"Patrick and I have to be at the Larchmont yard early in the morning," said Lucia.

"Let's go dancing," said Christian.

365

"Don't you have to work tomorrow?" asked Patrick.

"I don't need much sleep."

"Like mother like son," said Lucia, with a laugh. But she turned to Pia. "Are you coming?"

"Just for an hour or so," said Christian. Though he was not quite sure why, he felt too agitated to go home and sleep.

"Just for a little while," said Pia.

There was no point arguing, Lucia knew. She leaned over and kissed her daughter's cheek. "Don't be too late, darling. Goodnight, Christian."

"She doesn't like me," said Christian.

"She's just afraid you'll make me unhappy."

"Could I?"

"Yes," said Pia. "Very."

Christian watched Milena, carrying her precious balalaika, flushed with happiness, with success, leave with Mark and Katrinka, Rick Colins holding her arm, talking nonstop into her ear. Turning back to Pia, Christian raised his hand, brushed her hair back from her face, and kissed her ear, letting his lips trail along her cheek until they reached her mouth. "What do you see in me?" he asked.

"What do you see in *her*?" responded Pia. Milena was pretty enough, and without doubt talented. But she was so shy, so naive and unsophisticated, so obviously incapable of coping with someone as difficult and complex as Christian.

"When I was a child, I always wanted the toy I was not allowed to play with," he said with unusual honesty.

"Don't you think it's time you grew up?"

"Maybe you wouldn't love me if I changed. And then what would I do? Without my Pia to love me?"

Pia had no idea whether or not he was serious. Neither, for that matter, did Christian.

"Come on," he said. "Let's go."

Milena did two performances on Saturday and Sunday. On Monday she appeared on Rick Colins's television show, introduced as New York's newest sensation. By the following Friday, the hostess was turning people away at the door. Though Milena understood on some level how much of her success she owed to Katrinka—for giving her the opportunity to sing in the Starlight Club, for introducing her to people who could help make her famous—she still did not find any of what was happening to her particularly strange or unusual. It was exactly as she had dreamed success would be, sudden and brilliant.

Milena loved singing; she loved having people admire her voice. What Katrinka paid her seemed an enormous amount of money, and that she enjoyed, spending a lot of it on clothes: a chic little Betsey Johnson flowered top and skirt, an Anna Sui black lace chemise—all young and sophisticated and sexy. She was having the time of her life.

But despite Mark's fears, Milena's head was not turned. Remembering how grateful they had been for every gift that had arrived over the years from Katrinka, she sent part of what she earned home to her parents. Except for an occasional interview, she continued the quiet routine she had settled into before her debut at the Starlight, exploring the city, dining with Katrinka and Mark, allowing Christian to take her to an occasional concert or play, rehearsing for long hours every day. She did not accept dates from the strange men who approached her after each performance. Instead, watched by concerned hotel personnel, she returned to the suite in the hotel provided for her by Katrinka so that she would not have to venture out alone into New York streets so late at night. In a way it was a lonely life, but Milena had never been happier.

When she was performing, Milena was aware of an audience only as a group, as a large featureless body emanating waves of love and appreciation that she returned to them in a song. She saw no faces, recognized no friends. Her subconscious carried her through the repertoire without thought, without anxiety. And when she was finished, and the applause started, it took a few seconds for her to adjust, as if her eyes were switching focus from light to dark, from near to far.

Which was why she did not recognize Adam Graham when he came up to her after a performance, two weeks after she had begun singing in the club. "You don't remember me," he said, sounding a little hurt.

"Oh, yes, yes I do. I'm sorry, Mr. Graham. . . ."

"Adam," he corrected.

"Adam," she repeated, blushing. "I just am very . . ."—she searched for the word—"distracted when I sing."

"I've been hearing so much about you, from everyone, I had to come see for myself what the fuss was all about."

"Did you enjoy it?"

"Very much," he said. "You're very good."

She blushed again. "Thank you."

"Are you rushing off somewhere or can you stay awhile and have a drink with me?"

She looked quickly around the room, searching the tables for his party of friends. Where was Christian? she wondered. He usually stopped by to see her last show. Then she remembered he had gone to East Hampton for the weekend. "I'm not rushing anywhere," she said.

"Good." He took her arm and led her to a booth not far from the stage. No one else was seated there.

"You're alone?" she said, surprised. She always imagined the rich in large, expensive groups.

"That's what happens to bachelors in New York on summer weekends. Everyone else has left for the Hamptons."

Milena nodded. "Katrinka and Mark left early this afternoon. And Christian, too."

"You mean you've been deserted?"

"Oh, I like it. There's so much to do all day. And at night, of course, I'm here."

He signaled a waiter and they ordered drinks: white wine for Milena, a scotch with a splash of water for Adam.

"And how are you planning to keep yourself busy tomorrow?" he asked, when the waiter had gone.

Milena outlined her plans for him: they included a trip to Bloomingdale's, a stop at the Frick, a walk through the zoo, if it wasn't too hot, and a movie.

"What movie?"

"I haven't decided yet. I thought maybe *Lethal Weapon Three*."

"Good choice," said Adam.

"Have you seen it?"

"Not yet."

"What are you doing?" From anyone else it might have sounded like an invitation. From Milena, it was a simple expression of curiosity.

Adam shrugged. "Working, I suppose." The waiter returned with their drinks and Adam took a sip of his scotch and said, "I work too much, people are always telling me."

"Do you agree?"

"Sometimes. Like now." He smiled at her. "What if I play hookey?"

"Play what?"

"Hookey," he said, explaining the expression, feeling suddenly as if he were trapped in a time warp. He had spent the first few years of his marriage to Katrinka explaining just such expressions to her. "What if I take the day off? Will you keep me company?"

"You?"

"Sometimes I think I work so hard just so I won't be lonely."

She could not believe this man, so elegant and handsome and successful, did not have a long list of women eager to help him fend off loneliness. "Well . . ."

"We could go sailing. Have you ever been?" She shook her head. "You'll love it. We can drive up to Larchmont. It's only half an hour away. I keep a boat there. Several boats."

Perhaps because he had been Katrinka's husband and therefore was almost related to her, perhaps because he and Katrinka still seemed to be on such comfortable terms, perhaps because he was an attractive man, smiling coaxingly at her with a sweet, boyish grin, Milena was tempted. "I would be back in time for the show?" she asked.

"I promise."

"Well, then, yes, thank you. I think I would like that very much."

"So would I," said Adam, making a mental note to call his mother in the morning and tell her he would not be visiting her in Newport tomorrow after all.

The
Past

❦

Fall, 1992

Thirty

HER EXPERIENCE LIMITED TO EXPERIMENTAL KISSING AND FURTIVE GROPING WITH SCHOOLBOYS AS SEXUALLY inept as she, Milena had no adequate defenses against someone like Adam Graham, who had been playing the seduction game for thirty years or so and was rich enough to do it in a grand style.

When Adam invited her to go sailing, Milena assumed that he was momentarily at loose ends, perhaps a little lonely, just being kind to Katrinka's young cousin, left all on her own in New York. Any thought that he might be sexually attracted to her she pushed away: it made her uncomfortable. And she did not, at first, stop to look too deeply into her own feelings. As far as she was concerned, she had agreed to go because it sounded like fun. But by the time they had returned from their afternoon on Long Island Sound, Milena knew she wanted to see Adam again. By the end of lunch the next day, she was infatuated with him.

It took Adam two weeks to coax Milena into bed. And he might have done it more quickly had a business trip to the European shipyards not taken him away from New York for eight of the fourteen days.

While he was away, Adam phoned at least once a day; baskets overflowing with exotic flowers arrived in Milena's suite every morning. Gradually, it occurred to her that he might want her. The idea left her restless, uneasy, in a state of barely repressed sexual excitement that she mistook for the thrill of performing live, on stage, in front of an

373

audience of appreciative fans. The two became interwoven in her mind, adding to the confusion about her own and everyone else's motives. One night, when Christian escorted her back to her suite after a performance, she let him follow her in, help himself to a drink, kiss her. She was both searching for satisfaction and experimenting with her emotions. But, though Christian was skilled, gentle, passionate, everything that a woman might want in a lover, though he stopped as soon as she asked him to, the encounter left Milena feeling both frustrated and, for reasons she could not rationally explain, more than ever wary of Christian. Still, she repeated the experiment a few nights later. When she pushed him away again, Christian, doing his best to conceal his growing anger at her indifference to him, asked why; and, not knowing how to explain her behavior, Milena fell back on an age-old excuse. She told him that she was a virgin. It was the truth, and so much easier to say then the equally true alternatives: I don't love you; I don't want you.

By the time Adam returned from Europe, Milena's emotions were in a state of continual turmoil. To make matters worse, he overwhelmed her with gifts: cotton sundresses from Greece, perfume from Paris, a Stuart tartan kilt from Scotland. The flowers and phone calls continued. He gave her Hermès scarves, Judith Leiber handbags, Godiva chocolates, diamond earrings from Harry Winston. Even more impressively, he talked of the record company executives whom he had come to know during his days as head of Olympic Pictures, the Hollywood agents, the film producers, the directors. Though he made no promises, Adam let her see the advantages of a relationship with someone like him. Women with far more experience than Milena would have had their heads turned.

Milena was not mercenary, nor particularly ambitious. If Christian had offered her the same gifts as Adam, she would have refused them. Christian frightened her. His temperament was too uncertain, his moods too volatile. He reminded her of television newscasts she had seen of Mt. Pinatubo erupting. She could not rid herself of the idea that he was dangerous.

Adam, on the other hand, seemed to Milena to be stable, generous, attractive, attentive, and very good company. He went out of his way to please her, to reassure her, to keep her entertained. How was she to know that his dark side went veiled in wasp light, that generations of "good" breeding had produced a model gentleman, with all feelings, all passions—good and bad—buried beneath a structure composed of intelligence and reason, style and elegance, good humor and perfect manners? It was as if a nuclear reactor were concealed not behind the

stark walls of Chernobyl or Three Mile Island, but in the cellars of the Smithsonian or the cathedral at Chartres.

In her conscious mind, Milena saw her time in New York as a brief, exciting interlude. She planned to return to Czechoslovakia, go to university, and perhaps afterward, if she did not marry first, begin to think seriously about a career as a musician. Falling in love was not part of her agenda for the summer in New York. Having a lover, while romantically appealing, was something to daydream about, not do. Since girls of her age, where she was from, generally did not have lovers, she felt neither backward nor deprived. She rejected the notion with no more than a fleeting, wistful regret.

Her subconscious, however, had embarked on a different adventure. With every day that passed, with every gift she was presented, the idea of a lover became more and more exciting, more and more possible. A girl in her class at school had slept with a boy she had worked with during the hop harvest the year before and had become a glamorous figure, an object of envy to the rest of her schoolmates. What was it like? everyone wondered. Now Milena had a chance to find out. Wouldn't it be foolish not to take it? Wouldn't it be the perfect end to a perfect summer?

The first time Adam kissed her, seriously kissed her, Milena was ready to fall into his arms. She knew she was in love. When she felt his tongue in her mouth, his fingers on her breast, she had no desire at all to push him away, but moved closer against him, letting her hands wander through his crisp, short hair, down his back, stopping at his trim waist because she dared go no further. Adam didn't suffer from the same inhibitions, but as he reached under her skirt and began to lift it slowly, suddenly the image of Katrinka materialized in Milena's mind and she stopped him, holding his wrist as she twisted out of his arms. When he asked why, embarrassed to mention Katrinka's name, she gave him the same excuse she had given Christian a few nights before.

Adam didn't push the issue. He knew it was only a matter of time.

Milena cried herself to sleep that night. She didn't know what to do. She had fallen in love with Adam, but it seemed wrong to her to become romantically involved with her cousin's former husband, especially since she wasn't sure how Katrinka would feel about it. The last thing in the world she wanted to do was hurt Katrinka, who had done so much for her, who deserved nothing but her gratitude.

But, of course, Milena could not keep away from Adam. She was hooked. And he had no intention of throwing her back into the sea. When he called the next morning to ask her out, she agreed to meet him. He continued to shower her with gifts, bought her lunch at expensive restaurants, attended her performances with flattering regularity, and when Milena tentatively raised the question of his former wife, pointed out to her what was perfectly obvious: that Katrinka was remarried, that she had a child, that she was completely happy, that her relationship with Adam was friendly, that she wished him nothing but good, that she could have no possible objection to his spending time with Milena. What Adam did not suggest was that she ask Katrinka to confirm his reading of the situation.

If Milena suspected that Katrinka would not like her dating Adam, Adam was certain of it. It was perhaps his main reason for pursuing the affair and why he took some precautions to see that Katrinka did not find out—yet. The places he took Milena, while hardly dives, were not the ones usually frequented by Katrinka and her friends, or by his own friends for that matter. There was always a risk, in New York, of running into people you knew, but years of clandestine affairs had taught him that, if he confined himself to traveling by limo and kept well away from the hot spots, the odds were in his favor. His only real worry was that he might run into someone, Christian Heller in particular, in the Starlight Club, during one of Milena's performances, but even there his luck held.

Annoyed with Milena, Christian had stopped dropping in at the club, thinking that a little neglect might help his suit. On the one night he did stop by to let Milena know that he was taking the Concorde to Paris and flying from there to Venice to spend a long weekend with the Hellers at their palazzo, Adam had a late meeting at the Hartford shipyard and was not expected.

"Is Pia going with you?" asked Milena.

"No, of course not," said Christian, cheered a little by the question. "Why do you ask?"

"You spend a lot of time together, don't you?"

"We're just friends," said Christian firmly, thinking perhaps he had found the root of his problem. When he returned, he promised himself, he would make sure that Milena understood that he was interested in no one but her—at least for the moment. "I'll come see you Tuesday, as soon as I get back."

"Have a good time," she said politely, relieved at the prospect of a few days without his disturbing presence lurking in the background.

On her one night off, Adam took Milena to see Mariah Carey in concert, assured her that she was just as talented, then brought her home to his apartment for a late supper. She had never been there before and was a little nervous at the prospect, but Adam insisted, saying that he wanted her to see where he lived.

The sleek modernism of the apartment, its stripped-down functionalism, had an odd effect on Milena. There was nothing cozy about it, nothing familiar, and its strangeness increased her excitement, enhancing the feeling she had that she was about to embark on a great adventure. Only Carter's reassuring presence, serving them, kept the steadily building pressure from exploding. By the time he disappeared, leaving coffee and miniature Italian pastries for them in the sitting room, Milena was almost relieved.

Adam took off his jacket, stretched out on the contoured gray sofa, and pulled Milena down to rest against his chest. For a long while they just sat together, drinking coffee, not talking, listening to the voice of Frank Sinatra spill into the room from the four giant, carefully placed speakers. Finally, Adam bent his head to kiss the nape of Milena's neck. She turned in his arms, bringing her head around, so that her mouth met his. He took the cup from her hand and placed it with his on the coffee table, then adjusted their positions so that they lay side by side. "Not still frightened, are you?" he asked a few minutes later, his knee between her legs, his fingers moving up the inside of her thigh.

"No," she said. Fear was only a part of what she was feeling, a very small part.

"Let's go inside," he said, his mouth against her throat, his hand rubbing gently against the layers of nylon guarding her clitoris. He was thinking not only of comfort, but of the possible damage to his new sofa. "All right?" When she nodded, he stood up, pulled her to her feet, and kissed her again, letting his palms rest a moment against the sides of her small breasts. Could he do it? he wondered, estimating her weight and the distance to the bedroom. Certainly, he decided, as he swung her up into his arms.

Her arms tightened around his neck. "I love you," she said.

Christian returned from Venice late on Monday, and on Tuesday he stopped by at the end of Milena's first show and accompanied her back up to her suite, where she usually retreated to eat and rest between performances. He saw the change in her instantly. The complete ease she exhibited on stage always disappeared at the end of the set, but that night Milena seemed less shy than preoccupied. Instead of nervous and restless, she seemed animated and happy. Her eyes shone, her face glowed; she even moved differently, with an unfamiliar hesitancy in her lower body that, when he asked her about it, made her blush. It was nothing, she told him. He was imagining it. How could she admit to him that she ached all over, inside and out, from making love? Or that the soreness itself, a sense memory, provided her with a constant erotic thrill.

"Will you have supper with me tonight," he asked, as she handed him a glass of white wine. "After your last show?"

"No, I'm sorry. I can't."

She sat in one of the armchairs, while he sat across from her on the sofa. "Tomorrow?"

"I'm busy all week. Next week perhaps?" Adam was leaving on another trip, and she would have time then to be polite to Christian.

But he looked at her with surprise. "It's the beginning of September. Aren't you supposed to be returning home next week?"

Because the prospect of leaving spoiled her perfect happiness, she had stopped thinking about it. She had not even discussed it with Adam yet.

"Well," insisted Christian, "aren't you?"

Milena shook her head. "No," she said.

"Why not?"

"I don't want to," she responded belligerently. "I'm enjoying myself."

"Have you told Katrinka this?"

"Not yet. But don't tell her. Let me," she pleaded, looking like a worried, strangely erotic child in her ruffled Azzedine Alaia dress, her long red hair surrounding her lovely face in soft, delicate wisps.

Christian's first reaction was relief that she was staying—it gave him more time. But relief was followed immediately by suspicion. "Why have you decided to stay? I don't understand."

She spread her arms. "This is all like a dream come true. How can I leave?"

He was not quite convinced. "You're seeing someone, aren't you?"

"What?" Again, Milena blushed.

"A man. That's why you want to stay."

"Yes," said Milena finally, almost relieved to admit it.

"Who is it?"

"I don't have to tell you."

"Who is it?" He stood up and moved closer to her, hovering over her threateningly.

"It's none of your business."

"Tell me who it is!" He grabbed her by the arms, pulled her to her feet, shook her.

"I won't," she shouted at him.

The doorbell rang, startling them both. "Room service," said Christian, letting her go.

She nodded and went to the door, opening it to admit a smiling elderly waiter, pushing a cart. "Good evening, Miss Čermák. Mr. Heller," he said. Everyone knew Katrinka's son.

They mumbled a greeting and waited impatiently until the waiter had set up the cart and left. "I want you to go," said Milena as soon as the door had closed.

Christian nodded. "I'm sorry," he said, bowing formally and turning away.

"Don't tell Katrinka," she pleaded to his retreating back. "Please. I want to do it myself."

"Good night," was all he replied.

Worn out from the weekend in East Hampton, Katrinka and Mark had decided to spend the evening at home, alone. Their choice of houseguests had been unwise. Carey Powers and his family were usually easy enough company, but Carey and Mark were both so preoccupied with the growing problems of van Hollen Enterprises that they spent most of the time discussing business with each other and what little remained trying to avoid discussing anything but sports with Neil Goodman, who seemed to be in big trouble with the SEC. Adding to the general air of strain was the obvious fact that the Goodman marriage was failing rapidly. Alexandra was openly disdainful of her husband, and Neil was both bewildered and hurt by her attitude. Their two children, when not watching their parents with panic-stricken faces, picked fights with the Powers's children. And, with amazing skill, Alexandra managed to drag Gabriel de Mellor's name into every conversation, making everyone uncomfortable except Neil, who seemed not to understand that his wife and her lover were anything but the good friends she claimed. All in all, the weekend had been hell.

Mark and Katrinka were in the library, the television on, watching CNN's recapping of the day's presidential campaign, discussing Paul Zeiss's news that Monica Brand had finally returned to London and was under surveillance, when they heard the faint sound of the front doorbell ringing. The three dogs lying at their feet lifted their heads, pricked up their ears, and looked warily at the door. Mark groaned.

"No one is expected," said Katrinka.

"Maybe it's someone looking for Kelly," said Mark hopefully. Their dog walker had an active social life, though usually anyone wanting her rang the staff bell. But a few moments later, the dogs lumbered up slowly, and Mark heard the sound of footsteps in the corridor. "No such luck," he added.

There was a knock on the door and the dogs' tails began to wag. "Who is it?" called Katrinka.

"Me," said Christian, as he entered, stopping to pat the dogs who had moved in on him, blocking his progress. "Sorry to disturb you," he added. He pushed past the dogs and leaned over his mother to kiss her cheek. "I wanted to talk to you," he said in German.

"Obviously," she said.

"I hope it's not an inconvenient moment," he continued in English, looking at Mark.

"Would you like me to leave?"

Christian considered saying yes, then decided against it. Why irritate Mark any more than necessary? "No, not at all. It's Milena I want to talk about."

"Milena?" said Katrinka. "What about Milena?"

"Do you know what man she is seeing?" he asked, sinking into one of the deep armchairs.

"She is seeing someone?" asked Katrinka. She had spoken to the girl just before leaving for the Hamptons on Friday and Milena had mentioned nothing about a boyfriend.

"Why shouldn't she be?" asked Mark, using the remote to turn off the television. "She's young, beautiful. Every guy who passes through that lounge must ask her out. It's not surprising she says yes sometimes."

"But she won't say who it is," said Christian.

"Maybe she thinks it's none of your business," said Mark, who clearly thought the same.

"And she is not returning to Czechoslovakia next week."

"Shit!" muttered Mark. "I knew it."

Katrinka turned to him and said warningly, "Don't tell me, 'I did say so.'"

"I wasn't planning to," he replied, frowning, ignoring the mangled quote.

"You think she means it?" asked Katrinka, beginning to share some of Christian's concern.

Christian nodded. "What are you going to do about it?"

"What do you think we should do? Drag her by her hair to the plane and take her back whether she wants to go or not?" asked Mark. Katrinka and he were flying to Corfu early next week to attend Jean-Claude's wedding to Thea Papastratos. On the way, they had planned to stop in Prague, both to check on the state of the new hotel and to return Milena to her parents.

"František will kill me," said Katrinka.

"I'm sure he expected this. It's why he didn't want her to come in the first place."

"You don't mean you'll let her stay?" Christian sounded appalled by the idea.

"If she wants to, I don't see what we can do about it," said Mark.

"You could fire her. You could make her leave the hotel. You could insist she go home." Christian had focused his attention completely on his mother, hoping to convince her to do as he wanted. He knew he didn't have a prayer with Mark.

"Yes," said Katrinka, weighing the suggestion. "Why you think I should do that?"

Knowing that Christian would never admit jealousy as a reason, Mark waited for the answer.

"She's young. She's inexperienced. God knows what kind of trouble she would get into. And if she's not prepared at least to be honest with you, I think you should wash your hands of her."

"Maybe," said Mark, "she's just not prepared to be honest with you."

"Perhaps," said Christian grudgingly, his eyes flicking briefly to Mark before returning to his mother for an answer.

"I will talk to her in the morning," said Katrinka.

"Good." Christian stood up and went to his mother to kiss her good-bye. When she stroked his cheek softly, he took her hand and kissed that, too. Then, he bowed slightly to Mark and headed for the door. "Again, I'm sorry I intruded on your evening. But I was concerned."

"Don't be silly, *miláčku*. You're always welcome here. I'll speak to you tomorrow."

"Yes, please. Let me know what she tells you," he said.

As soon as Christian left, Mark said, "He's jealous, that's all. Otherwise he would not think any of this was serious."

"I know. But still, Milena is my responsibility. I do have to know what is happening with her."

"Yes," agreed Mark.

Katrinka sighed. "And I did think everything was going so well."

When Katrinka phoned Milena the next morning, there was no reply from her room. At eight in the morning, there were a few places Milena could reasonably be: in the shower; in the dining room; taking a walk.

But for someone who had done a late show the night before, it did not seem likely she would be anywhere but in her bed. If Katrinka had had any hope that Christian might be mistaken, it was instantly crushed. She left a message for Milena to call.

It was not Milena's having a lover that bothered Katrinka. After all, she had not been much older when her own affair with Mirek Bartoš had started. But she felt a sense of responsibility to her cousins, who, whatever their attitude about their daughter's having an affair might be, most certainly would not like anything that threatened the possibility of her returning home.

Like any decent fairy godmother, Katrinka had done her best to make Milena's dream come true. If she had not planned on Prince Charming making an entrance quite yet, it was only because Milena hadn't either. But now Katrinka understood, as Mark always had, that the invitation to New York had set Milena on a course that could not be reversed. It was unclear yet where the girl was headed, but it almost certainly was not Brno University.

Milena seemed to be on everyone's mind that morning. During an early meeting in her office at the Praha, the general manager of the Ambassador pointed out that the recent increase in bookings at that hotel was certainly due to the publicity generated by Milena's success in the club, a fact that he thought would please his employer, but instead seemed to annoy her. When she asked for ideas on how to improve occupancy rates at the other hotels, Michael Ferrante suggested (and he was only half joking) opening cocktail lounges in all of them and booking Milena round-robin. Katrinka, who normally had a good sense of humor, was not amused. The girl was not a secret weapon, she pointed out, and furthermore was expected to return home in a few days. At that, the Ambassador's manager grew pale and asked if there was any possibility that Milena might be encouraged to stay a while longer. "I do think," said Katrinka, ignoring the question, "that we should concentrate on some new promotions."

"The Planned Parenthood Ball is scheduled here later in the month," said Michael. "That should be good for some publicity. And your usual Children of the Streets Gala in December."

"It's not enough," said Katrinka.

"Maybe if Milena would entertain at the ball?" suggested someone. "That should attract some press attention."

"Maybe," said Katrinka, again ignoring the reference to Milena, "we should try again to work out a package deal with British Airways."

"That would help," agreed Michael. "Losing the Graham Marine package hurt us badly."

The arrangement between Adam's cruise ship line and Katrinka's hotels had ended with the divorce and Katrinka had so far found no way to replace the lost revenue. "Maybe this time, since we have the hotel in Prague to offer, BA would be more interested." Never one to waste a minute, Katrinka buzzed Robin on the intercom and told her to set up a meeting with the new head of British Airways, Sir Colin Marshall, a man she had known socially for years. "I'll stop in London on my way to Corfu," she said, "if he's available then. Or on the way back. But don't forget about Prague," she added, reminding herself again of the problem with Milena. When she finished the quick revision of her itinerary, she returned her attention to the group in front of her. "Now, let's think of a backup plan," she said.

It was eleven before Milena returned her call, claiming she had been shopping at Bloomingdale's. That was at least partially true, thought Katrinka, since she doubted the girl would lie to her. But she had not been at Bloomingdale's at eight in the morning. When Katrinka suggested they meet for lunch, Milena stammered an apology: she already had a lunch date, she said. "Then come by afterward," said Katrinka firmly. "I'll be here."

To Katrinka's surprise, the time passed quickly. She cleared the pile of correspondence on her desk, returned her phone calls, then talked to Zuzka, who had received another offer from Carla and was more torn than ever torn about what to do.

"Settle," advised Katrinka, not for the first time.

"But the lawyer says we would get much more if we go to trial."

"He will get more, certainly, if not from the settlement, from the fees you're paying him," replied Katrinka in her rapid-fire Czech. "The only thing you will get for sure is a lot more heartache."

"That's what Martin and Tomáš say."

"With the economy the way it is, the business can't be growing." Zuzka had been temporarily restrained from interfering in the company by court order. "Maybe soon, Carla will have less to give you than more."

"She's living with that girl," said Zuzka. "She's bought a house with her in North Carolina."

"Zuzka, zlatíčko, get on with your life."

Zuzka sighed. "I know you're right."

"Why should you make your lawyer rich, if it makes you miserable?"

Zuzka managed something resembling a laugh. "I'll think about it," she said. "You know, Katrinka, I don't think I love Carla now. I can't believe I ever did. Our whole affair, our life together, it's like a dream.

But I can't seem to wake up. I can't seem to let go. I don't know what else there is for me."

"Let go and you'll find out." What Zuzka needed, thought Katrinka, was a little distance from her problems. "We're stopping in Prague for a few days next week. Why don't you come?" she suggested. "You can see your family. It will cheer you up a little."

"I can't leave the house."

"Zuzka, settle," repeated Katrinka, her impatience obvious.

There was a long silence; then Zuzka said, "Maybe I will." She sounded more optimistic than she had in months.

As soon as Katrinka replaced the receiver, the intercom buzzed and her secretary announced that Milena had arrived. "Tell her to come in," said Katrinka. She got up from behind her desk and started toward the door. She greeted Milena in Czech, then said, "Do you want something to drink?"

"No, nothing, thank you." Milena seemed more ill at ease than Katrinka had ever seen her.

Katrinka requested some tea for herself, then settled on one of the sofas, indicating that Milena should sit opposite her. The girl did, an awkward smile fixed firmly on her face, her eyes skittering nervously from Katrinka's to objects in the room and back again. "That is a very nice outfit you're wearing," said Katrinka. It was a three-piece multicolored, striped Moschino suit with a scoop-neck T-shirt.

"Thank you," said Milena, showing no particular pleasure at the compliment.

"You like to shop?"

"Oh, yes. The clothes here are so beautiful."

"And you have such good taste. And real style. Everything you buy suits you very well."

Finally, Milena smiled. "Do you think so?"

Katrinka nodded. "Your parents won't believe their eyes when they see you."

Milena's smile was replaced instantly with a look of panic; but before she could reply, the door opened and the secretary entered with a pot of herb tea and two cups. Katrinka thanked her, then turned to Milena. "You're sure you don't want some?" Milena shook her head and Katrinka poured some for herself, then sat back and said, as casually as she could manage, "I suppose you'll be sorry to leave New York." It had seemed wiser to Katrinka not to involve Christian in the conversation.

"Yes," said Milena softly.

"It's always sad when an adventure comes to an end."

"Yes." Milena's voice was barely audible.

"I wanted to discuss travel plans with you," said Katrinka, distorting the truth only a little. "That's why I wanted to see you today."

Milena nodded. She had guessed as much, assuming that Katrinka would have said something on the phone earlier if Christian had confided his suspicions to her. "When are you planning to leave?"

"We are leaving Tuesday," said Katrinka firmly, emphasizing the "we" slightly. "We stop in London for a day. You'll enjoy that, though you won't have much time there. Then we go on to Prague." Since the wedding in Corfu was Saturday afternoon, Mark and she would take off again late on Friday. The itinerary did not allow much leeway for error, but for the first time Katrinka was leaving Anuška behind and did not want to be away a moment longer than necessary. She smiled cheerfully. "You'll be home by Thursday afternoon."

Milena sat silent for a moment, then said quickly, "I don't want to go."

"I can understand that," said Katrinka reasonably. "I know how much you've been enjoying yourself, but your parents are expecting you. You'll only have a few days with them as it is before you have to leave for Brno."

"I don't want to go home. I don't want to go to university." She sounded like a child close to tears.

"And your parents?" said Katrinka.

"Of course I want to see them. Just not now. Not when everything is going so well."

"When I suggested you sing in the club, you knew it would be just for a few weeks—"

"I don't care if you fire me," said Milena, interrupting. "I'll find work somewhere else." Adam had convinced her of this over lunch, when she had explained her problem to him. He had been very reassuring. In fact, he had promised to bring a top executive from MCA Records to hear her sing the following week.

"I'm sure you will," said Katrinka calmly, not prepared to argue that point. "You've attracted a lot of attention. But are you sure this is what you want?"

"Yes," said Milena passionately. "Yes!"

"And if your parents don't approve?"

"You'll explain it to them," said Milena. "You'll make them understand."

"But how can I, when I don't?"

"I can't leave," insisted Milena, beginning to cry.

Getting up, Katrinka joined Milena on the other sofa. She took her hand and said, "Milena, *andelíčku*, what has happened? Why have you changed your mind about university?"

"Why do I have to go?" she asked, forcing the words out between sobs. "What good is getting a degree? I am already doing what I want."

That was unarguably true, but Katrinka was now certain there was more to Milena's refusal to return home than the promise of a singing career. "That's your only reason?" she asked.

For a moment, Milena considered saying yes. But the truth was bound to come out eventually, and she could not bear the idea that Katrinka, on top of everything else, would then consider her a liar. "No," she said finally.

"Milena, can't you tell me?"

"I'm in love," said Milena.

Katrinka smiled reassuringly. "Well that's good, isn't it?" Milena nodded. "For the first time?" Again, Milena nodded. "It happens to everybody, sooner or later," said Katrinka. "But you have to be sure, before you turn your whole life upside down, that it's for the right person."

"I'm sure."

"Who is it? Anyone I know?" If he was someone responsible, thought Katrinka, her normal optimism taking hold, maybe she would try to smooth things over with František and his wife. Mark wouldn't like it, but really what else could she do? After all, what could be more normal than a young girl falling in love? And Milena's career was off to such a good start that it did seem a pity to bring it to a full stop. "Milena, who is it?" repeated Katrinka.

Milena took a deep breath, looked her in the eye, and said, "Adam. Adam Graham."

Thirty-One

As Milena babbled on about Adam's kindness, his generosity, his intelligence, his attractiveness, Katrinka's emotions passed rapidly from stunned disbelief to rage. "I know," she snapped finally, ending Milena's apparently endless stream of justifications for her behavior. "I was married to him, remember?"

"I'm sorry," sobbed Milena. She had seen flashes of Katrinka's temper before, but never anything like this. "You've been so good to me. I'm so sorry if I've hurt you."

"Hurt me? It's you I'm worried about, you silly girl. It's you who are going to get hurt."

But no, protested Milena, Adam would never hurt her: he loved her. And Katrinka, who soon saw the impossibility of proving her point when the girl was so obviously head-over-heels infatuated, stopped trying. Getting herself quickly (if temporarily) under control, she set to work calming the girl down, assuring her that she no longer harbored any romantic feelings for Adam, and that he was free to make love to whomever he liked. As he always has, added Katrinka bitterly, to herself.

"That's what he told me," said Milena. "Otherwise . . ."

"I know," said Katrinka soothingly, though she suspected Adam could have convinced Milena to walk over her dead body in the name of their love. "Why don't you go back to the hotel and rest for a while?

387

We'll talk later about what you're going to do, all right? When we've both had time to think."

Milena nodded, dabbed at her eyes and nose with a handkerchief, then stood up, apologizing steadily to Katrinka, who walked her to the door, anxious to be rid of her so that she could indeed think. But within seconds of Milena's departure, the rage Katrinka had carefully contained boiled over and she buzzed her secretary to ask that the car be brought around to the front of the hotel. Five minutes later she was on her way to the Seagram Building.

Adam was in a meeting when Katrinka arrived. His secretary, Debbie, tried to stop her from interrupting, but, brushing past the protesting woman, Katrinka threw open the door to the inner office and, finding only Mac with Adam, asked the CFO to leave. Though Katrinka clearly would not take no for an answer, Mac still looked for confirmation toward Adam, who nodded, saying, "We'll continue our conversation later," handing Mac the sheaf of papers with the latest figures on the van Hollen takeover.

"Good to see you, Katrinka," said Mac cheerfully, holding the papers so that no part of them was visible to her as he walked past. "You're looking great."

Katrinka ignored him, her attention focused entirely on Adam. "To what do I owe the honor?" he asked.

"You bastard," said Katrinka as Mac closed the door behind him.

"Would you like to sit down? Would you like something to drink before you tell me what this is about?" said Adam calmly.

"What you think it is about?" said Katrinka, leaning over his desk and glaring at him. "Milena!"

"She's told you?"

"How you could do it?"

"Don't you think you're being a little melodramatic?" asked Adam, trying to stifle the surge of pleasure he felt. He had wanted Katrinka to pay attention, and she certainly was.

"She's a child!"

"She's a very beautiful woman. Talented. Sweet . . ."

"Innocent . . ."

"Yes," agreed Adam. "It's one of her most endearing qualities."

"I didn't think even you would sink so low. To take advantage of her like this . . ." Katrinka backed away from the desk, then stood her ground, her anger, her contempt evident in her face.

"Milena has no complaints about the way I've treated her," said Adam coolly. "I don't see why you should."

388

"She's my responsibility."

"She's eighteen years old. If I remember correctly, you had a lover at her age. A married man, wasn't it? And a child you never bothered to tell me about."

"What I did is not the point," said Katrinka angrily. "We do talk about what you did. New York is full of girls. Why you did have to choose Milena? *Why?*"

"The heart wants what it wants," he replied smugly, quoting Woody Allen, whose face had been plastered all over the tabloids for weeks.

"Because you knew it would upset me, that's why!" shouted Katrinka, ignoring his remark.

"Now, wait a minute," said Adam, pretending an anger he didn't really feel. "You have nothing to do with this. Nothing at all. I was *attracted* to Milena. Who wouldn't be? She's so young . . ." There was a slight, pointed emphasis on the last word. "And so very lovely."

"You're a snake."

"My intentions are completely honorable. If Milena gets pregnant, I might even marry her. Which is more than your lover could do for you!"

"Pregnant! You can't make anyone pregnant! You did blame me for years for not having a child. You and your mother, you did make me feel like a failure. But it wasn't my fault. It was yours!" No matter how furious she had been with him before, knowing how lethal it was, she had never used that attack. Her resorting to it was a measure of her rage.

"You know that's not true," replied Adam, finally as angry as she. During the long years of trying to have a child, the evidence of a teenage girl he had once made pregnant had been dragged out time and time again as proof of his own fertility.

"I do have two children," said Katrinka. "Where are yours?"

"For all I know, I've got little bastards littering the country. And, with any luck, I'll soon have another."

Who are you trying to kid? Don't make me laugh. Give me a break! The words were on the tip of Katrinka's tongue, but she swallowed them, took a deep breath, and tried to regain some semblance of calm. Enraging Adam was no way to get him to do what she wanted. "You did have your fun, Adam," she said finally. "Now, leave her alone. Let her go back home next week."

Adam shrugged and said quietly, "Milena's free to do what she wants. And I don't think she wants to go."

"She will, if you end this stupid affair."

"I have no intention of doing that."

"She's supposed to start university in a few weeks, to study for a degree in music. With that, no matter what happens, she'll be secure. If she doesn't succeed with a career singing, she can teach. You're turning her life upside down, all for some stupid, selfish game you're playing."

"No. What I'm doing is giving her a new life, better than the one she had before. I did the same for you, remember? And don't tell me you have any regrets about that, because I won't believe you."

"Milena's not me," said Katrinka.

Adam laughed. "You don't have to tell me that. I can't imagine that you were ever so shy and sweet and so very agreeable."

"I won't allow this, Adam."

"And what do you plan to do to stop it? Take her back to Czechoslovakia by force?" he asked, echoing Mark. "I'll only go after her."

He would, too, thought Katrinka, if only to prove a point.

When Katrinka didn't reply, Adam smiled broadly. "Face it, Katrinka. This is one battle you can't win. I've got the advantage."

"Temporarily," said Katrinka. "But don't you count on keeping it."

Adam watched her as she turned and walked out of the office, her back straight, her head erect. She was jealous, he was certain of it, and that gave him a great deal of pleasure, which increased when he thought of how Mark van Hollen must feel seeing his wife still so emotionally involved with her former husband. He wouldn't like it at all. Chances are, he wouldn't stand for it. How ironic it would be, thought Adam, if the innocent Milena should succeed in breaking up the van Hollen marriage when all the wiles of Monica Brand had failed.

As usual, Adam underestimated Mark, who understood perfectly that Adam could have fucked every contestant in the Miss Universe contest and Katrinka would not have given a damn. It was not jealousy but concern for Milena that was upsetting his wife. Nevertheless, he did come close to fighting with Katrinka when he failed—in her opinion—to show sufficient outrage about Adam's seduction of the girl.

"You do think it's all right what he did?" asked Katrinka, her head emerging through the top of her cocktail dress, her voice holding enough outrage for both of them.

"I didn't say that," replied Mark impatiently. She looked a knockout, he thought, in a dress she had bought in Paris during the July couture collections. A Valentino, he remembered, a leopard-spotted silk chiffon print with a black bodice. His wife was beautiful, desirable, and he loved her. But there were times when he longed for the solitude of a mountain top or his house in the Hebrides—where he might have enough quiet to figure out how to save his company. His board of directors that day had made it clear that they were less than delighted with him, and with present corporate earnings, and would consider a takeover offer should one be made. The idea of a takeover, which many had at first dismissed as Mark's paranoia, was now taken very seriously. The company's stock continued to climb. Speculation on the street was growing. No one was certain yet who was behind the move, but it was obvious someone wanted VHE. Goddamn the whole board to hell! "What I said is that Adam's right: there's not a lot you can do about it now."

"I would like to kill him," said Katrinka in Czech, for the moment forgetting that Mark could understand her. "Cut his balls off. Feed them to pigs."

Mark laughed. "Katrinka, baby, try and be reasonable."

"I'm not supposed to be upset? She's my cousin!"

"I'm sure that added quite a bit to Adam's enjoyment of the situation."

"That's why he did it. I know it."

"It doesn't matter why. It's done. Milena, the little idiot, is in love. And Adam is sitting on top of the world. There's not a thing you can do to change that."

Mark was right, she knew, though accepting the fact was not easy. "You did expect all this to happen," said Katrinka finally, turning her back to him so that he could do up the zipper of her dress. They were going to a political fund-raiser neither was in the mood to attend.

"Something like this. Adam, I admit, came as a complete surprise."

"What am I going to tell František?" she asked, turning to face him. One of the most wonderful things about Mark, she thought, as she waited for his answer, was that no matter how worried he was about his own problems he never ignored hers.

"Would you listen to a little advice?" he asked.

"What?" she responded, her appreciation turning instantly to wariness.

"Let Milena tell him. Let her take the heat. It's her life, after all."

"All right," said Katrinka finally. "But it won't make any difference. He'll never forgive me."

Wanting to wait until she had herself more under control, Katrinka avoided speaking to Christian until the next morning, when he phoned and caught her still at the breakfast table. A long string of German expletives greeted her news. Aware of Christian's interest in Milena, knowing how much her son hated not getting what he wanted, Katrinka had expected him to be upset, but not like this. He was like a child, throwing a temper tantrum. His fury at having been outmaneuvered was frightening.

"Christian," said Katrinka sharply. "Christian, stop this minute. Do you hear me?" When the tirade at the other end of the line continued unabated, Katrinka repeated loudly, "Christian, listen to me! Stop it!" If she had been in the room with him, she would have slapped him.

Finally, Christian grew quiet. He apologized briefly, not sounding in the least sincere.

"I want you to calm down," ordered Katrinka, as if she were indeed speaking to a child. "This has nothing to do with you. Nothing. Do you hear me? I don't want you going near Milena." Her request was greeted with silence and she repeated, "You are not to go near her. Do you hear me?"

"Yes," said Christian, "I hear you."

"Good," said Katrinka, relaxing a little, assuming that what she had from him was a promise. "Now, go to work. Keep busy. That's the best way to keep your mind off things that don't concern you."

"Yes, Mother," said Christian. Back in his voice was the hint of sarcasm she had not heard since their time together in Prague.

Katrinka said good-bye, replaced the receiver, and looked across the breakfast table at Mark, who was studiously reading a newspaper, pretending he had not understood a word of her conversation, though his German was as good as her own. "When you get to the office . . ." began Katrinka.

"No," said Mark firmly, looking up from the paper.

"She's sweet and pretty, but she'd bore him in no time."

"You expect me to tell him that?"

Katrinka nodded and said, "Christian likes you. He respects you."

Mark grimaced. "Respects me, perhaps . . . Look, if I say anything at all, it will just get his back up."

Katrinka sighed. "It's so hard to know how to treat him. I'm never sure what I'm doing is right. Sometimes I think I give him too much. You know, like those silly parents who bribe their children to love them. And sometimes, I think I'm too hard on him. What right I have to tell him do this, do that, as if he was still a baby? I did give up that right when I put my name on the adoption papers."

"Christian is twenty-four years old. Even if you'd raised him yourself, you still wouldn't be able to tell him what to do."

"But then, at least, we'd have some kind of, what you do call it? A working relationship? This way, I don't know what we have. I'm so afraid of losing him. But I can't let him walk all over me and everyone else."

"You won't lose him," said Mark reassuringly. "Christian has no intention of letting you get away."

"I hope you're right. I love him so much." She smiled at Mark. "And you, too, in case I did forget to mention it lately."

Mark returned the smile. "It's always good to hear it." He stood up. "I better get going. I've got back-to-back meetings all day." He leaned over to kiss her good-bye and added, "I may be home a little late."

"Do you want me to cancel our dinner plans?" They were dining with Henry Kravis and Carolyne Roehm.

"No," said Mark. "That's how rumors get started. Anyway, I'd like to find out what Henry knows."

"You do think he's behind the move on VHE?" Henry Kravis's company had led the field in leveraged buyouts during the takeover-mad 1980s.

Mark shook his head. "No, I don't think so. I'm pretty certain it's Charles Wolf." He had not quite dismissed the Gettys as a possibility, but Wolf continued to seem the most likely raider. "Still, Henry may let something slip that could be useful to me."

"Not likely," said Katrinka. She touched the hand he had left resting on her shoulder. "You're so good," she said, "listening to all my problems when you do have so many of your own."

"I know," said Mark, grinning. "And I'll remind you of that when there's something I particularly want from you."

Having assumed that Katrinka would break the news to her parents, taking the brunt of her father's anger and her mother's anxiety, Milena at first refused to phone them. So adamant was she about not speaking to her parents herself that, for a few minutes, Katrinka actually began to hope that the girl would back down and agree to return home. But when Milena saw that Katrinka would neither make the call nor leave her hotel room before the matter was resolved, she reluctantly dialed the number of the farm and, when her father answered the phone, burst into tears and told him that she was staying in New York.

At that point Katrinka left for her office, but no sooner had she reached the Praha than Milena called to report on the conversation. She was hysterical. Her father was in a rage, but she was not going to give in. She didn't care what they did to her, she declared melodramatically, she was not going back to Czechoslovakia.

By the end of the day, Milena had spoken to her parents several times, and Katrinka had spoken to them once. František was, as she had expected, furious with her, and could not understand why Katrinka could not just ship the girl home. Katrinka did her best to explain how little there was she could do: if she refused to let Milena continue at the Ambassador, she would quickly get another job, thanks to the sensation she had become in New York's club scene; if she tried to have Milena's visa revoked, Adam would simply have it reinstated. The truth was, that as long as Milena had Adam to turn to, Katrinka's hands were tied. But František refused to believe that, as did Olinka, his wife. "What do you want me to do?" asked Katrinka finally. "Knock her out. Tie her up. Carry her to the plane?"

"Yes," said Olinka. "Once she is here, we can talk some sense to her."

"She's in love," said Katrinka. "There is no talking sense to her. Not now. In a little while, maybe." She did not bother to add that Adam had threatened to go after Milena and bring her back to New York.

"We should never have let her visit you," said Olinka bitterly. "Never!"

It was inevitable that they should blame her, Katrinka knew. "If any of us could see into the future," she said, "maybe we all would have acted differently." Of course, they all should have known what would happen. Turn a beautiful young woman loose in any city and she was bound to end up with a lover. "But we all did what we thought was best at the time," continued Katrinka.

"Talk to her, Katrinka, please," urged František, when he had calmed down a little. "Make her understand why she has to come home."

"I'll try," promised Katrinka, though she doubted she could say anything that would change Milena's mind.

The phone calls between New York and Mohelnice continued virtually nonstop for the next week. There were arguments, tears, ultimatums, pleas for forgiveness, refusals to budge from held positions. Milena begged Adam to talk to her parents, but since he suspected that a promise to marry Milena might be the only possible way to quiet their worries, he refused. She was a big girl, he told her. She ought to be able to handle her parents by herself. In any case, staying was her decision and, if she regretted it later, he did not want her blaming him for it.

"But why would I regret it?" she asked. "Don't you love me?"

"You know I only want to make you happy," he responded. Milena heard the remark as a declaration of undying passion.

Any feeble hope that Milena would change her mind and go home was lost two nights later when Adam brought the promised MCA executive to hear her sing. Red-eyed from crying, nose stuffy half an hour before the performance, on stage Milena seemed not to have a care in the world. Her problems had ceased to exist. Only the music had any reality for her. The executive was impressed and offered her a recording contract. Some changes had to be made in her repertoire; production and promotion would have to be handled carefully—after all, she did not quite fit into any easily exploitable mold. Still he was convinced that this beautiful redhead with an angelic voice and magical stage presence could be a star.

Milena was ecstatic. And once she told her parents and they understood that the recording contract was real, their opposition to her staying in New York began to weaken. Hardheaded, hardworking Czechs, they knew a good opportunity when they saw one. And Katrinka, acknowledging silently that it was a chance Milena would have been crazy to pass up, congratulated her and stopped making any attempt at all to change her mind.

Word about the contract hit the street within hours. The next day, Rick Colins called Milena to ask her to make a repeat appearance on his television show, to which she happily agreed; and Sabrina's column was headlined, "Playboy Tycoon Bouncing New Czech . . . on His Knee." Accompanying the story of breathless passion (Sabrina's source for this one was Adam himself) was a picture of Adam holding an obviously smitten Milena on his lap.

It was a tasteless photograph, one guaranteed not to meet with his mother's approval. And when she had finished letting Adam know the full extent of her anger, Nina Graham Luce showed up unannounced at Katrinka's office demanding to know all about this new "Czech person" and how Adam had become involved with her. "One of you really was quite enough," she snapped. "Even for Adam, I would have thought."

"I have been trying to convince him of the same thing," said Katrinka. "Maybe you will have better luck."

"How on earth could you have been so stupid as to introduce them?"

The two women stood glaring at each other, neither prepared to give an inch.

"Because even knowing what a low, sneaky, dishonest person he is, I didn't expect him to take advantage of her. She's nothing but a child. Completely without experience."

"How dare you speak about my son that way!"

"Why not? All I am saying is the truth!"

"Even if he is fool enough to involve himself with every grasping, conniving little tart who comes his way—"

"Who you are talking about?" said Katrinka, interrupting. Her voice was low, her pale blue eyes glinted coldly, her back was ramrod straight.

"Not you, certainly," said Nina, with a wave of her elegant hand, dismissing Katrinka's outrage. Retreating from the desk, she sat on the wide sofa and said, in a much more reasonable tone, "I have asked him repeatedly not to get himself into the papers with the election so near. It's the least he could do for me, you'd think." She had no idea that her son had long ago given up any hope of pleasing her and instead took every opportunity presented to do just the opposite.

"Nina, believe me, I don't like this any better than you do. Adam is the last person in the world I want Milena involved with. When you meet her, you will see why. She is so naive. So innocent. She won't know how to cope with him."

Nina looked at her speculatively. "You're telling me the truth?"

"Of course," said Katrinka. "Why I should lie?"

In spite of herself, Nina had over the years developed a grudging respect for Katrinka's judgment. "She's how old, did you say?"

"Eighteen. And a very sweet girl."

Looking slightly more cheerful, Nina said, "Well, I suppose if she manages to get pregnant, this whole mess won't have been a complete disaster. Adam can always put a stop to that record contract, if he has to marry her." She was seeing Milena in a new light—that of brood mare—and the image pleased her enormously. "So sorry to have interrupted your work, my dear." Her smile was as apologetic as she could make it as she stood and offered Katrinka her cheek to kiss.

But Katrinka was again choked with rage. For a moment she was tempted to repeat the accusation she had hurled at Adam, but when she could speak finally she didn't. It would be sinking to Nina's level, laying blame just for the pleasure of it, not an attractive personality trait.

"Now, don't sulk, dear," said Nina, withdrawing her unkissed cheek. She wagged a finger at Katrinka. "You must learn to find a silver lining in every cloud," she advised, as if she were not in the habit of predicting storms to darken everyone's sunny day. "With any luck, this may all just turn out for the best," she said.

"Not for Milena, I'm afraid."

"Don't be ridiculous," said Nina, heading for the door. "It's not every little farmgirl who ends up married to a Graham. If it happens, your cousin will count herself lucky. As I'm sure you did."

On Tuesday, Katrinka and Mark left for Europe, as scheduled, and without Milena. Accompanying them was Zuzka, who had settled her case with Carla and was looking relaxed and happy again. Their first stop was London, where Mark met with his senior staff to try to quiet the fears raised by the continuing takeover attempt, while Katrinka worked out an agreement with Sir Colin Marshall for a package deal between British Airways and her hotels.

Cocktails with Carlos was less satisfactory for Katrinka. Although he was flying to Prague about once a week and had managed to complete the redecoration of the new apartment, Carlos was so completely preoccupied with Alex Holden-White's problems that the work on the hotel was falling behind schedule. The tabloid press had had a field day with the story of the esteemed curator's sexual involvement with an underage boy, and the scandal had cost Alex his job, his pride, and his social standing. As hurt, angry, and betrayed as Carlos felt, he was determined to stick by the beleaguered Alex until the court case was resolved, both to avoid making it seem that he believed the evidence (the lawyers had entered a plea of not guilty) and to keep Alex from breaking down completely. The tension was tearing Carlos apart. "Thank God for Rick," he told Katrinka. "He makes me laugh. He keeps me sane." The two former lovers now spoke at least once a day. "As soon as this damn trial is over, I'll leave for Prague. I swear I'll make up for lost time," he promised.

"Don't worry," said Katrinka, trying to curb her usual impatience. "A few days late won't matter. Just take care of yourself."

But things in Prague were not so bad as Katrinka had expected—at least not with regard to her property. The new apartment had turned out exactly as she had imagined it. Furnished in the Biedermeier style, with most of the antiques imported from Austria and Germany, the apartment was spacious and comfortable. Carlos had even found a temporary skeleton staff to run it. Mark thoroughly approved, settled himself in the room designated his study, and spent his days on the phone taking care of business.

The hotel, too, was further along than Katrinka had feared and, with her on the scene for two days, the workers made up even more time. But the city itself had slowed down in its rush for economic redevelopment—and the country with it. With Václav Havel's resignation in July, Slovakia's push for independence, and the government's preoccupation with weeding out former collaborators from positions of power, the national focus had splintered and progress seemed, at least temporarily, stalled. Still, the small group Katrinka had helped to establish continued to make some headway, importing a steady stream of advisers to supply the more adventurous with advice and expertise on how to build a business. There had been some small but notable successes, despite the continuing obstacles, and Katrinka remained optimistic that the political situation would resolve itself quickly and the continuing stream of foreign investment would, in the meantime, keep the economy from totally disintegrating.

On their first night in Prague, Katrinka and Mark took a few friends to the Golden Prague for dinner. Among the guests were Zuzka, who was leaving the next day to visit her parents; Daisy and Riccardo, who had come from Florence in order to fly with the van Hollens to Corfu for Jean-Claude's wedding; Mirek's daughter, Zuzanka, and her husband. It was a relaxed, happy evening, the most enjoyable that Katrinka had spent since Christian's arrival at the New York house with news about Milena's affair.

The next night, however, was far from pleasant, though not nearly so bad as it might have been. František and Olinka drove to Prague from Mohelnice and, though Mark had suggested that Katrinka tackle them alone, he did in the end join them for dinner, which Katrinka had decided should be at home to avoid any scenes in public. He saved the situation. Not emotionally involved himself, Mark managed to keep everyone else discussing the matter calmly and, by the end of the evening, had allowed them all to convince themselves that young girls inevitably fell in love; that Adam had much to recommend him; that Milena was undoubtedly happy; that a singing career was a real possibility for her; that her life, in short, was far from ruined. When František and Olinka left for home the next morning, they were feeling much more optimistic about Milena's future. If taking chances had turned out so well for Katrinka, wouldn't they be foolish to prevent their daughter from doing the same?

"Thank you, *miláčku*," murmured Katrinka when they had left. "Thank you. I could never have calmed them down all by myself."

"Who knows?" said Mark, with unusual pessimism. "With a little luck, Milena's future may be just as rosy as we painted it."

Unfortunately, neither Mark nor Katrinka figured Christian into their calculations of Milena's future. Of course he had not stayed away from Milena as his mother had asked. He was too frustrated, too angry to behave sensibly, though Milena would not have suspected that from their many telephone conversations, so charming was Christian when they spoke, congratulating her on the record contract, asking if he could see her, telling her he wanted to buy her dinner to celebrate.

Even with Pia, Christian was on his best behavior. Too proud to let her know just how much he minded, he carried on as if Milena's relationship with Adam was of interest to him only because of his concern for her welfare.

Pia believed him because she wanted to. And when he asked her to move in with him, she took it as a sign that all his previous coldness to her, the erratic way in which their relationship repeatedly stopped and started, had been Christian's way of lurching toward intimacy, not an easy state to achieve for either of them, given their histories. She agreed immediately.

Martin, when she told him, said that she was crazy to believe a word that Christian said, he was such an obvious manipulator. But Pia wrote Martin's reaction off as jealousy. And her mother's objections she also dismissed as unreliable. If anyone was a manipulator, it was Patrick Kates, and, if Lucia couldn't see the truth about her own lover, how could she be trusted to recognize the faults in anyone else's? As they had done frequently since Pia's move to New York, mother and daughter quarreled, each saying things about the other's man that neither was likely to forgive too soon.

The night before Pia moved in with him, Christian finally had his date with Milena. While Adam was in New York, she had refused his invitations, but a few days after Mark and Katrinka had left for Europe, Adam had to return to Los Angeles to move out of his Malibu house. Milena had not been able to go with him because she refused to miss a performance. And though Adam claimed to be disappointed about her decision, he was, in fact, relieved. He needed a break from romance. The bodies of naive young girls might stop the heart, but their conversation frequently numbed the brain.

Christian arrived at the hotel after Milena's late performance. He was carrying a bouquet of long-stem white roses and a magnum of champagne. The concierge who saw him as he passed greeted him by name, as did the elevator operator who took him up to Milena's floor. When he rang the doorbell to the suite, Milena opened the door immediately, and what a maid saw as she pushed her cart past was Christian kissing her hello, then Milena exclaiming over the beauty of the flowers before the door closed, shielding the two of them from her view. What a lovely couple, she thought enviously, wondering how the papers had got it all wrong about Milena and Adam Graham.

"I thought we were going out for dinner," said Milena, who had expected Christian to phone her from the lobby.

"We are. I thought we would have some champagne first."

"Oh, yes, of course," said Milena politely. She had intended never to let Christian into her suite again.

Christian opened the champagne and poured them each a glass as Milena put the flowers into water. When she finished, she took her usual seat in an armchair, a safe distance away from Christian, who sat on the couch. He never mentioned Adam, but asked her about the recording contract. As she told him about the plans MCA had for her, seeing Christian's interest and enthusiasm, she began slowly to relax, beginning to wonder as he filled her glass again and again with champagne why she had been so afraid of him. Really, he was very kind, she thought, catching sight of the flowers he had brought.

"We should go," said Christian finally. He had made reservations for them at Cafe Metro, one of New York's recent hot spots, where the food was not nearly so interesting as the restaurant's celebrity diners.

Getting to her feet, Milena stumbled. "I'm a little drunk, I think," she said.

Christian reached out to steady her. "Not used to champagne?"

"Not yet," she said, giggling.

It was nothing he had planned, or at least not consciously, but as soon as Christian touched her, he knew he would not leave that suite without making love to Milena. He moved closer to her, pulling her into his arms.

"No," she said, trying to move away from him.

"Why not? You're not a virgin anymore."

Her brain was so slow that for a moment his argument almost made sense to her. She felt his lips against her hair, her ear, her cheek. Finally, they came to rest against her mouth. She thought of a response. Tipping her head back, so her lips were free again, she said, "I don't love you."

"How do you know?" he asked, forcing her head toward him with his hand. "Maybe if you give me a chance, you'll like me better than Adam." He took her bottom lip between his teeth and bit until she opened her mouth to scream, then thrust his tongue inside.

Her hands pushed against him, tried to hit him, but in his state each tiny blow felt like a caress. Once she managed to kick him, but he dragged her back to the couch, pushed her down, and got on top of her, pinning her beneath his body, one hand holding hers out of the way above her head. "Stop, please," she begged. "You're hurting me." There was terror in her voice.

He put his mouth over hers again to stop her crying, then reached under her short ruffled skirt to drag down her hose and panties. She tried to twist her body away from his, and for a moment Christian seemed to oblige, lifting himself slightly, but it was only to let her shift beneath him enough so that he could jam his leg between her thighs. He was hard. He had never been so hard in his life, he thought, as he unzipped the fly of his pants. "You'll like it," he murmured. "You will. I know you will . . ."

Thirty-Two

"You've had enough," said Adam.

Natalie lifted her wineglass and held it out to him. "Three little glasses," she said. "That's nothing."

It was true she didn't seem in the least high, but Adam knew, from recent unpleasant experience, that Natalie's descent from high-spirited dinner companion to belligerent shrew to self-pitying drunk could take less time than a free-fall from the top of the Empire State Building. "How much did you have before I picked you up?" he asked.

"*Ouff*," said Natalie with a shrug of her shoulders. "Not much." She smiled. "Just one more. Please?"

"This is it," he said, reassessing the habit of remaining friendly with former girlfriends as he poured the last of the 1961 Château Lafite into her glass. In general, he liked the easy, relatively nondemanding intimacy of the relationships; and when the women were as beautiful (and useful) as Alexandra or Lucia, the benefits always outweighed the inconveniences. Natalie, however, was turning out to be far more trouble than he was willing to deal with.

They were dining at Spago, Wolfgang Puck's restaurant overlooking the Strip. Below them, visible through the picture window, lay Book Soup, Tower Records, and the Friday night traffic, cruising along Sunset Boulevard from Laurel Canyon to Doheny, growing heavier as the night progressed, easing again only in the early hours of the morning. Tables by the window were much in demand, though no one paid particular attention to the view: the stars scattered within the restaurant were of far more interest than any hanging in the heavens— which was just as well, since thanks to a combination of light pollution and smog, the latter were rarely visible.

"You should have ordered a Château Gillette," said Natalie, staring critically at the empty wine bottle. "It would have been a nice gesture." She checked her watch and smiled bitterly. "On Corfu, the wedding day dawns. To the happy bridegroom," she said, raising her glass. "*Cet espèce de salaud.*" When Adam didn't respond, she added, "The least he could have done was invite us."

Adam had received an invitation, but a business trip to the Athens shipyard ten days before had not been postponable, and a return to Greece for the wedding an unnecessary expense. A few years earlier, he wouldn't have thought twice about such things as the cost of jet fuel; but the days of carefree spending were over. "I think it's understandable," he said to Natalie, seeing no reason to correct her misunderstanding. "In your case, at any rate. Why make the bride jealous on her wedding day?"

"He never asked me to marry him, you know." Her green eyes filled with tears.

Adam saw the warning signs and signaled the waiter.

"I loved him. I was pregnant with his baby. And still he never asked me. I had an abortion because of him." The tears started to run down her face. "First I lost that baby. And now I've lost Aziz."

"You haven't lost Aziz," said Adam reasonably. "You can visit him any time you like."

The tears were ringing her eyes with smudged mascara, leaving faint dark furrows along her cheeks. "I've lost him," she repeated, lapsing into French, which Adam did not understand.

"Anything else, sir?" asked the waiter.

"No, nothing," said Adam. "Just the check, please. As quickly as you can."

"*Je veux du café,*" said Natalie.

He recognized the word for "coffee," and said firmly, "We'll have it at home." He cut short a protest by adding, "Your makeup is a mess. Wouldn't you like to go fix it?"

For a moment, Adam thought she was going to refuse, but instead she got unsteadily to her feet and said, in English, "I'll be right back."

Standing, Adam put a steadying hand on her arm. "Can you walk?"

"Yes," she said. "Of course."

He watched anxiously as she made her way across the floor to the rest rooms, but not only did she seem to have no problem keeping upright, she even stopped to say hello to Bruce Willis and Demi Moore, who shopped regularly at her boutique on Melrose. Considering the shape she was in, it was something of a miracle that she contrived to keep her business from going under, but the stores were doing well. Adam was beginning to believe the old proverb about God's taking care of children and drunks.

The waiter brought the check and Adam realized that he had been staring fixedly at the spot where Natalie had disappeared from view for some time. He checked the bill, then, as he gave the waiter his credit card, a flurry of activity at the door caught his attention. Looking over, he saw Sean Connery entering with his wife and another couple. Behind them he spotted Lori Havlíček with a young woman he did not recognize. When they were seated, Adam got up and went over to say hello.

"Oh, Adam, hi," said Lori, with what she hoped passed for enthusiasm. "What are you doing in Los Angeles?"

"Packing up the Malibu house," he said.

"A beautiful house," she said sympathetically.

"Yes," he agreed, staring at her dinner companion. "But it's outlived its usefulness."

"I'm sorry," said Lori, her lips curving in a delighted smile. These were the moments she loved. "B. D. Howe, meet Adam Graham—the man who didn't make your movie."

B. D. Howe was indeed Oriental, as Adam had expected. She was also young, somewhere in her late twenties, and incredibly beautiful, which—for no particular reason—he had not. She was tiny, with small, precise features. Her hair was black, thick, short, and spiked. Tiny pearl drops studded the most beautiful ears he had ever seen. "If you had introduced us before I passed," said Adam, extending his hand to the writer, "I might have made a different decision."

"My mistake," said Lori pleasantly.

"How do you do?" said the young woman, who found Adam's smile very appealing. Could this be the bastard she had heard Lori denouncing for months as a man with no taste or integrity?

"Will you forgive me, Miss Howe?"

"Beth," she said. "Why not? Everything's turned out for the best." She looked fragile as a flower, but her gaze was unwaveringly direct and her attitude strictly no-nonsense.

Adam turned his attention briefly back to Lori. "Tomáš started filming yet?"

She nodded. "Monday. In San Francisco. The dailies have been incredible." Dailies were uncut footage of scenes already shot—long, tedious, and dull, filling people with false hope and equally unjustified despair as they tried to guess how a scene would really play in a finished film. No one was experienced enough to be right even half the time. "At least two Oscar-winning performances, or I'll eat my favorite jeans. Another two for best screenplay and best director."

Adam laughed, turned to Beth, and said, "Now there speaks a happy agent."

"I'm trying not to let myself get too carried away," said Beth, with a fond look at Lori. Agents from CAA and ICM, who last year would not return her calls, were already phoning to talk to her about changing representation. But it was thanks to Lori that this film was getting made, and Beth did not intend to forget it.

"How's the baby?" asked Adam.

"Beautiful," said Lori. "Smart. The joy of our lives."

Out of the corner of his eye, Adam saw Natalie making her way back from the rest room. He leaned over and kissed Lori's cheek. "I'm glad everything's going so well for you. You deserve it."

"No hard feelings?" she said.

"None at all," said Adam. A little to his surprise, he meant it. If Tomáš had cost him the studio sale, then he'd be turning the world upside down looking for the right revenge. As it was, Tomáš's being happy was no skin off his nose. He held out his hand to Beth Howe. "I hope to see you again sometime."

Not certain how best to respond, Beth nodded politely, then watched as Adam returned to his table, picked up his credit card, put an arm around Natalie, and steered her to the door. "He's not what I expected," she said.

"No?" asked Lori, who had always been surprised by the effect Adam had on women. For some reason, he did not appeal to her at all. Or vice versa, she acknowledged ruefully.

"He's not married, is he?" asked Beth, not bothering to elaborate on her former statement.

"Didn't you see Sabrina's column the other day, and that disgusting photograph?"

"I don't read that shit."

"He's fucking his former wife's eighteen-year-old cousin."

"Nice," said Beth.

"Very," agreed Lori sourly. "If he calls you," she added, "hang up. And that's my last word on the subject."

Adam drove Natalie home, half carried her to her door, and, refusing her invitation to go in for a nightcap, turned her over to her waiting housekeeper. When he arrived back at the Malibu house, however, the gray-faced Carter greeted him with an apologetic expression and the information that Natalie was on the phone, wanting to speak to him. "I thought she'd have passed out by now. Bring me a brandy, Carter, would you?" he said, and went into the study, the nearest room with a phone, picked up a receiver, and listened with as much patience as he could muster to Natalie's weeping about Jean-Claude, Khalid, himself, Aziz, all the loneliness and disappointments of her life.

"Natalie, go to sleep," said Adam. "It's late. You're tired. We'll talk again in the morning." Finally, he convinced her to hang up and go to bed.

"Miss Čermák called from New York," said Carter when he brought Adam the requested brandy. Adam groaned. And Carter added, "She sounded quite upset."

"I've had enough of weeping women for one day," said Adam. "No more calls tonight, Carter. I don't care who they're from or what they're about."

Carter murmured his agreement, said good night, and left. Adam remained at his desk for a moment, then, carrying the brandy with him, began walking through the silent house. The art was packed and shipped. His clothes and the few personal possessions he had would be packed and sent the next day. He went out on the patio and stood for a while looking at the ocean, its wind-ruffled surface glinting like pewter in the moonlight. He had no regrets about selling the studio. He had enjoyed the glamour, the deal-making, the thrill of having a hit. The starlets had been as accommodating as he had expected. And few people licked boots as efficiently and satisfyingly as lackeys in Hollywood. But the unpredictability of the business had frustrated him, and movies were not his real passion. Boats were that. No, he had let the studio go without a pang. The house was another story.

It was a beautiful house, he thought as he made his way back inside, across the granite floors, and up the staircase to the stark simplicity of his bedroom. In many ways it was the perfect house for him, closer to his ideal than any he had lived in before; but even with the price of California real estate lower than it had been for a considerable time, his business interests now were all on the East Coast and in Europe. Property in Malibu was still too expensive to buy if you could spend no more than a couple of weekends a year there.

He would build himself a house in the Hamptons, he decided. Or maybe in Maine, somewhere he could get away to and relax—fish, sail, swim, think. Maybe he would ease up a bit on work after the takeover of VHE was completed, hopefully any day now, and do what Katrinka had suggested—design a boat and sail in the next America's Cup competition.

The phone rang and Adam came out of the bathroom cursing Carter for not having obeyed instructions. Then he realized it was his private line. He couldn't have been crazy enough to give Natalie that number, he thought, as he tried to decide whether or not to pick it up. It could be Mac or Debbie, with some business crisis, though since it was four A.M. in New York that seemed unlikely. Or his mother. Another groan escaped him, but then it occurred to him that she might be ill. She was, after all, almost seventy—hard as that was to believe. He picked up the phone. "Yes?" The greeting was almost a snarl.

"Adam . . . Adam . . ."

She was trying to get words out past the sobs that caught her breath, leaving her speechless, and it took him a few seconds to recognize her voice. "Milena? Is that you?"

"Yes. Adam . . ." Again she tried and failed to speak.

Jesus Christ, he thought, what the fuck is going on tonight? "Milena, stop crying," he said calmly, feeling like a broken record. "Tell me what's wrong."

"Christian . . ." she said, almost choking with the effort.

"What about Christian?" He heard a rush of Czech words, then more weeping. "In English, Milena. I can't understand you."

"He . . . he raped me," she said, her voice rising and breaking in a wail.

The Papastratos estate was in the northern part of Corfu, several kilometers inland from the seaside villages of Sidari and Roda. The nearest airport was in the town of Corfu and wedding guests were ferried from there to the house by helicopter, giving them spectacular views of old stone villages, the curved towers of the ancient churches, the craggy mountains, the sandy beaches, and the dense green of cypresses mingling with the silvery sheen of olive groves. Servants greeted the arriving guests, escorting them to their rooms in the mansion and in the guest houses scattered about the estate, or taking them by limo along the narrow mountain roads to hotels in the nearby resorts. One of the Niarchoses arrived by yacht and anchored at Sidari.

Mark and Katrinka were in a vine-covered, white stucco guest house with Daisy and Riccardo. It consisted of two bedrooms, each with its own bathroom, a sitting room, and small efficiency kitchen. In the sitting room was a bar. The furnishings were spare, but comfortable, in

407

cool colors punctuated by bursts of bright turquoise. In every room were large bouquets of fresh flowers.

Dinner on Friday night was informal: a barbecue held on the grounds of the estate, chicken and lamb shish kebab, and endless side dishes, including the world-famous Papastratos olives. A local group entertained with Greek music and from time to time groups of men would assemble and begin to dance. The guests included a son of King Constantine, two of the Niarchos brothers, the Mosbachers, the French minister of finance, his Canadian counterpart, an assortment of national and local government officials, several members of the minor European nobility, and other relatives, business associates, and close friends of both the bride and groom—three hundred in all.

In the morning, an early breakfast was served in the dining room. And at ten o'clock a procession led by the bride (in a Dior gown) and her attendants (several unmarried cousins) walked along the narrow lane (resurfaced for the event) from the mansion to the church in Karoussades, a nearby village, where a Greek Orthodox priest married the slightly pregnant Thea to the slightly dazed Jean-Claude. A Roman Catholic priest had married him to Hélène twenty years before, but an annulment had been granted on the grounds of Hélène's inability to have children—nonsense, of course. Jean-Claude had never wanted any and Hélène had been careful not to conceive.

The wedding lunch was served in an enormous tent erected in a field adjacent to the olive groves. Outside, whole lambs roasted on open fires. An army of servants scurried back and forth with trays of pastichio and spanakopita, stuffed grape leaves and moussaka, hummus and tabouli. Inside, a string quartet imported from Paris alternated with a rock band from London and local musicians playing traditional music. The guests danced on the planked square in the center of the tent. Tables were set with Irish linen, French porcelain, Buccellati silver, and Venetian glass. The champagne was Dom Pérignon, the wine Château Gillette. Garlands of pink roses hung in graceful loops from the ceiling and cascaded down the canvas walls. The wedding favors were turtledoves, designed for the occasion by Madame Marie-Claude Lalique. The entire affair was extravagant, expensive, exuberant, and a lot of fun—nothing like the bride at all.

"What's wrong?" asked Mark, leaning close to whisper in Katrinka's ear. Her face had a distant, almost mournful look, totally at odds with the atmosphere and unusual for Katrinka, who liked nothing better than a party.

"I keep thinking of Natalie. How different everything would have been for her, if . . ." She stopped speaking and shrugged. "No point crying over spilled water," she said.

Mark laughed. "None at all," he agreed. "Do you want to dance?" Chance, the English rock band, was playing.

"Yes," she said, beginning to smile. "That will cheer me up."

They joined the crowd on the dance floor and remained there, changing partners, Mark dancing with the bride, her cousins, Daisy, one of the Niarchos wives; Katrinka with Jean-Claude, Riccardo, a Bavarian prince, and finally with Tony Moreland. Jean-Claude had apparently bought some art from him over the years and they had become friends.

"Quite a bash," said Tony, as he escorted Katrinka back to her table.

Daisy, who had already returned to her seat, smiled and said, "Tony, darling, come sit by me. Have you seen Hélène recently?" she asked.

"Sometimes I think my wife loves gossip even more than she loves me," said Riccardo with a dramatic sigh. "È vero, cara?" he asked, kissing Daisy's hand.

"I'm just curious," said Daisy.

Tony laughed. "Hélène is fine. Enjoying her settlement. Glad to be rid of him, I suspect. Though I think she was shocked at first. Couldn't believe he actually meant to divorce her this time."

"I do hope he settles down now," said Katrinka.

"He better," said Daisy. "I get the feeling the new Mrs. Gillette won't put up with much nonsense."

"Oh, I don't know," said Tony. "The most unlikely women turn into the most complacent wives." He couldn't resist throwing a glance in Katrinka's direction and she suddenly remembered that his London flat was one of the places where Mark had run into Monica Brand.

"You do mean me?" she said pleasantly.

"Oh, no, my dear, of course not," he said smoothly.

"Why on earth should he?" asked Daisy, who could not imagine what Katrinka was getting at. Then she too remembered. "Oh, are we talking about Monica Brand?"

Tony laughed uneasily. "Really, you two have absolutely no discretion."

"You mean we don't act in the least English?" said Daisy.

"Not when people make remarks about my marriage," said Katrinka simultaneously.

"Who's making remarks about your marriage?" said Mark, finally returning from his stint on the dance floor. He saw Tony's face and said, "Leave the poor man alone, Katrinka. He looks as if he's facing a firing squad."

"I do just want to ask how he knows Monica Brand."

"I think I told Mark that I don't. She came to dinner with Cumber, as I remember."

"And you did never see her anywhere else?"

Tony nodded. "From time to time. Always with a different man. Rich, successful men usually."

"Like Mark?" asked Katrinka.

Tony looked at Mark apologetically, as if trying to explain how he had leapt to (possibly) the wrong conclusion. "Yes," he said; then he smiled. "Though not always so attractive."

"Thank you," said Mark dryly.

"Sounds like a hooker to me," said Daisy.

Mark and Katrinka exchanged glances. That's *exactly* what it sounded like, but it made absolutely no sense. Why would a hooker be pursuing Mark, who clearly had no intention of paying? "She didn't look like a hooker," said Mark doubtfully.

"Not in the least," agreed Tony Moreland.

"Neither did Sugar Benson—after she actually became one," said Daisy.

Katrinka laughed. "That's what Adam did always say."

But any further thought of Monica Brand and her possible profession was driven from their minds by the arrival of the elaborate wedding cake, a many-tiered structure decorated with icing roses and topped by papier-mâché turtledoves. There were toasts, speeches, more dancing. The party was clearly intended to go on through the night, as new musicians replaced those leaving and the chefs began to prepare a light supper for anyone who might grow hungry again before breakfast was served. Thea and Jean-Claude were not scheduled to leave on their honeymoon until the following week when they were sailing on Jean-Claude's yacht to the South Sea Islands. Guests were invited to remain until Monday.

By ten, Mark had had it and even Katrinka was beginning to feel the effects of too much of a good time. They made their excuses and left the tent, walking arm-in-arm back past the olive groves toward the guest house. "It's so beautiful here," said Katrinka, looking at the clear night sky, the brilliant stars, the lighted stucco villa glowing against a backdrop of lush cypresses.

"Maybe we can come back next year, with the baby," said Mark. "We can rent a yacht, explore the islands."

"Mmm," said Katrinka happily. "I would love that."

Daisy and Riccardo had left the party earlier and their bedroom door was closed when Mark and Katrinka arrived back at the guest house.

Set out on a table in the sitting room was a tray of fruit and cheese. Beside it was a message for Mark.

"It's from Carey," he said when he read it. He went into the bedroom, picked up the phone, and asked whoever answered in the house to put through a call to New York.

As she changed out of her clothes, Katrinka listened to the conversation, but since it consisted mostly of swearing on Mark's end she learned little. Some of it she lost when she went into the bathroom to remove her makeup, the running water drowning out the sound of voices. When she returned to the bedroom, Mark was seated in the rush chair by the narrow wooden table where the phone rested, making notes on a small notepad, still listening to whatever bad news Carey had to report. His jacket was off, his tie loosened, the top button of his shirt undone. He looked worried.

The covers of the bed had been turned down and Katrinka slid between the crisply ironed sheets of Greek cotton, rested against the pillows, and waited. Finally, Mark said, "First thing in the morning . . . Yeah. See you," and hung up. He looked across the room to Katrinka. "Charles Wolf filed his intention to take control with the SEC, then faxed an offer to the office late Friday night. The sonovabitch must have known I was out of town. Christian went into the office on Saturday, to work on some report. He found the fax, and called Carey."

"He faxed an offer?"

"Didn't have the guts to talk to me personally. The prick."

"What you do now?"

"Turn it down. But my board isn't going to like it. We have to leave in the morning, baby. I have to be there on Monday to handle this, or all hell will break loose."

Katrinka nodded. "Come to bed, then. You have to get some sleep."

"In a minute." He picked up the phone again and asked to be put through to a hotel in Corfu. Luckily, his pilot was in and Mark told him to make the arrangements for as early a departure as possible on Sunday morning and to send a helicopter to pick up Katrinka and him. Since Riccardo had just finished a major piece of sculpture, he and Daisy were planning to take a few days vacation and tour the island.

When Mark finished his phone call, he stripped down to his shorts, leaving his Brioni tux in a heap on the floor, and walked into the bathroom. When he came back into the room, he got into bed beside Katrinka and pulled her into his arms. "I could lose everything," he said.

It was only then that Katrinka understood how frightened he was. "You won't," she said.

Whatever happened, he would have Katrinka, the baby, and more money than he could ever possibly spend. But money was not the issue. He had built his company from nothing. He had started with a small bindery and slowly, carefully, had put together a multinational media empire. Because it would make him a rich man, he had gone public in the late seventies—a decision he had only recently come to regret, one he would rethink if . . . *when* he fought off this takeover. He had no intention of losing his company. Or anything that was his. He had had enough loss to last him a lifetime. He kissed her bare shoulder. "No," he agreed. "I won't."

The trip to New York was a nightmare. Neither Mark nor Katrinka was able to relax. They sat in facing leather armchairs, silent for the most part. Occasionally, Mark would ask Katrinka's opinion of a board member or advice about some strategy he was planning. Otherwise he sat scribbling notes on a yellow pad. Katrinka tried to work, then to read, but she was too concerned for Mark to concentrate. The attendants served them food, offered them drinks. Mark barely tasted the expertly prepared meals and drank only water. When Katrinka suggested they lie down and try to nap for a while, Mark snapped at her. She had never seen him like this before, so edgy and short-tempered, completely unlike his usual, reasonable self.

It was one o'clock in the afternoon when the van Hollen jet touched down at JFK. Within minutes the customs officials were aboard to clear them for arrival. Still Mark complained about the delay. Wisely, Katrinka said nothing.

Mark's driver was waiting for them just outside the customs hall. He took their briefcases and motioned the porter handling their luggage to follow him. "Traffic's not bad," he said, assuming that was the question uppermost in Mark's mind.

Neither Mark nor Katrinka paid any attention to the dull Queens landscape as they sat staring out the tinted window. Not used to their silence, the driver wondered if they had had a fight. Several times, he felt compelled to say something, anything, to lighten the mood, then decided against it. Half an hour later the car pulled to a stop in front of the town house. "Here we are," he said unnecessarily.

"You come inside," asked Katrinka, "or go right to the office?"

Mark had showered and changed clothes on the plane, before landing. "I want to see Anuška," he said, then turned to the driver. "I'll be ten minutes."

"Yes, sir," said the driver, as he held the car door open for them.

Josef, the butler, opened the door, took their coats, then went outside to help with the luggage. "Welcome back," said Anna, who had come into the front hall to greet them.

"Everything is okay?" asked Katrinka.

"Fine. No problems at all," said Anna. "Mr. Heller is here. Upstairs in the nursery."

Katrinka nodded and followed Mark into the elevator, wondering why Christian was visiting in the middle of a Sunday afternoon. But there was not a sound as they walked along the brightly colored corridor toward Anuška's suite. When they entered, they found the sitting room empty. So was the bedroom at first glance. Then Mark sprang across the floor, reaching the changing table before Katrinka even noticed the baby lying there unattended. "Goddamnit," muttered Mark. "Where the hell is she?" he asked as he picked the baby up. She was wearing only a diaper.

"Jiřina!" called Katrinka sharply.

Anuška began to cry and Mark, regretting the display of temper, began to soothe her as the nanny came running into the room, carrying a pile of baby clothes. "What is it? What's wrong?" she asked. Christian stood in the doorway behind her.

"Where were you?" asked Katrinka in Czech, her pale eyes glinting with fury.

"I went to get some clothes for her to put on." There was a small laundry room, just for Anuška and her nurse, at the end of the corridor.

"And you left her alone?"

"It was only for a minute," said Jiřina, beginning to cry.

"We weren't gone long," said Christian, guessing at most of the conversation.

"I want her out of here," said Mark softly, still cradling the now quiet Anuška in his arms.

"I left her only for a minute," wailed Jiřina. Katrinka took her by the arm and led her into the sitting room, closing the door behind them. "Please," said the nanny. "It won't happen again. Give me another chance."

Katrinka shook her head. Mark might forgive many things, and so would she, but not endangering the life of their daughter. "I'm sorry," she said.

"Mother," said Christian, "for heaven's sake . . ."

"Keep out of this," she snapped. She turned back to Jiřina and took the clothes from her arms. "Go away now. We'll talk more later about what's to be done."

The girl nodded and left the room. Christian frowned. "You can't mean you're really going to fire her?" asked Christian, in German.

"The baby could have broken her neck, if she'd fallen," said Katrinka coldly, laying the clothes on a side table.

Christian's frown deepened. "I didn't think," he said, after a moment. Whatever resentment he had felt for the baby before her birth had disappeared, he wasn't sure why, except that, since he had saved her life, he felt possessive of her.

"No. And neither did Jiřina. What are you doing here, anyway?"

"Not making love to the nanny in the laundry room," snapped Christian.

"Just flirting a little?"

Christian shrugged. "I didn't see any harm in it."

"Don't do it again."

"I don't suppose I'll get the chance."

"With any of my staff."

"Yes, Mother," said Christian, and again that unpleasant note of sarcasm was back in his voice.

Mark came out of the bedroom. "She's sleeping," he said. He looked around the room. "Jiřina?"

"In her room, I think."

"I don't want her near the baby."

"Neither do I," snapped Katrinka.

Mark put his arms around her, and kissed her cheek. "I know, I've been a bear all day." He let her go and said, "I'll call you later, when I have some idea when I'll be home."

"I stopped by to see if you would like me to spend some time at the office today," asked Christian. "If I could be of some help."

Mark shook his head. "Thanks. Not right now. But I'll give you a call later, if I need you. Will you be around?"

"At my place," said Christian.

Mark left and Katrinka turned to Christian and said, "That was nice of you to offer."

"No," said Christian. "That's how all young executives get ahead, by toadying to the boss."

Katrinka shook her head and smiled. "I still don't know when you're serious and when you're not."

"I'm always serious," said Christian. Then the sulky look vanished from his face as he smiled and said, "Seeing Mark was only half my reason for stopping by."

"And the other half?"

"To see you, of course."

"Why?"

"Because I missed you." When Katrinka raised a disbelieving eyebrow, he added, "And to tell you that Pia moved in with me yesterday."

Katrinka was surprised. "That was quick."

"We've been talking about it. And . . ." He shrugged. "Well, once we made a decision, it seemed silly to waste time. Don't you approve?"

"I like Pia," said Katrinka. "I just thought . . . well, I thought you were tired of her."

Christian shook his head. "I think I wasn't ready to make a commitment."

"And now you are?"

"Yes."

"If you're happy, *miláčku*," said Katrinka finally, "I'm happy."

"Oh, I am, Mother. Very happy."

Why, wondered Katrinka, didn't she believe him?

Christian left to return to his apartment to spend the afternoon with Pia, waiting for Mark's phone call, and Katrinka stopped in to talk briefly with Jiřina; then leaving one of the housemaids with the baby, she went down to her bedroom to shower and wash her hair. She felt exhausted, worried about Mark, and undecided about how to handle the nanny.

As she got out of the shower, Katrinka heard the phone ring. Thinking it might be Mark, she slipped into a terry robe and rushed into the bedroom to answer it, leaving wet footprints on the carpet.

"Mrs. van Hollen, Mr. Graham is phoning," said Anna.

"Tell him I'm not here."

"He said to tell you he knows you're at home and if you won't talk to him he'll come over and make you."

"Thank you, Anna," said Katrinka. She pushed the button of the lighted extension and said, "Adam, I'm in no mood for you right now."

"I've got Milena with me," said Adam. "There's a problem. And I want you to come over. Right away, Katrinka."

"What problem?" Katrinka recognized the tone of voice and knew whatever it was, it was serious.

"I'll tell you when you get here. Do you have the address?"

"No," she said. "Wait." She opened the night table drawer, took out a pad and pen. "Go on." When Adam had dictated the address, she tried again. "Is she sick?"

"No," said Adam. "I'll explain when you get here."

* * *

Katrinka's first sight of Adam's new apartment for a moment drove all thought of Milena from her mind. It was so completely his taste, beautiful in a cold way. She was very happy not to have to live there.

"Hello, Mrs. van Hollen," said Carter. "Mr. Graham's in the library. Shall I show you the way?"

"Thank you," said Katrinka. "How you doing, Carter?" she asked, as she followed the butler's slender form along the narrow hallway.

"Very well, thank you, Mrs. van Hollen. Thank you for asking. And yourself? And the baby?" he asked politely when Katrinka had assured him she was fine.

"Fantastic," said Katrinka. She smiled. "You should come by and see her some day."

Carter smiled. "I'll do that, madam. Thank you. It would be nice to see Anna again as well."

All Katrinka's good humor faded at the first sight of Milena, who was stretched out on the sofa, her body wrapped in a stretch jumpsuit, looking a little pale, but otherwise fine. She was reading a magazine. Adam was sitting in an armchair, looking through the Sunday papers. There was a scotch and water on a nearby table. When he saw Katrinka, he stood.

"What is going on?" Katrinka turned and looked accusingly at Adam. "What you are up to? Calling me, scaring me half to death. And here you are, both of you, enjoying a quiet Sunday at home."

Milena burst into tears and a fleeting expression of annoyance crossed Adam's face. It was replaced instantly by one of acute concern. He went to the sofa and sat down beside Milena, gathering her into his arms. "Tell her," he said.

Milena, sobbing, shook her head.

"Tell her," insisted Adam.

"Why you don't tell me?" asked Katrinka.

"I want you to hear it from her. So that you'll believe it." He turned back to Milena and said, "Tell her, sweetheart. She has to know."

Katrinka sat in a chair opposite Milena and said quietly, "What is it, Milena?"

Hanging on to Adam as if he were a life raft, Milena looked across to Katrinka. "It's Christian," she said.

Thirty-Three

WHAT GUILT CHRISTIAN FELT FOR HIS ACTIONS WAS QUICKLY BURIED BENEATH A THICK COVER OF rationalizations—Milena had been teasing him for weeks; her refusal to have sex was some sort of ploy, or game, or weapon, all part of a grand strategy of seduction; it wasn't as if he were a stranger, or she a virgin. Any regret about hurting her was overwhelmed by his need to protect himself. If he was sorry, it was because he had lost control. And when he called Milena on Saturday morning to apologize (as if what he had done was a lapse in manners rather than a criminal offense), it was more to assess the situation than to express contrition. What he managed to learn before she hung up on him was that she had not thought of calling the police or even of going to see a doctor.

That information was reassuring and slanted the direction of the story Christian was preparing. Not that he expected to be punished for his behavior, at least not in any significant way. From childhood, he had successfully managed to avoid paying the usual penalties for his misdeeds—by shifting blame, outwitting whatever authorities happened to be in charge, sometimes even by blackmail. At the very most, all he anticipated this time were one or two unpleasant scenes and a confrontation with Katrinka that would end with her believing any lie he would choose to tell.

But when almost forty-eight hours passed without a word from anyone, Christian began to think Milena had decided to say nothing. He was convinced of it when one casual conversation with Katrinka's housekeeper on Sunday afternoon confirmed that Milena had not called; and his mother's face, when she returned home from Greece, showed that she knew nothing. On reflection, he wasn't surprised. After all, what would Milena gain from making an issue of his behavior? (Even to himself, he did not use the word "rape.") She could not cause trouble for Christian without hurting herself, Katrinka, her parents. It seemed to him more and more unlikely that she would be willing to do that.

So the phone call from Katrinka late on Sunday, demanding to see him immediately, took Christian a little by surprise. Still, he managed to sound convincingly puzzled by her request and, by the time he returned to the town house, had the story he had been preparing for thirty-six hours or so polished to a blinding sheen.

When Katrinka confronted him with Milena's allegations, Christian declared himself outraged. He admitted he had gone to her suite Friday night: they had had a date for dinner, and he had brought her flowers and champagne to celebrate her recording contract. Somehow, he was not quite sure how, they had begun to quarrel about her relationship with Adam: it was no secret Christian didn't approve of it. The argument had become so heated that she had refused to go out with him and he had left. He was angry, yes, but the accusation that he had raped her was crazy. Why would he do anything like that?

When Katrinka, in turn, asked him why Milena would make up such a story, Christian offered several possible explanations: Milena loved being in the spotlight—perhaps this was just a way of attracting more publicity; perhaps she was crazy; perhaps Adam had put her up to lying? He was only dating Milena to aggravate Katrinka—so Katrinka had said—and what better way to hurt her than through her son?

None of it made any sense to Katrinka. She could not believe Christian guilty of rape or Milena able to lie so outrageously. And while she thought Adam capable of almost anything, she could not accept that he hated her enough to ruin her son. He was not so evil.

"You do believe me, don't you?" asked Christian.

"I don't know what to believe," said Katrinka.

But despite his mother's lingering doubts, when Christian left the town house, he felt invulnerable. Milena had no proof. What had happened in the suite that night was her word against his. And he never doubted that this time, as always before, he would be able to lie his way out of trouble.

* * *

Preoccupied with his own problems, Mark was no more able to help Katrinka sort out her tangled emotions than she was able to concentrate on his business problems. That evening they listened distractedly to each other's troubles, expressed sympathy, suggested that everything would turn out all right in the end, then lapsed into silence. Immediately after dinner, Mark, who was trying to marshal enough support to allow him to reject the Wolf offer, retreated to his study to call the board members he had failed to reach earlier in the day, and Katrinka went up to Anuška's room to check on the baby. Mark found her there two hours later, sitting in the dark—thinking, she told him, though she was no closer to deciding who was telling the truth.

Early the next morning Christian appeared at the VHE offices looking serious enough to demonstrate to Mark his concern about both Milena and the takeover bid, but not enough so as to appear at all worried or, worse, guilty. He set to work with his usual diligence, and though he had impressed both Mark and Carey Powers from the beginning with his ability to grasp and solve problems, by the day's end he had convinced them beyond doubt of his brilliance. While Mark, Carey, lawyers, investment bankers, and a few of the most loyal board members discussed strategy in the conference room, Christian on his own initiative worked up the available numbers on Charles Wolf's company and, by mid-afternoon, had discovered that, according to the figures, Wolf didn't have the money to cover his bid. Where was his financing coming from? asked Christian's covering memo. None of the investment banks he had contacted had any idea.

It was the weapon that Mark needed to put down any attempted revolt by his board and he was so grateful to Christian that he would then have appeared on the stand in any court of law to serve as a character witness. Why would any young man as intelligent as Christian, as handsome, as successful with women, stoop to rape? he asked himself. It didn't make any sense.

Ironically, it was this bit of cleverness of Christian's that prompted Adam to cause a little more trouble.

Adam's concern for Milena was genuine. So was his outrage at what had happened. Though what he felt for her at most was desire and affection, every possessive bone in Adam's body craved satisfaction. But it hadn't taken him much longer than Christian to realize that, without proof, there was no way to get Christian indicted, let alone convicted, of rape.

However, when Mark rejected Charles Wolf's offer on Tuesday morning, Adam also realized that bringing charges against Christian would drag not only Katrinka but Mark again into the limelight, and the resulting scandal would further weaken Mark's influence with his board. Christian might not go to prison in the end, but Mark would certainly lose his company, and that to Adam seemed fair enough. He suggested to Milena that she press charges.

Totally ignorant of the system of justice in the United States, having grown up in a communist country where even an unsubstantiated allegation could result in an unpleasant neighbor or irritating co-worker's being condemned to hard labor in a prison camp, Milena was not troubled by either the lack of evidence or the fear of what the system might do to her. In her experience, it was the accused—guilty or innocent—who suffered, not the accuser. And Christian was certainly guilty. Feeling helpless, bewildered, but most of all angry, she wanted him punished for what he had done. She wanted to prove to Katrinka, who seemed to be siding with her son, that she was telling the truth. Her only reservation was about her parents: she did not want them to know. And when Adam pointed out that they were thousands of miles away and would never find out unless she told them, Milena agreed to go to the police.

If the names of Graham and van Hollen had not been mentioned, New York's Finest might have tried either to coax or to bully Milena into agreeing to forget the whole thing. She had waited over three days to press charges; she hadn't gone to a doctor; the few bruises on her body proved nothing; as one of the investigating cops put it, she didn't have a shred of fucking evidence that would hold up in court. But two of the most powerful families in New York were involved, Milena passed a lie detector test, and the investigation began.

It got nowhere fast. Christian stuck to his story and Milena wouldn't budge from hers. Hotel employees who were questioned agreed that Christian was a perfect gentlemen and Milena a lovely young lady. They had been observed going out together from time to time, and Christian had been seen in her suite more than once, though he had not, as far as anyone knew, stayed overnight. Everyone thought that the two young people seemed to have a friendly relationship, though just how friendly no one was prepared to say. The desk clerk remembered seeing Christian pass by that Friday night, looking in a very good mood, carrying champagne and roses. The elevator operator recalled that Milena, when she opened the door of her suite, seemed to be expecting Christian; and one of the housekeeping staff said that she had seen them kissing hello and thought what a handsome couple they made. The waiter who had brought breakfast and the maid who had cleaned the suite on Saturday morning had seen no sign of a struggle and, aside from the fact that the usually cheerful Milena had been crying, noticed nothing peculiar. One of the room service staff did have some vague recollection of interrupting a quarrel a few weeks before; but, when pressed, he admitted that he had heard and seen nothing—it was just that the atmosphere in the suite had been a little tense when he had arrived with Milena's dinner. And that was the most damning evidence anyone could provide.

Thinking Christian couldn't possibly be as good as the hotel employees were painting him, the police investigated the possibility that they were covering up because his mother owned the hotel and they were afraid of losing their jobs. But Katrinka, when they questioned her, seemed genuinely concerned for Milena and anxious to get to the truth. At the request of the detective in charge of the investigation, she called a meeting in the hotel's ballroom and urged her staff to tell everything they knew. They all insisted they had.

The police, to their credit, left no possibility unexplored. They talked to Pia Cavalletti, hoping to uncover some history of violence in Christian's sexual relationships. But she came vehemently to his defense. He was the most romantic, the most considerate lover. He was intelligent, handsome, charming. Girls threw themselves at him, herself included. Why would he rape someone? It was inconceivable, ever, but especially then. He had just asked her to move in with him. They were in love, planning a future together. It didn't make sense.

It didn't, agreed the police, who nevertheless asked Lucia for a statement. Had her daughter ever complained of Christian's being violent in any way? And Lucia, as much as she disliked Christian, had to admit that Pia's only complaint, and hers for that matter, was that he sometimes didn't pay Pia enough attention.

Mark van Hollen, who did not seem the type to be blinded by his stepson's faults, summed it up for everyone when he said it was equally hard to believe Milena a liar or Christian guilty.

Some enterprising young reporter would have stumbled onto the story eventually, but Adam saved them all time and effort by leaking it. He made a call to Sabrina, a call to Rick Colins, a call to a few other columnists he knew. Items began appearing in the New York papers and, thanks to Sabrina's column, in the Midwest and California as well. Rick called Katrinka to tell her that he couldn't ignore the story. Milena was "his discovery," after all, and he would look like a fool if he failed to mention her accusations on his television show. He promised to handle it as delicately as possible. Katrinka said she understood. Otherwise, she refused to talk to the press. Adam, on the other hand, kept up a constant attack. Pia, whose loathing and fear of the press dated from her childhood when she had seen her father hounded, nevertheless overcame her desire to run for cover and issued statements in support of Christian, which had the peripheral effect of making her a celebrity of sorts and boosting the sale of her jewelry in the specialty boutiques that carried it. New orders came flooding in. And Christian, while managing to appear reluctant, never refused an interview, and always spoke sympathetically about Milena, who (he suggested) must have suffered some sort of nervous breakdown brought on by her sudden success. It was a masterful performance and convinced everyone except those who held the belief that where there was smoke inevitably there had to be fire.

While the story played out in the newspapers, Katrinka made several attempts to see Milena, who had stopped performing in the Starlight Club and moved to Adam's apartment. But each time Katrinka called there, Carter refused to put her through, insisting that Miss Čermák had asked not to be disturbed. Doubting that very much, Katrinka finally phoned Adam at his office and asked why he wouldn't let Milena speak to her. He, of course, denied influencing the girl in any way at all. "She won't talk to you," he said, "because she's hurt that you don't believe her."

"Whether I believe her or not," said Katrinka, unable to admit to Adam any doubt about her son, "I still want to help her."

"She doesn't need your help."

"She must see a doctor."

"You mean a psychiatrist?"

"Some sort of therapist."

"She's not crazy. It's your son who has the problem, not Milena." Adam had all the prejudice of his New England ancestors against any hint of mental weakness.

"If she's lying, she needs help—"

"She's not!"

". . . And if she's telling the truth," continued Katrinka, ignoring his interruption, "she needs it even more."

Adam thought about that a minute and then said, "I'll take care of it." He had realized the advantage of having Milena under psychiatric care.

"Adam called me this morning," Alexandra told Katrinka later that day. They were in her office at the Praha, running through last-minute changes in the menu for the Planned Parenthood Ball the following night. "He wanted to know if I could suggest a psychiatrist for Milena."

"Who did you tell him?" asked Katrinka, relieved that he had acted so quickly. Alexandra mentioned a name and Katrinka nodded. "I hear he's very good. I hope Milena will go see him."

"I expect she'll do whatever Adam tells her," said Alexandra. "What a mess this all is," she added, looking at Katrinka expectantly.

Alexandra wanted information. But Katrinka, as usual, had no intention of saying more than she had to. "A nightmare," she agreed briefly.

Alexandra smiled ruefully. "Nina must be having a fit about all the publicity. The election is less than six weeks away."

"When she gets nowhere with Adam, she calls me, as if I could stop the stories. She knows Adam does always do what he wants, no matter who gets hurt."

"He can be a good friend," said Alexandra loyally.

"Yes," agreed Katrinka. "But a terrible enemy."

In Alexandra's view—that of an old girlfriend and distant family member, Adam was nowhere near as black a character as others painted him. But defending ex-husbands to their former wives was a thankless task, so she let the matter rest and said, "I better get going." She began to gather up her papers. "I promised Gabriel I'd help him buy a painting this afternoon." While never actually admitting that she and the Argentinean were lovers, her tone always left no doubt that they were a couple. "On second thought, I do want the caviar hors d'oeuvres. I know they cost a fortune, but they're always such a big hit."

"If you do substitute the caviar for one of the shrimp dishes, it won't be much more."

"Will that be enough food?" asked Alexandra doubtfully.

"Plenty."

"Okay, then," she agreed as she stood up. "Did you find a new nanny yet?"

"Yes. A Salvadoran woman. Young, very political, very responsible. And Jiřina is in the trainee program at the Ambassador—far away from babies." She shook her head. "I never did see Mark so angry."

"Neil's the same about the children. So protective," said Alexandra, walking with Katrinka toward the office door. "God knows what he'd do if I tried to take them away from him. If I took them out of the country. He'd probably end up like Natalie," she added glumly. "I don't know what to do. I'm so confused." Her reasons for marrying

423

Neil had been complex: she had wanted his money and the social position that money could buy her, but she had loved him and been very attracted to him sexually, more so than to any other man she had ever known. But that had started to change even before Gabriel had entered her life. As Neil's hold on Knapp Manning had started to slip, so had his hold on Alexandra. As his power eroded, so did her desire. Now, Alexandra was no longer even sure that she loved him. Her blue eyes filled with tears. "Maybe it's time I paid a visit to that psychiatrist," she said as she opened the door leading out of Katrinka's office. "And tried to figure out what the hell it is I really want."

However confused about her future Alexandra may have been when she left the Praha, by that night she had made a decision. When she returned home from her afternoon with Gabriel, she found Neil waiting and upset. He had spent his day with the New York Stock Exchange's disciplinary committee, which, after months of investigating, had decided to censure him for failing to stop several of Knapp Manning's brokers from engaging in illegal business practices, including churning accounts to generate commissions, fraudulently luring clients into high-risk investments, and forging signatures on option and margin trading agreements. This censure might amount to no more than a slap on the wrist for him, unless he could be implicated more directly in the activities of the brokers. If he was, he would face federal prosecution for violation of SEC regulations. In either case, he would have to resign as CEO of Knapp Manning. His career was over.

What Neil wanted from his wife was sympathy, an unquestioning acceptance of his innocence, and a total belief in his ability to escape the clutches of the United States Attorney, who was investigating the case. What he got was contempt for his stupidity. Alexandra did not understand that such practices were common and that Neil, by ignoring them, had simply been following normal business procedure —if this had been 1984 instead of 1992 even the United States Attorney probably would have paid no attention.

One word inevitably led to too many; and before either quite realized what was happening, their marriage was in a worse shambles than Neil's business life. Not only did Alexandra tell him of her affair with Gabriel, but she announced that she was leaving him for the Argentinean. Neil reasoned, he pleaded, but Alexandra was adamant. Gabriel had been begging her for months to marry him and she had refused out of some loyalty, which she now saw as misguided, to her husband. As far as she was concerned, there was no longer any reason to refuse.

Neil left the house; and Alexandra, the deception over, felt relieved. When she called Gabriel to tell him the news, he was ecstatic and insisted on coming to the house to keep her company. They spent the entire night making plans for their future while waiting for Neil to return. He never did.

The next day Neil phoned his office at Knapp Manning to say that he would not be in that day. Alexandra, when she tried to reach him, was told by his secretary that she had no idea where he was. As the day progressed, Alexandra became more and more frantic. Not only was she worried, but the Planned Parenthood Ball was that night and she hated to think of the speculation that would arise if Neil failed to appear.

As it turned out, the press had more to occupy their minds than the condition of Neil and Alexandra Goodman's marriage. Two hours before the start of the ball, a pro-life group began to protest in front of the hotel. They were a large, noisy crowd—men, women, and children—carrying banners and chanting slogans. Security alerted Katrinka, who called Alexandra to tell her the problem. Uncharacteristically, Alexandra burst into tears. "That's all I need," she sobbed.

"Between my security and the police, I don't think there will be a big problem."

"I don't know where Neil is," said Alexandra. "We had a fight. I told him about Gabriel." She said nothing about the problems at Knapp Manning.

"You will deal with that tomorrow," said Katrinka sternly. "Tonight, concentrate on the ball."

But before Alexandra left the house for the hotel, Neil phoned. He was all right, he told her. He understood her feelings. He didn't blame her. He wouldn't be returning home. When she asked where he was staying, he told her she could reach him the next day at the office. He sounded like a ruined man.

By the time Katrinka returned to the hotel, accompanied by Mark, the protesters had been joined by television crews and print journalists, and the police were having a hard time keeping the street and sidewalk in front of the hotel clear for arriving guests. Trying to get her attention, the journalists shouted Katrinka's name as she walked by. "Look this way," called a photographer, who snapped her picture as she turned. "Do you have a comment to make about the protesters?" asked a television reporter, shoving a microphone into her face.

"I'm an American," said Katrinka. "I do believe in the First Amendment."

"Baby-killer," shouted someone in the crowd.

"Are you personally pro-abortion?" asked another reporter.

Thinking of her mother's miscarriages, the painful childlessness of friends, her own years of infertility, Katrinka made an impatient gesture. She hated the idea of abortion. That, however, was not the issue. "Nobody is pro-abortion," she said. "But I do believe whether it is good or bad, right or wrong in any particular case, that is a private, moral decision."

"Do you agree with your wife, Mr. van Hollen?"

"Certainly," said Mark. For once, instead of scowling, the cameras caught him flashing a smile that usually only his friends saw. "Wouldn't anyone who loves this country and its Constitution? That's enough," said Mark, the smile fading as questions continued to be hurled from the crowd. He steered Katrinka toward the entrance.

"There's Alexandra Goodman," someone shouted. A reporter from his paper, *The Chronicle*, Mark noted. She had kept a discreet distance when Katrinka was being interviewed. "Mrs. Goodman, can I have a statement, please?" she asked.

"Katrinka," shouted someone else. "Great gown. Who's the designer?"

Katrinka, not stopping to answer the question, followed Mark inside.

If the protest outside wasn't enough to keep the media happy, there was plenty of drama raging inside the ballroom for those members of the press who had been invited to the party. Rick Colins was there, a faint bruise under his left eye, acting as escort for a recently divorced socialite. Sabrina, in a strapless green Alan Platt gown that would have looked wonderful on someone twenty years younger and twenty pounds lighter, was with her constant companion, the designer himself. John Fairchild, Liz Smith, Richard Johnson, Cindy Adams, Billy Norwich, all were present.

Adam had insisted on bringing Milena, who looked pale and unhappy, embarrassed and shaken by the media gauntlet that had greeted her arrival at the hotel. It had been a hellish time for her—the endless grilling by the police, the photographs in the papers, the ugly insinuations about her character, the anguish of knowing that no one, with the exception of Adam, believed her. When Katrinka stopped to say hello, she ran crying to the ladies' room and Adam, after physically restraining Katrinka from following her, went in after her himself, trailed a moment later by Sabrina, who was always looking for ways to keep a story on the boil.

Christian had come with Pia, who spent the evening casting

accusing glances in Milena's direction, while Christian, depending on the audience, alternated between his role of victim of a vile campaign of slander and sympathetic defender of a deranged young girl.

One of the few men, aside from Adam, Milena would let near her was Martin Havlíček. They danced together several times, chatting comfortably in Czech. Once, Martin even succeeded in making Milena forget her troubles long enough to laugh.

"I don't know how you can even talk to her after what she's done," Pia said to Martin a little while later, when they were dancing.

"What *she's* done?" said Martin.

"You don't believe what she says about Christian?" said Pia, sounding outraged.

Martin hesitated a moment before answering. "Yes," he said finally. "I do."

Pulling away from him, Pia said, "I think you've been neglecting your date."

Martin had come with another of the new young investment brokers from Knapp Manning, a pretty young woman with a snub nose and freckles. They went out together occasionally, when they had time, to dinner or a movie. But it was nothing serious, at least not on Martin's part. He was still in love with Pia. Grabbing her arm, he stopped her from moving away. "Pia, he doesn't . . . he doesn't hurt you, does he?" It seemed inconceivable to him that Pia would put up with anything like that, but the newspapers every day were full of the most incredible stories, people doing things that in your wildest dreams you would never have imagined.

"You mean *hit* me?" she asked coldly. "No, he doesn't. He loves me. How could you believe he'd do anything like that, when you know him? How could you think I'd stand for it?" Embarrassed, Martin shrugged. "Excuse me," said Pia, twisting out of his grasp.

Catching sight of the argument between Martin and her daughter, Lucia felt a familiar wave of dismay wash over her. Martin was such a nice young man, steady and dependable. Attractive, too, like his father, with that roguish gypsy look. She knew she would feel much more optimistic about her daughter's future, if only she had fallen in love with him instead of Christian. But Lucia had not said a word on the subject since Pia had moved out. There was no point. Every time they discussed Christian, they quarreled. But at the first sign of trouble, she would drag her daughter home, by the hair if she had to. She didn't care who she upset by doing it.

"Three weeks, four at the most," said Adam. He turned to Lucia. "Do you agree?"

427

"Lucia," said Patrick Kates sharply, when she did not respond to Adam's question.

"What?" She had been so preoccupied thinking about Pia that she had completely lost track of the conversation.

"I was assuring Patrick that the work on his yacht would be completed by the end of October."

"I've been telling him that for days," said Lucia impatiently.

"Forgive me for not taking your word," said Patrick, leaning heavily on the sarcasm, "but what started out as a simple refitting seems to have taken you two forever to complete. You're already a month behind schedule."

"You know that's because you keep changing the plans," said Lucia.

"If you didn't spend so damn much time on your other projects . . ."

"We all have to make a living," said Adam. He turned again to Lucia. "Speaking of which, how did your meeting with Charles Wolf go?"

"Fine," said Lucia.

"Didn't you just complete a yacht for him? He can't want another this soon."

"Why not? You always do," said Adam.

"It's for his son," said Lucia, making peace. "A birthday present. He's turning twenty-one in a few months."

"How much money does the guy have? Making runs at companies, buying yachts as if they were toys? I heard he just bought himself a new corporate jet."

"I don't suppose he's using his own money," said Lucia. "At least not for the takeover. Only fools use their own money to finance business deals." She laughed. "Or so Nick used to say."

Both Adam and Patrick appeared startled by the remark. They stared at her for a moment, as if trying to read on her face exactly what she knew. Adam wondered if somehow she had guessed that he was backing Charles Wolf; Patrick thought she might suspect that he had sunk so much of his own money in the America's Cup race that he was very nearly broke. Then with slight, almost imperceptible shakes of the head, each of them dismissed her comment as completely innocent.

Adam smiled. "I better go look after Milena," he said, though in fact she seemed comfortable enough talking to Martin Havlíček and his date. He leaned toward Lucia and said softly, "Can't you get Pia to stop seeing that sonovabitch?"

"No," she said, her eyes flicking briefly to where Christian and Pia stood talking to Carey Powers and his wife.

"Like mother, like daughter," muttered Adam as he walked away.

"You know what I'd like to do?" said Patrick, his hand fondling her bottom. "Give a party. On the yacht. To show it off, just as soon as it's done."

"A great idea," said Lucia, her attention still focused on Pia.

"Will you plan it for me?"

"Sure," said Lucia, moving away from his wandering hand, wondering how she was going to fit that into her schedule. For the past year, she had been working harder for less money, taking on more and more commissions, some for much smaller projects than she was used to doing, trying keep her level of income from dropping too far. She knew she shouldn't allow Patrick to take up any more of her time or energy than he already did, but she couldn't help it. She loved him, or she thought she did. "I'd be happy to, darling," she said.

Hoping to repeat her Palm Beach success, Alexandra had decided to make an auction the centerpiece of her party, but this time not paintings but "objects of vertu" were on the block, including many gold and enamel snuffboxes, jeweled cigarette cases, French candlesticks, Dutch wall sconces.

"Having fun?" asked Alexandra as she danced past Margo and Katrinka, who were studying her with anxious faces. For one thing, Alexandra had obviously had far too much champagne. "I'm having a wonderful time."

"It's great," called Katrinka cheerfully, though she wished for nothing more than to be spending the evening quietly at home with Mark. That was happening a lot lately, and was not at all like her. It wasn't the social whirl that was getting to her, however, but the constant attention from the press. The papers were full of stories not only about Christian and Milena, but about Charles Wolf's bid for Mark's company. It was exhausting keeping up a pretense of not giving a damn.

"What does Alexandra think she's doing?" whispered Margo. "Everybody's talking." Alexandra, having decided that playing the part of the abandoned wife was much less satisfying than playing a gay soon-to-be-divorcée, had danced too frequently with Gabriel for it to escape anyone's notice.

"I don't think she does care right now," replied Katrinka, who filled Margo in on the little she knew.

"Where do you suppose Neil is staying?" asked Margo, when Katrinka had finished. "Do you think he has a girlfriend tucked away somewhere?"

"Neil?"

"Why sound so surprised? It does happen, you know."

"Yes," agreed Katrinka. "But not every man . . ."

"I wouldn't trust one of them as far as I could throw him," said Margo, looking to where her lover of two months, James Newman, who owned several Seventh Avenue design labels, was dancing with a girl young enough to be his daughter.

"Just because Ted—"

"He's coming," said Margo, interrupting Katrinka. "My daughter told me this afternoon." Her bright-red mouth curved into a delighted smile. "Apparently he doesn't like the idea of my seeing so much of James. Well, sauce for the goose . . ." She let the sentence trail off.

Seeing Margo's smiling face, Katrinka shook her head and said gently, "Don't count eggs before they're chickens, Margo."

Margo laughed and said, "I won't. I promise. Anyway, what the hell, I'm enjoying myself." Since meeting James, she had stopped caring quite so much that she had not been able to find a job, at least not yet. Something would turn up sooner or later, she was sure. And, if not, well, Ted would just have to cough up more money to keep her. It was half hers, after all.

"I'd like to ask one of you ladies to dance," said Rick, coming up to them. "But what will I do with the other?"

"Dance with Margo," said Katrinka. She had just caught sight of Sabrina, talking to Christian. "I have to go rescue my son."

"You don't have to worry about Christian," said Rick. "He can take care of himself." It was hard to tell whether or not he meant that as a compliment.

"What happened to your eye?" asked Margo, stepping into Rick's arms as Katrinka moved away.

"Walked into a door." Rick said it lightly. Some boy he had brought home from a bar a few days before had turned out to be a little rougher than Rick had expected.

"You should be more careful," said Margo, guessing what had happened.

"I intend to be," said Rick.

"Hello, Sabrina, how you doing?" said Katrinka cheerfully as she stepped between the columnist and Christian. "Lovely gown."

"It's one of Alan's," said Sabrina, pleasantly for her. The mention of Alan or his work always mellowed her.

"He's very talented," said Katrinka. "I did buy two ensembles from his last show."

"I'm sure they look wonderful on you."

Katrinka caught Christian's eye and, with a slight bow, he said, "If you'll excuse me . . ."

"He's charming," said Sabrina, watching as Christian made his way back toward Pia.

"Do you think so? Of course, I'm prejudiced."

"And Milena's such a sweet girl, don't you think?"

"Yes," said Katrinka, frustrating Sabrina's desire to get a nasty comment from her. "I hope this mess does blow over quickly for both of them."

Not a prayer, thought Sabrina, though her mouth curved into a smile. "Yes, I can imagine you've about had it with the press for the moment."

"I know you're all just doing your job," said Katrinka sweetly.

"My, how understanding you are. But of course you are married to one of the world's most powerful newspaper men . . . though not for long, I expect."

Sabrina was referring to the Charles Wolf takeover, Katrinka knew. She laughed. "But I do intend to be married to Mark for the rest of my life," she said, pretending to misunderstand. "If you excuse me, Sabrina, I think I should find out what my kitchen has done with the dessert." Katrinka was so anxious for the evening to end that even the Praha's impeccable service seemed slow to her that night.

"Did she mention Charles Wolf?" said Mark, grabbing Katrinka's hand as she went past him. At the moment, he was as eager as Sabrina for gossip. Wolf had responded to the turndown by raising his offer, though no one as yet could figure out the source of his financing.

"She did hint that soon he would have your company. That's all."

"Over my dead body," muttered Mark. That afternoon, VHE's lawyers had filed for an injunction, citing various antitrust statutes, to stop the takeover attempt. Mark had little hope that the ploy would work, but at least it would gain him some time.

"That's what I did tell her."

"You didn't!"

Katrinka smiled. "Of course not," she said. "I am always very nice to Sabrina. Now, if you let go of me, I will be on my way."

"Sorry," said Mark, smiling apologetically as he released her. He watched her for a moment as she continued across the floor, then, turning around, caught sight of Milena, who was sitting and talking with Rick Colins. Impulsively he went over and asked her to dance.

Her glance not quite meeting his, Milena refused. "I . . . uh, I hurt my ankle a while ago," she said. She had been using that as an excuse for the past hour.

"If you're in pain," said Mark sympathetically, though he didn't believe it was her ankle that was hurting, "maybe you should get Adam to take you home?"

"He says we can't leave until after the auction." She looked pale, vulnerable, very near tears.

"Why he thinks anyone cares . . ." said Rick.

"If you need us," said Mark, switching to Czech, "Katrinka or me, for anything, you only have to ask."

"You don't believe me," she said, her eyes filling with tears.

"We care about you," said Mark, evading the issue. He still wasn't sure whom or what to believe. "We'd do whatever we could to help. Remember that. See you, Rick," he added, switching to English.

"What did he say?" asked Rick, unable to restrain his reporter's curiosity even about someone he liked as much as Mark.

Milena shrugged. "It doesn't matter," she said.

"I hope you didn't say anything to upset Milena," said Adam, intercepting Mark as he crossed back to his own table.

"Why don't you get her the hell out of here, if you're so goddamned concerned about her feelings?"

"And let everyone think she has something to hide?"

"Who gives a fuck what anybody thinks? The girl's in agony."

"Temper, temper," said Adam genially. "You really shouldn't let your business problems make you so irritable."

The idea of throwing a punch at Adam Graham's smug face was extremely tempting. The thought of ending up on the front page of tomorrow's tabloids was not. Mark took a deep breath and said calmly, "Take her home, Adam."

"Do you think the court will grant you that injunction?"

"She'll break in a little while, if you don't get her out of here," said Mark, refusing to switch the conversation to business.

"You don't have a prayer," said Adam. "You can't stop Charles Wolf."

Adam's voice was still perfectly pleasant, but never before had Mark felt so strongly the other man's contempt for him. He recognized it for what it was: the upper class bully's terror that some tough new kid was going to beat the shit out of him. He had experienced it for most of his adult life. "I didn't know Charles Wolf was such a great friend of yours," he said.

"Not friend exactly. Business associate."

"Oh?" said Mark.

"I built his last yacht," said Adam quickly, afraid that by giving in to his desire to taunt Mark he might have revealed more than he had intended.

But Mark seemed satisfied with the reply. "Then maybe you can deliver a message for me?"

"I'd be happy to."

"Tell him if he doesn't back off, I'm going to break his company into little pieces and feed it to the sharks."

Like hell you will, thought Adam, watching Mark walk away, delighted to have seen even such a small crack in his cool facade. Smiling, Adam returned to the table where Milena sat talking to Sabrina and Alan Platt. Milena looked, he thought, like a victim being led to the slaughter. Mark was right: he'd better get her away before she fell completely apart. "You all look very serious," he said, coming to a stop behind Milena's chair, letting his hands rest on her shoulders.

"I was just trying to talk Milena into letting me design a wardrobe for her next stage appearance," said Alan.

"Sounds like a great idea," replied Adam, who had no intention of allowing that to happen. Not that he particularly disliked Platt's designs. He just considered the designer an unpleasant and manipulative little toad.

Milena twisted around slightly in her seat and smiled at Adam. "I told him it would probably be a while before I appear in public again."

Adam looked at Sabrina and nodded. "Milena's psychiatrist thinks she should avoid any unnecessary stress at the moment."

Sabrina's eyes grew bright with interest. "She's under psychiatric care?"

Adam stroked Milena's hair. "Poor little sweetheart," he said. "Ready to go?"

"Can we?" said Milena eagerly.

"Of course." Adam pulled back Milena's chair and helped her rise. "Good to see you, as always, Sabrina. Good night, Alan," he said.

"She's such a quiet little mouse," said Alan. "I don't know what he sees in her."

"The same thing I see in you, no doubt," said Sabrina coldly.

For a moment Alan Platt's eyes held nothing but loathing, and then he smiled. "You think she's that good in bed?"

"Don't flatter yourself," said Sabrina, enjoying her power. She had no worries at all that Alan might leave her. After all, where would he be without her to champion him as the new genius among American designers? Nowhere. Nowhere at all.

* * *

433

The auction was not the huge success that Alexandra had hoped it would be. The demonstration outside may have dampened the mood of the guests, or the various undercurrents in the room might have had their own negative effect. Or perhaps it was the general feeling that, despite the president's insistence that the economy was improving and one or two small indicators pointing to some growth, no one's mood was optimistic, no one felt like spending money, everyone was worried about what the effect on business would be if a Democrat was elected to the White House.

As she watched the various items go for much less than she had anticipated, Alexandra had the awful feeling that her bubble had burst, that her short stay in the New York sun was over, that—unless she was very careful—she would find herself slipping back into the genteel poverty of her youth. A terrifying thought! She clung to Gabriel, smiled at him adoringly, and told him in the little Spanish that he had taught her that he was her life, which was true enough.

As soon as the auction was over, the crowd began to thin. "Have lunch with me tomorrow?" begged Alexandra as Katrinka said good night to her.

Katrinka nodded, then looked in surprise at Mark who had deliberately avoided saying good-bye, which was a breach of good manners unusual for him. "What is wrong?"

"I keep getting an image of rats deserting a sinking ship," said Mark bitterly. It hadn't taken long for the rumors to start. Mark had heard from his investment banker about Neil's meeting with the disciplinary committee.

"You know something about Neil?"

"I'll tell you when we get home," said Mark softly.

Katrinka nodded, then left him for a moment to talk to the banquet captain.

"Mark?"

Turning, Mark saw Martin Havlíček, coat on, ready to go. He looked worried. Mark smiled and said, "Lost your date?"

"She's in the rest room." Martin didn't smile in return but looked around to be sure no one was near enough to overhear, then said, his voice serious, "Look, I probably shouldn't say anything. Loyalty to clients, and all that. But, uh, well, you and Katrinka have been very helpful to me. And I can't see what harm it would do to tell you. Or what good either, for that matter. But . . ."

"If this is something you could get into trouble for doing, Martin, I'd just as soon you didn't. I appreciate the thought, but, really, I can take care of myself."

"It's nothing illegal, if that's what you mean."

"In that case . . ." said Mark, with a reassuring smile.

Martin hesitated a minute and then said, "I was playing with the computer this afternoon, at the office. I do that sometimes when things are slow. Anyway, one of our traders is buying big chunks of VHE stock."

Not for Charles Wolf, Mark knew, since legally Wolf could not start buying stock for fifteen days from the date of his tender offer—or longer, if the injunction was granted. "For whom?"

"I didn't recognize the names."

"Names?"

"Two. Galahad, Inc., registered in the Isle of Man. And Hydra, registered in Switzerland."

"How many shares have they acquired?"

Martin told him and Mark whistled. Those shares combined with what Charles Wolf had acquired before making his offer would amount to close to fifteen percent of VHE stock, not enough to get control, but sufficient to cause even more problems. Were Galahad and Hydra operating independently, that was the question? If yes, Mark had to get to them before Wolf did. If not, then it looked as if Wolf might be involved in an illegal maneuver to conceal acquisition of shares. Either way, it was important for Mark to find out, as fast as possible, who controlled the two mystery companies. "Thank you, Martin," he said. "I'm very grateful."

Martin looked no happier than he had at the beginning of the conversation. It had been a hard call, trying to decide whether to respect a client's confidence or help a friend. He still wasn't sure he had made the right decision.

"Hey, cheer up," said Mark. "You didn't give away any state secrets."

"I suppose not," said Martin, smiling faintly.

For the first time since he had learned that someone was gobbling up his company's shares Mark felt confident, really confident, that he was in control of the situation. He had Martin to thank for that. He extended his hand and, almost reluctantly, Martin took it. The kid had a good, firm handshake, Mark noticed.

"If it's any consolation, I think you did the right thing."

"Yeah, well, you would," replied Martin, not sounding convinced.

Thirty-Four

MARK WOULD PROBABLY HAVE MENTIONED TO KATRIN-
KA AT SOME POINT BEFORE GOING TO BED THAT NIGHT
what Martin had told him about the companies acquiring VHE stock
except that, when they arrived home, they found Anuška running a
high fever. It had happened twice before and, even though the doctor
had assured them that such high temperatures were not unusual in
babies, still the feel of her small hot body and the sound of her crying
terrified them.

The new nanny, Marisol, apparently unflappable in a crisis, told the
worried parents that she had spoken to Anuška's pediatrician and was
following his recommendations exactly. She even hinted that it might
be a good idea if they were to go to bed and leave her to do what she
had to without interference. They didn't take the hint. After changing
into comfortable clothes, Katrinka and Mark returned to the nursery
and helped Marisol bathe the baby, change her bedding, feed her
bottles of water and juice, fetch one another cups of coffee and tea.

By three-thirty in the morning, to everyone's relief, Anuška's fever
broke. Exhausted, Mark and Marisol—at Katrinka's insistence—went
to bed for a few hours, while Katrinka, still tense with fear, curled up
on the sofa in the nursery sitting room, distractedly watching the Home
Shopping Network on cable television while she listened for sounds
from the baby. But Anuška was quiet, sleeping peacefully each time
Katrinka went back into her room to check.

It was at such moments, standing over her daughter's bed, feeling helpless and frightened, that Katrinka understood what her own mother must have gone through watching her daredevil daughter hurtle down ski trails, taking incredible chances in pursuit of medals and championships, never giving a thought to the neck she might break. I wish you could see her, *Mami*, she thought as she touched Anuška's tiny balled fist. The loss of her parents was an ache that never seemed to go away.

The next day, since she had no meetings scheduled, Katrinka, after taking the baby to the pediatrician, worked at home, spending the day running between the nursery and her cheerful second-floor study, keeping a wary eye on Anuška, while dealing with phone calls, correspondence, and the plans for the opening celebration for the hotel in Prague in mid-November. Every couple of hours Mark called for an update on the baby's condition, and finally Katrinka felt secure enough to laugh. "I do think we are the most nervous parents in the world," she said.

"Probably," he agreed, not bothering to point out that with their histories they were bound to be.

Late in the afternoon, Robin walked over from the Praha to deliver a folder full of reports and a Federal Express package of sketches and fabric samples from Carlos.

"What happened with Sir Alex?" asked Robin as Katrinka looked through the sketches. "Is the trial over?"

Katrinka nodded. Alex was serving a prison sentence in a place called Wormwood Scrubs, and Carlos was back in Prague at work on the last phase of the hotel's renovation.

"I don't know how Carlos could have stuck by him," said Robin disapprovingly.

Though she had little sympathy for Alex herself, Katrinka said, "When you love somebody, you can't just walk away when they need you. No matter how hurt or angry you are."

"But how can you love someone who'd do a thing like that? How old was the boy? Fifteen? It's disgusting."

The boy had been a practicing homosexual for years, and his encounter with Alex had not been his first exchange of sex for money; still, it was indeed disgusting, thought Katrinka. But love doesn't die in a minute—although it would be better for everyone if it did. Now, hopefully, with the trial over and Carlos having done what he considered the right thing, his feelings for Alex would continue to fade and the relationship would gradually come to an end.

The idea of that made Katrinka a little sad. The romantic in her preferred to think that love was eternal. The realist accepted that it was not—except perhaps where children were concerned. If Mark ever betrayed her, eventually she would stop loving him, just as she had stopped loving Adam. But nothing, nothing in the world, could ever kill what she felt for Anuška, or Christian.

The house phone rang and Robin, who was nearest to it, answered. Looking up, Katrinka saw her eyes widen in surprise, then her mouth pinch with disapproval. "She's got a hell of a nerve," she said. "All right, I'll ask." Taking the phone from her ear, she said, "It's Anna. Natalie Bovier is here. Do you want me to go down and get rid of her?"

"No, I'll see her." A few months before, Katrinka would have agreed immediately to Robin's suggestion, but the last of her anger toward Natalie had died at the time of the kidnapping. "Tell Anna to show her into the sitting room."

Grudgingly, Robin did as Katrinka asked, then gathered up her papers, shoved them into a folder, and accompanied Katrinka downstairs. Robin's pale, freckled face was wary, her slender body poised for trouble. Trailing Katrinka into the sitting room, she watched disapprovingly as Natalie, speaking incomprehensibly in French, launched herself from the beige sofa into Katrinka's arms.

Natalie had gained more weight. Though she was still far from fat, her face and body had the puffy, balloonlike appearance of someone who drinks too much. Dark roots were visible in her blond hair, her dress puckered unflatteringly at her waist, her nail polish was chipped —it was unbelievable how far she had let herself go. And Robin understood enough French to know that her words were slurred. It was barely five in the afternoon, and Natalie was very drunk.

Katrinka murmured to her soothingly, and, when she had convinced her to sit again, turned to Robin and said, "Please ask Anna to bring some coffee."

A few minutes later, when Robin returned, Katrinka was sitting next to Natalie on the sofa, holding her hand, listening to her babble in a mixture of English and French. They had been friends since their early twenties when they had met in Munich, where Katrinka was a model and Natalie a visiting buyer for Galleries Gillette. Neither had spoken the other's native language, but they had worked out a way of communicating that, while it often sounded confused to others, was perfectly clear to them.

Noticing Robin for the first time, Natalie smiled, despite the tears running down her face, and said, "Robin, *chérie* . . ."

"Hello, Natalie." Hearing the tone of Robin's voice, Natalie resumed

her weeping, and Robin looked at Katrinka and said, "Do you want me to stay?"

Katrinka shook her head. "No, thank you. I'll see you in the morning."

"There's an executive committee meeting at ten, at the Ambassador."

"I'll be there."

"Well," said Robin reluctantly. She felt she ought to stay, though it was perfectly obvious that Katrinka could handle the situation herself. "'Bye."

Just as Robin reached the door, Josef opened it, and Anna entered, carrying a silver coffee service, Sèvres cups, and a plate of cookies. Her glance locked for a moment with Robin's, before it shifted to the two women seated on the sofa. She clearly no more approved of this turn of events than Robin did.

"They hate me," murmured Natalie when she and Katrinka were alone again.

"Nobody hates you," said Katrinka, refilling Natalie's cup with strong coffee.

She had come east for business, Natalie told Katrinka, stopping first in Palm Beach, then coming north for a meeting with her bankers. The meeting had been scheduled for four and Natalie had not made it. This was not the first meeting she had missed. Sometimes she forgot; sometimes, like today, she was in no condition to attend. She could not make herself care about business any longer, about success, about money. Now that she had lost Aziz, she didn't care about anything. *"Je veux mourir,"* she said at last, very calmly. And when Katrinka protested, she repeated, "It's true. I want only to die."

With the clarity of hindsight, Katrinka could see that no healthy, self-respecting woman would have tolerated a relationship with the married Jean-Claude for as long as Natalie had; she would not have married, on the rebound, Khalid, a Moslem who already had two wives; she would not have had an affair with her best friend's husband. What had seemed, when they were very young, like high spirits and an interesting lack of conventional morality in Natalie now appeared neurotic and self-destructive.

The daughter of a laundress, launched into Parisian high society by a married lover, she had always felt out of her depth, like a fraud, tolerated because of her beauty, doubting the intelligence that was the real basis of her success, masking her insecurity with a veneer of sophistication. Though Katrinka had never realized it, Natalie had envied her friend's self-confidence, her resilience, the sure way in

439

which Katrinka climbed from success to success, the emotional stability of her life. It was envy that had made Natalie say yes to Adam, when
she knew she ought to say no. It was her attempt to grab some of that
security for herself, while destroying it for the woman who was her
best friend.

The failure of her relationships with Jean-Claude, with Khalid, and,
to a lesser extent, with Adam had further undermined Natalie's
self-confidence. More and more, she drank and took drugs for relief
from a nagging sense of failure that persisted despite her business
success. She had been drowning in despair when she learned that
Jean-Claude was going to marry Thea Papastratos. The loss of Aziz
pushed her under for the third time.

"You're my only friend," she said to Katrinka. "The only one who
understands."

Realizing there was no way to deal with her until she had slept off
the effects of the alcohol, Katrinka suggested that Natalie return to the
Plaza, where she was staying, and go to bed. But she refused to leave
and Katrinka, knowing Mark would be furious with her, took Natalie
upstairs to one of the guest rooms. "You have to get help," said
Katrinka, as she removed Natalie's shoes and settled her between the
crisp cotton sheets of the bed.

Natalie yawned. "You'll help me."

Torn between irritation and sympathy, Katrinka did not reply. She
had said over and over again, to Jean-Claude, to Khalid, to everyone,
that Natalie was not her problem, but here Natalie was, passed out in a
drunken sleep in her guest bedroom. What was she supposed to do
now?

After leaving Natalie, Katrinka went up to the nursery to see
Anuška, who seemed—with that incredible resilience of children—to
be completely recovered; then she returned to her study to work for a
while longer on the plans for the Prague opening, but she had no
sooner picked up her pen than the phone rang. It was Mark. "Everything under control?" he asked. And when Katrinka hesitated he
leaped instantly to the worst conclusion.

"Anuška's fine," said Katrinka quickly. "She does look as if she's
never had a thing wrong with her. But . . . well, Natalie Bovier came
by this afternoon. She was drunk. And . . ."

"And?"

"She's upstairs now, asleep."

"Jesus Christ, Katrinka, you are not running a fucking hostel for
wayward friends."

"What was I supposed to do?" said Katrinka, losing her temper. "Throw her out in the street?"

"Call a taxi and send her back to her goddamn hotel."

Mark, who was one of the most generous people in the world was, as far as Katrinka was concerned, completely irrational on the subject of house guests.

"I'll do that as soon as she does wake up. Meanwhile, I'll keep her out of your way."

"Good. I've had a rotten day, and I don't think I'll make a very gracious host."

"You didn't get the injunction."

"No."

"Oh, Mark, *miláčku*, I'm sorry. What you do now?"

"Make an offer for Wolf's company."

"But that's—"

"I know, crazy. Completely nuts." In essence, Mark was planning to counterattack, to put Wolf on the defensive. "But it may force him to back off."

"Can you do it?"

She meant, did he have the financing. He didn't, not yet at any rate, but he could get it. "Yes," he said.

"And if he doesn't back off?"

"Then we'll spend the next several years in court, trying to figure out who owns whom. That ought to be a lot of fun." Mark laughed, sounding almost as if he was enjoying the situation which, in a perverse way, he was. Fighting for your life—or your company's life—might be exhausting, it might be frightening, but it was also exhilarating. "What I called to tell you is that Paul Zeiss is stopping by tonight. At about nine. I invited him to have dinner with us."

"Paul Zeiss. He is here in New York?"

"He's coming in on the Concorde."

"He has news?"

"He wasn't giving much away on the phone. You know what he's like. But yes, I think he has news."

At nine exactly, the doorbell rang. Natalie was still upstairs sound asleep, to Mark's annoyance, and he and Katrinka were waiting for the detective in the sitting room. As the butler opened the door to usher him in, Mark got to his feet and crossed the floor to greet the slim, gray figure. "Monsieur van Hollen, Madame," said Zeiss, switching his leather attaché case to his left hand, extending his right to shake Mark's. He was incurably formal.

441

"Please, sit down," said Katrinka, as he shook her hand.

"Would you like something to drink?"

Zeiss smiled almost shyly and said, "A whiskey, if I may."

As Zeiss waited for his drink, he picked up his attaché case, put it on his lap, snapped it open, removed a folder, then closed the case again, returning it to the floor at his feet. When Mark handed him the whiskey, he took a sip, then placed the cut-crystal glass on the table in front of him, and opened the folder. "As you know, Monica Brand has been, for some time, in Hong Kong." Mark nodded and Zeiss continued. "While there, she was seen frequently in the company of a number of rich, influential businessmen, some married, some not. Her relationships with them were quite open. She accompanied them to the theater, to concerts, to parties, on trips—for both business and pleasure . . ."

"A beautiful, single woman having a good time," said Mark.

"Possibly," agreed Zeiss. "In the case of the single men, she would often return with them to their homes and spend the night there. The married men tended to pass an hour or two with her in her apartment at the end of an evening. Of course, there were times, in the middle of the day . . ."

"Well, she never struck me as being shy about sex."

"Daisy was right," said Katrinka. "She's a hooker."

"Yes, I think there's very little doubt about that. Miss Brand lives quite well, and, as far as we can determine, without any legitimate source of income. Her real name is Mona Brendzel. Does it mean anything to you?" he asked.

"No, nothing."

"She was born in Connecticut, someplace called Darien." But that information meant nothing to Mark or Katrinka, nor did anything else Zeiss told them about Monica Brand's background, hoping to find in it some clue about why she had been pursuing Mark. "I didn't expect any of that would mean much to you," he said finally. "But there is one certain connection. When she returned to London—"

"She's in London?" asked Mark.

Zeiss nodded and said, "She returned three days ago. And one of the first people she called in to see was Sugar Benson." Katrinka repeated Sugar's name, as if not quite sure of what she had heard, and again Zeiss nodded. "You know her, I believe?"

"Very well," said Katrinka, sounding a little dazed.

"This couldn't just be coincidence?" asked Mark, adding immediately, "No, I suppose not."

"We managed to trace the photographer who took the photographs of you and Miss Brand. He was paid by Madame Benson."

"But why would Sugar want to break up our marriage?" asked Katrinka.

"Indeed," said Paul Zeiss. "Could there be some other motive?"

"There's always the possibility," said Mark, grinning, "that Monica acted on her own initiative. She may just have found me irresistible." He reached for Katrinka's hand. "Some women do."

Pulling her hand away, Katrinka said, "This is serious, Mark."

"You didn't seem to think that . . . uh, passion was the issue when you asked me to investigate the matter."

"I still don't," said Mark, taking Katrinka's hand again and refusing to let go. "But I don't have a better explanation."

"All the publicity caused some problems within your company, I understand."

Mark thought the matter over for a moment, then said, "You mean someone who wanted to weaken my position with my board might have instigated the scandal?"

"It occurred to me as a possibility."

"Someone like Charles Wolf?" said Katrinka, getting the point immediately.

"It's possible, I suppose," said Mark. "But very farfetched."

"Someone certainly paid Sugar Benson for Miss Brand's services."

"But you don't know who."

"Unfortunately, not yet." One of the Zeiss "associates" had broken into Sugar's London office, had found whatever records were hidden there, and cross checked them with the files on the computer. That had turned up quite a lot of fascinating information—none of which Zeiss had any intention of revealing: he was not being paid to ruin Sugar Benson. "The person in question is listed only as 'Z' on the company books. We have not yet found a master client list, or a key code. But we did find quite a comprehensive address book and Charles Wolf's name does not appear in it."

"Why we don't just go to this Monica Brand and ask her what Sugar is up to?" asked Katrinka.

"That's a possibility," said Zeiss without enthusiasm.

"She wants money, we pay her."

"You don't think that will work?" asked Mark.

"I doubt that Miss Brand knows anything more than we do at this point," said Zeiss.

"You said there's an address book?" asked Mark. He did not bother to inquire how Zeiss had managed to get hold of it.

"Yes."

"If we could see it, we might recognize some of the names."

"I suspect you might recognize all the names," said Zeiss dryly. But showing them the book was out of the question as far as Zeiss was concerned: it violated his code of ethics, which required him to reveal to his clients only what they had paid him to discover.

"Goddamnit," said Mark, "if seeing that book—"

"I don't think you would be able to discover any more than I already have," said Zeiss, interrupting him.

"Then we are at a dead stop?" said Katrinka.

"No, not quite." He had wanted to see them, explained Zeiss, to find out if what he had so far discovered was enough or if they wished him to proceed.

Mark hesitated. Monica hadn't caused any trouble in months. Perhaps it was best to forget the whole thing, let sleeping whores lie, so to speak. But Katrinka wasn't willing to let the matter rest there. The idea of some secret enemy stalking her and her family was frightening.

The house phone rang. Katrinka answered it, listened for a moment, then said, "Thank you. We'll be right there. Would you please ask Anna to check on Miss Bovier and take a tray to her room, if she's hungry." Replacing the receiver, she stood. "Dinner is ready." As the two men got to their feet, she looked from one to the other. "I do want to know who this 'Mr. Z' is."

Zeiss looked at Mark, who nodded. "How long do you think it will take you to find out?"

"Not long, I think. We're very close."

"Funny little man," said Mark, when the detective had gone.

"But very good at his job."

They went together to say goodnight to Anuška, then Katrinka looked in on Natalie and found her still asleep, the tray of food untouched. Mark was already in bed when Katrinka returned to their room. She changed quickly into a silk teddy, washed her face, brushed her hair, and joined him. They were too exhausted even to think about making love, and lay for a while with their arms around each other, talking about Anuška, about Natalie, about the identity of Mr. Z, until they drifted off to sleep, again without Mark mentioning the two companies buying VHE stock.

"I don't know what to do," said Margo.

Katrinka was at her wit's end. She had to get Margo off the phone. "You do love him?"

444

"Of course I do."

"Then take him back."

"But . . ."

Now that his Gigi, tired of waiting for him to decide between his wife and his mistress, had fallen in love with someone else, Ted wanted Margo back. "But what about my pride?" wailed Margo.

"You would rather be jobless and alone in New York than in Monte Carlo together with Ted?"

"No." The answer was more of a whimper than a denial.

"All right then," said Katrinka impatiently.

"You really think I should take him back?"

"Yes. Now, Margo, I do have to go. We have a takeoff time in ninety minutes." When Katrinka had returned home from her meeting at the Ambassador, she had found Natalie in the nursery, playing on the floor with Anuška, Marisol watching them with an odd look on her face—surprise, pleasure, it was hard to tell. Katrinka had observed the scene for a moment and had made up her mind. When the baby had been put to bed for her nap, Katrinka invited Natalie into her study and had spent the next several hours trying to convince her to check into the Betty Ford Clinic. Finally, Natalie had agreed and Katrinka called the clinic, then Mark, who had (albeit grudgingly) offered her the VHE jet for the trip to Rancho Mirage.

"I think you're crazy," said Margo, forgetting her own problems for a minute.

"You think I don't know it. 'Bye. I will call you when I get back." She replaced the receiver and turned to Robin. "Let's go."

"I can't believe I'm doing this," muttered Robin.

"That does make two of us," said Katrinka, leading the way out of her study, heading for the stairs, Robin trailing her at a near run.

"He did what?" said Adam.

"You heard me," replied Charles Wolf, the fear obvious in his voice. The first thing that morning, VHE had filed a notice with the SEC that it planned to acquire a controlling interest in Charles Wolf's newspaper chain. That afternoon, it made a tender offer for the company, sending Wolf (as Mark had predicted) into shock. "What the hell am I supposed to do now?"

"Don't worry," said Adam, more than a little thrown himself. "You'll have control of VHE long before he can buy enough shares of your company for it to matter." He hadn't expected Mark to pull this crazy a ploy.

"But what if I don't?

How had he ever become involved with such a nervous Nellie? wondered Adam. "Just relax, and do what I tell you. One of your directors is also on the board of Chase Manhattan, right?"

"Yes."

"Well, Chase Manhattan is the trustee for the VHE employee stock option plan. Ask him to release the stock for sale. And when he does, buy it."

"He won't do that without van Hollen's consent, and he won't give it."

"For chrissake, Charles, be persuasive. Or you *will* lose your goddamn company."

"Yes, yes," said Wolf, sounding nervous. "And the money?"

"You'll have the money." It meant a little more juggling of funds, but the goal was so near now, it was worth the risk. "Keep me informed," said Adam.

"Yes, of course."

If he wimps out on me now, thought Adam, I'll ruin him. He replaced the receiver and stood staring blankly past the narrow blinds of his office window at the Racquet and Tennis Club across the street, thinking about the evening ahead of him without much joy. He was having dinner with Milena and the MCA executive, with a woman perched on the edge of hysteria and a fag record mogul. For the life of him, he couldn't imagine why he had become involved with Milena in the first place. Then he remembered: Katrinka.

He would go work out, he decided. That would relieve some of the tension he was feeling. But first he had to start transferring some money. As he turned to reach again for the phone, the intercom buzzed. It was Debbie. "Mr. Heller is here to see you," she said, not quite concealing her surprise.

"Christian Heller?"

"Yes."

"Tell him to come in."

Seeing no reason to be polite and go to greet his surprise guest, Adam sat and watched as Christian crossed the carpeted floor toward him. He was wearing a dark suit, Italian, probably Armani, thought Adam. His dark hair was carefully rumpled, a slight smile curved his full lips. His eyes were wary. But otherwise he looked cool, assured, certain of his welcome. He was a handsome bastard, admitted Adam, and an arrogant sonovabitch. "To what do I owe the pleasure?"

Christian sat in one of the leather armchairs facing Adam and said, "I stumbled on some information I wanted to share with you."

"What kind of information?"

446

"My stepfather asked me to try and find the ownership of two companies currently purchasing large quantities of VHE stock."

"I suppose this does have something to do with me."

"Oh, I think so. The companies are Galahad and Hydra."

Adam hadn't made a fortune by allowing his feelings to show on his face. "And?" he said calmly.

"I discovered that you control them." Christian was too certain of himself for Adam even to bother denying the fact. "And since the companies together own more than nine percent of VHE stock, you are seriously in violation of SEC rules."

"Am I?"

"And I suspect, though this I cannot prove—yet—that what you are doing is parking stock for Charles Wolf. Also illegal."

"You've told your stepfather this?"

Christian shook his head. "No."

"Why not?"

"Well, I thought you and I could use this information to our mutual advantage."

Adam laughed. "You really are something. You'd betray your mother, your stepfather, for what?"

"You will get Milena to say she was lying," said Christian calmly, ignoring the contempt in Adam's voice. That didn't matter to him. What did, was getting his name cleared, not because he was afraid of going to prison—there was no chance of that—but because he wanted Katrinka to believe him innocent. For that, Mark was well worth the sacrifice.

"That's it?"

"Not quite," said Christian. "Although my mother is an extremely generous woman, I find somehow I am always a little short of cash . . ."

Blackmail. Was it worth it? wondered Adam. But, really, he had no choice. He was too close to his goal to give up now. "And how will you keep Mark from finding out about Hydra and Galahad?"

"I think I can arrange for him not to discover the truth until it's too late to matter." Adam sat quietly for a moment, assessing the risk. "Is it a deal?" asked Christian finally.

Adam nodded. "It's a deal."

Neither man offered to shake hands.

447

Thirty-Five

 "WHAT IT COMES DOWN TO," SAID CHRISTIAN BITTER-
LY, "IS YOU BELIEVED MILENA AND NOT ME."
He was sprawled on the sofa in the town house library, staring
belligerently across at his mother, who was seated in an armchair
opposite him. They had not seen each other since before Katrinka had
left for Rancho Mirage with Natalie two days before. Christian had
been spending most of his waking hours in the VHE building on the
Avenue of the Americas, gathering information for Mark and his staff
to use fighting off Wolf's takeover attempt—at least that was what he
was supposed to be doing. In reality, he had been busily devising false
trails to conceal Adam Graham's involvement. And so far he had been
successful. But he didn't like the fact that Mark and the others were still
at work while he, for the first time in weeks, had left early in answer to
a summons from his mother. Milena's retraction had been printed in
all the major tabloids that morning.

Katrinka studied her son somberly, then shook her head and replied
quietly, in German, "Christian, you have to understand—"

But he cut her off. "Understand? Yes, I do. I understand that my own
mother thinks I'm a liar and . . . and worse."

"It was an impossible situation, having to choose between you and
Milena." Katrinka pointed to the stack of newspapers, lying on the
floor beside the sofa. "Who could believe she would make up
something so terrible?"

"But that I would do something so terrible, *that* you could believe?" The pain in Christian's voice was genuine. That Katrinka did not love him enough to believe completely in his innocence, that she did not trust him, hurt his feelings. It was irrational, even he knew that, given how little he deserved either to be loved or trusted; still, that was how he felt.

"It's finished now. At least for you." Immediately after seeing the papers, Katrinka had phoned Milena, to say what, she wasn't certain, but the girl still refused to speak to her. She would not recover from whatever had caused her strange, destructive behavior for a very long time. "Can't we just put it behind us? Forget it happened? Start over?" Christian remained slouched on the sofa, now staring at his outstretched feet, distant and sulky. When he didn't reply, Katrinka moved across to him. She touched his cheek with her hand. *"Miláčku, whatever happens, whatever you do, you're my son, and I love you."*

He lifted his head to look at her; his dark eyes were full of anger, pain, and something else—speculation, perhaps. "Enough to forgive me anything?"

Katrinka smiled. "You never make things easy for me."

"Would you?"

Katrinka didn't answer immediately. Finally, she said, "Love you, yes. Forgive you, yes. But let you get away with something I thought was wrong? No. I don't think I could do that."

"But you let Mark betray you with that woman, and you did nothing."

"He didn't betray me."

"You believed him," said Christian contemptuously. "That's worse. How could you be such a fool?"

There was no way to explain to Christian (or to herself, for that matter) why her trust in Mark was so instinctive and total, while her trust in her son was not. She said coldly, "I don't want to discuss Mark with you."

"Really? And do you also refuse to discuss me with him?"

"Now, you're being childish."

Christian stood up. "I really must get back to the office."

Katrinka reached out and took hold of his hand. "I'm sorry, *miláčku.* So sorry that I hurt you."

He took her hand, raised it to his lips, and kissed it. "I know."

"I do love you."

He wanted to say that he loved her too, but he couldn't. He wasn't completely sure it was true, which might not have stopped him, except that saying it seemed somehow like a defeat, and a surrender. Still holding her hand, he bent forward and kissed her cheek. "We'll do as you say. We'll forget this business with Milena ever happened."

"Yes," she said, hoping that it was possible. "That's best, I think."

Christian went upstairs to the nursery to see Anuška (his affection for his half sisters was the only uncomplicated emotion he seemed capable of feeling), then left, just missing a phone call from Pia, who had tracked him down, wanting to know what time he expected to be home. It was just as well. The call would have made him furious. He hated having to account for his actions.

"I'll talk to her," said Katrinka, when the butler told her who was on the line.

"And Mr. Graham called again."

"You told him I don't want to speak to him?"

"Yes. He said to tell you he only wants to know about Miss Bovier."

"Call his apartment, and leave word where she is. He can talk to her himself."

"Yes, madame," said the butler.

Katrinka picked up the other line. "Pia? How you doing?"

"Fine. Just fine, now that Milena's finally told the truth."

"Yes, we're all relieved."

"Christian's been so upset about it, though he tried not to let it show."

"You were good to stick by him, the way you did." Once the press got involved, Katrinka had half expected Pia to run back to Florence, to escape the onslaught.

Pia laughed. "Goodness had nothing to do with it. I love him."

"You're happy?"

"Yes. Happier than I've been in a long time. Everything's going so well. Between Christian and me, and every other way. There's going to be a piece in *Chic* next month, featuring my jewelry."

"That's wonderful." Katrinka had never heard the reserved Pia sound so exuberant.

"Now, if only Mother and I would stop fighting . . ."

"Well, I do believe that's normal," Katrinka teased.

"Yes, I suppose." Pia sighed, then continued, "She's stopped picking on me, but . . . well, I can't seem to leave her alone." Katrinka was someone she had known since childhood, someone she trusted enough to confide in—and there weren't many people like that in her life. "I can't stand that Patrick Kates. I really despise him. He's such a user." Trying to decide what to say, Katrinka was quiet for a moment, and Pia added anxiously, "Do you think I'm wrong?"

"No," said Katrinka finally. "But it's not necessary for you and me to like Patrick. If your mother loves him—"

Pia interrupted. "I know. I won't let anyone say a word against Christian. And look at the way you stood by Mark." She stopped suddenly, afraid that she had gone too far. "I mean . . ." Pia took a deep breath and continued, determined to make her point. "Well, sometimes you can go too far. Look at how my mother stuck by my father all those years, and she shouldn't have. I'm afraid she's doing the same thing with Patrick, refusing to see him for what he is, being loyal when she should dump him. Sometimes I think she's just afraid to be alone. And that's crazy. She's so beautiful, she can have her pick of men."

Katrinka did not point out that for middle-aged women, even beautiful ones, that "pick" was very limited. She said, "Even if you're right, there's nothing you can do about it. Nobody can talk us out of making our own mistakes."

"Yes, but—"

"Pia, what is the worst that could happen?"

"The worst? I don't know."

"Neither do I. But whatever it is, your mother can handle it. Trust her."

There was a brief silence and then Pia laughed. "That's what I keep saying to her. Trust me."

"It's very good advice." But the trouble with loving people, thought Katrinka, when she had said good-bye to Pia, was that you couldn't help wanting to do everything in your power to make sure that nothing would ever hurt them. It was an instinct very hard to resist.

"Mrs. van Hollen's butler called," said Carter as he placed the Perrier on the table at Adam's right hand.

Adam leaned back in his chair and frowned. "Her butler?"

"Yes. With a message from Mrs. van Hollen." Carter repeated the message and then said, "He left the clinic's number. Shall I try it for you?"

"No, thank you, Carter, not right now." Adam watched his butler's retreating form for a moment, then turned his attention to Milena, who was lying on the sofa, sipping a glass of white wine, reading *People* magazine, looking pale and miserable, a waif abused by the world. She had not wanted to make the retraction, and it had taken a great deal of bullying to get her to do it. Despite her lowered eyes, waves of reproach traveled toward him from across the room.

Finding that view depressing, Adam turned slightly so that he could

451

see out the window. It was raining, which suited him. There was something about rain (about water, really) that helped him to think clearly. Katrinka obviously had no intention of ever speaking to him again; he had caved in to her son, one way and another agreeing to pay the bastard an enormous amount of blackmail; and Charles Wolf, the gutless bag of wind, was on the verge of losing his nerve and pulling out of the VHE takeover. Could he force him to stay in? And if so, was it worth it? Was there another way to go?

Glass in hand, he turned over plans in his mind, losing track of time for a while, until, finally, the sound of Milena's sniffling penetrated the layers of preoccupation. It made him want to do nothing so much as strangle her. "What's wrong?" he snapped. He knew one of the things he had to figure out was a way to get rid of her fast.

"Nothing," she said, looking up from her magazine and fastening her unhappy eyes on him.

"Then why are you crying?"

"Nothing's wrong. I just . . . I'm not sure . . ."

"What?" he said sharply. It was unbelievable how much she had changed from the beautiful, the magical girl he had seen performing in the Starlight Club such a short time before.

"I went to the doctor today."

She went to the doctor every day, at one hundred and twenty-five dollars a session. As far as Adam could see, the psychiatrist was doing her no good at all. "And he said?"

"I'm going to have a baby."

He had not really been paying attention to her, so her words took a few seconds to register. And then he couldn't believe them. "What?"

"You know how sick I've been feeling, in the mornings?" Adam had not noticed the mornings particularly. Lately, it had seemed to him that Milena was ill at all hours of the day and night. Nevertheless, he nodded, and Milena explained that her psychiatrist, who had obviously been paying more attention—as he should at those prices—had recommended that she see a gynecologist. "I went today, and she said I'm pregnant."

"He's certain?"

"She," corrected Milena. "Absolutely certain." Her sniffling increased in intensity. "I wanted to tell you as soon as you got home, but you were so . . . you seemed so worried, I didn't want to bother you. I didn't know how you'd feel."

Feel? How did he feel?

"I didn't know what you'd want to do."

"What do you mean, *do*?" He sat in his chair, staring at her, knowing he ought to get up and go to her, comfort her somehow. But he was frozen in place, stunned, apparently incapable of thought, of emotion.

Milena tried to get control of herself. She knew what a sad, pathetic picture she was presenting, and she didn't like it any more than Adam did. But she could not seem to help herself. Until her arrival in New York, she had led a very sheltered life: she had been loved, protected, admired. She had adored her family, trusted her friends, sung for the pleasure of it. Her talent had not made her arrogant; she had had dreams but not ambitions. She had made no enemies. Nothing bad had ever happened to her. Her disposition had always been optimistic, cheerful. My little sunbeam, her grandmother had always called her. Now, Milena hardly recognized herself. She seemed to be carrying a great, heavy weight on her heart. When she wasn't crying, she wanted to. She wiped the tears from her eyes with a handkerchief and said, "I didn't know whether you'd be happy or not. Whether you'd want the baby."

Want the baby? Suddenly, without any conscious decision, Adam was out of his chair and beside Milena on the couch. "Of course I want the baby," he said, gathering her into his arms. All thought of packing her off to Czechoslovakia was forgotten. All thought of Christian and his possible involvement in this pregnancy was pushed firmly out of Adam's mind. "How could you even ask?" Hoping that Milena would become pregnant, he had all along insisted that she not use any protection. He never used any himself. Joy began to push through the shock, the disbelief, elbowing doubt out of the way. This was his baby. And no one was going to say otherwise. "We'll get married," he said. "We'll fly your parents here for the wedding. Your brothers, too. Would you like that?"

"Oh, yes," said Milena. "They were so upset when I didn't go home. Now, they'll understand why."

The wedding would be in Newport, Adam decided; as soon as possible. His mother would make his life a living hell if he got married again in Europe. Anyway, this time he was in the mood for a big celebration. He was going to be a Father!

Adam had planned to dine at home that evening, but the good news had changed his mind. He felt better than he had in weeks. So did Milena. The dying mouse look was gone from her face; she positively glowed with happiness. She changed into a black leather skirt and corset jacket; Adam told Carter to call ahead for a reservation, and, when the driver (who had been expecting the night off) returned with the car, they headed downtown along the East River Drive to Brooklyn Heights for dinner at the River Café. Afterward, they went back to midtown, to Tatou, to dance, something they had not done in weeks. Inevitably, they ran into people they knew, including Lucia di Campo and Patrick Kates. The music was deafening and it was impossible to carry on a prolonged conversation, but Lucia had known Adam long enough to read his moods. "You look very pleased with yourself," she said into his ear as they walked back from the dance floor.

"We're getting married," he told her, leading her into the bar, where it was a little quieter. Milena and Patrick were still dancing.

"You and Milena?" To say Lucia was shocked would have been to put it mildly. Not only had she been convinced that Adam was bored with Milena, she also could not imagine his marrying anyone who had created a world-class scandal by falsely accusing his former wife's son of rape. Nina Graham Luce was, after all, his mother. And Adam, when he wasn't deliberately trying to provoke her, did share her respect for the Graham name and the family's position in society.

"She's pregnant."

Well, that explained it. Lucia summoned a smile. "Congratulations."

"The wedding will be in Newport. As soon as Mother can get it organized. Right after the election, I suppose."

"She'll be ecstatic."

"Briefly," said Adam, with a laugh.

"There you are," said Patrick unnecessarily, as he led Milena toward them.

Adam faked a welcoming smile, then said, "We better get going," not wanting to spend any more time than necessary in Patrick's company.

"The party's set for the thirteenth," said Patrick, slipping an arm around Lucia's waist.

"What party?"

"The relaunch of my yacht. Assuming you'll have it ready in time."

"It will be ready," said Lucia reassuringly.

"The thirteenth? Isn't that a Friday?"

"Mark it down," said Patrick.

"Not a lucky day."

Patrick shrugged. "Who's superstitious? Not me. Sweet girl," he added, as he watched Milena and Adam make their way toward the door. "Hard to believe she could make up such a whopper of a lie."

"Yes," agreed Lucia. In fact, if Milena had not admitted it herself, Lucia never would have believed her capable of it.

"She must hate that little prick a lot." Patrick had no more affection for Christian than Lucia did. "I wonder what he did to her." Lucia shrugged. She couldn't imagine. Patrick nuzzled his face into her neck. "But then, we all have our dirty little secrets, don't we?"

"Do we?" said Lucia coldly, pulling away from him.

"Oh, not you, my little angel," said Patrick, his voice heavy with sarcasm. He raised his arm from her waist and slipped his hand inside the bodice of her sequined slip-dress to fondle her breast. "You're too good to be true. Beautiful, talented, loyal." She tried to move away but he gripped her more firmly and she felt her nipples rise. Part of her hated it when he treated her like this, fondling her in public, like a whore. Part of her was turned on by it. "Let's go home," he said.

She nodded and he released her. "I'll get my coat," she said.

There was a message from Sugar Benson, who was in London, awaiting Adam when he and Milena returned home. Instead of announcing it aloud, the trustworthy Carter discreetly handed him a note. It was marked urgent. But somewhere in the course of the evening, it had occurred to Adam that he and Milena had not made love in weeks. Remedying that situation had become a top priority for him. Returning the note to Carter, he told him he would take care of it in the morning, then he hurried Milena down the hall to the bedroom. Her laced leather top at first seemed daunting, but he found the zipper. Hurriedly, he stripped her of her skirt and panty hose. She wore no bra and only a thin strip of silk bikini.

"I thought you didn't love me anymore," she said, as she watched him remove his clothes.

"You were upset. I didn't want to bother you," he lied, stretching out beside her on the bed, half covering her body with his own. His lips moved from her mouth, to her throat, to her breasts. She could feel his wet tongue circling her nipples, his hand stroking her flat stomach. "Is this all right?" he asked finally. "I don't want to hurt you."

"Oh, you won't," she assured him, though she was far from certain. She no longer enjoyed sex. Her body, instead of yielding, tensed, and where there should have been pleasure, she felt either nothing or pain. "You won't. I love you. I love you so much."

At six the next morning, Carter entered the bedroom, wakened Adam quietly so as not to disturb Milena, and handed him a piece of paper with Sugar Benson's name scrawled boldly across it. Swearing softly under his breath, Adam got up, slipped into a robe, and padded down the corridor to his study. "What the hell is so important it can't wait for a reasonable hour?" he snarled into the receiver, too tired to be polite.

Sugar had spent most of the night on the phone with clients in all parts of the world; she was worried, tired, and she got immediately to the point. "Someone broke into the office in New York last night."

"So?"

"There was also a burglary in the London office a few nights ago. Whoever did it found the master client list, the list of employees, the key to the code we use keeping accounts. They even took some of the computer disks."

"Police?"

"I doubt it. Either here or in New York, they would have come in daylight, with a search warrant."

"Then who?"

"Someone looking for blackmail targets, I expect."

"They must have found plenty."

Sugar smiled wanly. Heads of state, government leaders, prominent businessmen, you name them, they were on the master list. When she had first learned of the break-in, her instinct had been to say nothing. Whoever had stolen the records knew what they were doing, had understood that the information from one office was useless without supplementary information from the other, which meant that the thefts were not coincidental. It also meant that the information would be used sooner or later. However, there would be no way to trace any revelations back to her. She could have denied all knowledge, all responsibility. But some sense of loyalty to the men (and women) who had helped make her rich, a feeling of good fellowship toward her companions in fun and games, had made her want to warn them about possible trouble ahead. "Adam, I swear I took every precaution. I really thought my system was foolproof. I can't tell you how sorry I am that this could end up causing you trouble."

Adam realized that Sugar had not had to make the call. He also realized, with all humility, that on the list of her clients he was comparatively small potatoes. Someone looking for prime candidates to blackmail would undoubtedly choose first the government officials, the ones with the most to lose, not someone like himself who might possibly not give a damn. In any case, what would cross-checking all Sugar's complicated lists eventually reveal: that he had paid for the services of a beautiful hooker named Monica Brand? Even his mother wouldn't give much of a damn about that. He could afford to be gracious. "I can take care of myself," he said, as always a little surprised by how much he actually liked Sugar. "I just hope this doesn't cause you too much trouble."

"That, honey, makes two of us. And thanks for being so understanding," she added before she hung up.

Two hours later, Paul Zeiss phoned Katrinka and Mark asking to see them as soon as possible, and half an hour after that he was seated across the breakfast table from them, his briefcase at his feet, sipping a cup of coffee laced with milk and sampling a croissant, which could in no way compare to those he usually enjoyed at home with his café crème. Again, he did not go into detail about his methods, though he was quite satisfied with how easily the last phase of this operation had reached its conclusion. "We have managed to locate the key code and the master client list," he said, managing to sound businesslike and not at all too pleased with himself. "Which is why I asked to see you."

"You've found out who the mysterious Mr. Z is?"

"Is it Charles Wolf?" asked Katrinka.

"No," said Zeiss. "Mr. Wolf's name does not appear on any list."

"Well, who is it?" asked Mark impatiently.

Casting a quick glance at Katrinka, Zeiss hesitated a moment. Then he said, "It seems to be Adam Graham."

"That's ridiculous," said Katrinka. "There must be some mistake. Why would Adam do such a thing?"

Zeiss shrugged. "The possibility of a mistake always exists. Yet, the lists do seem to be conclusive."

"May we see them?" asked Mark.

"I'm afraid not," said Zeiss. "There is more information on those lists than any of us ought to know. But I assure you, Adam Graham is the one responsible."

Zeiss's word might not stand up in a court of law, but neither Mark nor Katrinka had any doubt that he was right. They sat in stunned silence, trying to work out the implications of what they had just learned. Then, a terrible thought began to take form in Mark's mind. He turned to Katrinka and said, "Do the names Galahad or Hydra mean anything to you?"

For a moment she could not think what Mark was talking about. Why was he asking irrelevant questions when Zeiss had just exploded this bombshell about Adam. But the names did sound vaguely familiar. She thought a moment and then said, "Yes, I think I did hear Adam talk about them, a long time ago. I think they are companies of his, holding companies, registered abroad."

"That goddamn sonovabitch," said Mark. "He's been behind everything, from the beginning."

Thirty-Six

KNOWING TWO AND TWO MAKE FOUR AND PROVING IT ARE NOT THE SAME THING, MARK POINTED OUT TO Katrinka, whose immediate impulse was to phone Adam and confront him.

"But we do have to make him stop," said Katrinka.

Mark assured her that he had enough maneuvers at his disposal to protect his company for the next few weeks while they gathered the necessary evidence.

"Weeks!"

"Maybe less," said Mark soothingly, knowing that patience was not one of his wife's virtues. "But we have to be able to prove, first, that Adam controls Galahad and Hydra; and, second, that he entered into a secret agreement with Charles Wolf to acquire VHE illegally. It'll take time."

Paul Zeiss, as expected, came down on Mark's side, counseling caution, and Katrinka reluctantly agreed. Saving Mark's company was the issue, not venting her rage.

Zeiss left and Mark went up to the nursery to say good-bye to his daughter. On his way out, he stopped into the bedroom where Katrinka was changing from the jumpsuit she had worn at breakfast to a Ralph Lauren pin-striped coat dress suitable for the long day of meetings ahead. She still look worried. "Why Adam is doing this?" she

458

asked Mark as she handed him a strand of pearls to fasten around her neck.

"Why? Because he hates me."

She felt his lips brush her nape but didn't pause to enjoy it, spinning around to face him. "What you did ever do to him?"

Mark laughed. It wasn't a cheerful sound. "How did I piss him off? Easy. I didn't stay in the gutter where I belonged. And I not only climbed out, I got rich. I crashed his clubs, hung out with his buddies, got invited to the White House for dinner. I married his ex-wife. You want me to go on?"

"You think he's so jealous of you?"

"No. It's nothing as simple as jealousy. It's more like class warfare."

One of the first things Katrinka had discovered when she married Adam Graham was how much disdain the old money aristocracy had for those whose fortunes were newer (and often larger) than theirs, turning up their aristocratic noses at these "nouveaux riches," excluding them from parties, from clubs, from whatever they dared, though they never hesitated to accept contributions for the right charitable or political causes. It was not the money they despised, just the money-makers. With few exceptions, Katrinka had found the Grahams and their friends to be unwavering snobs. But she never would have believed them capable of trying to ruin someone just because they did not approve of his background. She never would have believed Adam capable of it.

"Most of them wouldn't have the guts to try," said Mark, his voice full of contempt. "But Adam's another story. He's got guts to spare, and enough ruthlessness to make Andrew Carnegie look like Mother Teresa."

On his way to the office, as he sat in the back of his car mulling over the revelations of the morning, another disturbing possibility occurred to Mark, one he was not prepared to share with Katrinka unless he absolutely had to. And when he had filled Carey Powers in on what had been discovered so far, and given his CFO a few minutes to relieve himself of every four-letter word in his vocabulary, Mark asked him if it was Christian who was trying to track down the Galahad and Hydra connections.

Carey nodded. "He's brilliant at seeing the kinds of connections the rest of us sometimes miss," he said, suddenly feeling—though he could not imagine why—that he had to defend his choice.

"Yeah, there's no arguing with that. He's one smart kid."

"You have a problem with him? I mean, a real problem. Not just some stepson/stepfather shit."

Mark smiled. "You think that's not bad enough?"

"You're the one who suggested we hire him. And I admit at first I had my doubts. But, frankly, now I think we were lucky to get him."

"Call it a gut feeling . . ." Carey frowned. Lately, Mark's gut feelings had turned out to be a little too accurate. "I don't want you to say anything to Christian," continued Mark. "Let him do what he's been doing. Just put someone else you trust to work tracking the same information."

"How am I supposed to keep that secret? You know all our computers interface."

"Try, okay?"

Carey had begun by admiring Christian and ended by considering him something of a protégé. He nodded reluctantly. "Whatever it is you're thinking, I think you're wrong. But I'll do it."

"Who're you going to use?"

Carey thought a minute. "My assistant. She hates Christian's guts."

Mark smiled. "Good choice."

Mark was not the only one plagued by unpleasant thoughts that morning. Katrinka had her share as well.

Shortly after she arrived at her office, Lucia di Campo stopped in unexpectedly. "What is it? What's the matter?" said Katrinka, getting up from her desk to greet her.

Lucia was wearing a long-skirted tweed Oscar de la Renta suit with a fitted jacket. Her petite figure was trim, her auburn hair perfectly colored and coiffed, her short nails expertly polished. She looked too well put together for disaster to have struck, but her face looked grim, and she never would have appeared at the Praha if something terrible had not happened. None of the friends ever just dropped in on one another at work.

"Is something wrong with Pia?"

"No. I'm sorry. Bursting in on you like this . . ."

"Don't be silly. Just sit down and tell me what's going on."

"It's Adam," said Lucia as she settled herself on the sofa.

Katrinka groaned. What she did not want to hear that morning was anything more about him.

Startled, Pia looked at Katrinka and said, "You've heard?"

There was a brief knock at the office door and, when it opened, Katrinka's secretary entered, carrying a tea service. When she had poured them each a cup and left, Katrinka said warily, "Heard what?" She was not prepared to discuss Adam's involvement with Sugar Benson and the VHE takeover.

"About Milena," said Lucia with equal caution.

"Milena?" What more could there possibly be to know about Milena and Adam? Then Katrinka relaxed a little. "Adam's left her," she said with conviction, feeling both relief and sympathy.

"No. In fact, they're getting married. Milena's pregnant."

"She's what?" It couldn't be. It was impossible. "You're certain?"

"Adam told me himself. Last night. They'll be married in Newport, right after the election."

She should have been pleased for Adam, thought Katrinka, knowing how much he wanted a child. She should have been relieved for Milena that Adam cared enough to marry her. But she was neither pleased nor relieved. Something about the news bothered her terribly.

The look of concern on her face deepening, Lucia said, "I just didn't want you to read about it in the papers."

Katrinka nodded. She searched for something to say, but could think of nothing.

"Are you all right?"

"A little shocked," said Katrinka finally. "That's all. Thank you for telling me."

"Better me than Sabrina, I figured."

Katrinka was even more grateful to Lucia when Nina Graham Luce called her to gloat. "Oh, you *know*," she said, sounding disappointed that her information had failed to shock. "I suppose Adam phoned you even before he did me."

"I haven't spoken to Adam for weeks, and I don't want to."

"Now, my dear, you mustn't take this to heart," said Nina, sounding for once in her life almost like a mother—before she ruined it all by adding, "It is just as I said from the start. The two of you simply were not compatible, genetically speaking. You mustn't blame yourself too much."

"I don't blame myself at all."

"Good, I'm delighted to hear it. All those years wasted, for you as well as my son, well, it's best not to think of them now." Katrinka didn't reply and Nina continued, "Now if that darling girl would just produce a son, my life would be perfect, absolutely perfect."

"I'm so happy for you," said Katrinka, unable for once to keep the sarcasm from her voice.

She finished her conversation with Nina with the same relief she always felt to be rid of the woman—at least until the next time. But the news about Milena and the baby continued to disturb her. Something about it worried her, and she could not put her finger on exactly what, though she recognized disbelief and shock as elements. After all, she had felt the same when she had discovered herself to be pregnant with Anuška after all those years of being unable to conceive. But there was something else, something her mind could not quite come to terms with. What it was eluded her and finally she decided to stop thinking about it and try to concentrate on work.

The news about Milena's pregnancy made Sabrina's column the next day, but since Rick Colins had reported it on his television show the preceding evening, the columnist did not give the expected happy event much play. Her own scoop came a few days later and it was a blockbuster, bigger than any story she had previously broken.

Among the people Sugar Benson had notified about the theft of the records from her office was the designer Alan Platt, who had been a steady client of the agency's for years, first in Europe, then in New York. The idea of someone he didn't know, a stranger, an enemy, running around with the sort of information contained in those records terrified Alan. He had spent years building his label, trying to gain recognition as a designer. And just when he was beginning to feel as if he had achieved his goal, he stood in danger of losing everything. His reputation wasn't securely enough established, or so he feared, to withstand a scandal. And what a scandal it would be if the story got out. It wasn't just that Alan Platt trafficked with hookers. If that were his total offense against public morals, he would not have been so worried. But he liked to play with men as well as women, and sometimes everybody all together. He was a true follower of Sugar Benson's creed of Benetton sex.

Noticing her lover's air of acute anxiety, Sabrina of course asked him what was wrong. Alan at first tried to placate her with tales of a creative crisis—plans for his next show were not going well, he claimed. But Sabrina had watched him preparing collections since long before they had become lovers and never had she seen him in such a state of near hysteria. She didn't believe him, and not one to stop asking questions because someone refused to answer, she kept at him until Alan caved in and told her more than she had ever hoped to know.

It was not just that he broke under the pressure of Sabrina's relentless interrogation, but Alan genuinely, if mistakenly, believed that he would wake up one morning to find his name bandied about the media and his reputation in tatters. (If it could happen to Woody Allen, how could he be safe?) He also believed that, since Sabrina had built his reputation, she could somehow save it. Alan wanted her help.

And Sabrina wanted the story of her life. She worked quickly through her pain, her outrage, her feelings of betrayal, to a clear view of what Alan's confession really meant for her. Like Senator Joe McCarthy hunting communists in 1954, Sabrina saw a way to achieve the gossip columnist's hall of fame in 1992 by hunting sinners. After all, "family values" was a hot issue in the presidential campaign—or at least some people thought it was. She asked Alan Platt to name names, and he did.

Some of the names were of people Alan knew for a fact to be clients of Sugar's because they'd been bedmates of his; others he assumed to be because he had seen them over the years at a wide variety of social events with Sugar's girls—and boys. Quite a few of the names were of people who had often done favors of one kind or another for Sabrina and toward whom she normally displayed some loyalty and restraint. But this was too big for those kind-hearted sentiments to apply. She was prepared to spare only those who were not well known enough to matter—minor executives who enjoyed illicit fun and games while away from the wife and kiddies, for example. CEOs of leading corporations were another and much better story, as were heads of state, government officials, media stars, socialites, and anyone with a title.

With so much good material, Sabrina felt it would be a waste to squander it all in one column. She did a four-part series, called "Sugar After Dark," in which she hinted that she had received copies of the stolen records (and claimed First Amendment rights when the vice squad came asking for a look); did a biographical sketch of Sugar covering her "rise up the ladder" from poor girl to porn star to socialite to madam; and slowly, in a world-class tease, revealed the names that Alan Platt had revealed to her. Television news shows featured the stories, which almost succeeded in pushing the three presidential candidates from center stage as one television star was dropped from a series and the head of a large automobile company took early retirement as a result. The foreign press picked up the story and ran it, which caused, among other things, the resignation of an English MP, the suicide of a Bavarian prince, and another crisis in the Japanese government. Alan Platt, as a reward, appeared anonymously as "a reliable source"; and Adam Graham, whose relationship with Sugar was not known, was not mentioned at all.

Unfortunately, his stepfather was. "Luce Likes the Ladies . . . and Gentlemen," ran the subhead of Sabrina's column on the last day of the series. The East Coast establishment rocked with the story, as if an earthquake had shuddered along a fault line from Kennebunkport, Maine, to Bal Harbour, Florida. According to Sabrina, when not

463

tenderly caring for his dying first wife or laboriously tending to matters of state, Russell Luce III, honorable member of the United States Senate, had been cavorting with Sugar's guys and gals. "A reliable source tells me," said Sabrina, "that Senator Luce's style has not been unduly cramped by his recent marriage to the former Nina Graham." If Sabrina was grateful for anything, it was this chance to get even with the grande dame whose contempt for her had been obvious at every encounter.

What resulted was Nina Graham Luce's idea of hell—her name and photograph splashed across the pages of the tabloids, every bit of dirt in the family history swept out from under the carpet for everyone to get a look at. She asked Russell once if the story was true; his denial did not convince her, and she packed her bags and left their Virginia home for the Graham mansion in Newport, where Edward, the butler, stood guard, not allowing access to the numberless journalists clamoring for a statement. Within forty-eight hours Nina had filed for divorce and Russell Luce had withdrawn from the Senate race.

There had been times, over the years, when Nina had been at her most scornful about Katrinka and Adam's ability to attract publicity, that Katrinka had wished for her mother-in-law to experience firsthand just how awful it was to live in the media's spotlight. But now that it had happened, Katrinka—to her surprise—felt something like compassion for the woman, and she phoned her to sympathize.

"It's so humiliating," confessed Nina.

"Don't read the papers," advised Katrinka. "Don't watch television."

"I wouldn't dream of touching one of those ghastly papers, or turning on the television. But I know what they're saying, and that's quite awful enough."

"Try not to think about it."

"How could he do this to me? How?" As unimaginable as it was, Nina seemed close to tears.

"Maybe you should go away for a while, until all the publicity does die," said Katrinka, offering Nina the use of the Villa Mahmed.

"That's very sweet of you, my dear. But I couldn't possibly leave now." She sniffed a little, as if trying to get control, then said, "Not with the wedding in just a few days."

"The wedding?" With Nina's world falling apart, Katrinka had thought the wedding would be postponed.

"Oh, yes. Adam doesn't want to wait, and I shouldn't imagine

Milena does. We've decided to move it up, in fact. It's going to be a very quiet affair, given the circumstances at the moment. Just the two families present." There was a brief pause and then Nina added thoughtfully, "I suppose one could say that includes you."

"I'm leaving for Prague," said Katrinka quickly. "My new hotel opens next week. But thank you for the thought."

"Well, to be perfectly honest, I had no intention of inviting you. Think how odd it would look."

"Very peculiar," agreed Katrinka.

"Come and see me when you get back."

There was a note of pleading in her voice that Katrinka could not resist. "I will," she promised. Nina suddenly seemed to her less like an old dragon than a sad old lady.

"No wonder Zeiss didn't want us to see that client list," said Mark. He lay stretched out on the bed, hands behind his head, watching Katrinka pack. It was something she always did herself, not trusting even Anna, who had been with her for years, to know exactly what she would need when traveling. "Who do you suppose gave it to Sabrina?"

"Not Zeiss," said Katrinka firmly.

"Nope, definitely not him." Mark considered the evidence for a moment. "Maybe somebody on Sugar's staff who needed money. Or someone on the list? Someone Sugar told it was stolen."

"But why?"

"For money? Sabrina would have paid for the information, and she would have paid plenty, if she had to. Whoever it was could have figured that, since the list was stolen, the information could never be traced to him—or her."

"Maybe. But this time we know it wasn't Adam."

"We do?" said Mark.

Katrinka nodded. "Your name and Monica Brand's would have been everywhere, if it was him. Your board would have tried to remove you and the stockholders would have yelled like crazy until your company was sold to Wolf."

Mark laughed. "Who said I didn't marry you for your brains?" He reached out, grabbed hold of her arm, and pulled her down on top of him. "I'm going to miss you."

"I wish you could come."

"So do I." But there was no way he could leave New York with Adam Graham and Charles Wolf still running loose. He kissed her. "In addition to everything else, I'd like to see the hotel."

"How close are you to proving Adam owns Hydra and Galahad?" Mark shrugged and Katrinka asked, "Well, what does Christian say?"

Mark hesitated a moment and then replied, "When someone goes to a lot of trouble to conceal ownership of a company, it takes a while to blow his cover."

"And Wolf still won't back down?"

Mark's counteroffer had scared Wolf, but not enough. The phone calls, the meetings, the bargaining had gone on day after day since then, but Wolf had still not conceded. "He's weakening. It's just a matter of time."

"Time," said Katrinka impatiently.

"Don't worry so much."

"I'm not worried. I'm mad."

Mark pulled her closer. "When this is over, I'm taking the company private again. I never want to have to live through another takeover attempt." His lips moved up her throat, along the line of her chin, to her ear.

She shivered slightly, then put all thoughts of packing out of her mind. Shifting her weight to her knees, she began to unbuckle his belt. "How I do miss you when I'm away."

"Miss me, or this?" he asked, stroking the wool of her skirt over her bottom and legs until he reached its hem.

"Both."

"Then don't stay away too long," he said.

The next day was Election Day. Katrinka, after spending some time in the nursery with Anuška, went with Mark to vote. Then Mark's driver dropped him off at his office and took Katrinka on to the airport, where the VHE jet was fueled and ready for takeoff. When she borrowed the corporate plane, as she did often, she reimbursed VHE for the cost, so that neither the stockholders nor the IRS had cause for complaint. One less grievance for Mark's board to consider.

Robin was already on board when Katrinka arrived, as were Michael Ferrante, the general manager of the Praha, and his wife. Margo and Ted Jensen, who were in the first tentative stages of a reconciliation, arrived soon after. Looking as awkward and embarrassed as a schoolboy who had been caught with his pants down, Ted kissed Katrinka hello and murmured that it was good to see her again. Margo, her hair teased to a frizzed halo around her pale face, alternated between seeming wary and blissful.

Most of Katrinka's friends had been invited to the opening of the hotel, but not all could attend. Tomáš was still filming. Zuzka, who had been in Czechoslovakia with Katrinka in September, preferred to stay in New York, where she had moved, to plan the business she wanted to start with the money from her settlement. Daisy had phoned from Florence to say that Riccardo, to his great annoyance, had the flu and was in a vile temper because he was too sick either to travel or to work. Neil Goodman was too involved with lawyers preparing a defense; and Alexandra, overlooking how upset her children were at the breakup of their parents' marriage, had decided to accompany her lover to Argentina for a few weeks, which was not as selfish as it sounded since her main objective was to provide them with a secure future.

The Ferrantes, who had never been to Czechoslovakia before, were thrilled to have been asked to the opening of the hotel, and all were looking forward to seeing it. So was Katrinka, who felt happy, excited, and only marginally apprehensive, not about the party, which she was sure would be a success, but about the hotel's economic prospects. The signs were good. Despite the imminent secession of Slovakia from the union, tourism was booming, not only thanks to the legendary beauty of Prague, but because it was far cheaper to vacation there than in Paris or Madrid, where prices were astronomically high. Certain that the name recognition of her hotels would give her a significant bite of the tourist pie in Prague, she hoped that would help boost the hotel chain's overall profitability, which was still sagging in spite of the deal with British Airways. But as optimistic as Katrinka felt, she was also realistic enough to know that she was at the mercy of largely unpredictable political and economic factors. Since the stunningly unexpected fall of the Berlin Wall and the collapse of communism, no one felt able to forecast the future with any confidence.

However, the hotel itself lived up to all Katrinka's expectations. The newly renovated baroque exterior was painted a pale green trimmed in white, with boxes of scarlet geraniums decorating windows at regular intervals. Inside, the rich baroque palette was continued, the main rooms done in creamy yellows, the suites and bedrooms in rose, sand, green, pumpkin, and ochre, all trimmed with beige and gold, decorated with reproduction antiques and Oriental carpets. Like all her hotels, the Ambassador was elegant and luxurious, without being in the least grand or stuffy. It was wonderful, declared her guests, who congratulated Carlos for pulling off another success.

"Rick is here," Carlos told Katrinka when he snatched five minutes alone with her in her office.

She nodded and said, "He would never miss one of our openings."

Rick had written articles about all their joint ventures and was doing a piece on the Prague Ambassador for *Architectural Digest*. "You do mind?"

"No," said Carlos. "I'm happy to see him." Rick had made it clear that he was offering friendship, and nothing more. And, still bruised from the end of his relationship with Alex Holden-White, Carlos was grateful for that and glad to have Rick nearby to make him laugh again.

"Where he is staying?"

"Here."

"Good," said Katrinka, glad that Carlos had not invited his former lover to stay at his apartment. They were two bruised souls who needed rescuing, but Katrinka was not sure either of them was emotionally stable enough at the moment to be of any real help to the other. "I hope we did give him a nice room."

"Are you kidding?" said Carlos, with mock outrage. "Every room is wonderful."

Even Jean-Claude and Thea Gillette, who were there as much to celebrate the opening of the specialty boutiques as the hotel itself, pronounced themselves pleased with the accommodations. At least Jean-Claude did. Thea was rarely pleased.

The Prague Ambassador's opening night party was as big a success as Katrinka had hoped. Officials from the national and city governments attended in force, along with foreign ambassadors, artists, writers, filmmakers, entertainers, leading figures from the business world, as well as friends. Everyone Katrinka knew and liked or needed who could crowd into the Ambassador's ballroom had been invited, and most had accepted. Although the wine was exclusively Château Gillette, typical Czech food was served and a band played traditional waltzes and polkas for dancing. For days afterward photographs of Katrinka in her strapless red Scaasi, flanked by Jean-Claude, by Carlos, by the mayor of Prague, by the president of the republic, appeared in newspapers and magazines around the world. Bookings began to climb steadily. The hotel was off and running.

The day after the opening, the Ferrantes took a commercial flight to New York and the Jensens returned to their home in Monte Carlo to put it up for sale, pack their belongings, and leave for good. The small tax haven was too full of unpleasant memories for them to continue living there, though they had no idea as yet where they would settle permanently. One suggestion was Liechtenstein, another Cap Ferrat. A third possibility was to bite the tax bullet and return to the United States, possibly to Miami, which was turning into quite an interesting cosmopolitan city. Only New York was off the list, as Margo had resigned herself to the likelihood that, at her age, nobody would hire her. Luckily, she didn't need a job.

Katrinka remained in Prague an extra day for a committee meeting to review the program, make necessary changes, and plan future seminars. Then, since Mark continued to assure her that he and Anuška were fine, she left with Robin for London, not only to take care of business concerning the hotel and casino, but, at Mark's request, to meet privately with the top VHE officials there and reassure them about the eventual failure of the takeover bid—without, however, being too specific about what Mark was planning. After her last appointment, a dinner at Le Caprice, she called Mark from the Chapel Street house and told him that, despite all her efforts, everyone was still nervous.

"As long as they don't panic and offer their stock to Wolf, that's okay."

"They won't do that. They all did say, if they decide to sell, they would give you first refusal."

"Good."

"How much longer is this going to take?"

"Not much," said Mark.

"A week? A month?"

"Not a month," said Mark, adding, "The papers here are full of stories about the wedding." It had taken place the day before.

"Here, nobody cares. There was only one little mention in Nigel Dempster's column."

"Adam's going to spend the early years of his marriage behind bars," said Mark, "if I get my way."

"It does have to go that far?" said Katrinka.

"Don't tell me you're starting to feel sorry for him?"

Was she? Perhaps. She had loved him once, after all. "I do feel sorry for Milena anyway," said Katrinka, not responding directly to Mark's question.

"She's better off without him," said Mark firmly. Then, his tone softening, he asked, "How soon can you get back here?"

"I do have meetings all day tomorrow. The day after—at the latest."

"Good. I miss you."

It was just after six in the morning when Mark finished his conversation with Katrinka. He changed into sweat clothes and went jogging in the park with Anuška's bodyguard, the dog trainer Kelly, and the six Alsatians—a group to make any potential mugger think twice. He returned home, showered, dressed, had a light breakfast, went up to the nursery to play with Anuška for a while, and then left for the office, where he found a message that Carey Powers wanted to see him as soon as he got in.

A few minutes later, Carey entered Mark's office, accompanied by his assistant, who was holding a file, which she offered to Mark. Inside were detailed the long, complex, devious histories of both Galahad and Hydra, which ultimately controlled both Adam's tanker and cruise ship lines and surprisingly listed Katrinka, not Adam, as owner, though Katrinka certainly had no knowledge of the fact. Adam had either forgotten to make the necessary changes after the divorce or had not thought it worth the trouble.

"Can we prove that it's Adam who gives the orders?" asked Mark.

"It will take a few more phone calls, but yes," said Carey.

Mark looked at the assistant. "You'll keep your mouth shut about this?"

"Oh, absolutely, sir," said the nervous young woman.

"Thank you. Now, if you wouldn't mind, I'd like a word with Carey."

"Of course." The woman stood, made a tentative gesture toward the folder, realized that Mark had no intention of relinquishing it, blushed slightly, and left.

"She did a good job."

Carey nodded in agreement and then said, "You think Christian knew this and kept quiet about it, don't you?"

"That's what I think," said Mark.

"I still can't believe it."

"That's because you don't know him as well as I do."

"What are you going to do about him?"

Mark shrugged. "Worry about him later. First, I have to take care of Adam Graham."

One option was to wait patiently while the SEC went to work, gathered evidence, and put an end not only to Wolf's attempted takeover of VHE, but of Charles Wolf himself and his partner-in-crime, Adam Graham. But Mark did not want to sit twiddling his thumbs while the wheels of justice ground on in their exceedingly slow way. Too much time had passed already. He wanted the takeover stopped immediately.

After an hour's discussion, Mark and his CFO decided that Carey would get on a plane to Chicago to have a talk with Charles Wolf while

Mark stayed in New York to deal with Adam. It was important to get to Adam first, since they did not want to give him any time to try to cover his tracks. Wolf, they knew, would cave in at the first hint of exposure.

Adam, however, was not available for meetings that day, his secretary informed Mark's secretary when she called: he was in Mustique with his bride, having a brief honeymoon, and was scheduled to return late that afternoon. Debbie refused to make an appointment without speaking to Adam first, especially since Mark's secretary would not tell her what the subject of the meeting was to be.

"He'll probably be at Kates's party tonight," said Mark, when Josh had told him the outcome of the phone call.

"Are you going?" asked Carey.

"I hadn't planned to, since Katrinka is away, but now I think I will."

The party was on board Patrick Kates's redesigned yacht, anchored offshore near his Greenwich home, which did not have a mooring deep enough to accommodate its draft. Guests were ferried to the boat by cigarettes and Patrick Kates, with Lucia at his side, stood under heat lamps on deck greeting them as they came aboard.

"I'm so glad you could come," said Lucia, when she saw Mark. "I thought with Katrinka away you might not."

"I couldn't resist seeing your latest work," he lied cheerfully. Mark had made certain to arrive early, so as not to miss Adam.

Lucia smiled. "I'm flattered you could tear yourself away from your daughter long enough."

"Yes, well, I admit it wasn't easy. I'm nuts about her."

"Come on," she said, taking a glass of champagne from the tray of a passing waiter and handing it to him. "I'll give you the guided tour myself."

"Where are you going?" asked Kates, as Lucia started to move away.

Without looking at him, she said, "Be right back."

The yacht could accommodate sixteen guests and seven crew. It had a helipad on top and a range of close to four thousand miles, Lucia pointed out proudly. Its hull was mahogany and its bridge mahogany and aluminum. That motif was repeated in the cabins with red leather used for both seating and furniture trim. Before, the interior design of the yacht had been rather fussy—mirrors and gilt (Patrick had bought it from a Lebanese arms dealer), but Lucia had stripped away all the clutter, leaving a subdued but luxurious feel throughout.

"It's beautiful," said Mark, and it was, though he preferred something a little cozier himself.

"It's a bit stark for most people, but Patrick likes it." She looked around critically. "Those aren't right," she said, pointing to some framed posters on the cabin wall. "We still haven't found exactly the paintings we want. Patrick was so anxious to have this party, there was no time."

"I don't know about paintings. I think maybe lithographs would fit the decor better."

Lucia mulled over the idea, then said, "What a good idea." She smiled. "You see, your visit wasn't a complete waste of time."

Mark returned the smile and said cheerfully, "I never thought it would be."

She studied him a moment, then said, "I like you, Mark."

Considering Lucia's taste in men, that was not necessarily flattering, but Mark took it in the spirit in which it was meant. "You had your doubts?"

"A few." The primary one had been named Monica Brand, but now, alone with him, without all the noise and distraction of crossed conversations, Mark seemed so completely decent and trustworthy to her, Lucia was suddenly sure that he hadn't been having an affair. "But they're all gone." And, as she returned with Mark to the deck, for the first time she began to think seriously about leaving Patrick Kates.

Most of the guests were people Mark didn't know—friends of Patrick, fellow sailors, people who had sponsored his races over the years, a handful of neighbors. Taking another glass of champagne, Mark put on his best social manner and mingled. After an hour, he had learned more than he really cared to know about Patrick Kates, but still there was no sign of Adam Graham. He spotted Liz Smith in the crowd and, since he genuinely liked the smart, friendly Texan, went over to say hello and ended by offering her a job. "I suppose that means you're planning to hold on to your newspaper," she said with just a hint of a drawl.

"That's exactly what I'm planning," he assured her.

"Well, if I'm ever unhappy where I am, you'll be the first to know."

Mark heard the sound of disco music and drifted toward the main saloon, where an area had been cleared for dancing. There were a few couples on the floor, among them Pia and Christian. For a moment, Mark stood watching them, his attention focused entirely on the girl. In another world as always when she danced, she seemed unaware of her own beauty and grace, and of the effect that her body, wrapped tightly in a studded jumpsuit that caught the light as she moved, was having on the men observing her—with one exception, Mark noted finally. Christian seemed less appreciative than annoyed by Pia's performance. Probably because, when she danced, Pia forgot he existed.

Finally, Christian had had enough and pulled Pia from the dance floor. They stopped for a moment to talk with Mark, who managed not to show either his dislike or his distrust of his stepson while he answered questions about Anuška, about Katrinka's return, even about the takeover. You have to admire his chutzpah, thought Mark, as Christian pumped for information. Only when he apologized for not having come up with any useful information about Galahad and Hydra, did Mark's control slip. "Don't lose any sleep over it," he said coldly. "I think I've got what I need to win."

Christian began to press him for the details, but Mark excused himself with as much politeness as he could manage and moved away, as Pia turned to Christian and asked what he had done to make Mark angry.

"Nothing," said Christian, his eyes fastened on Mark's retreating back, wondering why his stepfather had reacted to him so strangely. Lately, he had begun to think that he had actually gained Mark's respect. "I have been of great help to him through this whole business. He just dislikes me. I don't know why, except perhaps that he is jealous."

"Jealous? Of what?" Pia sounded doubtful.

"My relationship with my mother."

"Mark isn't like that."

"How would you know?" snapped Christian. "Some men are very possessive. They don't like sharing affection, or attention." He caught Pia's look and smiled. "Yes," he said, "like me."

As if to prove he had no purpose in being at the party except to admire the yacht and enjoy himself, Mark continued to drift through the crowd, stopping occasionally to chat until, finally, he saw Adam arrive, apparently alone. He began to make his way toward him in what he hoped was not too obvious a way.

Christian got there first. "Hello, Adam," he said, extending his hand.

Managing a brief smile as they shook hands, Adam said hello, then switched his attention to Pia. "You look sensational," he said, kissing her cheek, adding as he put an affectionate arm around her waist, "I still have a hard time believing you're all grown up. How's the business going?"

Adam had been a part of Pia's life for as long as she could remember.

473

She had liked him—loved him, really, until he had begun making false accusations about Christian. Moving away from him slightly, forcing his arm to drop, she said coolly, "Very well, thank you."

"Christian's forgiven me. Don't you think you can?"

Surprised, Pia looked at Christian, who nodded. "We're the best of friends, aren't we?"

"Without a doubt," said Adam dryly.

"Where is Milena tonight?"

"She wasn't feeling well and decided to stay home."

"Oh, yes." Christian's mouth curved in a smile that was not in the least friendly. "I heard that she was pregnant."

The thought of hitting Christian was very tempting, but Adam had not yet drunk enough to consider brawling in public. "Yes," he said curtly.

"Congratulations." There was an infuriating smugness in his voice.

Questions flooded through Pia's mind, which she decided not to ask now or later, partly for fear of annoying Christian, partly because she really didn't want to know what was going on between him and Adam. "Yes, and on your wedding, too," she said politely. "I hope you'll both be very happy." She linked her arm through Christian's. "Come on. We haven't seen much of the yacht." Looking at Adam, she added, "Mother says it's her best work yet."

"Close to it anyway. Run along and I'll see you both later."

Christian nodded his head and swiveled in his usual abortive bow, then let Pia lead him away.

As soon as they had gone, someone else claimed Adam's attention. Mark took another glass of champagne, exchanged a few words with another of the guests, and waited his chance. Finally, he saw it, that brief pause between one conversation's end and another's beginning. He stepped in front of Adam, blocking his path. "Good evening," he said.

"Is it?" Adam looked around and asked, "Where's Katrinka?"

"In London. Until tomorrow."

"And Milena's home, not feeling well. So, here we are, two temporary bachelors."

"I'd like to talk to you. Privately."

"My secretary said you'd called for an appointment. Can't it wait?"

"No."

"It's that urgent."

"I think so."

Adam shrugged, then said, "The master cabin is as good a place as any, I suppose. It's comfortable and the door locks." He grabbed a bottle of champagne from a waiter and led the way. As they passed Lucia, who cast a worried look in their direction, Adam stopped to kiss her bare shoulder. "Don't look so scared. We're not about to do each other in."

"At least not tonight," said Mark grimly.

"That's reassuring," said Lucia dryly. "If you're not back in ten minutes, I'm coming to get you."

"Make it twenty," said Mark.

The master cabin was, as Adam had said, large. It had built-in wall-to-wall, floor-to-ceiling mahogany cabinets with inset mirrors, a king-sized bed trimmed in red leather, and two red leather armchairs. Adam locked the door behind them, took a seat in one of the chairs, poured himself a glass of champagne, put the bottle on the table next to him, crossed his legs, and said, "Well?"

Mark sat opposite him and said, "Do the names Galahad and Hydra sound familiar to you?"

Adam started in surprise, but didn't even try to bluff. He was too angry. "That double-crossing sonovabitch," he said.

"It wasn't Christian who told me," said Mark, any hope that he had been wrong about his stepson completely shattered.

"Then who?"

"What does it matter? I know. That's the point. About Galahad and Hydra. About your deal with Charles Wolf." He hesitated a moment and then smiled. He had the upper hand finally and he was enjoying it. "About Sugar Benson and Monica Brand. About everything you've been up to these past eleven months."

"Jesus Christ!" muttered Adam, not quite believing what was happening. "How? Oh my God, you're the one who stole Sugar's records."

Mark shrugged. "The question it seems to me is not how I know, but what I am going to do with my vast store of knowledge."

"Yes," said Adam. He felt trapped in a bad dream. "What are you going to do?"

"Hang you out to dry."

"You don't have any proof," said Adam, trying to regain enough calm to negotiate his way out of the mess.

"I have enough. And what I don't have, I'm certain the SEC will be able to find."

Adam jumped up quickly, knocking the chair over. Looking ready to kill, he covered the few feet between himself and Mark.

"That's right, hit me," Mark said easily. "Give me the excuse I want to take you apart."

The cool words stopped Adam, making him think, giving him time to remember that Mark hadn't been raised to fight politely, observing the Marquess of Queensberry's rules. "And what if I take you apart?" he asked.

"If you could, it wouldn't save your ass. I'm not the only one who knows."

"Does Katrinka?"

"Yes. And others."

Adam returned to the table, poured himself another glass of champagne, and took a sip. Then he said, "Look, there's got to be a way we can settle this, without bringing the SEC into it."

Mark stood up. "I can't think of one." He walked to the door, unlocked it, then turned and said, "I gave you too much credit, Adam. I never took you for a fool."

Mark left, and Adam sat watching the closed door, thinking back over the past months, trying to figure out where he had made his mistake. What had led Mark van Hollen to Hydra and Galahad and eventually to him? Luck, he decided finally, which was not altogether wrong. That Mark's intelligence might be a match for his own did not bear thinking about.

Finishing the bottle of champagne, Adam considered going upstairs for another. Usually, he didn't drink much, but tonight he felt the need. He got up, headed for the door, then spotted the cabinet which, he remembered from studying Lucia's designs, was the bar. Eureka, he thought, as he opened it and found a full supply of liquor. He poured a shot of scotch into his champagne glass, then took the bottle back with him to the bed where he sat, leaning against the leather headboard, the bottle on the night table within easy reach, trying to think of something to do to save his ass. Nothing came immediately to mind and he poured himself another drink.

On deck, the party gradually wound down, the guests heading in groups back to shore in the cigarettes, until only Patrick Kates and Lucia remained. "Check all the cabins. Make sure everyone's safely off, then lock up," said Patrick to the chief steward. "Don't leave any strays behind."

"Yes, sir."

"We'll take her out in the morning. About eight," continued Patrick as he followed Lucia down the gangplank to the waiting cigarette.

"Make that nine," said Lucia. She turned to Patrick and added, smiling, "I need my beauty sleep."

"Do you think it will help?"

"Bastard," she muttered.

"Bitch," he returned softly.

Lovely couple, thought the steward as he turned away to supervise the cleaning up. An hour later, it was impossible to tell that a party had ever occurred on board. The crew began to leave, as the steward began a final check of the cabins to see that no one was left behind.

Oh shit, he thought as he recognized Adam, who was passed out on the bed in the master cabin. He tried to wake him and failed. The prospect of carrying him to the deck, loading him into a cigarette, then figuring out how to get him ashore, and home, was not a happy one. Leaving him to sleep it off seemed much more sensible. It meant getting back by eight at the latest to get him away before Mr. Kates turned up for his morning cruise, but it was worth it not to have to deal with the situation then. His decision made, the steward removed Adam's shoes, maneuvered the blankets out from under his inert form, covered him, adjusted the pillow under his head, turned out the light, and left.

Two hours later, Adam woke up. His head aching, his thoughts confused, it took him a while to remember where he was. Gradually, it all came back to him. Getting up, he went into the bathroom, splashed cold water on his face, then put on his shoes and went prowling through the boat, searching for the crew. The yacht was deserted. Obviously, he'd been left behind. Returning to the master cabin, he took off his rumpled jacket and lay down again on the bed, trying to decide what to do. Waiting until someone came back in the morning seemed the most sensible plan. He picked up the phone, called his apartment, told Carter what had happened, and refused to speak to Milena.

"She is very upset, sir," said Carter. "Frantic, one might say."

"You explain. Tell her I'll see her in the morning." Adam replaced the receiver, removed his shoes, and tried to think of some way to stop Mark van Hollen from ruining his life. Eventually, he thought of one: Katrinka. She would help him. She would stop Mark from going to the SEC. For old times' sake, if nothing else. Getting up again, he rummaged in his jacket pocket, found the electronic notebook he always carried with him, and looked up her London phone number. It seemed to take forever for the call to go through and when it did, it was Robin who answered, not Katrinka. "I want to talk to her," he said.

"It must be the middle of the night there," said Robin.

"Put her on the goddamn phone," said Adam.

"I'll see if she's in," said Robin in her most efficient voice.

A moment later, Katrinka spoke into the phone, her voice angry. "What you want now? Why you are bothering me? Why you can't leave us alone?"

But before Adam could reply, an enormous explosion ripped through the boat. It picked him up and hurled him against the wall, which caved in, burying him beneath the shattered lengths of beautifully finished mahogany.

"Adam," called Katrinka. "Adam, where are you? What has happened? Answer me. Adam?"

The Present

Fall, 1992

Thirty-Seven

 "FEELING BETTER?" THAT WAS ALEXANDRA'S VOICE. "YES," SAID KATRINKA. "MUCH BETTER."

"Maybe a cup of tea?" That was Robin, sounding worried.

"Oh, yes, of course." A man's voice—one Katrinka did not recognize.

"No, thank you. I'm all right." She opened her eyes, started to rise, then sank back into the chair, and closed them again.

"Just stay quiet for a few more minutes." That was Lucia.

"Here, drink this."

Robin pressed a paper cup into Katrinka's hands. Opening her eyes, she took a sip, saw the strange man hovering solicitously nearby, forced a reassuring smile, and said, "I never faint." She looked around at the small, comfortably furnished room and realized that they were in a private parlor of the Campbell Funeral Chapel. The man was the funeral director.

"It was the shock," said Lucia.

"I fainted myself when I heard the news," said Alexandra. She had returned from Argentina for the funeral.

Lucia began to weep, then turned away to hide it, so as not to upset the others more than they already were. Katrinka again started to rise and this time Robin put a steadying hand under her elbow. "I'm all right now," said Katrinka, taking a step forward to prove it. "We should go inside." Her voice was full of dread.

481

"Oh, God, I don't think I can bear it," wept Lucia, as Alexandra slipped a comforting arm around her waist.

Former lovers of Adam's, always his good friends, what would Lucia and Alexandra think, wondered Katrinka, if she were to tell them the terrible things he had done to her, and to Mark? Forgive him, probably, as she had done, now that he was dead.

The funeral director stepped to the door and opened it, then let the four women precede him through it, into the parlor where what remained of Adam Graham's shattered body lay in a closed flower-draped coffin as friends and relatives paid their final respects. The rows of fiddleback chairs were mostly empty, the crowds having come the preceding night. A heavy, sweet smell permeated the air.

Nina Graham stood not far from the bier, her lovely face drawn with pain, but otherwise controlled and regal, her hand on her new daughter-in-law's arm, as if trying to infuse some of her own strength into the frail girl, who looked ready to collapse under the weight of her grief. Katrinka went immediately to them, to offer her condolences.

"Are you feeling better?" asked Nina, who sounded less concerned than disapproving of Katrinka's unseemly display of emotion. Real women didn't faint.

"Yes," said Katrinka.

"Too bad your husband couldn't be here with you." It was clear that Nina felt Mark's absence was in very poor taste.

Katrinka and Mark had quarreled about his attending the funeral. Mark had said he was not hypocrite enough to pretend he was sorry to see the last of Adam Graham, not even for Katrinka, who wanted him there for support. "You'll have plenty of friends around," said Mark. "You won't need me." And instead he had taken off for Europe, to re-exert control over his companies there now that Charles Wolf had withdrawn his tender offer. Katrinka understood his position, but understanding didn't seem to lessen the anger she felt at him for not being with her when she needed him.

But none of that anger showed as Katrinka responded to Nina. "Unfortunately, he had to leave for Europe." She smiled grimly. "I do think Adam would understand," she said, and turned to Milena, adding in Czech, "*Zlatíčko*, I'm so sorry. If I can help you, in any way . . ."

Before she could finish, the weeping girl threw her arms around Katrinka and sobbed. "I don't believe it. It's so terrible. How can I believe it? What am I to do?"

Nina frowned, but said gently, "Milena, my dear, do try to get a grip on yourself."

Milena's family, who had remained in New York for a brief holiday after the wedding, had still not returned to Czechoslovakia and were seated in a corner, out of the way. But, seeing her daughter break down again, Olinka got to her feet, cut through the room full of strangers, acknowledged Katrinka with a brief nod, then put an arm around Milena. "*Andelíčku*, come, sit down," she murmured in Czech. "*Mami* is here. *Mami* will take care of you."

As Olinka tried to lead her away, Milena looked questioningly at Nina, as if seeking her approval. But before Nina could speak, Katrinka said gently, "It's all right. Go with your mother."

Nina's frowned deepened but she nodded, then watched as Olinka led Milena toward the family group in the corner. "She wants to go home, to Czechoslovakia," said Nina.

"Maybe it's best, for a little while."

Nina shook her head and said, her voice firm, "I intend to have my grandchild born here, in the United States, like all Grahams, from the seventeenth century on." Neither the scandal surrounding her coming divorce nor the death of her son had managed to break her spirit.

Others hovered, waiting for a word with Nina, and Katrinka moved on, stopping to speak with Adam's sister, Clementine, her husband, and their two sons, all of whom treated her presence at his funeral with the same dismay as they had her marriage to Adam. How would poor Milena cope with them, wondered Katrinka, as she went to join her cousins, the last of whose anger with her had vanished with their daughter's wedding.

Katrinka sat beside Aunt Zdeňka for a while, holding the bewildered old woman's hand, surveying the room for familiar faces. Neil Goodman was there, with his first wife. Since leaving Alexandra, he had been staying with her, in their old home in Scarsdale, and the pleasant, matronly woman seemed delighted to have him back.

Alexandra had gone to sit with Daisy and Riccardo, who had arrived from Florence the day before. Both looked worn out and grief-stricken. Seeming almost as upset, his face pale with disbelief, was Patrick Kates, who sat beside Lucia, silent, separate, as if walled up in his personal grief. No one had imagined that he felt so deeply about Adam, and some cynics hazarded the guess that it was actually the destruction of his prized yacht he was mourning.

To his producer's horror, Tomáš had suspended shooting for a day and he and Lori had taken the red-eye in from the West Coast to attend the funeral. They would return as soon as the service was over.

Zuzka was there, Martin beside her, both looking shocked and saddened. All the Havlíčeks, even Tomáš who had come to blows with him often, had remained devoted to Adam, grateful for all the help he had given them over the years.

He could be a very good friend, Katrinka reminded herself.

Only the Jensens were missing; and Natalie, to whom Katrinka had spoken the day before to urge her not to come. Her emotional state was still too precarious for her to leave the clinic.

From the chapel, the funeral cortege lumbered to St. James Church. Christian and Pia, who had not put in an appearance at the funeral home, joined Katrinka in her pew for the service. Pia's face, as usual, was impassive, but her eyes were full of shock and sorrow. When she was little, she had adored Adam. Her head, since she had heard about the explosion, had been full of images of him, of the times he had taken her sailing in a sunfish off the *Lady Katrinka,* of the year he had taught her to swim in the pool at the Villa Mahmed. Christian's expression was harder to read; but, when Nina, in one of those quick reversals of attitude that had infuriated her over the years, asked Katrinka, as a favor, to go with the family to Newport for the burial, he insisted on accompanying her.

Afterward, Katrinka wondered if things might have turned out differently had she refused his offer.

The funeral cortege consisted of eight cars, including Katrinka's gray Mercedes. The farther north they traveled, the more beautiful the afternoon became—cold, clear, the sun shining, the sky a brilliant blue above the bare branches of the trees. Most of the passengers in the cars did not notice; most of those who did were afflicted with a momentary guilt for being alive to enjoy the scenery when Adam was not; a few felt an intense rush of pleasure for exactly the same reason.

Katrinka and Christian sat, for the most part, silent in the back of the Mercedes, Katrinka lost in memories, Christian studying his mother, trying to understand what was going on in her mind, wondering why she should be so upset about the death of the man who had made her so miserable. Her willingness to forgive the men who hurt her was something he could not understand. Unless he happened to be its object, Christian did not see forgiveness as a virtue.

Dusk was closing in as the cortege reached the cemetery, the light fading, dulling the colors, except for the blue of the sky, which seemed to deepen. As the pallbearers removed the massive mahogany coffin from the hearse, the family climbed out of their cars, assembling awkwardly, then following in procession to the crypt. Adam was to be buried in the Graham vault, with his father and grandfather, and all the generations of Grahams who had gone before him.

The bearers placed the coffin on a draped trolley, and an Episcopal bishop—a second cousin, Katrinka remembered—spoke a few words of eulogy and murmured a prayer, punctuated by the sound of Milena's weeping. At the end of the brief service, the bearers carried the coffin inside, slipped it into the space prepared for it, then came out, closing the vault's giant doors. Milena's cries grew louder and again Olinka pushed through the line of people separating her from her daughter and put her arms around the girl, whispering words of comfort in Czech, as Nina stood her ground, not prepared to relinquish the mother of her grandchild to anyone.

Gradually, everyone made their way back through the growing dark to the cars. Nina, as she was about to enter hers, caught sight of Katrinka and motioned to her. "You'll come back to the house?" she asked when Katrinka, followed by Christian, drew near. It was less a request than an order. A funeral supper was waiting at home and Nina wanted to make sure that her former daughter-in-law, whom she now instinctively regarded as a sort of emotional security guard, as a second line of defense against weakness and grief, would not try to slip away without joining the family in this final burial rite.

But in the split second while Katrinka was choosing between making an excuse or doing as Nina asked, Milena screamed. At first, everyone thought it was just another, louder phase of her endless weeping. But she pulled away from her bewildered parents, who had been leading her toward the limousine, pushed past Nina and Katrinka, and flung herself at Christian, slapping his face, punching his chest. "Go away," she screamed, "Go away. You have no right to be here. Go away." Oblivious to everything but her own pain, she had not noticed him in the church or by the crypt. It was only when he had stood next to Nina that she had finally seen him.

Christian grabbed her hands to stop her hitting him, and she began to kick. Katrinka tried to pull her away, but Milena, in her fury, was too strong. She was shouting obscenities in Czech, words her father had never heard her use before. František grabbed her by the shoulders, swung her around, and slapped her face. Sobbing, Milena collapsed against him. "Tatí, Tatí . . ."

"Sssh," murmured František, "it's all right. I'm here." His eyes came to rest for a moment on Christian, and he said, "I apologize for my daughter." Then, looking at Nina and Katrinka, he continued in Czech, "She's hysterical, poor little thing. She doesn't know what she's doing."

But Katrinka was very afraid that her cousin was wrong. She looked briefly at her son, who stood with ashen face and blank eyes, staring at the girl crying in her father's arms, then she turned to Nina and said, "I'm sorry, I must get back to New York."

"Don't be foolish," snapped Nina. "The girl is hysterical."

"Yes," agreed Katrinka, adding firmly, "I will come back to see you in a day or so."

Nina was about to lodge another protest, but then thought better of it. She bowed her head graciously and said, "Please, do," then allowed her chauffeur to help her into her car. Milena, in another breach of protocol, accompanied her parents into theirs. Katrinka, ignoring the whispers of Clementine and the assorted cousins, turned away and headed for her own car, where Luther, seeing her approach, opened the door for her. As she settled herself in the far corner, Christian climbed in and sat, his eyes still blank, his face composed, waiting.

It was not until they had left the cemetery that Katrinka turned to him and said quietly, in German, "Tell me."

"You expect me to explain the actions of an hysterical girl?" replied Christian, his voice ice cold.

"Tell me," she said sharply. She could see Luther start to turn his head, surprised by her tone, then look straight ahead again, pretending he had heard nothing. "And don't lie," she added, grateful that her driver did not understand German. There was no way she could have remained quiet until Christian and she were alone.

Christian shrugged, but said nothing.

"You did rape her, didn't you? She was telling the truth all along."

"Just because a grieving widow starts screaming—"

"Yes," said Katrinka. "Just because. She wasn't thinking about you today; she wasn't plotting; she had no energy left to lie, to pretend. She hates you, and you must have given her a good reason for that."

"It wasn't rape," said Christian quietly. He wasn't quite sure why he was admitting even that much, except perhaps that it was the only way left to get Katrinka to believe him.

"Then what was it?"

"It was the way I told you. We started to argue, about Adam. I was trying to calm her down, and one thing led to another."

"Did she ask you to stop?" Again Christian shrugged. "Did she tell you to go?"

"Maybe, I don't remember."

Katrinka heard a moan and then realized she was making the sound. The pain was excruciating, different from anything she had ever felt before—a mixture of love, shame, loathing, and anger. "How could you do it?"

"I was angry. I lost control."

"Lost control!" snapped Katrinka. "What are you, an animal?"

"Don't talk to me like that," said Christian, his voice full of fury. "What do you know about me? What I'm like. How I feel? How could you possibly know?"

"I know Milena is a young girl, inexperienced and naive, and that you hurt her. I know that she was my responsibility. I know that I trusted you. What a fool I was!"

Luther, not liking the angry sound of raised voices in the back, slowed the car slightly, preparing to stop, to go to Katrinka's aid, if she needed him.

But Christian's voice when he replied was quiet again. "Yes," he agreed. Furious, Katrinka raised her hand to slap him, but he grabbed her wrist. "Don't," he said. "I've had enough of that for one day." Her arm went limp, and Christian released her. "In any case, I no longer allow any of my parents to hit me." His voice was full of the sarcasm she hated. "I haven't since I was six, when I warned them I would tell everyone they molested me, unless they left me alone."

Katrinka's eyes widened in horror. "Did they?"

Christian smiled at her and said, "Yes. Well, my father, the esteemed ambassador, did." It was impossible to judge whether or not he was telling the truth. "That's why my mother made him send me away to school." He looked at her, his face no longer blank, but expectant, curious. "Do you believe me?"

Katrinka folded her hands in her lap and noticed they were trembling. "I don't know," she admitted. Her son liked to shock; he liked to appear interesting; he liked to create effects. But would he go this far?

"I know it's difficult. Such things are always hard to believe."

Katrinka's head was beginning to ache. She closed her eyes. Then she opened them again. "Why did Milena retract her story?"

"Still harping on that?"

"Why?"

"I don't know," he lied. "I suppose Adam decided the publicity was bad for her. And with a baby on the way . . ." He shrugged, as if that explained it all.

And Katrinka finally understood what it was that had been bothering her since discovering that Milena was pregnant. She had never really believed the child was Adam's. Never. "The baby is yours," she said.

Christian smiled faintly. "It's possible."

"Oh, my God." She closed her eyes again. Her head was reeling with everything she had heard. Conflicting emotions tore at her insides:

anger at Christian; rage at the Hellers; revulsion for all of them for the pain they had caused; sympathy for Milena, the innocent victim; pity for her son, who needed it whether he was lying or telling the truth. Her body ached, as if she had been beaten. "You will apologize to Milena," she said finally.

"I already have. The next day. You see how she has forgiven me."

"You will again. We both will. It's not enough, but I don't know what else to do."

Katrinka told no one, not even Mark when he phoned, about her conversation with Christian. She needed to be sure of what she wanted to do, sure of what her feelings were before she confided them to anyone else, even to her husband. And she knew the relationship between Mark and her son was not an easy one. She was reluctant to make it worse, if she didn't have to.

Christian was not so careful. When Pia, in one of her endless attempts to get past his guard, to feel close to him, to try to understand his shifting moods, his sudden melancholy, his unhappiness, pressed him hard about what was bothering him, he told her. At first she didn't believe him. It was still inconceivable to her that he could be guilty of anything as terrible as rape, or that he would lie so outrageously to escape punishment. Only when, furious at her constant questions, he lost complete control and turned on her, did she realize how violent he could be. Before he hurt her, she ran, leaving the apartment with nothing, not even a purse. Luckily, her mother was home and paid the taxi driver. Pia told her that Christian and she had quarreled, about what she wouldn't say, that he had frightened her and she'd left him. Not giving her a chance to change her mind, Lucia booked them both on a flight to Florence, then returned to Christian's to pack her daughter's things. He sat soberly in an armchair watching her. Neither said a word. And the next day, just before they left for the airport, Lucia called Katrinka to tell her that she and Pia were going. Although she knew she ought to, she did not say why. She could not quite muster the courage to tell her friend that she thought her son was sick.

"Let me talk to Pia," said Katrinka. Reluctantly, Lucia agreed, and after listening to Pia's evasions for a few minutes, Katrinka asked, "Did he hurt you?"

"No," said Pia, her voice unsteady. "But he wanted to."

Still, Katrinka felt relief. Christian hadn't hurt her. He didn't always lose control.

Lucia took the phone away from her daughter and said, "I don't know how long we'll be away." Immediately after Adam's funeral,

Lucia had ended her relationship with Patrick. It had not been as difficult as she had expected: there was nothing like a brush with death to convince a person to stop wasting time. And Patrick was so dazed by what had happened that he did not even pretend to care.

"Just stay in touch," said Katrinka.

"I will," promised Lucia.

Katrinka hung up and phoned Christian, at VHE, where he still reported dutifully to work every day, though he noticed Carey Powers's attitude toward him had shifted from open admiration to distrust. Had something gone wrong? wondered Christian. Surely, if they suspected his involvement with Adam, Mark would have mentioned it by now?

"We are going to Newport tomorrow, to see Milena," Katrinka told him.

"I don't think I can get away."

"Do you want me to call Carey?"

He could hear there was no point arguing. "I'll speak to him."

"Pia's leaving today for Florence." Katrinka's voice was cold, angry.

"I didn't touch her."

"So she said."

The next day, Katrinka drove with Christian to Newport. Her cousins were still there, though the boys were anxious to go, and Nina to be rid of them all, even going so far as to ask Katrinka, during a brief moment alone, to convince them to leave, which she agreed to do if Nina would stop pressuring Milena and let her return home with her parents, at least for a while. Reluctantly, Nina gave her consent. The cousins were delighted; and, taking advantage of the improvement in mood, Katrinka asked to see Milena, who had kept to her room during the entire visit.

At first Milena refused, but when František insisted that she owed her cousin the courtesy of a good-bye, she reluctantly said yes. And though, when Christian followed Katrinka into her suite of rooms, Milena looked frightened, and opened her mouth as if to scream again, she did not. She was more firmly in control of her emotions than she had been for some time.

Katrinka closed the door behind them and said, "We have both come to say how sorry we are. Christian for what he did. Me, for not believing you." She turned to Christian and waited.

"I'm sorry," he said. "I hope by now you can believe that. I regret what I did very much. If I could undo it, I would."

Milena's hands instinctively closed over her stomach, which was no more yet than a slight mound. "Have you told anyone?" she asked.

Katrinka hesitated a moment and then answered truthfully, "Pia knows."

"She won't tell anyone else?" It was as if she had realized the threat such knowledge could be to the future of her unborn child.

"I don't think so."

"No," said Christian firmly. He studied Milena a moment and then added, "If you ever need me, for . . . well, for anything, you must let me know."

For a single moment, Katrinka believed she saw something resembling real concern in her son's eyes. Milena didn't reply and the look faded, to be replaced slowly by one of complete indifference to the fate of Milena and her child.

"If you can forgive us, Milena, we would both be grateful." Milena, too, was a battleground of conflicting emotions and, not being certain of what she wanted to say, again she said nothing. Katrinka went to her and kissed her cheek. "Maybe someday," she said.

Milena's only response was a slight nod.

When they were back in the car, Katrinka leaned heavily against the leather seat, as if exhausted, and said, "You got off easy this time."

"There won't be a next time," Christian assured her.

"I hope not."

"Why is it?" he said, his voice full of pain, "you can ask Milena to forgive you, when you can't forgive me? Why is it that you can forgive everyone but me?"

Katrinka turned to him. "Everyone?" She didn't know what he was talking about.

"Adam. You forgave him, no matter what he did. And Mark."

"That's not true."

"It is." His voice was like a child's, full of incomprehension and pain. "Don't try to deny it. I've watched you. And you expect me to believe that you love me? What a joke!"

He meant it, that much Katrinka knew for certain. His hurt was genuine. Unable to accept responsibility for the consequences of his own actions, he blamed her for not loving him enough to forgive him for them. "Oh, *miláčku*," she said, taking his hand, "what am I going to do with you?"

Thirty-Eight

WITHIN DAYS OF ADAM'S DEATH, THE RUMORS BEGAN CIRCULATING, NOT ONLY IN THE TABLOIDS BUT IN respected newspapers like *The Wall Street Journal* and *The New York Times.*

The damage to Patrick Kates's yacht had been severe and it had sunk where it stood at anchor, off Greenwich. Had Adam Graham not been aboard at the time of the explosion, a fact testified to by the chief steward who had left him asleep in the main cabin, by Adam's butler, and by Katrinka, who happened to be speaking to him when the blast shattered the boat, the investigation might not have been so thorough and the event written off as an accident. However, he had been on board, and that seemed too coincidental to some. And when further investigation revealed that the explosion had been caused by two small bombs set with timing devices, the major question on everyone's lips became, who had been trying to kill Adam Graham and why?

As happens when journalists start asking questions, they began to get answers no one expected. From a variety of sources (brokers at Knapp Manning, investigators at the New York Stock Exchange, someone at the SEC), they got a hint here, an off-the-record statement there, and gradually learned of Adam's illegal involvement in the takeover attempt of van Hollen Enterprises. They uncovered a complicated and equally illegal diversion of funds from the pension plans of some of the publicly held Graham companies, presumably to help

491

finance that takeover. And since it was no secret that Mark van Hollen had been present at the party on board the yacht the night of the explosion, that he and Adam Graham had gone off together for a long, private discussion, and that Charles Wolf had withdrawn his bid for VHE the next day, *The Wall Street Journal* asked whether Graham, fearing public exposure of his crimes, had taken his own life. Privately, some people speculated that Adam had not been drunk but drugged and left to die, presumably by Mark van Hollen. Why? Revenge, jealousy, to save his company—imaginations ran riot. Perhaps Katrinka was involved as well. That she should be on the phone with Adam at the moment of the explosion seemed highly suspicious, as was the fact (also revealed in newspaper accounts) that, since she was the nominal owner of the two companies involved in the VHE takeover, Hydra and Galahad, it appeared she would gain control of them at his death. Add to that a long history of marital discord and the trouble Adam had caused for Christian Heller just a few weeks earlier, and it seemed to many that Katrinka van Hollen also had ample reason to want her former husband dead.

Adam's death, the continuing revelations about his criminal business dealings, the nasty insinuations about herself and Mark, the endless questions from the police and the press, often made Katrinka feel as if she were in the middle of a guerrilla war, under fire from shadowy enemies who would appear and disappear with amazing ease. "Thank God nobody does know about Adam's link to Monica Brand," she said to Mark a few days after his return from Europe, "or we would both by now be dead in the electric chair."

"Locked up for life," corrected Mark. "There's no capital punishment in New York State—at least not while Cuomo's governor." Then they both started to laugh. "At least we haven't lost our sense of humor," he said.

And the talk would have been much worse, they agreed, if Sabrina had been writing about the mess. But with Charles Wolf's fortunes sinking, she had jumped ship. After accepting an offer from Mort Zuckerman, which would give her the wider circulation she wanted, she had gone to Grand Cayman Island, on a sort of working holiday, to visit a rock star who was—to put it mildly—publicity mad. For the first time in years, she was traveling without Alan Platt. Though she had kept Platt's name out of her "Sugar After Dark" series, she was afraid that the stolen files would surface sooner or later, exposing those like Platt who had escaped Sabrina's pen. The thought of what rival columnists would say then about her liaison with the bisexual design-

492

er, whose reputation she had single-handedly built, made her shudder. Sabrina didn't like being gossiped about.

Sugar Benson was also worried that her files would fall into the wrong hands. But while the publicity had driven away her clients, forcing her to shut up shop—at least temporarily—so far she had escaped the clutches of the IRS, the Inland Revenue, and various other government agencies who would be after her with all guns blazing if they ever managed to get hold of her records. Thinking it best to lie low until the threat of danger blew over, Sugar went on an extended visit to a former lover in Rio, a city that provided ample scope for her talents. Monica Brand remained in London, free-lancing.

As for Alan Platt, or so some of the gossip ran, he was keeping ex-Senator Russell Luce company at his retreat in Maine, where the disgraced aristocrat had gone to hide out until the memory of his scandal was wiped out by another, more interesting one. That had happened sooner than anyone had expected; and, to his great satisfaction, plunged his soon-to-be-divorced wife Nina back into the spotlight she loathed.

Rick Colins, seeing an opportunity of a lifetime, called Katrinka at her office to ask her to intercede with Nina for him. "Tell her she can trust me," he pleaded.

"She'll never agree to an interview," said Katrinka.

"If I could just talk to her for five minutes. But I can't get past that snotty butler of hers. You know how charming I can be," he added, when she refused.

"Have you talked to Carlos?" asked Katrinka, to change the subject.

"Yes. He's moving back to New York. Did he tell you?" Katrinka said that he had and asked how Rick felt about it. "Delighted, of course. But . . . well, it did take a lot of bricks falling on my head, but I've finally realized you can't go back." He had spent enough time with Carlos recently to know. They both knew. The friendship had survived but there was no passion left, on either side. Neither was particularly happy about it, but so it was.

"That's not what Neil Goodman thinks," said Katrinka.

"Can you believe it!" said Rick, laughing. "And that first wife of his is such a frump."

"She's very sweet."

"Yes, you're right. And that is a *very* important quality in a woman. So, why won't you be sweet to me and call Nina Graham?"

Katrinka laughed. "You do never give up! No. Absolutely no." She knew Rick didn't have a malicious bone in his body and normally she wouldn't hesitate to do him a favor, but not this time, not with Nina Graham.

"Poor love, you really are overwhelmed with everything at the moment, aren't you?"

"Yes."

"You can count on me," he promised.

Katrinka hung up and, trying to put both Adam Graham and his mother out of her mind, turned her attention to the Children of the Streets fund-raising gala, which was scheduled for the following week. But Rick had no intention of letting go of such a potentially good story. He sat in his apartment on Thompson Street, in the cramped, untidy room that served as his office, and went through his address book, looking for another link. From old New England stock himself, he knew plenty of people who knew Nina Graham, and soon found a way to reach her, through a friend of one of his aunts.

First, Rick got Nina to agree to an interview for the coffee table book on the "first families" of the United States that he had spent the past several months trying to write; and, when that went well, managed to coax her into an appearance on his television show by convincing her that it would help quiet all the terrible stories about Adam.

A camera crew went to Newport; Nina conducted Rick on a guided tour of the house and grounds; she looked beautiful, regal, composed, a model of integrity. The charm, which made all but her children overlook her difficult, demanding personality, was at its most seductive. Looking straight into the camera, her voice steady, she told of the Graham family's proud heritage, of the heros who had defended their country in every war from the French and Indian to the Second World War, and denied that her son could ever have been involved in anything shady. She even tried to do a good turn for Katrinka (or fire the first shot in a legal battle, depending on your point of view) by claiming that the legal ownership of Galahad and Hydra would take a team of lawyers and a judge a considerable amount of time to determine. It was a good performance and, if the evidence against Adam had not been so overwhelming, it might have done some good. As it was, all the interview did was add more spice to the gossip stew as the stories surrounding Adam's death continued to grow more and more complicated, more and more extravagant.

Though Katrinka and Mark found the speculations about their personal involvement disturbing, they did not take them seriously. The stories were too wild, too inconsistent, did not make much sense when examined closely. And though the insurance and police investigators repeatedly questioned them both, it was clear that no one believed the rumors that were currently the major source of entertainment at business meetings and dinner parties.

The van Hollens brazened it out, keeping to their usual social schedule so as not to give the gossips a chance to accuse them of hiding. Katrinka's friends, as always, rallied around. Rick, true to his word, pointed out the absurdity of the stories linking the van Hollens to Adam's death. Zuzka, who was still in New York and in the early stages of setting up her own sports merchandising business, threatened the guests at two lunches and one dinner with unspecified dire consequences if they did not stop slandering Katrinka and Mark. The phone calls came daily from all over: from Tomáš, who was in San Francisco in the last weeks of principal photography on the film that he knew, with absolutely certainty, was finally going to earn him his Palme d'Or at Cannes; from Margo Jensen, house-hunting in Miami with Ted; from Daisy, either at her farm on the outskirts of Florence or the chesa in St. Moritz; from Lucia in Fiesole. She and her daughter were each at work designing new commissions, enjoying each other's company, trying to use what they called their "mutual disability," their uncanny knack for always getting involved with the wrong man, as a basis for reestablishing their relationship, which—before Christian and Patrick—had been a close one. "Martin Havlíček is spending Christmas with us," said Lucia at the beginning of December. She considered Pia's extending the invitation to Martin a sign that one of them at least was on the way to recovery. And Martin, on the basis of it, had decided to leave Knapp Manning to work with his mother. A great deal of mobility forbidden to a junior executive was allowed a company partner, and Martin intended to do a lot of traveling until Pia was ready to return to New York. "We'll either be here or at Daisy and Riccardo's in St. Moritz," continued Lucia. "What are you and Mark doing?"

"So much is happening, we haven't talked about Christmas," said Katrinka.

"Come spend it with us," urged Lucia.

Katrinka promised to think about it, but it was hard to plan ahead to Christmas when each day still brought new, sometimes terrible, revelations. A few weeks after Adam's death, Neil Goodman, along with several of his brokers, were indicted on various charges of security violations—none of them as yet having to do with Hydra or Galahad. Claiming that he had neither known about nor approved the violations, Neil nevertheless resigned from Knapp Manning, which the following week filed for protection from bankruptcy under Chapter 11. Neil's days as a respected player on the Street were over, his reputation ruined, any hope of a comeback wiped out. Someone else might have contemplated a leap out the window, but not Neil. He was already looking forward to the future, the brightest spot of which was his planned remarriage to his first wife when his divorce from Alexandra was final.

It was speculated that John MacIntyre, Adam's CFO, would also be indicted shortly for securities violations; and Charles Wolf as well. Those rumors sent the stock of Wolf's company plummeting and for a while Mark considered carrying through on his threat to buy the newspapers, but decided that he would rather keep his debt burden under control and spend what capital reserves he had bringing VHE, or at least the publishing part of it, private again. The paper mills and binderies he was prepared to lose in a takeover, but not the heart of his business, the newspapers and magazines, and certainly not his newest creation, *The International,* which was earning more advertising revenue with each issue as the magazine's approach to reporting and the quality of its writing gained both critical approval and a growing list of subscribers.

Mark, in fact, would have been feeling very pleased with his life at that moment, except for one problem he had not yet solved: Christian. He could neither allow someone he distrusted to continue working for him, nor figure out how to move his stepson out of VHE without telling his wife what Christian had done. For someone who prided himself on being open and honest, Mark found the weight of the secret he was keeping from Katrinka oppressive. It made him unusually short-tempered, something his wife could not fail to notice, though for a long time she assumed his mood was due to the amount of publicity they were both attracting. If there was one thing Mark hated, it was seeing his name and photograph splashed across the pages of newspapers and magazines.

For Katrinka, the subject of Christian was even more complicated. Keeping secrets had been a way of life for her, and though she had been uncharacteristically open with Mark throughout their relationship, when it became a question of "betraying" her son, even to her husband, it was easy for her to slip back into old behavior. Without ever consciously making the decision, she had not told Mark the truth about Milena's rape. But, unlike other times, this time her silence was disturbing to her. She wanted to confide in Mark. She wanted to ask his advice about how to handle her difficult son. Still she said nothing. And because Katrinka's reserve was hidden behind an apparently open and optimistic facade, it was always difficult to tell when something was troubling her, if she chose to conceal it. Mark never suspected that Katrinka was worried about anything beyond the ugly repercussions of Adam's death.

It took close to a month for matters to come to a head.

They were in the small garden room of the town house having breakfast about nine o'clock one Saturday morning when the house phone rang. Mark picked it up, listened while the butler told him who was on the line, then said to Katrinka, "It's the insurance investigator. Probably with more goddamn questions." He sounded unusually irritable. Switching to the outside line, Mark said good morning, asked when the harassment was going to stop, then, surprisingly, said, "Wait a minute. I want my wife to hear this." He handed Katrinka the phone. "I'll pick up the extension in the library." Both Katrinka and the investigator remained silent until they heard Mark's voice. "I'm here. Go on."

"Like I said, we've discovered who set the explosion."

"Who?" asked Katrinka.

"Patrick Kates."

Mark muttered an obscenity and Katrinka, sounding as if she found it very hard to believe, said, "But he just paid all that money to have the yacht completely redone. Why he would blow it up?"

That, explained the investigator, was how Patrick Kates had hoped everyone would react. What they had learned over weeks of investigation and two days of questioning was that Kates had put most of his own money in the America's Cup race and lost the rest in a number of high-risk investments. He had had nothing left but his house in Connecticut and his yacht. The house was heavily mortgaged, but the yacht was not. It was insured for millions, and no one, he was certain, would accuse him of sabotaging it after having taken such care with its renovation. Patrick had expected the investigation to be cursory, and the insurance money to be paid without much fuss. That money was his bankroll to a more prosperous future.

Patrick had tried to make sure that no one would be hurt in the accident. Knowing that the death of even one member of the crew would cause endless complications, he had ordered that no one was to remain aboard the yacht that night, giving his most trusted employee responsibility for making sure his order was carried out. In any case, while Patrick was unquestionably larcenous, he was not a killer. Adam's death in the explosion had weighed heavily on his conscience.

Though his guilt had not sent him running to confess, as the evidence began slowly to point in his direction, as he felt the net closing in on him, Kates had begun to panic. When the investigators confronted him with their suspicions, he bluffed for thirty seconds, then caved in and called his lawyer, who immediately began to plea-bargain.

"We've got him," said the investigator, who had just saved his company millions and was sounding justifiably pleased with himself.

Mark thanked him for phoning to let them know what had happened, then hung up as Katrinka asked what would happen to Patrick. "They're going to prosecute. He'll go to prison," she told Mark when he returned to the garden room.

Mark shrugged. "He's guilty of fraud. And manslaughter. Maybe this will get our names out of the papers," he added.

"Oh God, I do hope so. I still can't believe it," she said, overwhelmed by another wave of grief for Adam, whose life had been ended by Patrick Kates's greed, whose reputation had been ruined by his own. Then she thought of Lucia and felt worse. How would she take knowing Patrick had deliberately destroyed the work she was so proud of, and had killed one of her best friends doing it? She had fallen apart when she realized Nick was involved with the Mafia, and this—because it was more immediate and personal—seemed somehow so much worse. "I have to tell Lucia, before she does read it in the newspapers," said Katrinka as she picked up the phone again.

"Better call Daisy, too. Lucia may need some moral support." Mark poured himself another cup of coffee and sat, his face glum, watching her dial.

Over the next few days, as the stories about Patrick Kates and Adam Graham continued to expand, those about the van Hollens began, to their relief, to dwindle. Neither Mark's mood, nor Katrinka's, however, seemed to improve very much. And one night, after a performance of *Lucia di Lammermoor* at the Met, which both had been too distracted to enjoy, Mark said, "Would you like to tell me what's bothering you?"

"Bothering me? Nothing," said Katrinka. "I'm fine." She pulled a cashmere robe on over her silk teddy and disappeared into the bathroom.

Mark watched her a moment, then went into his dressing room, took off his clothes, hung up his suit, left his shoes out for one of the staff to polish, and wearing only his shorts continued on into his bathroom. From Katrinka's he could hear faintly the sounds duplicating those in his own: the flush of the toilet, the running water, the opening and closing of the cabinets, the scrape of toothbrush against teeth. Maybe nothing was bothering her, he thought, except possibly his own bad mood. Returning to their comfortable, peaceful cream-colored bedroom, he climbed between the sheets that the housemaid had turned down earlier, picked up a book from the bedside table, but made no attempt to read. Part of his mind was engaged in trying to relax, the other in working out a way to get rid of his stepson, the cause of Mark's continuing irritability and, therefore, it seemed to him, the source of the current tension in the van Hollen marriage.

Katrinka came out of the bathroom, took off her robe, slipped into bed beside her husband, and cuddled against him. He let the book fall to the floor and put his arms around her. "It is a year today I went to Kitzbühel to find Christian," she said, as if in response to his earlier question.

"Do you have any regrets?" he asked.

"No," she said fiercely. "None. I had to know where he was, *how* he was."

"He hasn't been easy for you to deal with," said Mark cautiously, searching for a path through the minefield to his goal.

Smiling ruefully, Katrinka shook her head. "No, Christian is not easy." Pulling away from Mark, she sat up. Even the faint smile had disappeared from her face. "You know what he did tell me? That Kurt Heller abused him when he was little. If it's true, I'll never forgive myself . . ."

"*If* . . ." repeated Mark.

Katrinka studied his face for a moment, then said, "You don't trust him." She had to stop herself from adding the word "either."

Mark hesitated. "No," he said finally.

Though it was not a thought she liked to dwell on, Katrinka had always known that Mark did not care for Christian in the way that she wanted him to. But he had seemed to respect him and to value his work at VHE. "Why?" she asked.

"Who knows?" said Mark evasively. "Feelings aren't always rational."

"You want him to leave VHE?"

Mark nodded. "I think that would be a good idea. Yes."

Katrinka lay down again, this time well away from Mark. She closed her eyes. She wasn't angry. She was thinking, trying to make sense of what was happening.

"Baby," murmured Mark, "I'm sorry. You know I don't like hurting you." He took her hand.

Not saying anything for a moment, she let him hold it, then asked, "Was it Christian who did find out that Adam was in control of Hydra and Galahad?"

"Yes," said Mark, reluctant to expand on the statement.

But to Katrinka it was inconceivable that Christian could have

499

provided Mark with the information that had saved his company and that Mark would not be grateful for it. She opened her eyes so that she could see Mark's face. "He was the one who did tell you about it?" she said, rephrasing the question.

Mark hesitated a moment. He had never lied to Katrinka before and had no intention of starting now. But it wasn't, in this case at least, so easy to tell her the truth.

His hesitation was answer enough. "He didn't tell you. But why? Why?"

"I haven't discussed it with him," said Mark. "To me, it doesn't matter why."

Sitting up again, she turned and looked at him. "How you did find out about the companies?"

"Carey's assistant did a computer search."

"You had both of them working on it?" Mark nodded and Katrinka looked at him accusingly. "You didn't trust Christian, from the beginning." She knew her attitude was unreasonable, but she couldn't help herself: it was her son they were talking about.

"That's not true," said Mark. "Somewhere along the way, I just got this gut feeling . . ." He stopped and then said irritably, "Oh, fuck . . . I didn't want to have this discussion with you. I didn't want to have to accuse your son, or defend myself. I just want him out of my company." He got out of bed and sat in an armchair, facing her. "He's got to go. I can't have him working with me."

"I know." She sounded numb.

"Jesus Christ, Katrinka . . ."

"I understand," she said quietly. "I do. I agree with you. It's just . . ." She began to cry and Mark returned to the bed and gathered her into his arms. "He's so bad," she said. "Worse than you think." She started to tell him about Milena, about the rape, and the baby, but even then she couldn't. "I'll tell him he has to go," she said instead.

"I'll do it," volunteered Mark. "It's my job to do it. He works for me." Now that Katrinka knew, Mark was looking forward to confronting Christian.

"No, I want to," she insisted.

"You're sure?"

Katrinka nodded. Shifting in his arms, she reached to the bedside table for a Kleenex, then wiped her eyes with it. "But I don't want to lose him," she said. "Still, I love him."

The next morning Katrinka called Christian and arranged to see him after work. At his apartment, she insisted when he offered to meet her at either her office or the town house. It was the only place they could really be alone.

From the tone of his mother's voice, Christian knew that their meeting would not be pleasant, but he was certain that he could deal with whatever was bothering her. He always had so far.

When he got home from work, he changed out of his suit into a pair of slacks and a cashmere turtleneck. He checked the apartment to be sure that everything was neat and tidy, though a cleaning woman came in every day to make certain that it was. She did his laundry too, as well as ironing and minor repairs. Once or twice, she had even cooked for him. A perfect gentleman, she thought him. And handsome as the devil, with his dark hair and brooding eyes.

Christian was in the kitchen, opening a bottle of wine, when he heard the house phone ring. His mother was on the way up, the doorman informed him. He put the wine in a bucket of ice, carried it into the sitting room to the bar, poured himself a small scotch, then heard the bell ring and went to answer the door. "Come in, come in," he said, as if having her visit him was the greatest pleasure life allowed. He kissed her. "You look beautiful," he added admiringly.

"Thank you," she said. "May I have a glass of wine?"

"Of course. Please, sit down." He poured her a glass of wine and brought it to her. "You look very serious." He sat on the opposite end of the sofa and turned a little to face her. "I assume that means I've done something to upset you?"

"You have no idea what it could be?"

"I didn't think there were any secrets left between us."

"Neither did I." She took a sip of wine, then looked around the apartment, remembering how optimistic and happy she had been while furnishing it for him before his arrival in New York.

"It's a lovely apartment," said Christian. He had expected to receive the deed to it for Christmas. Now, that didn't seem likely. "You have been so generous to me."

"Yes. And Mark, too."

Christian was not sure whether it was a statement or a question. "Of course. Mark has been the best of stepfathers," he said, unable to control the slight edge of sarcasm in his voice.

"Then, tell me why you didn't let him know that Adam was behind the takeover attempt?"

Christian paled. How the hell had she discovered that? "What makes you think I knew?"

"Didn't you?"

"No."

"You're lying," she said.

"You can think what you want. I clearly can't stop you." Getting up from the sofa, he went to the bar and freshened his drink. He hadn't drunk half of it yet, but he needed something to do.

"If you imagine I *want* to think you did something so terrible . . ."

Both Mark and Carey had been behaving coldly to him at work, keeping him at a distance, making sure he did not attend certain meetings or receive confidential memos. But since neither had confronted him, he had assumed that whatever suspicions they had were slight, unprovable. He had never dreamed that Mark would go running to Katrinka with them. "He accuses me and you believe him, just like that."

"Mark wouldn't lie to me."

"And I would?"

"Yes. I hate to say it. I hate that it's true. But yes."

She didn't know about his deal with Adam, thought Christian, or she would have said something. She didn't know about the money or the stocks. He came back toward her and slumped into the armchair across from her, his face sullen. "If that's how you feel, I can't stay here," he said, playing what he thought was his trump card. He didn't believe she'd ever let him leave.

But to his surprise she nodded and said quietly, "I agree. I think it's best if you go."

She did not mean, he realized, just the apartment. He was stunned. "Leave New York?"

"I don't want to see you for a while. And if you go back to Germany, we won't have to explain to anyone why that is." She stood up. Resisting the urge to go to him, to smooth back his hair, to comfort him, she said, *"Miláčku*, this is breaking my heart."

"You see," he said bitterly. "I was right. You do forgive everyone but me."

"I love you. But I can't allow you to make trouble in my life. I can't allow you to hurt the people who are close to me."

"You think by sending me away you can stop it?"

Katrinka recoiled slightly. For the first time, she felt afraid of him, afraid of her own son, her flesh and blood. But that was ridiculous, she thought. He didn't mean what he was saying. He was just so angry. "You're a grown man, Christian. I can't tell you what to do—"

"You can't control me, that's why you're so upset. You only like to have people around you can control."

"But when you return to Munich," she continued, ignoring his interruption, "I think it would be a good idea . . ."

"Don't say it. I spent my childhood seeing psychiatrists. And a lot of good it did."

"You're older now. You understand more. Don't you want to find out why you need to hurt the people who care about you? Don't you want to stop doing it?" When he didn't answer, not able to resist finally, she went to him and smoothed back the lock of hair that had fallen across his high forehead. "Take care of yourself, *miláčku*."

He smiled bitterly. "That's one thing you don't have to worry about." He watched her as she walked to the door. "Tell Mark I'll stop by in the morning, early, and clear out my desk." Turning to look at him for what she knew would be the last time for a long while, Katrinka nodded. "And I'll leave New York by the end of the week." Again she nodded. "Good-bye, Mother," he said.

"Good-bye," she said, then left quickly, closing the door behind her.

When Mark got home, he found Katrinka in the nursery, holding Anuška, who had fallen asleep in her arms before quite finishing the plastic bottle of apple juice now resting on a nearby table. Katrinka looked up as he entered and smiled. "I think she said 'mama' before."

"Babies don't talk at her age. They just make sounds," said Mark as he dropped to the floor at her feet.

"So all the books say. But it did sound just like it."

They sat for a moment in silence, enjoying the luxury of being alone together, just the three of them. Mark reached up and touched the baby's hand. She looked flushed and contented, her long body wrapped in a bright quilt, her blond hair falling in ringlets against her head, a red bow tied into one curl. Even he could see that she was the image of him, except for the slanted pale blue eyes like Katrinka's. She was going to be knockout. She *was* a knockout. "Did you see Christian?" he asked. Katrinka nodded, not certain she could speak. "And?"

"He'll be out of VHE first thing in the morning, and he'll leave New York by the end of the week." Her voice was a little unsteady.

"I'm sorry, baby," he said, letting his head rest against her knee.

"I know." She moved one hand from Anuška's round thigh to Mark's graying hair.

Reaching up, Mark grabbed it, brought it back to his mouth, and kissed it. "We have each other," he said.

Mark had lost so much, his first wife, his sons, and still he had managed to find happiness again, in her and in Anuška. Could she do the same? wondered Katrinka. Yes, she was certain of it, though it was hard to believe now, when the pain of losing Christian was so great.

But she hadn't lost him forever. Katrinka tried to console herself with the thought. He would change. It was possible. And at the first sign of his wanting to, she would be there to help him. Did her son understand that? she wondered, and realized that of course he did, on some level. Despite all his destructiveness, Christian was too smart not to know when someone had his best interests at heart.

Slowly, Katrinka felt the heavy weight lifting from her spirits. The feeling of despair that had enveloped her since the night before began to give way before her natural optimism. If Adam Graham, who was no insignificant adversary, had failed in his plan to destroy Mark and end their marriage, who could do it? No one. Only themselves, if they allowed it, if they let bitterness and mistrust and fear rob them of their happiness. But they wouldn't, Katrinka was certain of that. And her certainty made her feel suddenly invincible, made her feel free, free to love without the fear that had haunted her since her parents' death.

She had Mark and Anuška. She would win Christian back. Leaning forward, she kissed the top of Mark's head. "I do love you."

"I should hope so," he said, relieved to hear her sounding a little happier. He let go of her hand and turned to look at her. She was absolutely beautiful he thought, sitting there, holding his daughter. "What do you want to do for Christmas?"

"Go skiing," she said.

Mark laughed. The mountains were where, like him, Katrinka had gone all her life to heal her pain, regain her energy, gather the strength to fight the next set of battles. "Of course," he said, "we'll go skiing."